Lily the Thief

Janne Kukkonen

Color by
Kévin Bazot

:01
First Second
New York

On the dark day of rising,
From their lairs they'll come knocking,
Scratching a crack in the calm.
Beware, then, all that is bright,
Even the palest moon's light.

1

The **Urn**

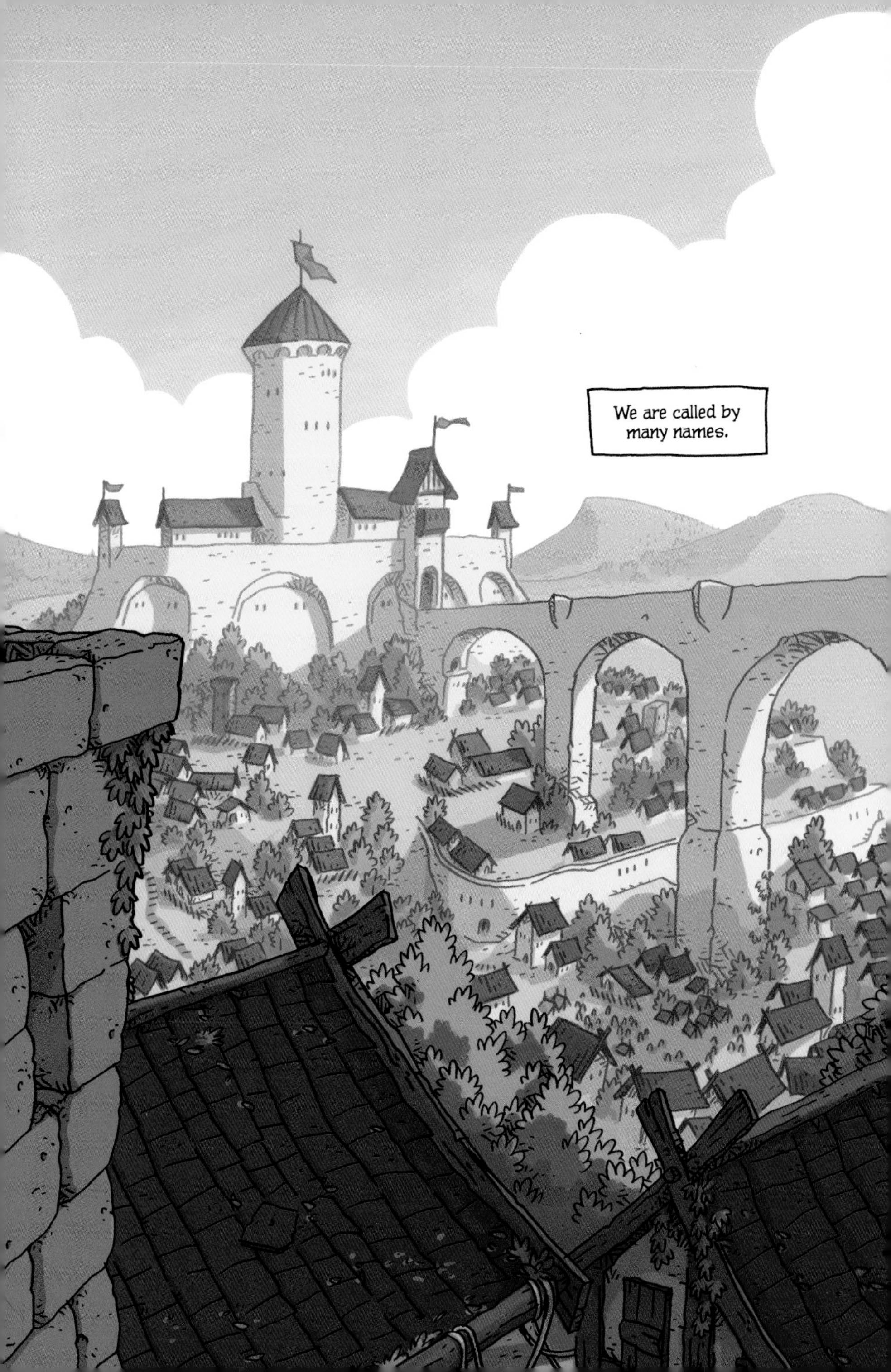
We are called by many names.

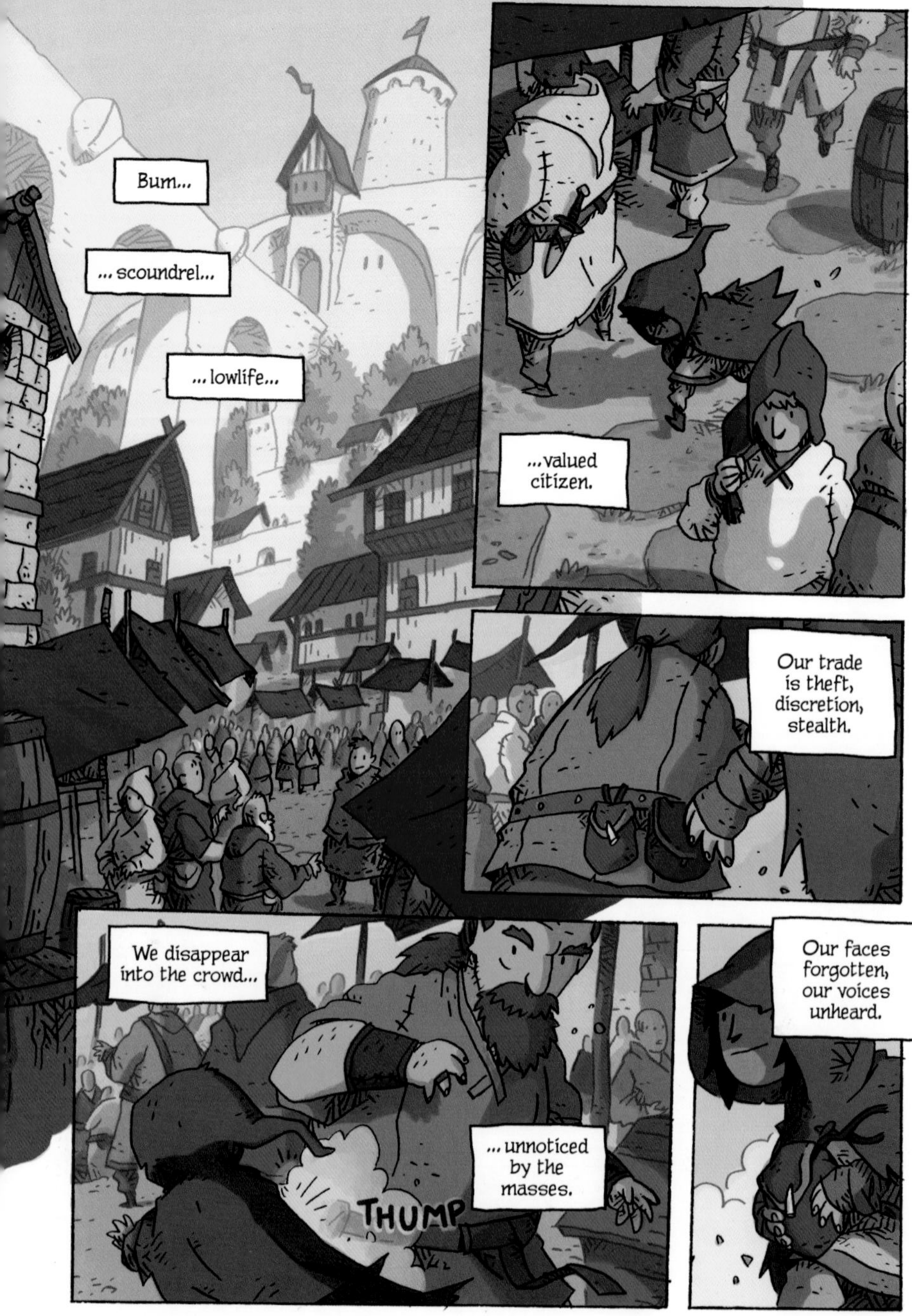
Bum...
... scoundrel...
... lowlife...
...valued citizen.
Our trade is theft, discretion, stealth.
We disappear into the crowd...
... unnoticed by the masses.
THUMP
Our faces forgotten, our voices unheard.

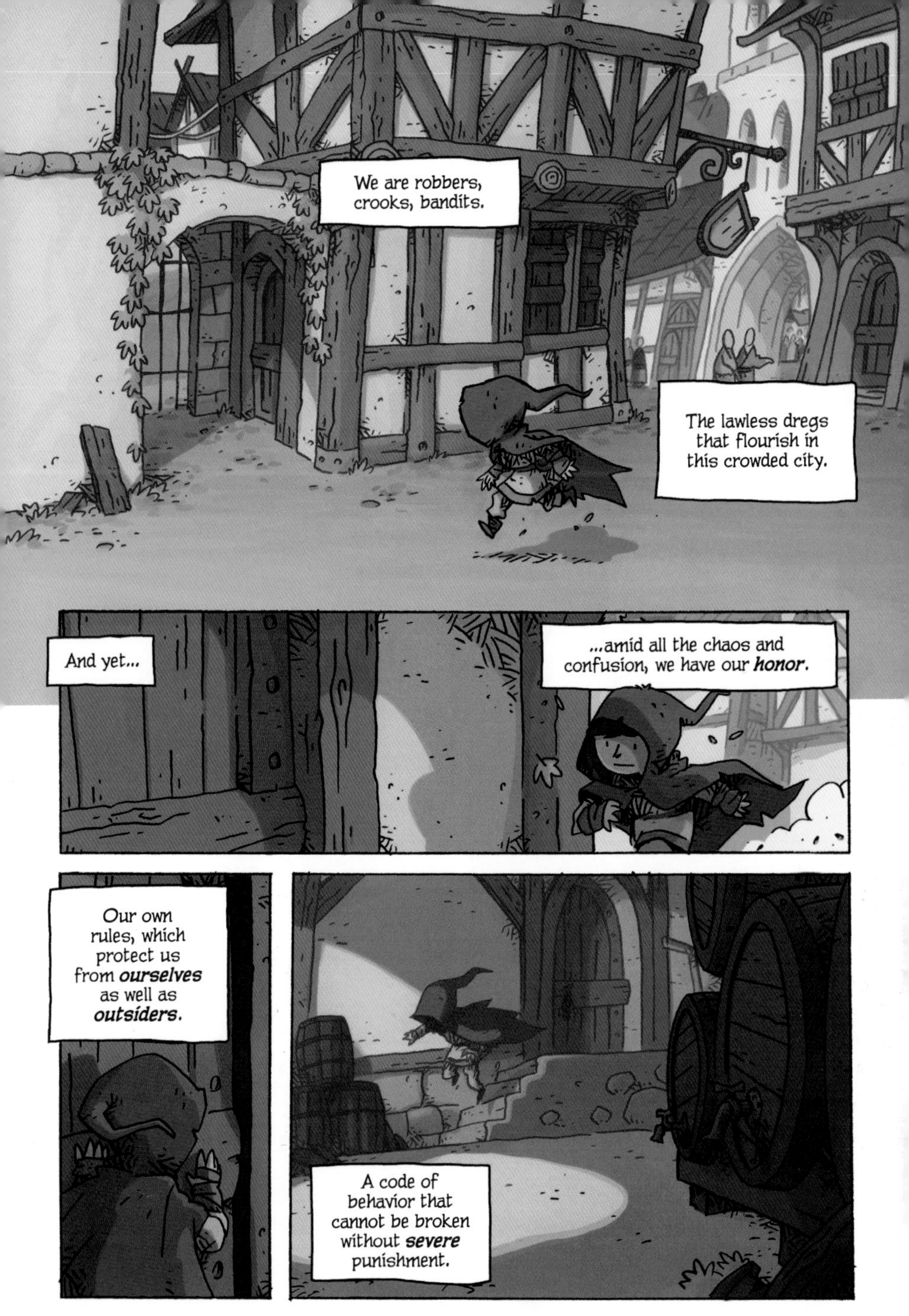

We are robbers, crooks, bandits.
The lawless dregs that flourish in this crowded city.
And yet...
...amid all the chaos and confusion, we have our ***honor***.
Our own rules, which protect us from ***ourselves*** as well as ***outsiders***.
A code of behavior that cannot be broken without ***severe*** punishment.

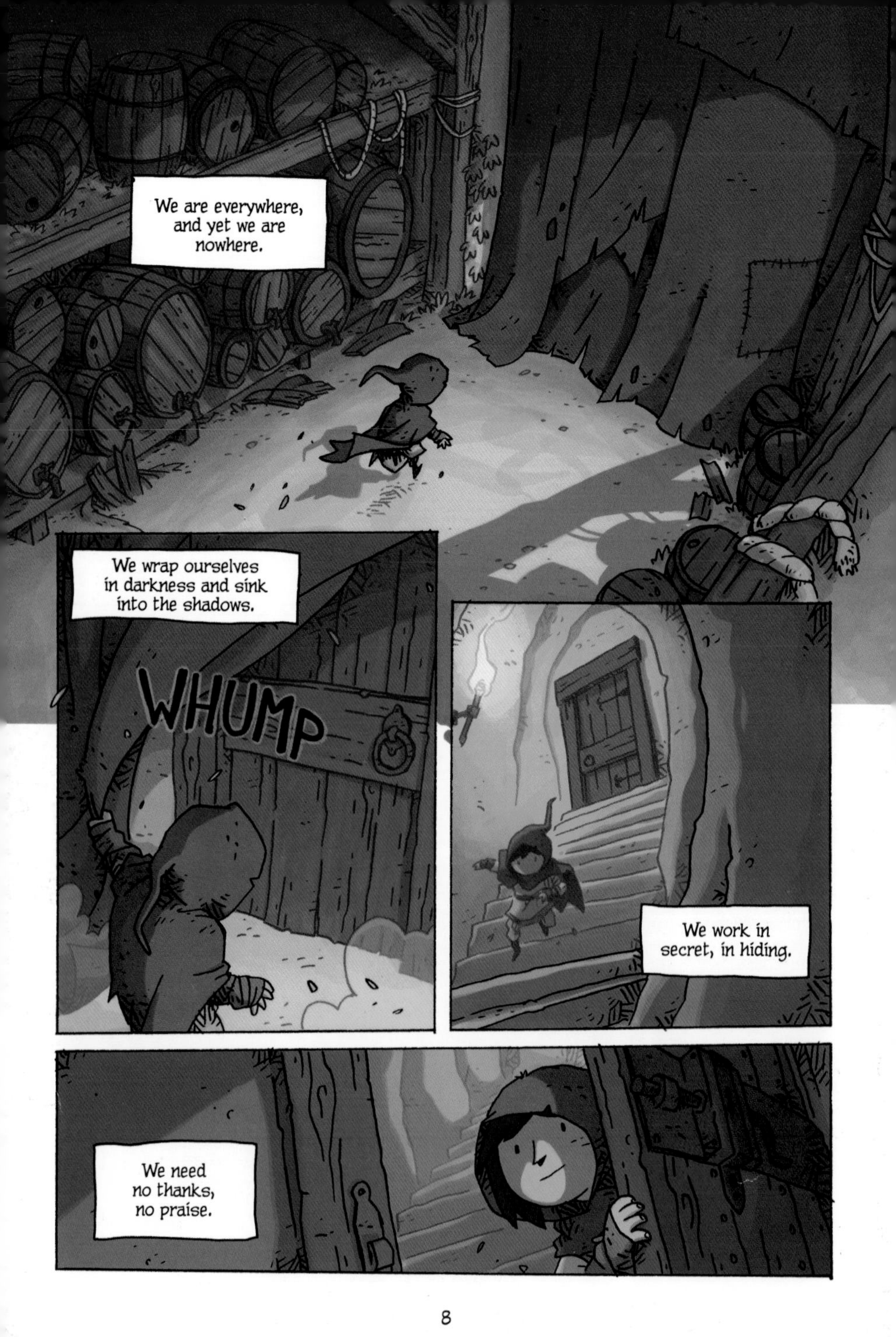

We are everywhere, and yet we are nowhere.
We wrap ourselves in darkness and sink into the shadows.
WHUMP
We work in secret, in hiding.
We need no thanks, no praise.

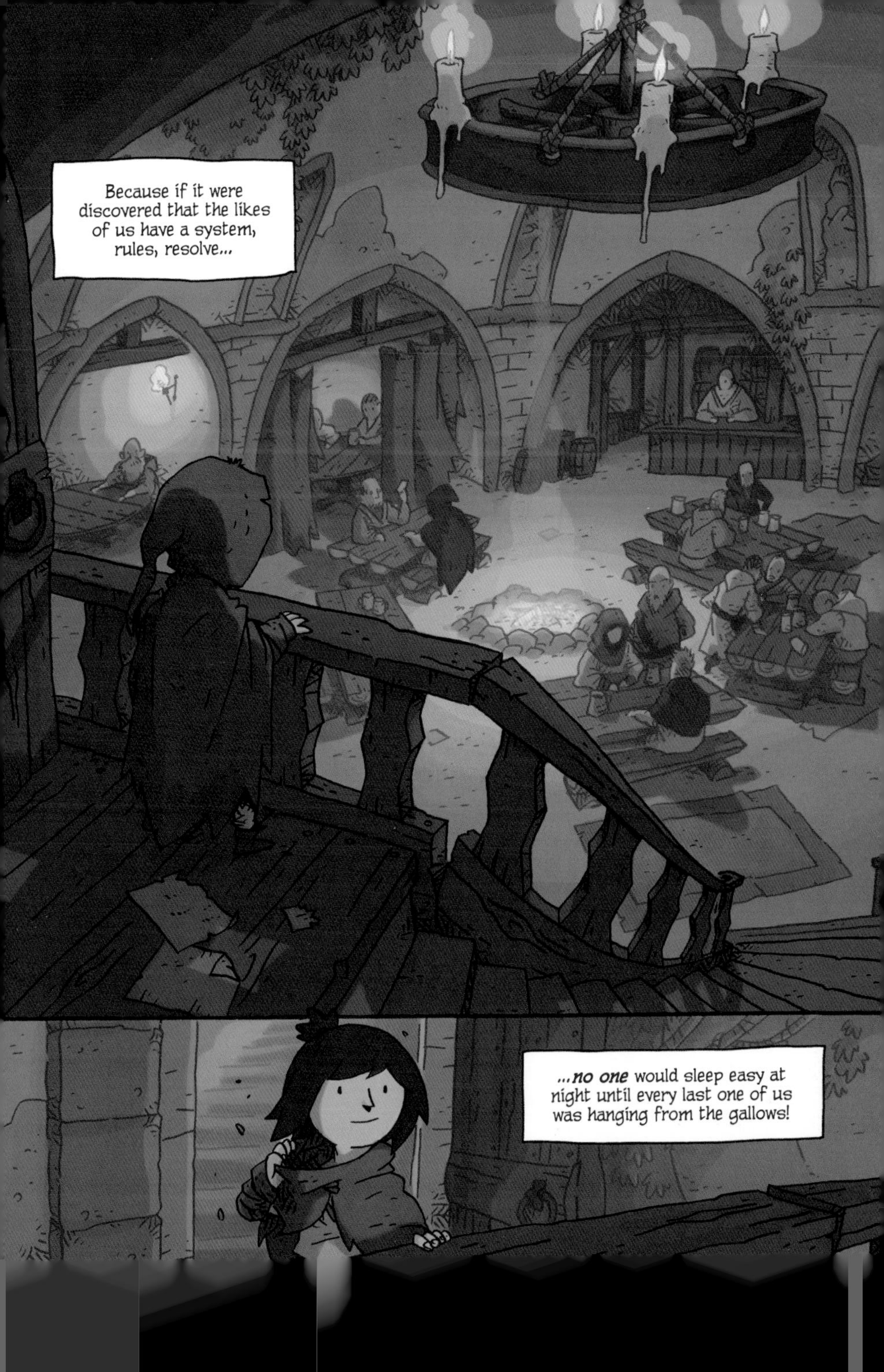
Because if it were discovered that the likes of us have a system, rules, resolve...
...*no one* would sleep easy at night until every last one of us was hanging from the gallows!

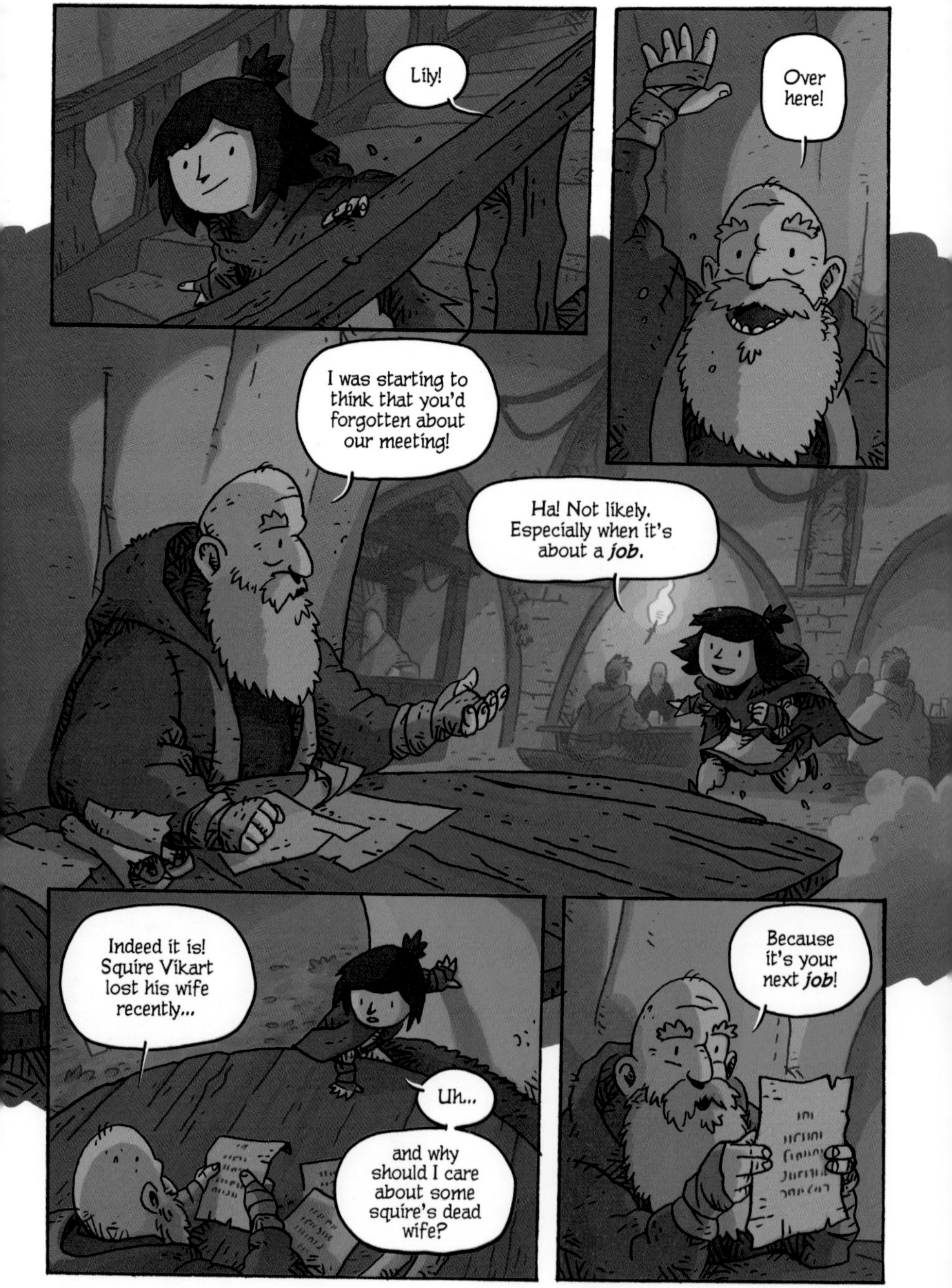
Lily!
Over here!
I was starting to think that you'd forgotten about our meeting!
Ha! Not likely. Especially when it's about a *job*.
Indeed it is! Squire Vikart lost his wife recently...
Uh...
and why should I care about some squire's dead wife?
Because it's your next *job*!

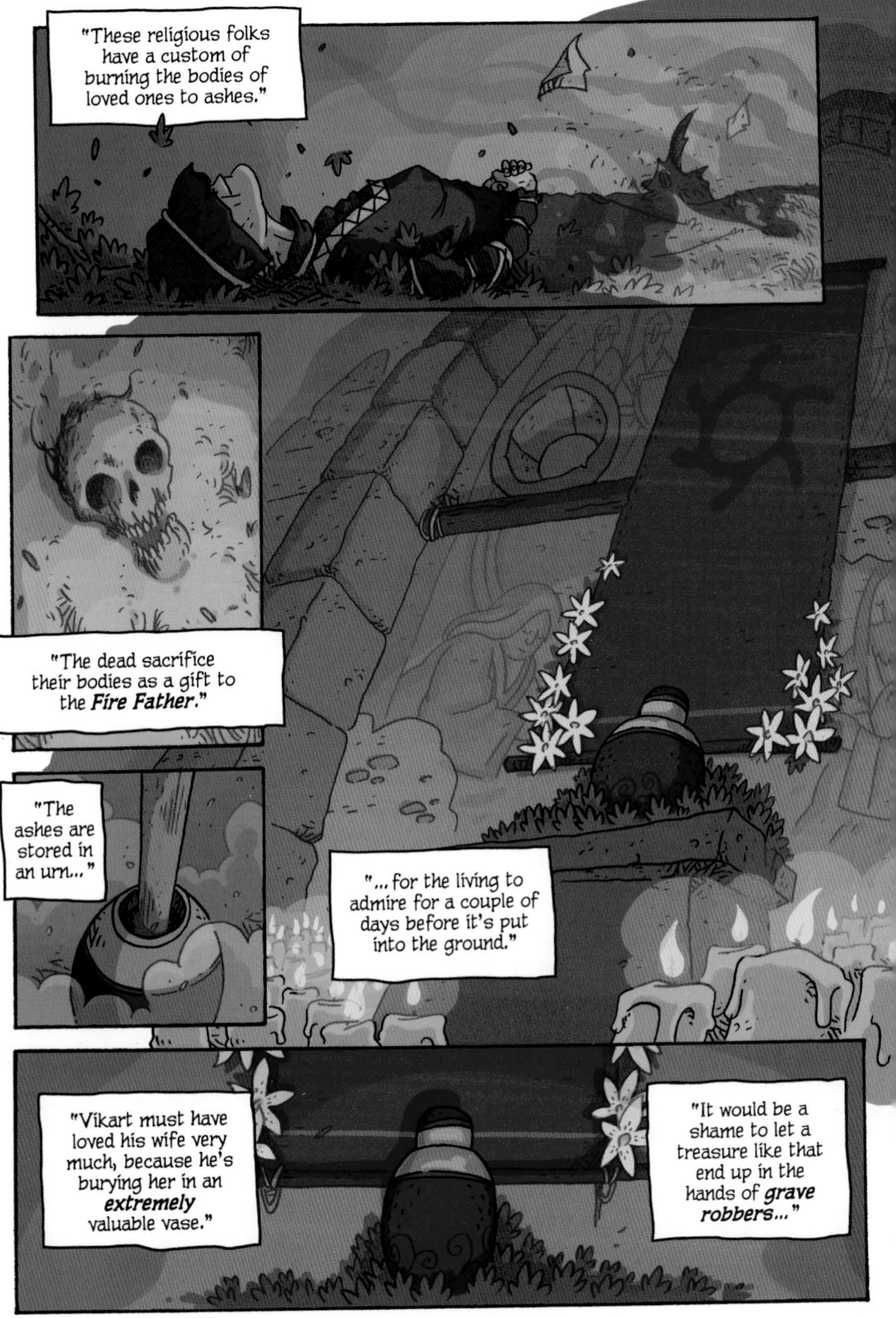
"These religious folks have a custom of burning the bodies of loved ones to ashes."
"The dead sacrifice their bodies as a gift to the ***Fire Father***."
"The ashes are stored in an urn..."
"... for the living to admire for a couple of days before it's put into the ground."
"Vikart must have loved his wife very much, because he's burying her in an ***extremely*** valuable vase."
"It would be a shame to let a treasure like that end up in the hands of ***grave robbers***..."

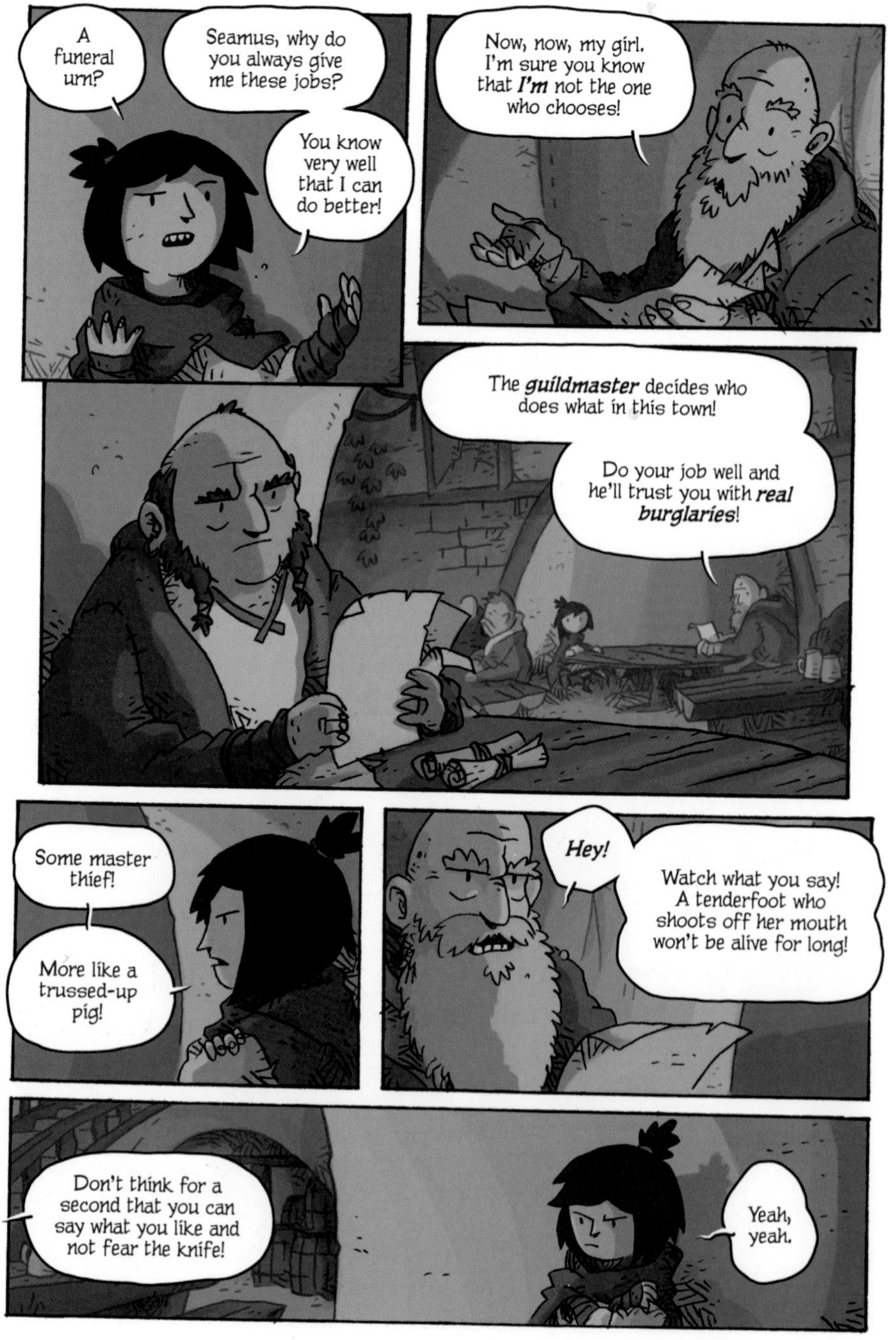
A funeral urn?
Seamus, why do you always give me these jobs?
You know very well that I can do better!
Now, now, my girl. I'm sure you know that *I'm* not the one who chooses!
The **guildmaster** decides who does what in this town!
Do your job well and he'll trust you with **real burglaries**!
Some master thief!
More like a trussed-up pig!
Hey!
Watch what you say! A tenderfoot who shoots off her mouth won't be alive for long!
Don't think for a second that you can say what you like and not fear the knife!
Yeah, yeah.

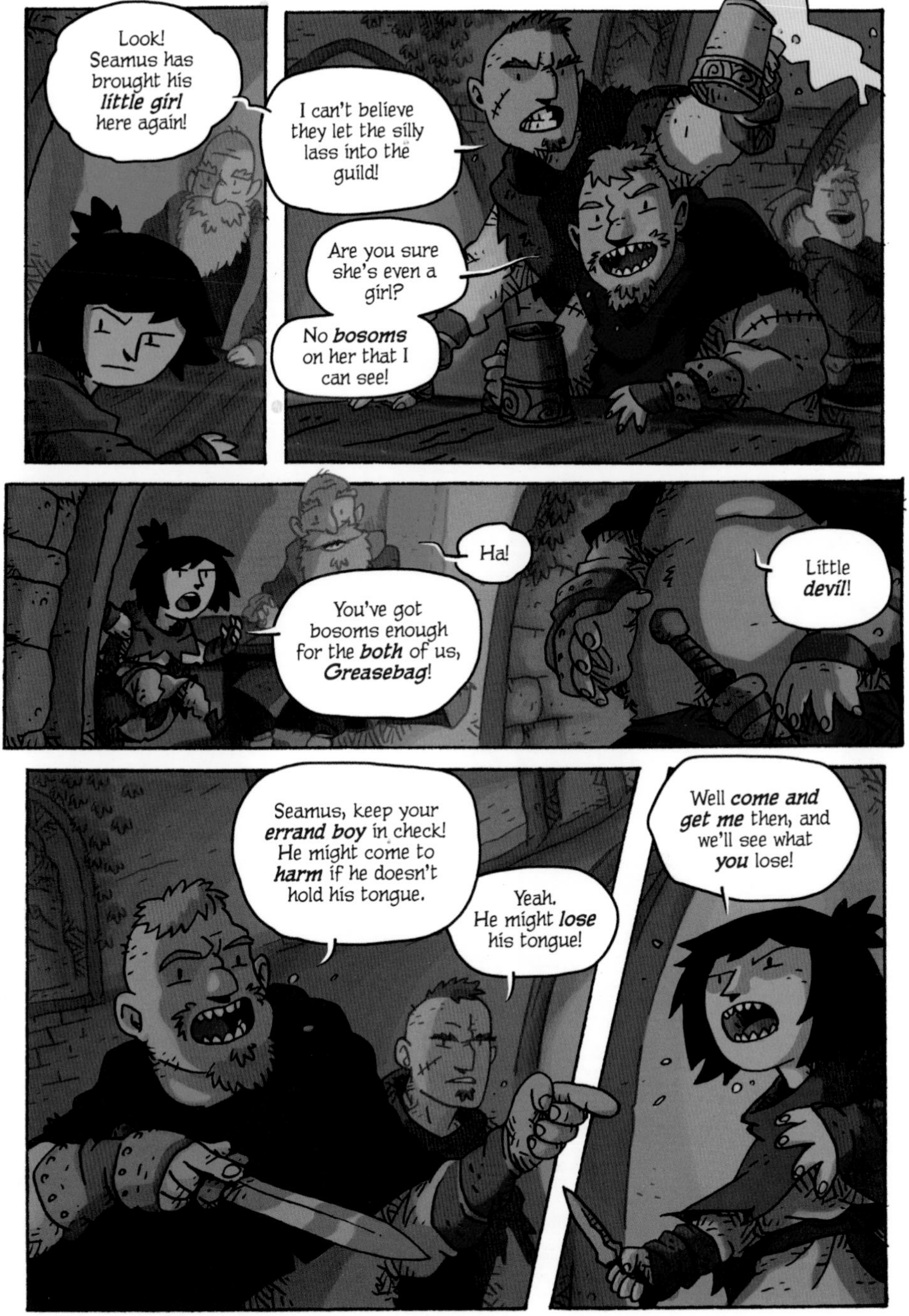

Look! Seamus has brought his ***little girl*** here again!
I can't believe they let the silly lass into the guild!
Are you sure she's even a girl?
No ***bosoms*** on her that I can see!
Ha!
You've got bosoms enough for the ***both*** of us, ***Greasebag***!
Little ***devil***!
Seamus, keep your ***errand boy*** in check! He might come to ***harm*** if he doesn't hold his tongue.
Yeah. He might ***lose*** his tongue!
Well ***come and get me*** then, and we'll see what ***you*** lose!

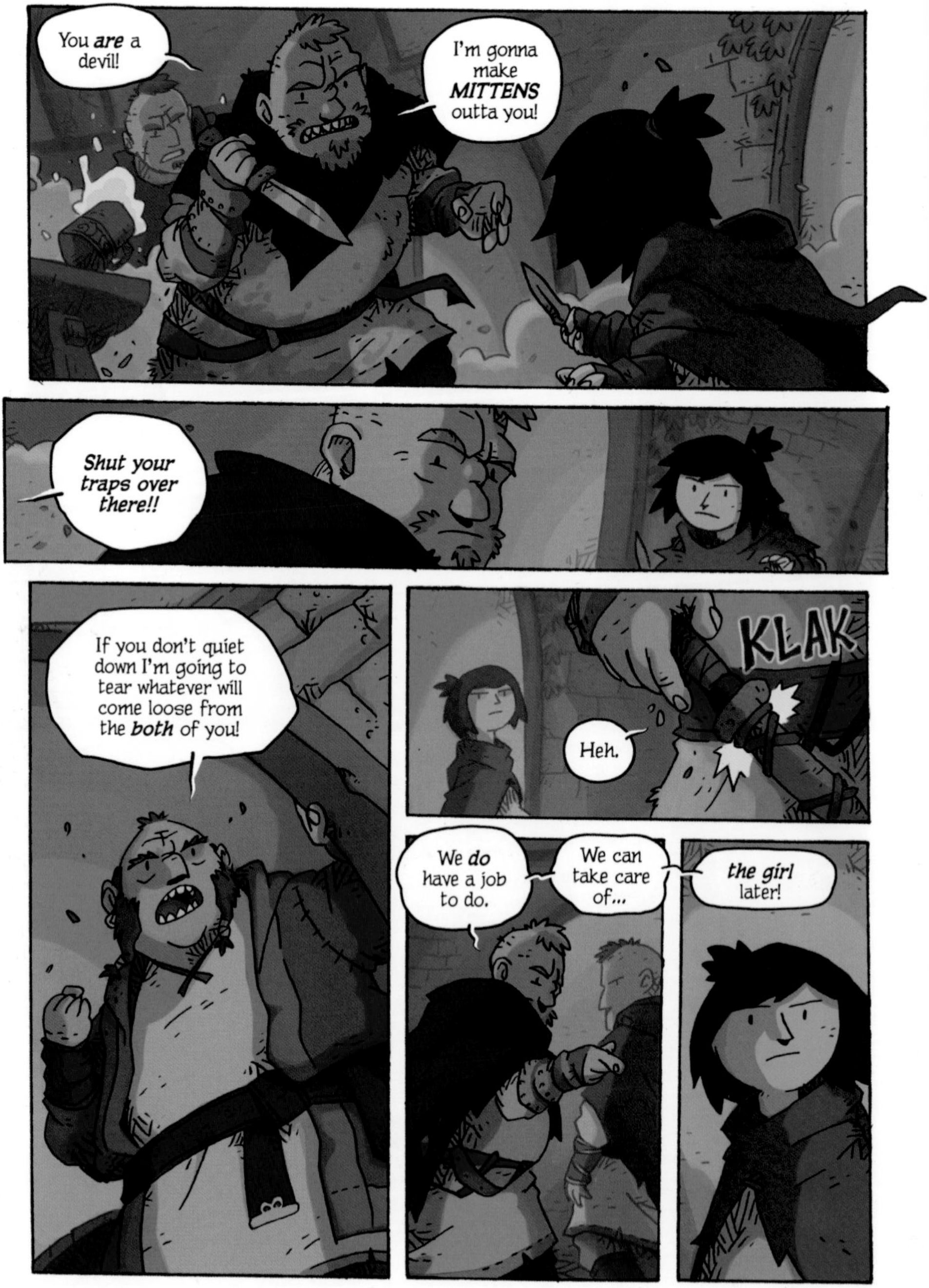
You *are* a devil!
I'm gonna make **MITTENS** outta you!
Shut your traps over there!!
If you don't quiet down I'm going to tear whatever will come loose from the ***both*** of you!
KLAK
Heh.
We *do* have a job to do.
We can take care of...
the girl later!

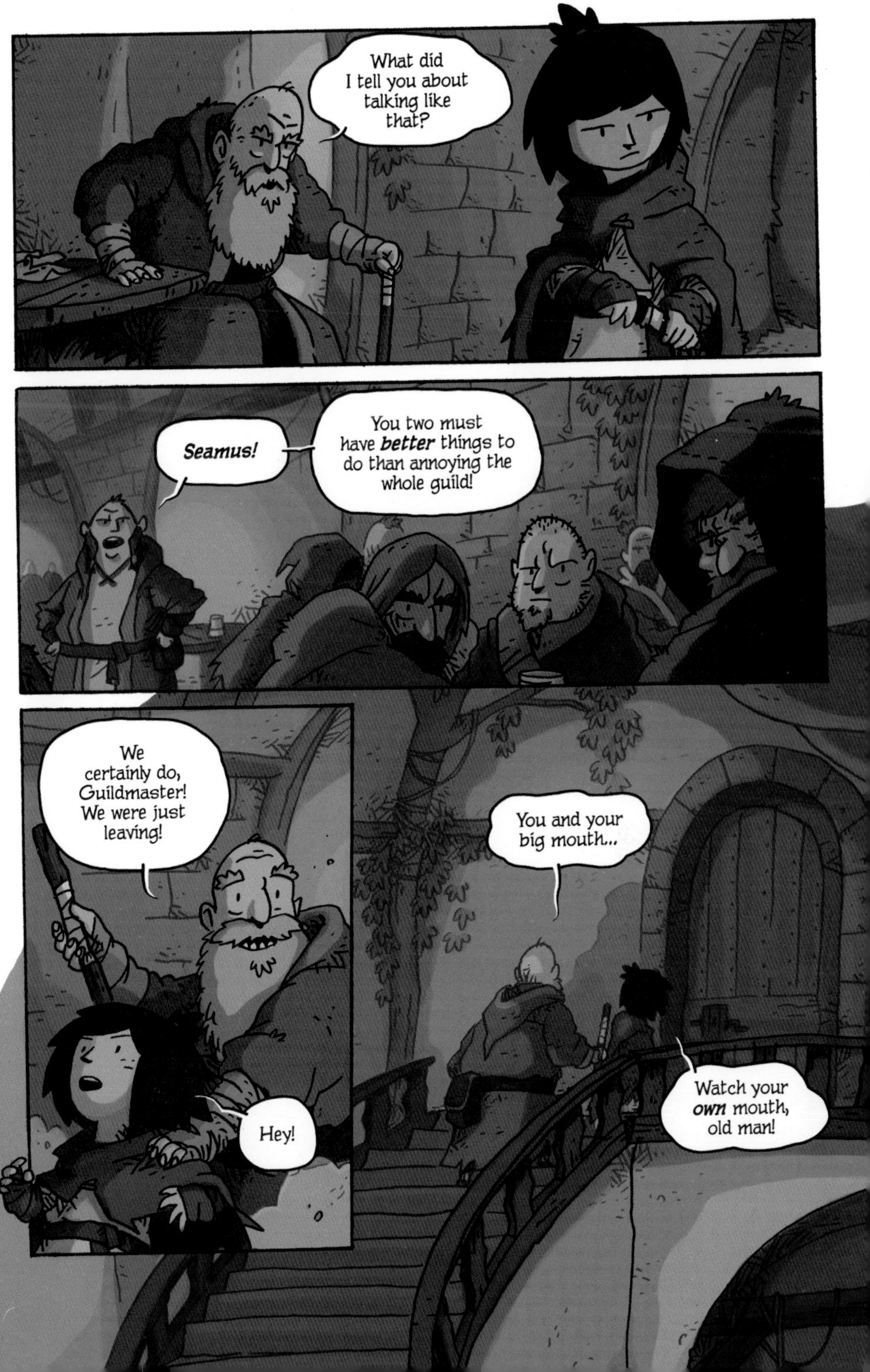

What did I tell you about talking like that?
Seamus!
You two must have **better** things to do than annoying the whole guild!
We certainly do, Guildmaster! We were just leaving!
Hey!
You and your big mouth...
Watch your **own** mouth, old man!

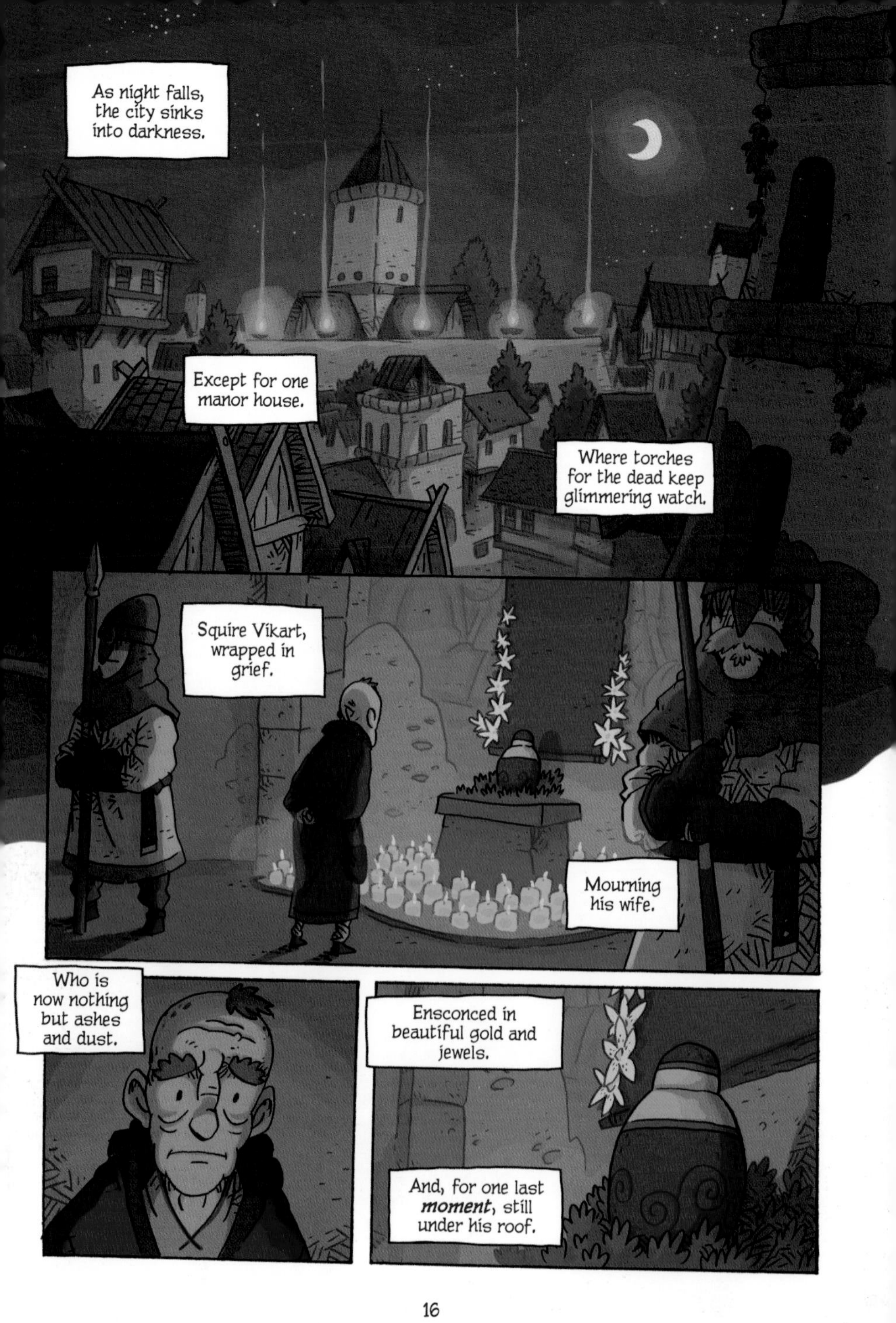

As night falls, the city sinks into darkness.
Except for one manor house.
Where torches for the dead keep glimmering watch.
Squire Vikart, wrapped in grief.
Mourning his wife.
Who is now nothing but ashes and dust.
Ensconced in beautiful gold and jewels.
And, for one last ***moment***, still under his roof.

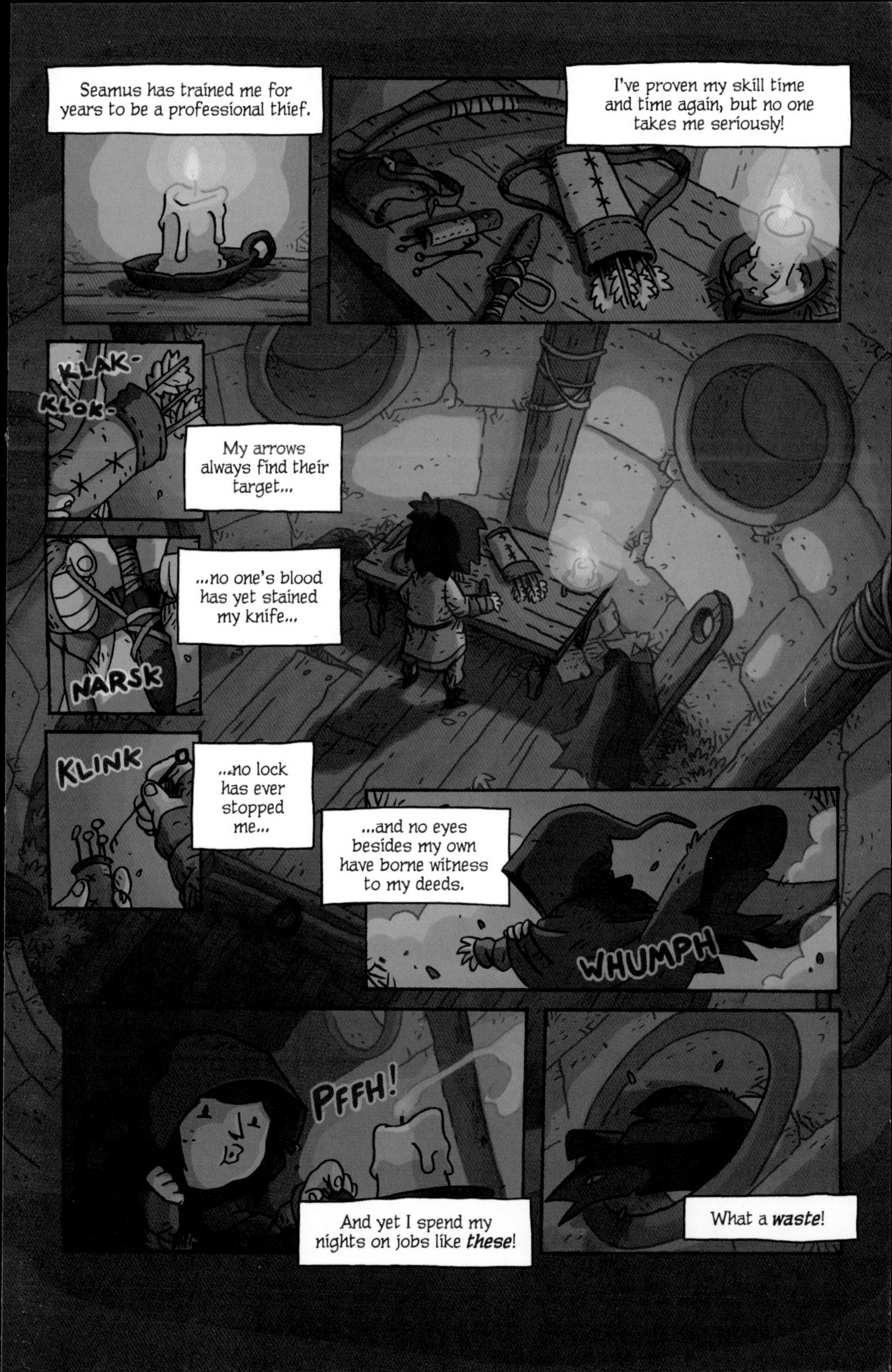
Seamus has trained me for years to be a professional thief.
I've proven my skill time and time again, but no one takes me seriously!
KLAK-KLOK-
My arrows always find their target...
...no one's blood has yet stained my knife...
NARSK
KLINK
...no lock has ever stopped me...
...and no eyes besides my own have borne witness to my deeds.
WHUMPH
PFFH!
And yet I spend my nights on jobs like *these*!
What a *waste*!

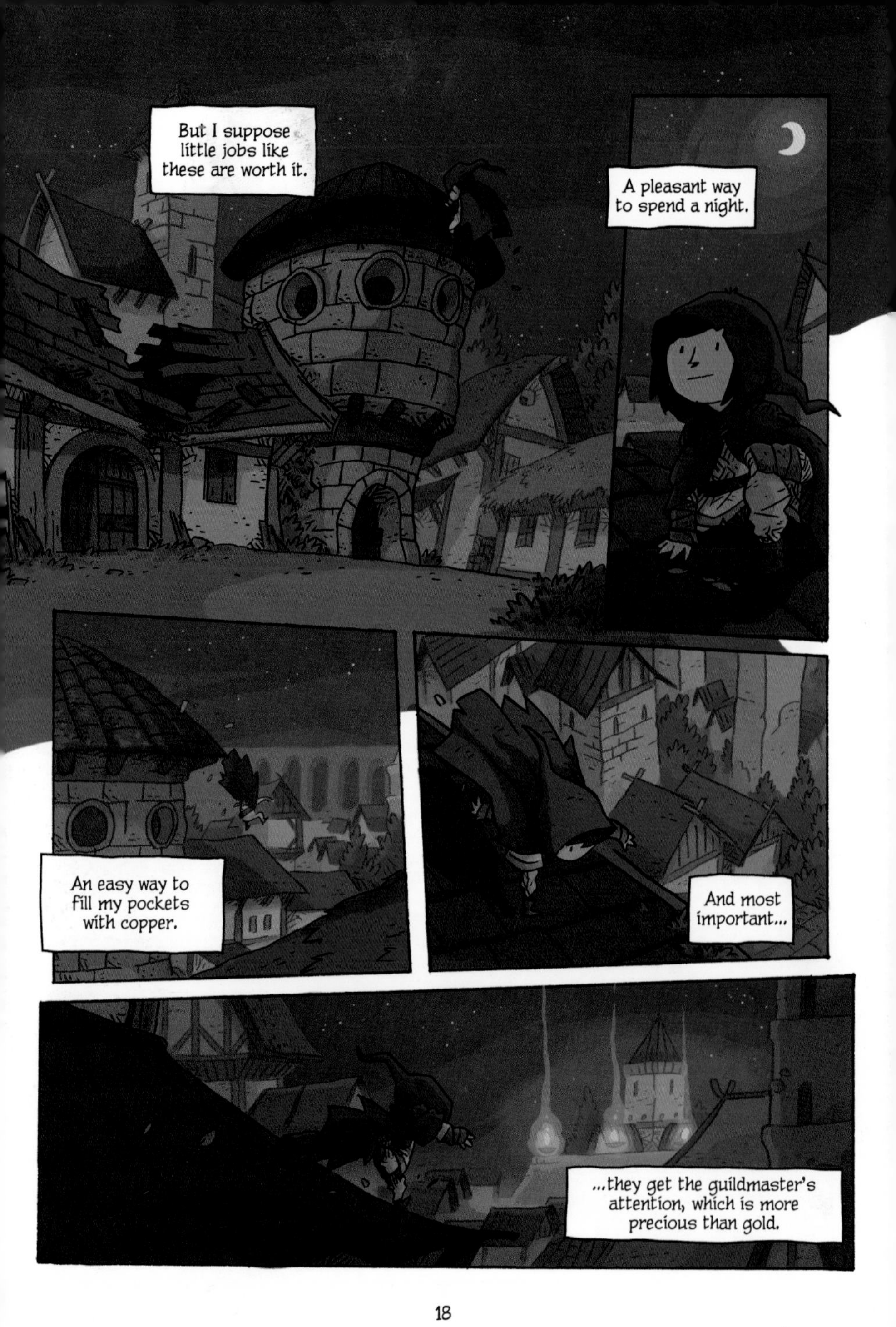
But I suppose little jobs like these are worth it.
A pleasant way to spend a night.
An easy way to fill my pockets with copper.
And most important...
...they get the guildmaster's attention, which is more precious than gold.

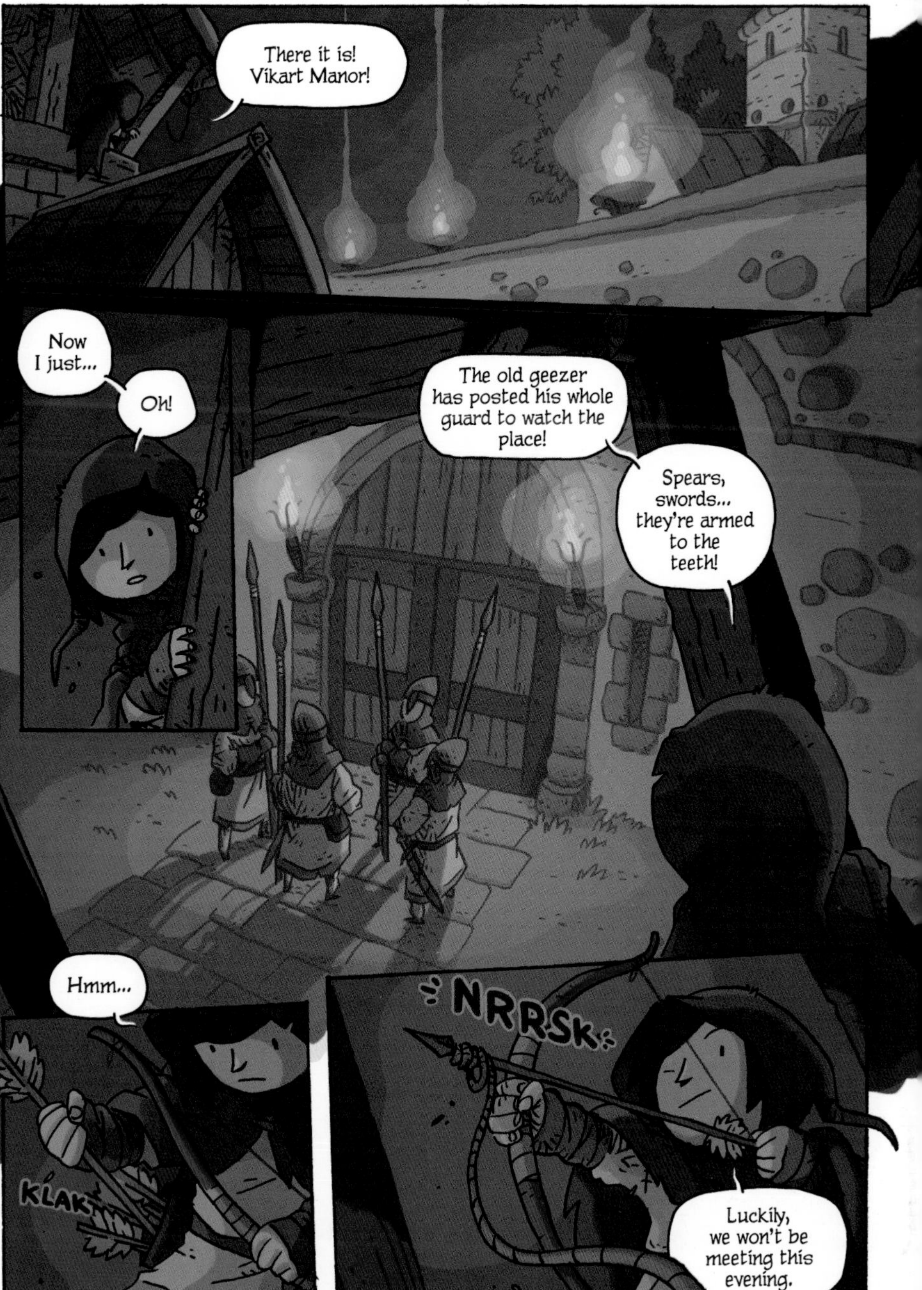
There it is! Vikart Manor!
Now I just...
Oh!
The old geezer has posted his whole guard to watch the place!
Spears, swords... they're armed to the teeth!
Hmm...
KLAK
NRRSK
Luckily, we won't be meeting this evening.

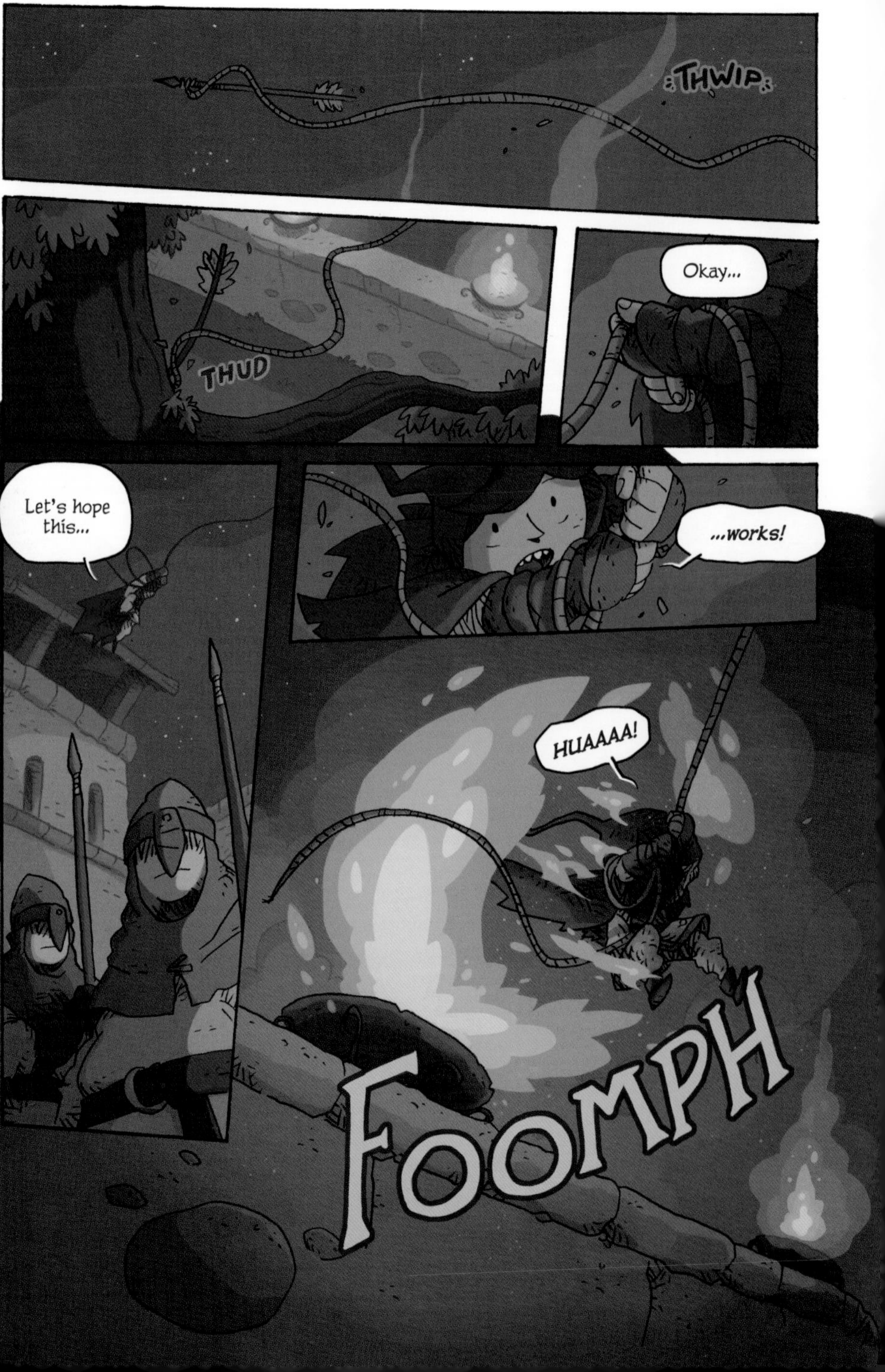
THWIP
THUD
Okay...
Let's hope this...
...works!
HUAAAA!
FOOMPH

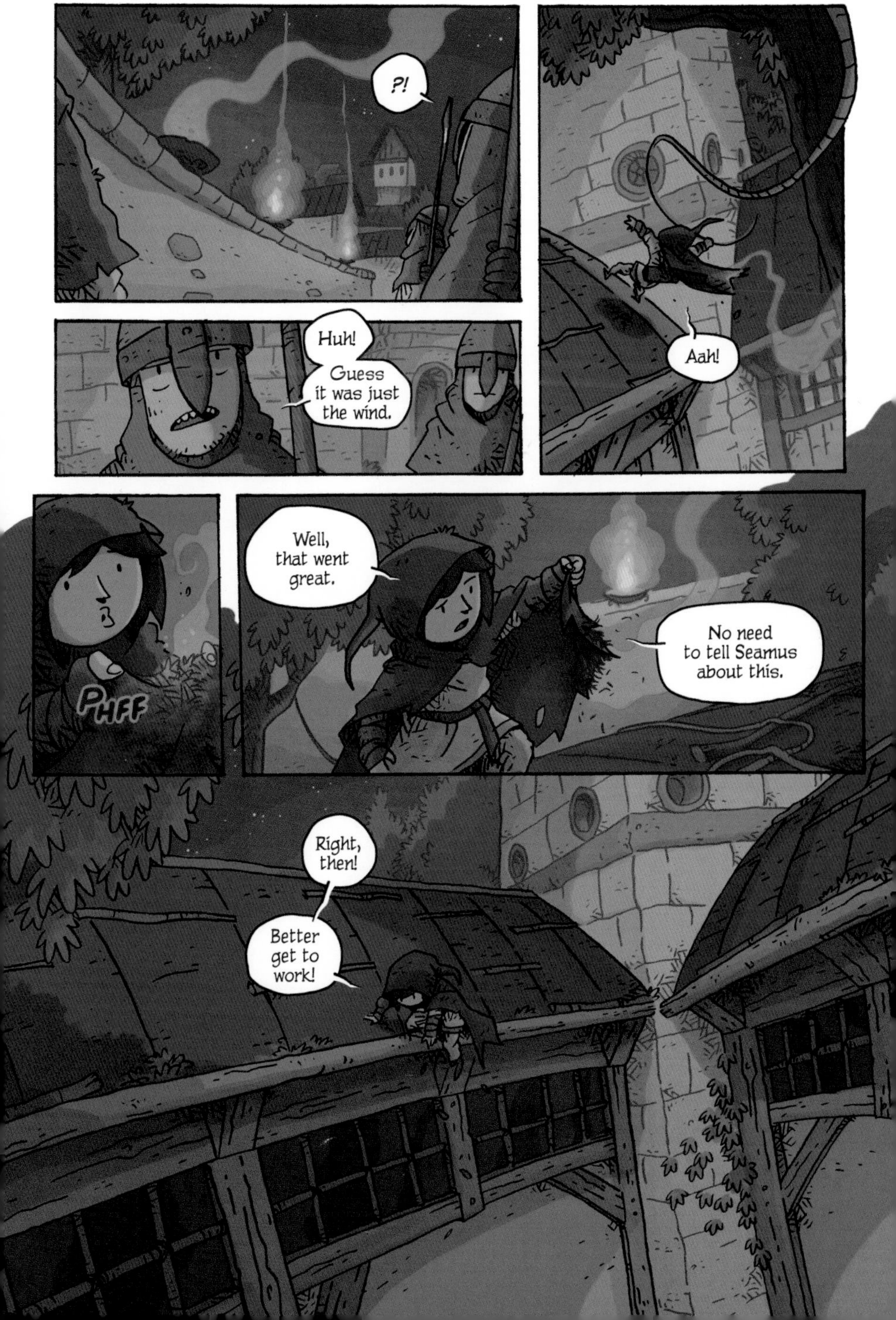
?!
Huh!
Guess it was just the wind.
Aah!
PHFF
Well, that went great.
No need to tell Seamus about this.
Right, then!
Better get to work!

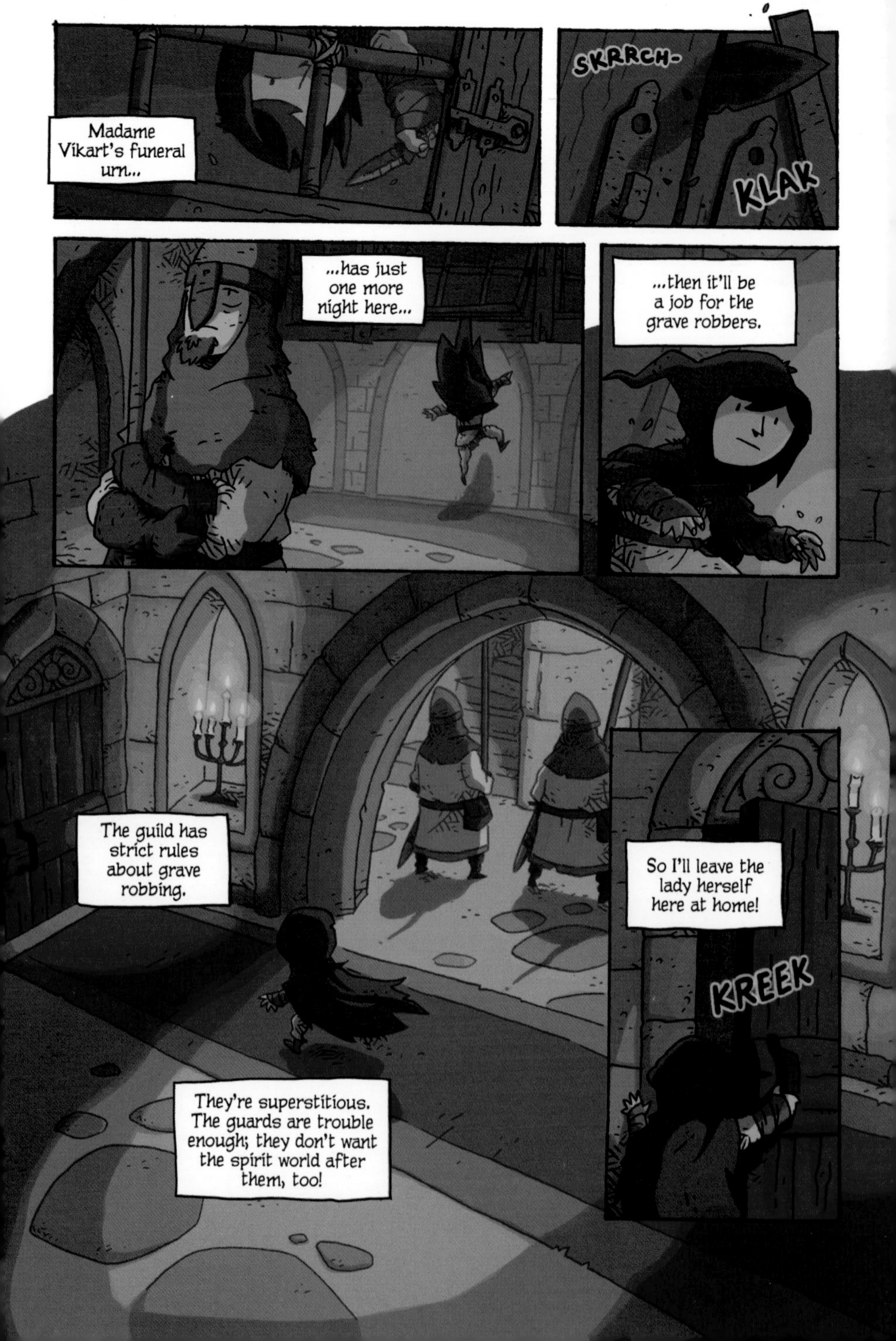
Madame Vikart's funeral urn...
SKRRCH-
KLAK
...has just one more night here...
...then it'll be a job for the grave robbers.
The guild has strict rules about grave robbing.
They're superstitious. The guards are trouble enough; they don't want the spirit world after them, too!
So I'll leave the lady herself here at home!
KREEK

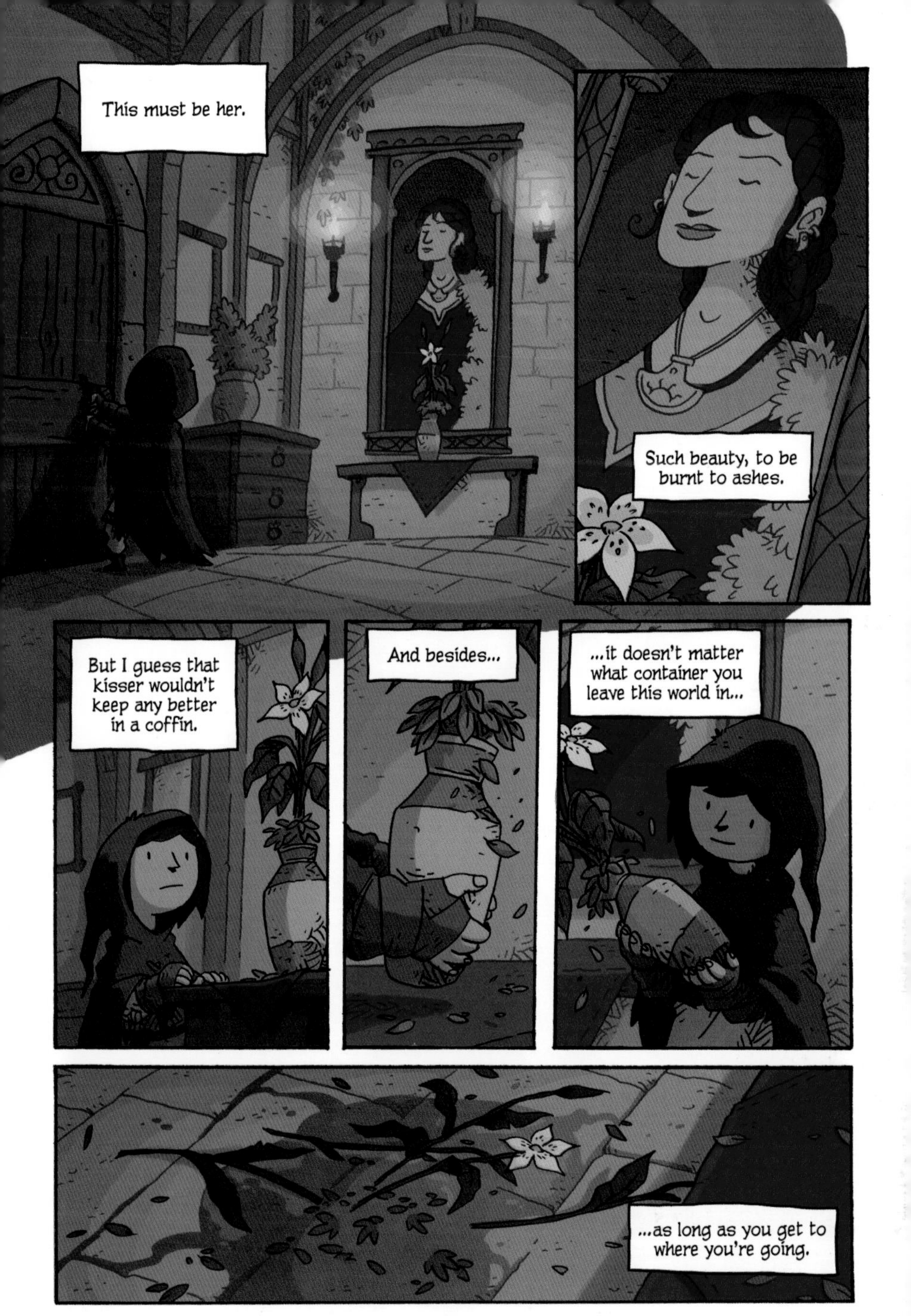
This must be her.
Such beauty, to be burnt to ashes.
But I guess that kisser wouldn't keep any better in a coffin.
And besides...
...it doesn't matter what container you leave this world in...
...as long as you get to where you're going.

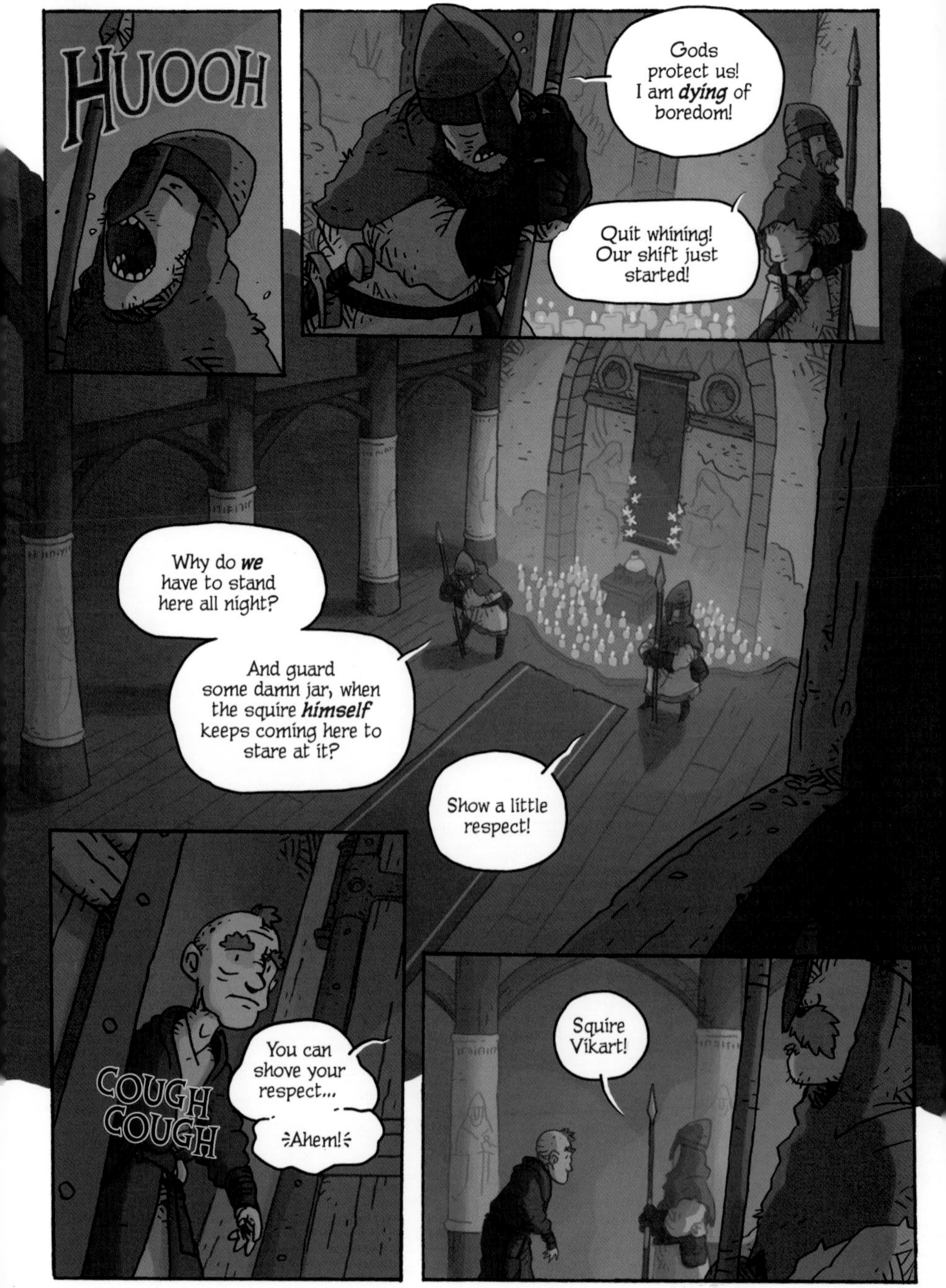
HUOOH
Gods protect us! I am *dying* of boredom!
Quit whining! Our shift just started!
Why do *we* have to stand here all night?
And guard some damn jar, when the squire *himself* keeps coming here to stare at it?
Show a little respect!
COUGH COUGH
You can shove your respect...
Ahem!
Squire Vikart!

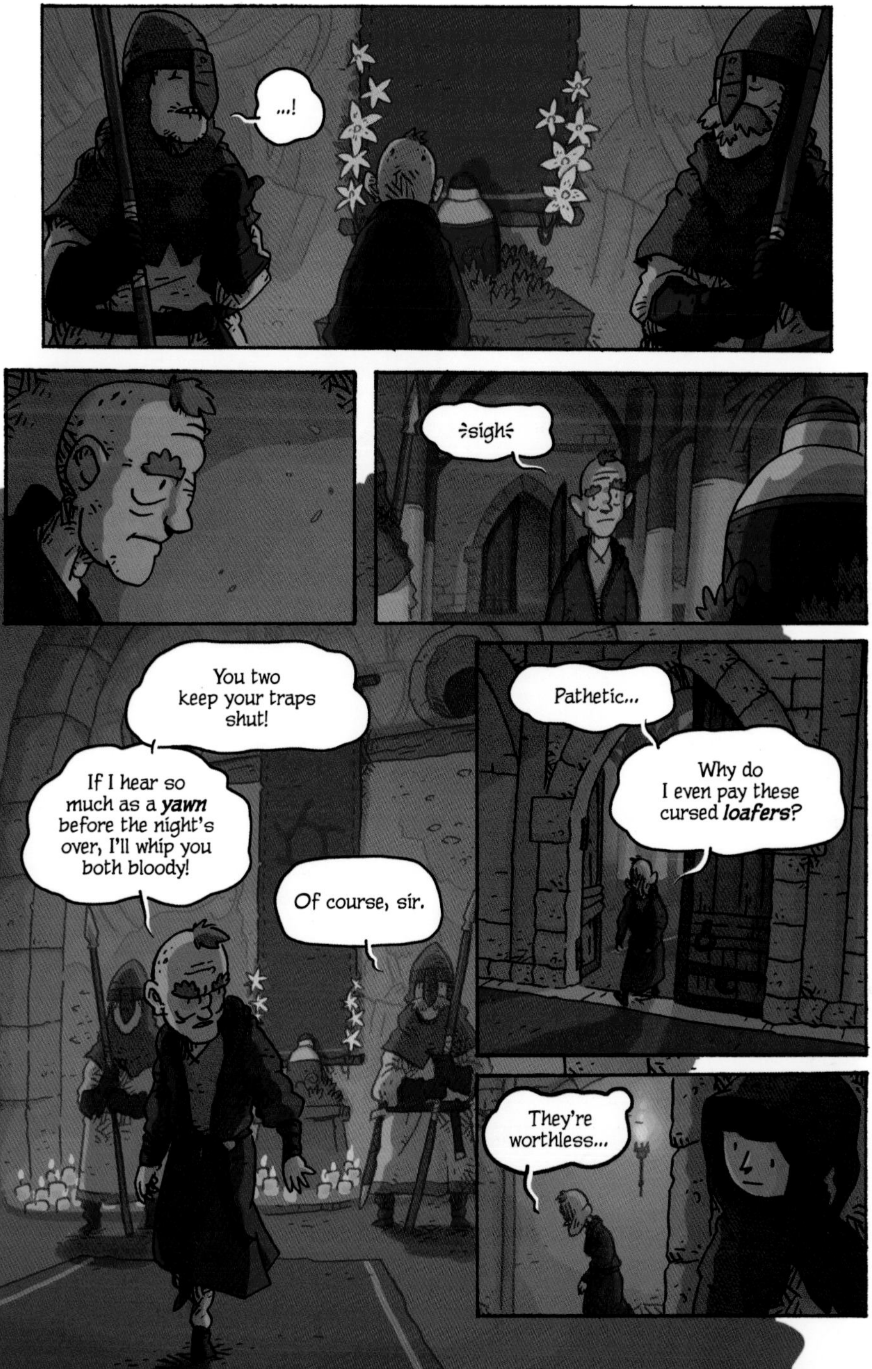
...!
⇍sigh⇏
You two keep your traps shut!
If I hear so much as a *yawn* before the night's over, I'll whip you both bloody!
Of course, sir.
Pathetic...
Why do I even pay these cursed *loafers*?
They're worthless...

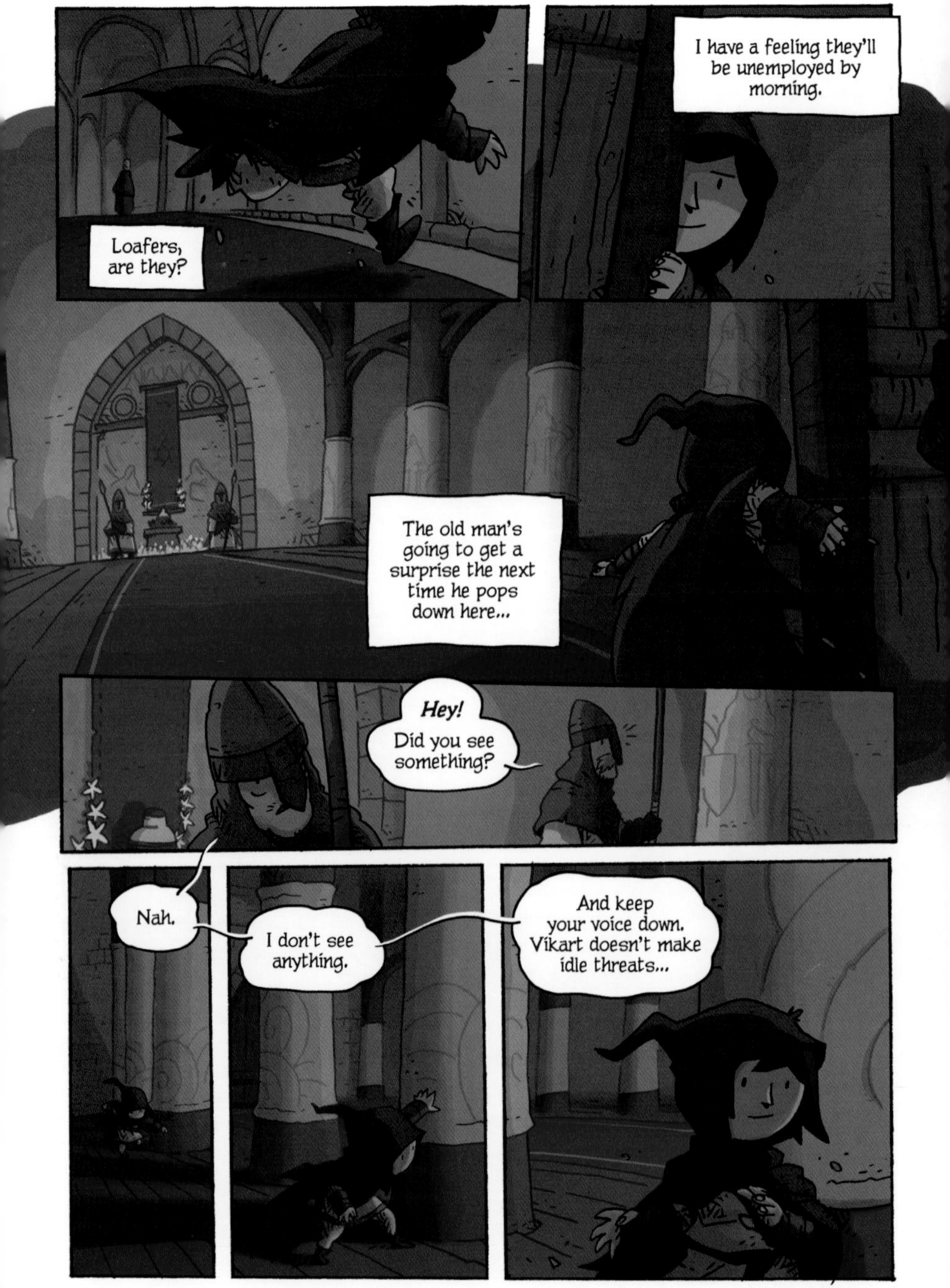
Loafers, are they?
I have a feeling they'll be unemployed by morning.
The old man's going to get a surprise the next time he pops down here...
Hey! Did you see something?
Nah.
I don't see anything.
And keep your voice down. Vikart doesn't make idle threats...

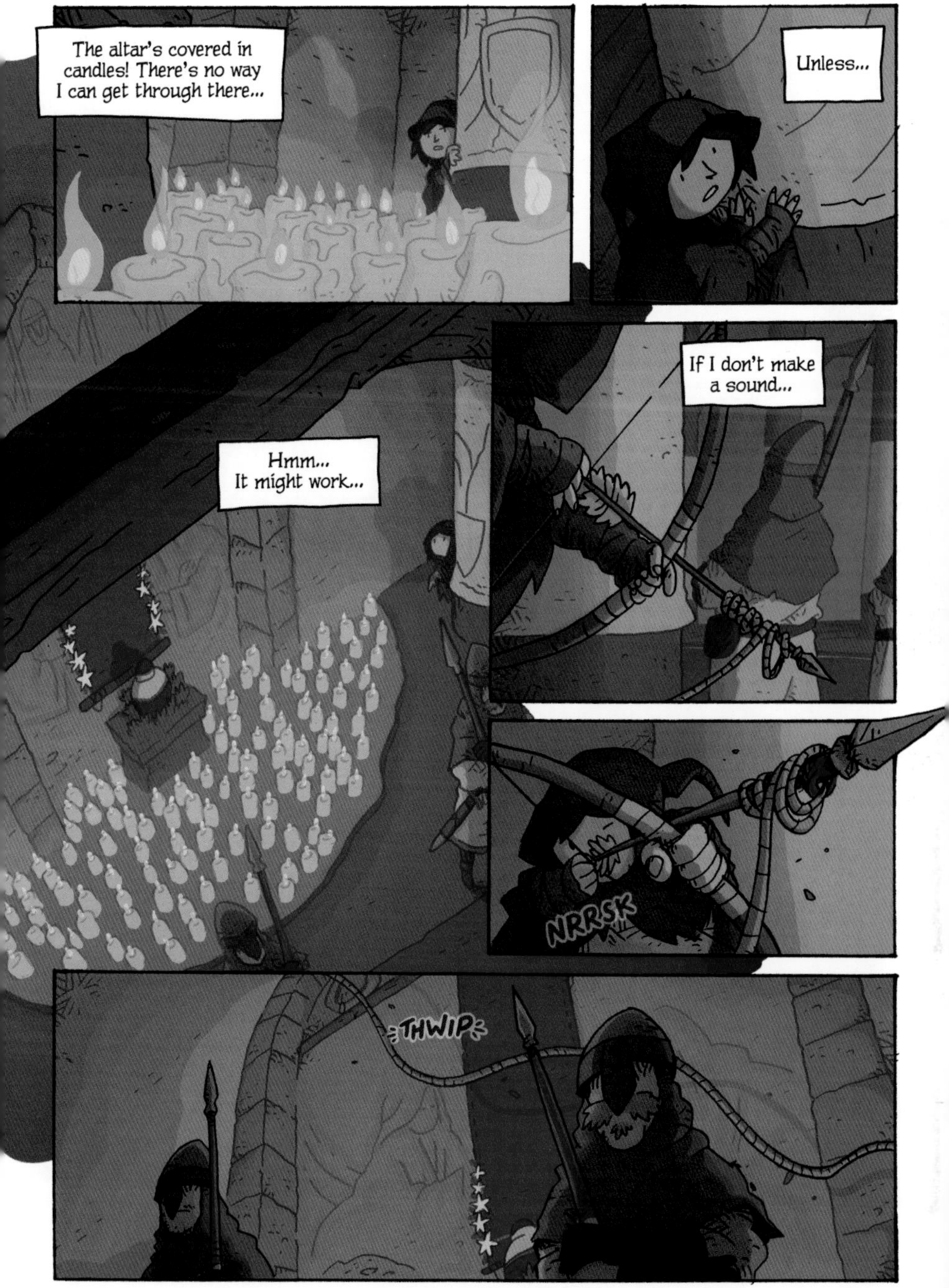
The altar's covered in candles! There's no way I can get through there...
Unless...
Hmm... It might work...
If I don't make a sound...
NRRSK
THWIP

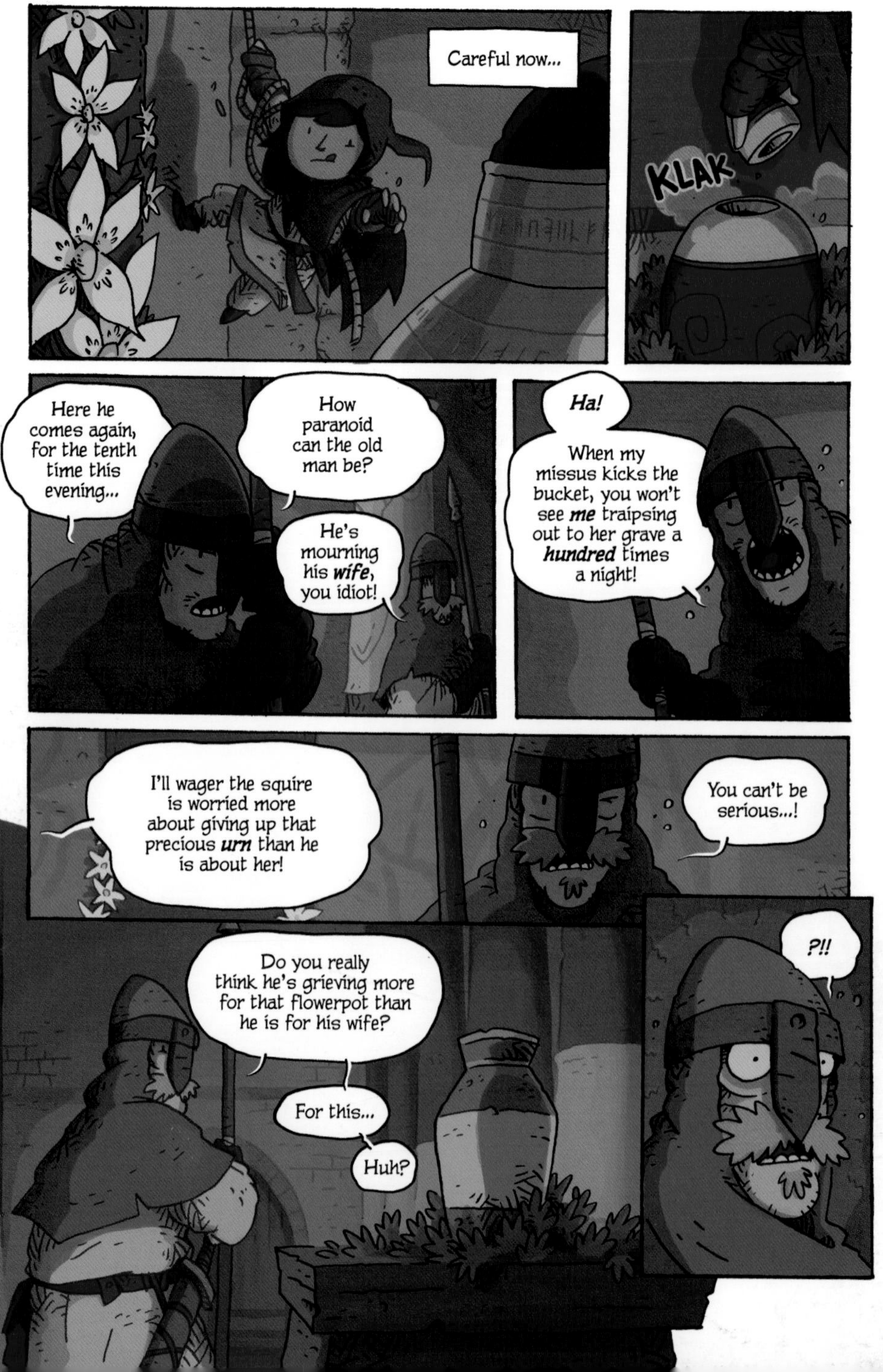
Careful now...
KLAK
Here he comes again, for the tenth time this evening...
How paranoid can the old man be?
He's mourning his *wife*, you idiot!
Ha!
When my missus kicks the bucket, you won't see *me* traipsing out to her grave a *hundred* times a night!
I'll wager the squire is worried more about giving up that precious *urn* than he is about her!
You can't be serious...!
Do you really think he's grieving more for that flowerpot than he is for his wife?
For this...
Huh?
?!!

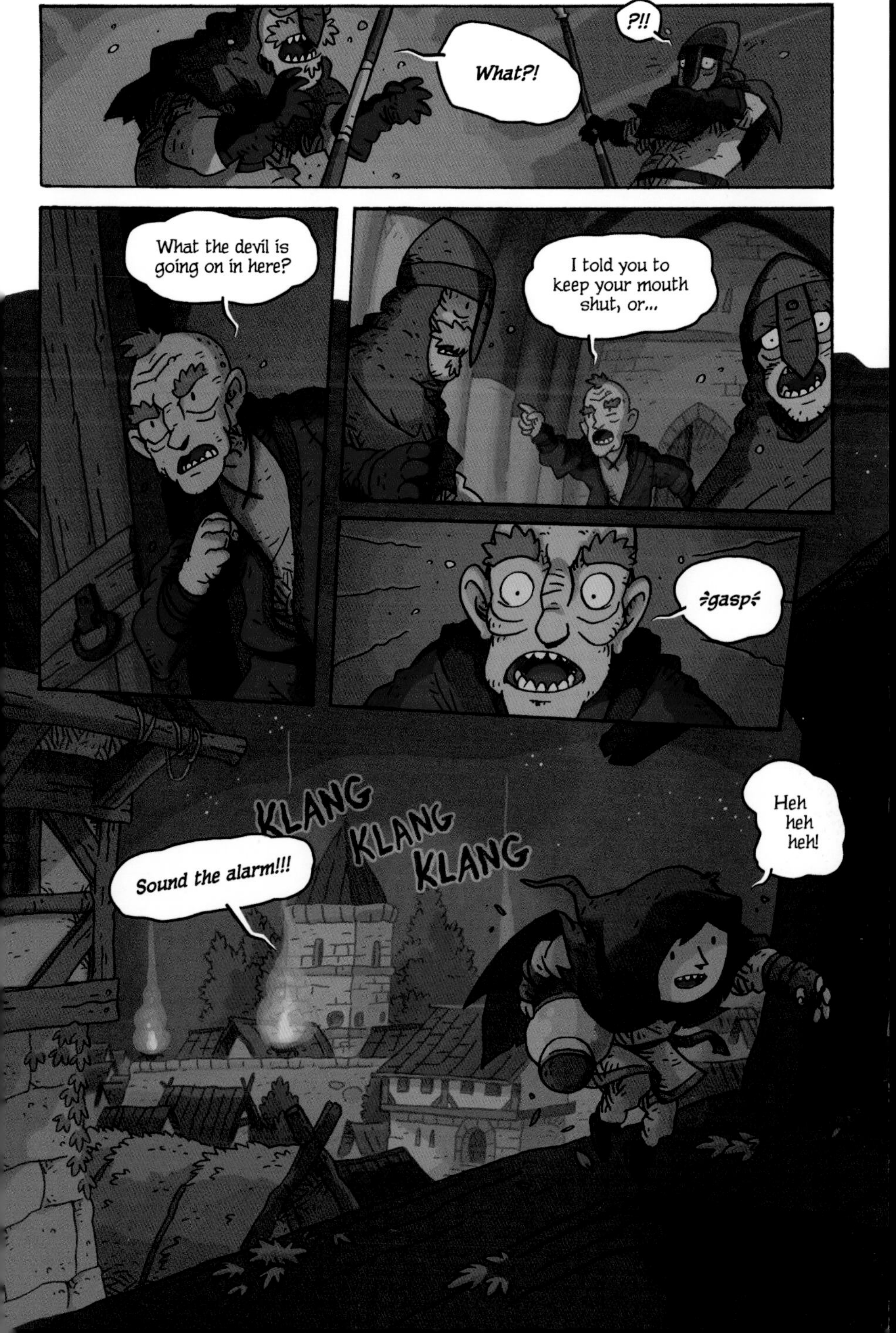
What?!
?!!
What the devil is going on in here?
I told you to keep your mouth shut, or...
gasp
KLANG
KLANG
KLANG
Sound the alarm!!!
Heh heh heh!

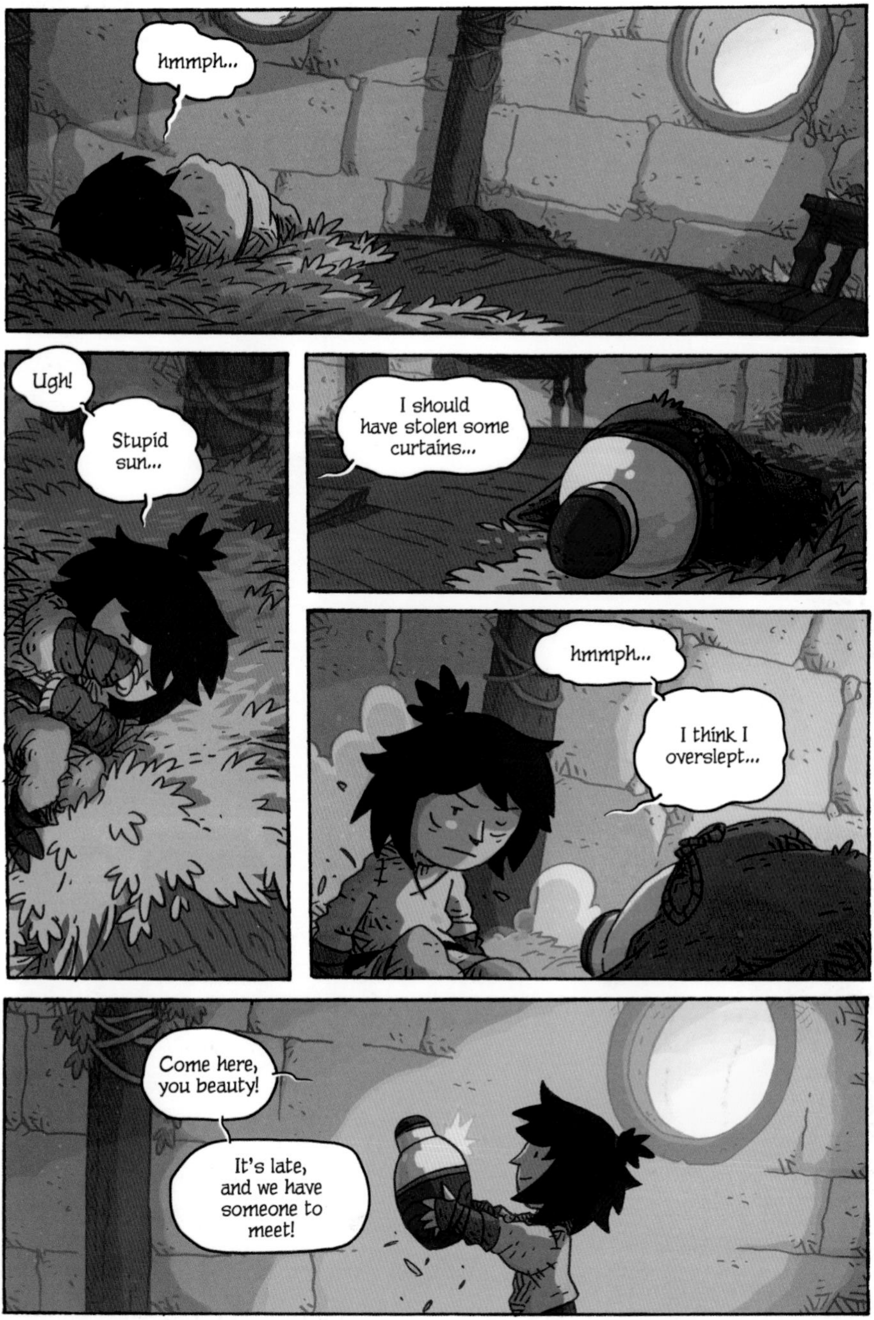
hmmph...
Ugh!
Stupid sun...
I should have stolen some curtains...
hmmph...
I think I overslept...
Come here, you beauty!
It's late, and we have someone to meet!

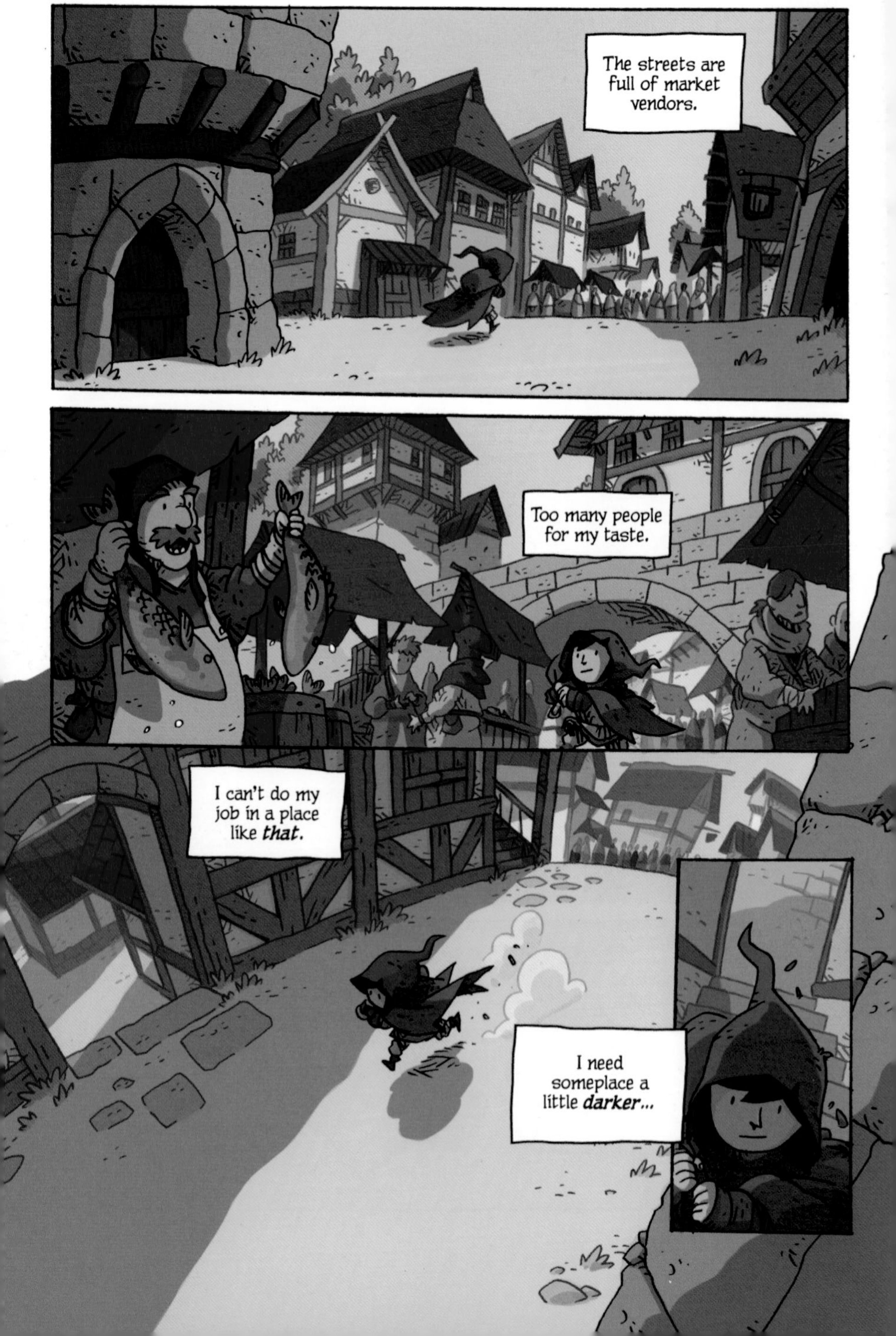
The streets are full of market vendors.
Too many people for my taste.
I can't do my job in a place like ***that***.
I need someplace a little ***darker***...

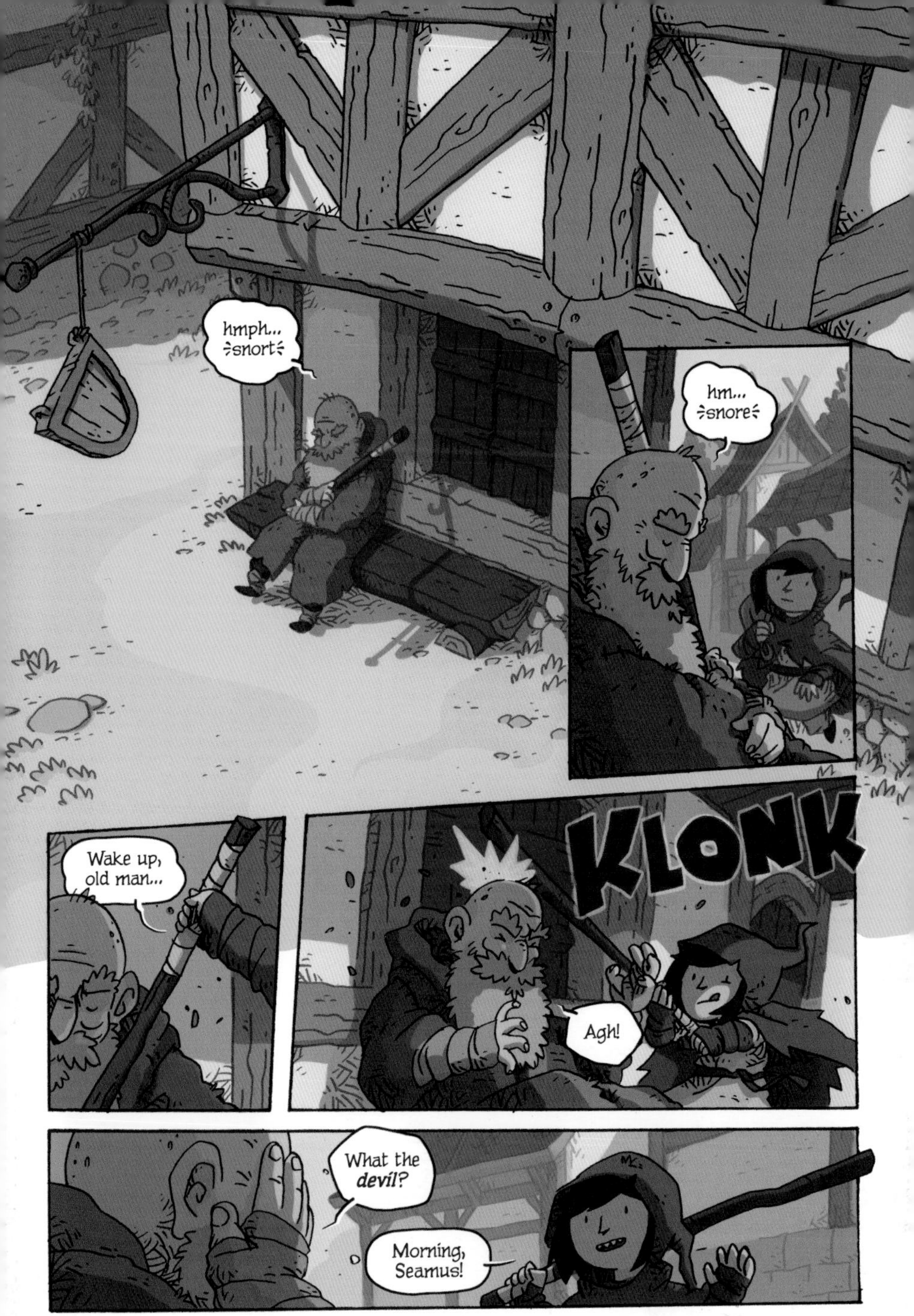
hmph... snort
hm... snore
Wake up, old man...
KLONK
Agh!
What the *devil*?
Morning, Seamus!

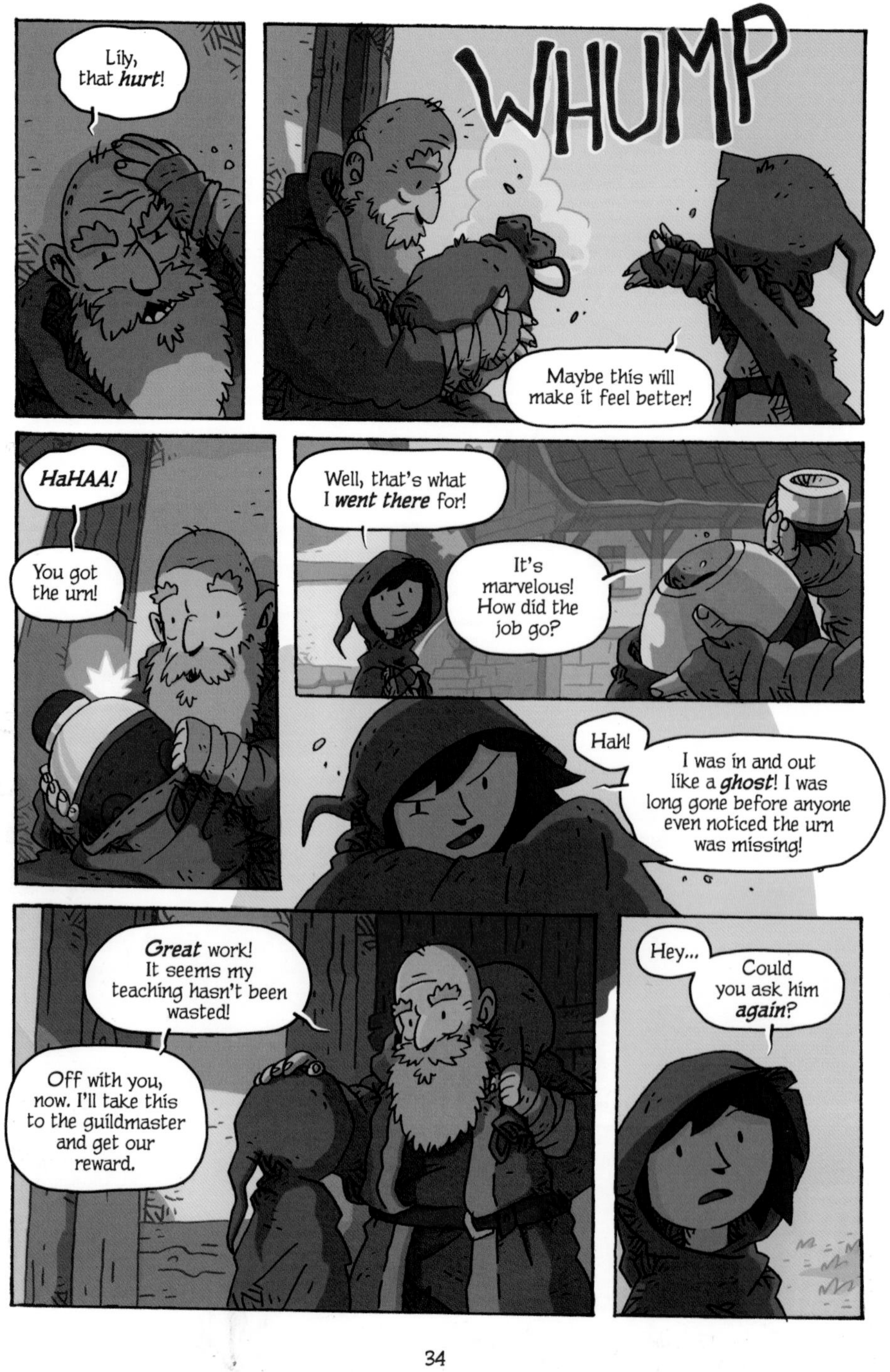
Lily, that **hurt**!
WHUMP
Maybe this will make it feel better!
HaHAA!
You got the urn!
Well, that's what I **went there** for!
It's marvelous! How did the job go?
Hah!
I was in and out like a **ghost**! I was long gone before anyone even noticed the urn was missing!
Great work! It seems my teaching hasn't been wasted!
Off with you, now. I'll take this to the guildmaster and get our reward.
Hey...
Could you ask him **again**?

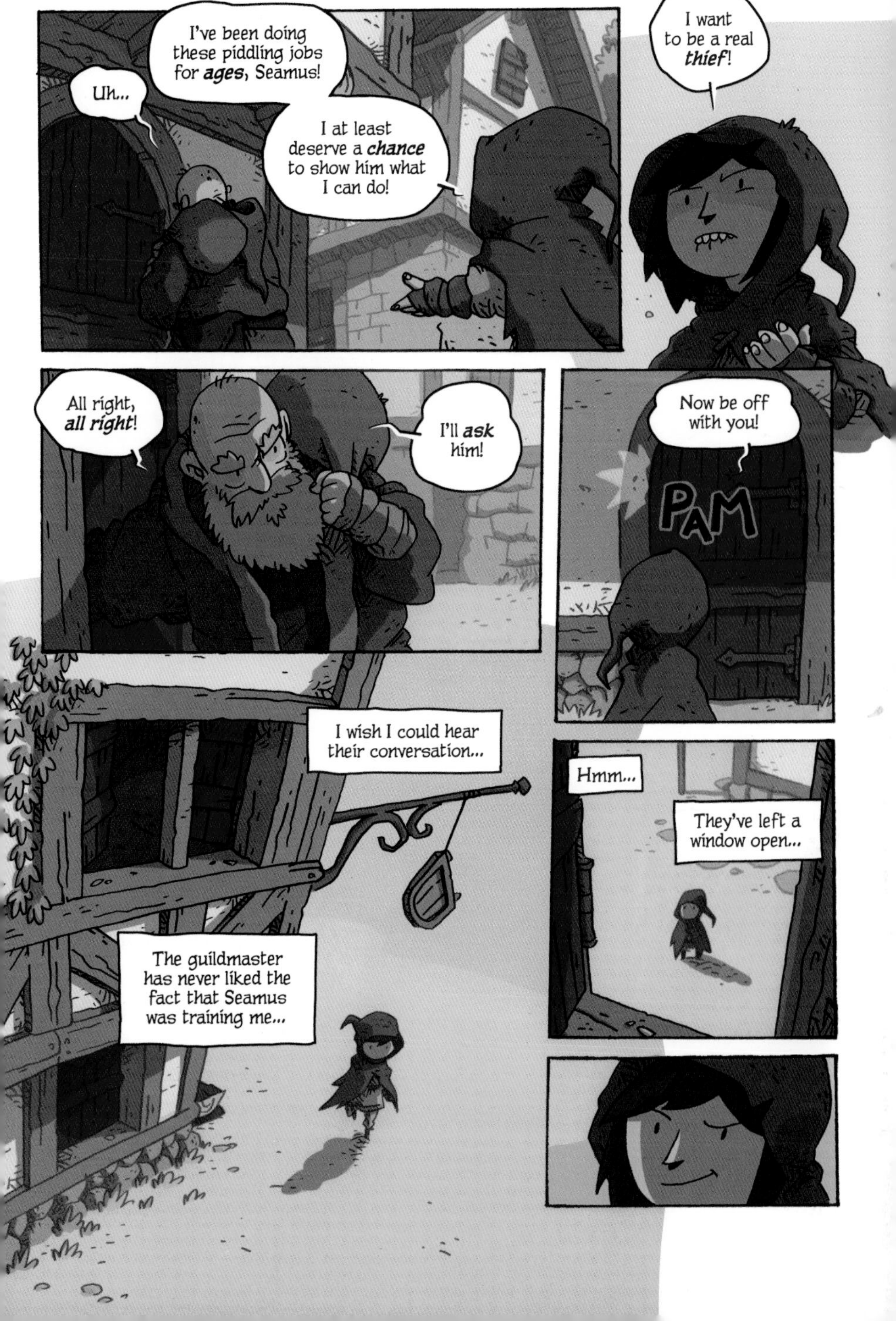
Uh...
I've been doing these piddling jobs for ***ages***, Seamus!
I at least deserve a ***chance*** to show him what I can do!
I want to be a real ***thief***!
All right, ***all right***!
I'll ***ask*** him!
Now be off with you!
PAM
I wish I could hear their conversation...
The guildmaster has never liked the fact that Seamus was training me...
Hmm...
They've left a window open...

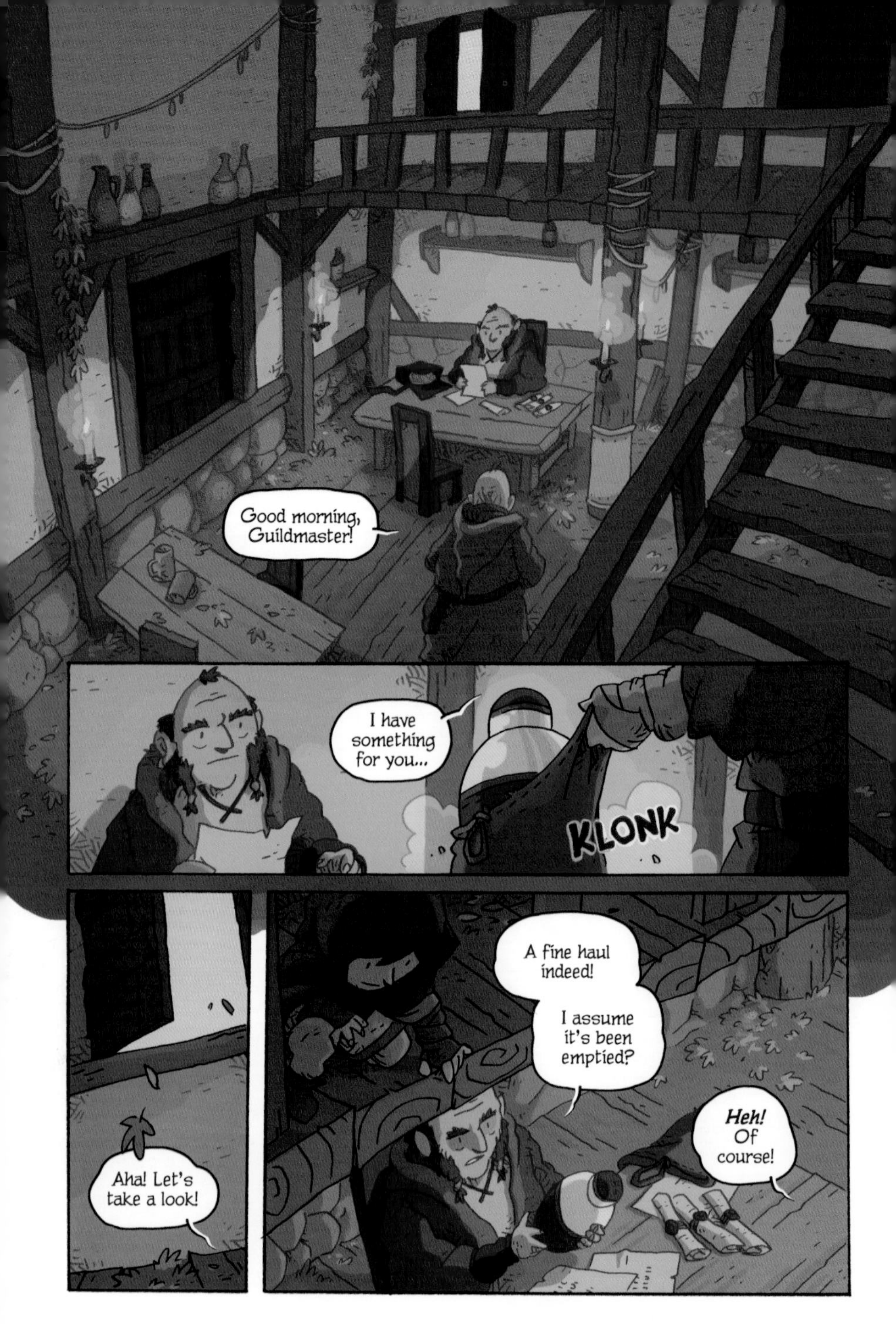
Good morning, Guildmaster!
I have something for you...
KLONK
A fine haul indeed!
I assume it's been emptied?
Heh! Of course!
Aha! Let's take a look!

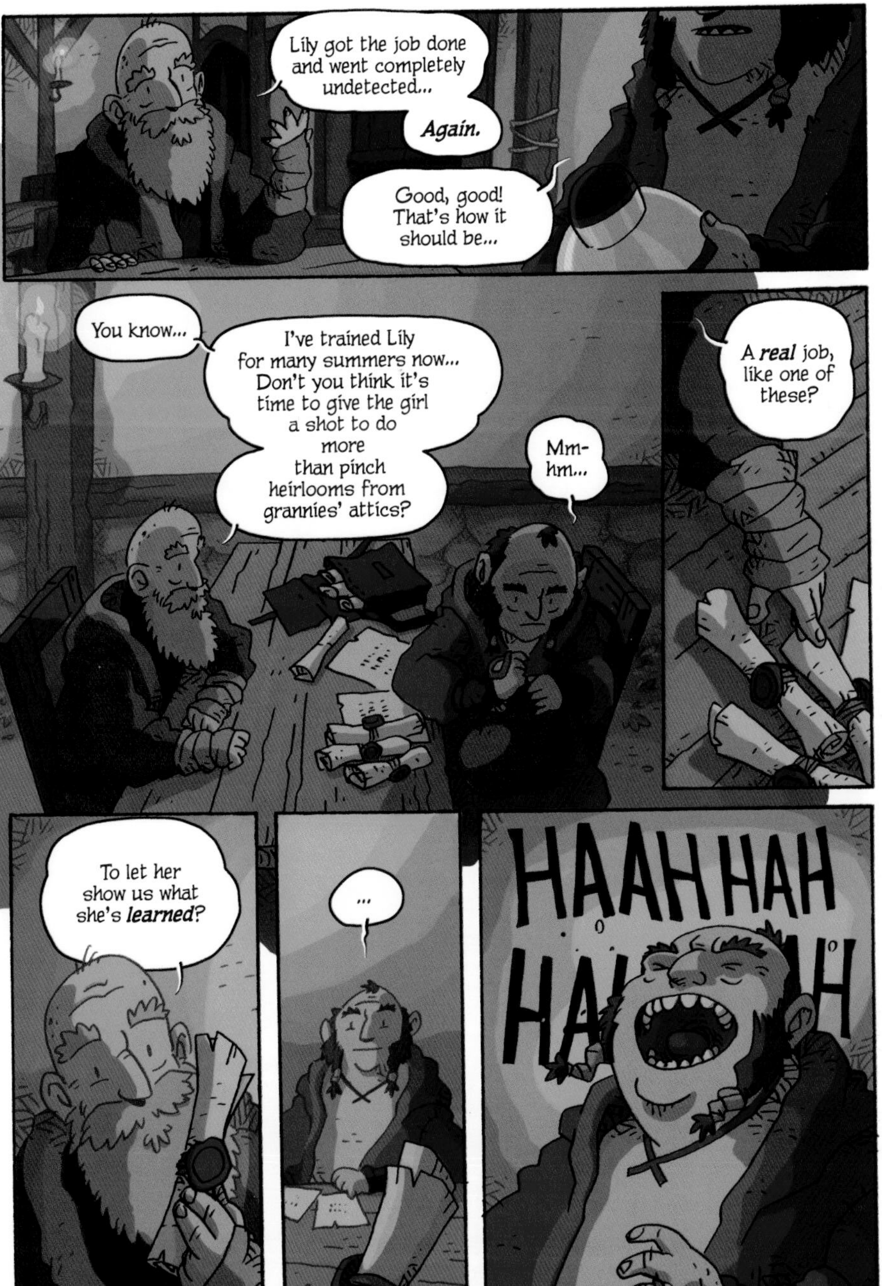
Lily got the job done and went completely undetected...
Again.
Good, good! That's how it should be...
You know...
I've trained Lily for many summers now... Don't you think it's time to give the girl a shot to do more than pinch heirlooms from grannies' attics?
Mm-hm...
A ***real*** job, like one of these?
To let her show us what she's ***learned***?
...
HAAHHAH
HA

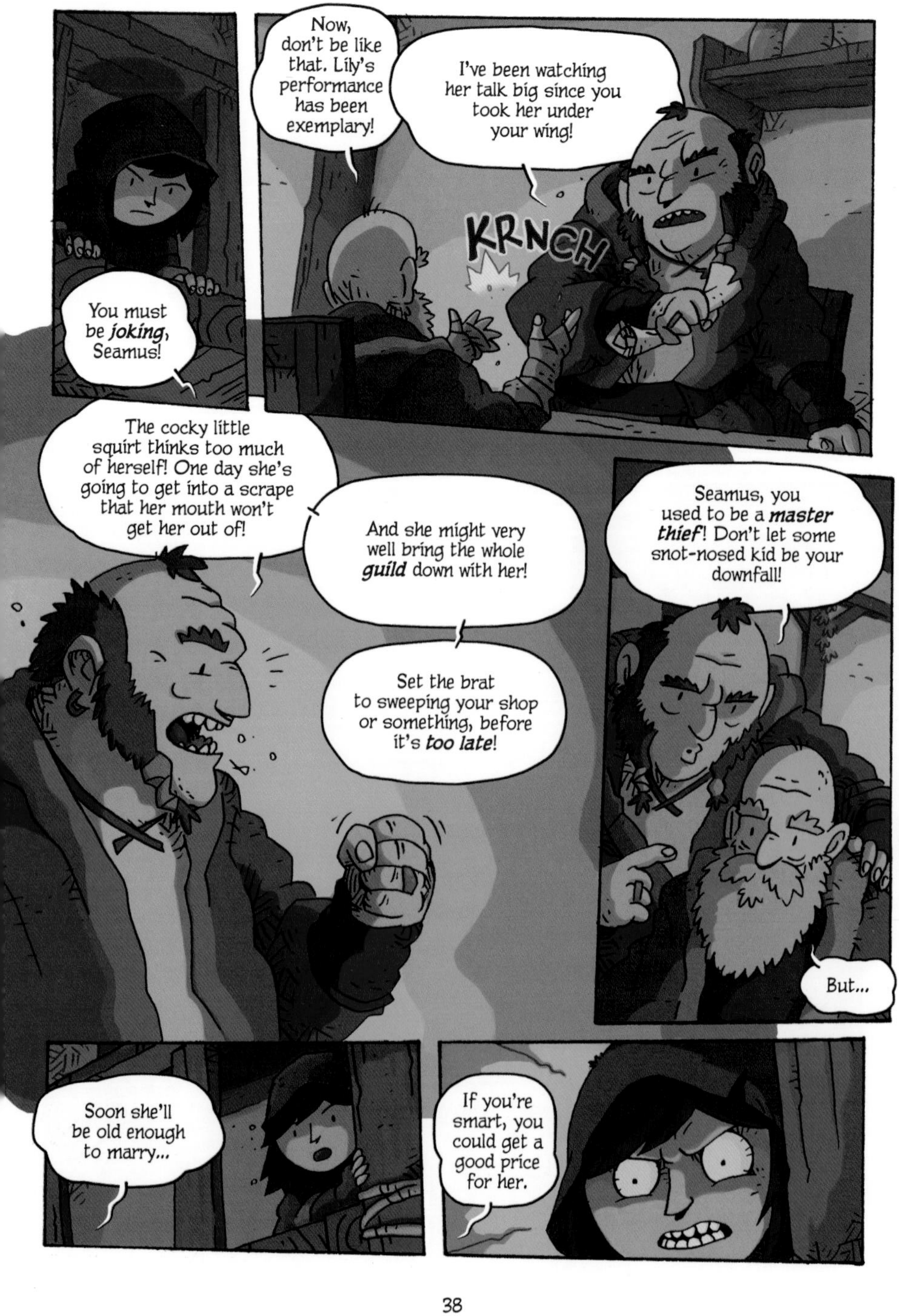
Now, don't be like that. Lily's performance has been exemplary!
I've been watching her talk big since you took her under your wing!
KRNCH
You must be *joking*, Seamus!
The cocky little squirt thinks too much of herself! One day she's going to get into a scrape that her mouth won't get her out of!
And she might very well bring the whole *guild* down with her!
Set the brat to sweeping your shop or something, before it's *too late*!
Seamus, you used to be a **master thief**! Don't let some snot-nosed kid be your downfall!
But...
Soon she'll be old enough to marry...
If you're smart, you could get a good price for her.

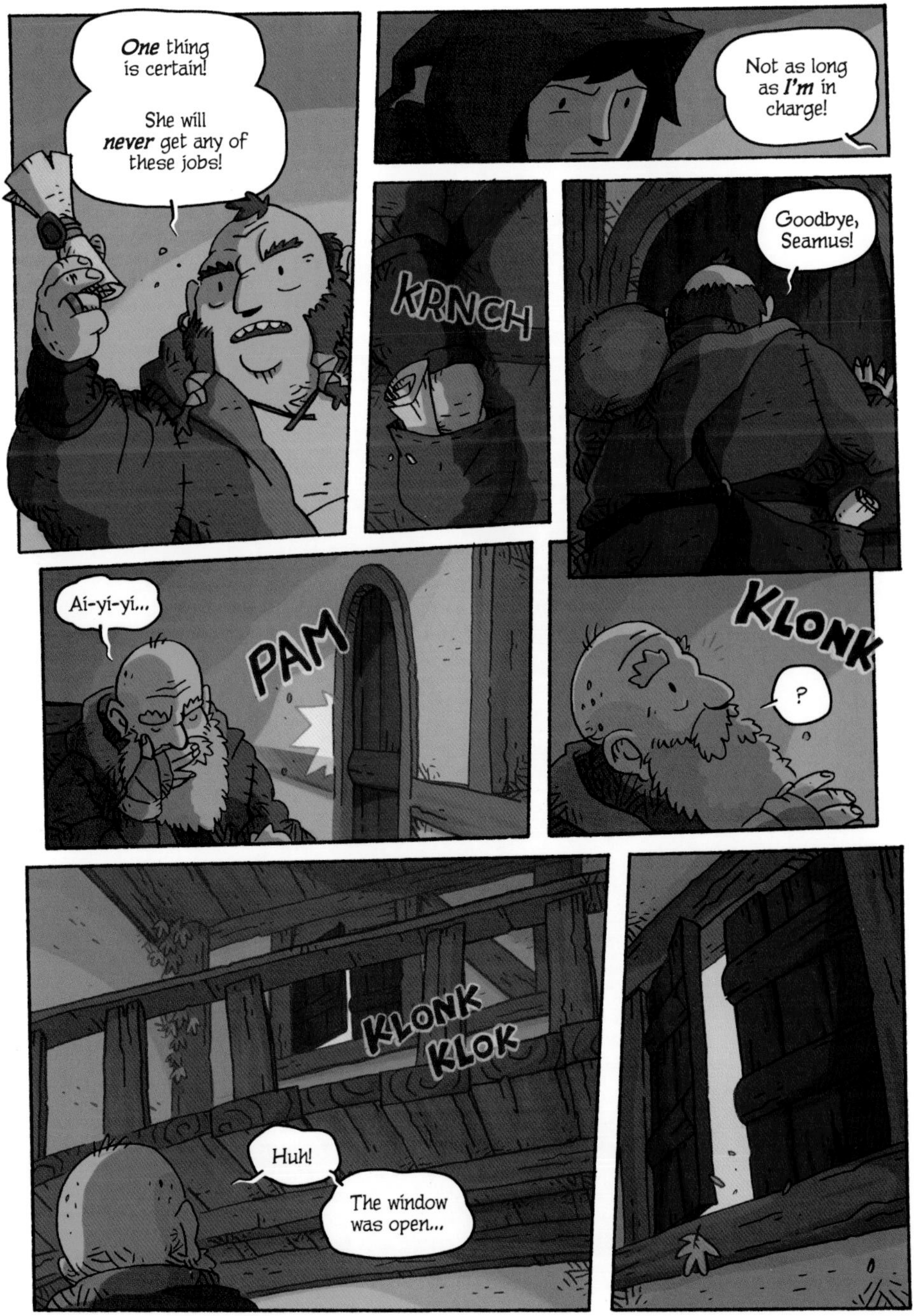
One thing is certain!
She will never get any of these jobs!
Not as long as I'm in charge!
KRNCH
Goodbye, Seamus!
Ai-yi-yi...
PAM
KLONK
?
KLONK
KLOK
Huh!
The window was open...

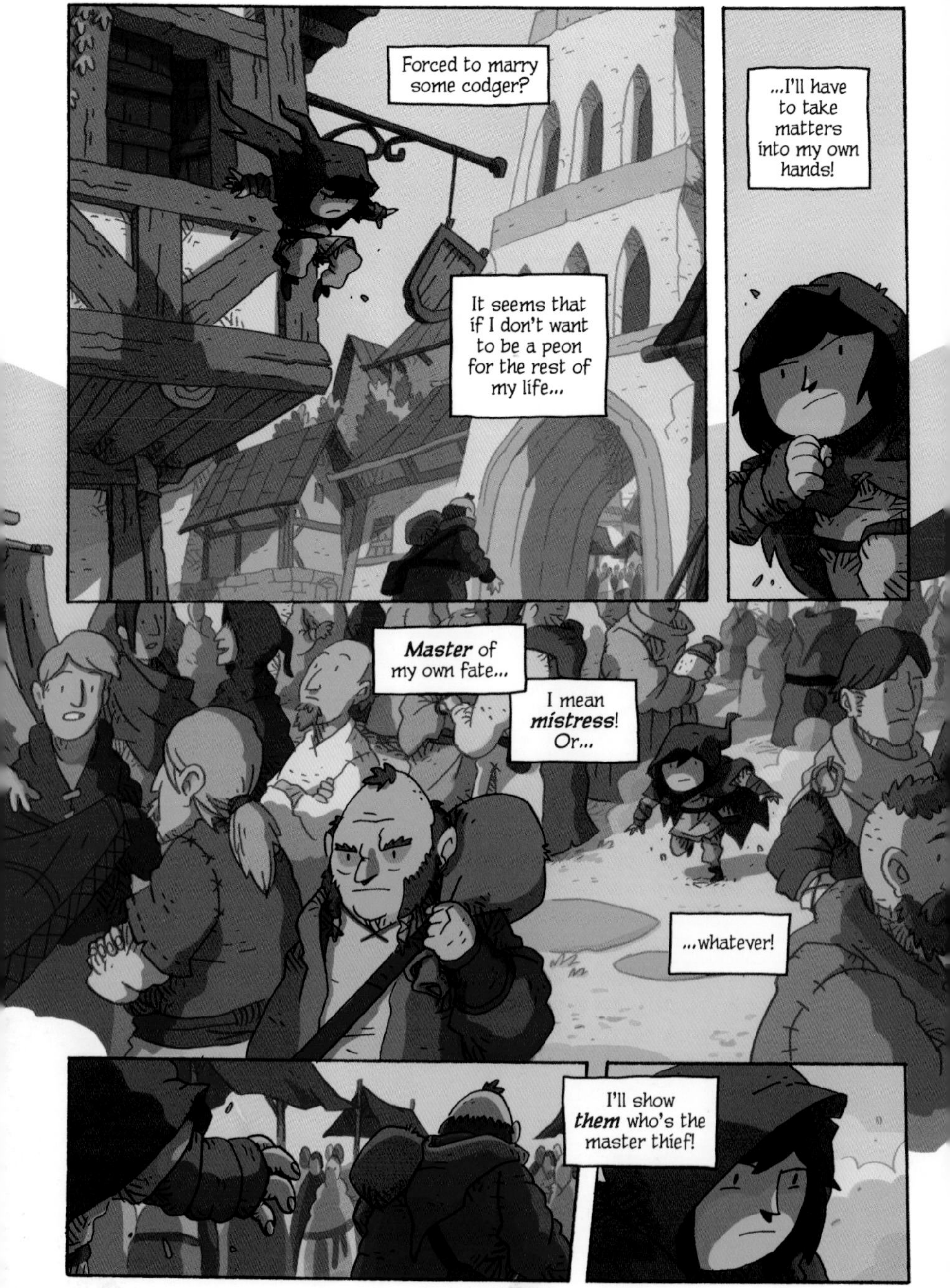
Forced to marry some codger?
It seems that if I don't want to be a peon for the rest of my life...
...I'll have to take matters into my own hands!
Master of my own fate...
I mean mistress! Or...
...whatever!
I'll show them who's the master thief!

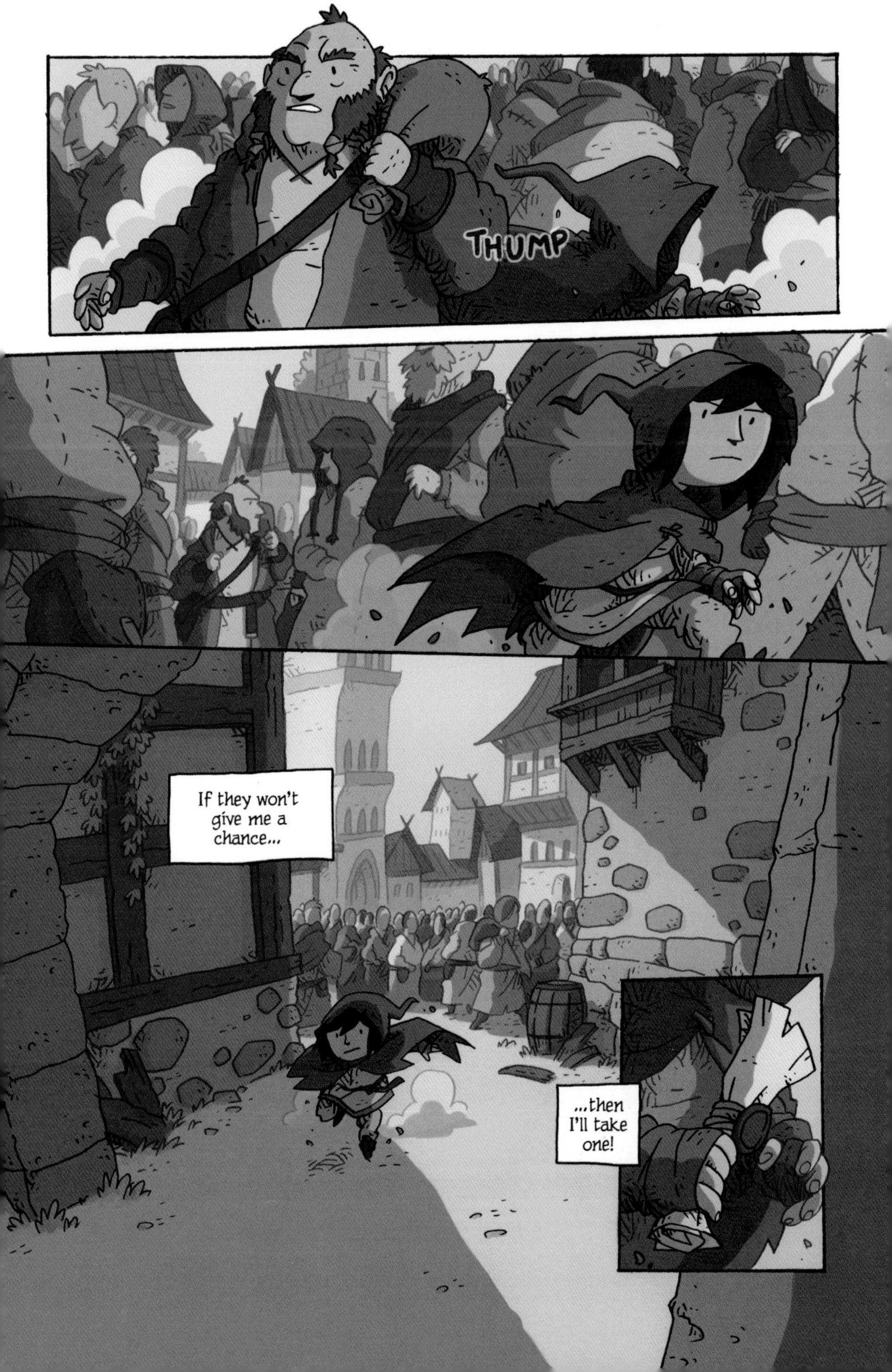
THUMP
If they won't give me a chance...
...then I'll take one!

Long ago three mighty kings,
Went down into the mines,
With jeweled cloaks upon
their backs,
And riches of every kind.

2

The Relic

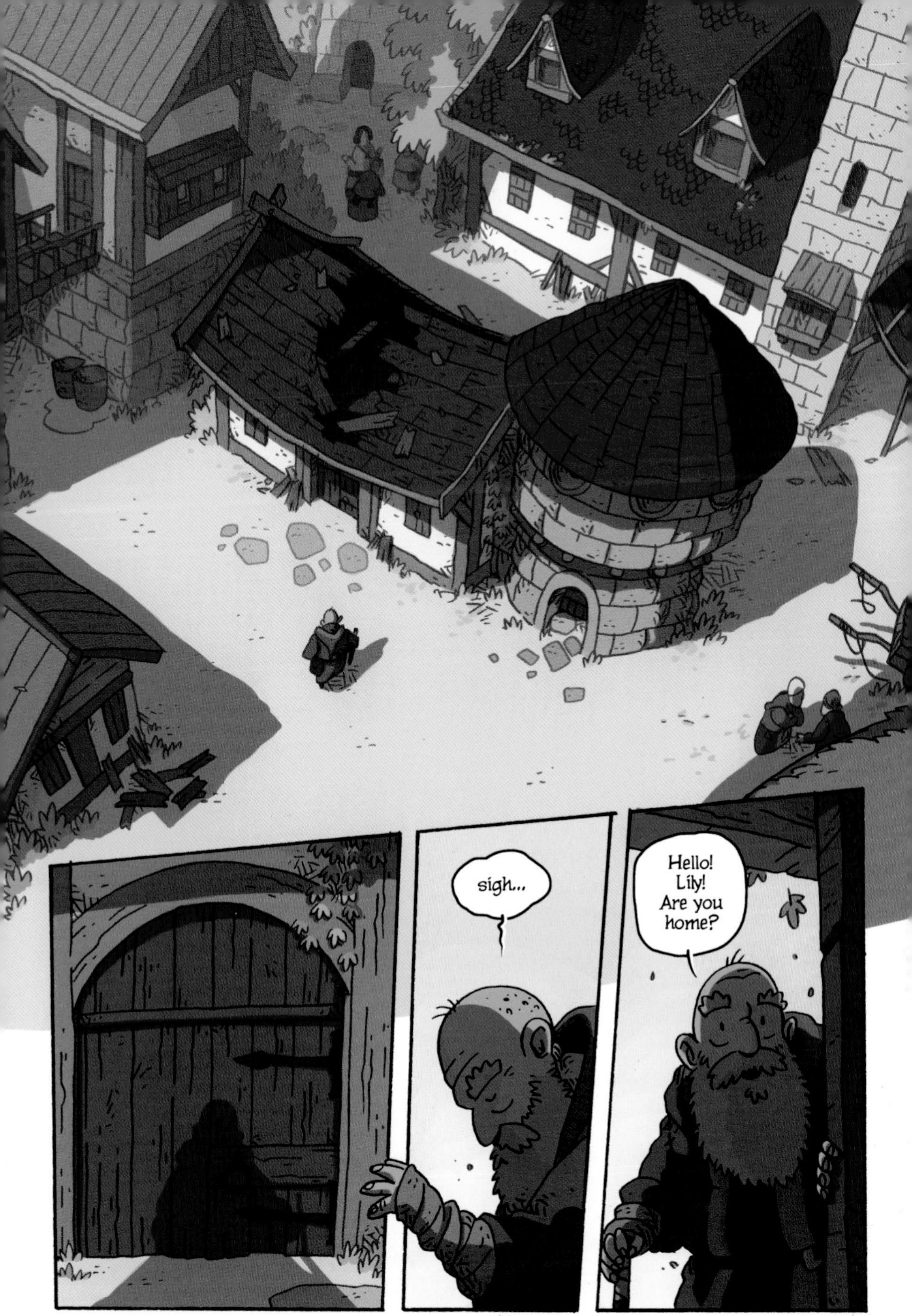
sigh...
Hello! Lily! Are you home?

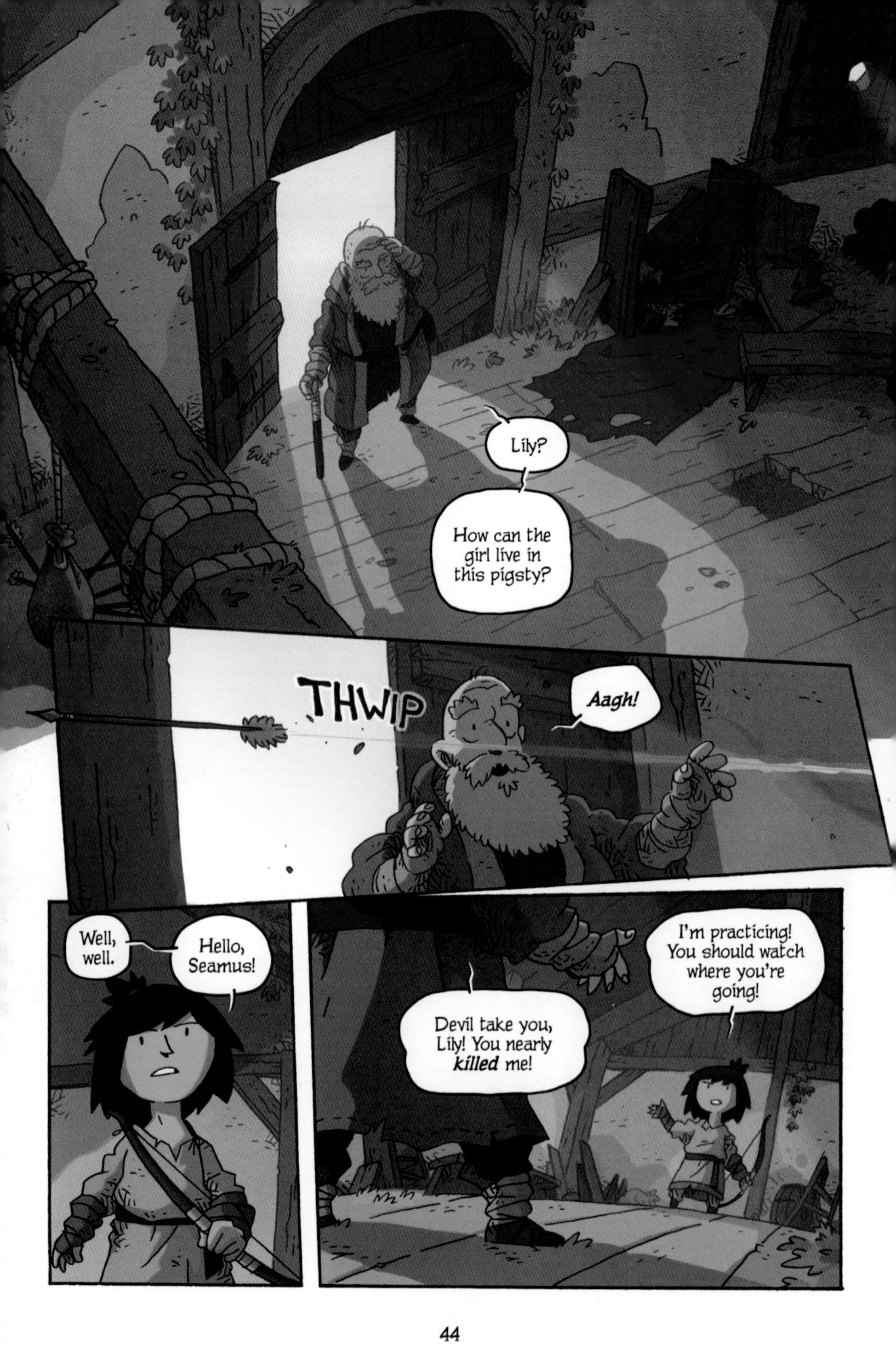

Lily?
How can the girl live in this pigsty?
THWIP
Aagh!
Well, well.
Hello, Seamus!
Devil take you, Lily! You nearly ***killed*** me!
I'm practicing! You should watch where you're going!

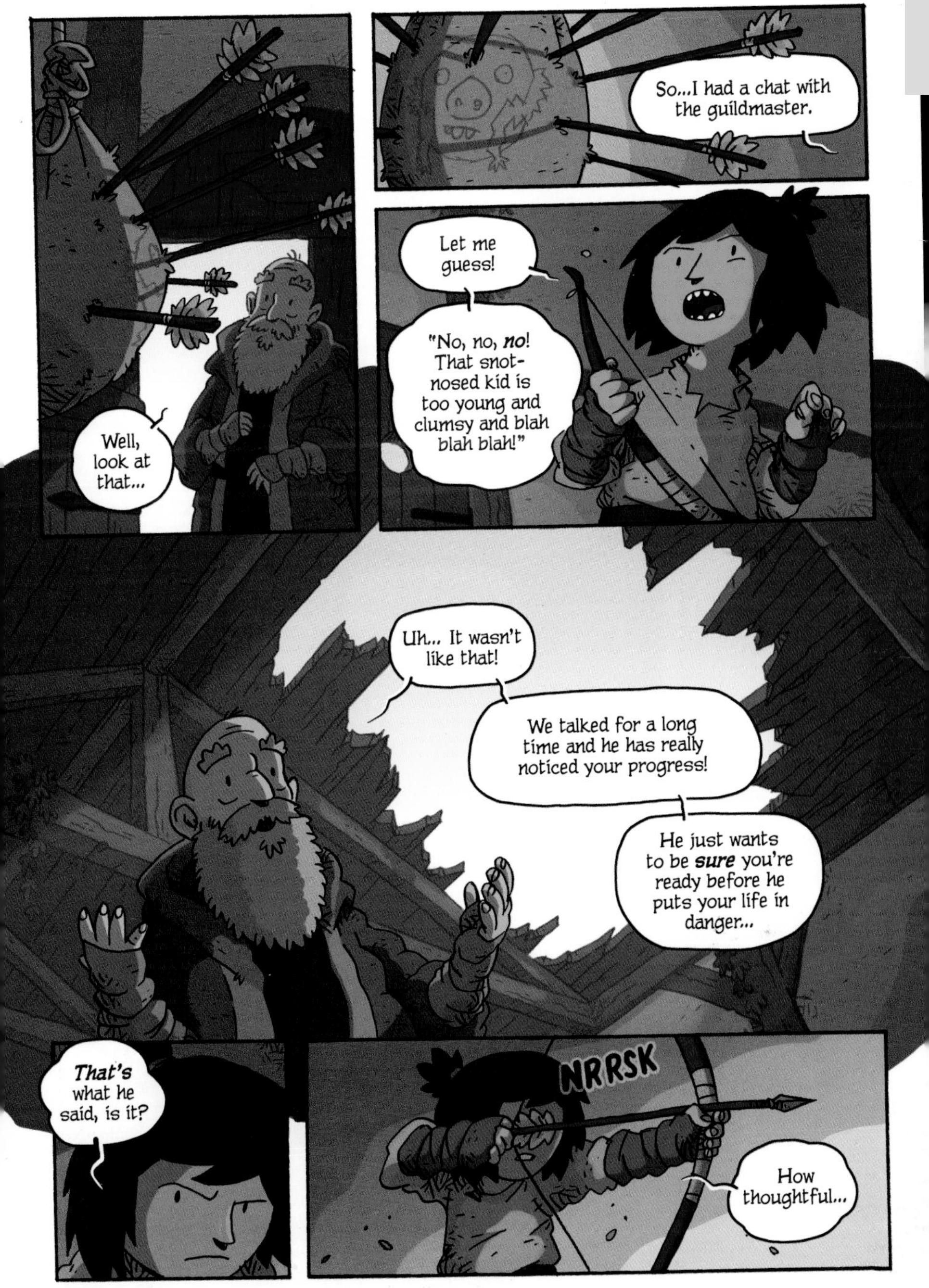
So...I had a chat with the guildmaster.
Well, look at that...
Let me guess!
"No, no, *no*! That snot-nosed kid is too young and clumsy and blah blah blah!"
Uh... It wasn't like that!
We talked for a long time and he has really noticed your progress!
He just wants to be *sure* you're ready before he puts your life in danger...
That's what he said, is it?
NRRSK
How thoughtful...

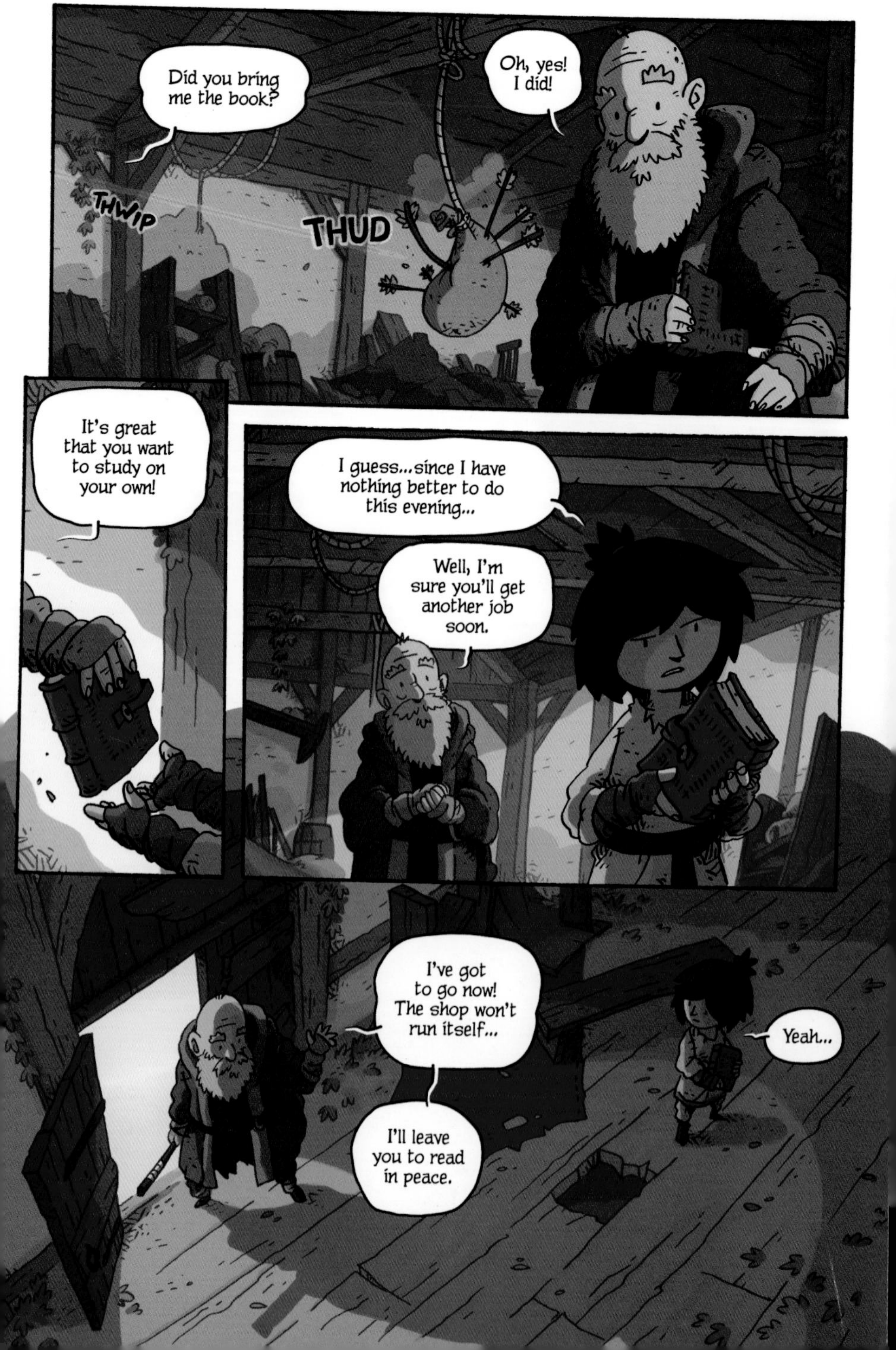
Did you bring me the book?
THWIP
THUD
Oh, yes! I did!
It's great that you want to study on your own!
I guess...since I have nothing better to do this evening...
Well, I'm sure you'll get another job soon.
I've got to go now! The shop won't run itself...
I'll leave you to read in peace.
Yeah...

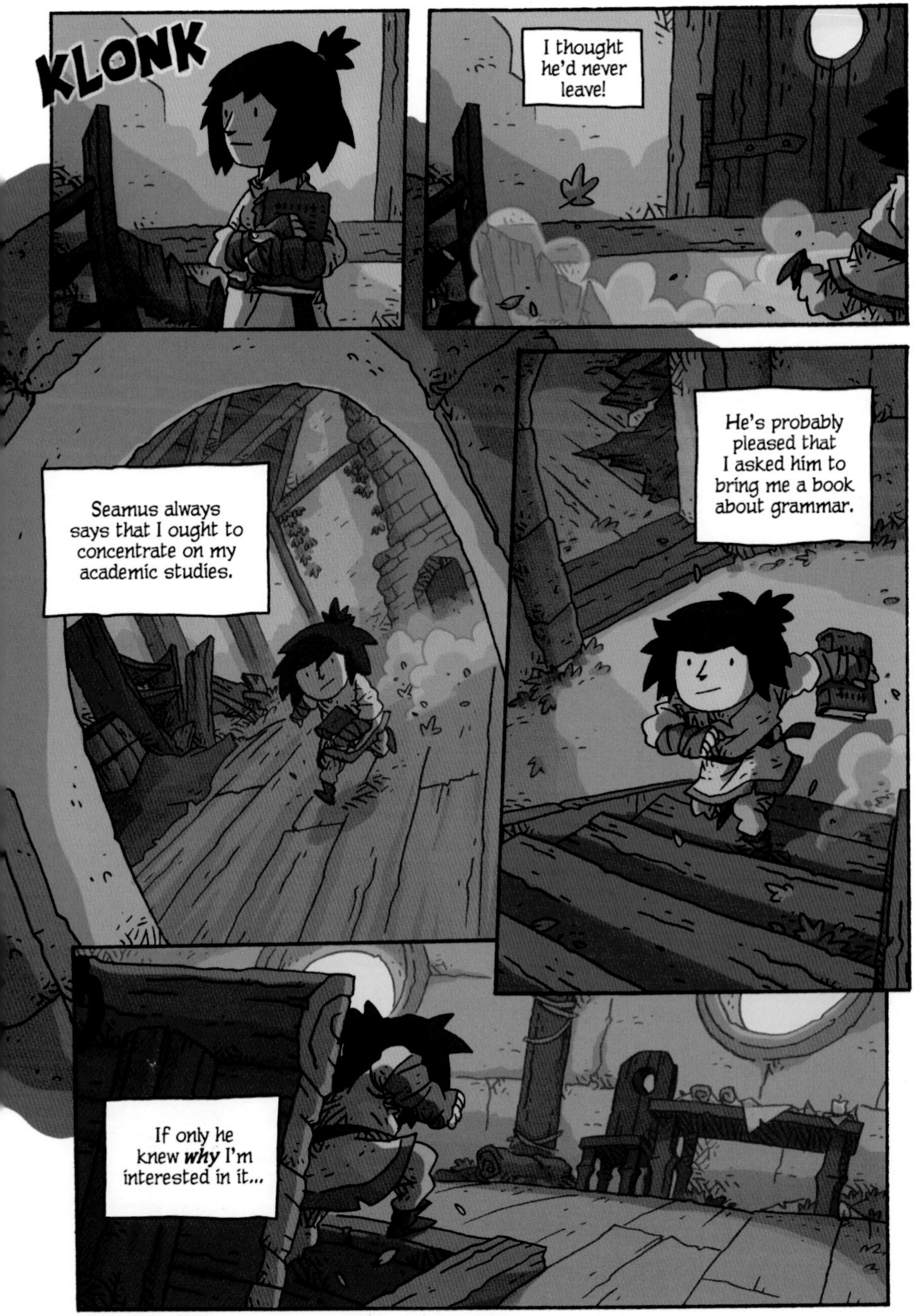
KLONK
I thought he'd never leave!
Seamus always says that I ought to concentrate on my academic studies.
He's probably pleased that I asked him to bring me a book about grammar.
If only he knew *why* I'm interested in it...

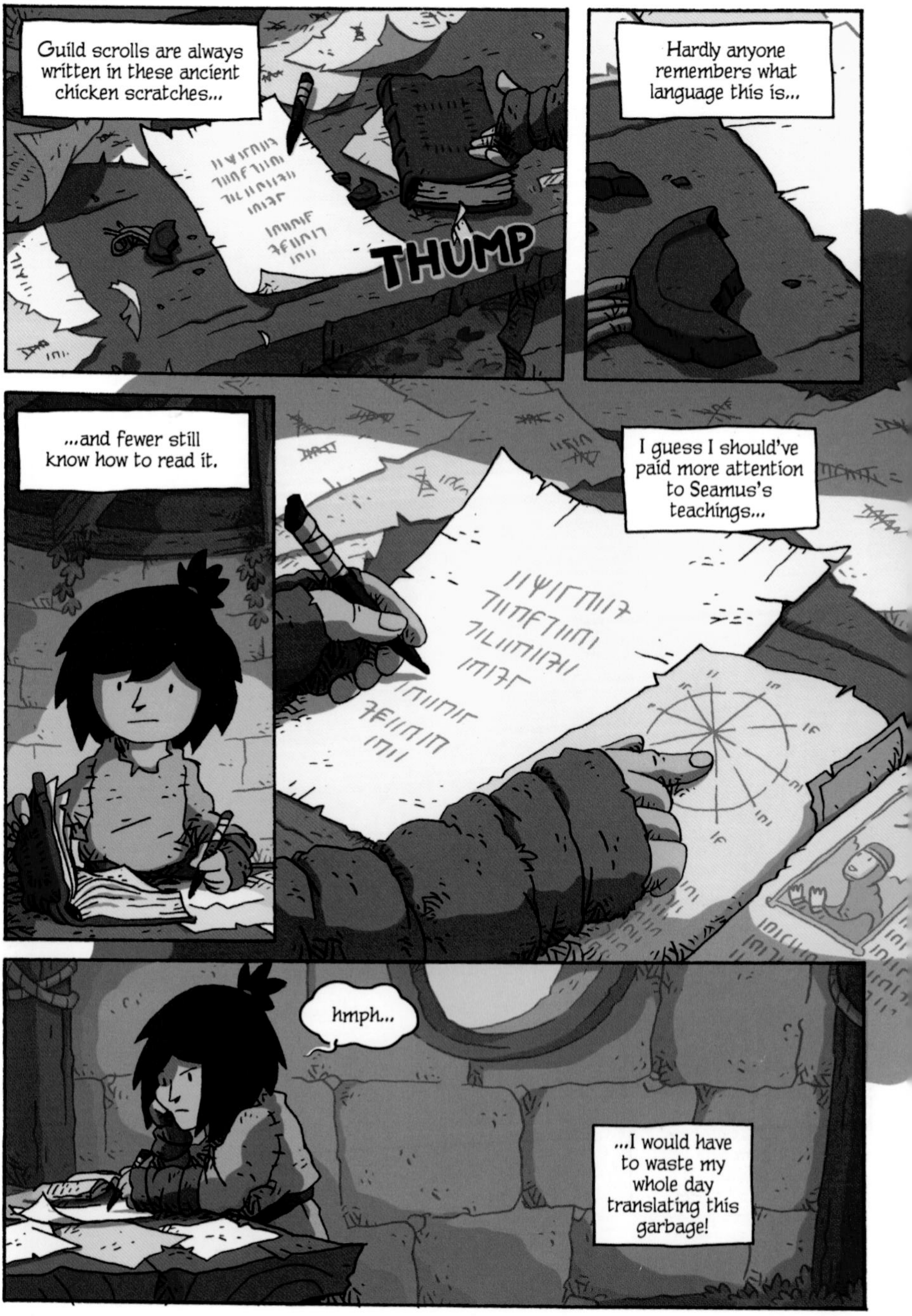

Guild scrolls are always written in these ancient chicken scratches...
THUMP
Hardly anyone remembers what language this is...
...and fewer still know how to read it.
I guess I should've paid more attention to Seamus's teachings...
hmph...
...I would have to waste my whole day translating this garbage!

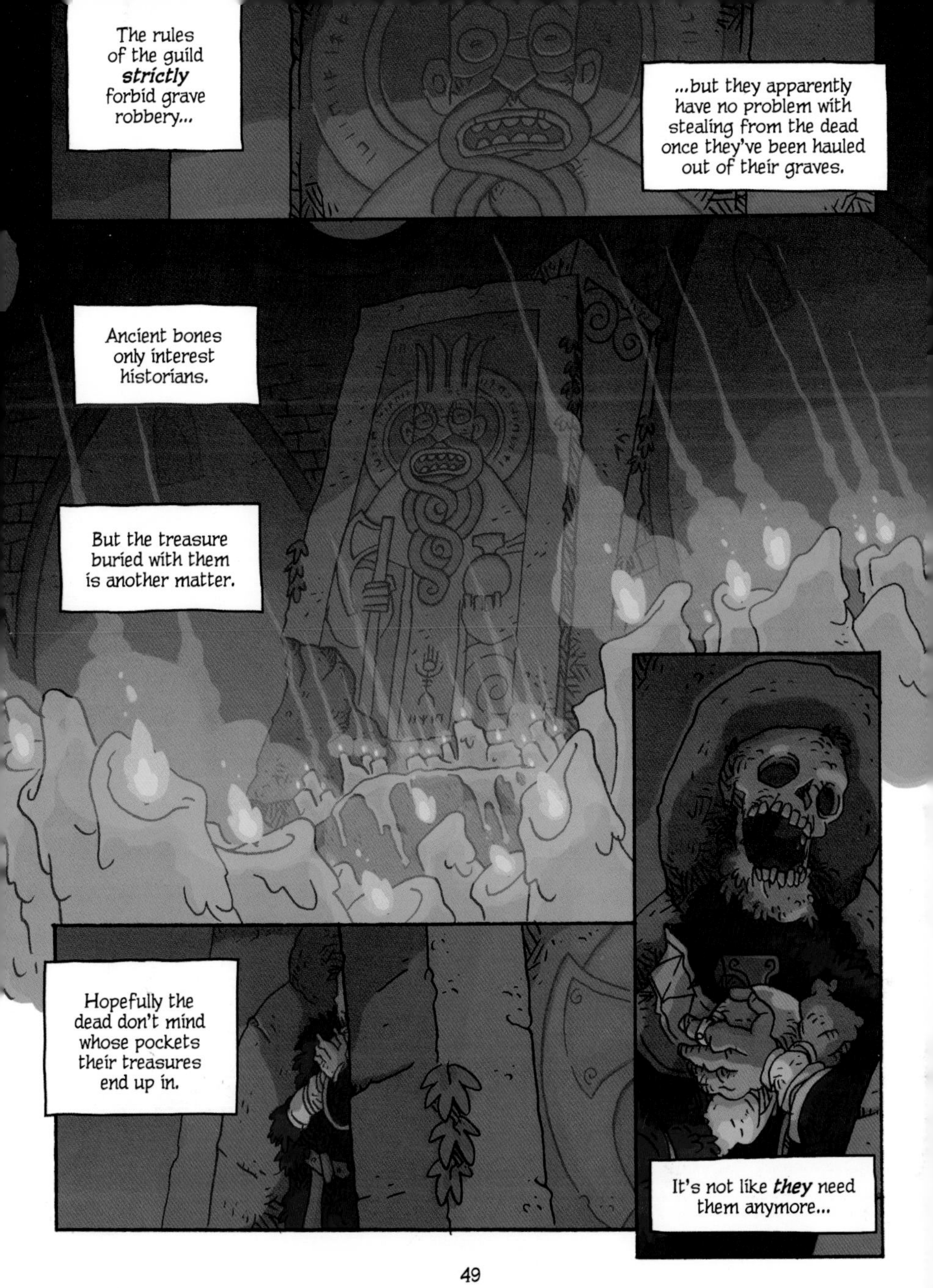
The rules of the guild **strictly** forbid grave robbery...
...but they apparently have no problem with stealing from the dead once they've been hauled out of their graves.
Ancient bones only interest historians.
But the treasure buried with them is another matter.
Hopefully the dead don't mind whose pockets their treasures end up in.
It's not like **they** need them anymore...

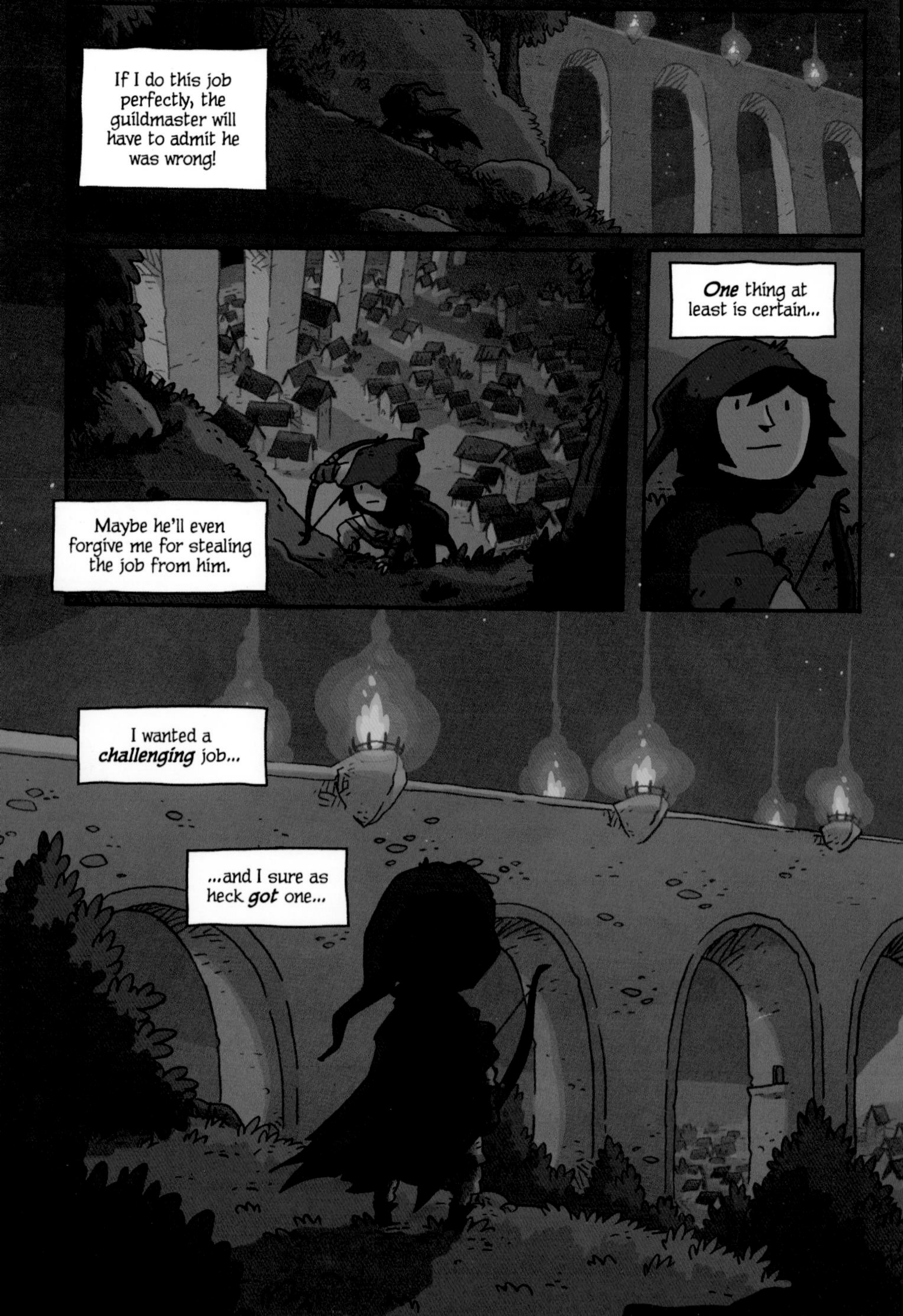
If I do this job perfectly, the guildmaster will have to admit he was wrong!
Maybe he'll even forgive me for stealing the job from him.
One thing at least is certain...
I wanted a *challenging* job...
...and I sure as heck *got* one...

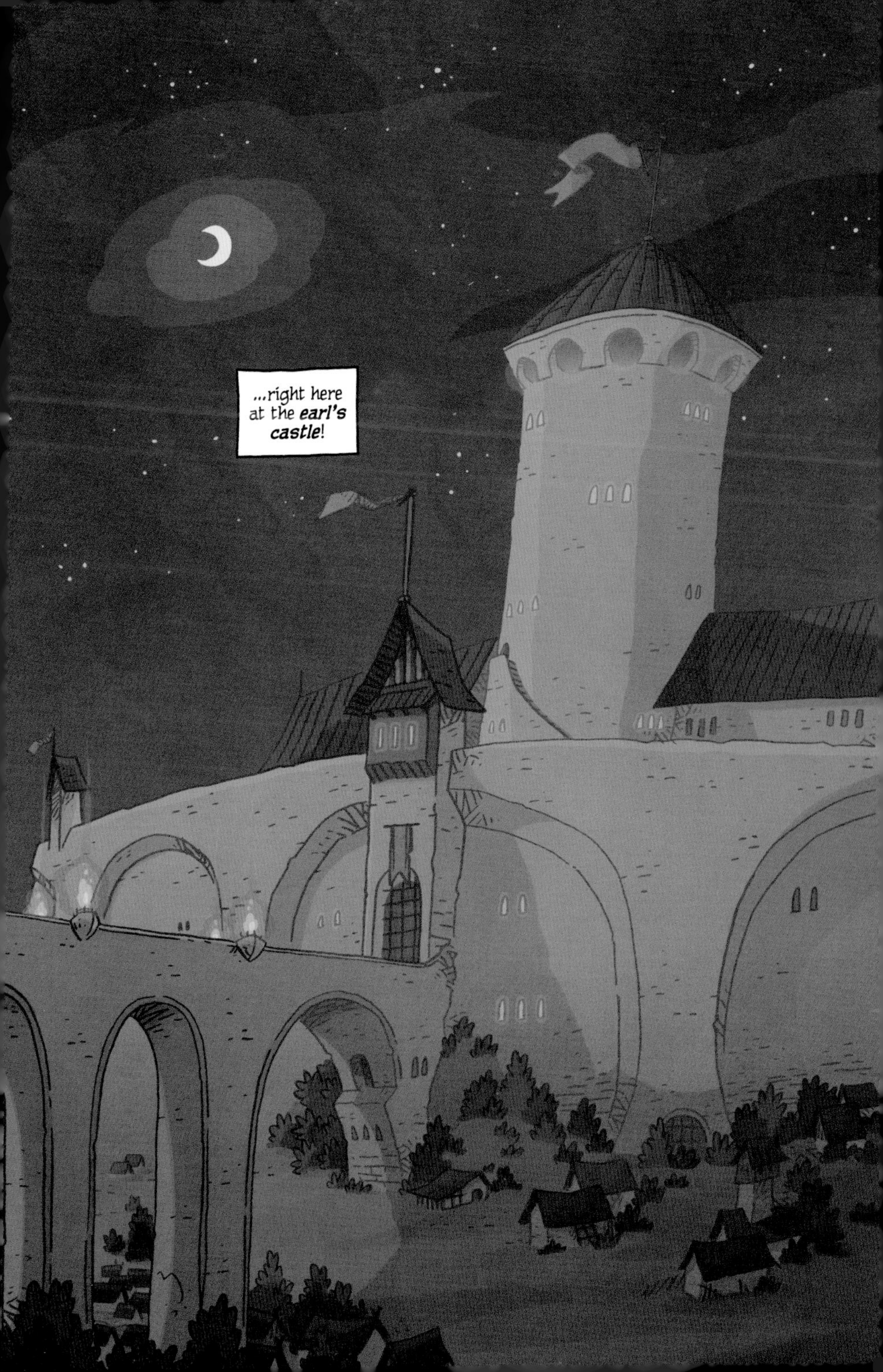
...right here at the earl's castle!

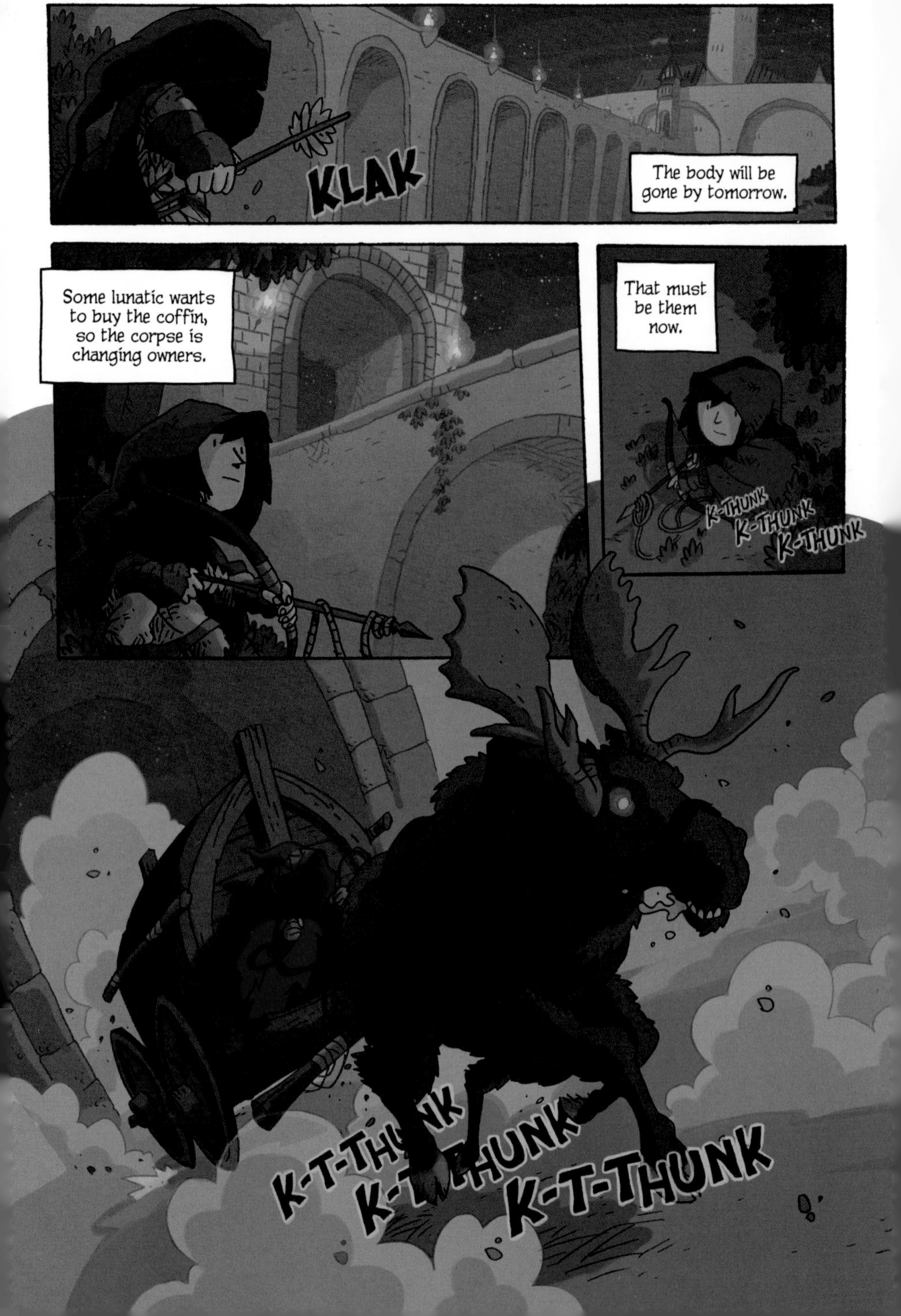
KLAK
The body will be gone by tomorrow.
Some lunatic wants to buy the coffin, so the corpse is changing owners.
That must be them now.
K-THUNK
K-THUNK
K-THUNK
K-T-THUNK
K-T-THUNK
K-T-THUNK

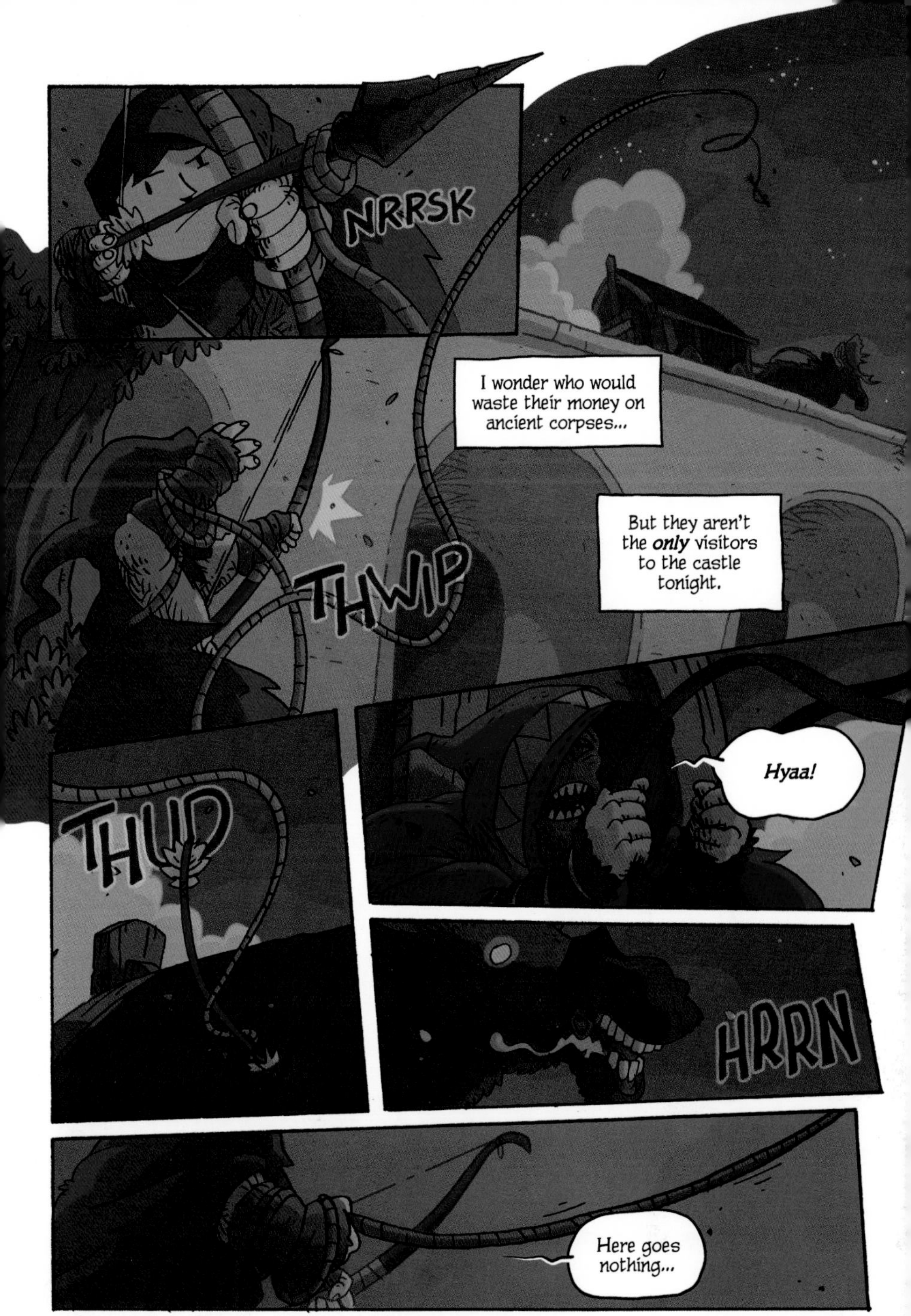
NRRSK
I wonder who would waste their money on ancient corpses...
THWIP
But they aren't the *only* visitors to the castle tonight.
THUD
Hyaa!
HRRN
Here goes nothing...

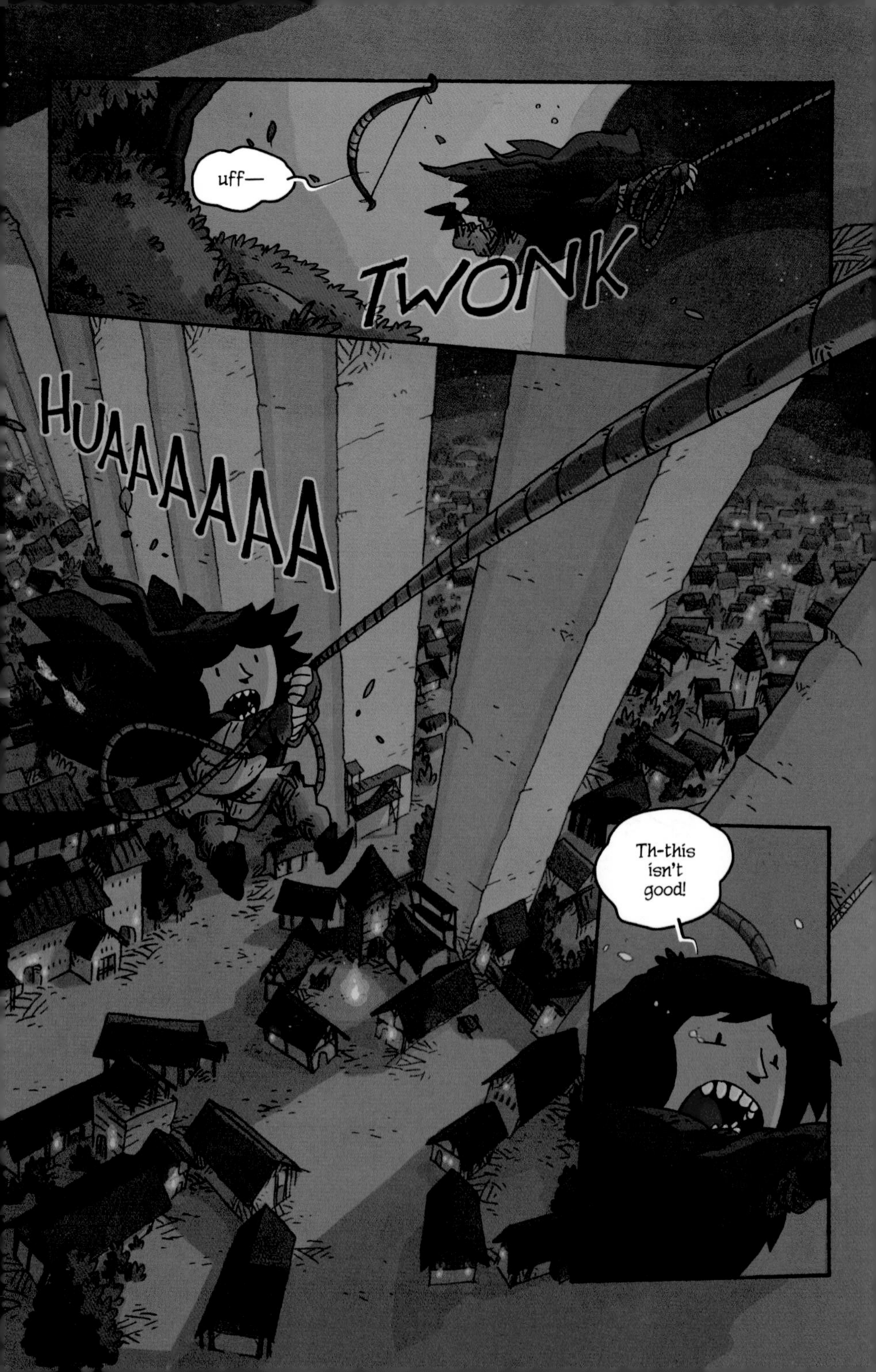
uff—
TWONK
HUAAAAAAA
Th-this isn't good!

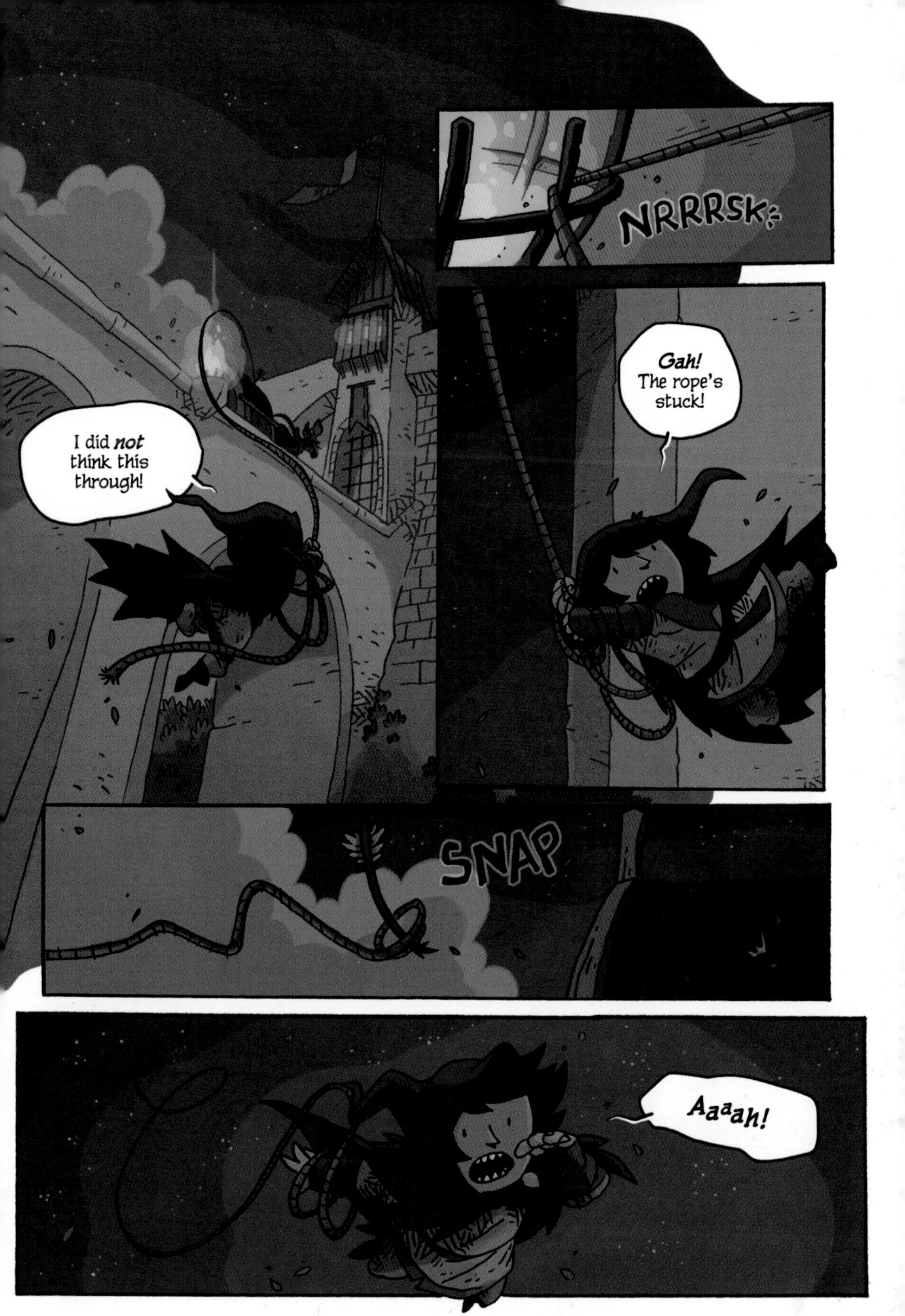

NRRRSK
I did *not* think this through!
Gah! The rope's stuck!
SNAP
Aaaah!

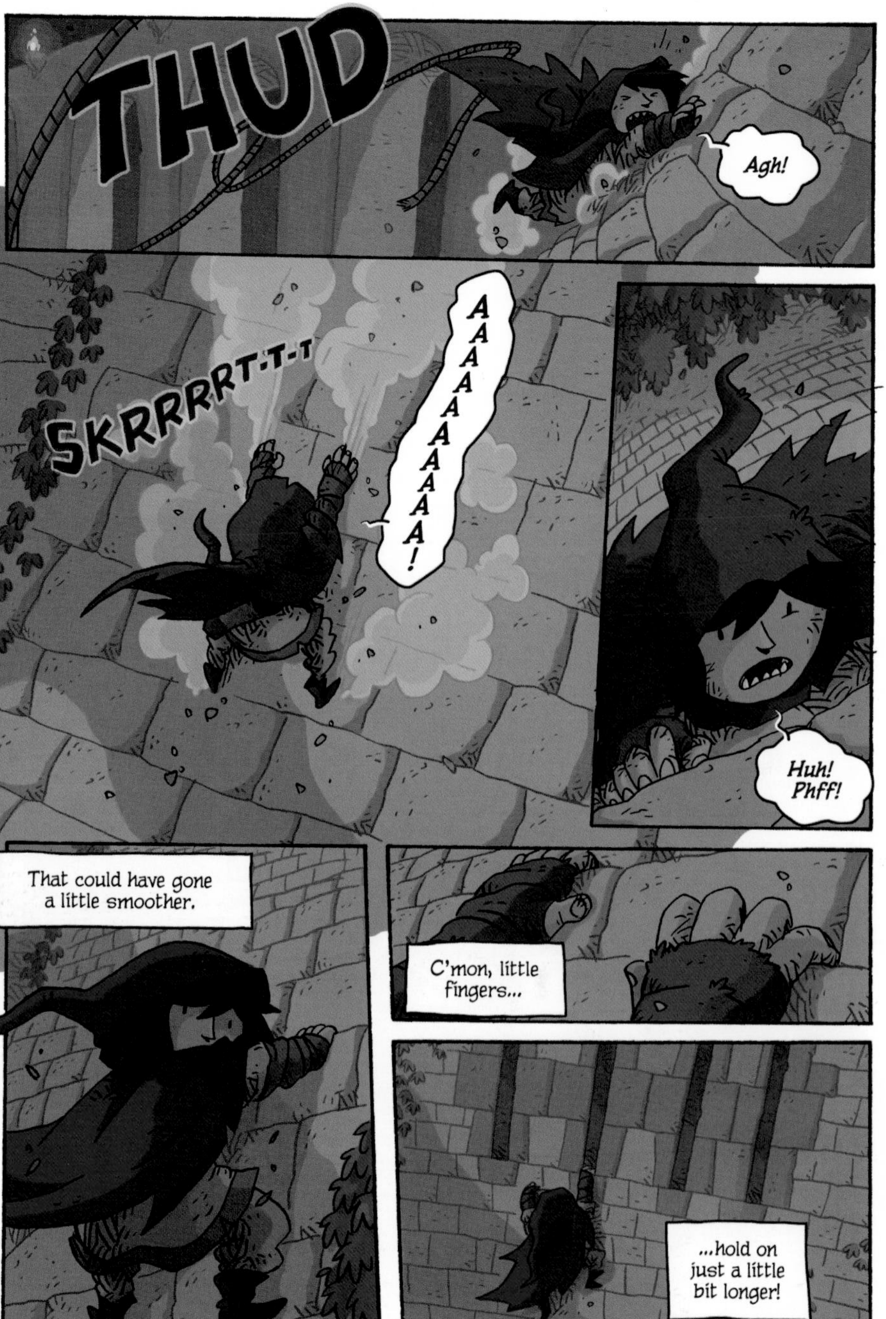
THUD
Agh!
SKRRRRT-T-T
AAAAAAAAAAAA!
Huh! Phff!
That could have gone a little smoother.
C'mon, little fingers...
...hold on just a little bit longer!

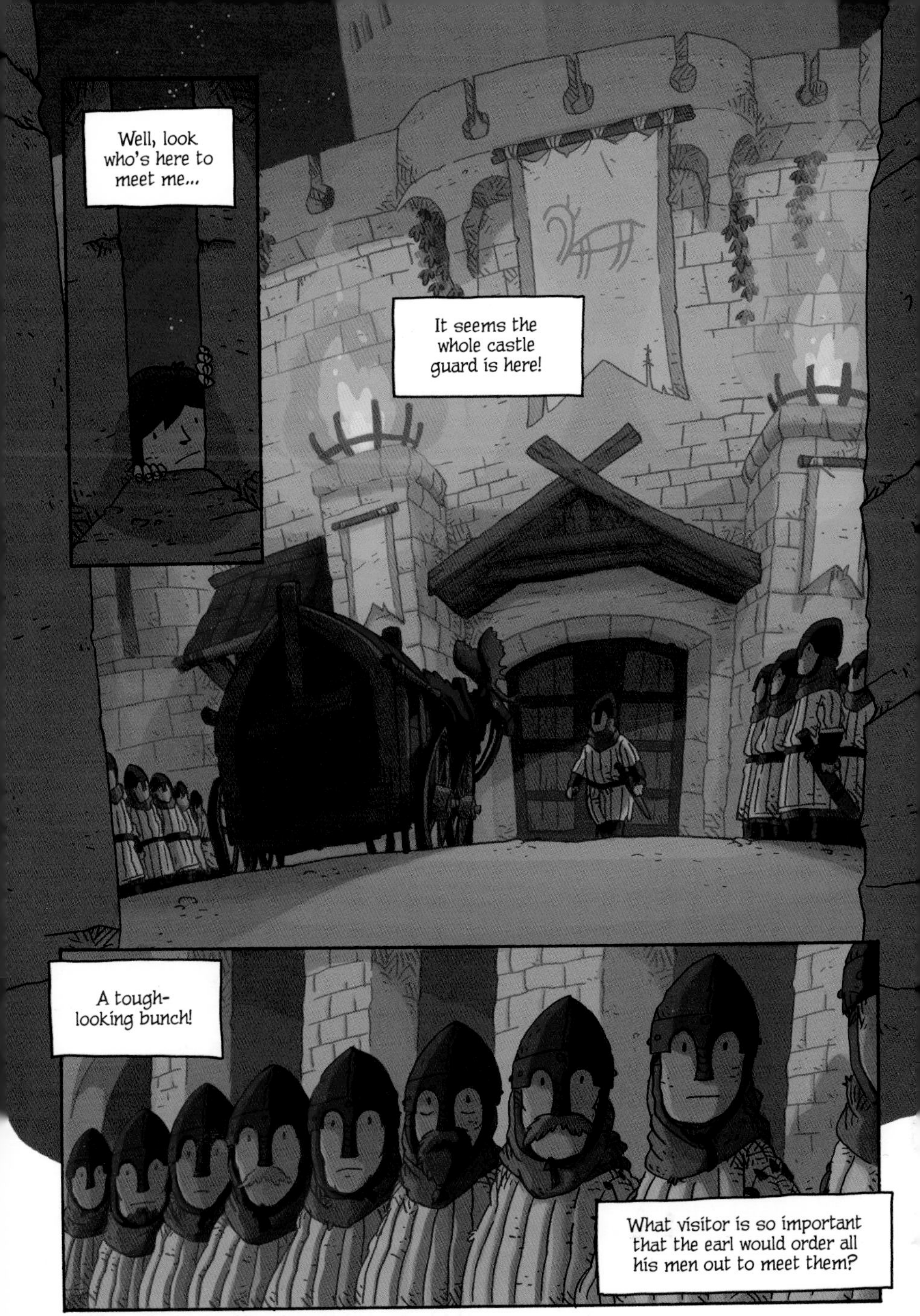
Well, look who's here to meet me...
It seems the whole castle guard is here!
A tough-looking bunch!
What visitor is so important that the earl would order all his men out to meet them?

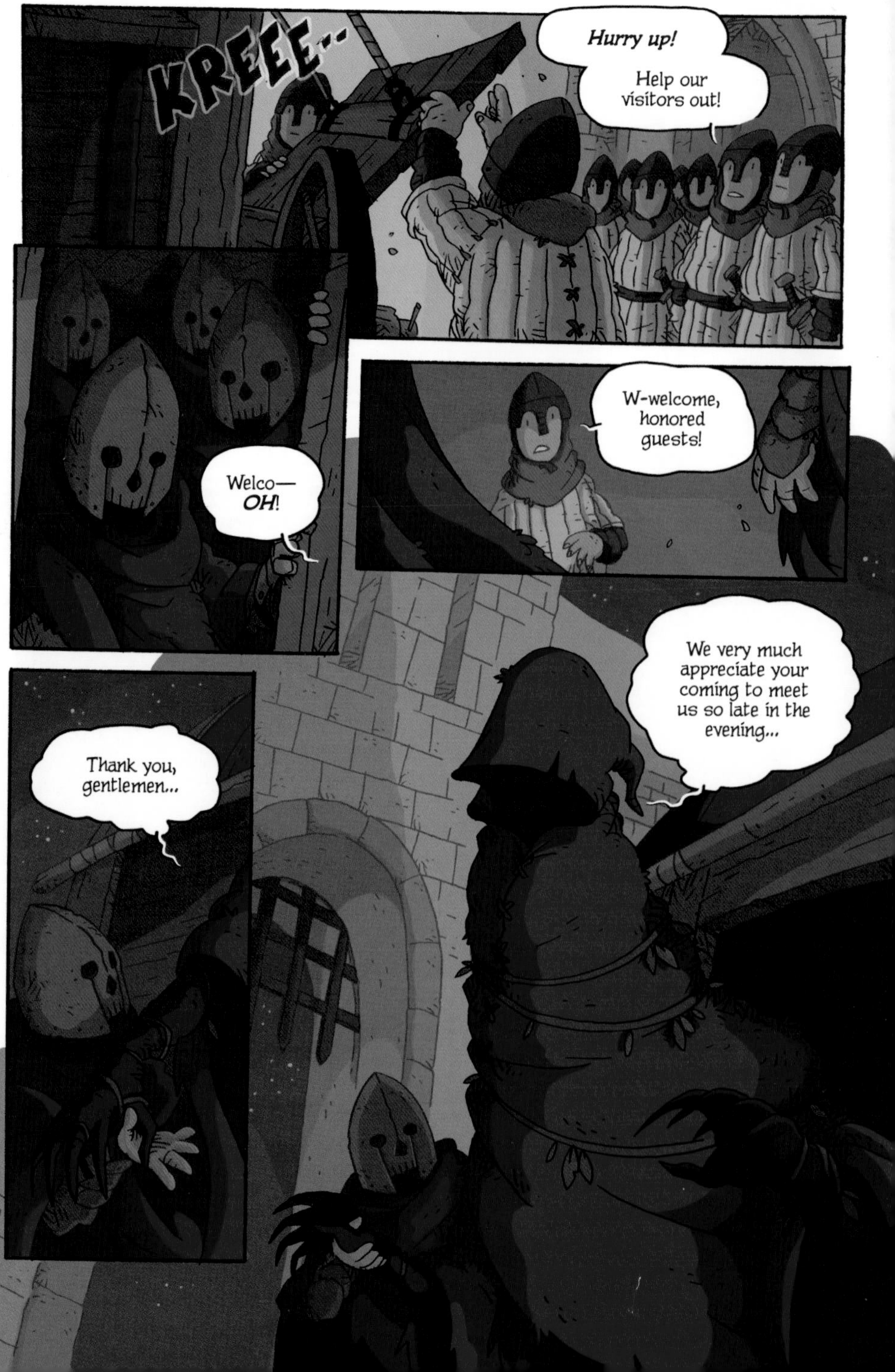
KREEE..
Hurry up!
Help our visitors out!
Welco— OH!
W-welcome, honored guests!
We very much appreciate your coming to meet us so late in the evening...
Thank you, gentlemen...

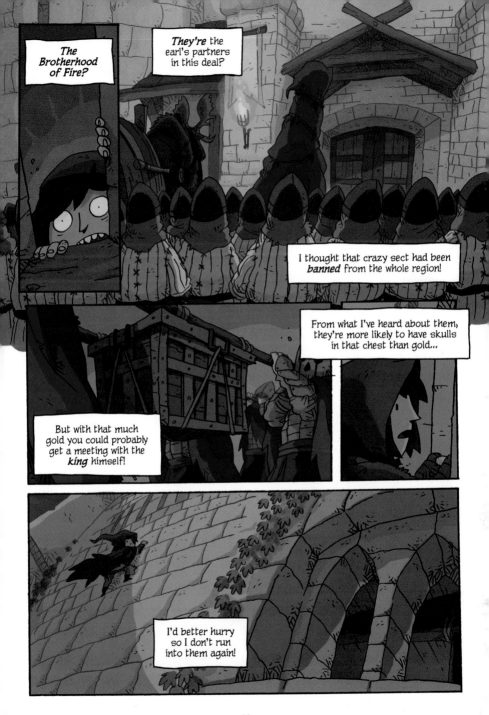

The Brotherhood of Fire?

They're the earl's partners in this deal?

I thought that crazy sect had been *banned* from the whole region!

From what I've heard about them, they're more likely to have skulls in that chest than gold...

But with that much gold you could probably get a meeting with the *king* himself!

I'd better hurry so I don't run into them again!

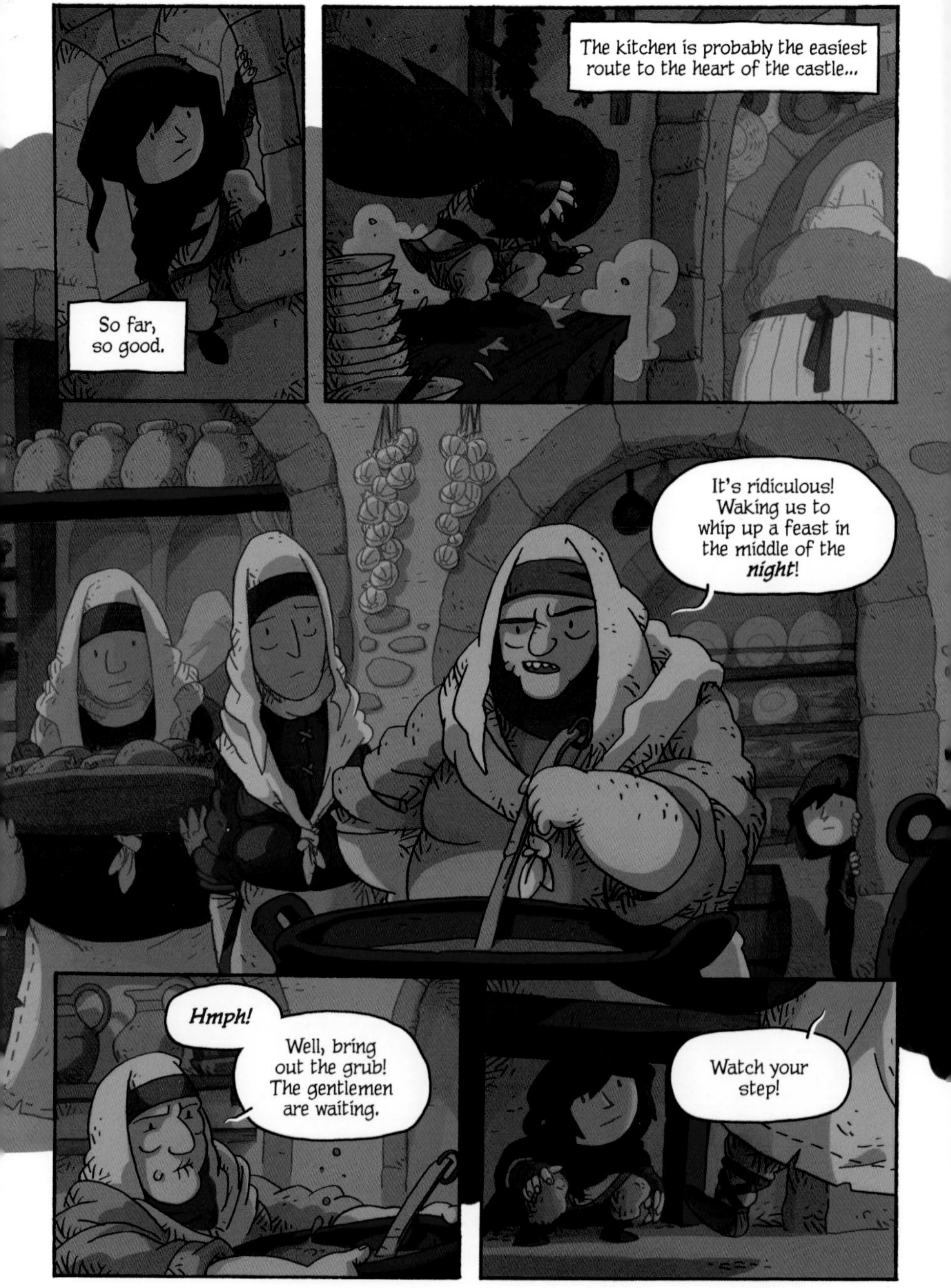
So far, so good.
The kitchen is probably the easiest route to the heart of the castle...
It's ridiculous! Waking us to whip up a feast in the middle of the *night*!
Hmph!
Well, bring out the grub! The gentlemen are waiting.
Watch your step!

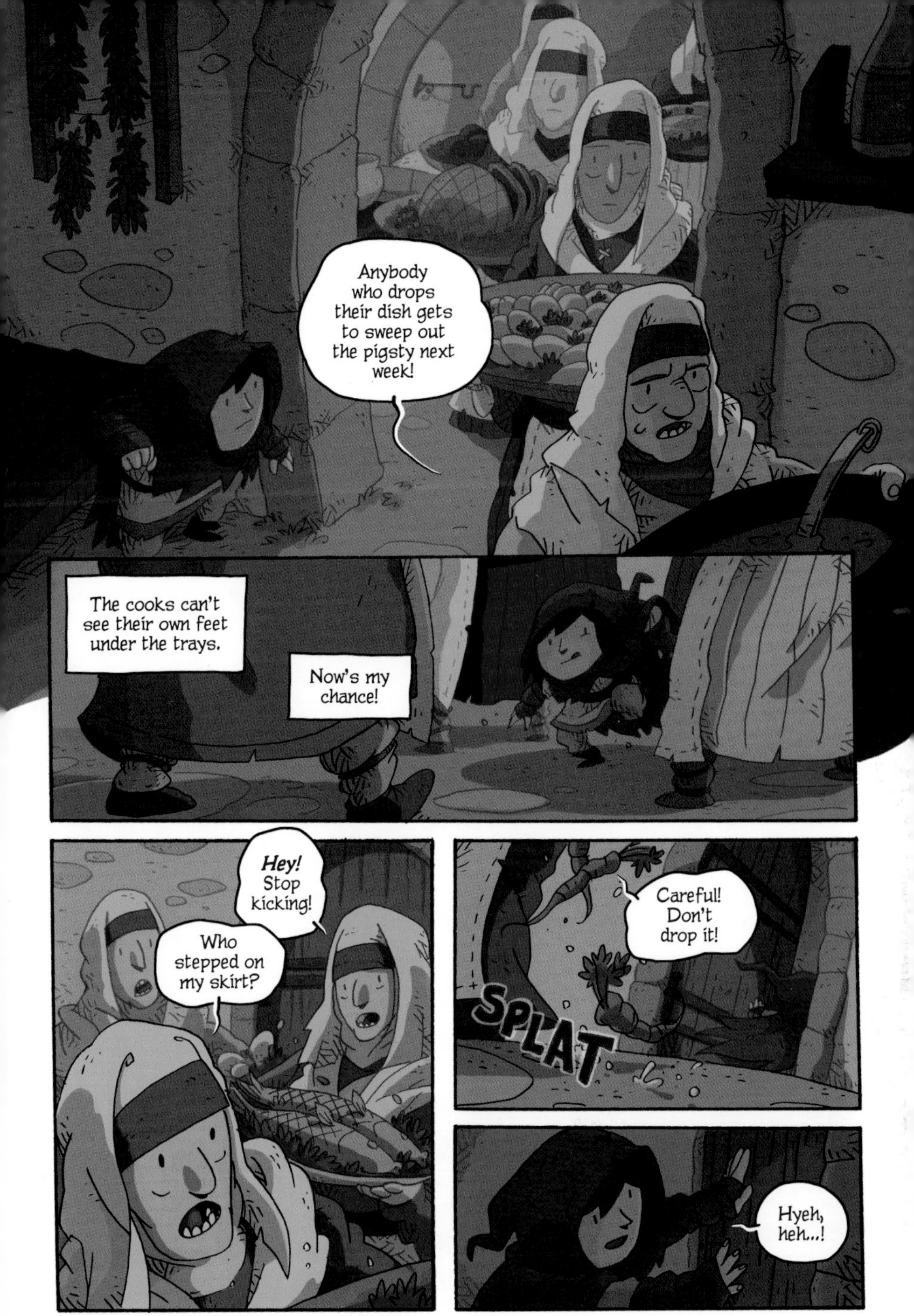
Anybody who drops their dish gets to sweep out the pigsty next week!
The cooks can't see their own feet under the trays.
Now's my chance!
Hey! Stop kicking!
Who stepped on my skirt?
Careful! Don't drop it!
SPLAT
Hyeh, heh...!

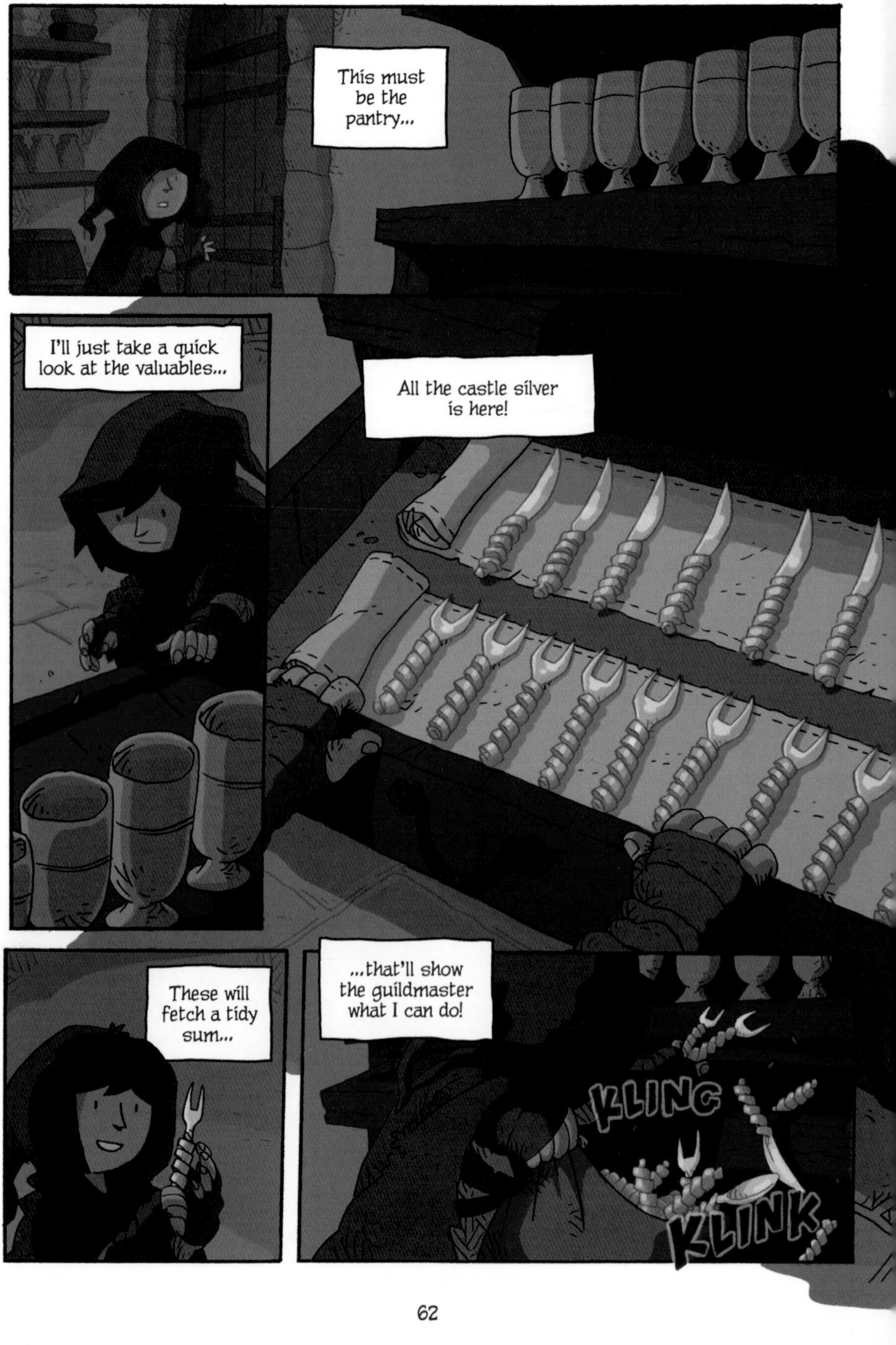

This must be the pantry...
I'll just take a quick look at the valuables...
All the castle silver is here!
These will fetch a tidy sum...
...that'll show the guildmaster what I can do!
KLINC
KLINK

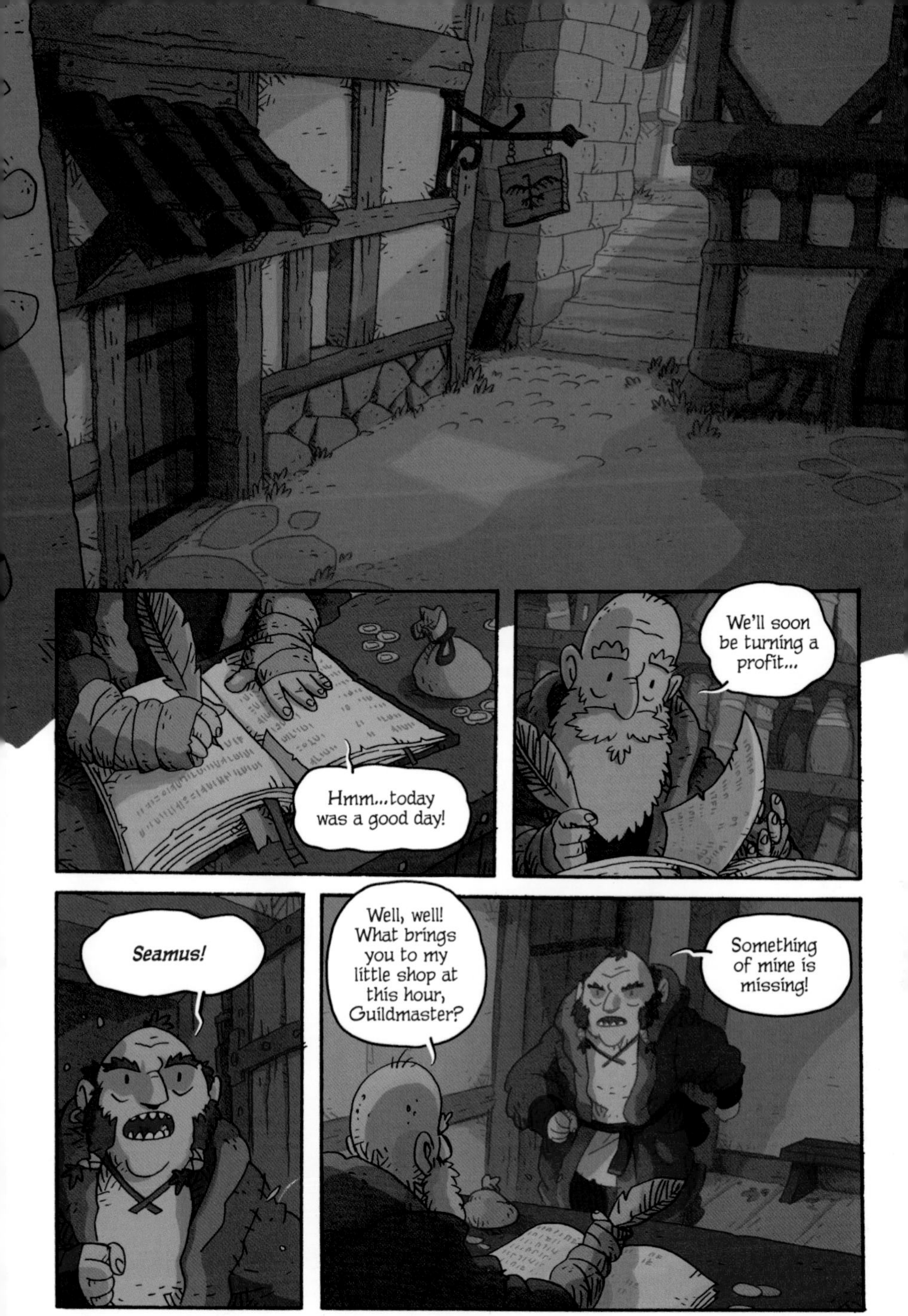
Hmm...today was a good day!
We'll soon be turning a profit...
Seamus!
Well, well! What brings you to my little shop at this hour, Guildmaster?
Something of mine is missing!

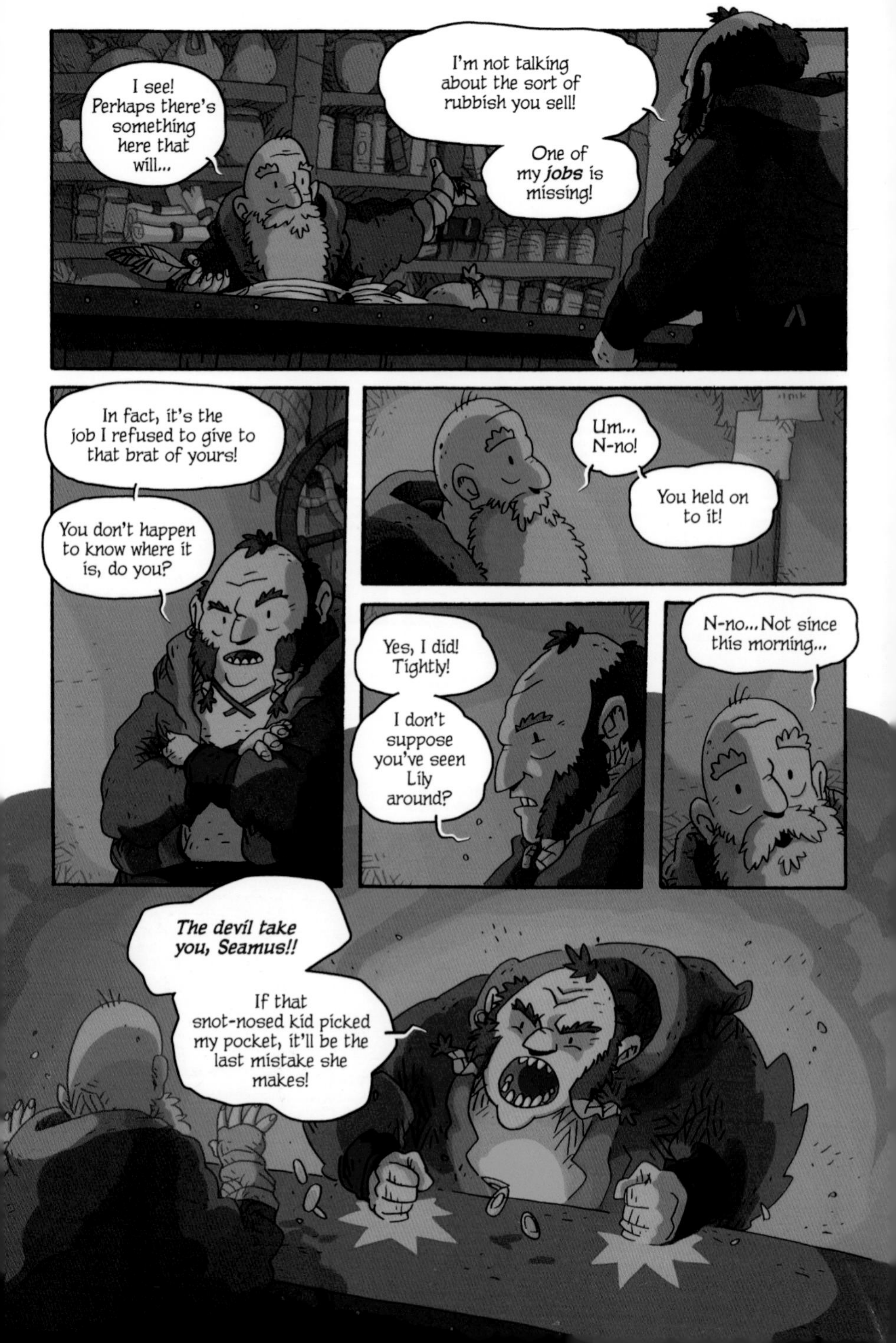
I see! Perhaps there's something here that will...
I'm not talking about the sort of rubbish you sell!
One of my *jobs* is missing!
In fact, it's the job I refused to give to that brat of yours!
You don't happen to know where it is, do you?
Um... N-no!
You held on to it!
Yes, I did! Tightly!
I don't suppose you've seen Lily around?
N-no... Not since this morning...
The devil take you, Seamus!!
If that snot-nosed kid picked my pocket, it'll be the last mistake she makes!

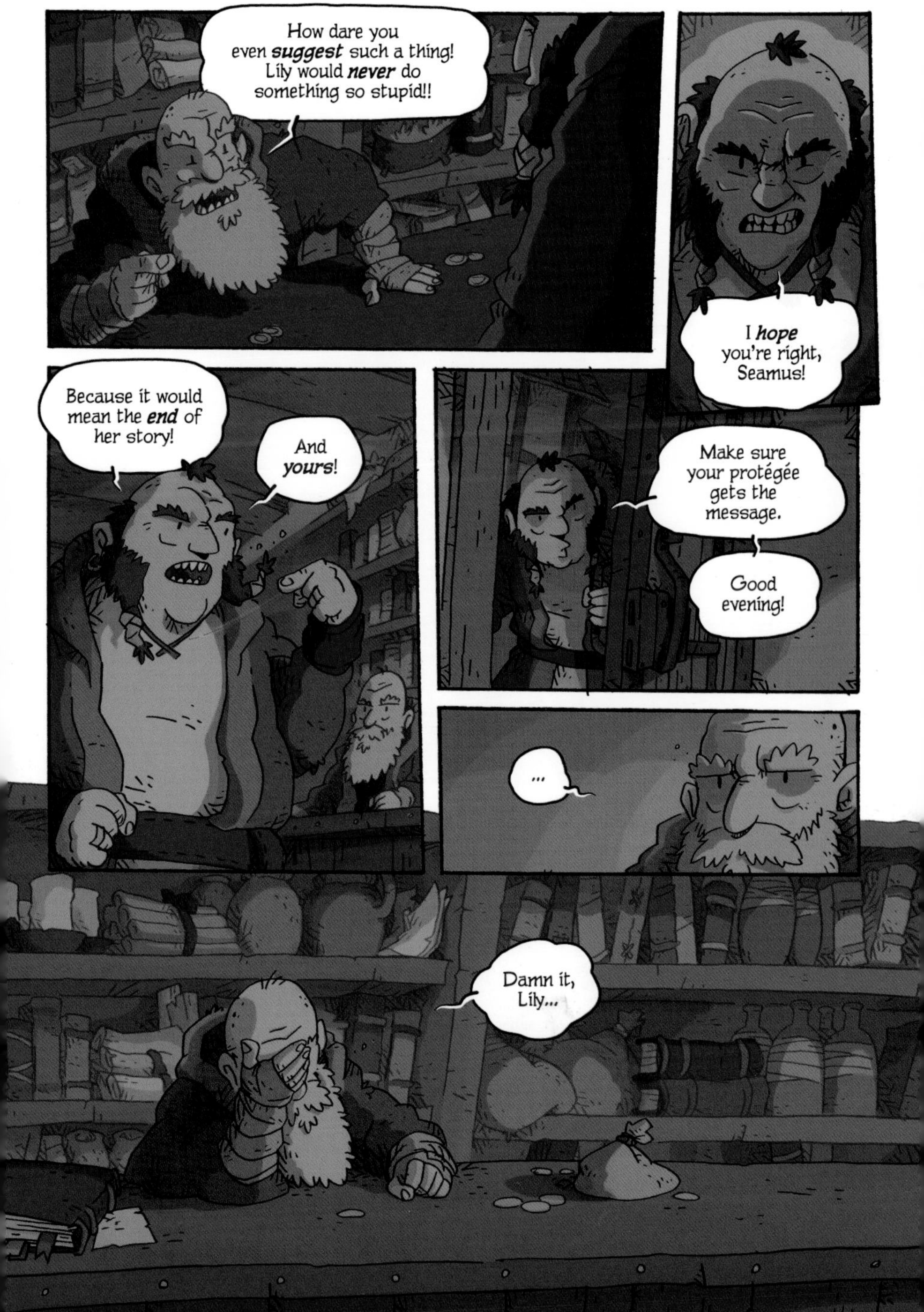
How dare you even ***suggest*** such a thing! Lily would ***never*** do something so stupid!!
I ***hope*** you're right, Seamus!
Because it would mean the ***end*** of her story!
And ***yours***!
Make sure your protégée gets the message.
Good evening!
...
Damn it, Lily...

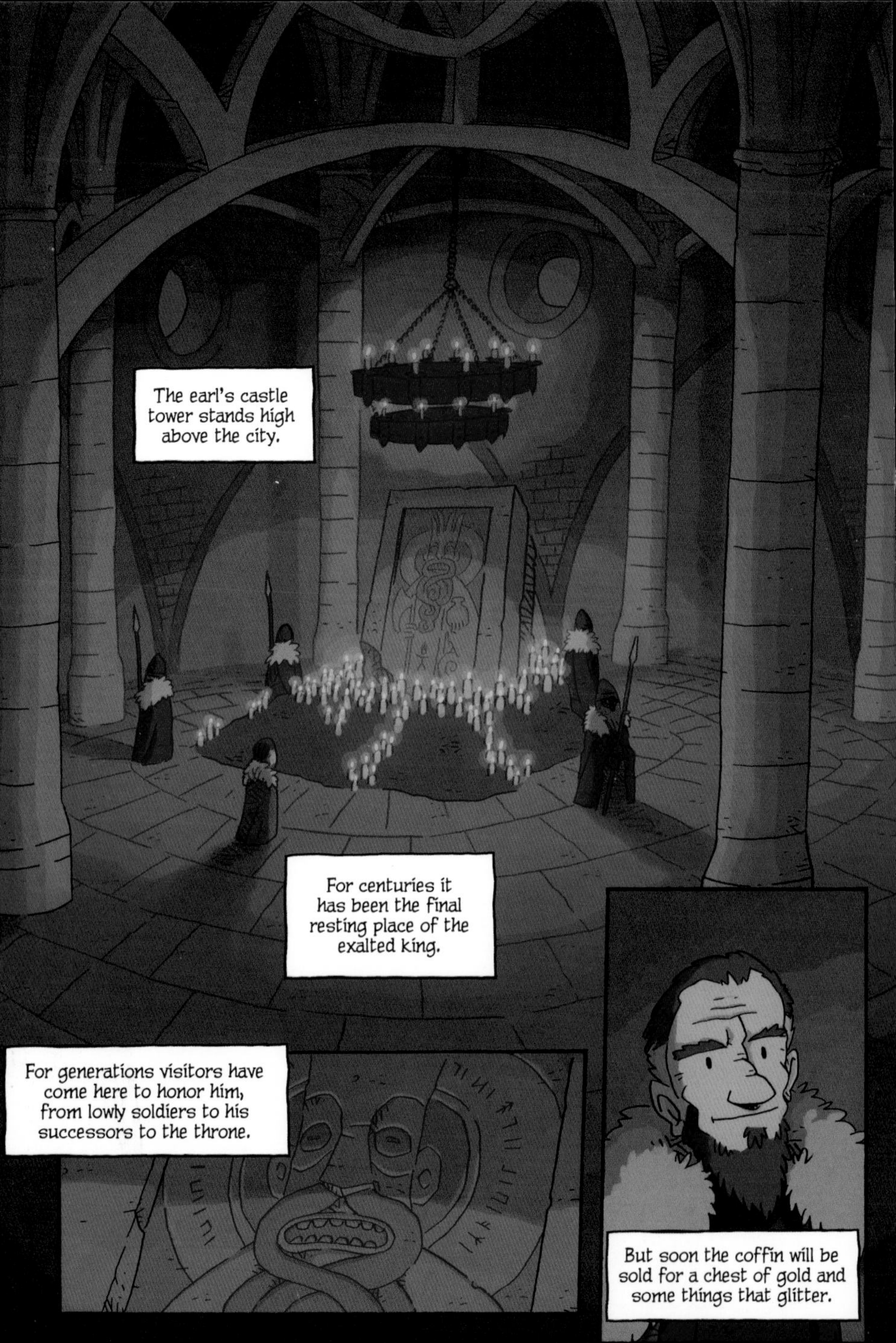
The earl's castle tower stands high above the city.
For centuries it has been the final resting place of the exalted king.
For generations visitors have come here to honor him, from lowly soldiers to his successors to the throne.
But soon the coffin will be sold for a chest of gold and some things that glitter.

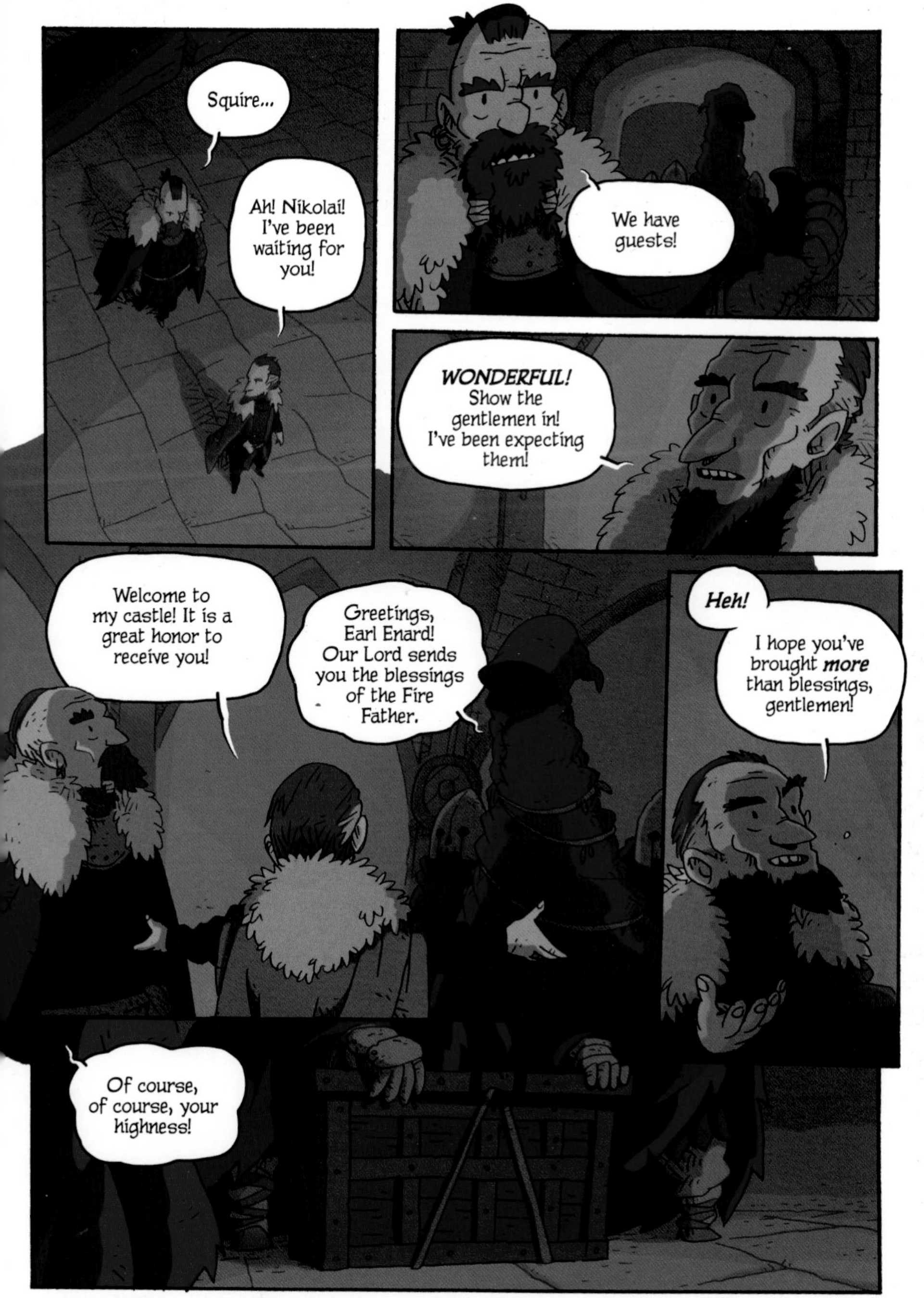
Squire...
Ah! Nikolai! I've been waiting for you!
We have guests!
WONDERFUL! Show the gentlemen in! I've been expecting them!
Welcome to my castle! It is a great honor to receive you!
Greetings, Earl Enard! Our Lord sends you the blessings of the Fire Father.
Heh!
I hope you've brought more than blessings, gentlemen!
Of course, of course, your highness!

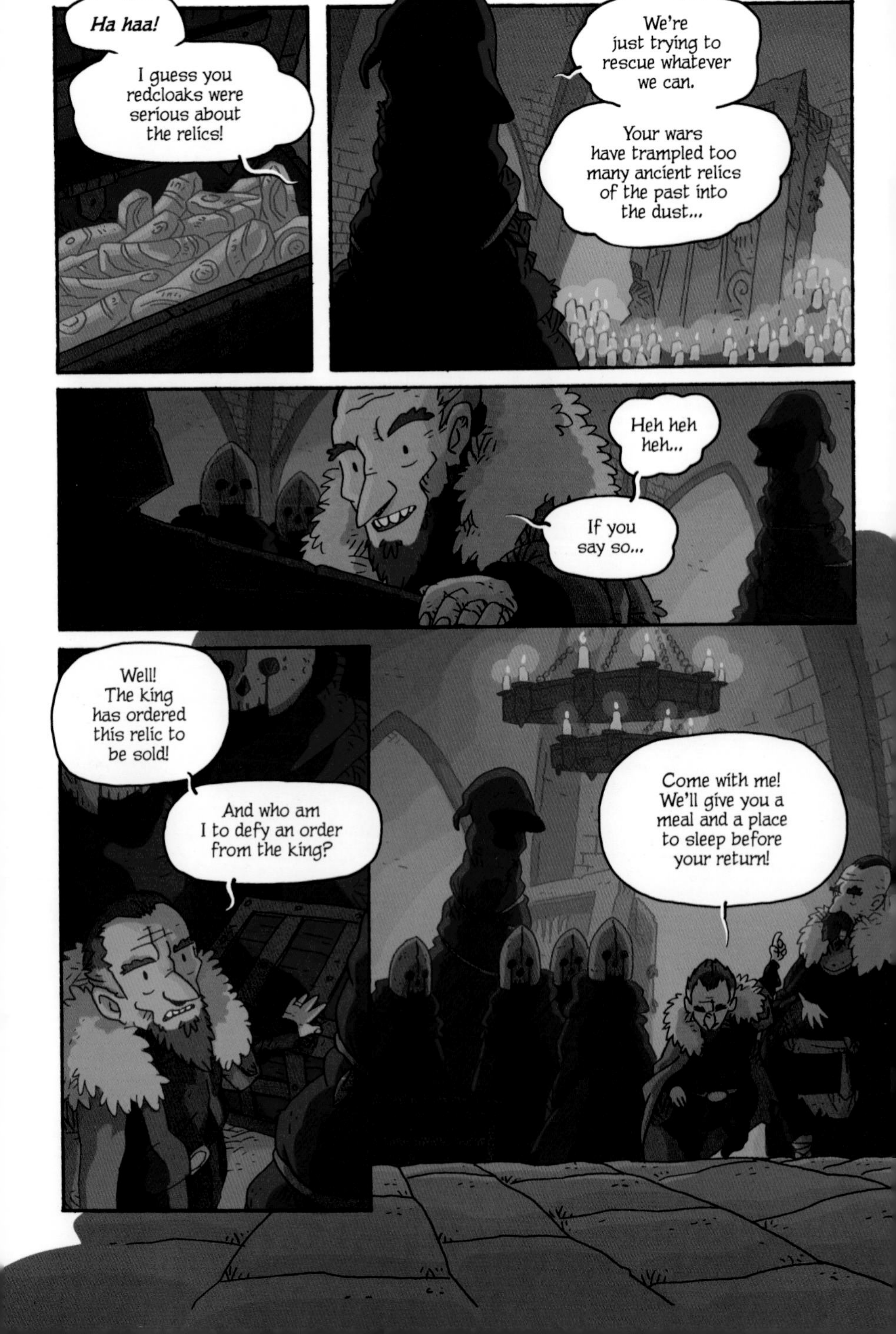
Ha haa!
I guess you redcloaks were serious about the relics!
We're just trying to rescue whatever we can.
Your wars have trampled too many ancient relics of the past into the dust...
Heh heh heh...
If you say so...
Well! The king has ordered this relic to be sold!
And who am I to defy an order from the king?
Come with me! We'll give you a meal and a place to sleep before your return!

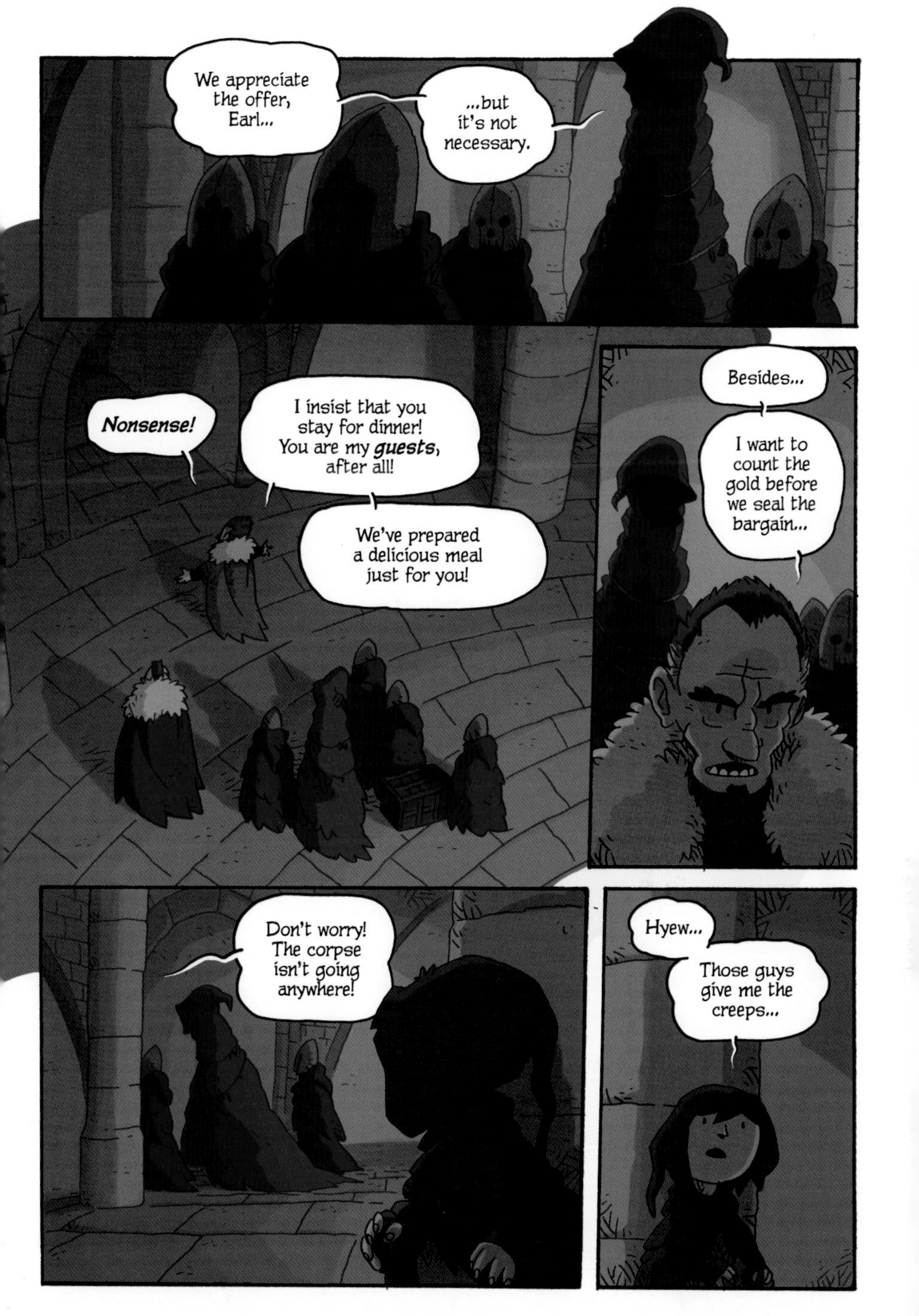
We appreciate the offer, Earl...
...but it's not necessary.
Nonsense!
I insist that you stay for dinner! You are my guests, after all!
We've prepared a delicious meal just for you!
Besides...
I want to count the gold before we seal the bargain...
Don't worry! The corpse isn't going anywhere!
Hyew...
Those guys give me the creeps...

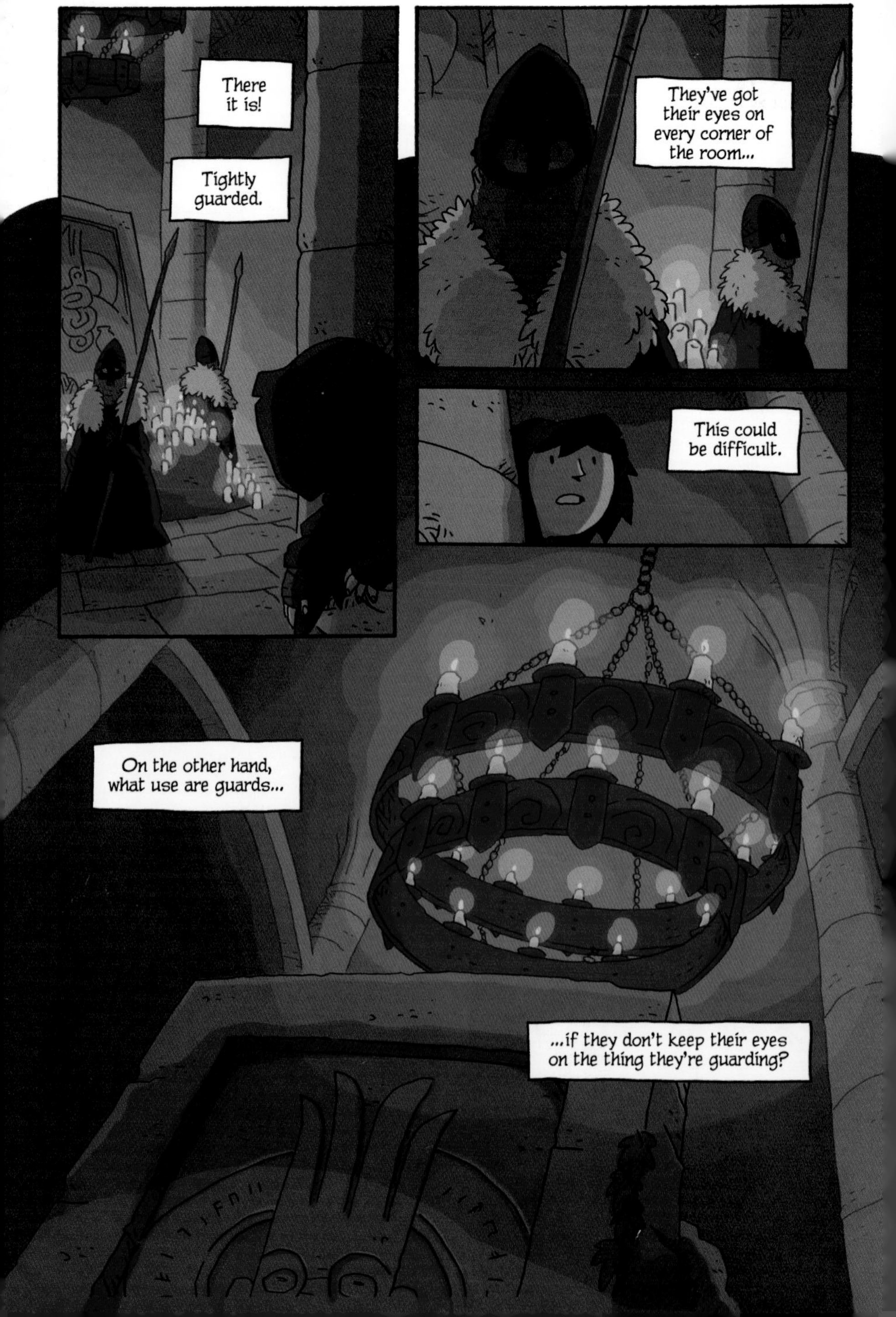
There it is!
Tightly guarded.
They've got their eyes on every corner of the room...
This could be difficult.
On the other hand, what use are guards...
...if they don't keep their eyes on the thing they're guarding?

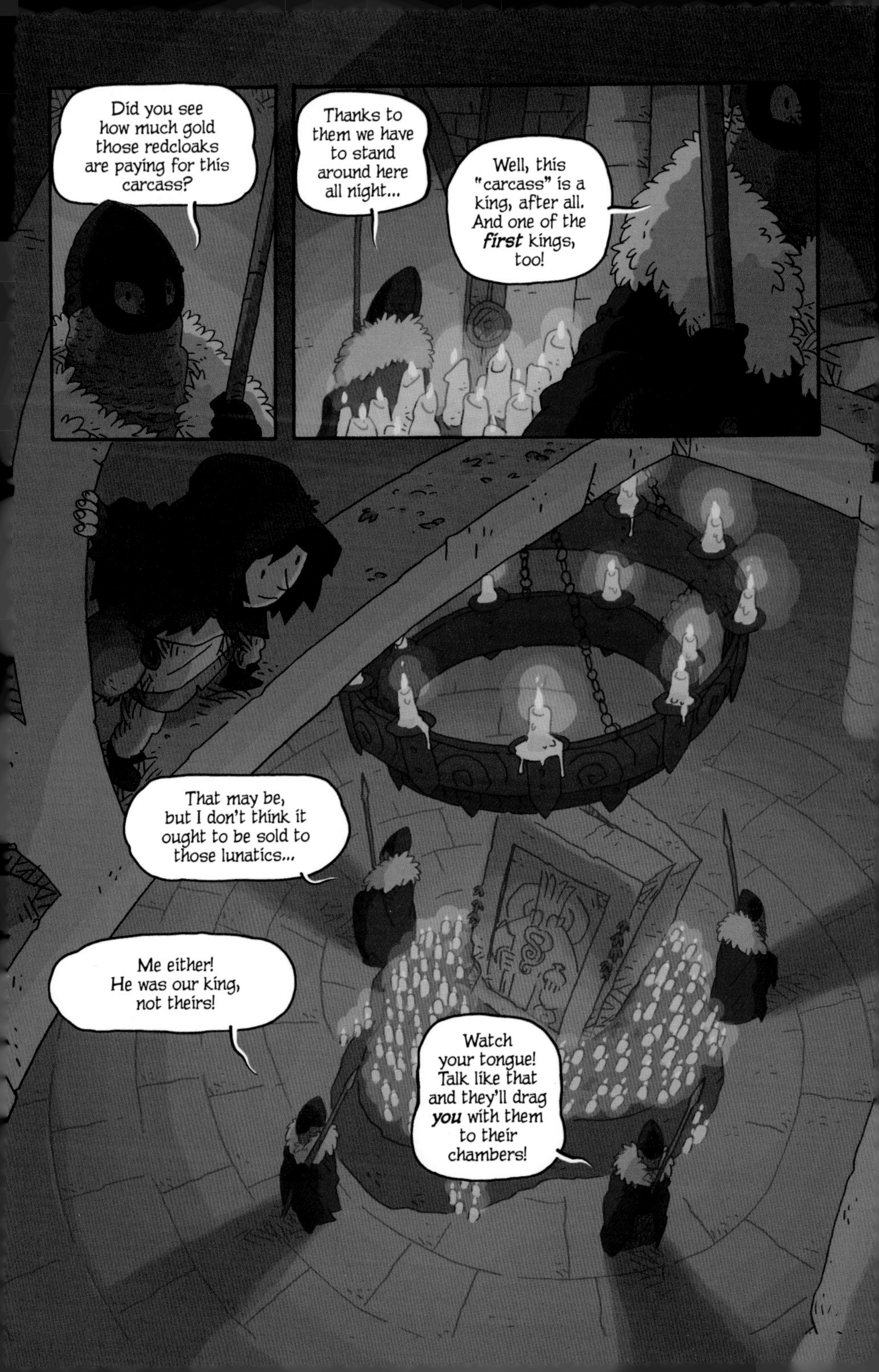
Did you see how much gold those redcloaks are paying for this carcass?
Thanks to them we have to stand around here all night...
Well, this "carcass" is a king, after all. And one of the *first* kings, too!
That may be, but I don't think it ought to be sold to those lunatics...
Me either! He was our king, not theirs!
Watch your tongue! Talk like that and they'll drag *you* with them to their chambers!

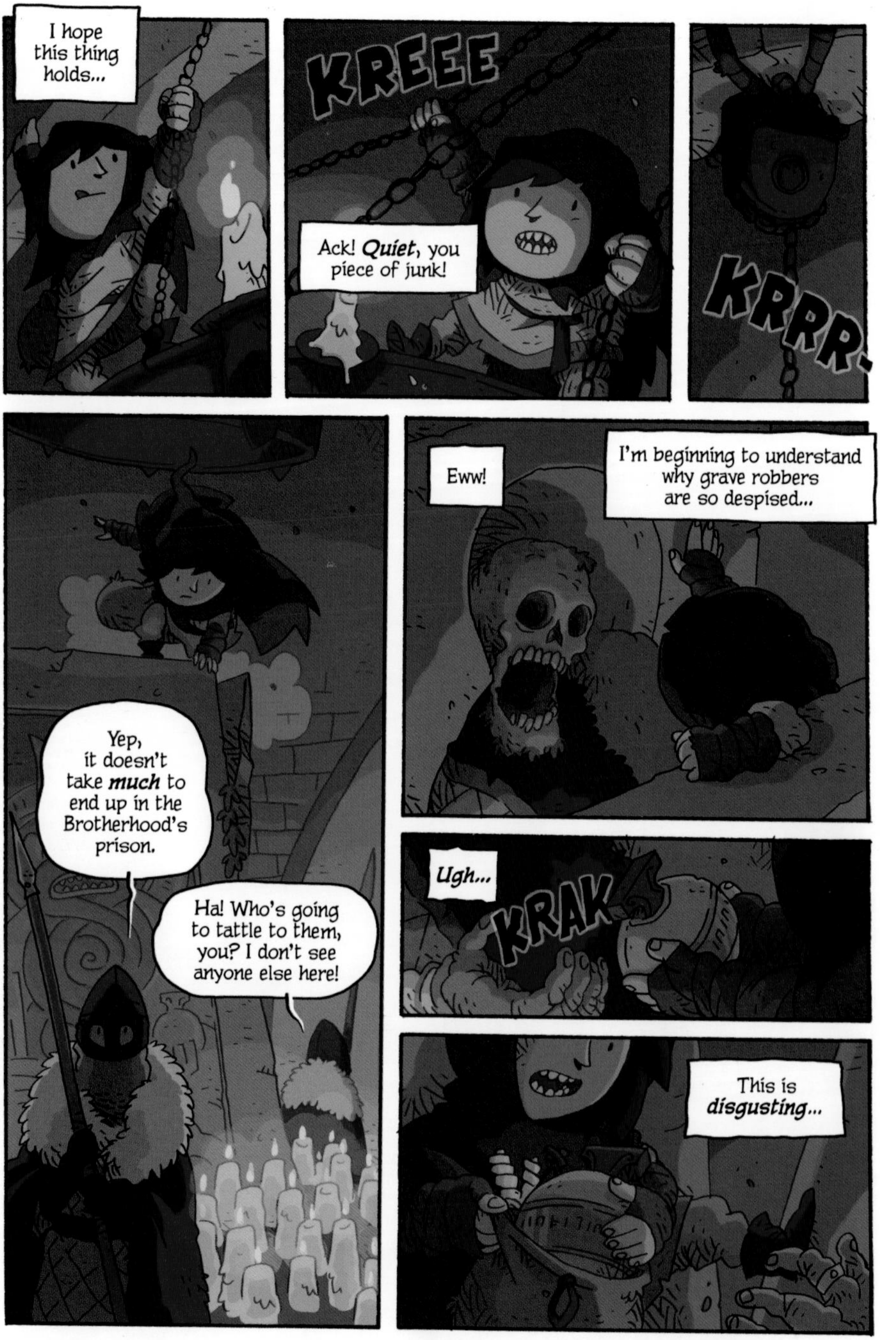
I hope this thing holds...
KREEE
Ack! *Quiet*, you piece of junk!
KRRR-
Yep, it doesn't take *much* to end up in the Brotherhood's prison.
Ha! Who's going to tattle to them, you? I don't see anyone else here!
Eww!
I'm beginning to understand why grave robbers are so despised...
Ugh...
KRAK
This is *disgusting*...

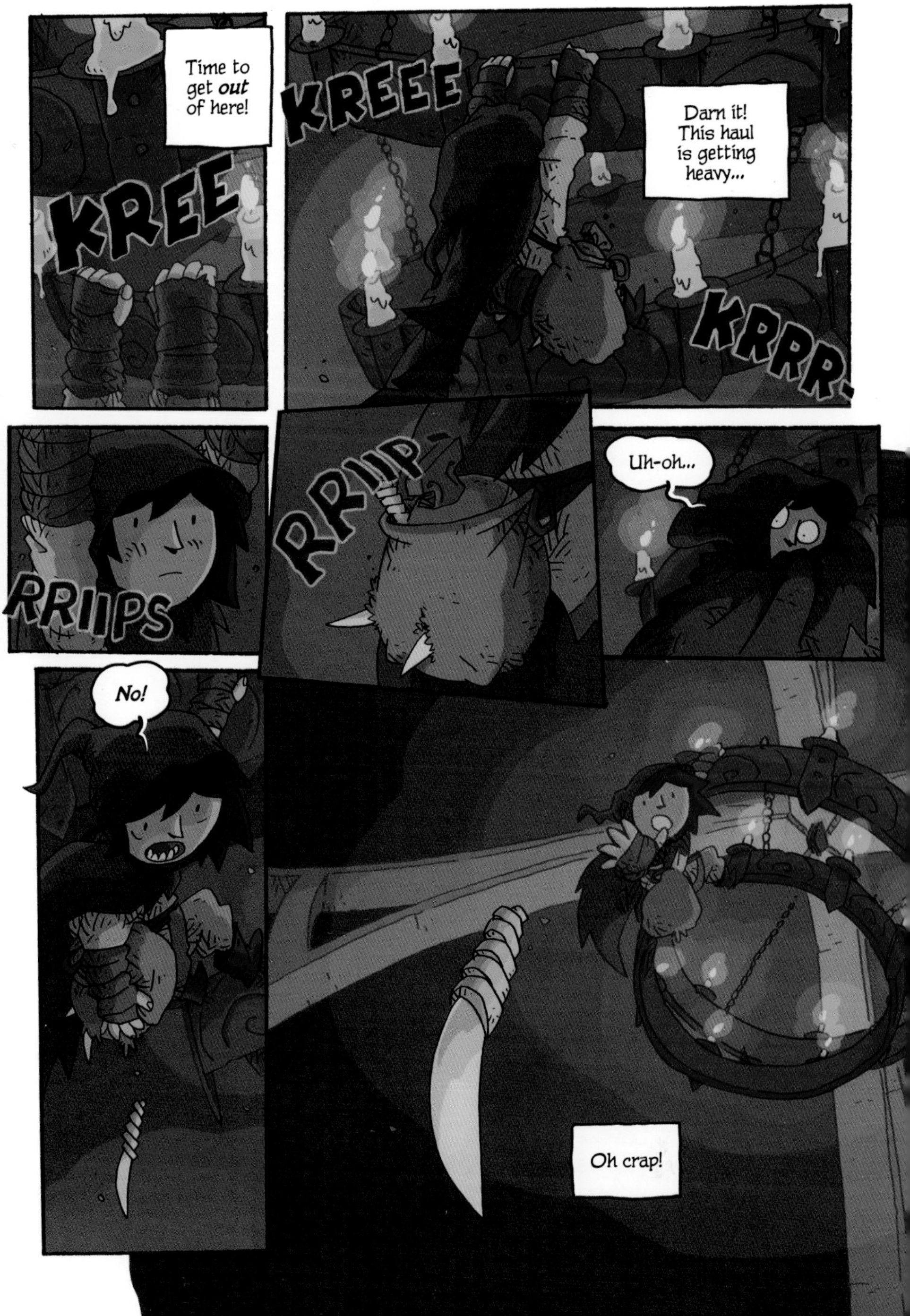
Time to get *out* of here!
KREE
KREEE
Darn it! This haul is getting heavy...
KRRRR-
RRIIPS
RRIIP
Uh-oh...
No!
Oh crap!

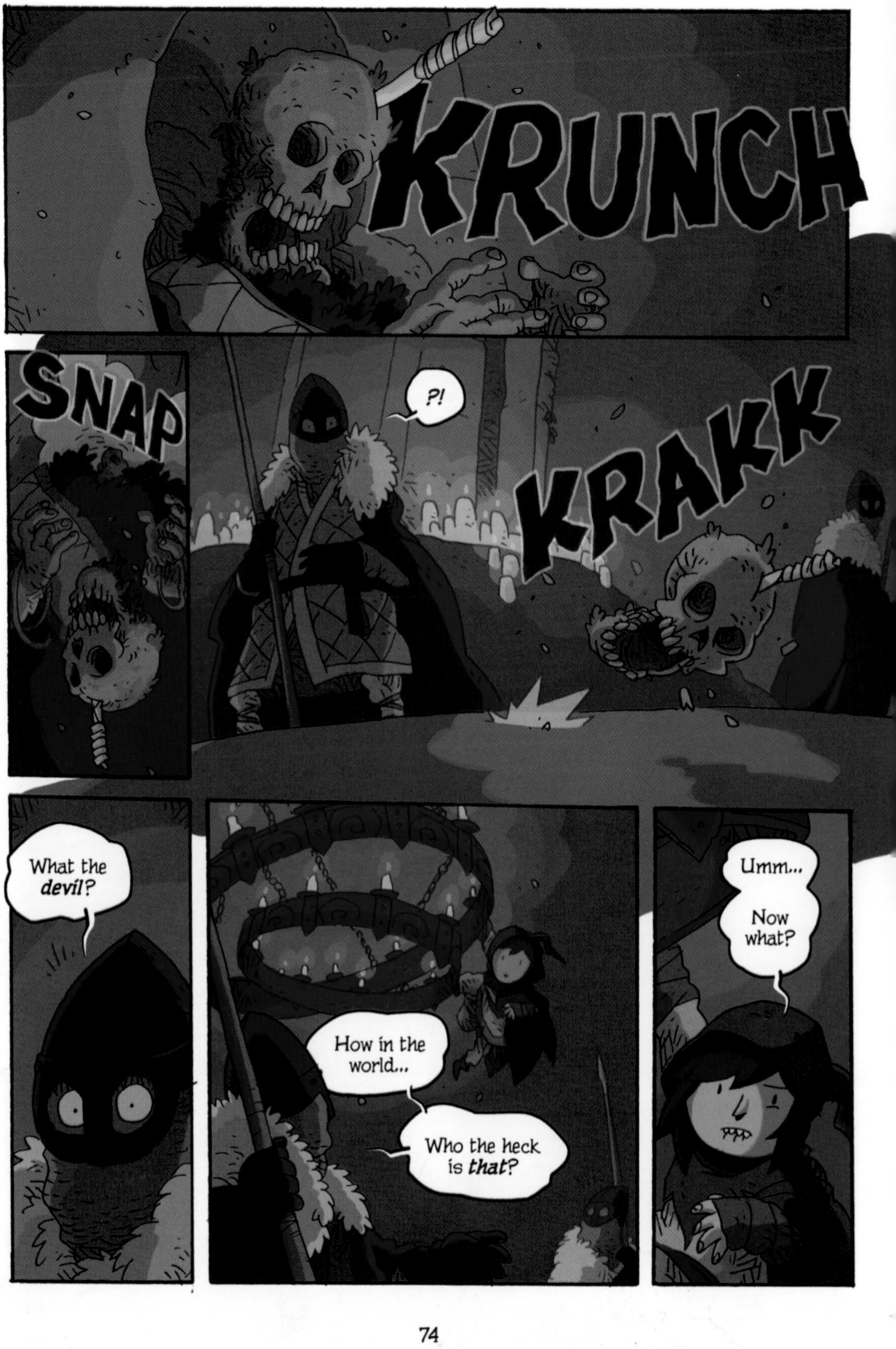
KRUNCH
SNAP
?!
KRAKK
What the *devil*?
How in the world...
Who the heck is ***that***?
Umm...
Now what?

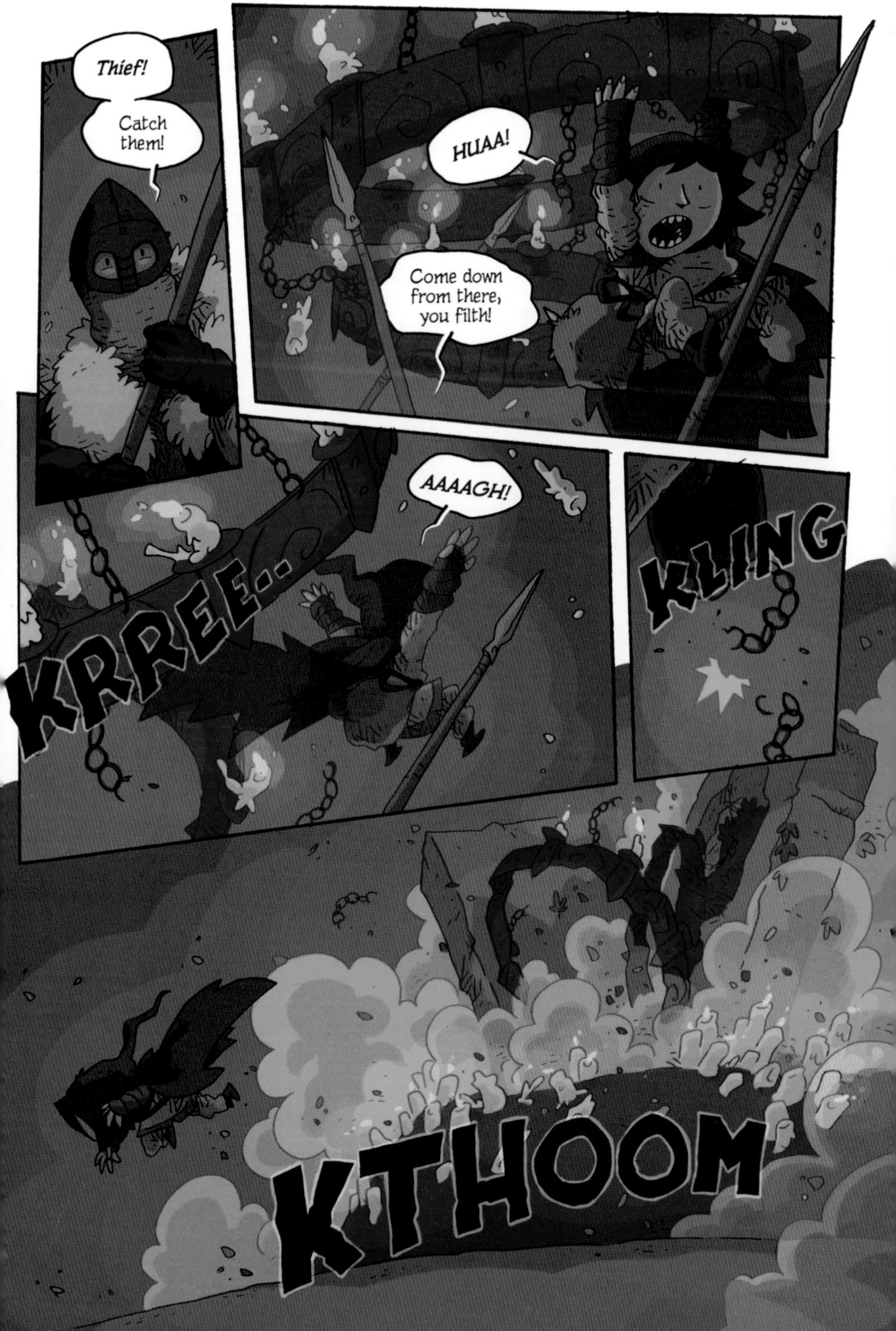
Thief!
Catch them!
HUAA!
Come down from there, you filth!
AAAAGH!
KRREE..
KLING
KTHOOM

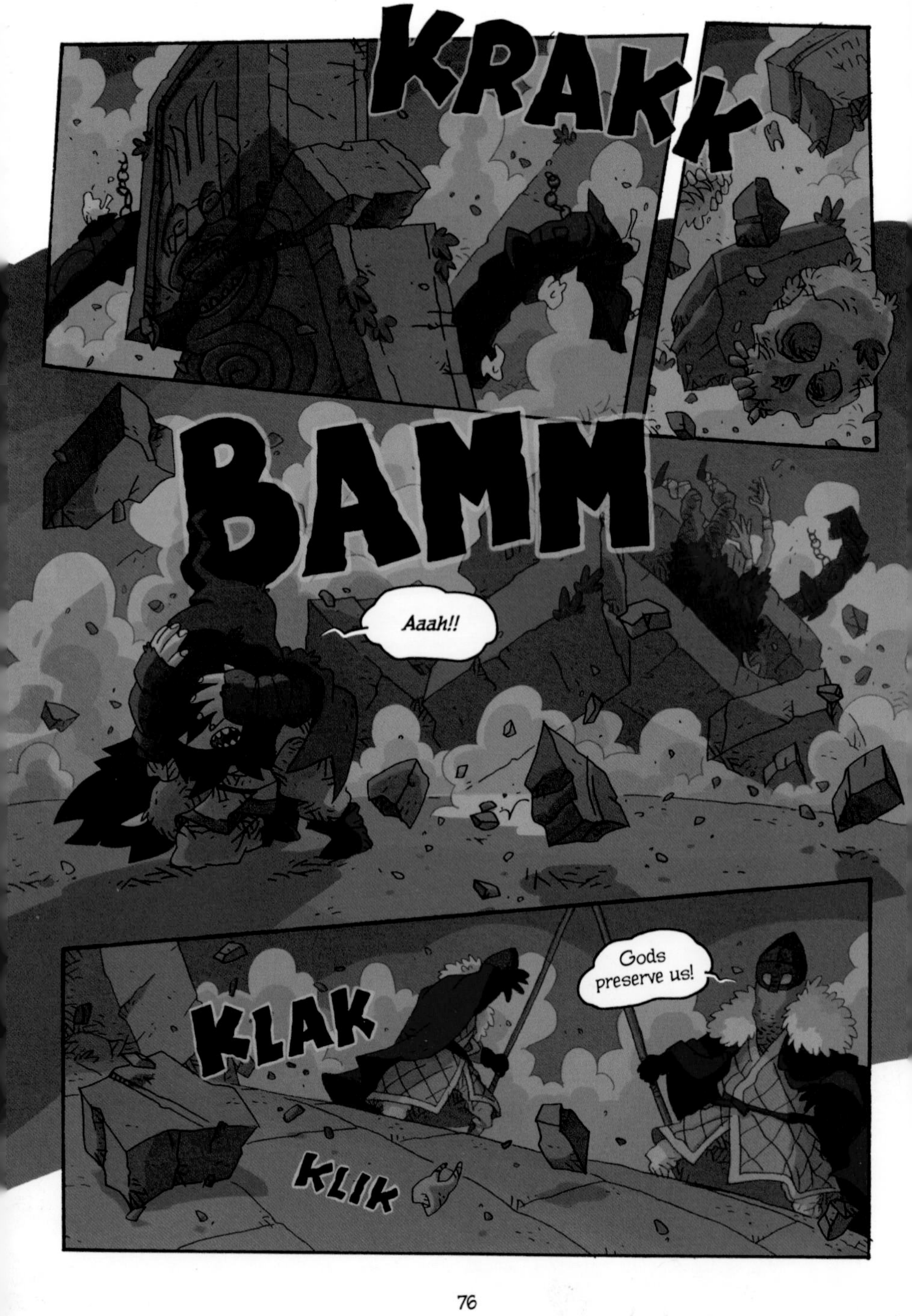
KRAKK
BAMM
Aaah!!
Gods preserve us!
KLAK
KLIK

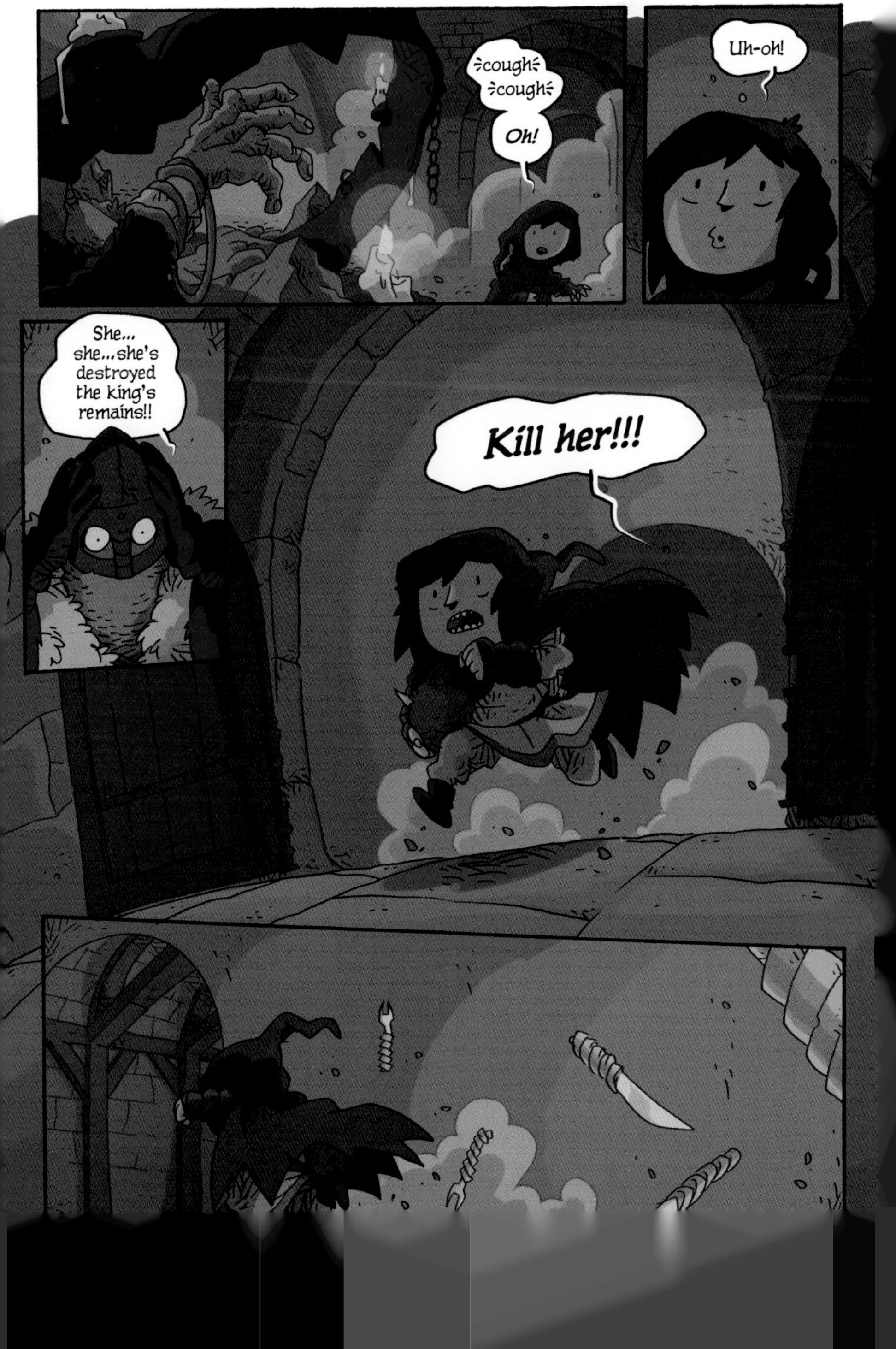

cough
cough
Oh!
Uh-oh!
She... she...she's destroyed the king's remains!!
Kill her!!!

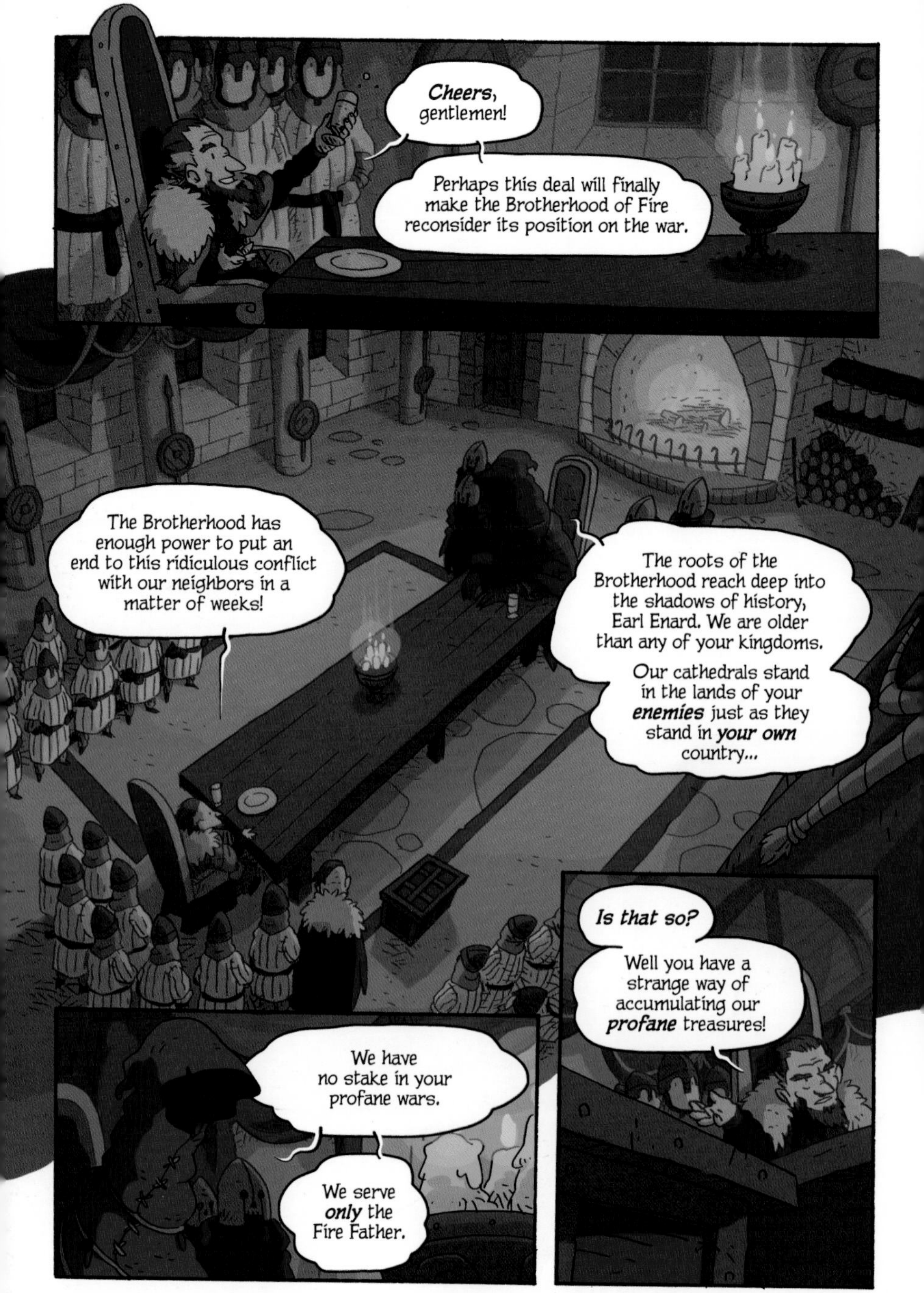

Cheers, gentlemen!
Perhaps this deal will finally make the Brotherhood of Fire reconsider its position on the war.
The Brotherhood has enough power to put an end to this ridiculous conflict with our neighbors in a matter of weeks!
The roots of the Brotherhood reach deep into the shadows of history, Earl Enard. We are older than any of your kingdoms.
Our cathedrals stand in the lands of your enemies just as they stand in your own country...
We have no stake in your profane wars.
We serve only the Fire Father.
Is that so?
Well you have a strange way of accumulating our profane treasures!

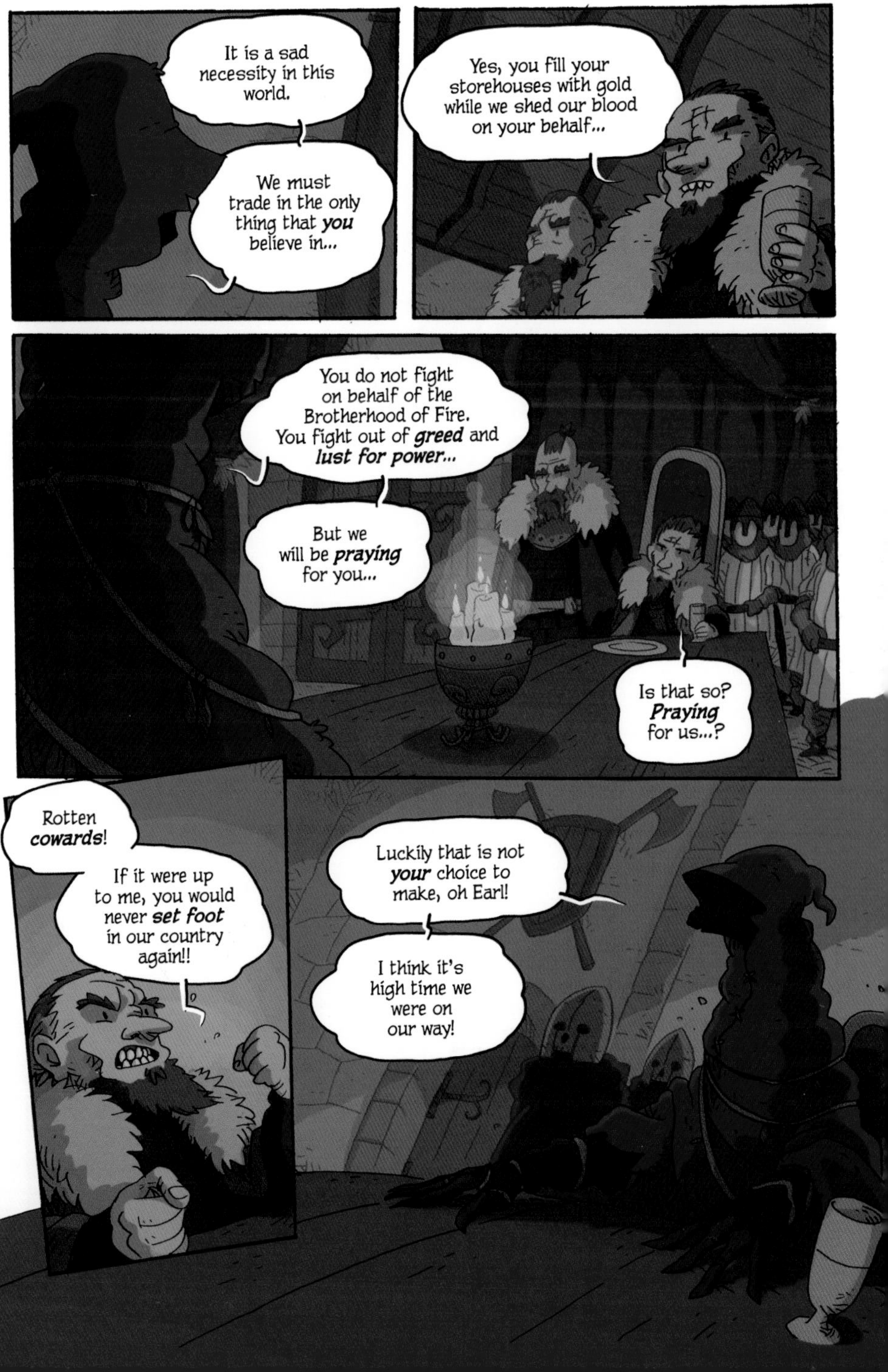
It is a sad necessity in this world.
We must trade in the only thing that *you* believe in...
Yes, you fill your storehouses with gold while we shed our blood on your behalf...
You do not fight on behalf of the Brotherhood of Fire. You fight out of ***greed*** and ***lust for power***...
But we will be ***praying*** for you...
Is that so? ***Praying*** for us...?
Rotten ***cowards***!
If it were up to me, you would never ***set foot*** in our country again!!
Luckily that is not ***your*** choice to make, oh Earl!
I think it's high time we were on our way!

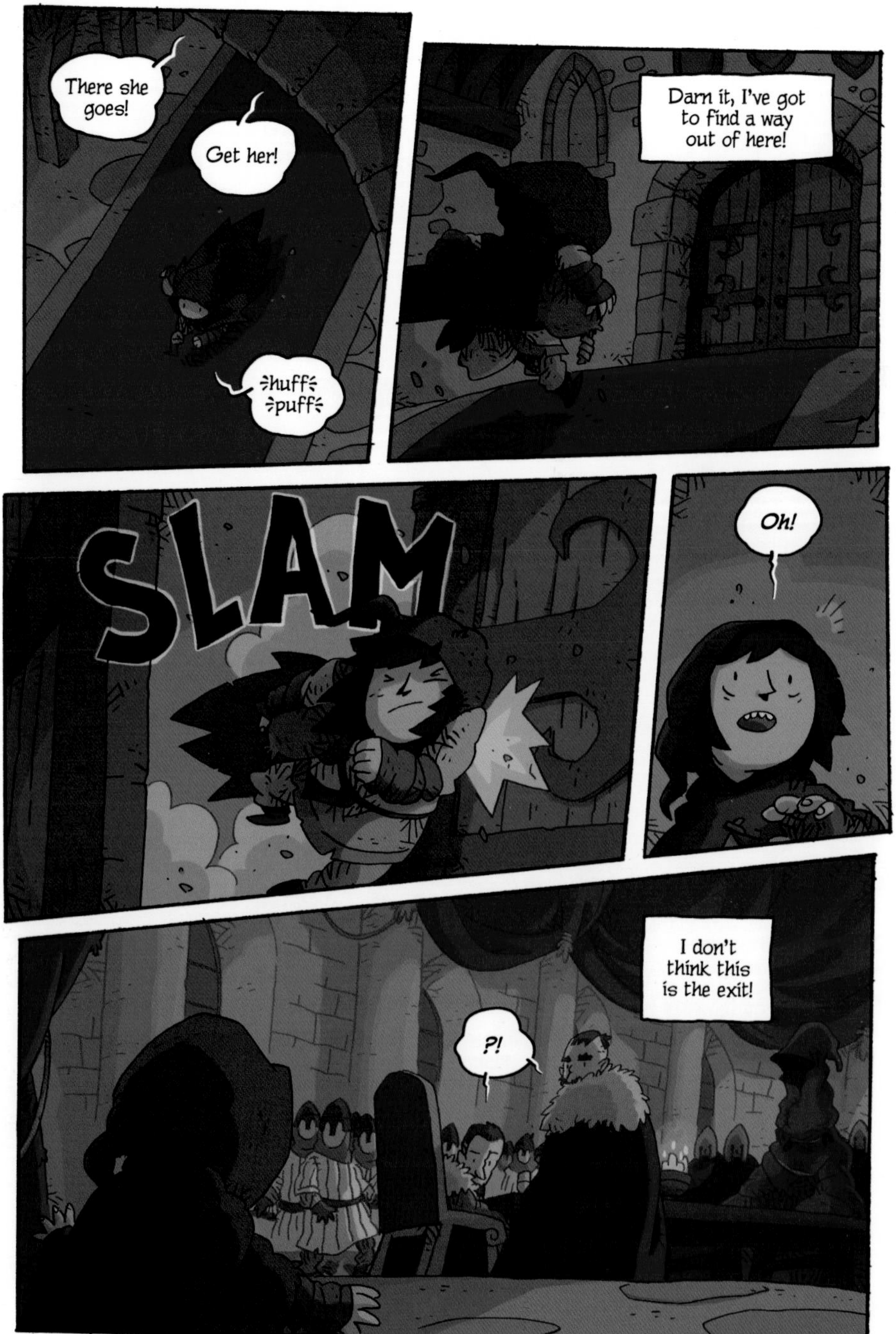
There she goes!
Get her!
huff puff
Darn it, I've got to find a way out of here!
SLAM
Oh!
I don't think this is the exit!
?!

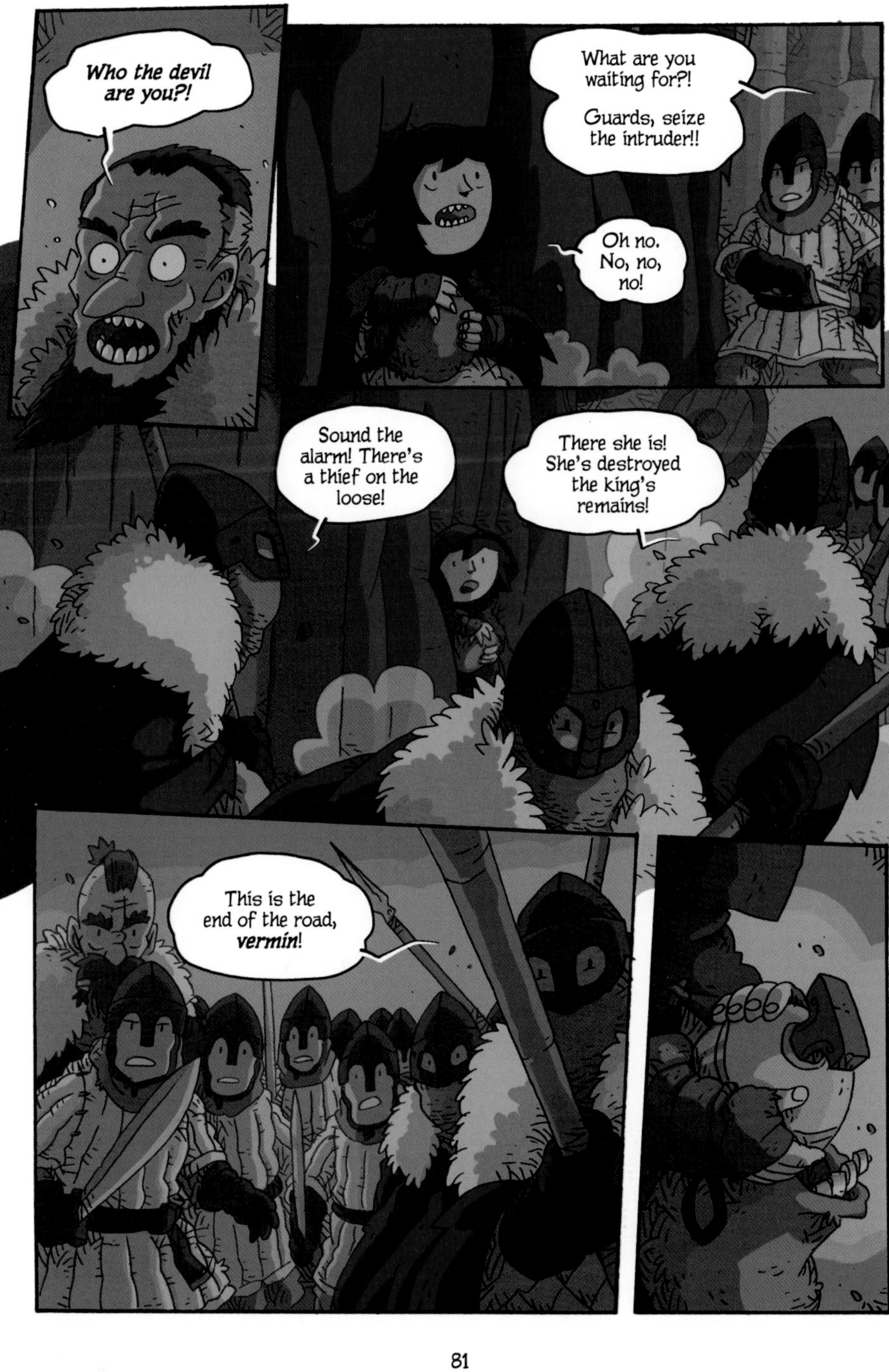

Who the devil are you?!
What are you waiting for?!
Guards, seize the intruder!!
Oh no. No, no, no!
Sound the alarm! There's a thief on the loose!
There she is! She's destroyed the king's remains!
This is the end of the road, ***vermin***!

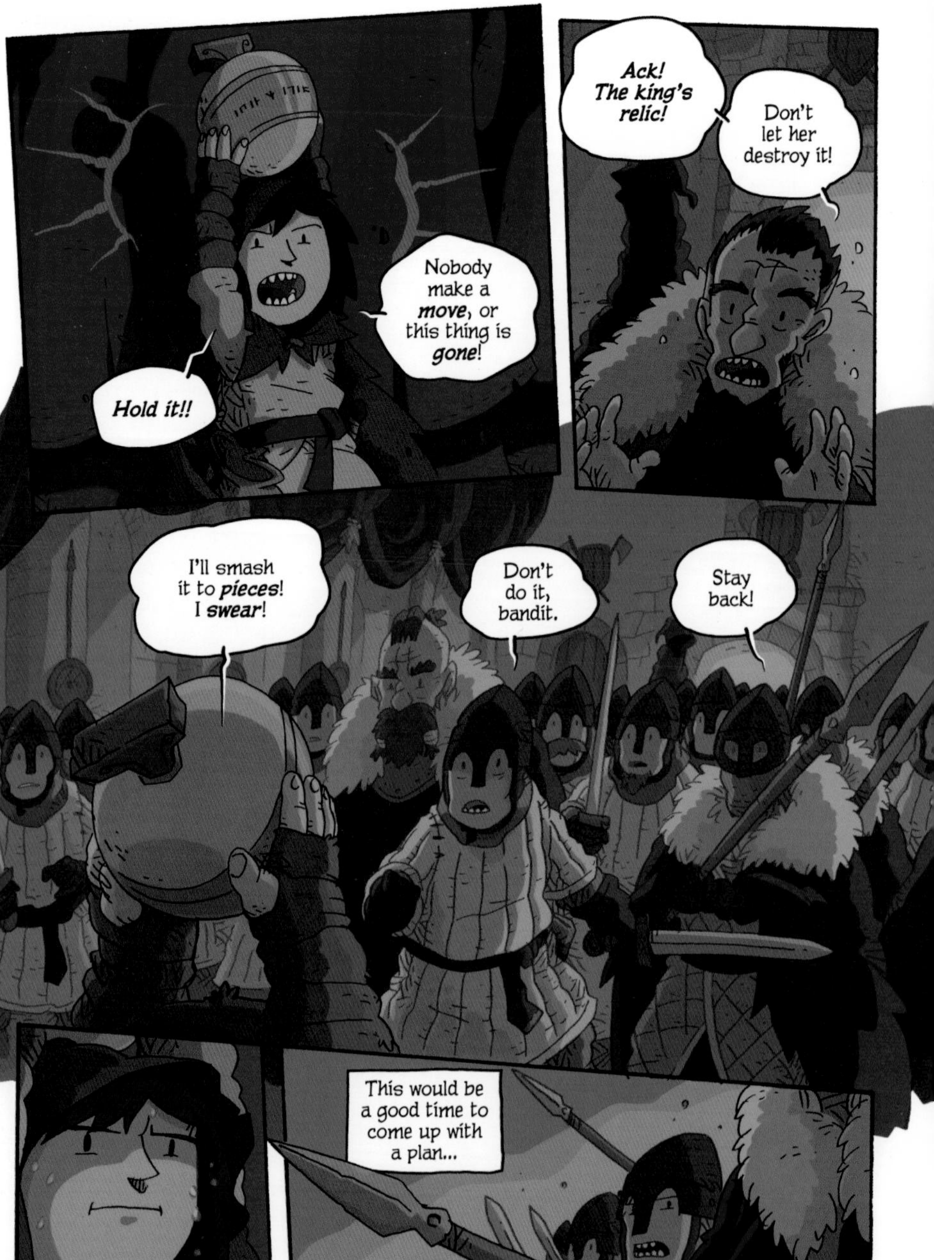
Hold it!!
Nobody make a *move*, or this thing is *gone*!
Ack! The king's relic!
Don't let her destroy it!
I'll smash it to *pieces*! I *swear*!
Don't do it, bandit.
Stay back!
This would be a good time to come up with a plan...

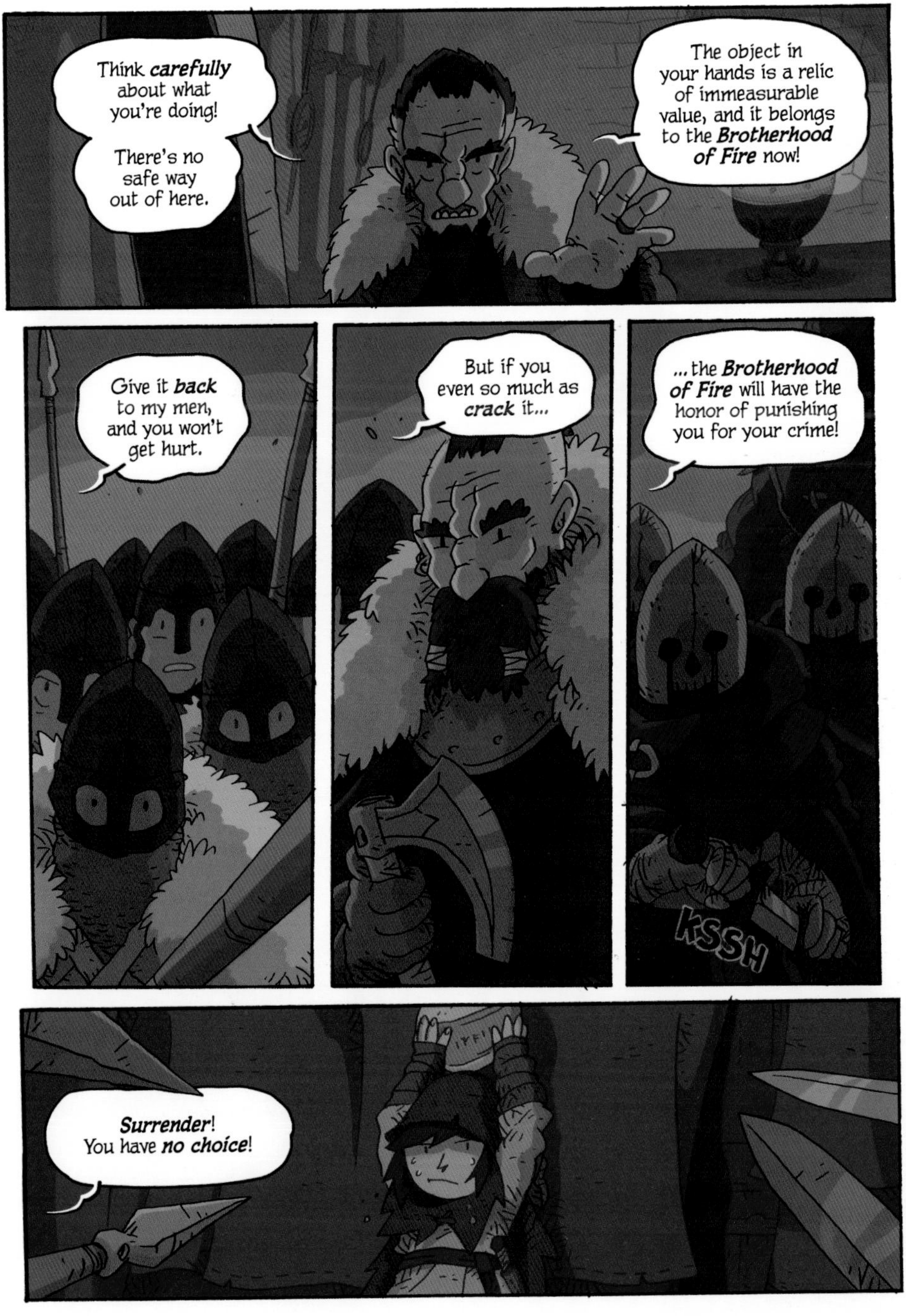
Think *carefully* about what you're doing!
There's no safe way out of here.
The object in your hands is a relic of immeasurable value, and it belongs to the *Brotherhood of Fire* now!
Give it *back* to my men, and you won't get hurt.
But if you even so much as *crack* it...
...the *Brotherhood of Fire* will have the honor of punishing you for your crime!
KSSH
Surrender! You have *no choice*!

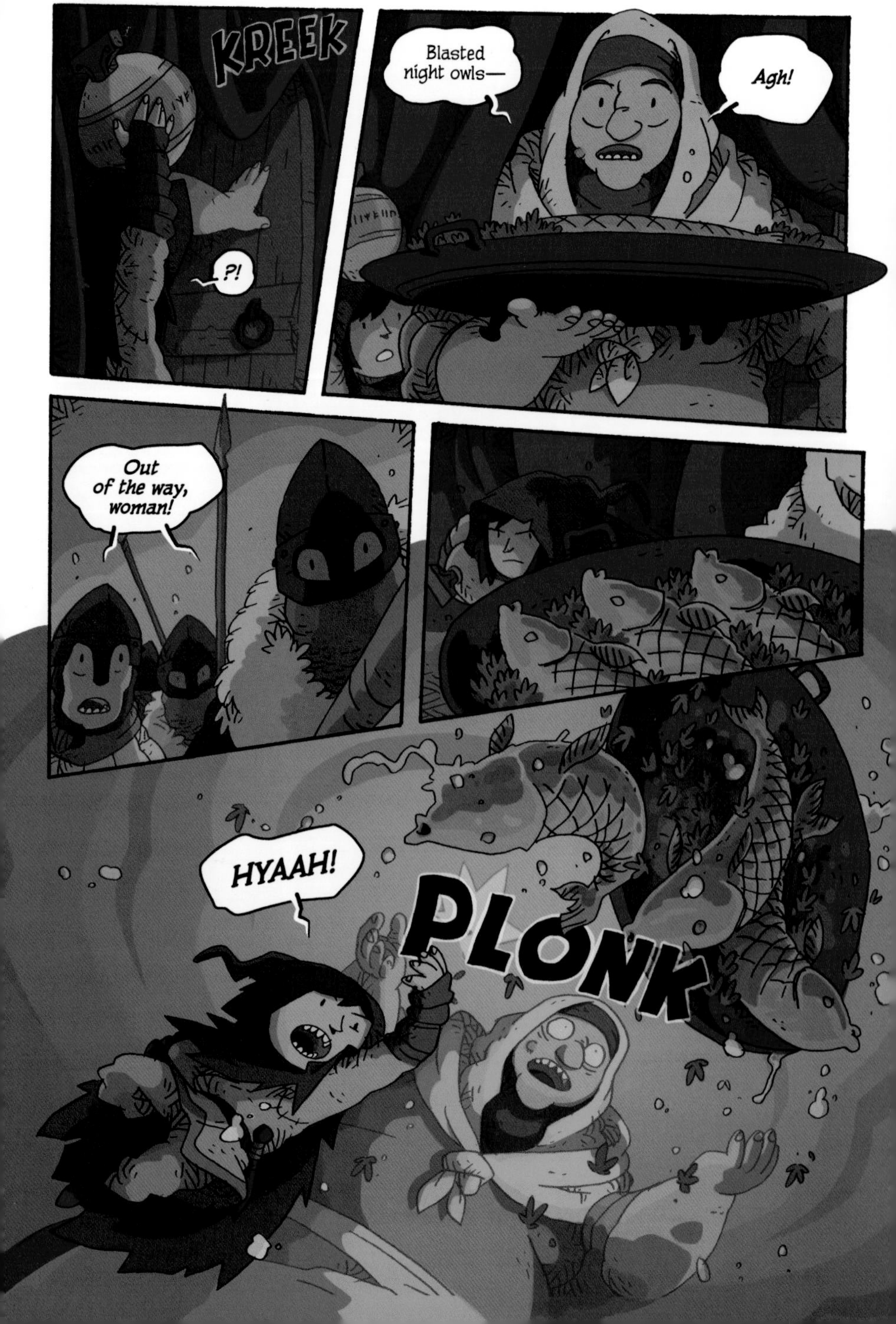

KREEK
?!
Blasted night owls—
Agh!
Out of the way, woman!
HYAAH!
PLONK

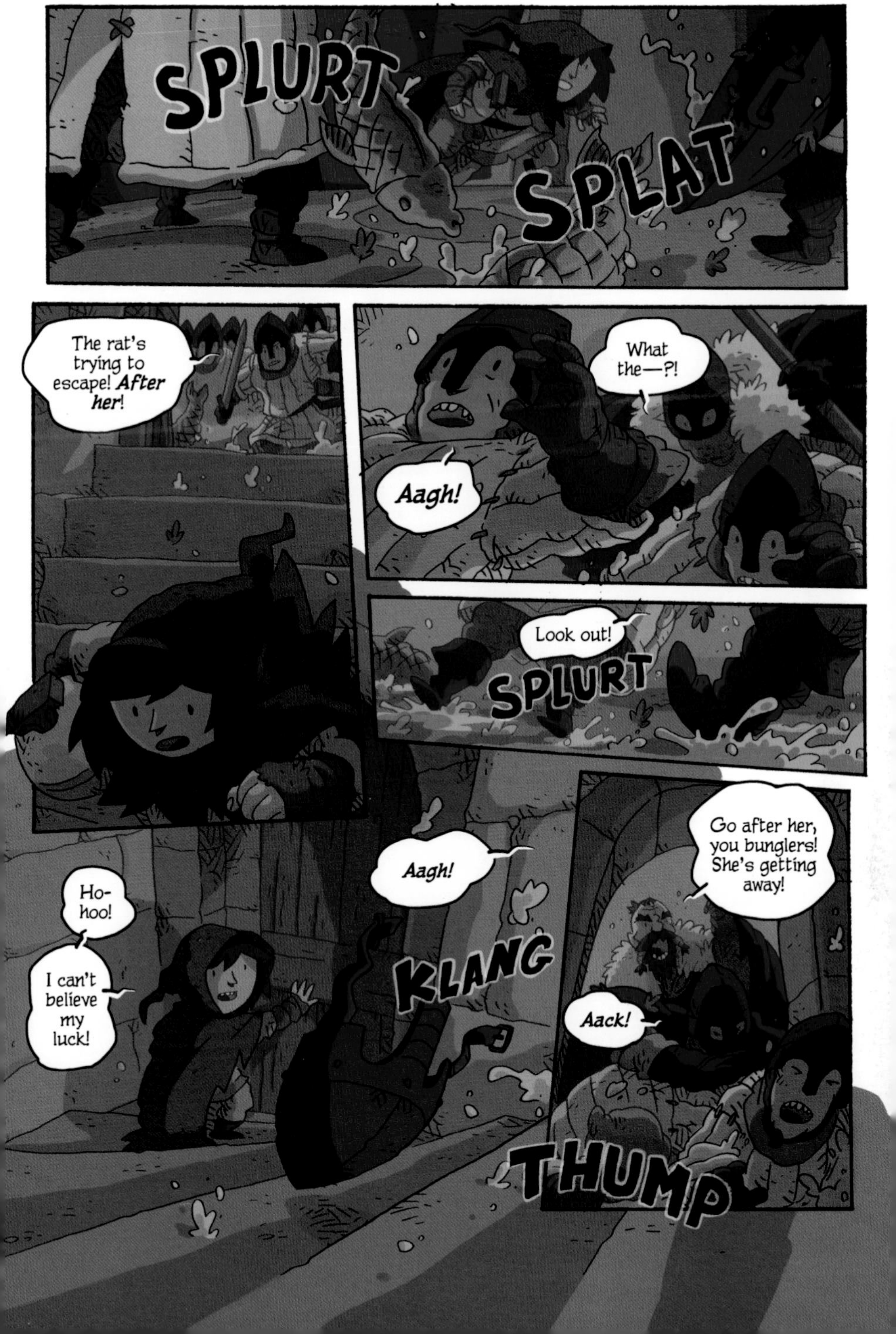
SPLURT
SPLAT
The rat's trying to escape! **After her**!
What the—?!
Aagh!
Look out!
SPLURT
Go after her, you bunglers! She's getting away!
Aagh!
Ho-hoo!
I can't believe my luck!
KLANG
Aack!
THUMP

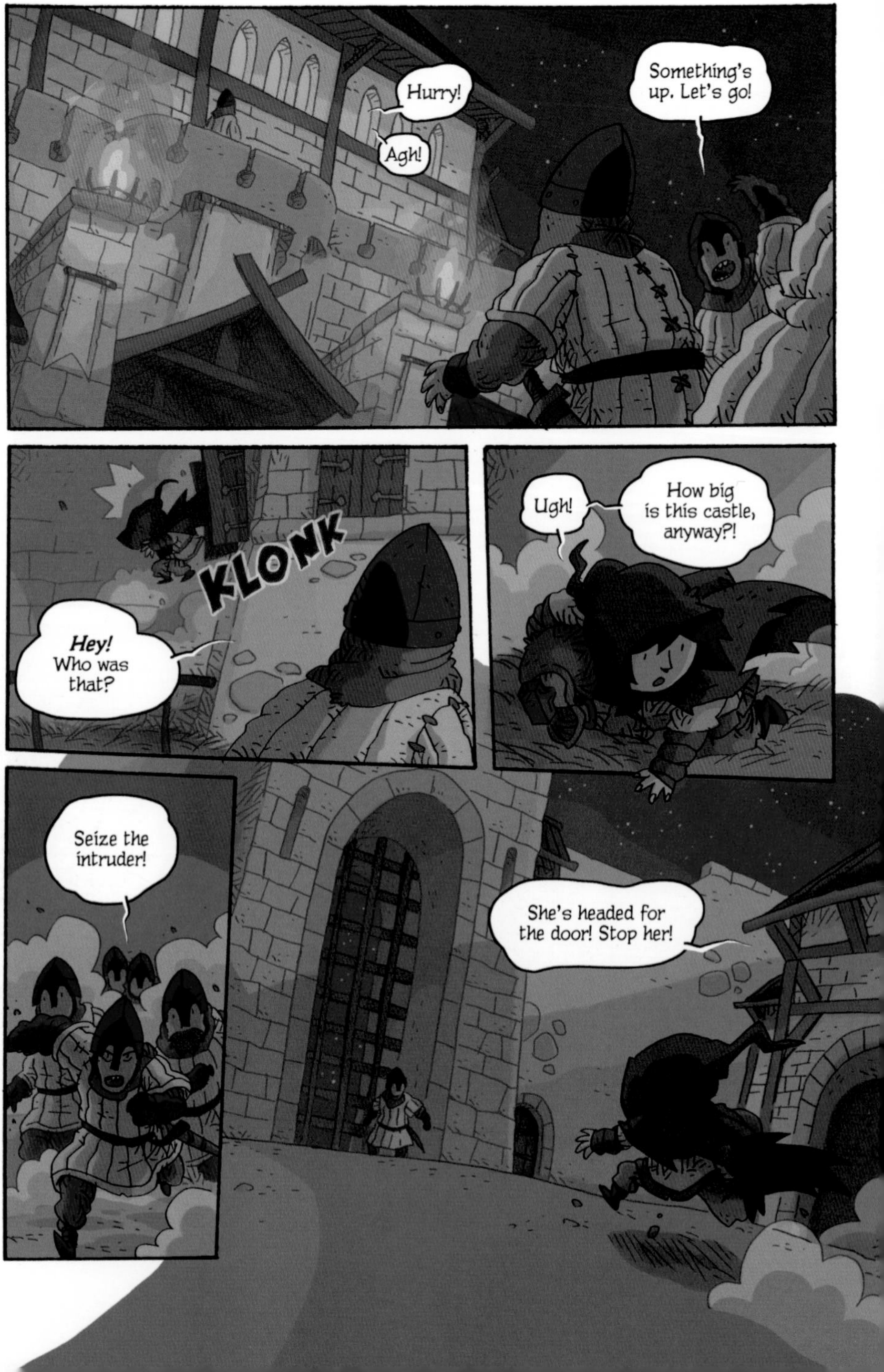
Hurry!
Agh!
Something's up. Let's go!
KLONK
Hey! Who was that?
Ugh!
How big is this castle, anyway?!
Seize the intruder!
She's headed for the door! Stop her!

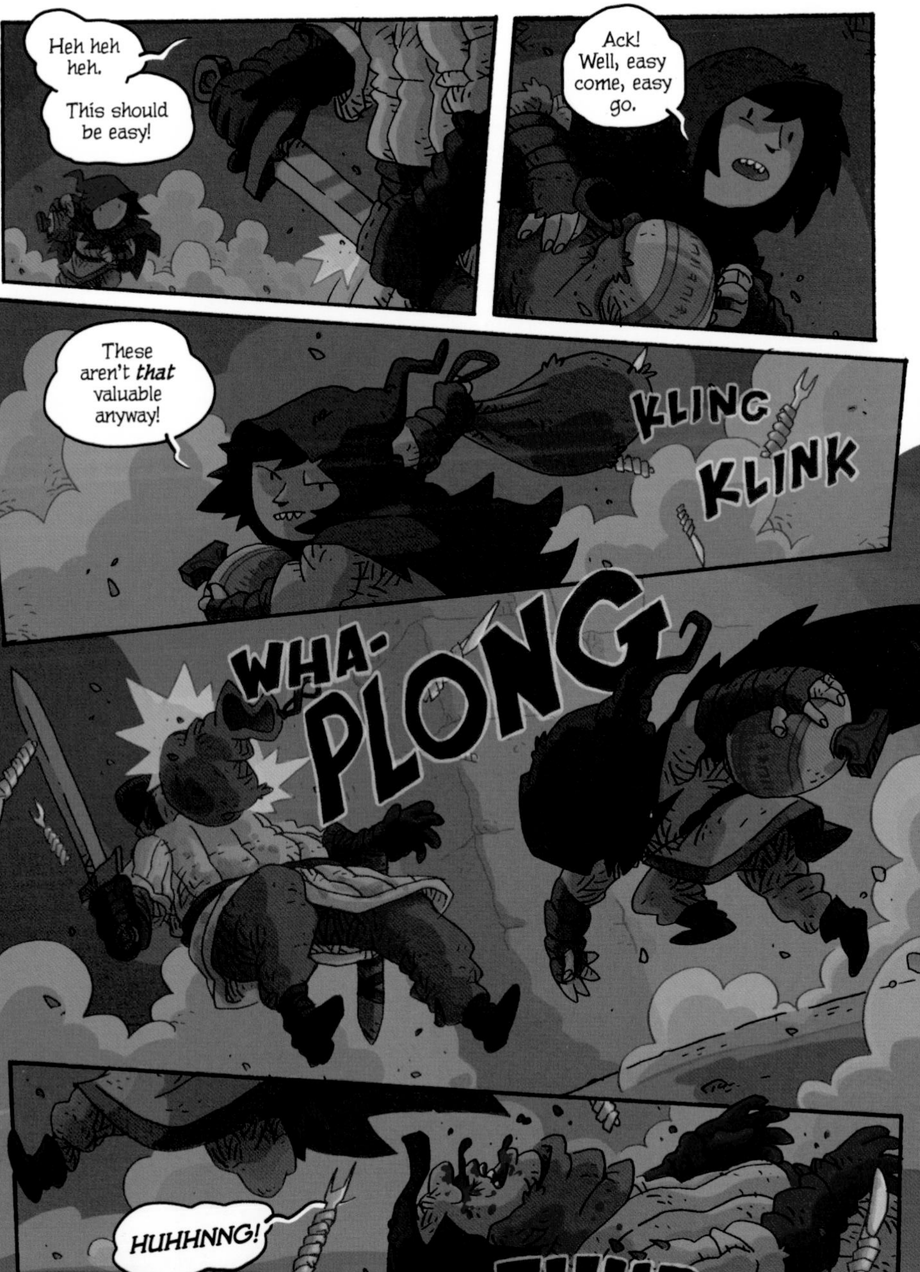
Heh heh heh.
This should be easy!
Ack! Well, easy come, easy go.
These aren't *that* valuable anyway!
KLING
KLINK
WHA-PLONG
HUHHNNG!
THUD

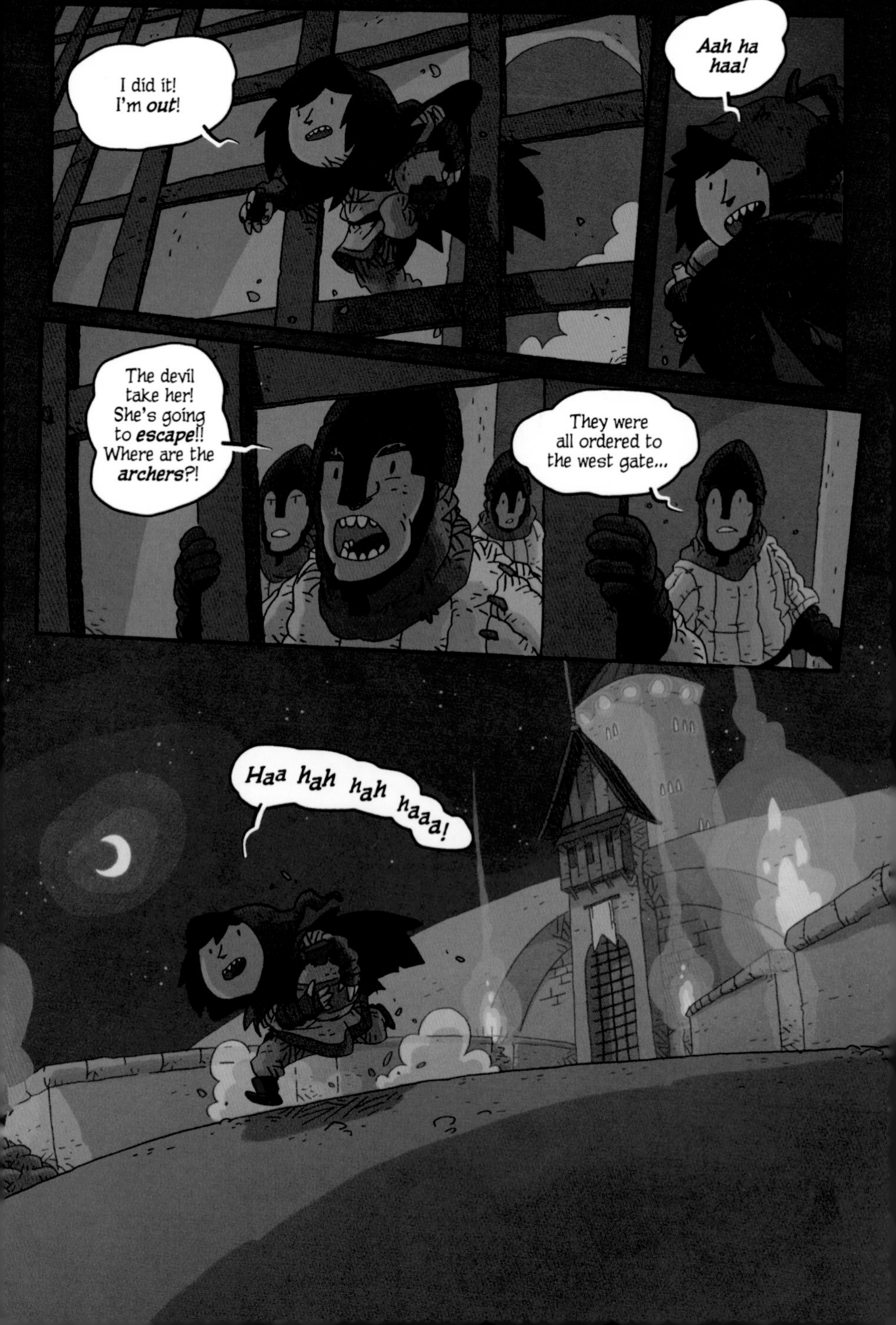
I did it! I'm *out*!
Aah ha haa!
The devil take her! She's going to ***escape***!! Where are the ***archers***?!
They were all ordered to the west gate...
Haa hah hah haaa!

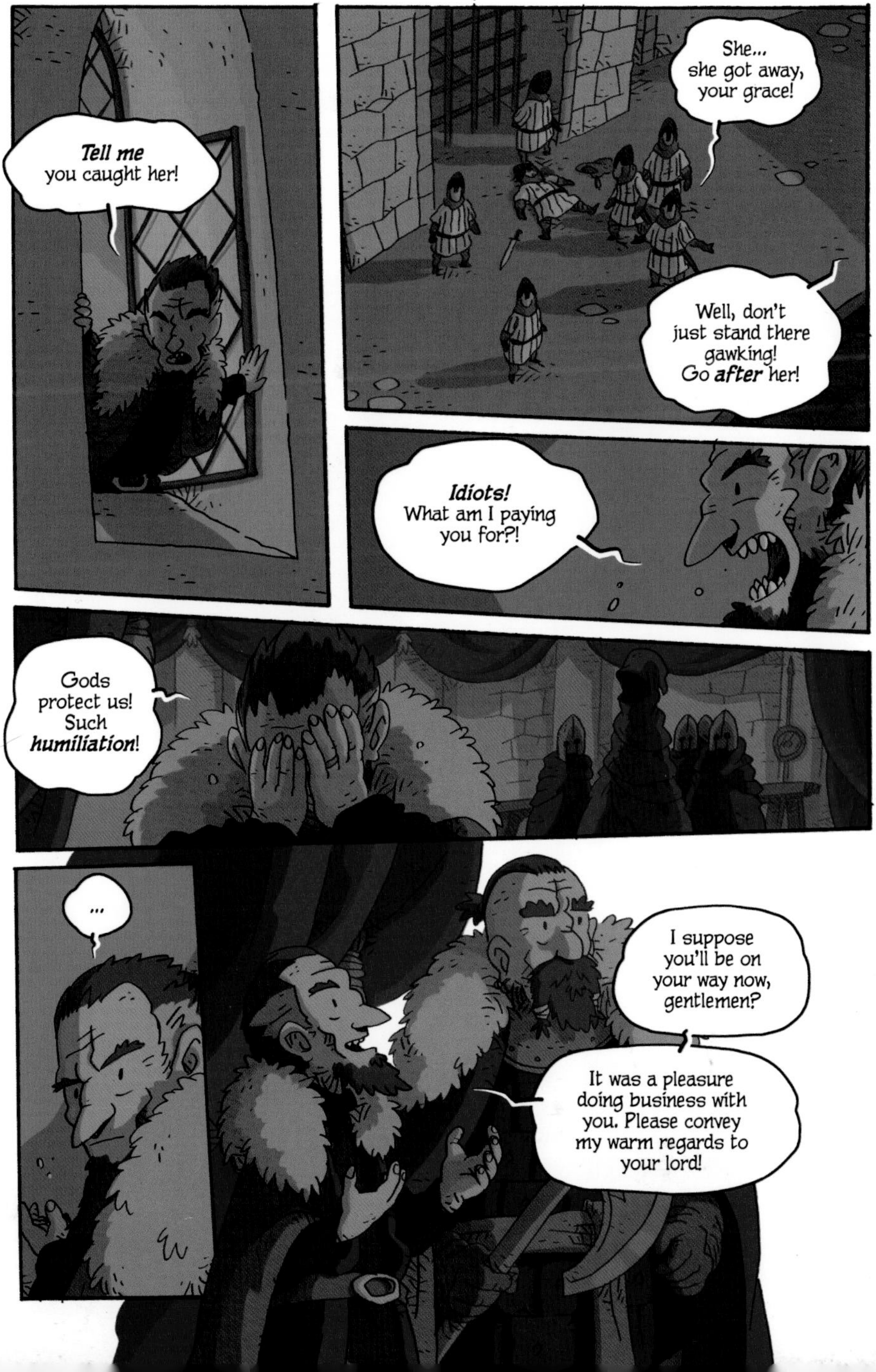
Tell me you caught her!
She... she got away, your grace!
Well, don't just stand there gawking! Go *after* her!
Idiots! What am I paying you for?!
Gods protect us! Such *humiliation*!
...
I suppose you'll be on your way now, gentlemen?
It was a pleasure doing business with you. Please convey my warm regards to your lord!

Secrets deep are whispered,
Of where a faint light flickers,
Upon a gleaming treasure,
Riches beyond measure,
Golden, upon gold.

The **Three Locks**

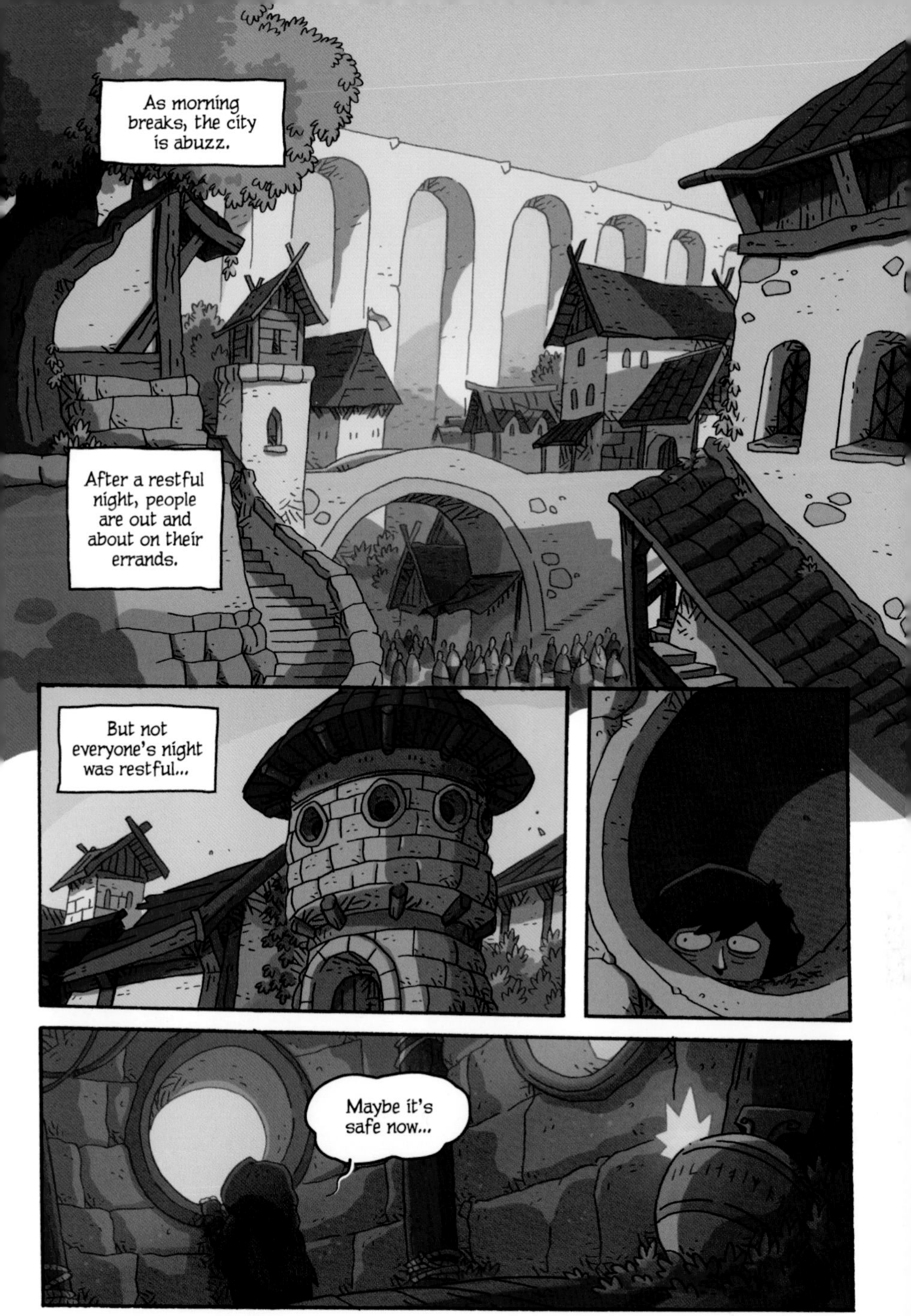
As morning breaks, the city is abuzz.
After a restful night, people are out and about on their errands.
But not everyone's night was restful...
Maybe it's safe now...

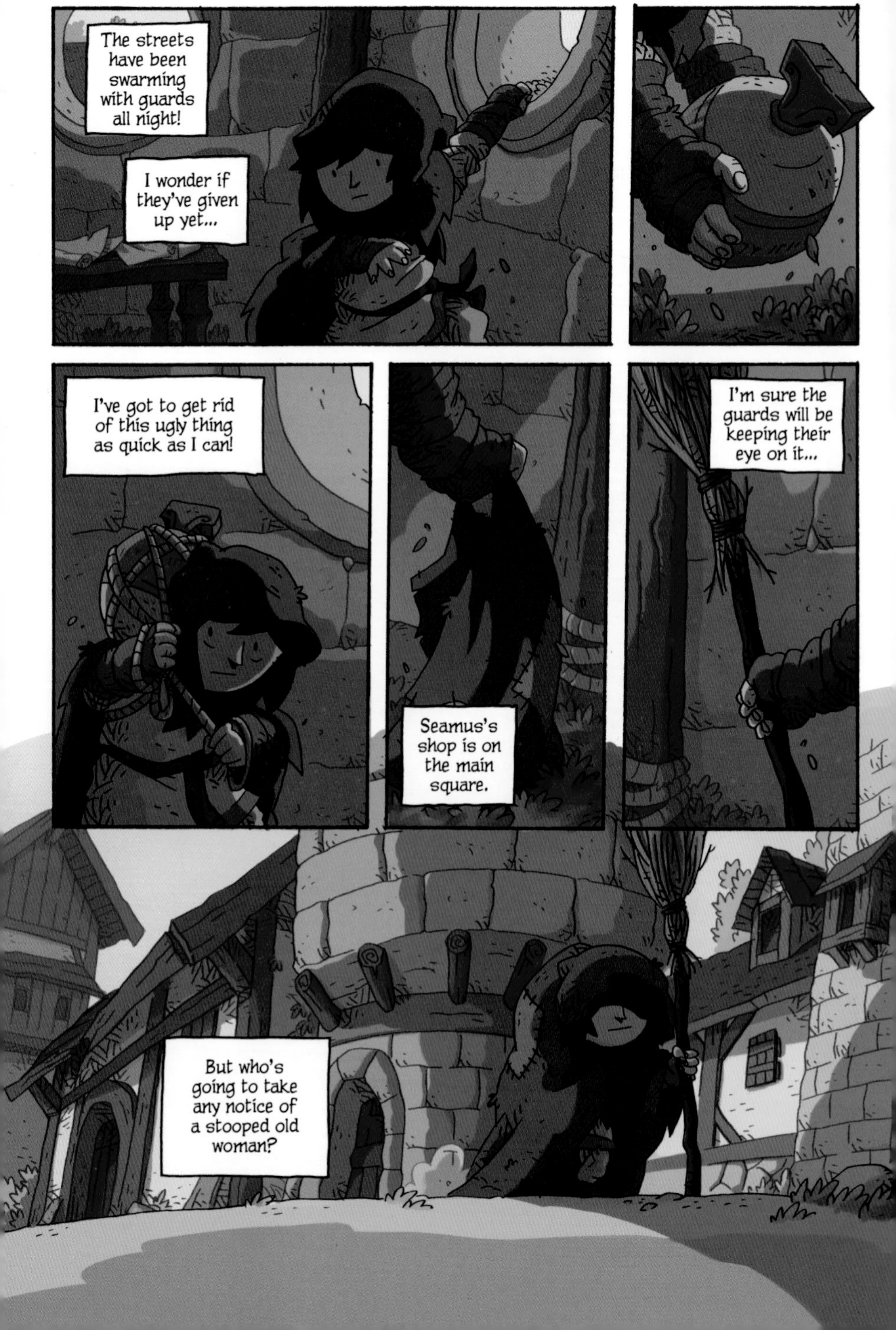
The streets have been swarming with guards all night!
I wonder if they've given up yet...
I've got to get rid of this ugly thing as quick as I can!
Seamus's shop is on the main square.
I'm sure the guards will be keeping their eye on it...
But who's going to take any notice of a stooped old woman?

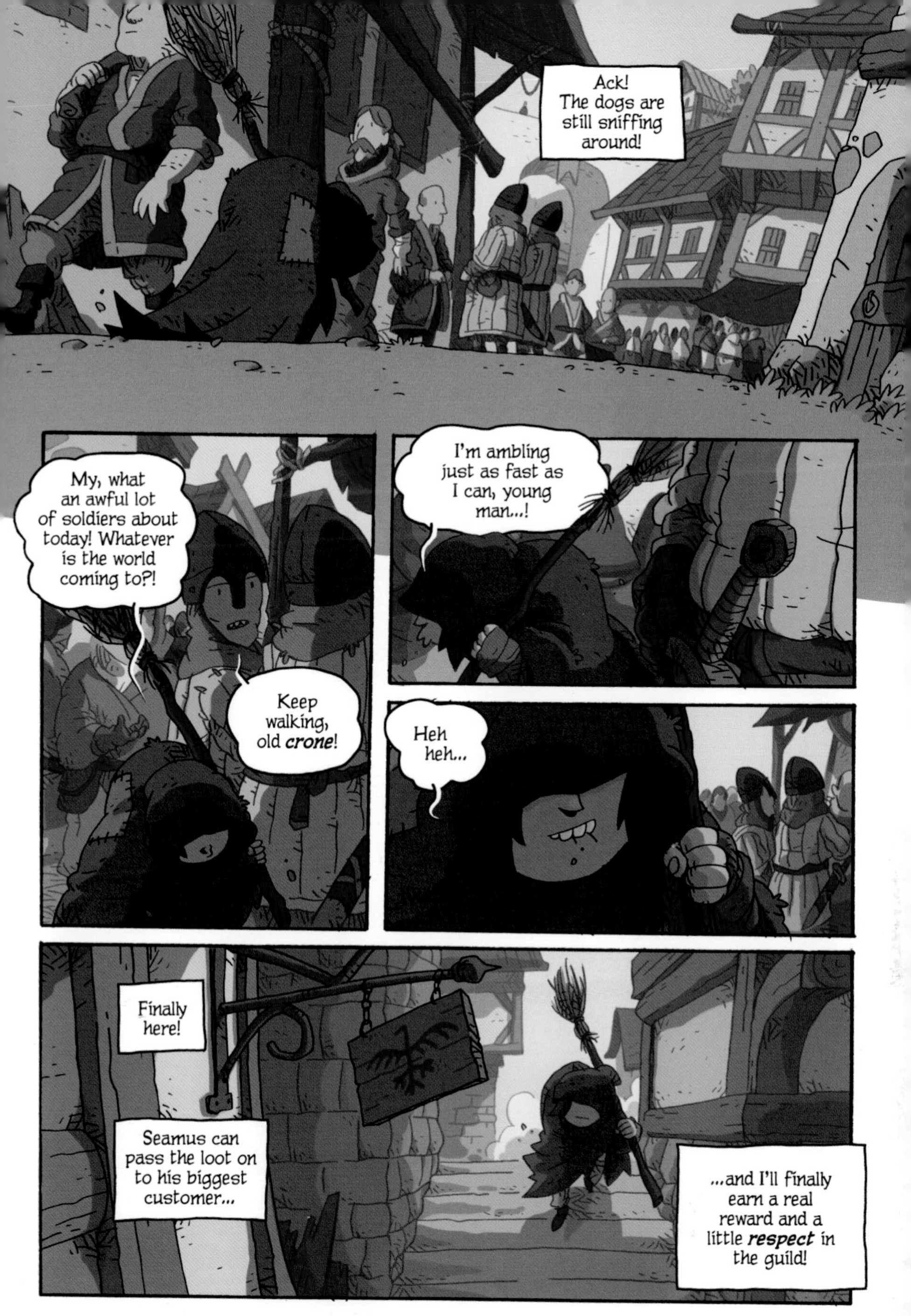
Ack! The dogs are still sniffing around!
My, what an awful lot of soldiers about today! Whatever is the world coming to?!
Keep walking, old *crone*!
I'm ambling just as fast as I can, young man...!
Heh heh...
Finally here!
Seamus can pass the loot on to his biggest customer...
...and I'll finally earn a real reward and a little *respect* in the guild!

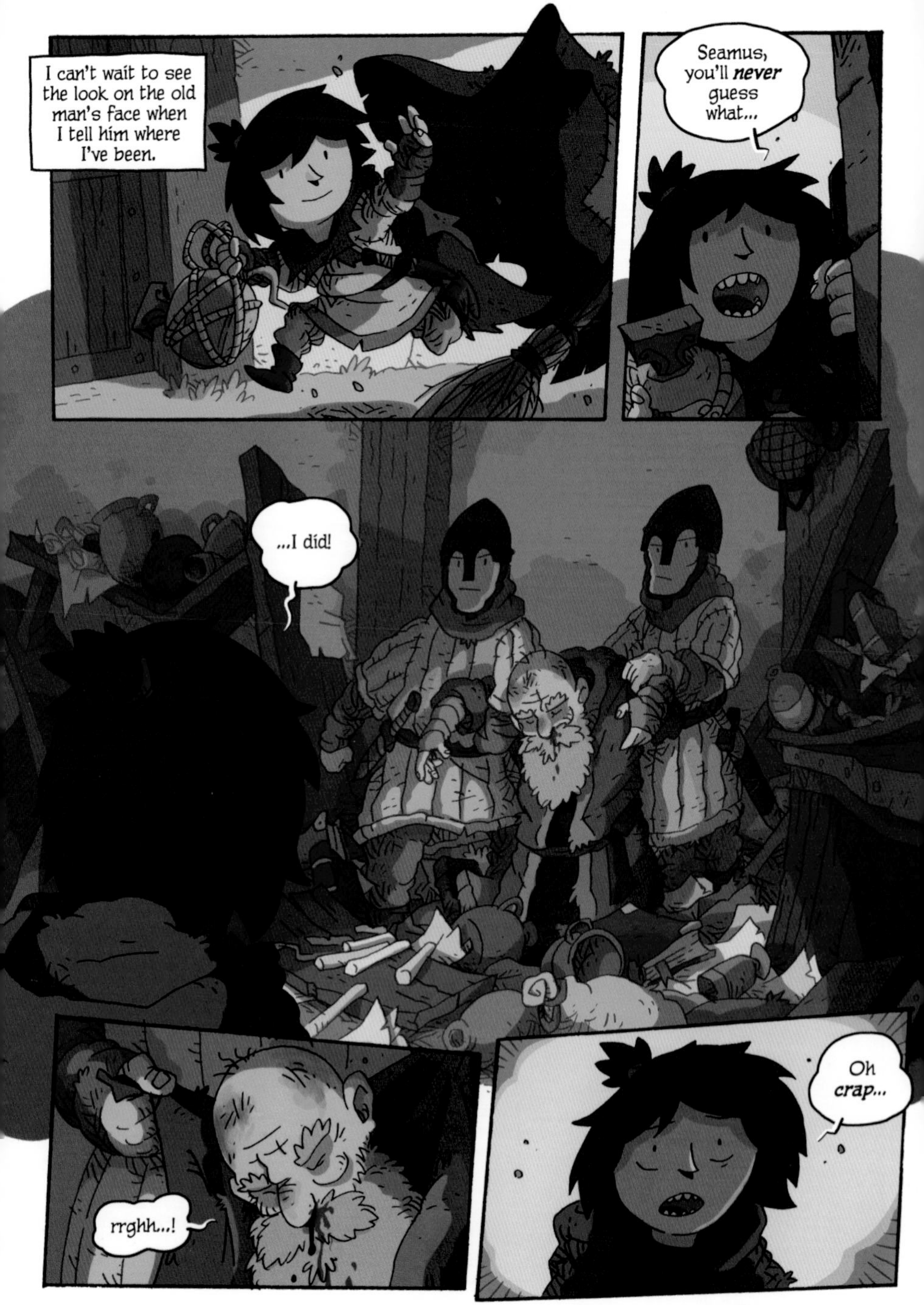
I can't wait to see the look on the old man's face when I tell him where I've been.
Seamus, you'll ***never*** guess what...
...I did!
rrghh...!
Oh *crap*...

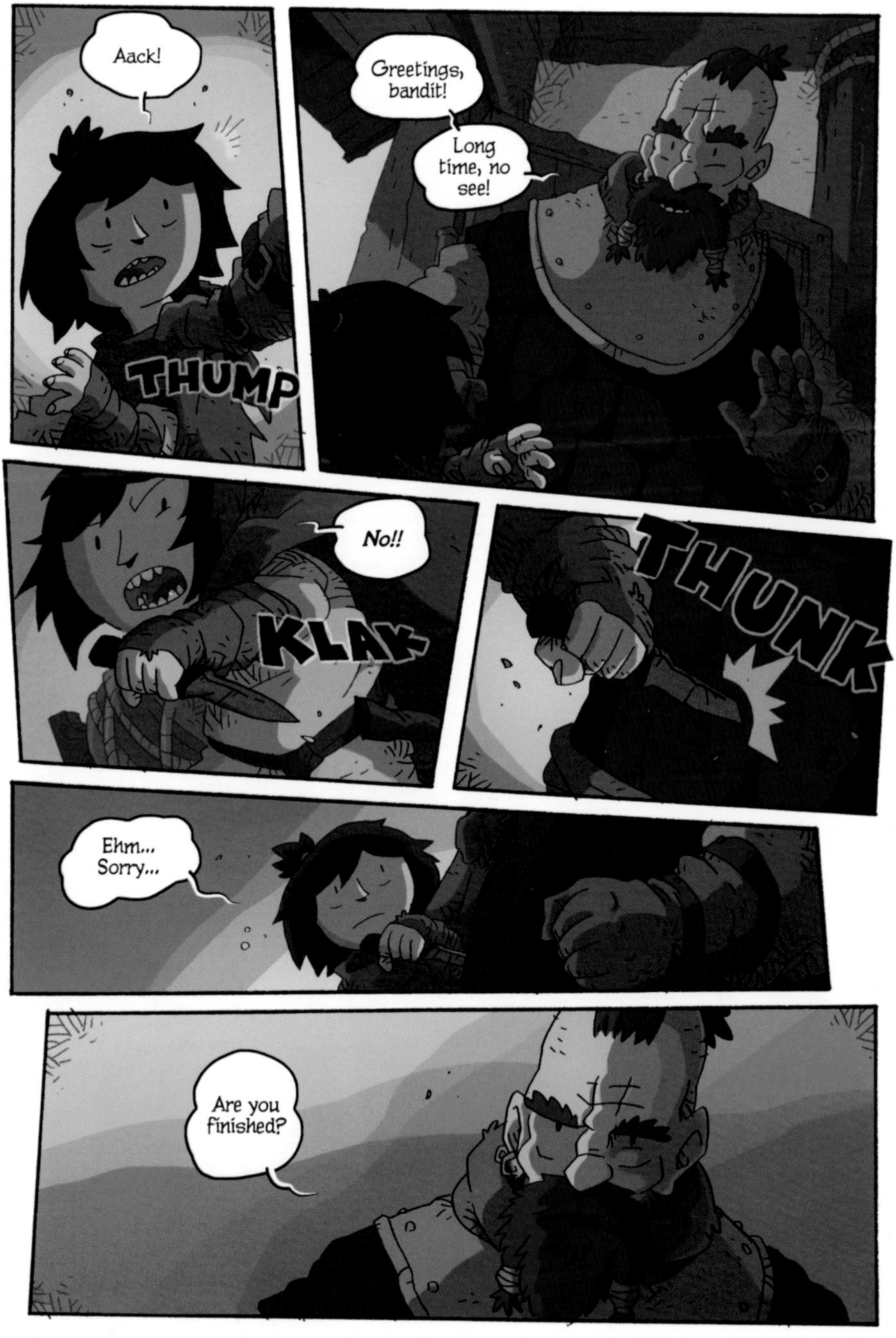
Aack!
THUMP
Greetings, bandit!
Long time, no see!
No!!
KLAK
THUNK
Ehm... Sorry...
Are you finished?

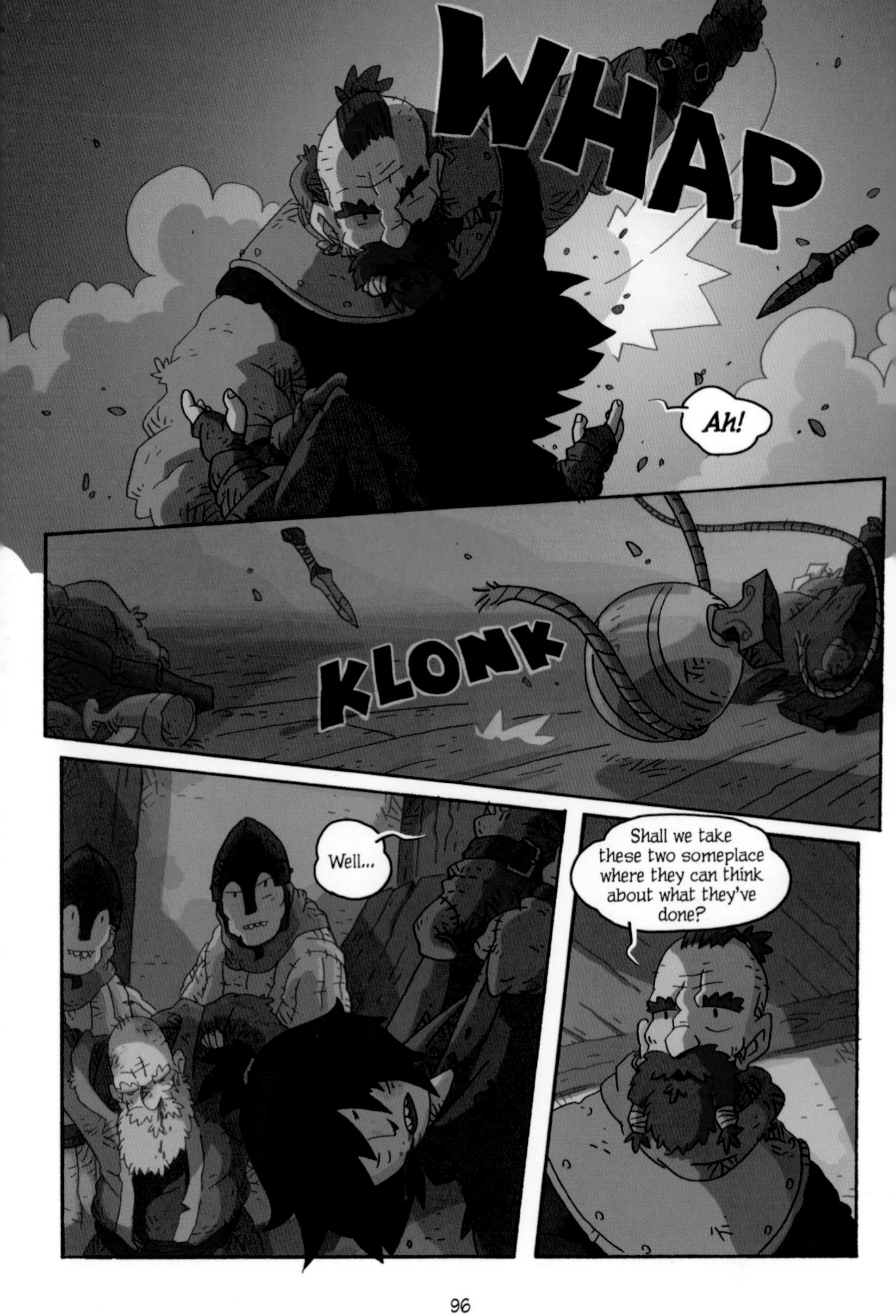
WHAP
Ah!
KLONK
Well...
Shall we take these two someplace where they can think about what they've done?

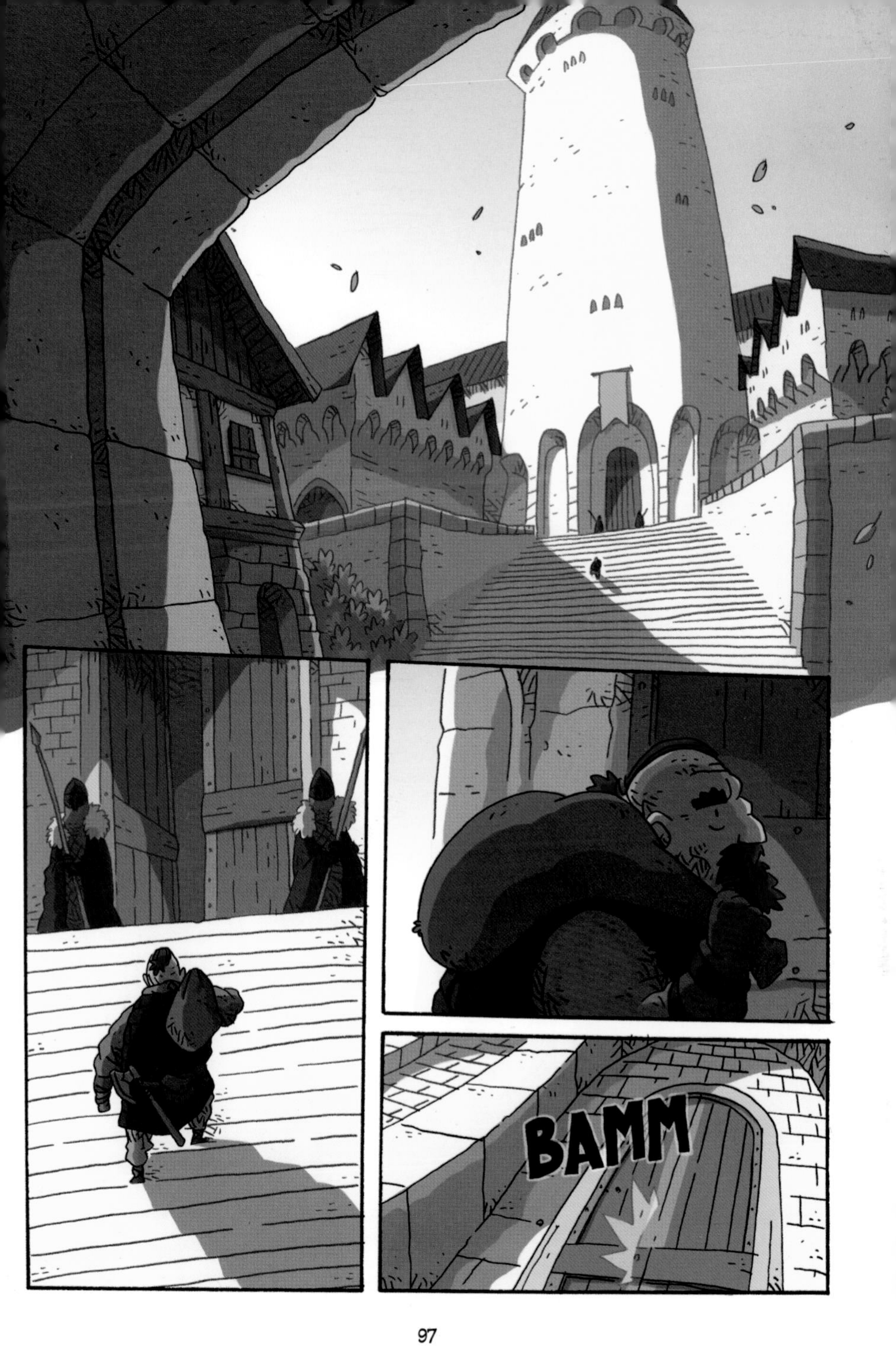
BAMM

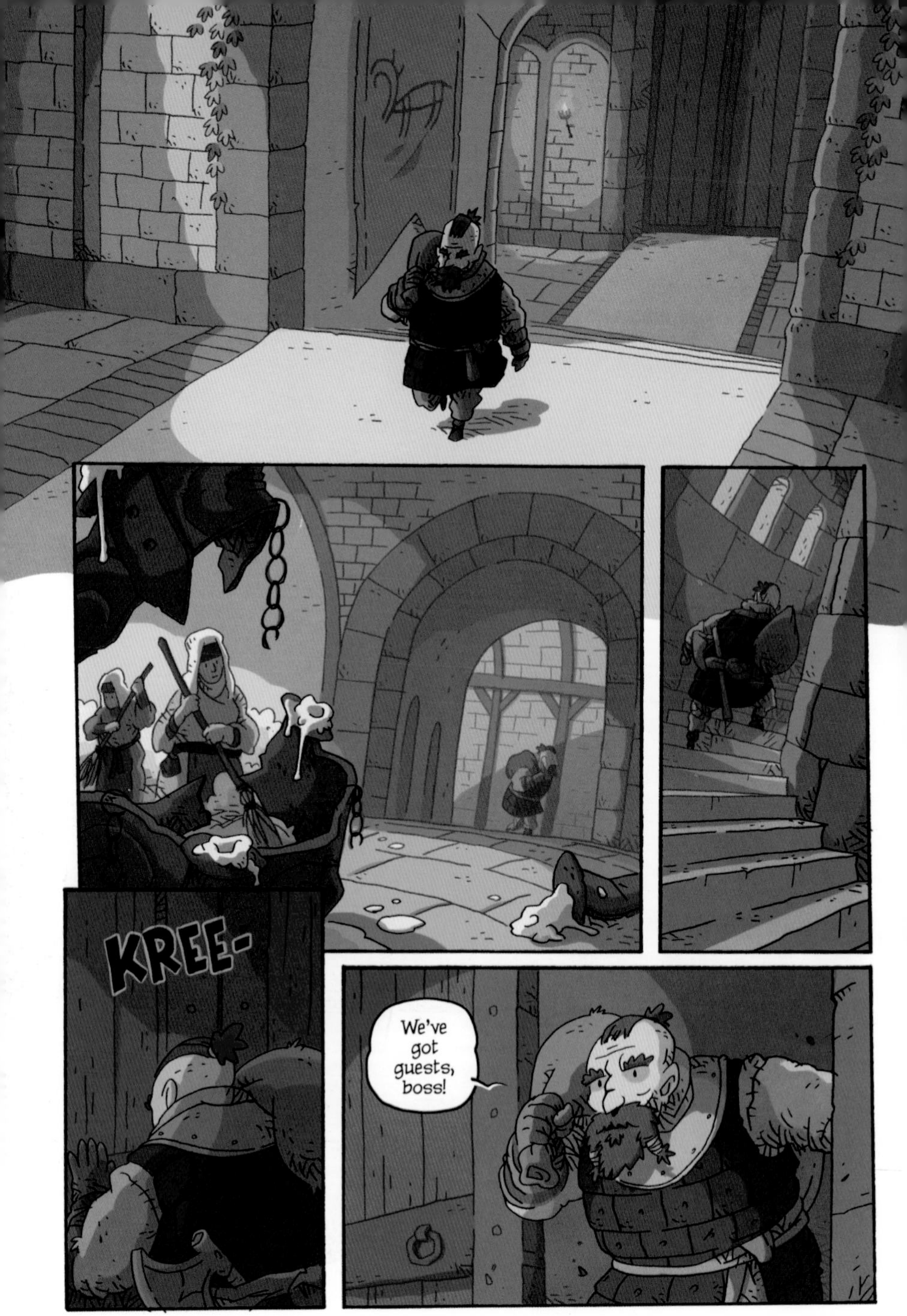
KREE-
We've got guests, boss!

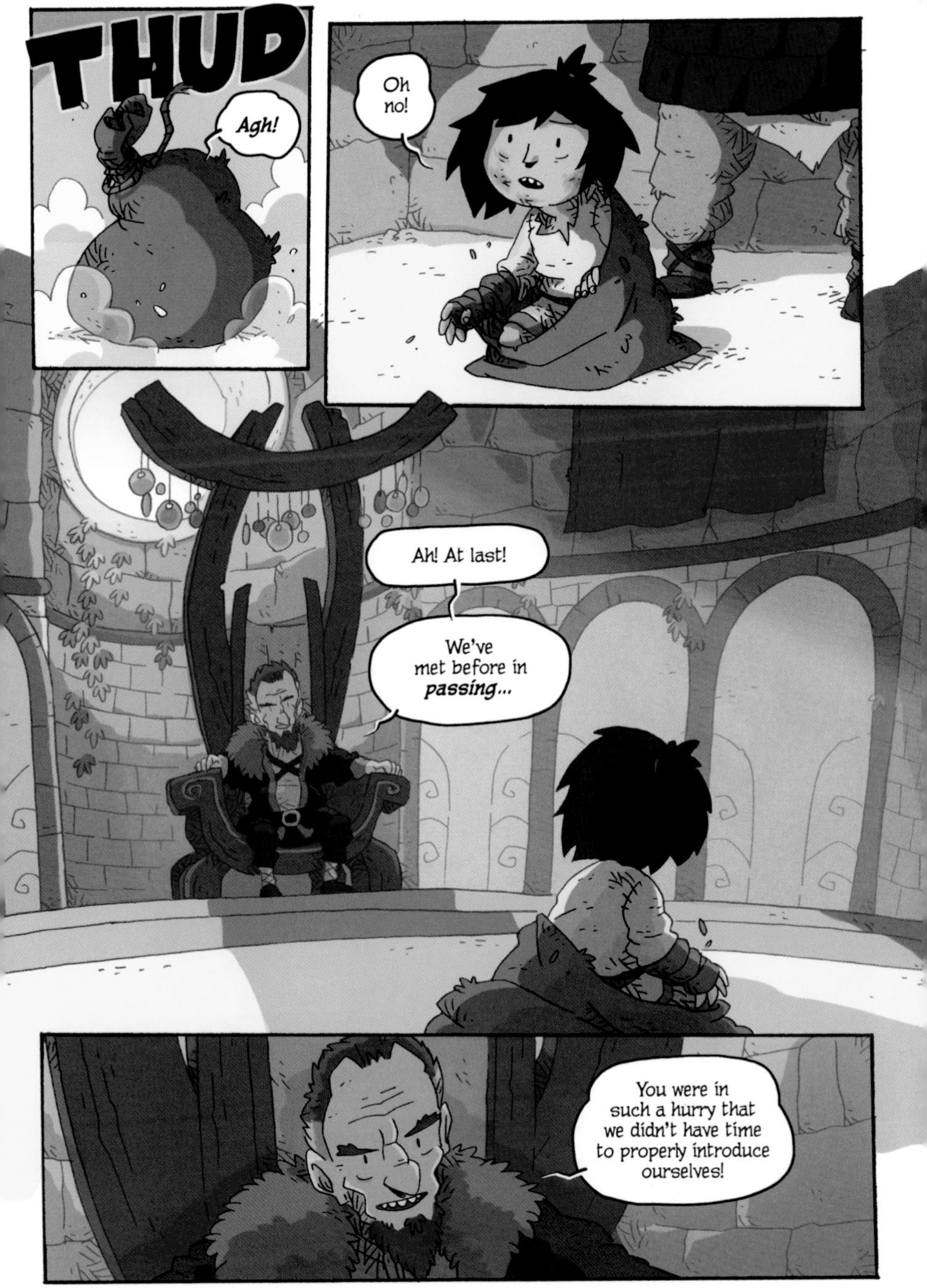
THUD
Agh!
Oh no!
Ah! At last!
We've met before in *passing*...
You were in such a hurry that we didn't have time to properly introduce ourselves!

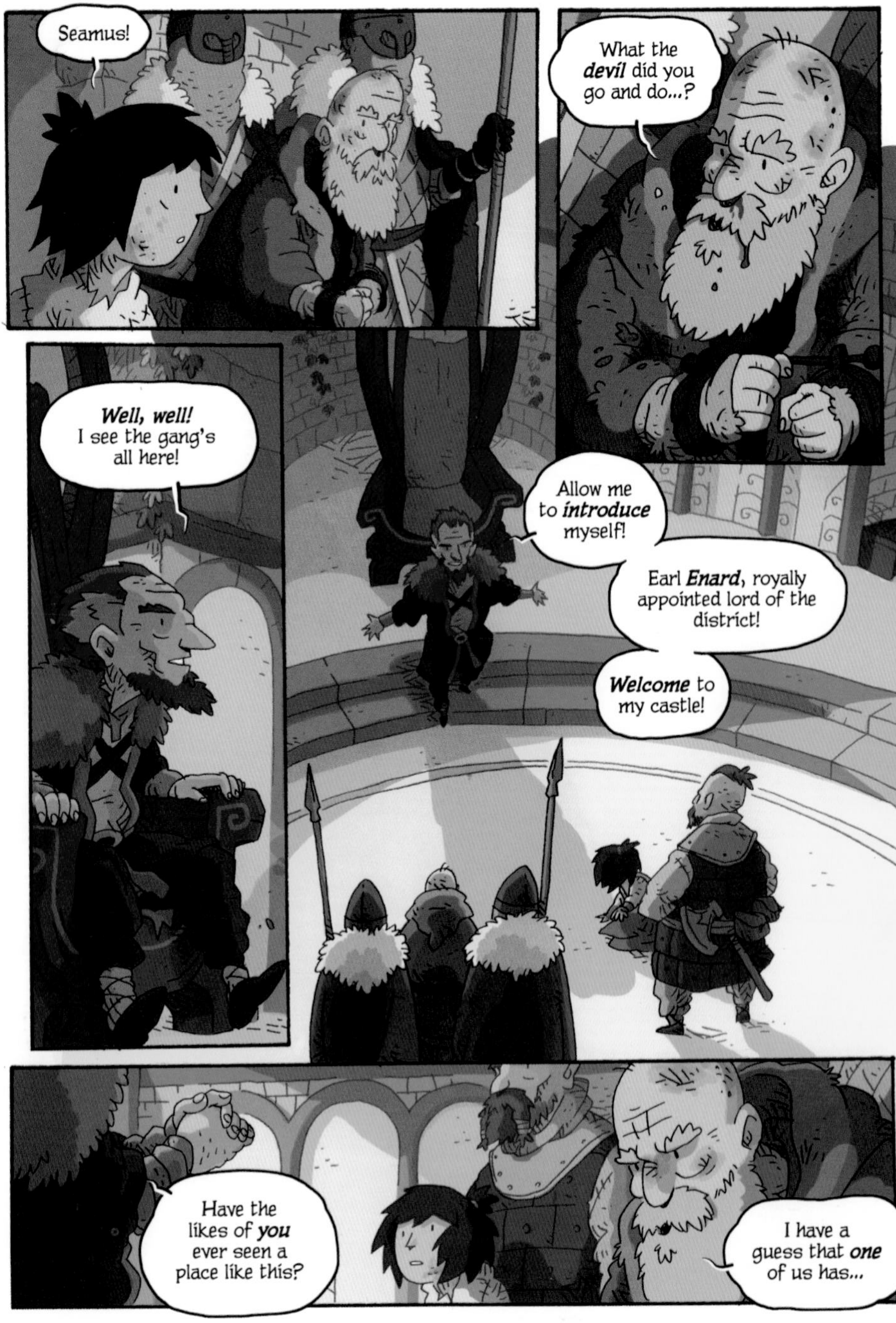
Seamus!
What the *devil* did you go and do...?
Well, well! I see the gang's all here!
Allow me to *introduce* myself!
Earl *Enard*, royally appointed lord of the district!
Welcome to my castle!
Have the likes of *you* ever seen a place like this?
I have a guess that *one* of us has...

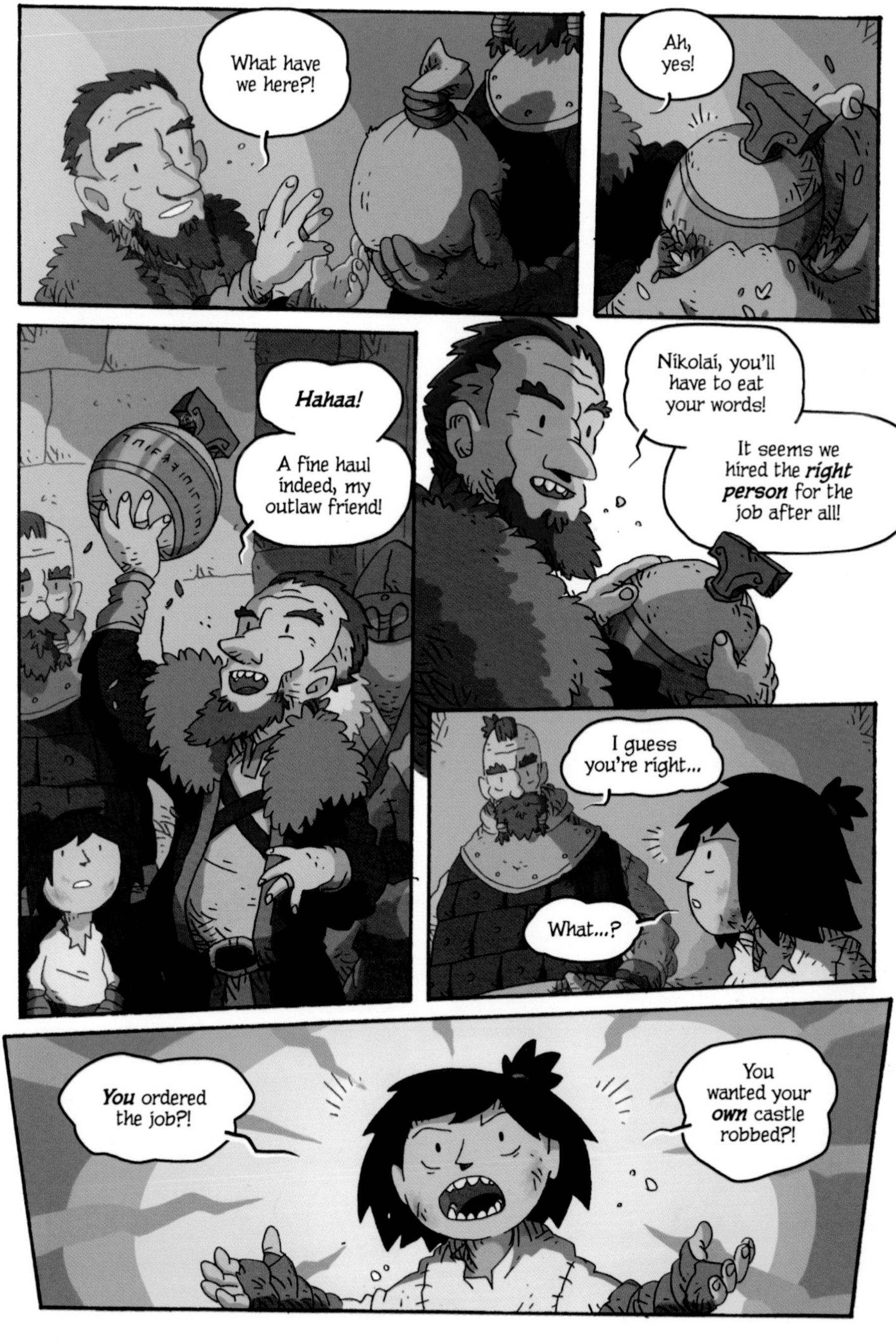
What have we here?!
Ah, yes!
Hahaa!
A fine haul indeed, my outlaw friend!
Nikolai, you'll have to eat your words!
It seems we hired the **right person** for the job after all!
I guess you're right...
What...?
You ordered the job?!
You wanted your ***own*** castle robbed?!

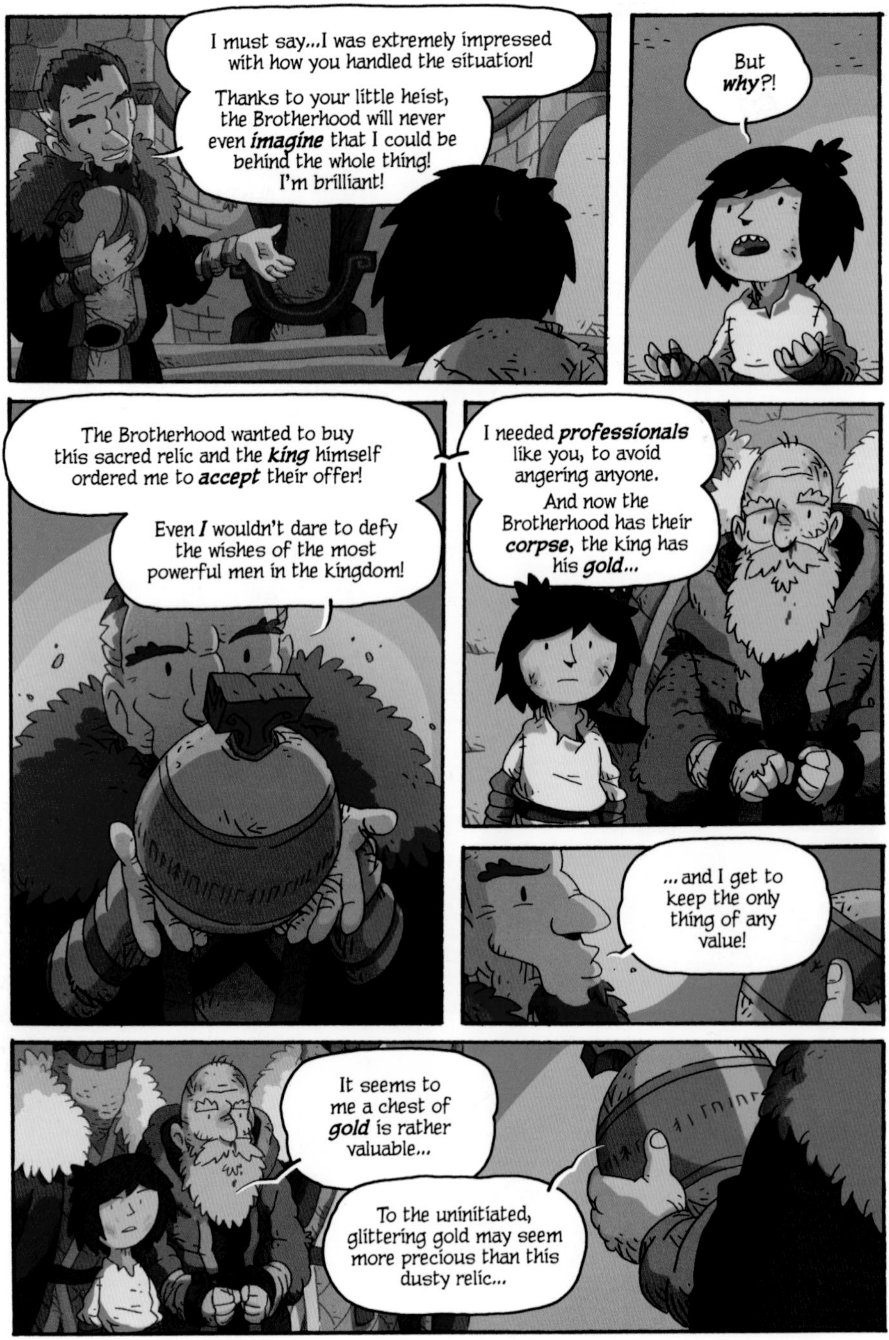
I must say...I was extremely impressed with how you handled the situation!
Thanks to your little heist, the Brotherhood will never even *imagine* that I could be behind the whole thing! I'm brilliant!
But *why*?!
The Brotherhood wanted to buy this sacred relic and the *king* himself ordered me to *accept* their offer!
Even *I* wouldn't dare to defy the wishes of the most powerful men in the kingdom!
I needed *professionals* like you, to avoid angering anyone.
And now the Brotherhood has their *corpse*, the king has his *gold*...
...and I get to keep the only thing of any value!
It seems to me a chest of *gold* is rather valuable...
To the uninitiated, glittering gold may seem more precious than this dusty relic...

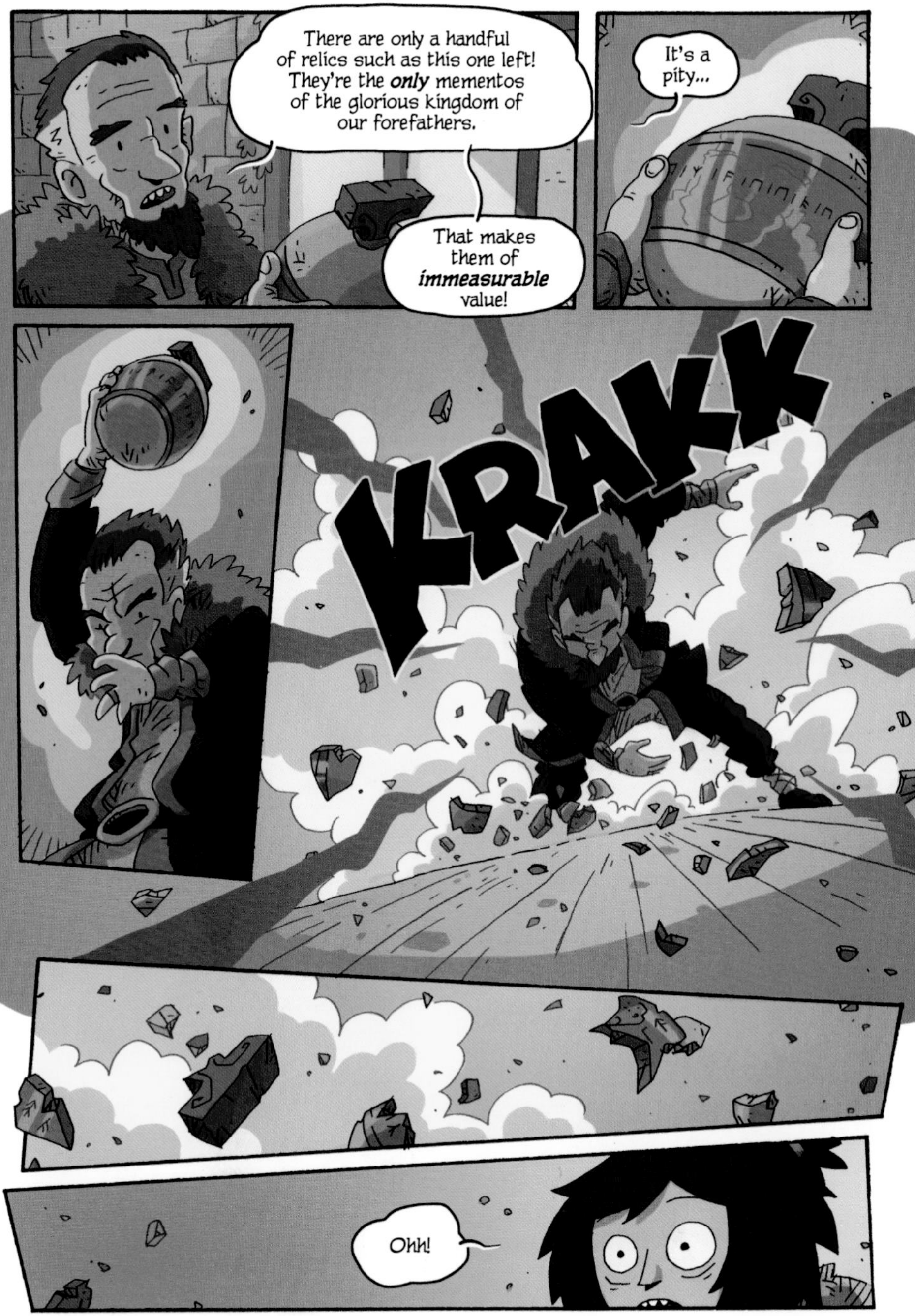
There are only a handful of relics such as this one left! They're the ***only*** mementos of the glorious kingdom of our forefathers.
That makes them of ***immeasurable*** value!
It's a pity...
KRAKK
Ohh!

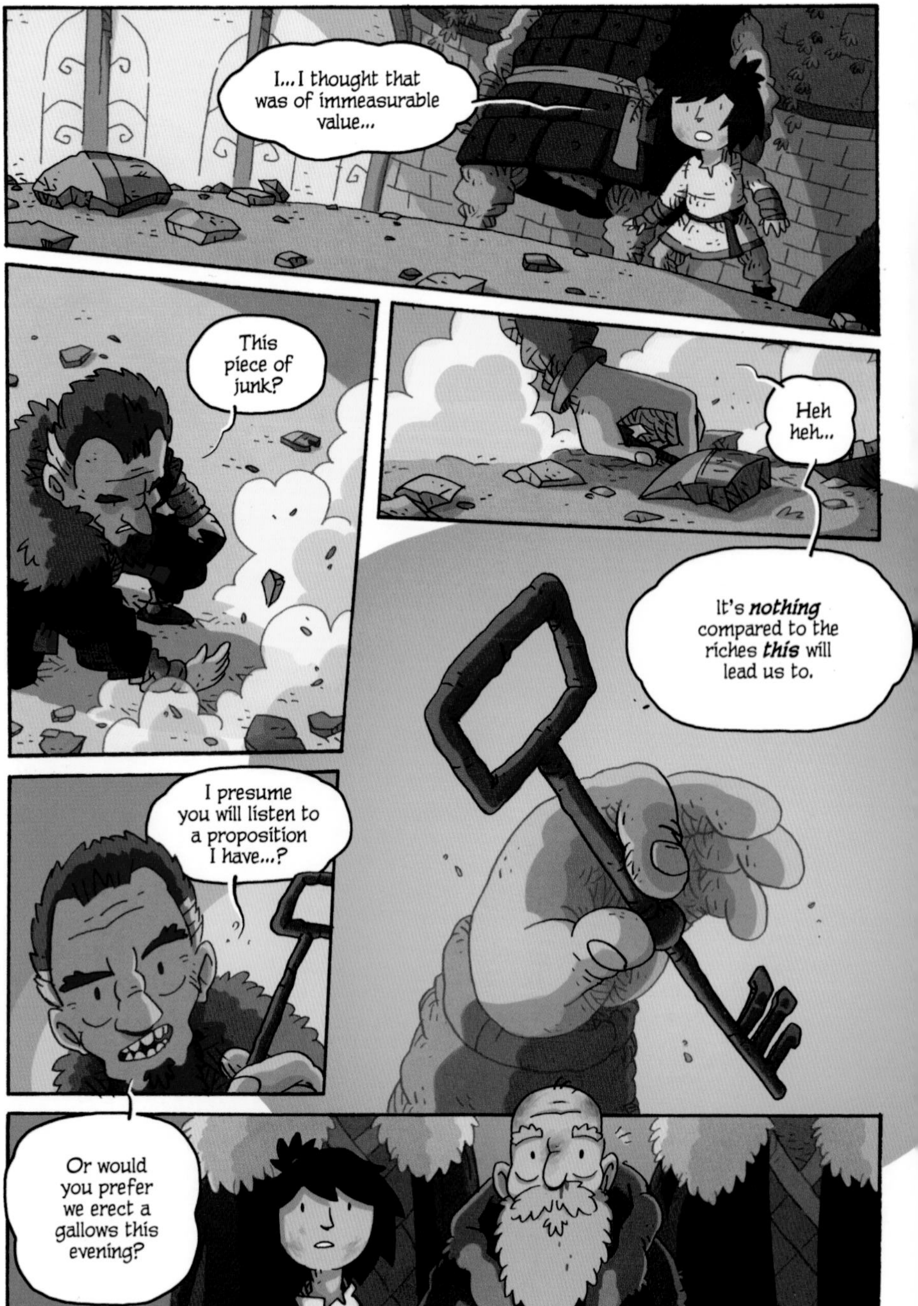
I...I thought that was of immeasurable value...
This piece of junk?
Heh heh...
It's ***nothing*** compared to the riches ***this*** will lead us to.
I presume you will listen to a proposition I have...?
Or would you prefer we erect a gallows this evening?

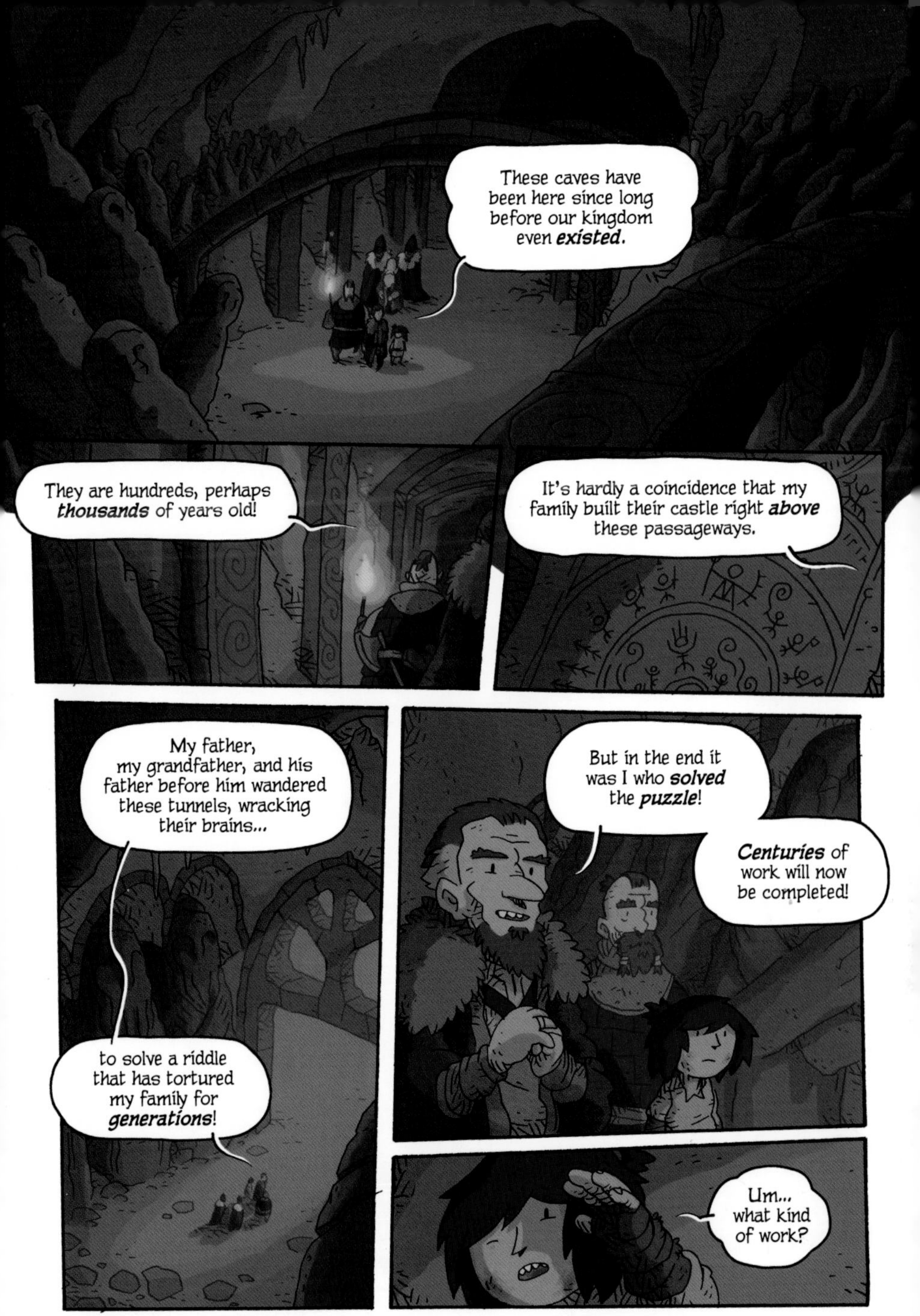
These caves have been here since long before our kingdom even **existed**.
They are hundreds, perhaps ***thousands*** of years old!
It's hardly a coincidence that my family built their castle right ***above*** these passageways.
My father, my grandfather, and his father before him wandered these tunnels, wracking their brains...
to solve a riddle that has tortured my family for ***generations***!
But in the end it was I who ***solved*** the ***puzzle***!
Centuries of work will now be completed!
Um... what kind of work?

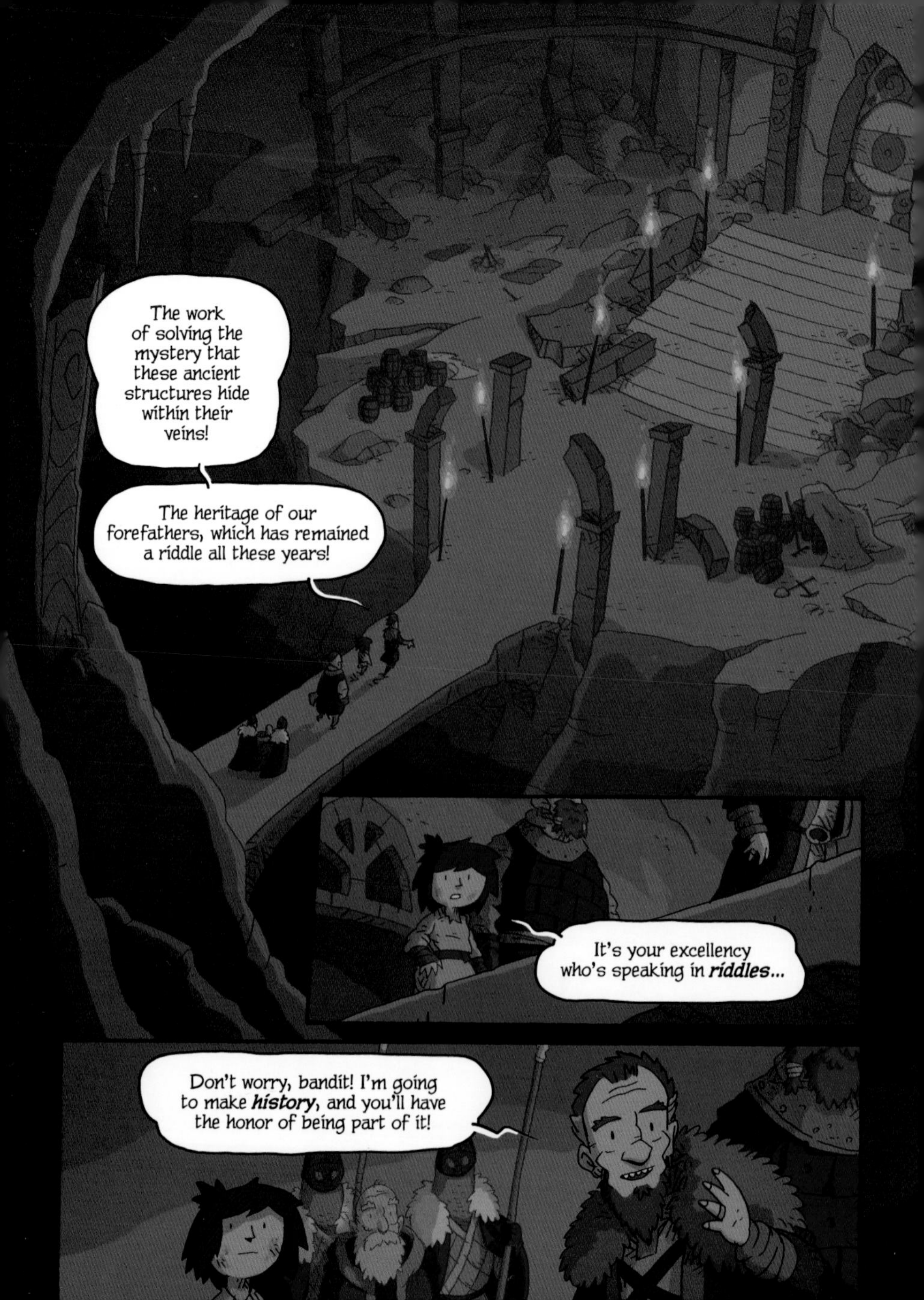
The work of solving the mystery that these ancient structures hide within their veins!
The heritage of our forefathers, which has remained a riddle all these years!
It's your excellency who's speaking in ***riddles***...
Don't worry, bandit! I'm going to make ***history***, and you'll have the honor of being part of it!

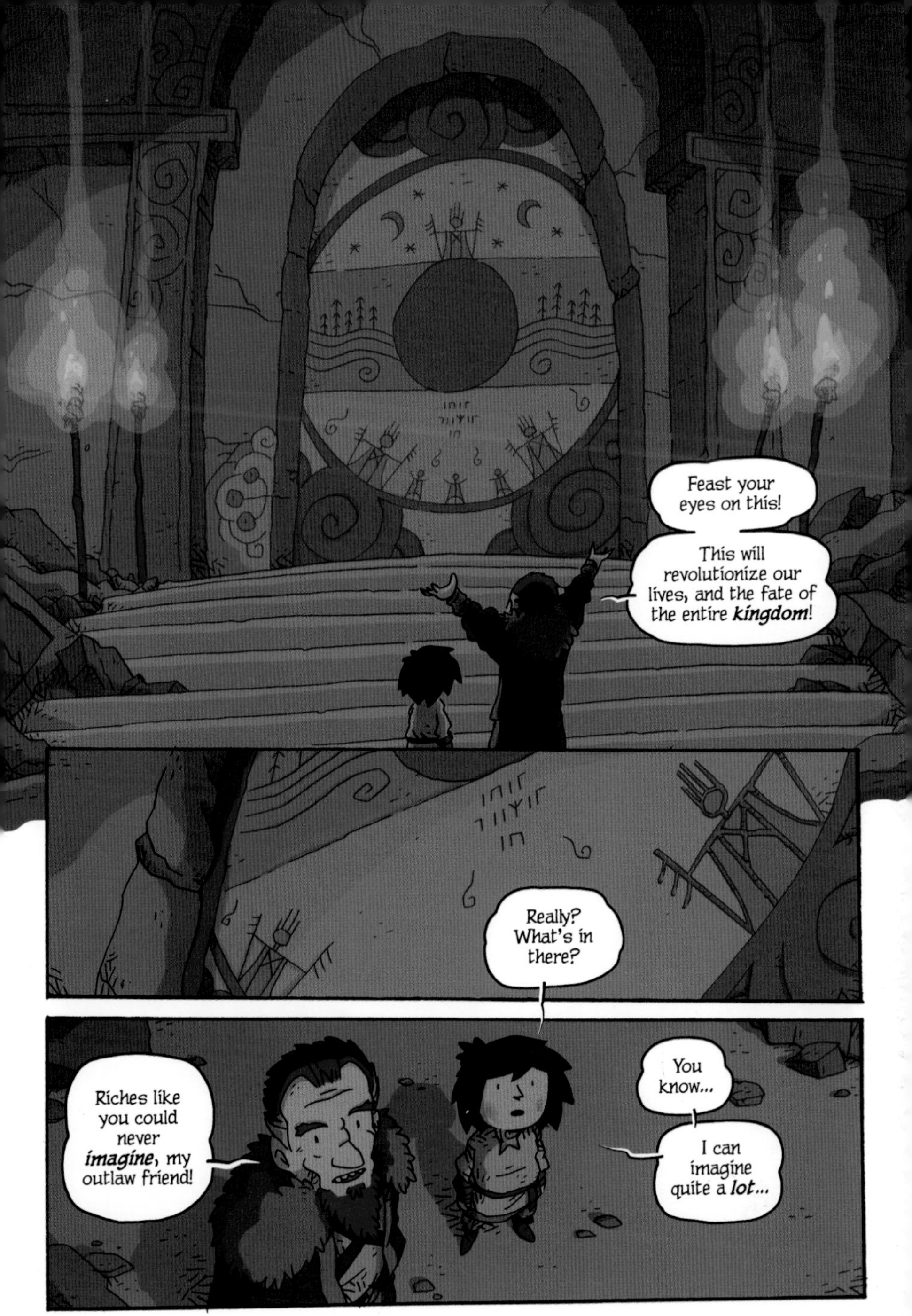
Feast your eyes on this!
This will revolutionize our lives, and the fate of the entire **kingdom**!
Really? What's in there?
Riches like you could never ***imagine***, my outlaw friend!
You know...
I can imagine quite a ***lot***...

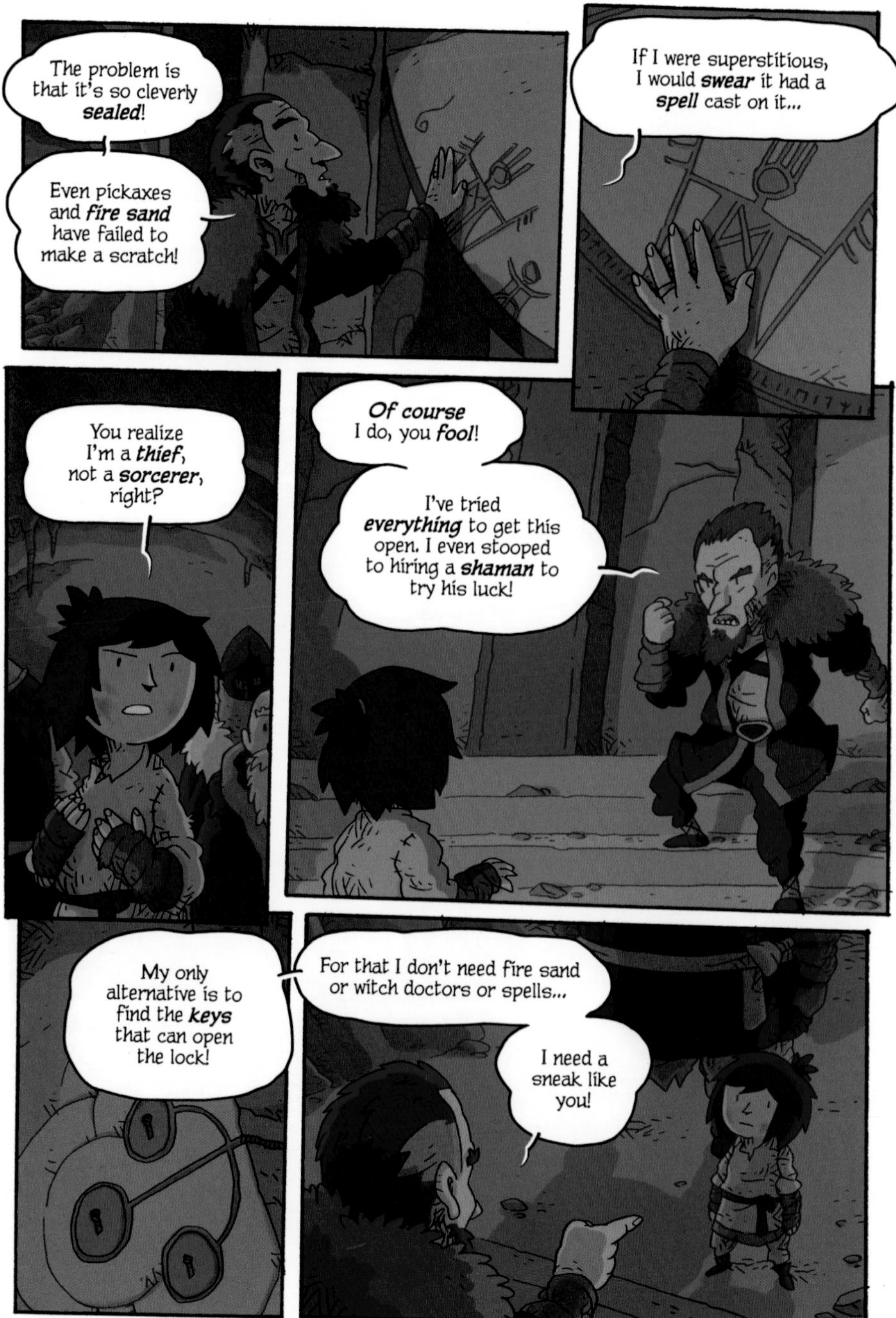
The problem is that it's so cleverly **sealed**!
Even pickaxes and ***fire sand*** have failed to make a scratch!
If I were superstitious, I would ***swear*** it had a ***spell*** cast on it...
You realize I'm a ***thief***, not a ***sorcerer***, right?
Of course I do, you ***fool***!
I've tried ***everything*** to get this open. I even stooped to hiring a ***shaman*** to try his luck!
My only alternative is to find the ***keys*** that can open the lock!
For that I don't need fire sand or witch doctors or spells...
I need a sneak like you!

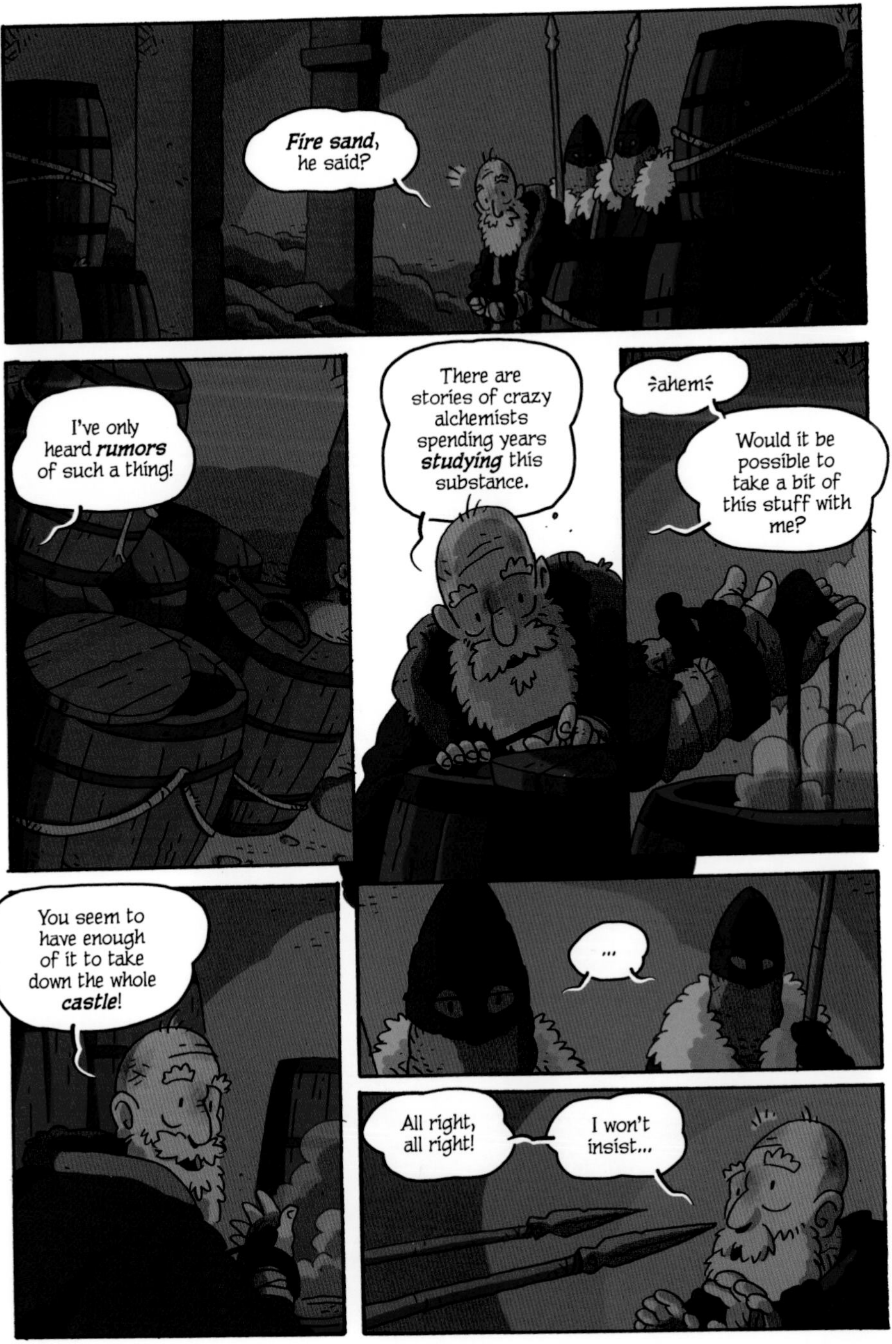

Fire sand, he said?
I've only heard ***rumors*** of such a thing!
There are stories of crazy alchemists spending years ***studying*** this substance.
ahem
Would it be possible to take a bit of this stuff with me?
You seem to have enough of it to take down the whole ***castle***!
...
All right, all right!
I won't insist...

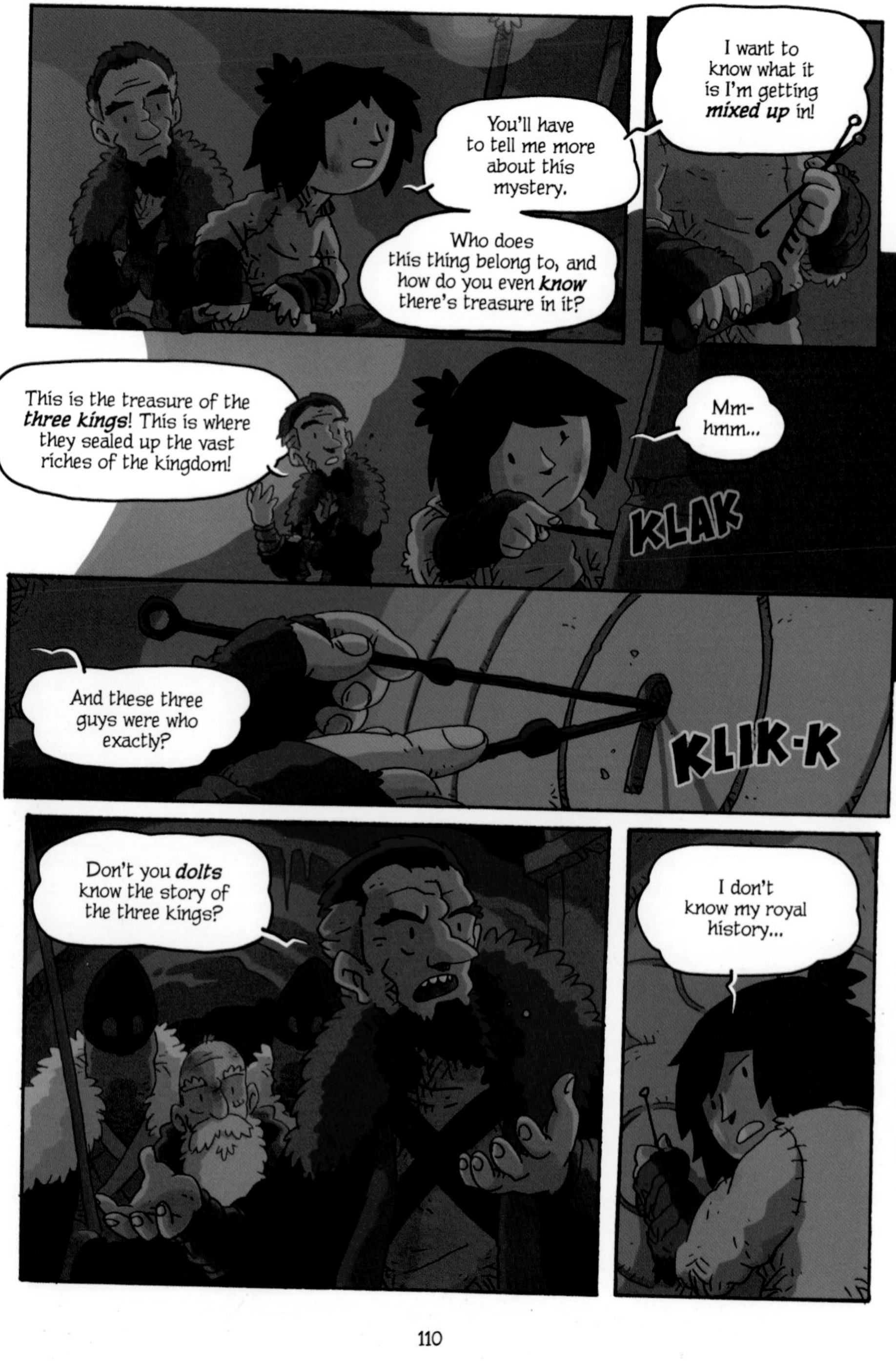
You'll have to tell me more about this mystery.
Who does this thing belong to, and how do you even *know* there's treasure in it?
I want to know what it is I'm getting *mixed up* in!
This is the treasure of the *three kings*! This is where they sealed up the vast riches of the kingdom!
Mm-hmm...
KLAK
And these three guys were who exactly?
KLIK-K
Don't you *dolts* know the story of the three kings?
I don't know my royal history...

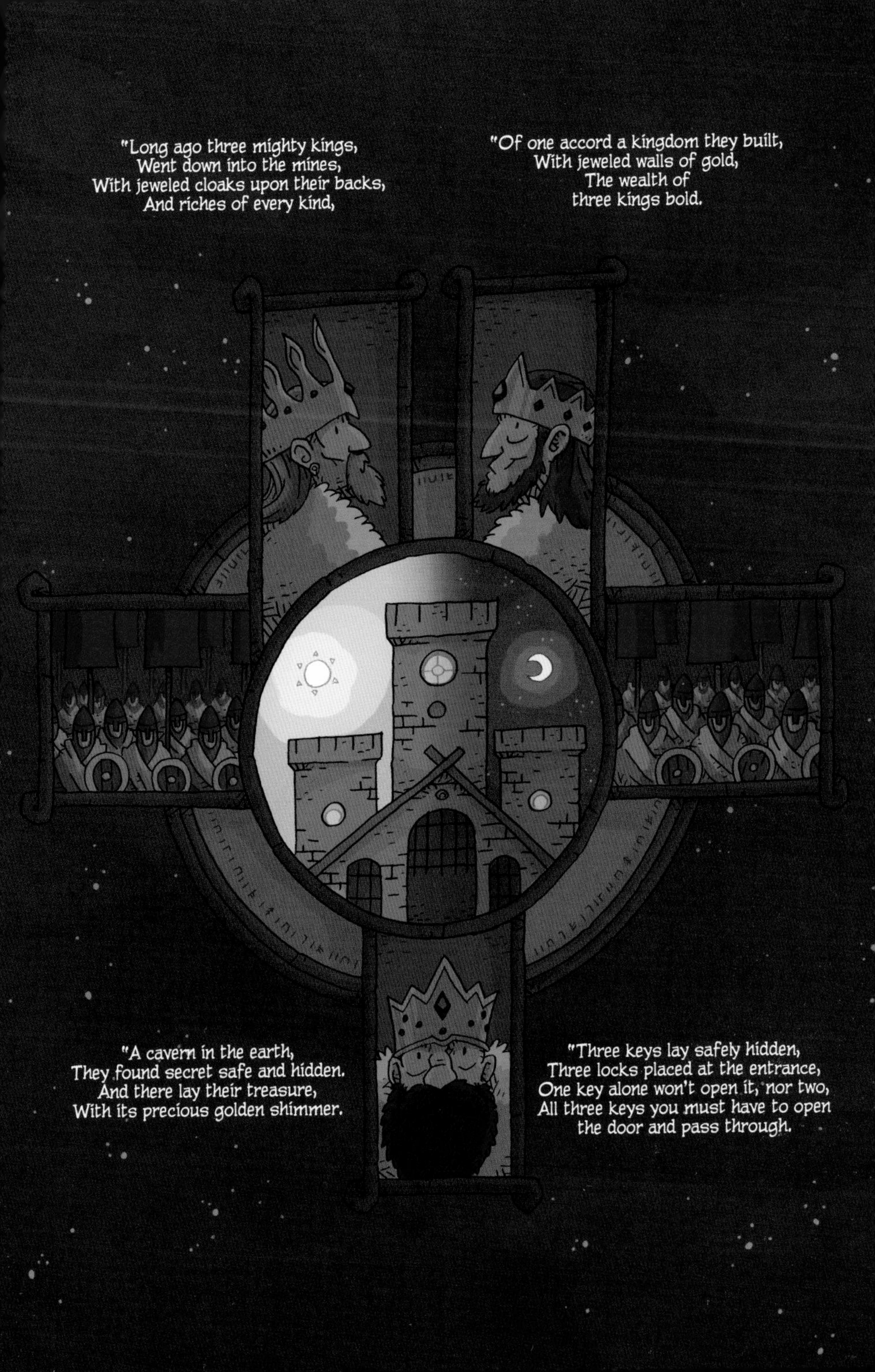
"Long ago three mighty kings,
Went down into the mines,
With jeweled cloaks upon their backs,
And riches of every kind,
"Of one accord a kingdom they built,
With jeweled walls of gold,
The wealth of
three kings bold.
"A cavern in the earth,
They found secret safe and hidden.
And there lay their treasure,
With its precious golden shimmer.
"Three keys lay safely hidden,
Three locks placed at the entrance,
One key alone won't open it, nor two,
All three keys you must have to open
the door and pass through.

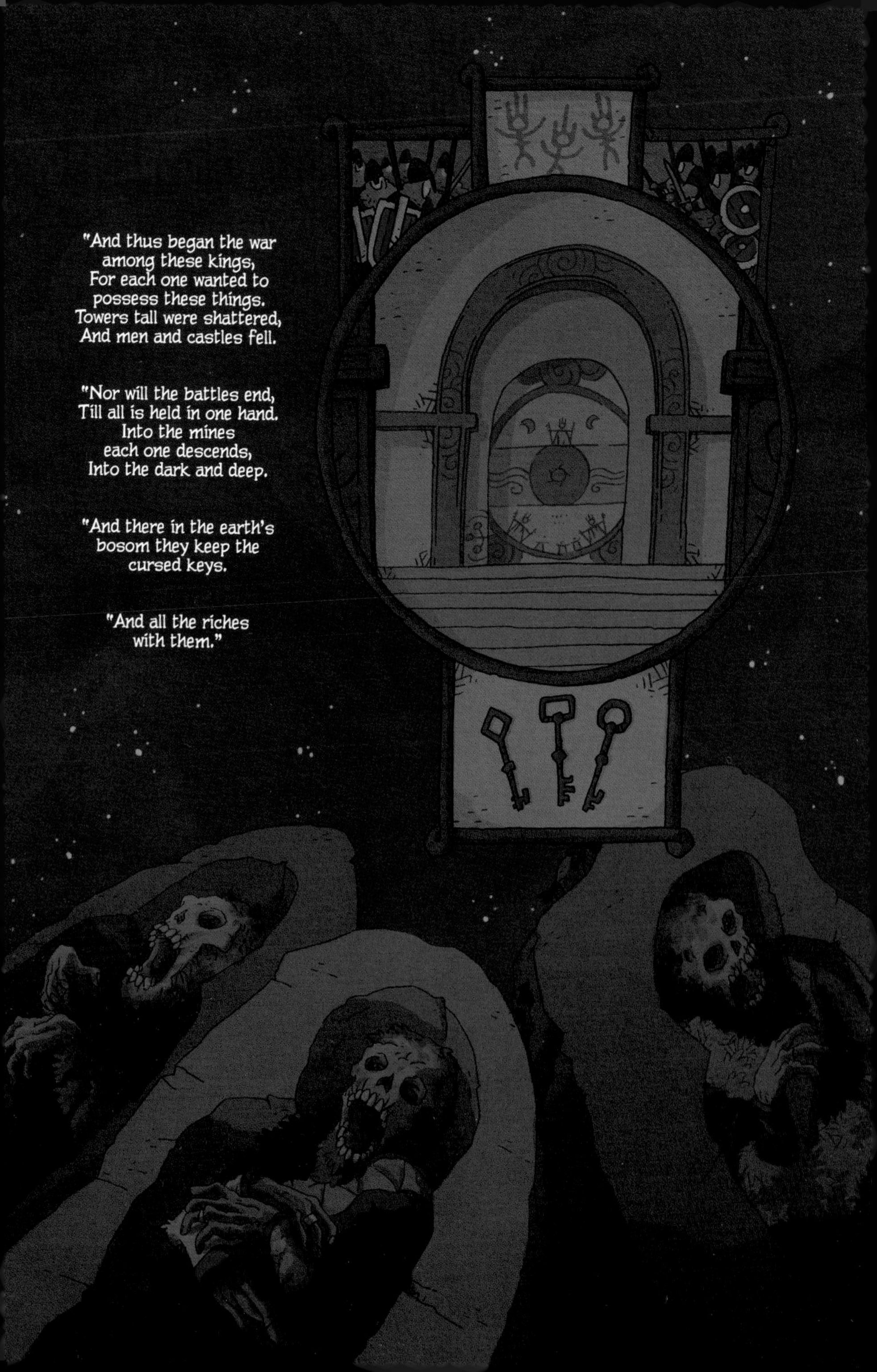
"And thus began the war
among these kings,
For each one wanted to
possess these things.
Towers tall were shattered,
And men and castles fell.
"Nor will the battles end,
Till all is held in one hand.
Into the mines
each one descends,
Into the dark and deep.
"And there in the earth's
bosom they keep the
cursed keys.
"And all the riches
with them."

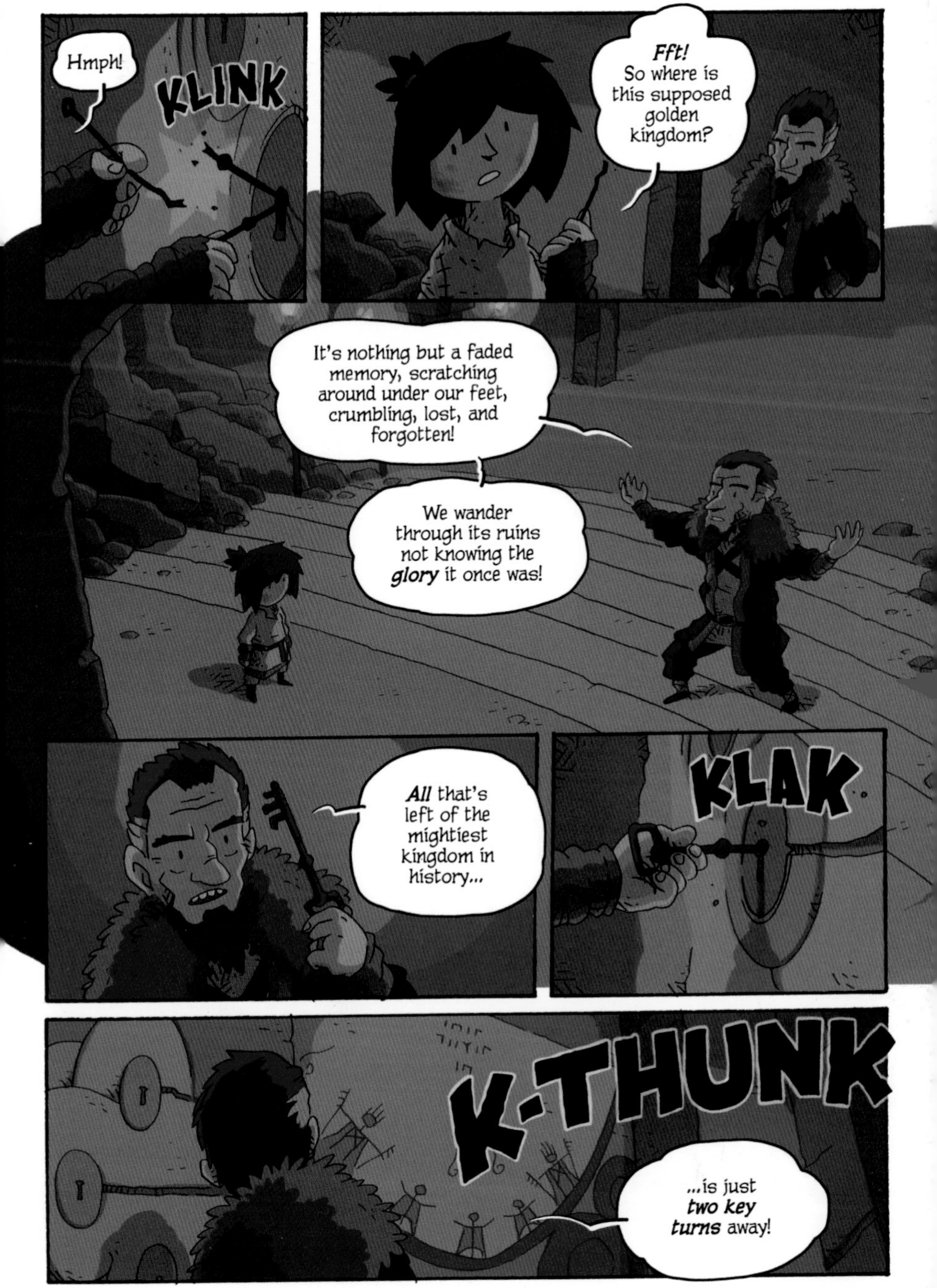
Hmph!
KLINK
Fft! So where is this supposed golden kingdom?
It's nothing but a faded memory, scratching around under our feet, crumbling, lost, and forgotten!
We wander through its ruins not knowing the ***glory*** it once was!
All that's left of the mightiest kingdom in history...
KLAK
K-THUNK
...is just ***two key turns*** away!

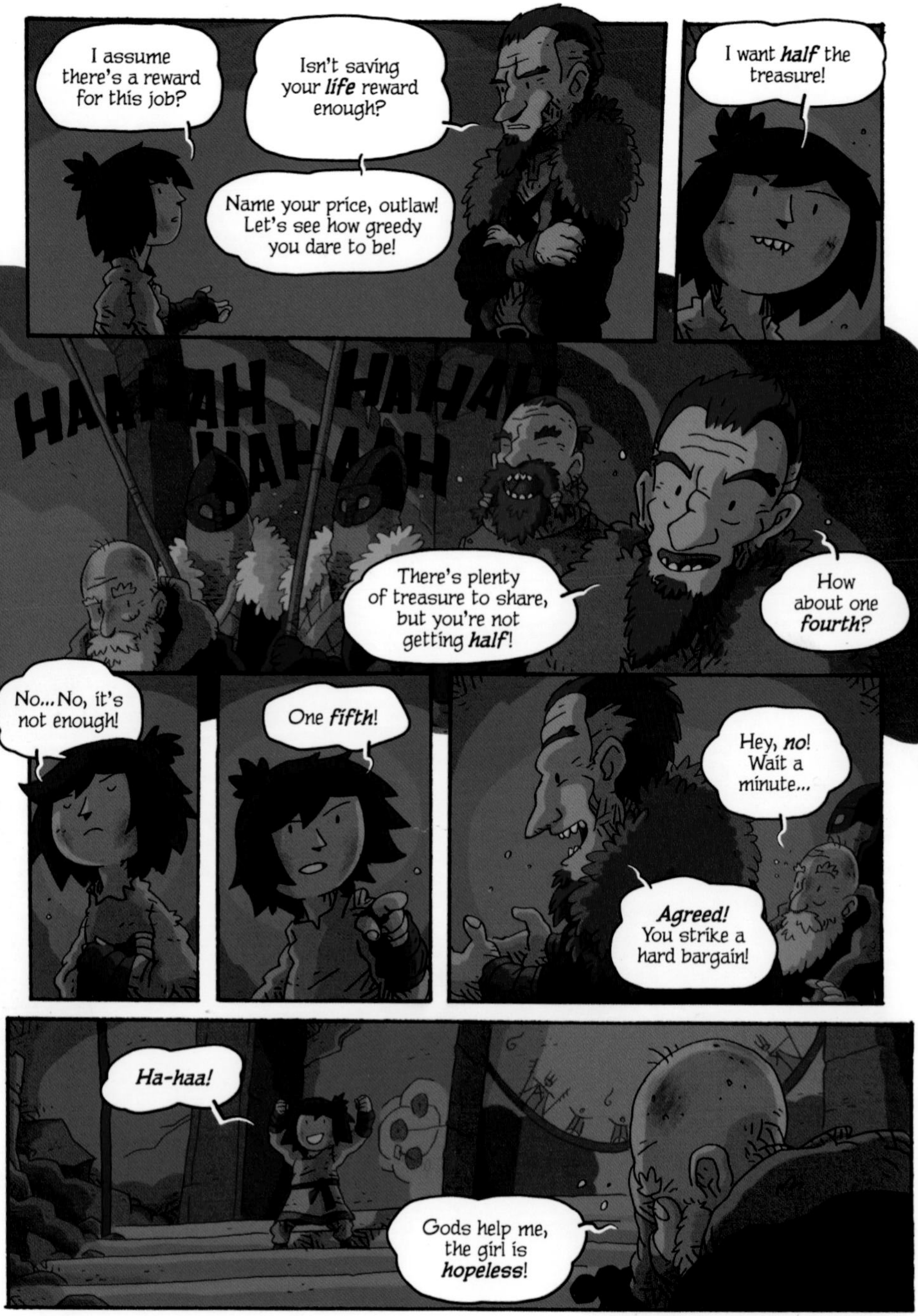
I assume there's a reward for this job?
Isn't saving your *life* reward enough?
Name your price, outlaw! Let's see how greedy you dare to be!
I want *half* the treasure!
HAHAHAH HAHAH HAHAAH
There's plenty of treasure to share, but you're not getting *half*!
How about one *fourth*?
No... No, it's not enough!
One *fifth*!
Hey, *no*! Wait a minute...
Agreed! You strike a hard bargain!
Ha-haa!
Gods help me, the girl is *hopeless*!

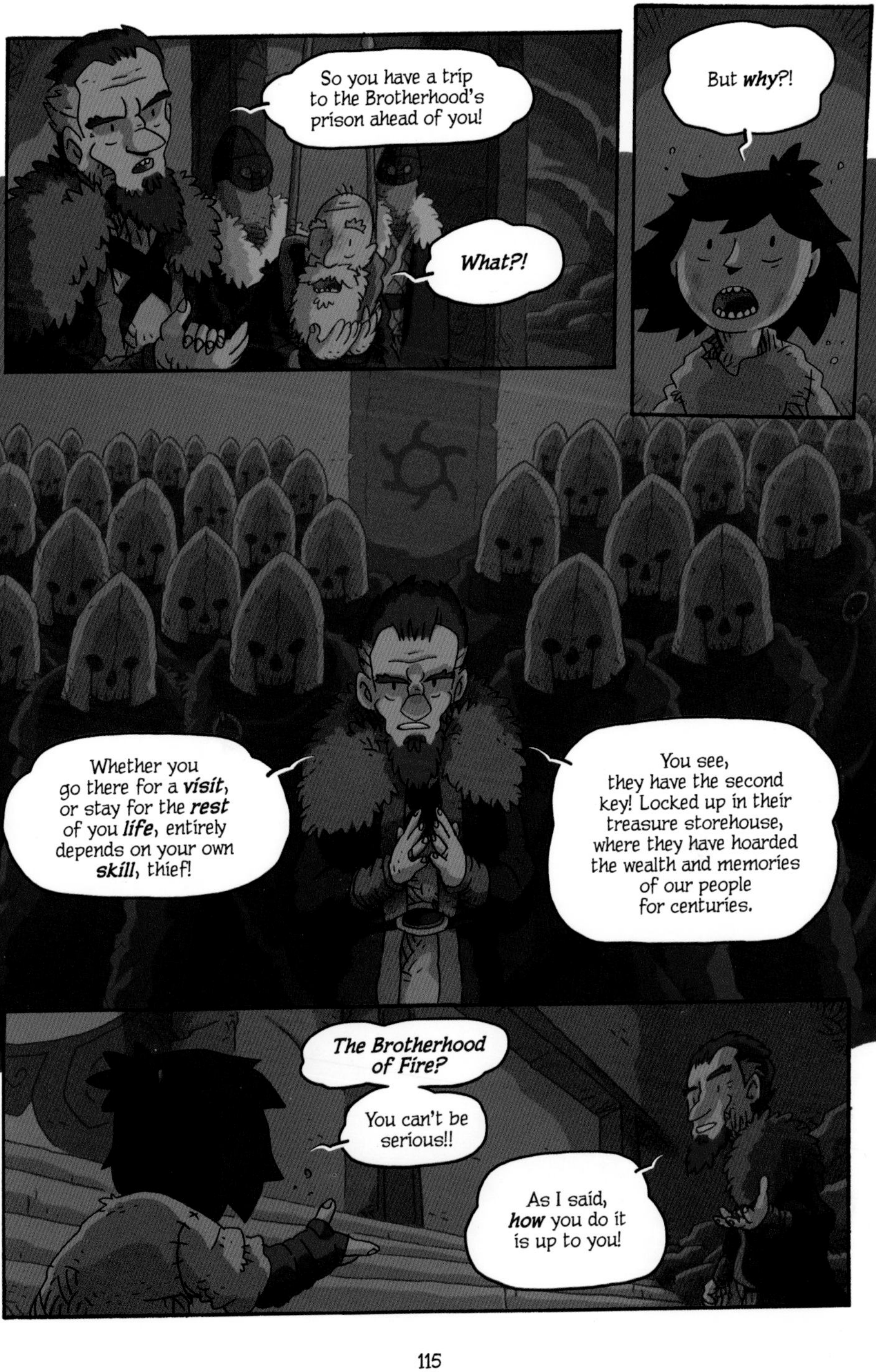
So you have a trip to the Brotherhood's prison ahead of you!
What?!
But why?!
Whether you go there for a visit, or stay for the rest of you life, entirely depends on your own skill, thief!
You see, they have the second key! Locked up in their treasure storehouse, where they have hoarded the wealth and memories of our people for centuries.
The Brotherhood of Fire?
You can't be serious!!
As I said, how you do it is up to you!

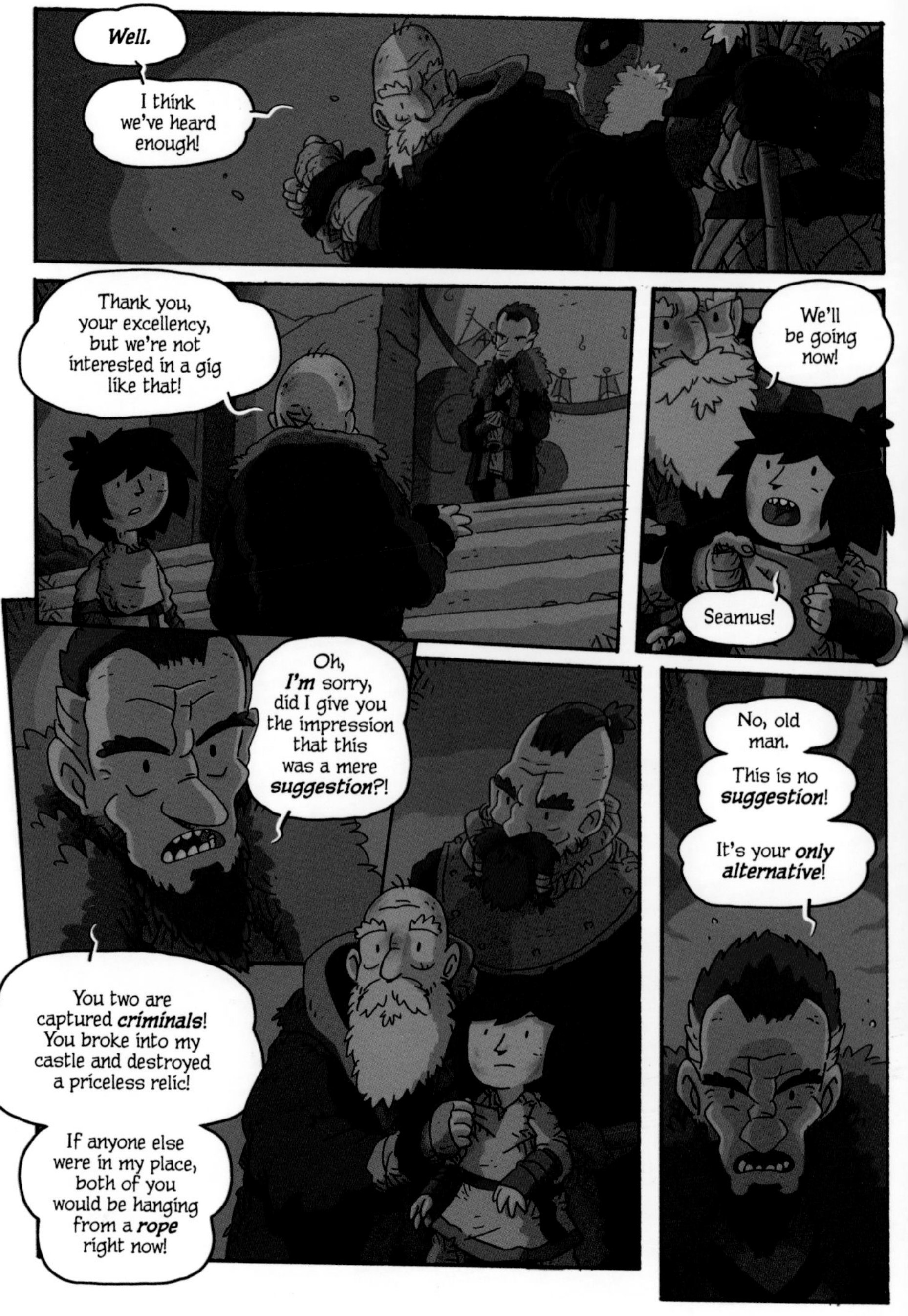
Well.
I think we've heard enough!
Thank you, your excellency, but we're not interested in a gig like that!
We'll be going now!
Seamus!
Oh, I'm sorry, did I give you the impression that this was a mere suggestion?!
You two are captured criminals! You broke into my castle and destroyed a priceless relic!
If anyone else were in my place, both of you would be hanging from a rope right now!
No, old man.
This is no suggestion!
It's your only alternative!

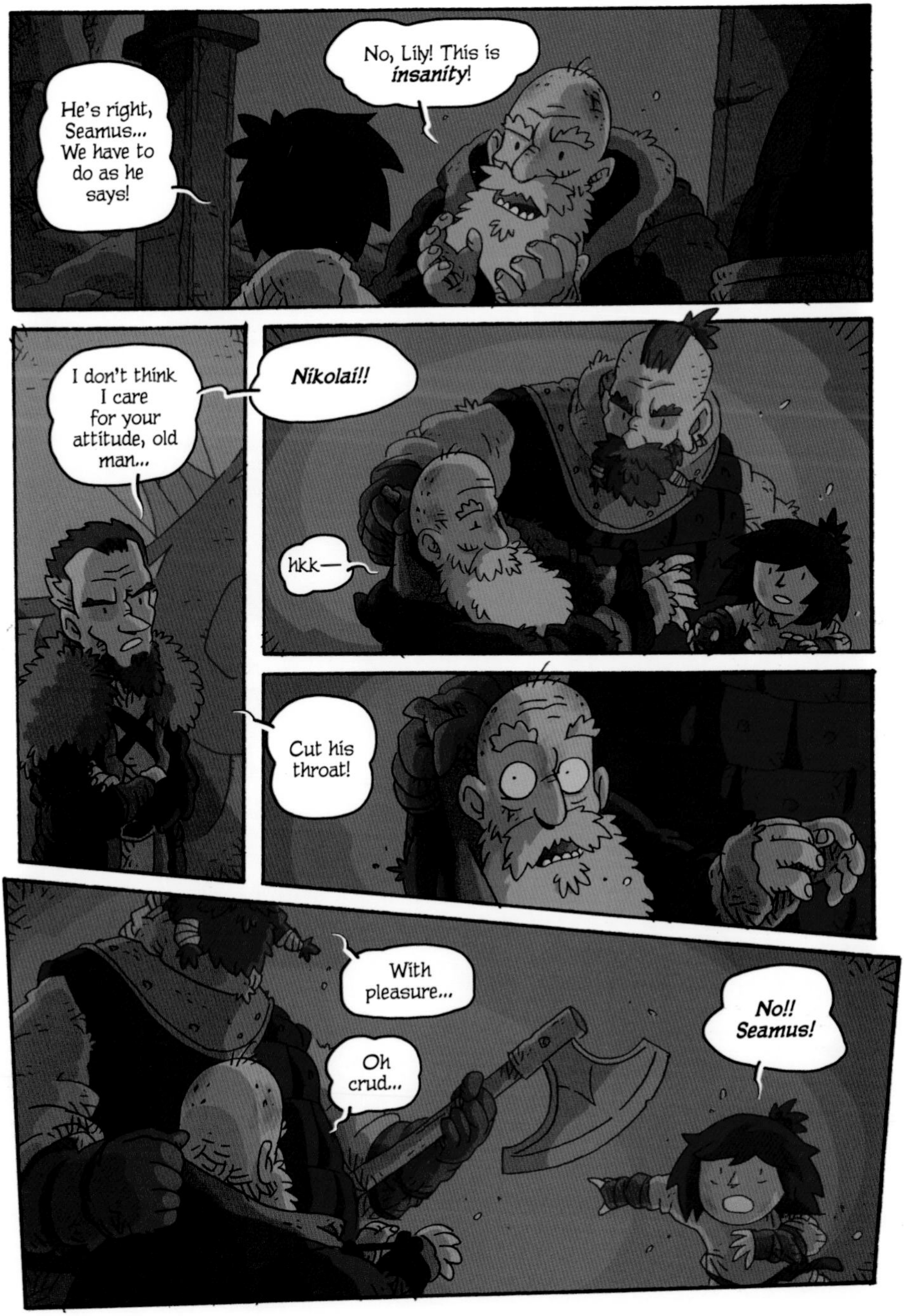
No, Lily! This is *insanity*!
He's right, Seamus... We have to do as he says!
I don't think I care for your attitude, old man...
Nikolai!!
hkk—
Cut his throat!
With pleasure...
Oh crud...
No!! Seamus!

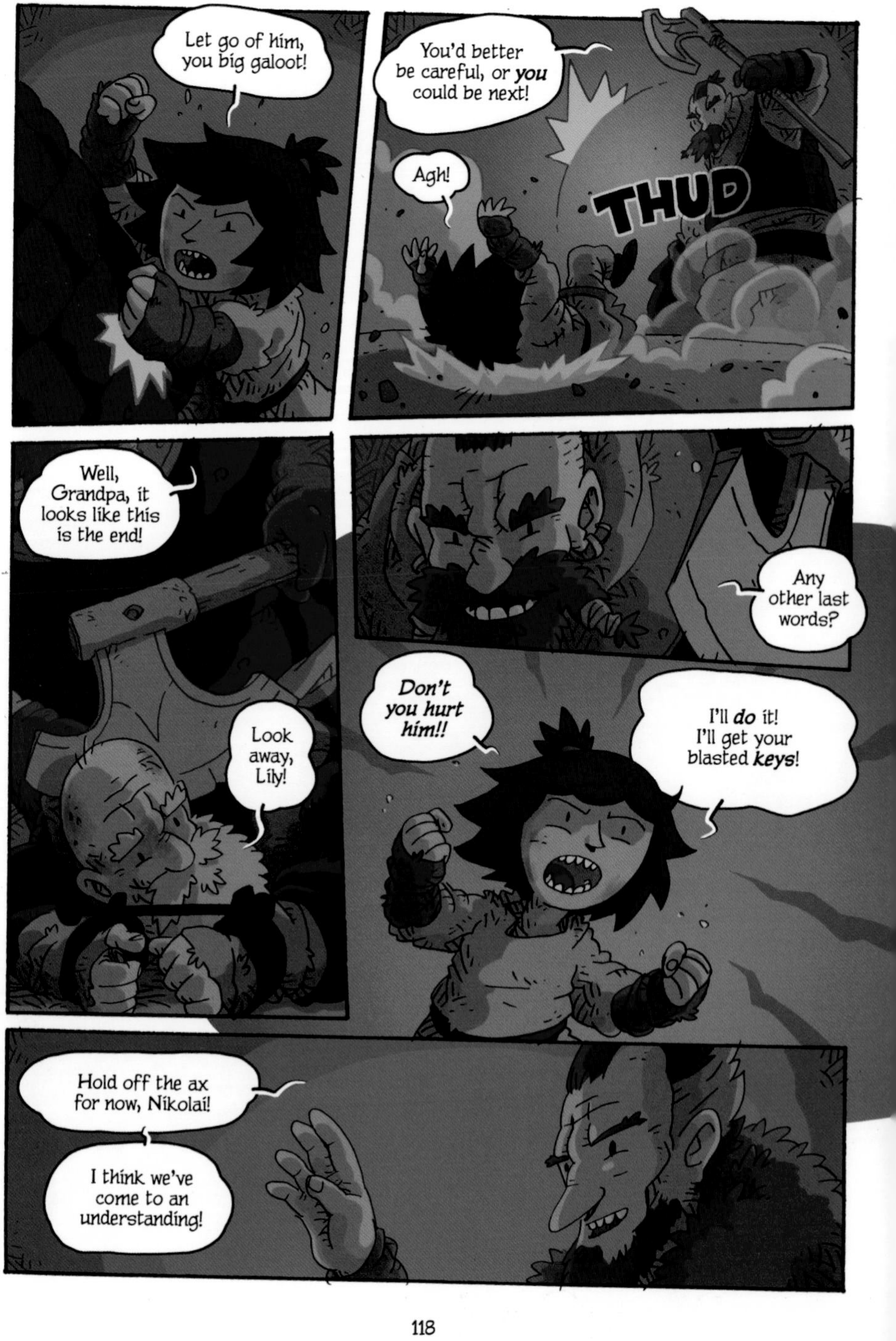
Let go of him, you big galoot!
You'd better be careful, or **you** could be next!
Agh!
THUD
Well, Grandpa, it looks like this is the end!
Look away, Lily!
Any other last words?
Don't you hurt him!!
I'll ***do*** it! I'll get your blasted ***keys***!
Hold off the ax for now, Nikolai!
I think we've come to an understanding!

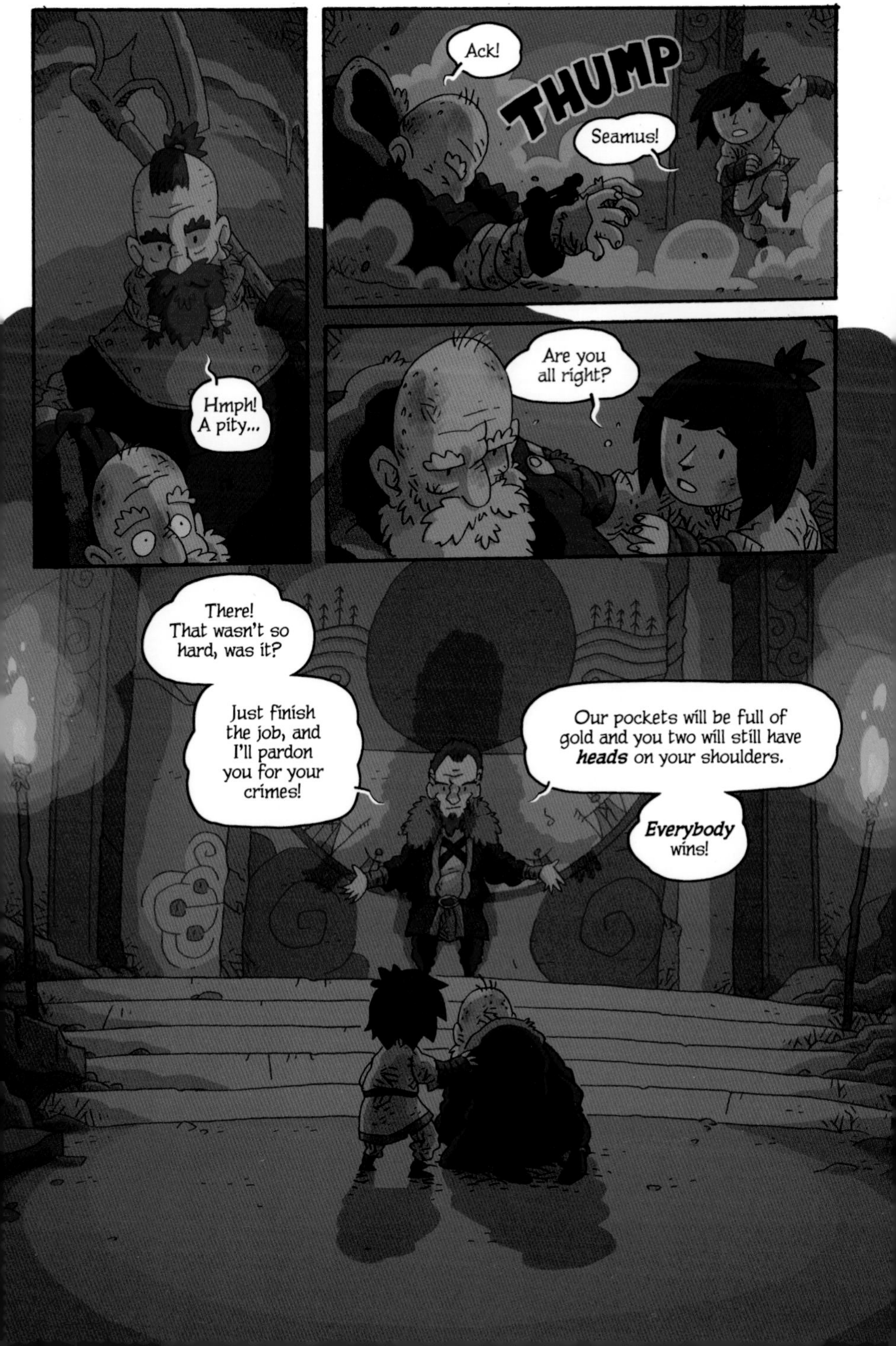
Ack!
THUMP
Seamus!
Hmph! A pity...
Are you all right?
There! That wasn't so hard, was it?
Just finish the job, and I'll pardon you for your crimes!
Our pockets will be full of gold and you two will still have ***heads*** on your shoulders.
Everybody wins!

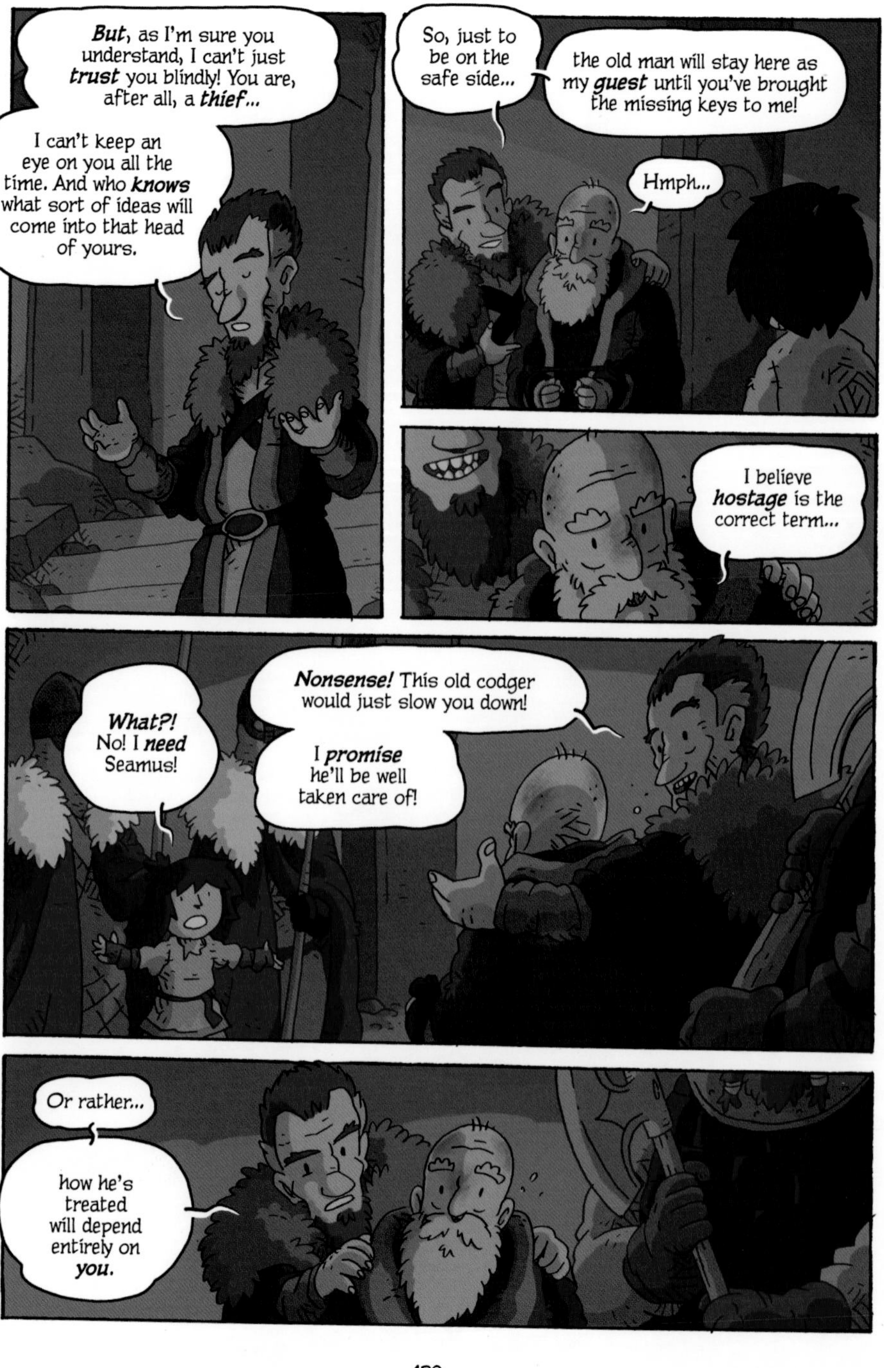

But, as I'm sure you understand, I can't just ***trust*** you blindly! You are, after all, a ***thief***...
I can't keep an eye on you all the time. And who ***knows*** what sort of ideas will come into that head of yours.
So, just to be on the safe side...
the old man will stay here as my ***guest*** until you've brought the missing keys to me!
Hmph...
I believe ***hostage*** is the correct term...
What?! No! I ***need*** Seamus!
Nonsense! This old codger would just slow you down!
I ***promise*** he'll be well taken care of!
Or rather...
how he's treated will depend entirely on ***you***.

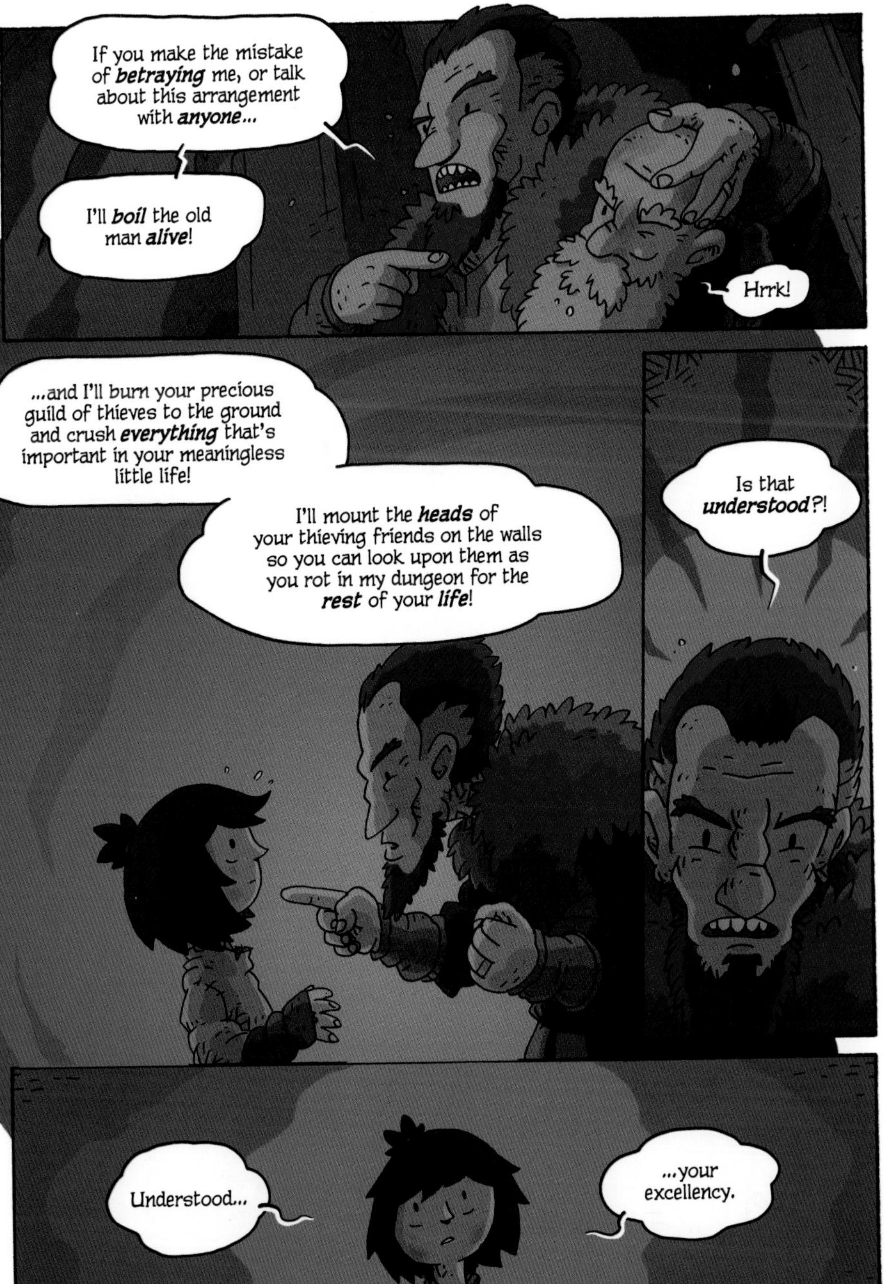
If you make the mistake of *betraying* me, or talk about this arrangement with *anyone*...
I'll *boil* the old man *alive*!
Hrrk!
...and I'll burn your precious guild of thieves to the ground and crush *everything* that's important in your meaningless little life!
I'll mount the *heads* of your thieving friends on the walls so you can look upon them as you rot in my dungeon for the *rest* of your *life*!
Is that *understood*?!
Understood...
...your excellency.

Gleam of steel,
Glow of coals,
Chase wickedness away,
Out the evil goes.
The breath of the Brotherhood,
Blows life upon the embers.

The Dungeon

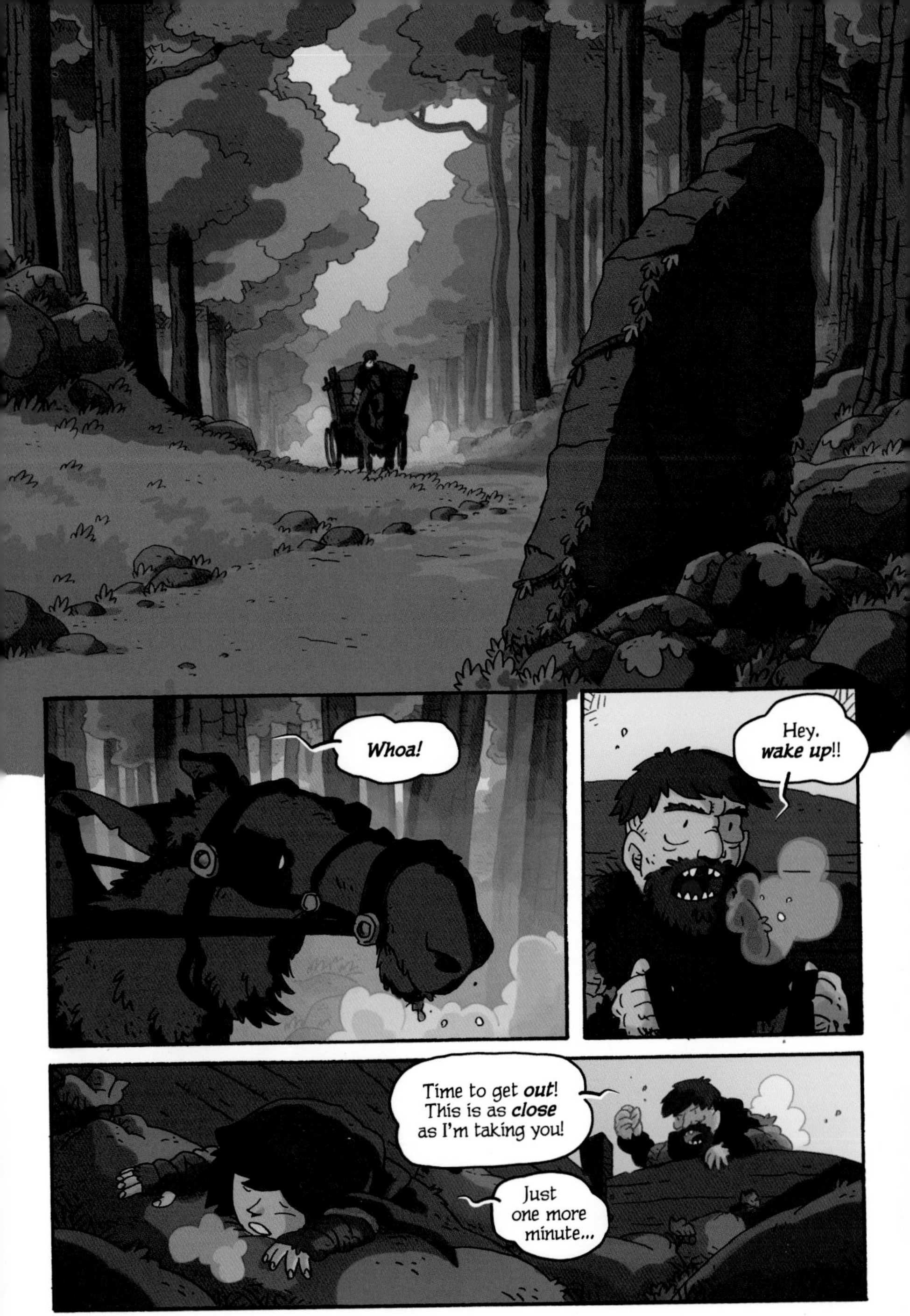
Whoa!
Hey. *wake up*!!
Time to get *out*! This is as *close* as I'm taking you!
Just one more minute...

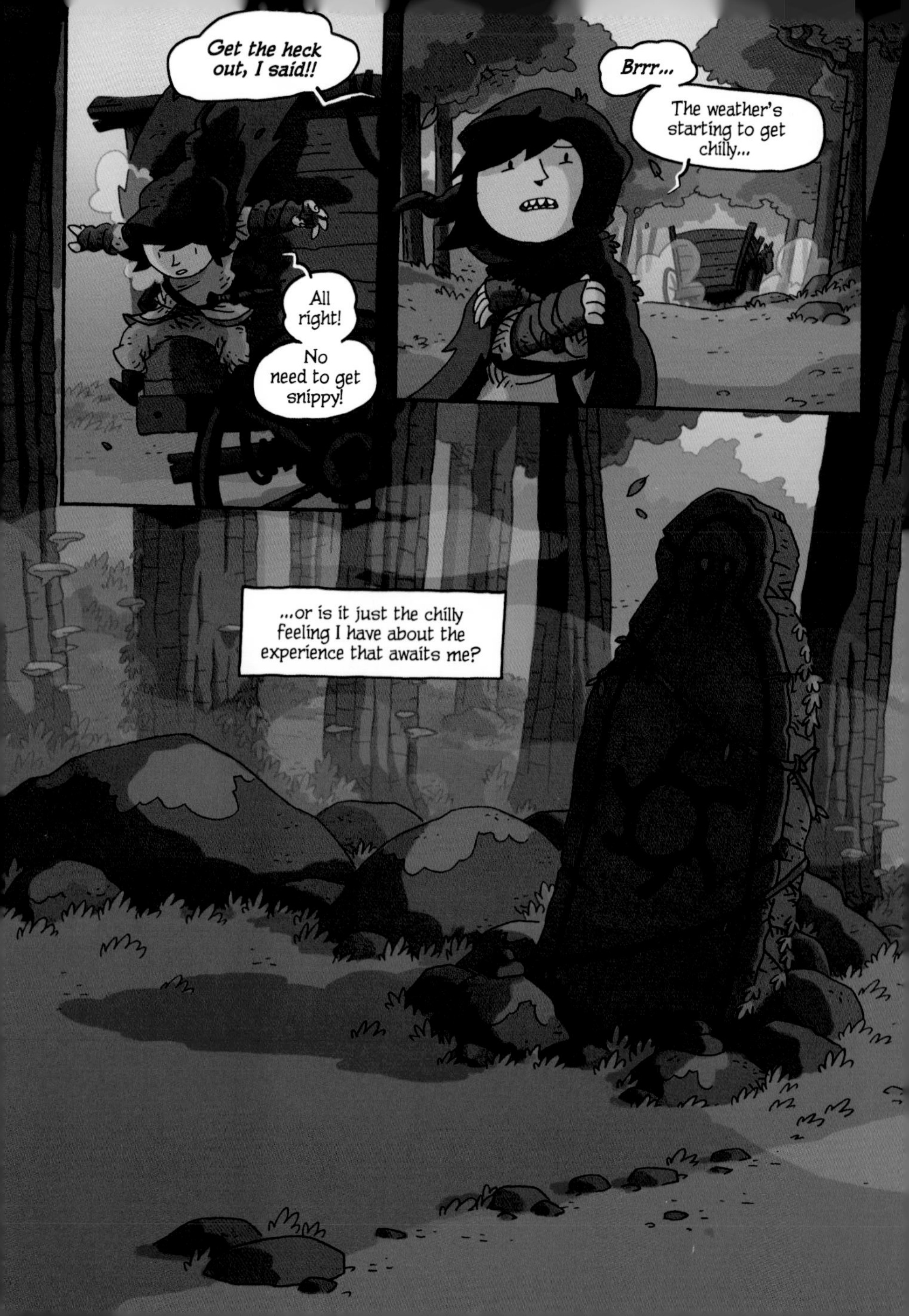
Get the heck out, I said!!
All right!
No need to get snippy!
Brrr...
The weather's starting to get chilly...
...or is it just the chilly feeling I have about the experience that awaits me?

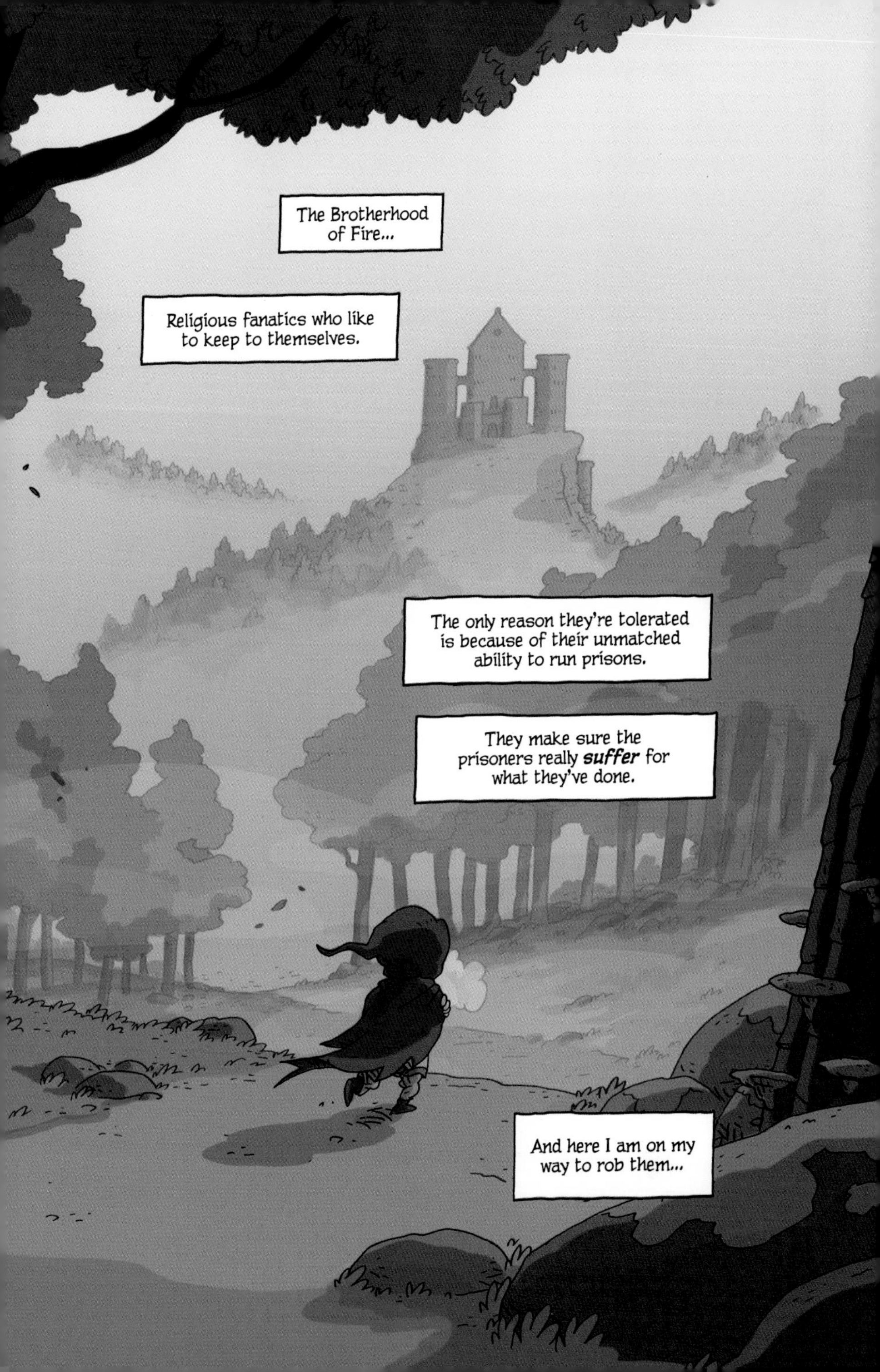
The Brotherhood of Fire...
Religious fanatics who like to keep to themselves.
The only reason they're tolerated is because of their unmatched ability to run prisons.
They make sure the prisoners really ***suffer*** for what they've done.
And here I am on my way to rob them...

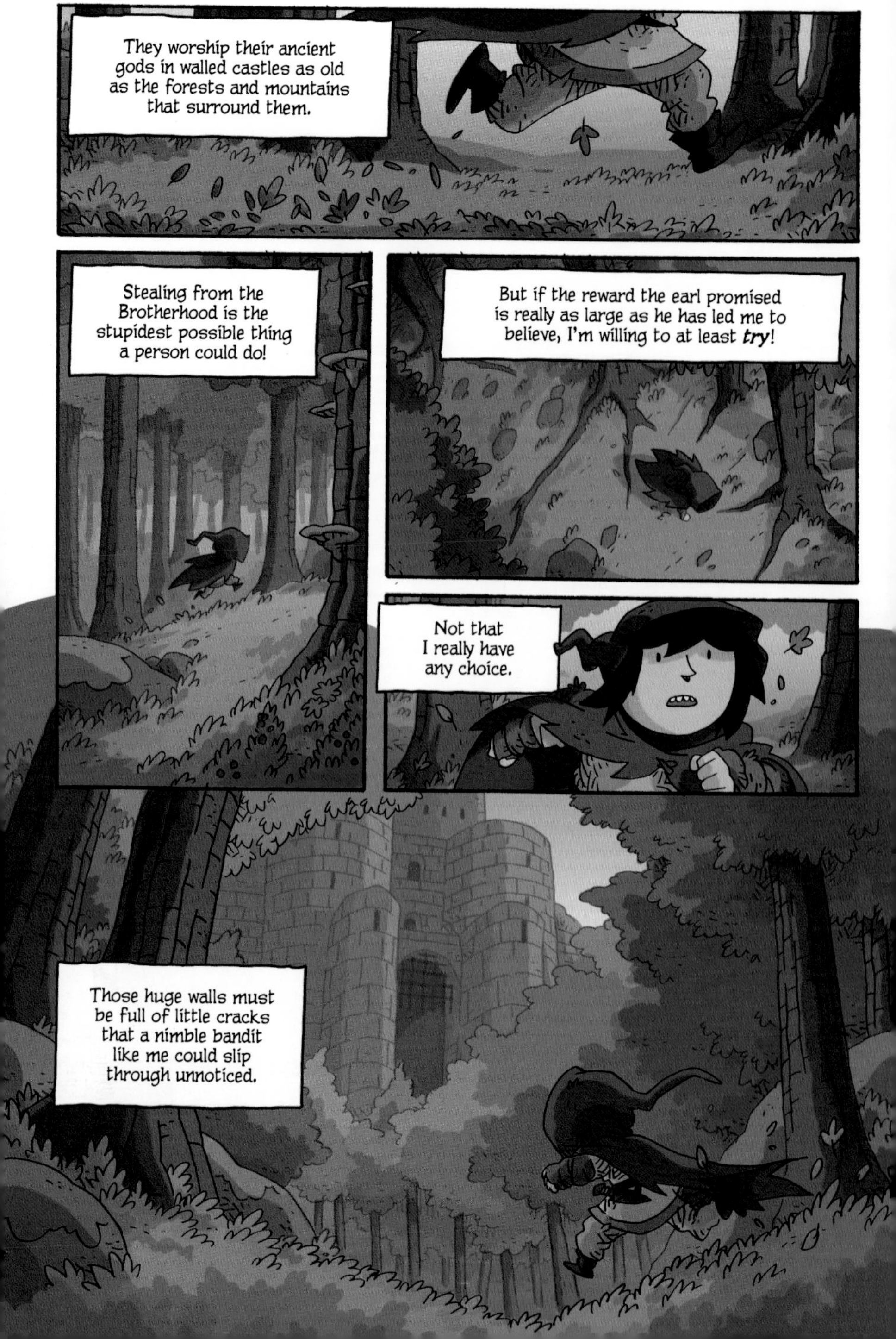
They worship their ancient gods in walled castles as old as the forests and mountains that surround them.
Stealing from the Brotherhood is the stupidest possible thing a person could do!
But if the reward the earl promised is really as large as he has led me to believe, I'm willing to at least *try*!
Not that I really have any choice.
Those huge walls must be full of little cracks that a nimble bandit like me could slip through unnoticed.

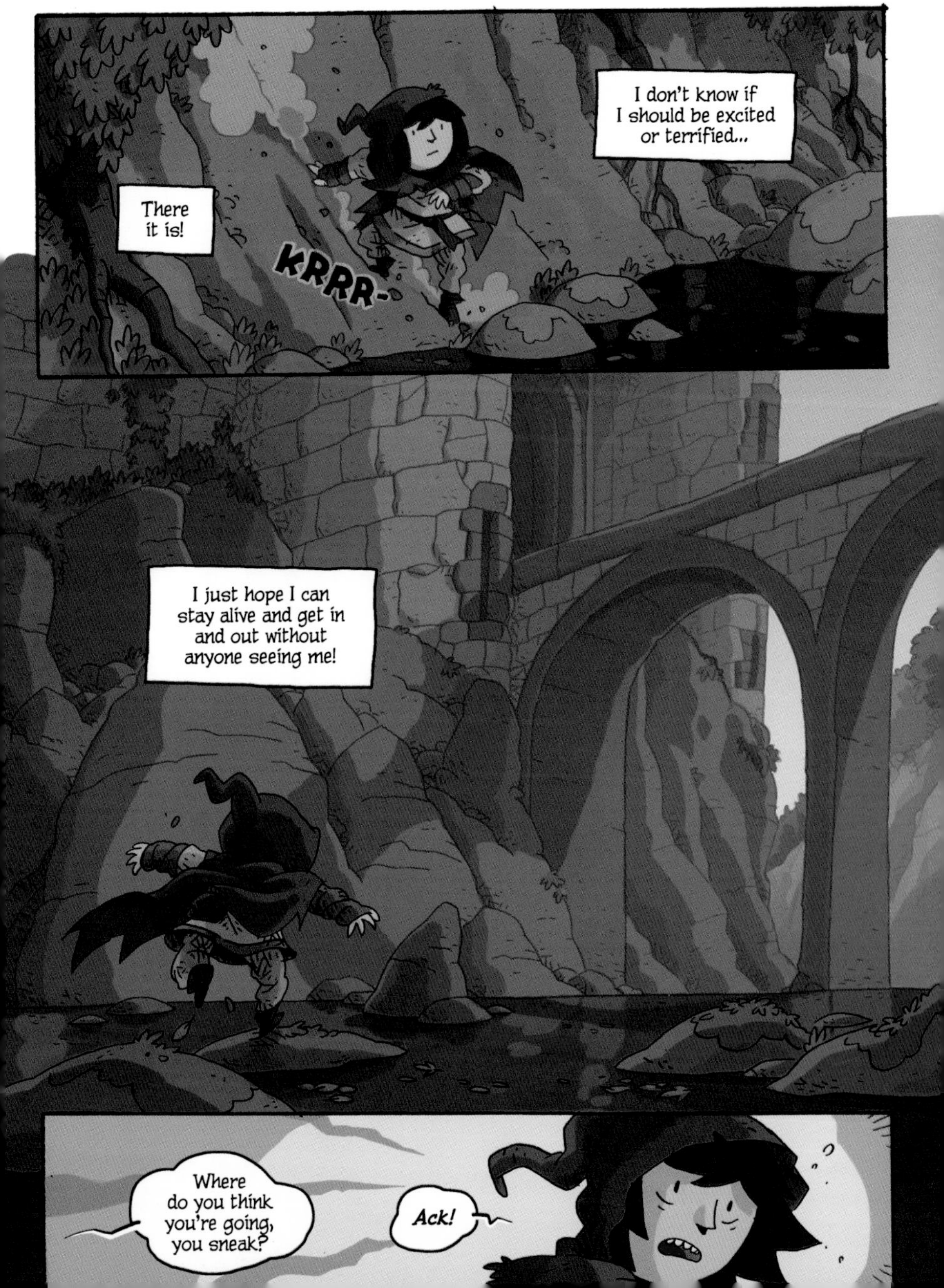
There it is!
I don't know if I should be excited or terrified...
KRRR-
I just hope I can stay alive and get in and out without anyone seeing me!
Where do you think you're going, you sneak?
Ack!

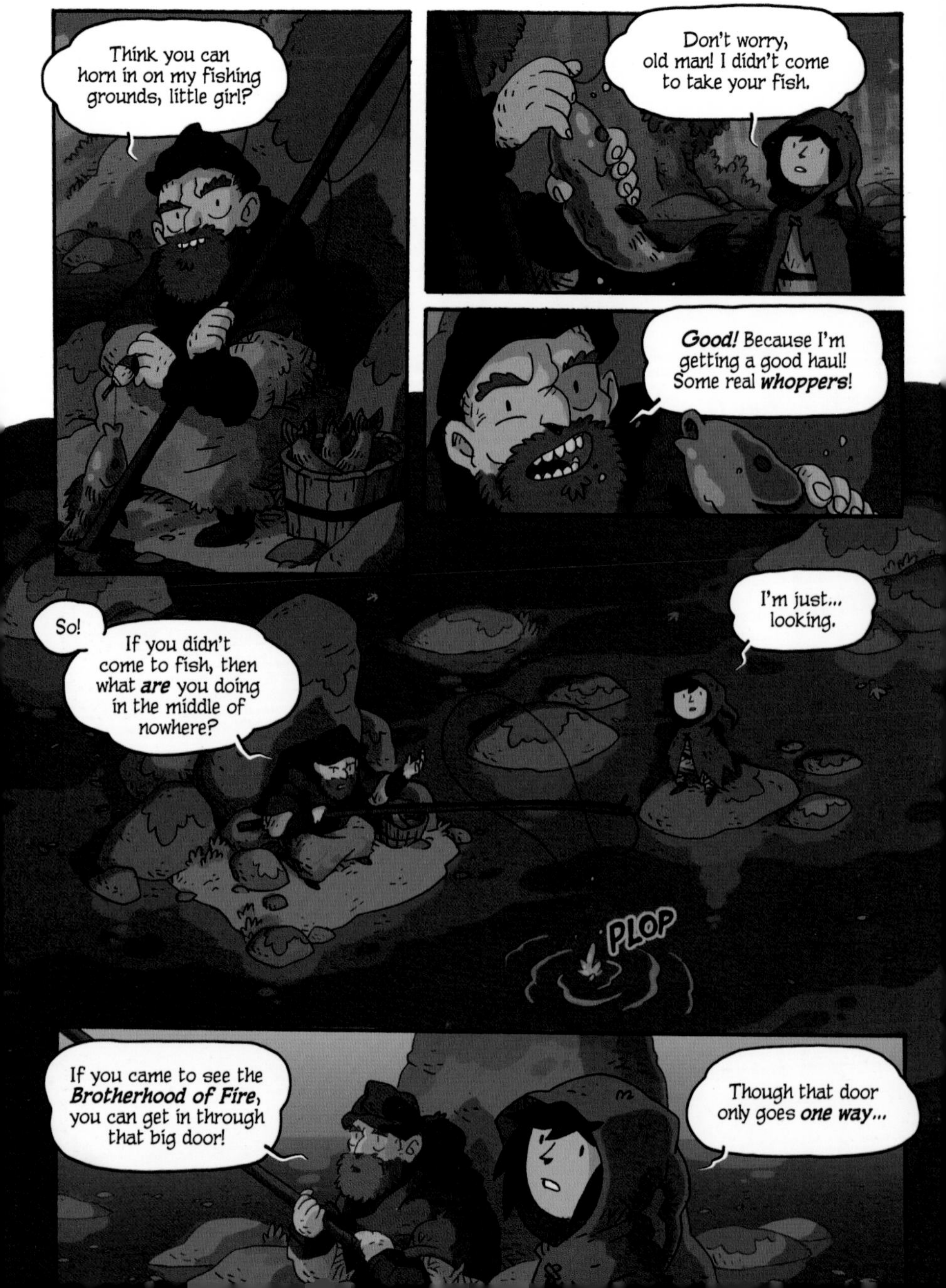
Think you can horn in on my fishing grounds, little girl?
Don't worry, old man! I didn't come to take your fish.
Good! Because I'm getting a good haul! Some real *whoppers*!
So!
If you didn't come to fish, then what *are* you doing in the middle of nowhere?
I'm just... looking.
PLOP
If you came to see the *Brotherhood of Fire*, you can get in through that big door!
Though that door only goes *one way*...

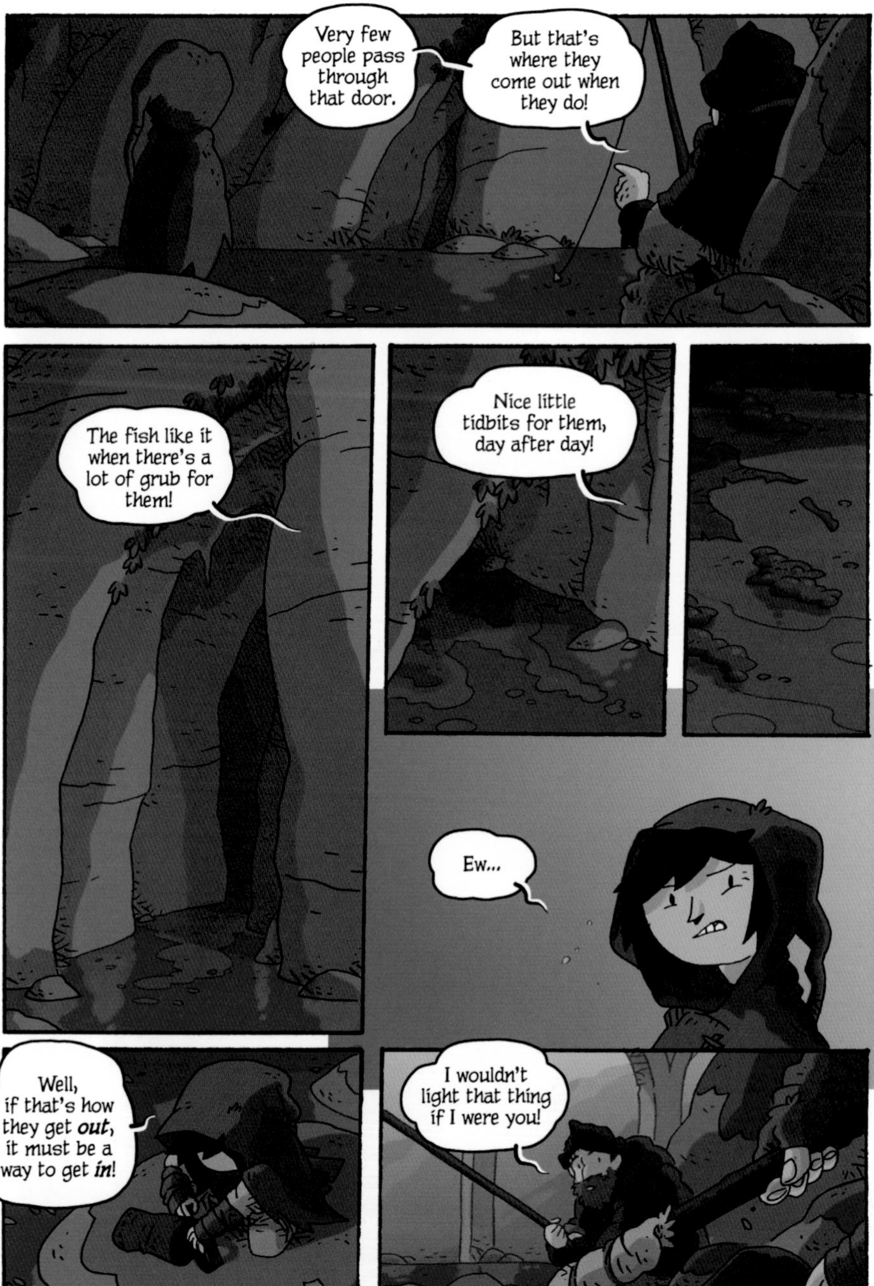

Very few people pass through that door.
But that's where they come out when they do!
The fish like it when there's a lot of grub for them!
Nice little tidbits for them, day after day!
Ew...
Well, if that's how they get *out*, it must be a way to get *in*!
I wouldn't light that thing if I were you!

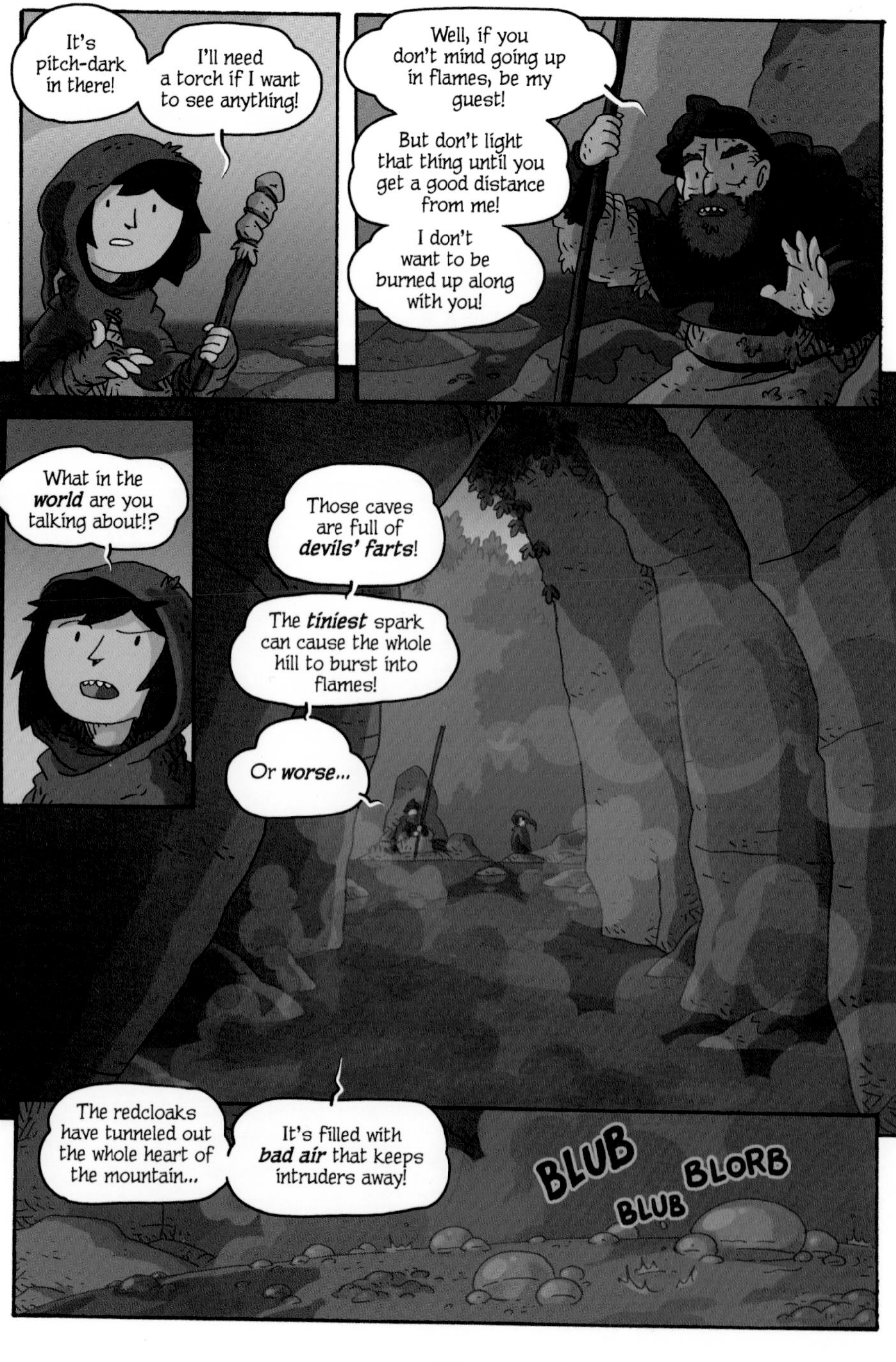
It's pitch-dark in there!
I'll need a torch if I want to see anything!
Well, if you don't mind going up in flames, be my guest!
But don't light that thing until you get a good distance from me!
I don't want to be burned up along with you!
What in the *world* are you talking about!?
Those caves are full of ***devils' farts***!
The ***tiniest*** spark can cause the whole hill to burst into flames!
Or ***worse...***
The redcloaks have tunneled out the whole heart of the mountain...
It's filled with ***bad air*** that keeps intruders away!
BLUB
BLUB
BLORB

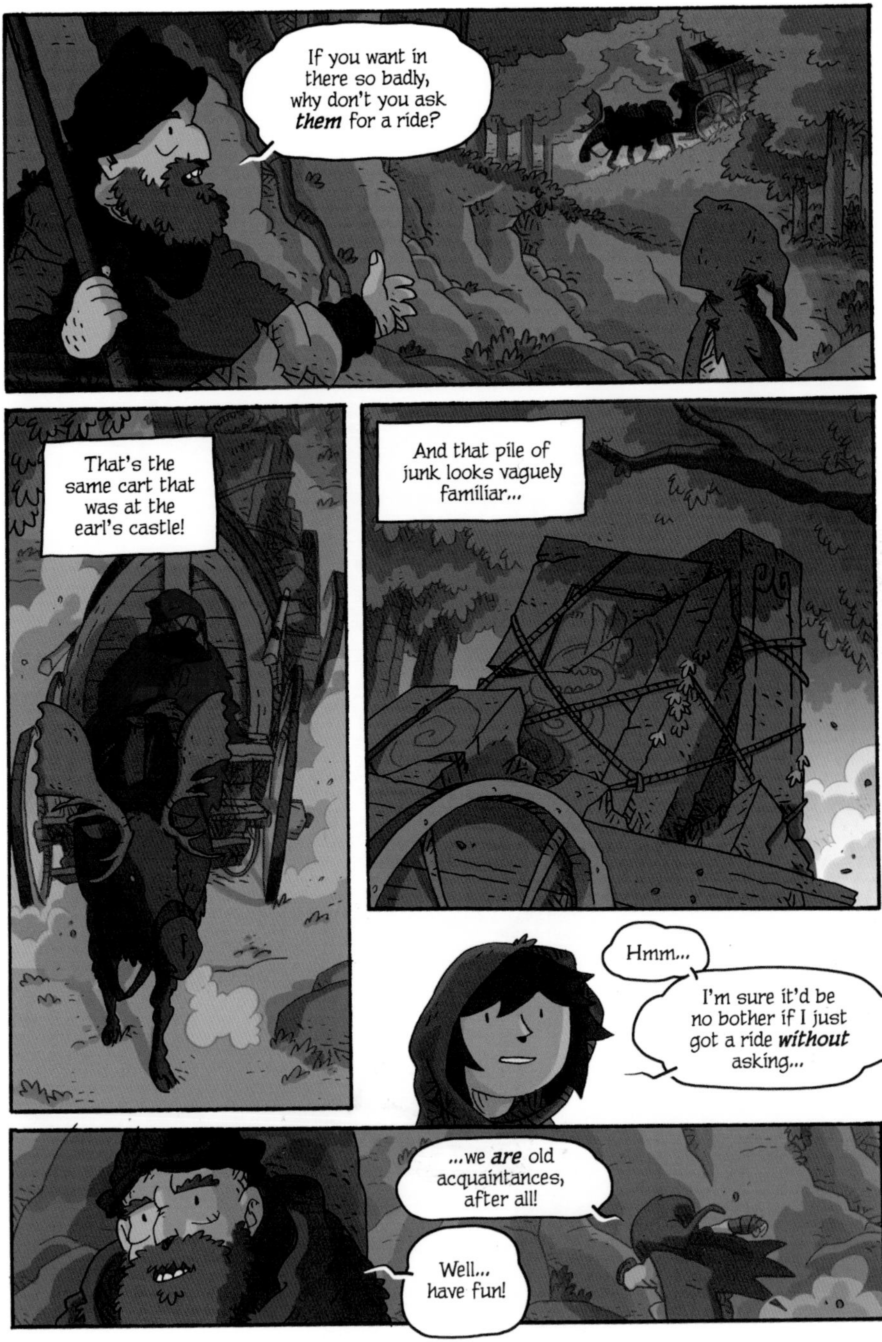
If you want in there so badly, why don't you ask ***them*** for a ride?
That's the same cart that was at the earl's castle!
And that pile of junk looks vaguely familiar...
Hmm...
I'm sure it'd be no bother if I just got a ride ***without*** asking...
...we ***are*** old acquaintances, after all!
Well... have fun!

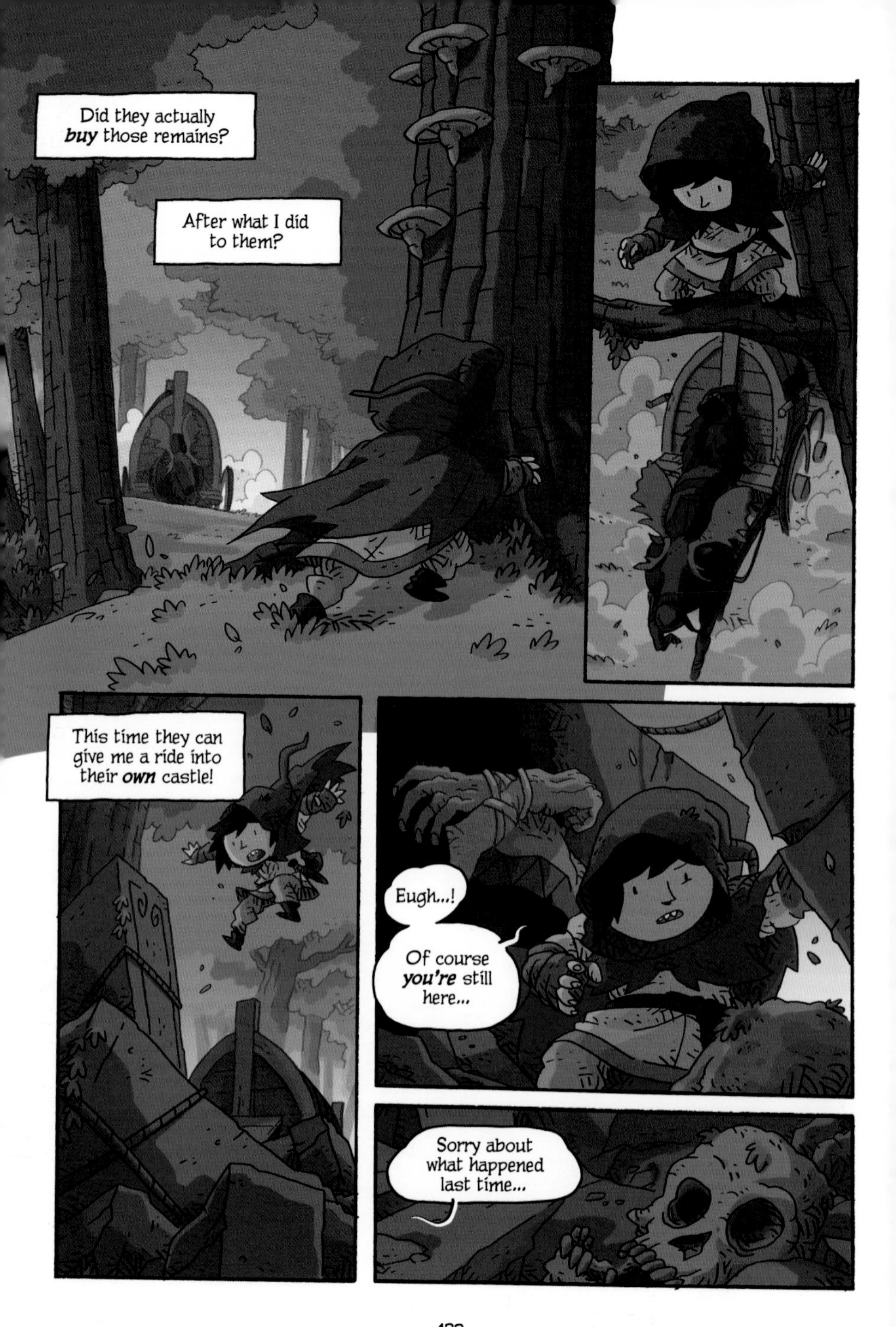
Did they actually *buy* those remains?
After what I did to them?
This time they can give me a ride into their *own* castle!
Eugh...!
Of course *you're* still here...
Sorry about what happened last time...

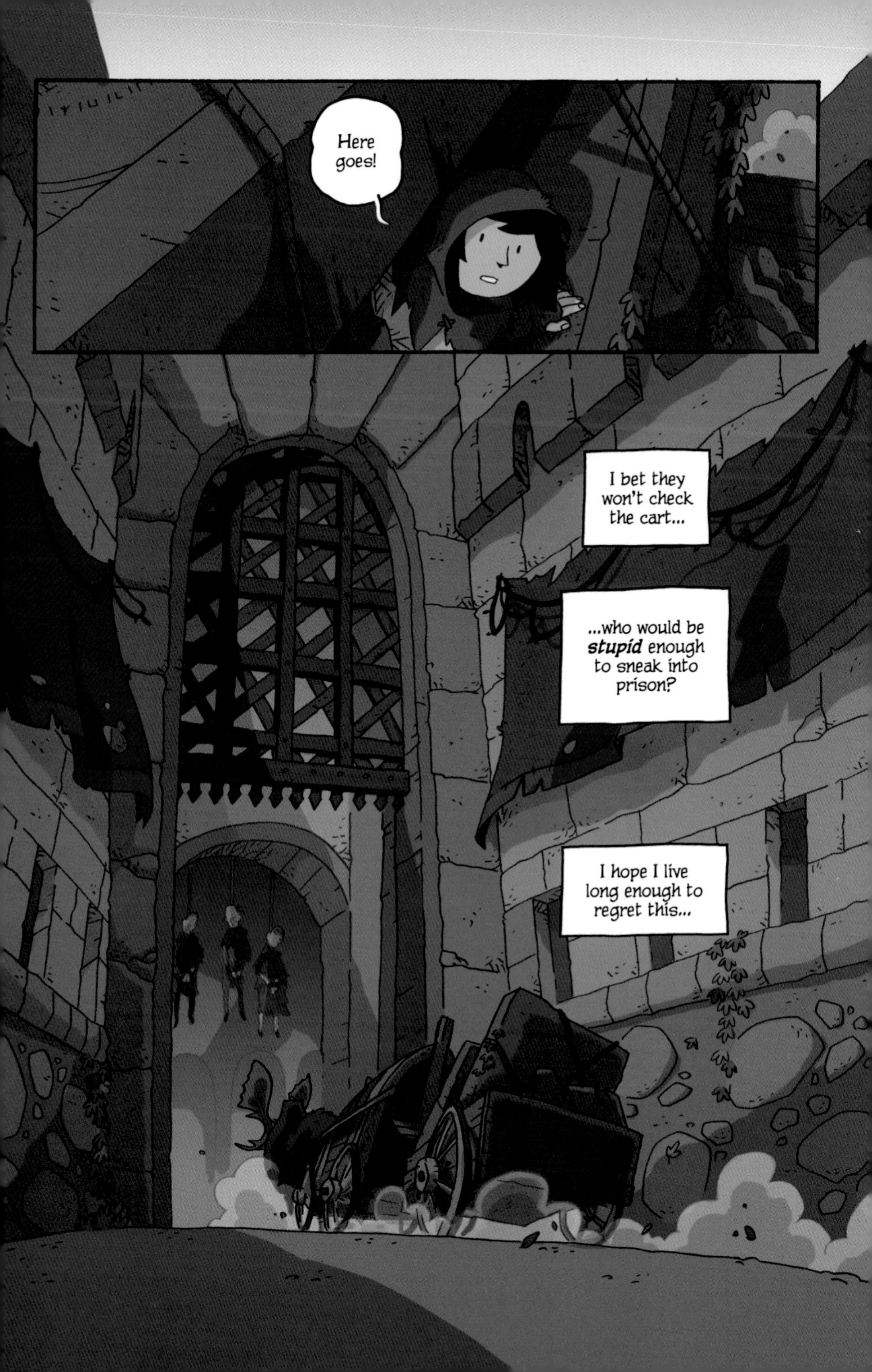
Here goes!
I bet they won't check the cart...
...who would be *stupid* enough to sneak into prison?
I hope I live long enough to regret this...

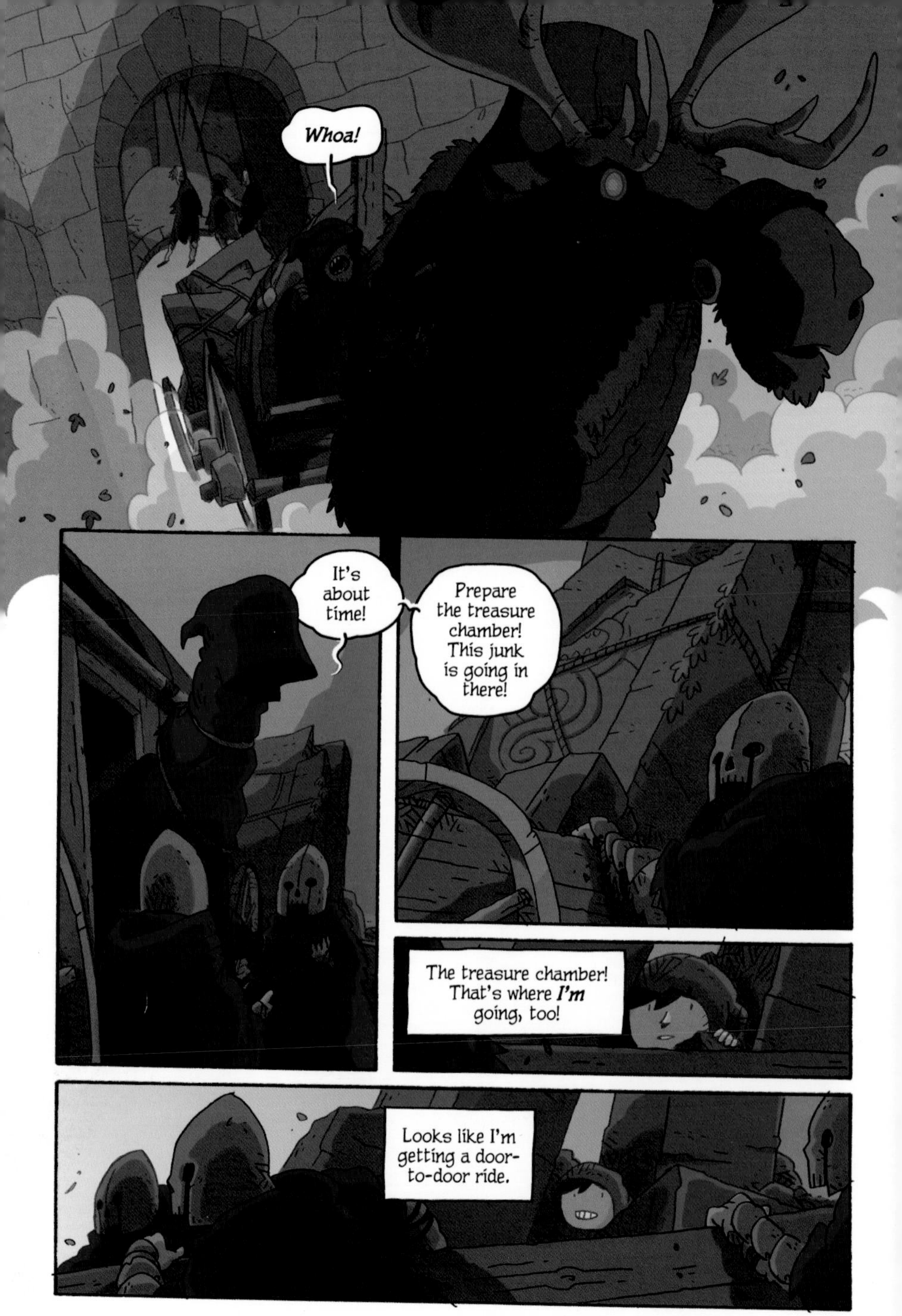
Whoa!
It's about time!
Prepare the treasure chamber! This junk is going in there!
The treasure chamber! That's where ***I'm*** going, too!
Looks like I'm getting a door-to-door ride.

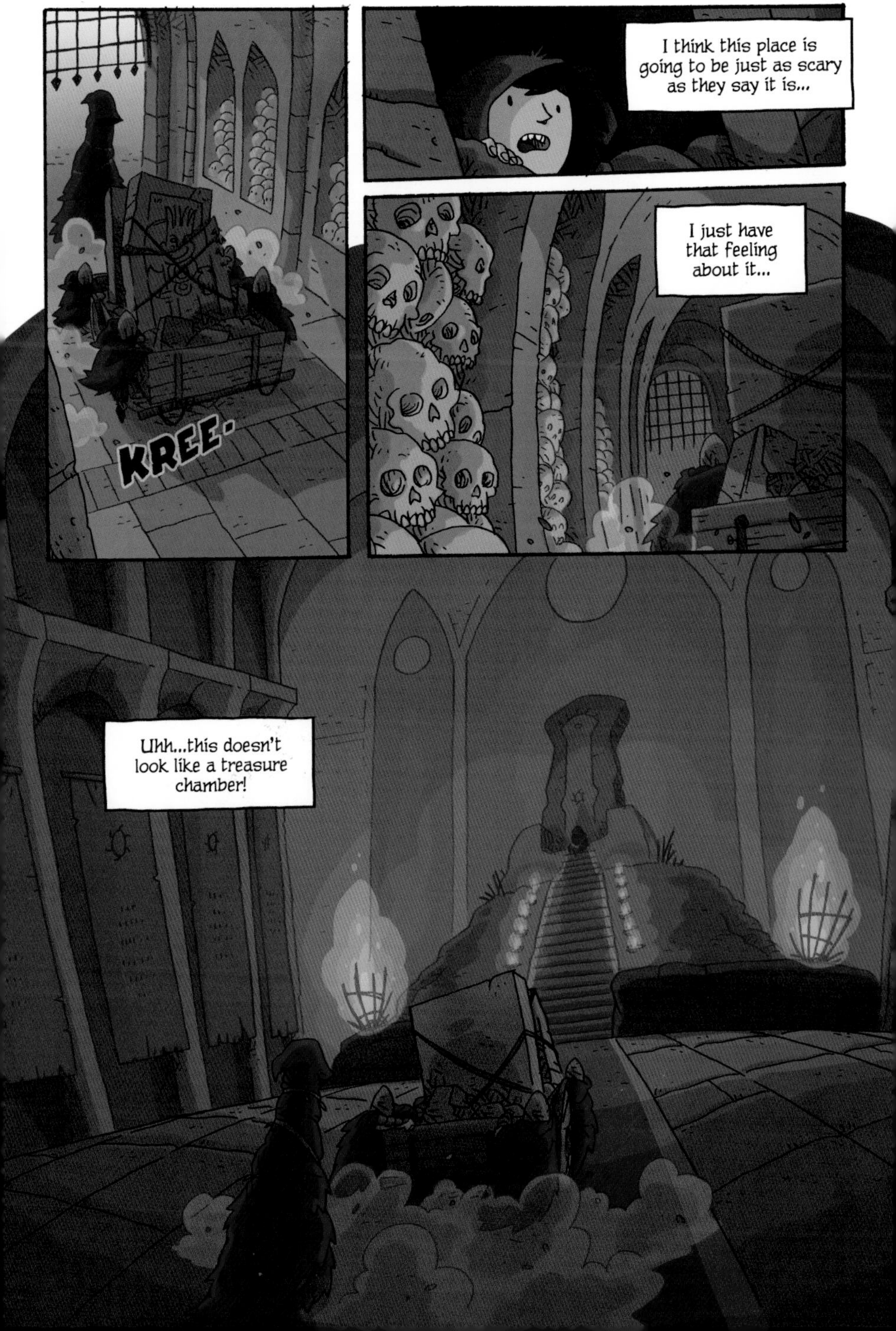
KREE-
I think this place is going to be just as scary as they say it is...
I just have that feeling about it...
Uhh...this doesn't look like a treasure chamber!

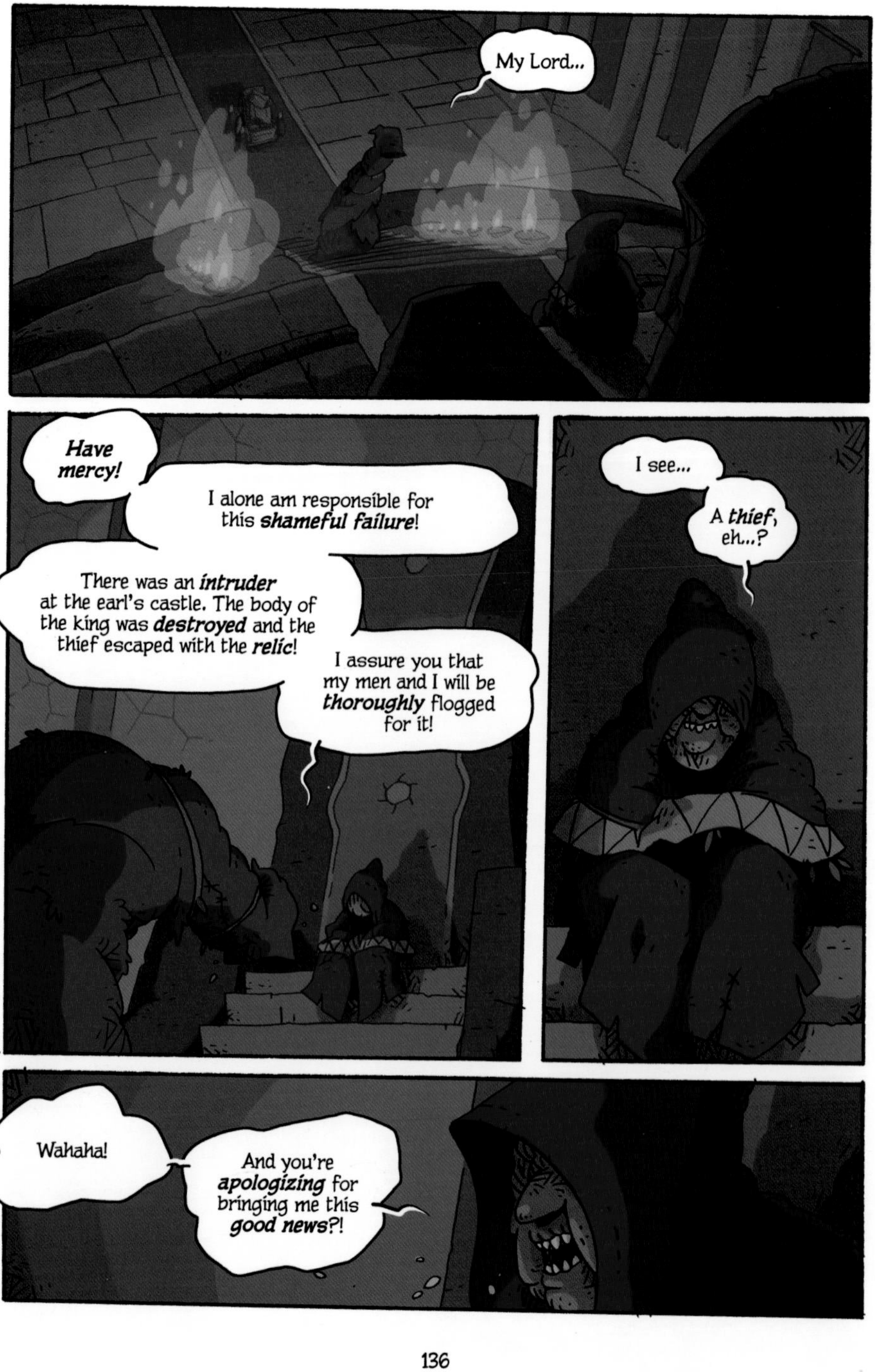
My Lord...
Have mercy!
I alone am responsible for this shameful failure!
There was an intruder at the earl's castle. The body of the king was destroyed and the thief escaped with the relic!
I assure you that my men and I will be thoroughly flogged for it!
I see...
A thief, eh...?
Wahaha!
And you're apologizing for bringing me this good news?!

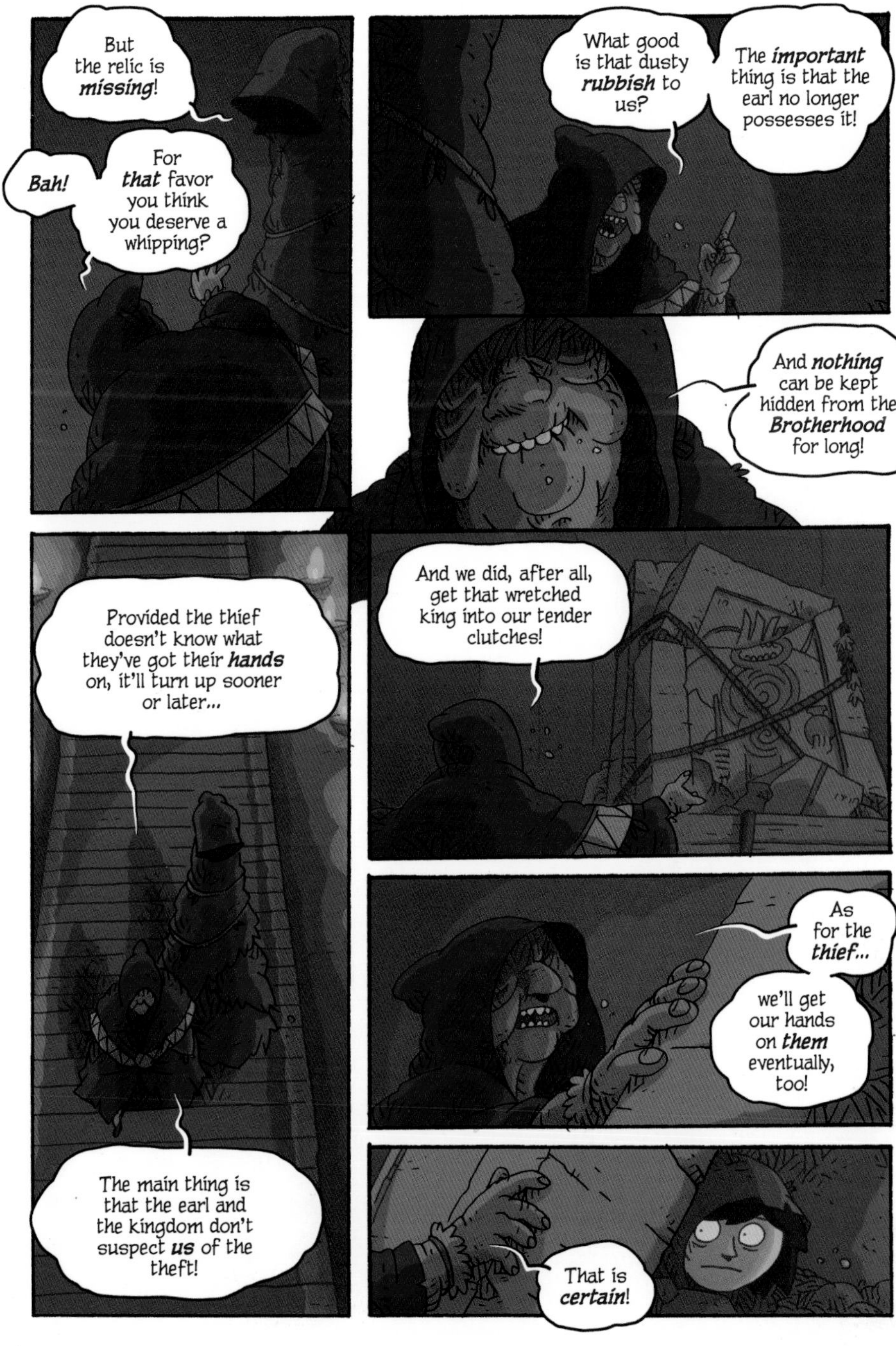
But the relic is ***missing***!
Bah!
For ***that*** favor you think you deserve a whipping?
What good is that dusty ***rubbish*** to us?
The ***important*** thing is that the earl no longer possesses it!
And ***nothing*** can be kept hidden from the ***Brotherhood*** for long!
Provided the thief doesn't know what they've got their ***hands*** on, it'll turn up sooner or later...
The main thing is that the earl and the kingdom don't suspect ***us*** of the theft!
And we did, after all, get that wretched king into our tender clutches!
As for the ***thief***...
we'll get our hands on ***them*** eventually, too!
That is ***certain***!

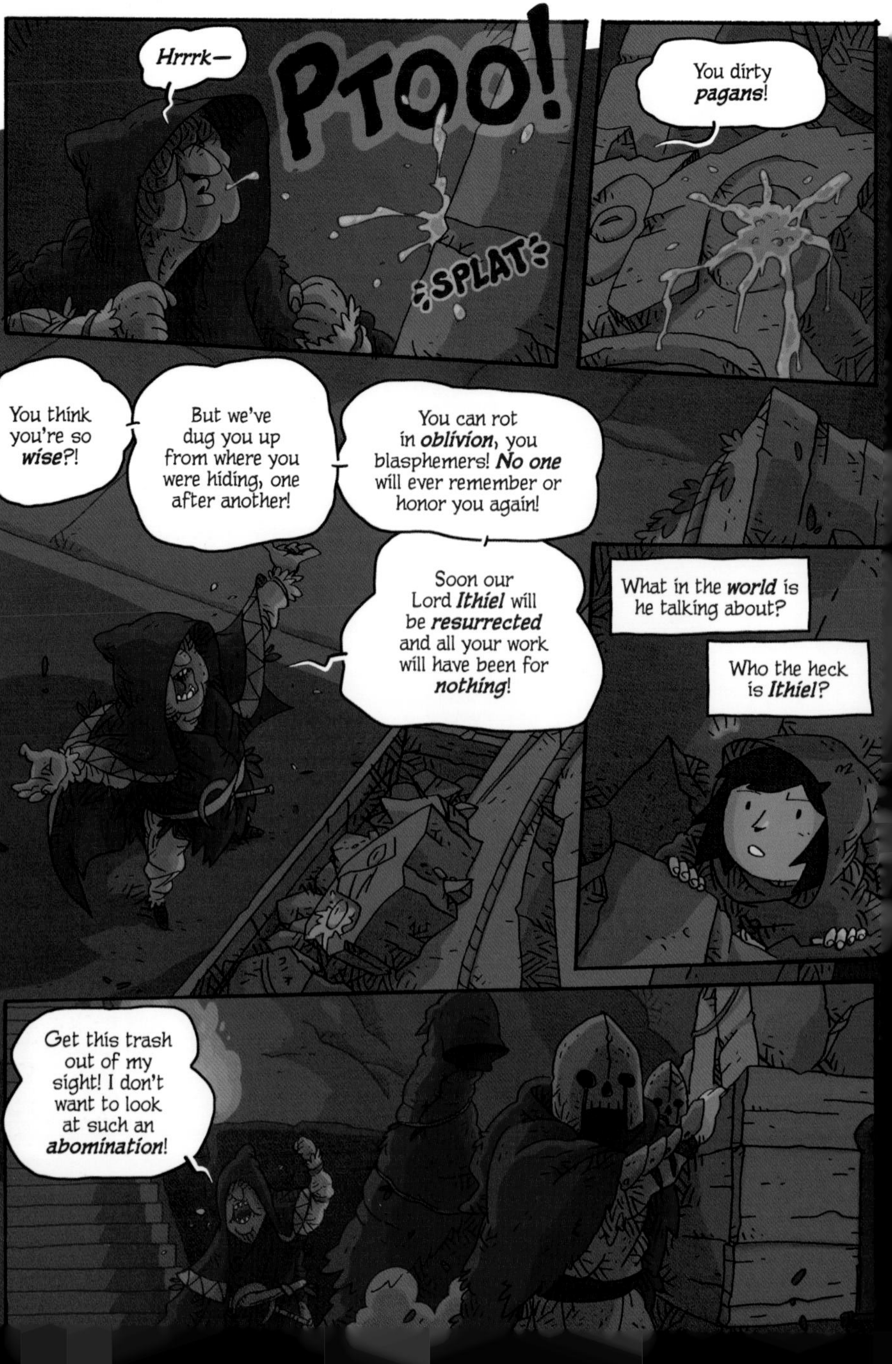
Hrrrk—
PTOO!
SPLAT
You dirty pagans!
You think you're so wise?!
But we've dug you up from where you were hiding, one after another!
You can rot in oblivion, you blasphemers! No one will ever remember or honor you again!
Soon our Lord Ithiel will be resurrected and all your work will have been for nothing!
What in the world is he talking about?
Who the heck is Ithiel?
Get this trash out of my sight! I don't want to look at such an abomination!

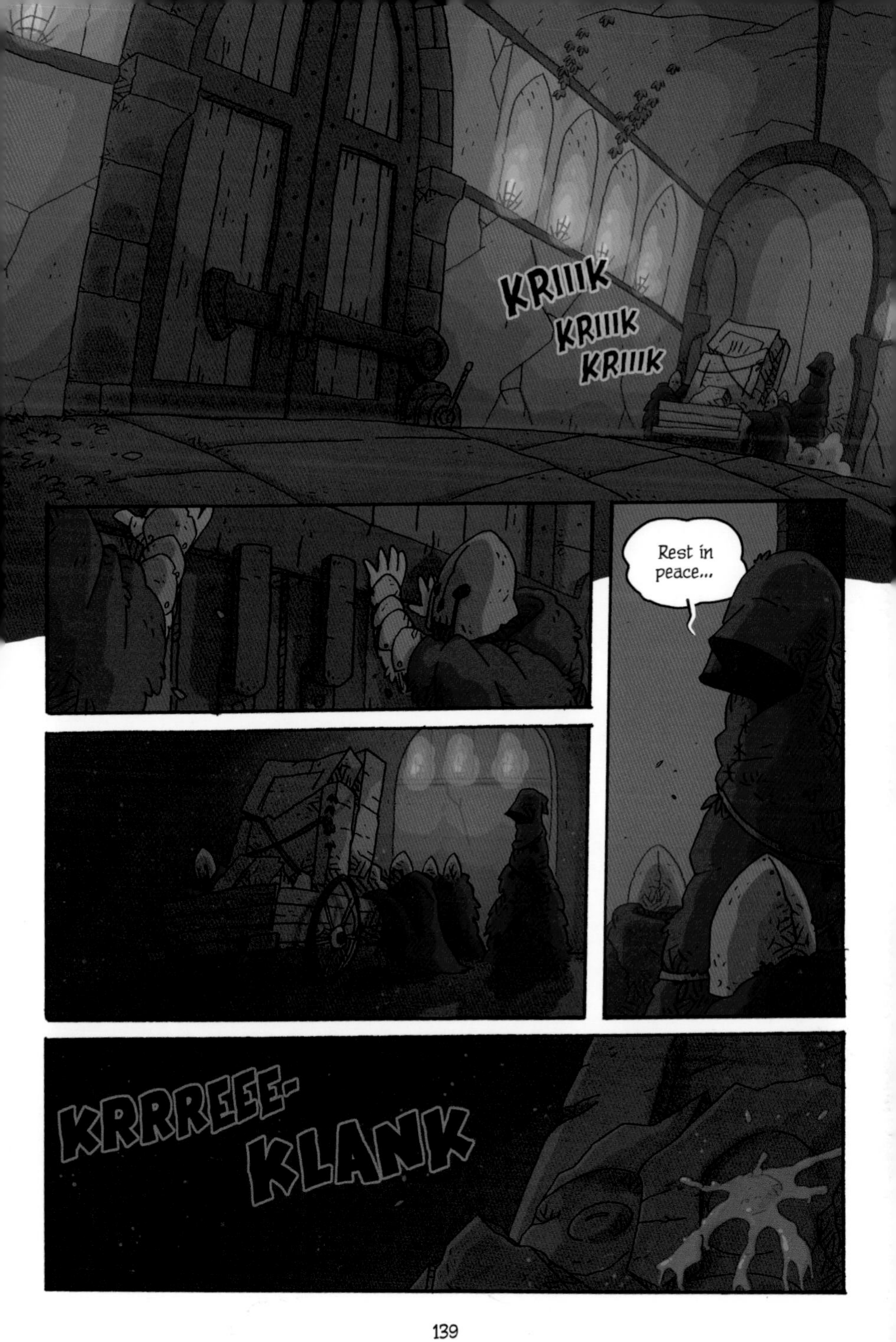
KRIIIK
KRIIIK
KRIIIK
Rest in peace...
KRRREEE-
KLANK

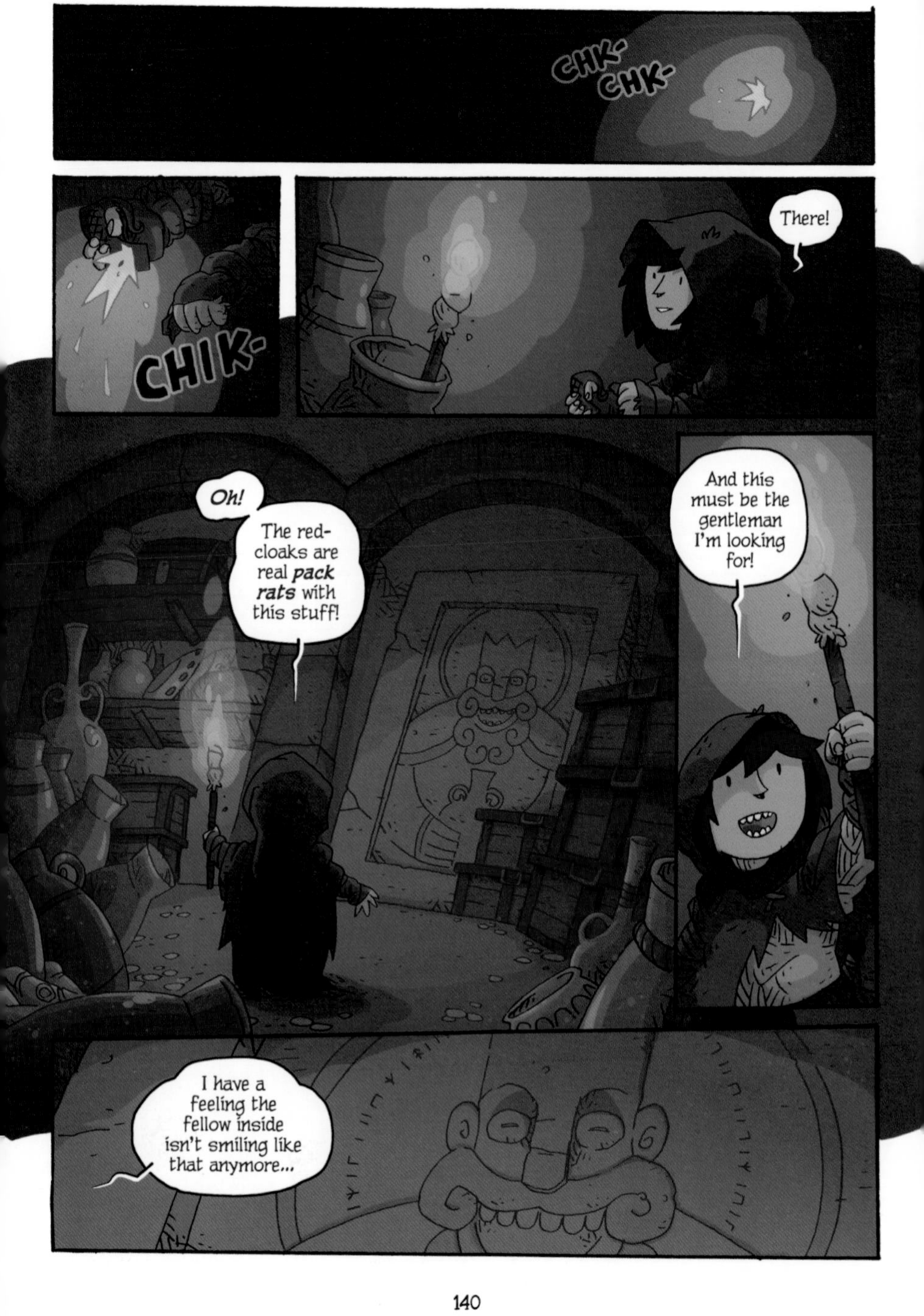
CHK-
CHK-
CHIK-
There!
Oh!
The red-cloaks are real ***pack rats*** with this stuff!
And this must be the gentleman I'm looking for!
I have a feeling the fellow inside isn't smiling like that anymore...

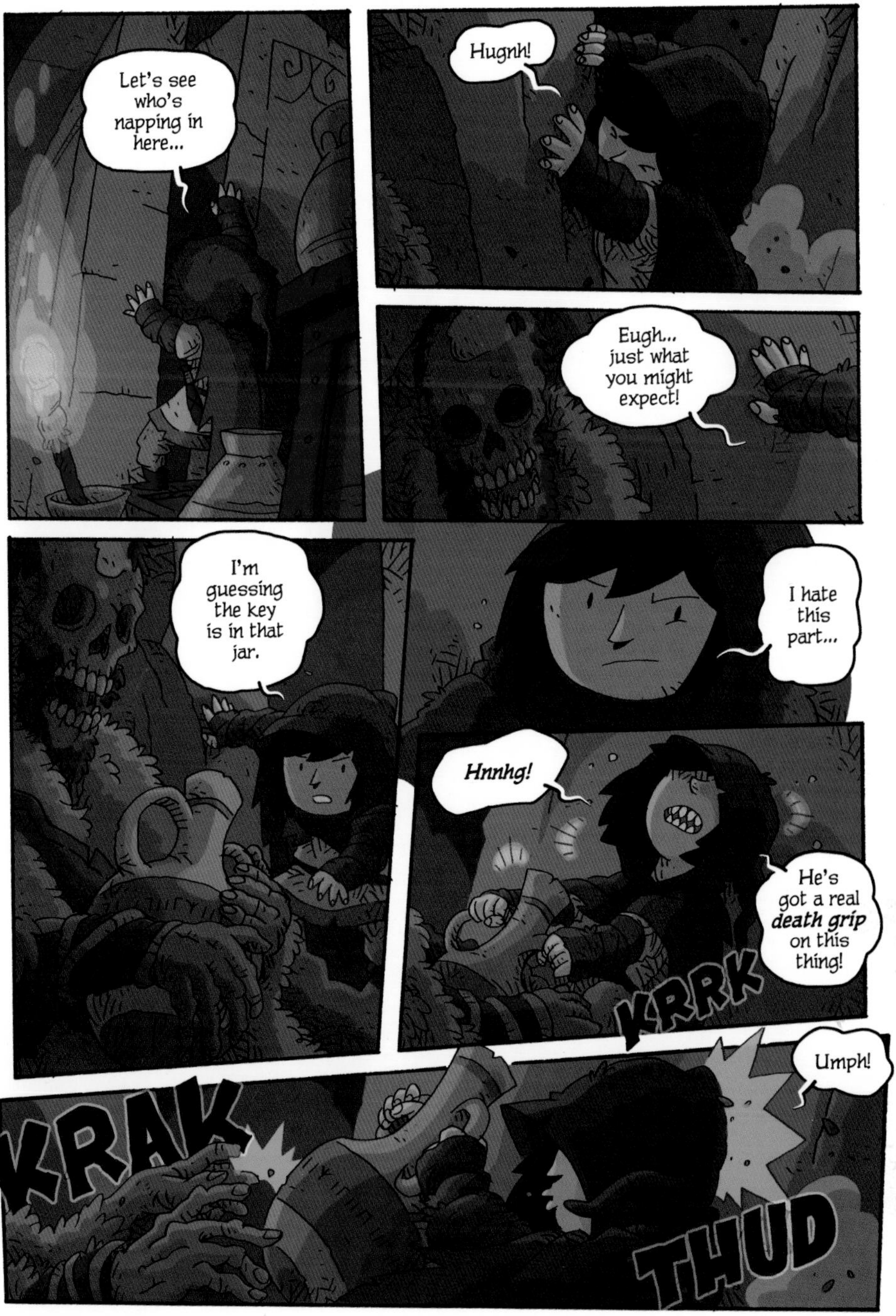
Let's see who's napping in here...
Hugnh!
Eugh... just what you might expect!
I'm guessing the key is in that jar.
I hate this part...
Hnnhg!
He's got a real ***death grip*** on this thing!
KRRK
Umph!
KRAK
THUD

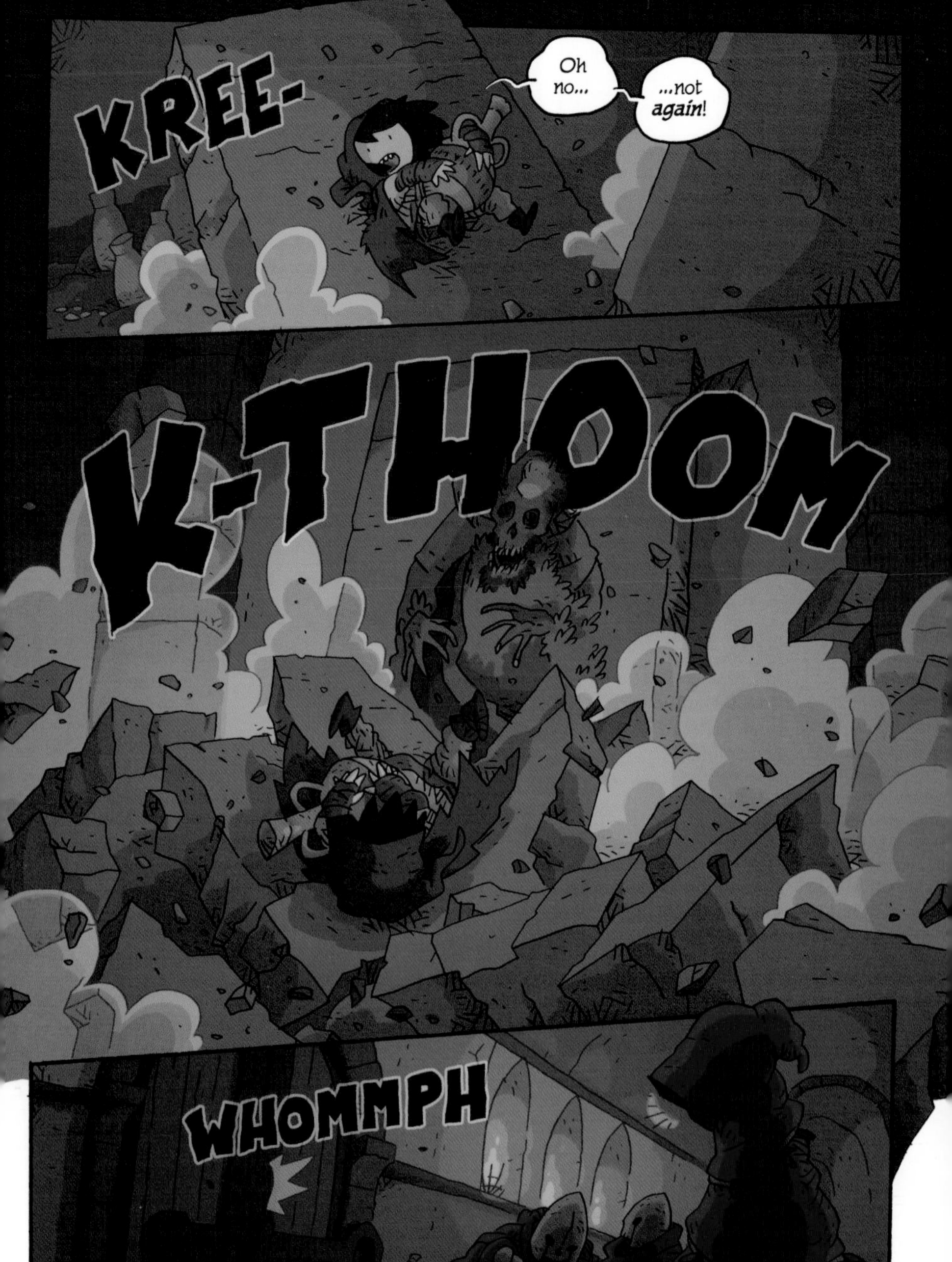
KREE-
Oh no...
...not *again*!
K-THOOM
WHOMMPH

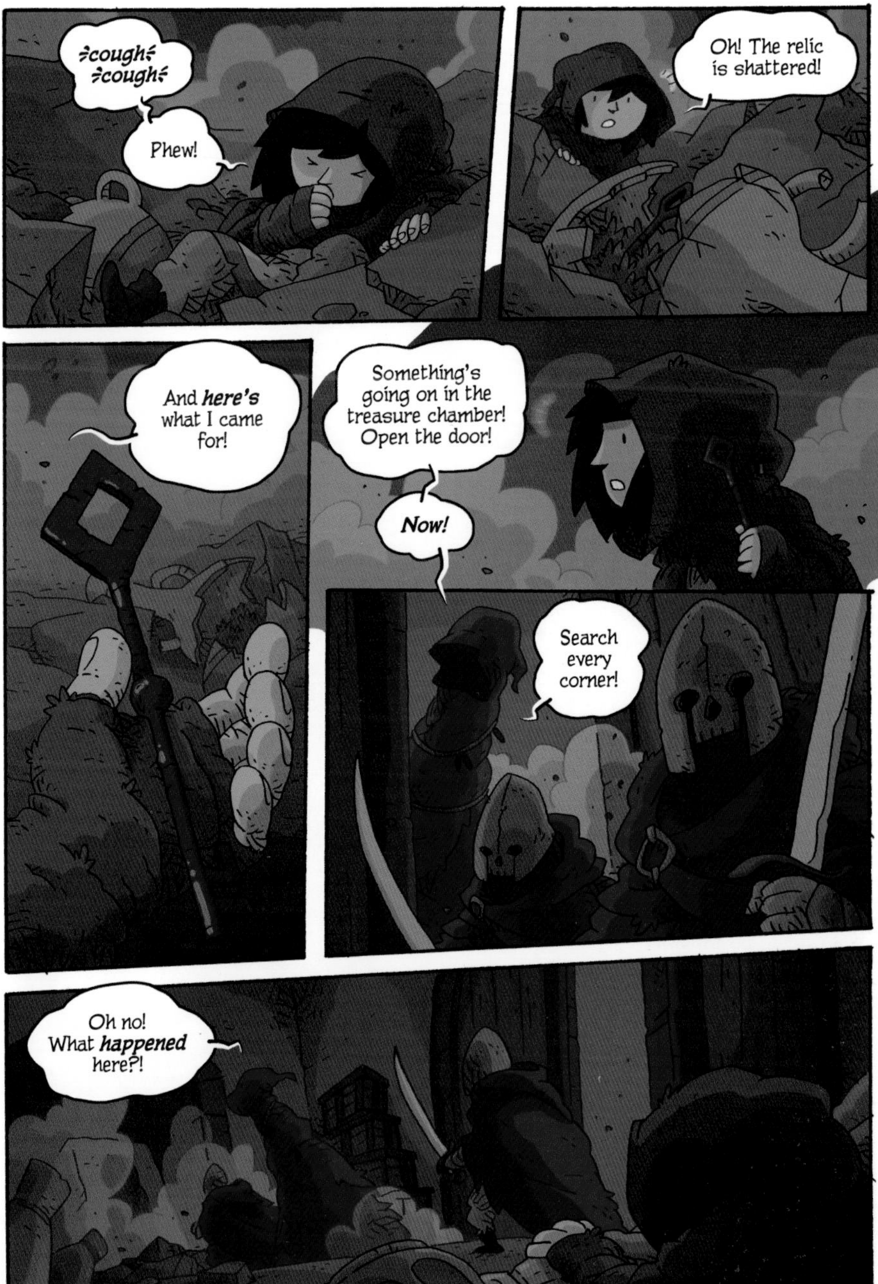

cough
cough
Phew!
Oh! The relic is shattered!
And ***here's*** what I came for!
Something's going on in the treasure chamber! Open the door!
Now!
Search every corner!
Oh no! What ***happened*** here?!

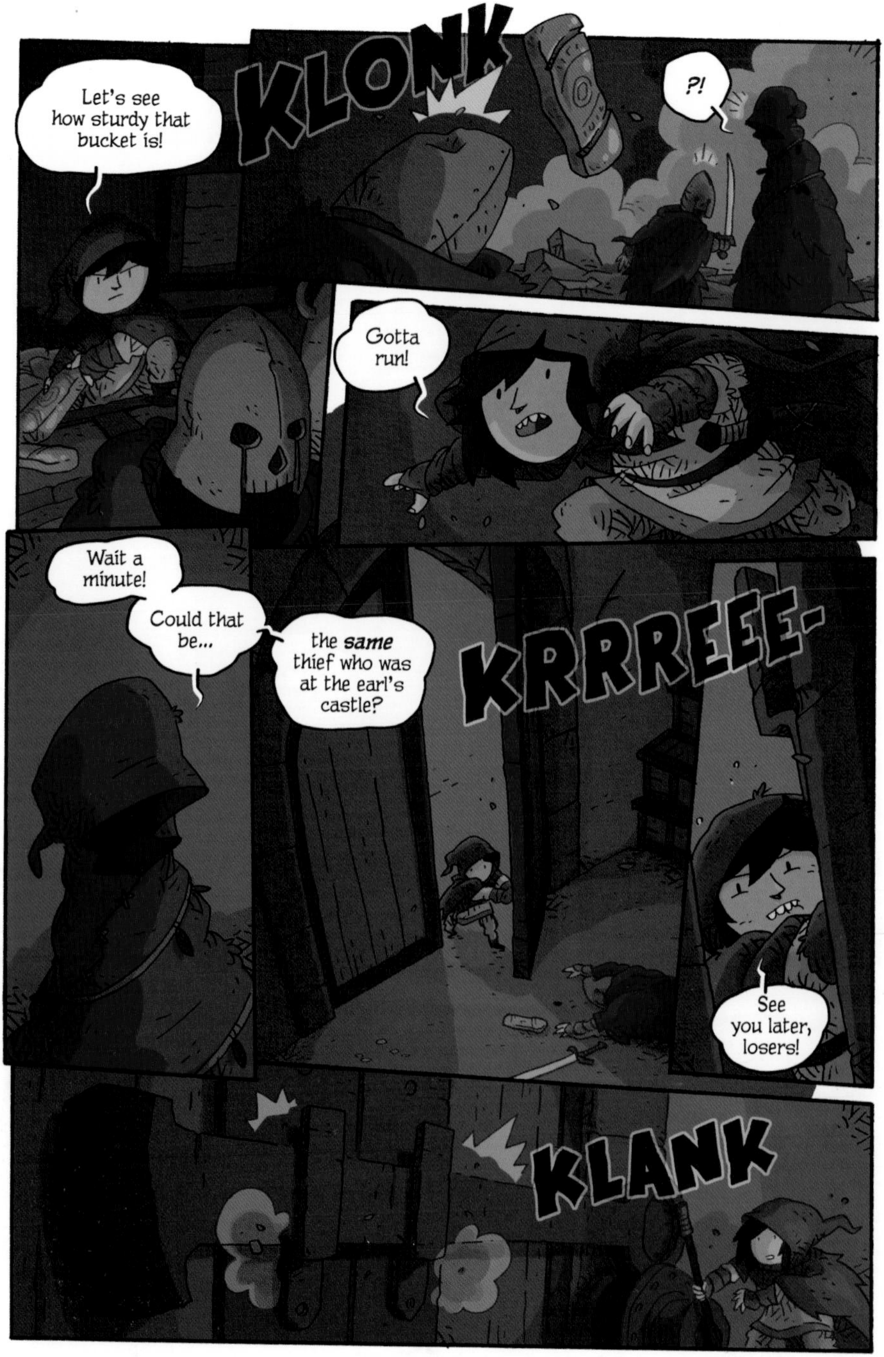
KLONK
Let's see how sturdy that bucket is!
?!
Gotta run!
Wait a minute!
Could that be...
the *same* thief who was at the earl's castle?
KRRREEE-
See you later, losers!
KLANK

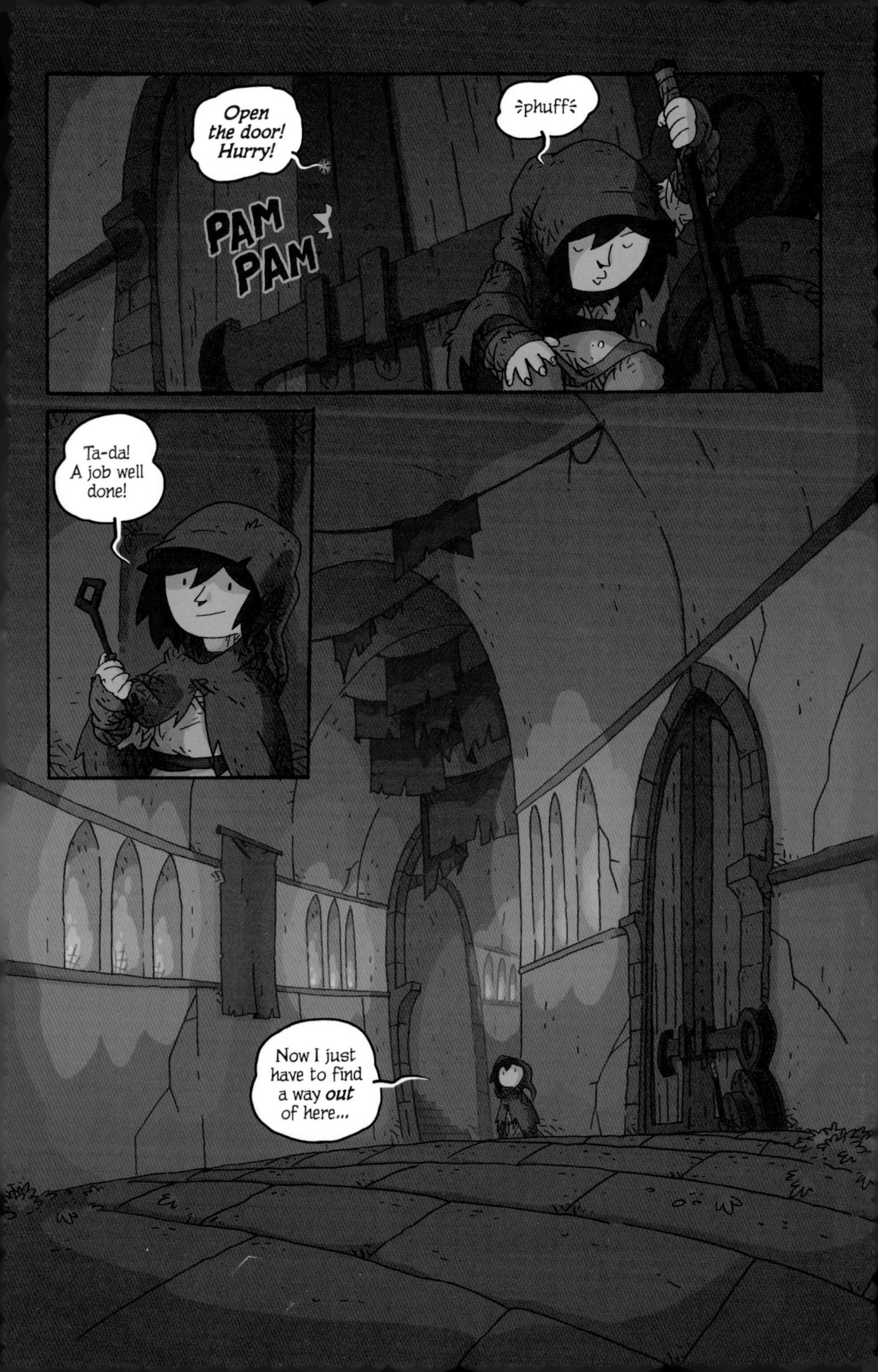
Open the door! Hurry!
PAM PAM
phuff
Ta-da! A job well done!
Now I just have to find a way *out* of here...

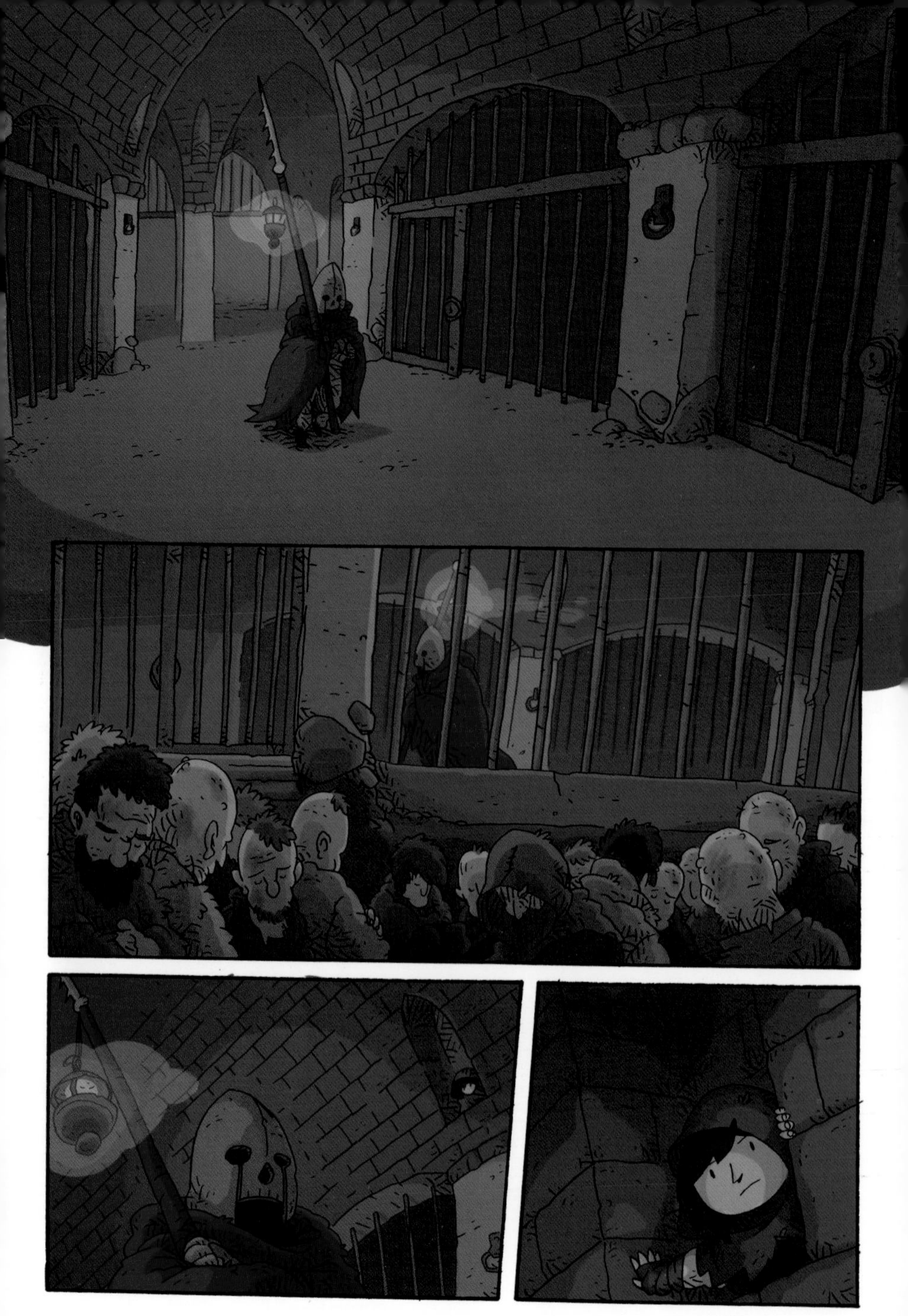

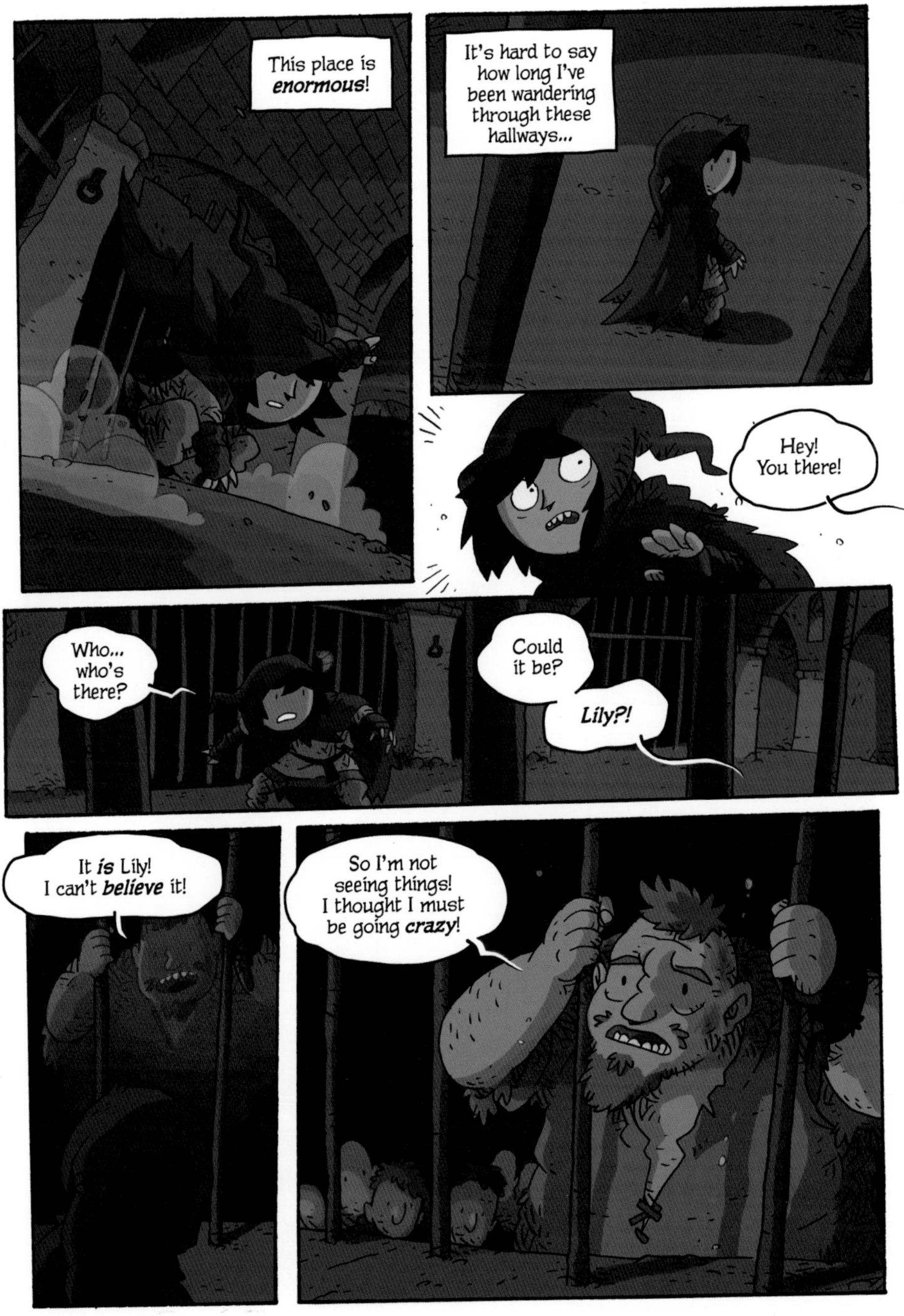
This place is *enormous*!
It's hard to say how long I've been wandering through these hallways...
Hey! You there!
Who... who's there?
Could it be?
Lily?!
It *is* Lily! I can't *believe* it!
So I'm not seeing things! I thought I must be going *crazy*!

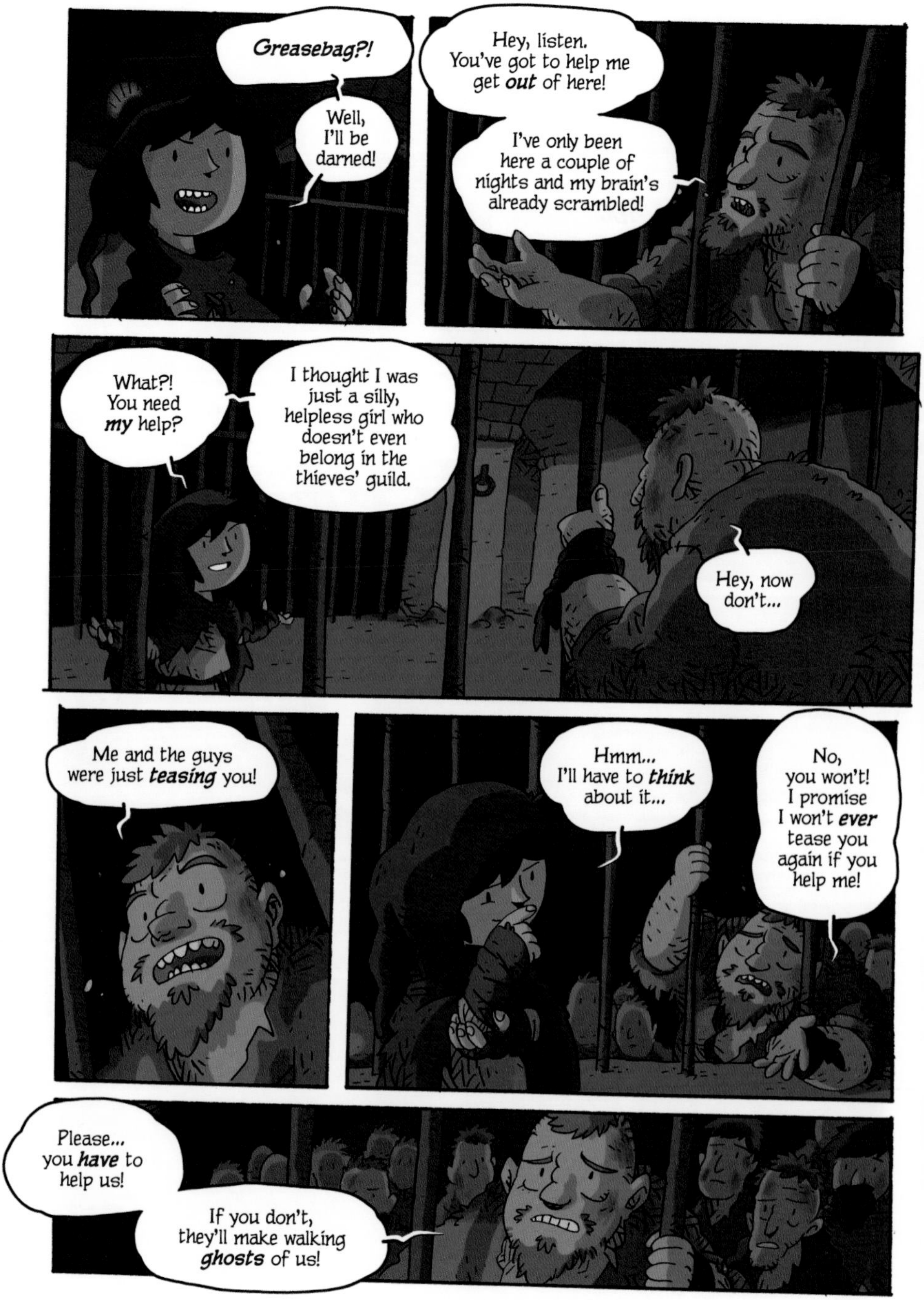
Greasebag?!
Well, I'll be darned!
Hey, listen. You've got to help me get out of here!
I've only been here a couple of nights and my brain's already scrambled!
What?! You need my help?
I thought I was just a silly, helpless girl who doesn't even belong in the thieves' guild.
Hey, now don't...
Me and the guys were just teasing you!
Hmm... I'll have to think about it...
No, you won't! I promise I won't ever tease you again if you help me!
Please... you have to help us!
If you don't, they'll make walking ghosts of us!

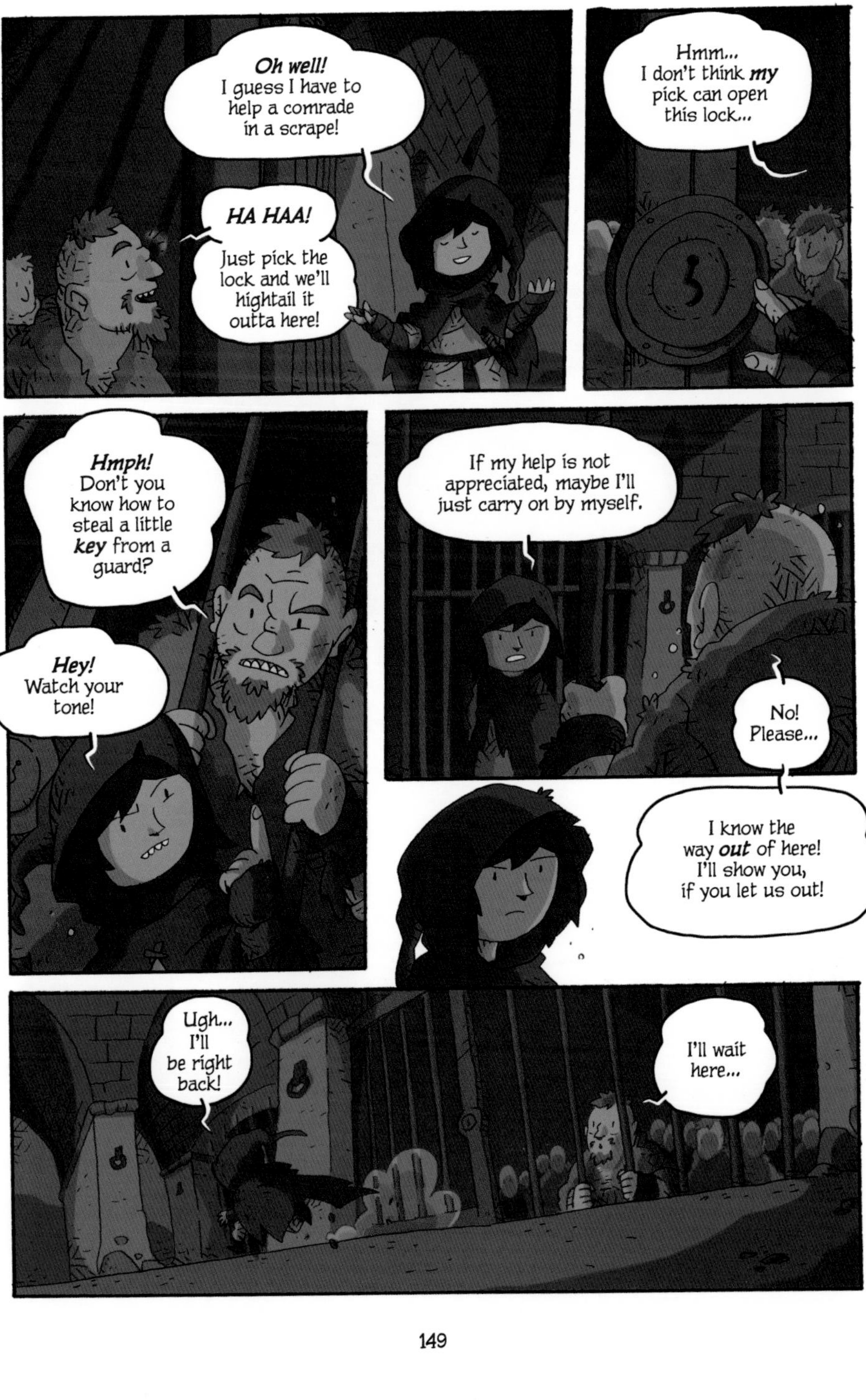
Oh well! I guess I have to help a comrade in a scrape!
HA HAA!
Just pick the lock and we'll hightail it outta here!
Hmm... I don't think my pick can open this lock...
Hmph! Don't you know how to steal a little key from a guard?
Hey! Watch your tone!
If my help is not appreciated, maybe I'll just carry on by myself.
No! Please...
I know the way out of here! I'll show you, if you let us out!
Ugh... I'll be right back!
I'll wait here...

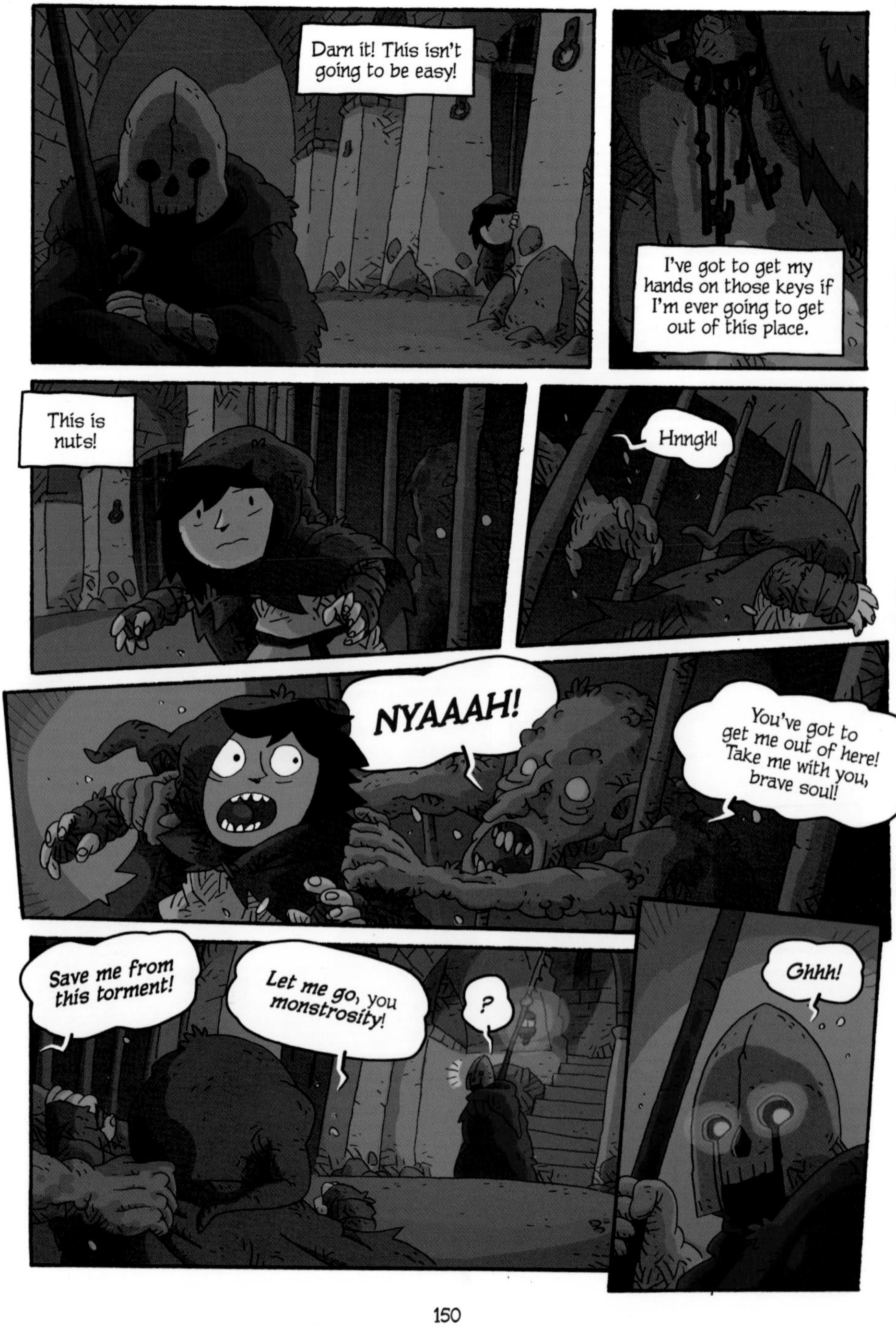
Darn it! This isn't going to be easy!
I've got to get my hands on those keys if I'm ever going to get out of this place.
This is nuts!
Hnngh!
NYAAAH!
You've got to get me out of here! Take me with you, brave soul!
Save me from this torment!
Let me go, you monstrosity!
?
Ghhh!

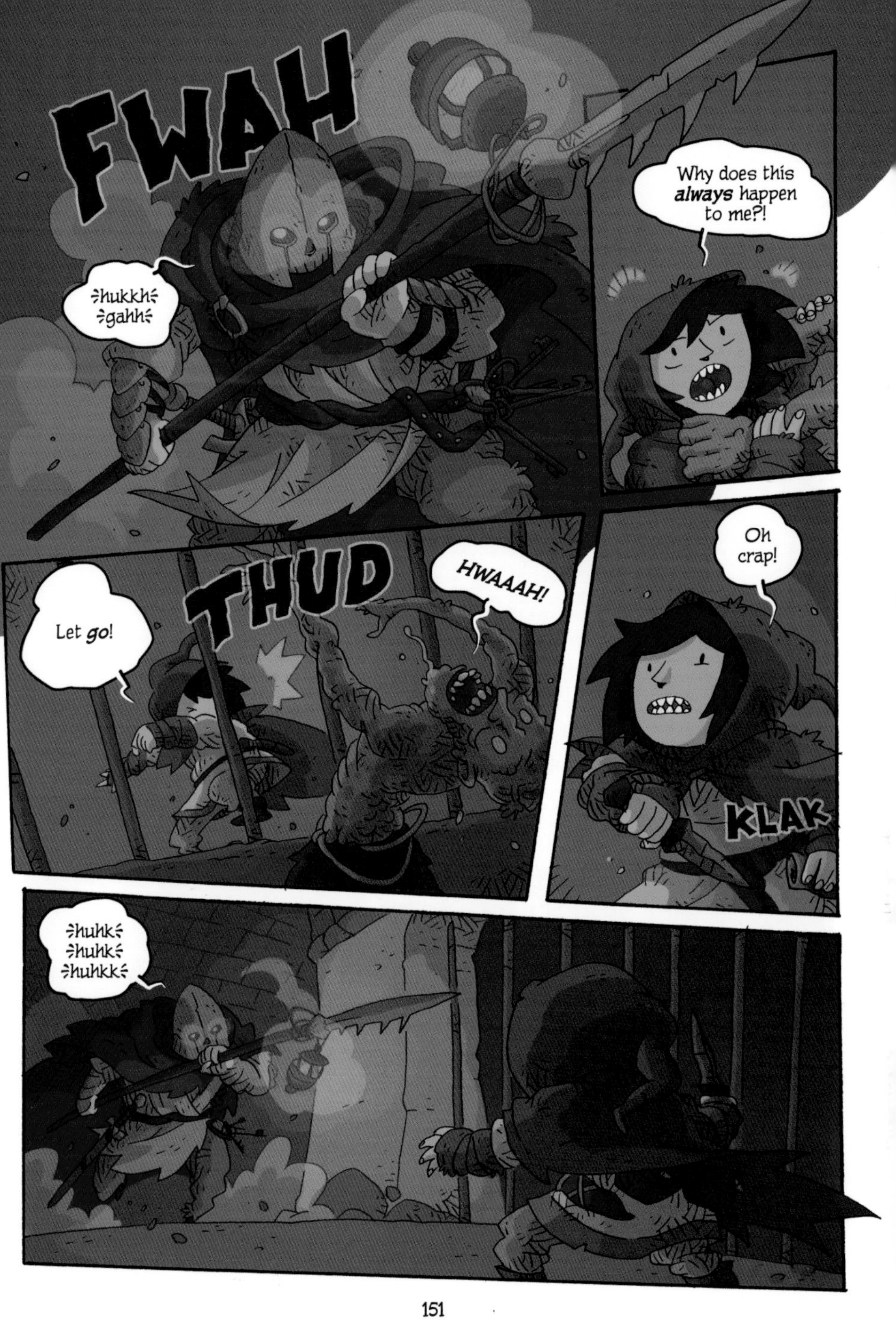
FWAH
~hukkh~ ~gahh~
Why does this **always** happen to me?!
THUD
Let **go**!
HWAAAH!
Oh crap!
KLAK
~huhk~ ~huhk~ ~huhkk~

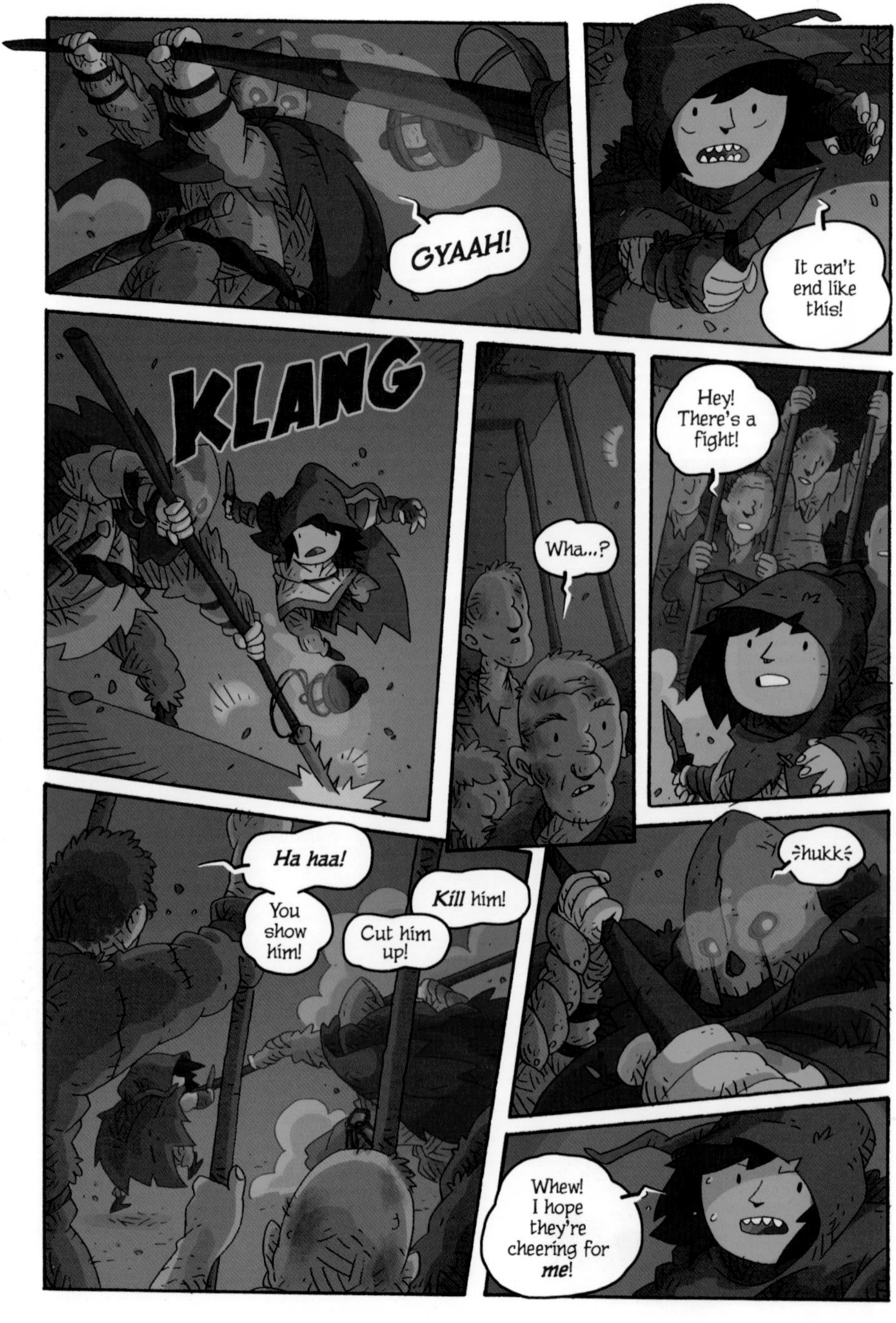
GYAAH!
It can't end like this!
KLANG
Wha...?
Hey! There's a fight!
Ha haa!
You show him!
Kill him!
Cut him up!
hukk
Whew! I hope they're cheering for *me*!

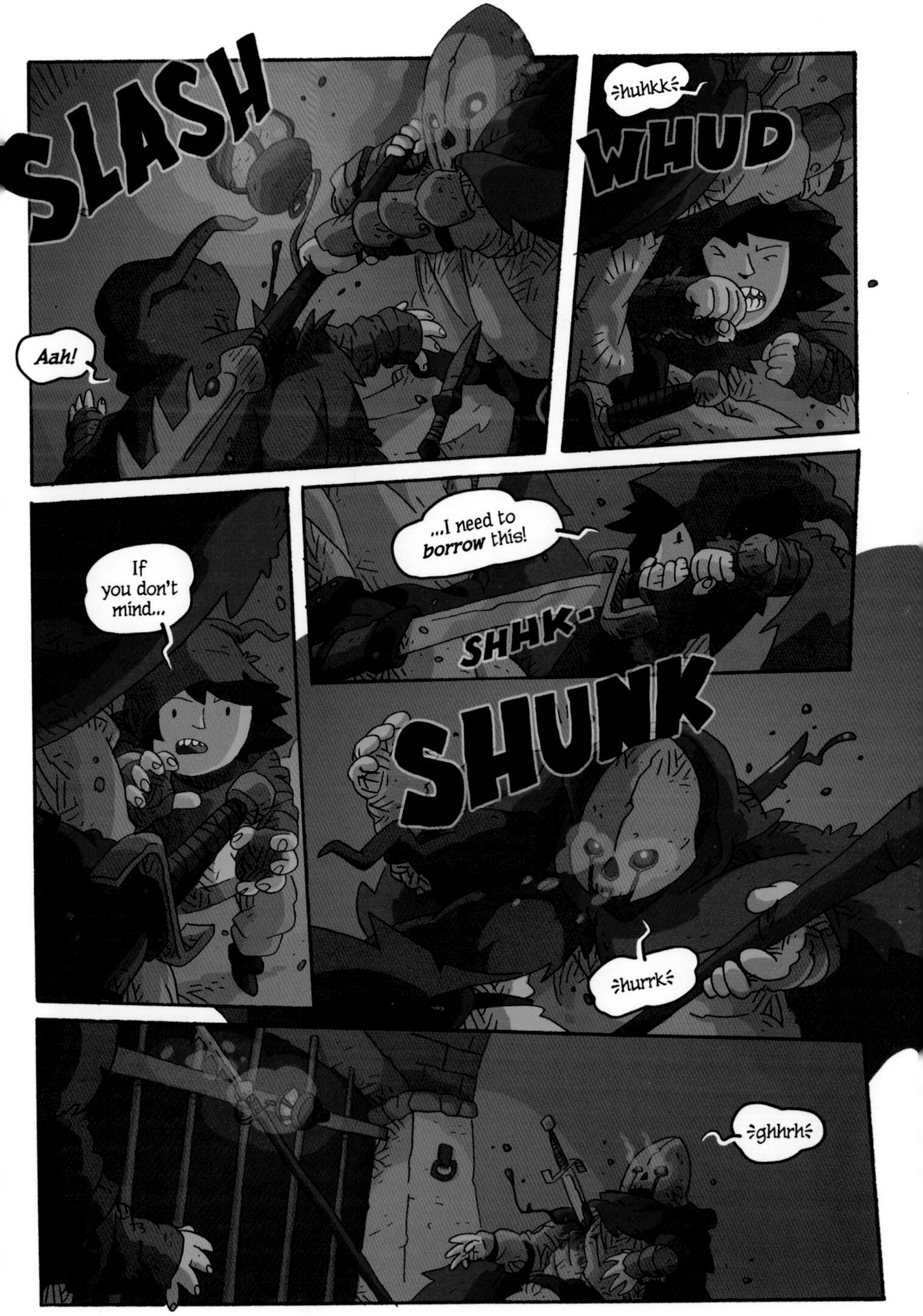
SLASH
Aah!
≑huhkk≑
WHUD
If you don't mind...
...I need to borrow this!
SHHK-
SHUNK
≑hurrk≑
≑ghhrh≑

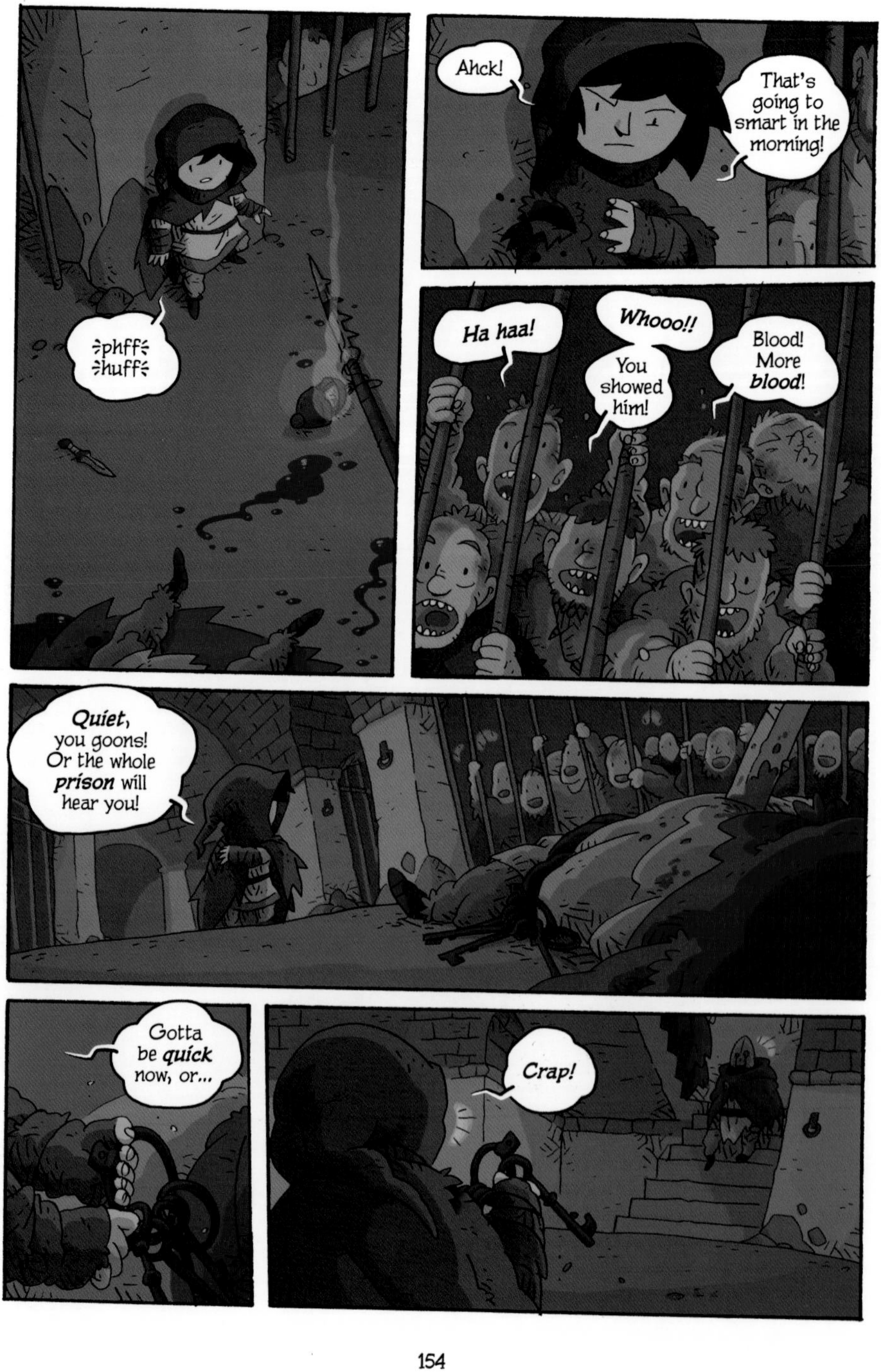

phff huff
Ahck!
That's going to smart in the morning!
Ha haa!
Whooo!!
You showed him!
Blood! More *blood*!
Quiet, you goons! Or the whole *prison* will hear you!
Gotta be *quick* now, or...
Crap!

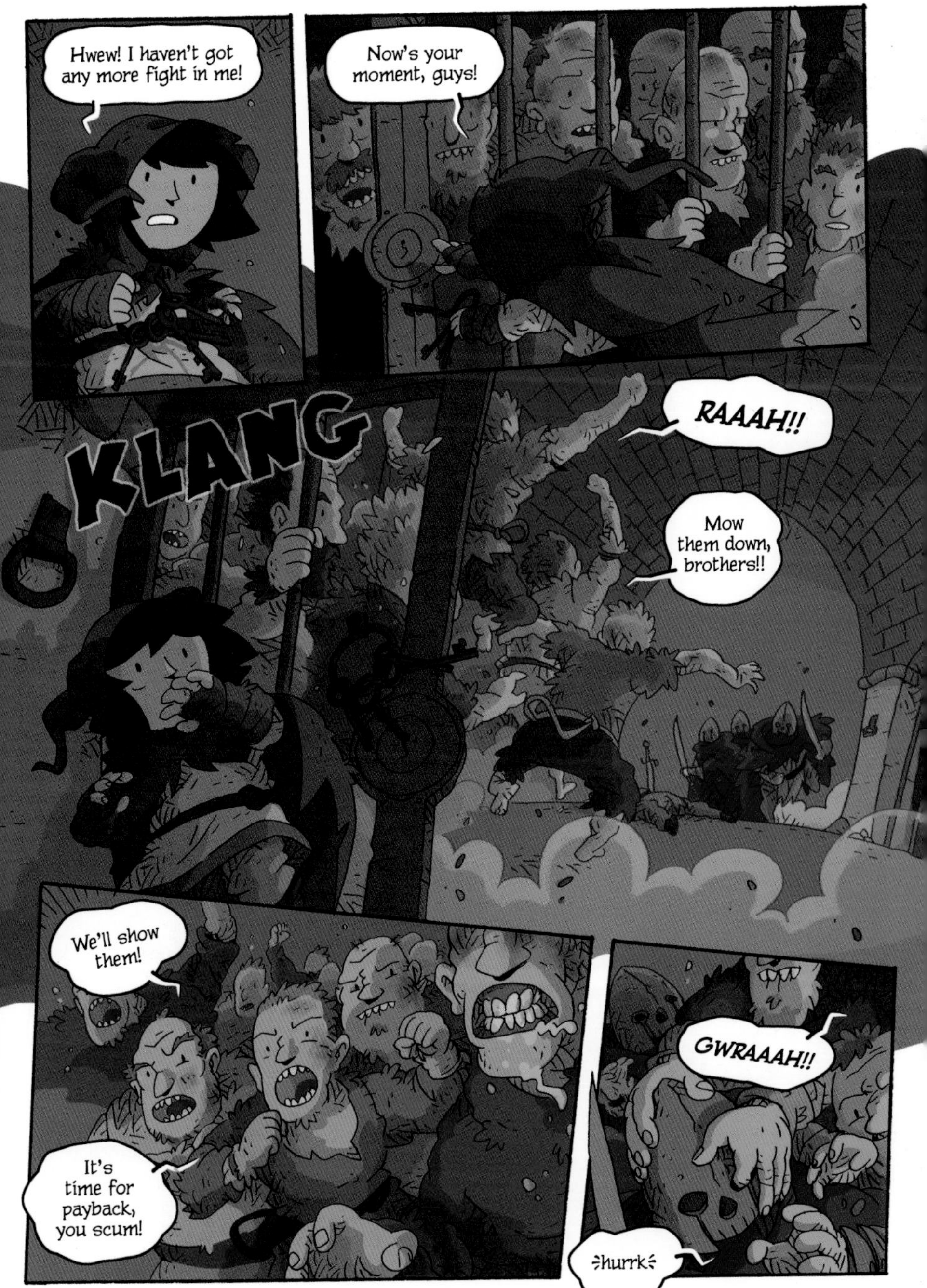
Hwew! I haven't got any more fight in me!
Now's your moment, guys!
KLANG
RAAAH!!
Mow them down, brothers!!
We'll show them!
It's time for payback, you scum!
GWRAAAH!!
hurrk

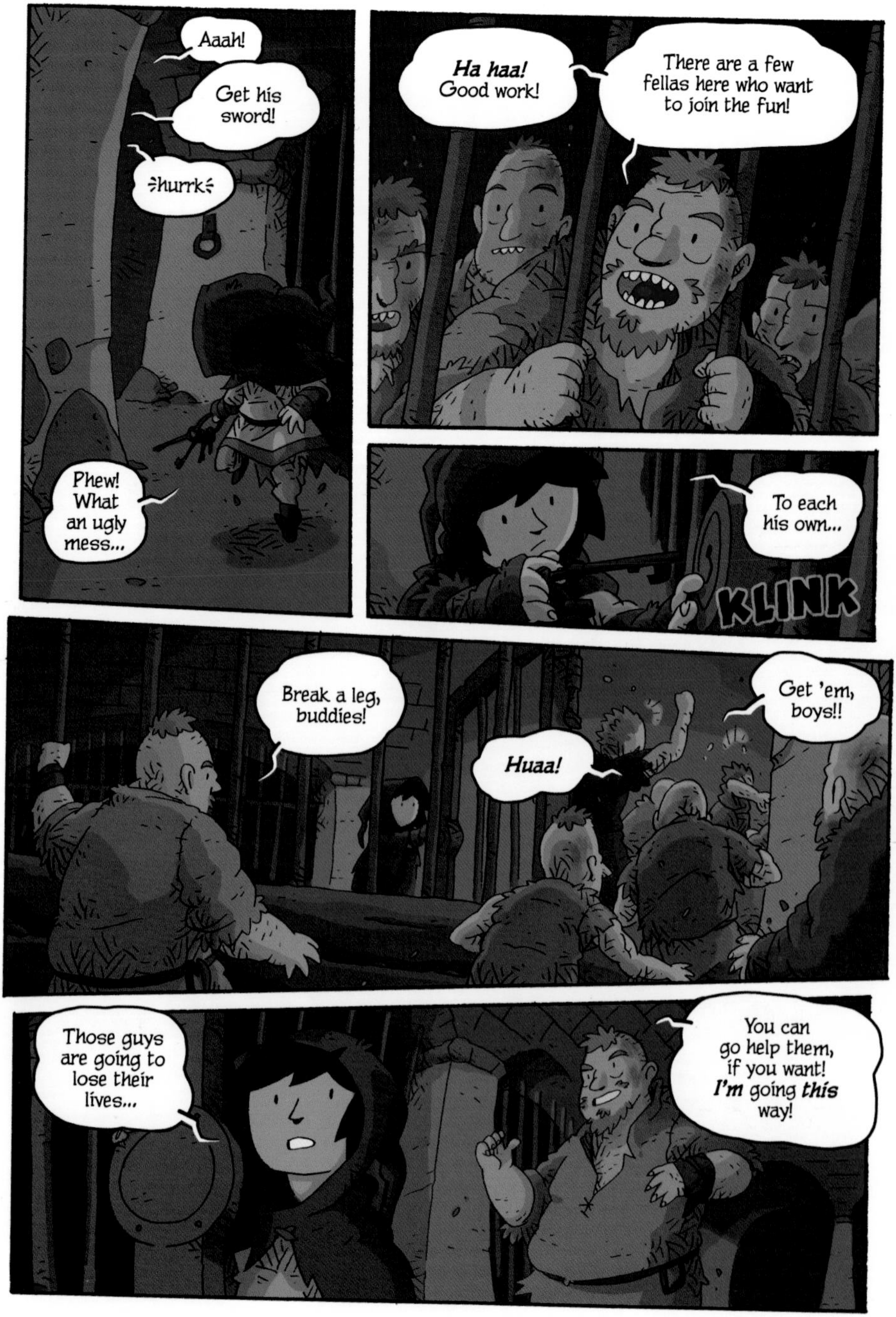
Aaah!
Get his sword!
hurrk
Ha haa! Good work!
There are a few fellas here who want to join the fun!
Phew! What an ugly mess...
To each his own...
KLINK
Break a leg, buddies!
Huaa!
Get 'em, boys!!
Those guys are going to lose their lives...
You can go help them, if you want! I'm going this way!

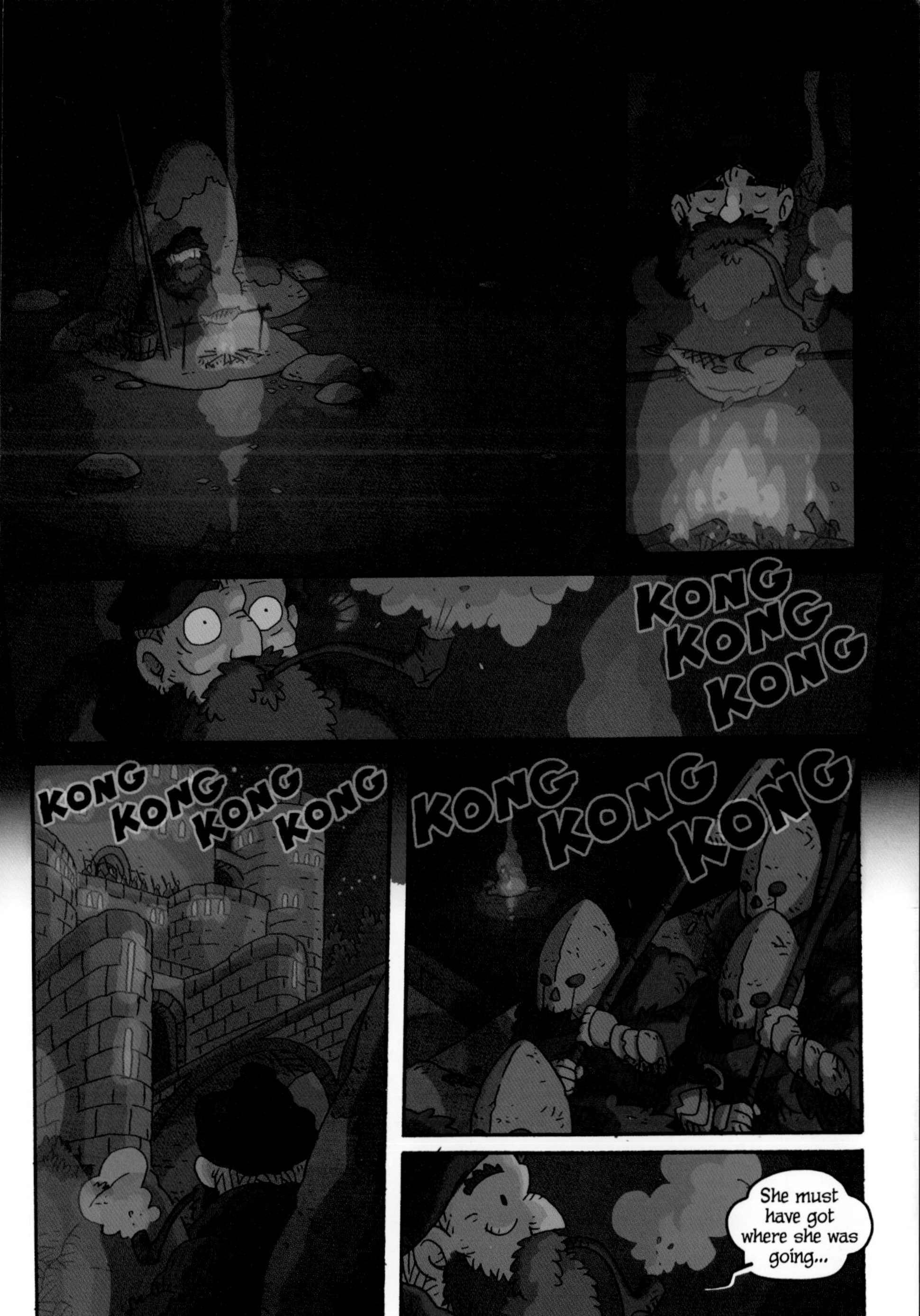
KONG
KONG
KONG
KONG
KONG
KONG
KONG
KONG
KONG
KONG
She must have got where she was going...

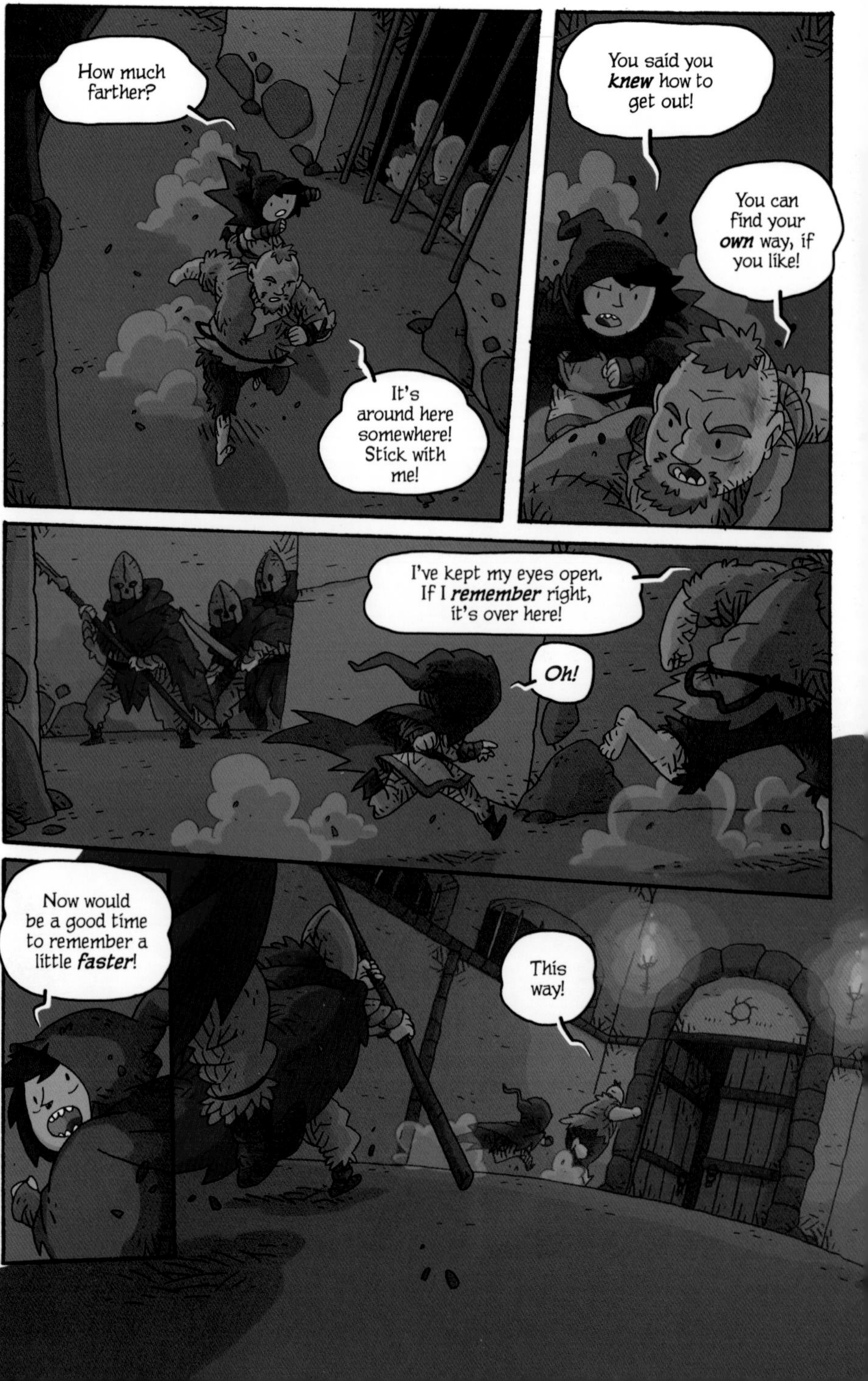
How much farther?
It's around here somewhere! Stick with me!
You said you **knew** how to get out!
You can find your **own** way, if you like!
I've kept my eyes open. If I **remember** right, it's over here!
Oh!
Now would be a good time to remember a little **faster**!
This way!

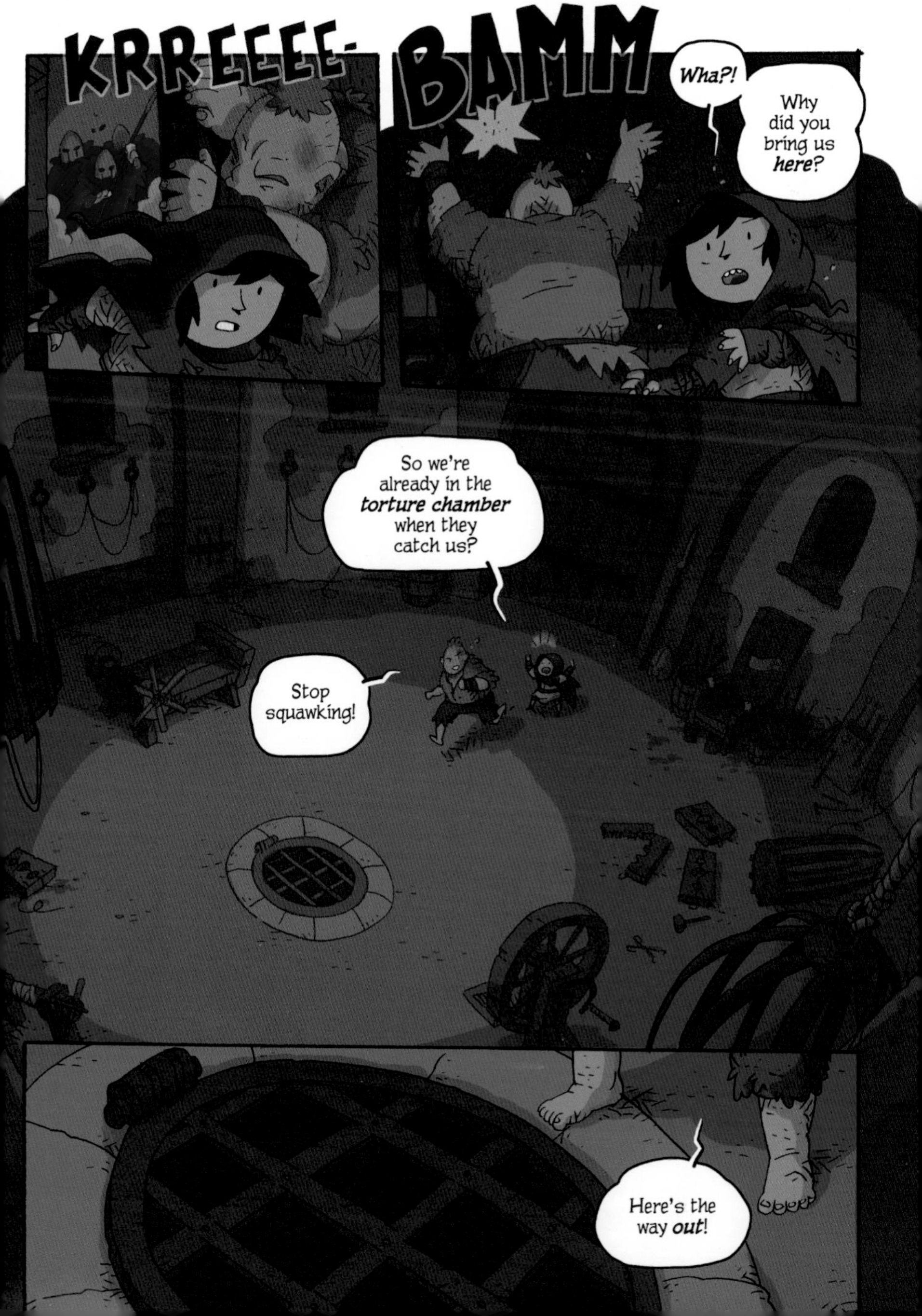
KRREEEEE-
BAMM
Wha?!
Why did you bring us *here*?
So we're already in the *torture chamber* when they catch us?
Stop squawking!
Here's the way *out*!

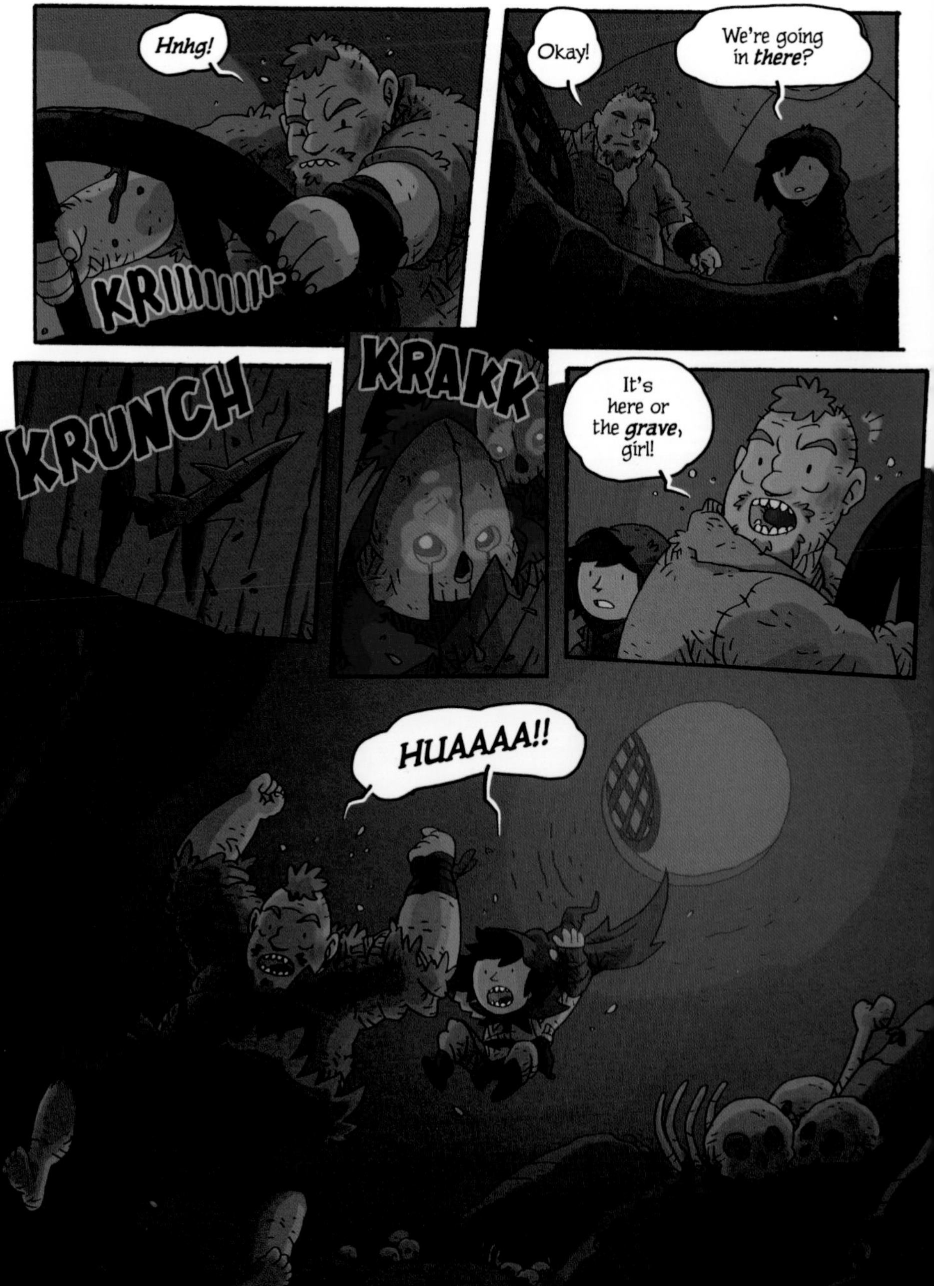
Hnhg!
KRIIIIIIIII-
Okay!
We're going in *there*?
KRUNCH
KRAKK
It's here or the *grave*, girl!
HUAAAA!!

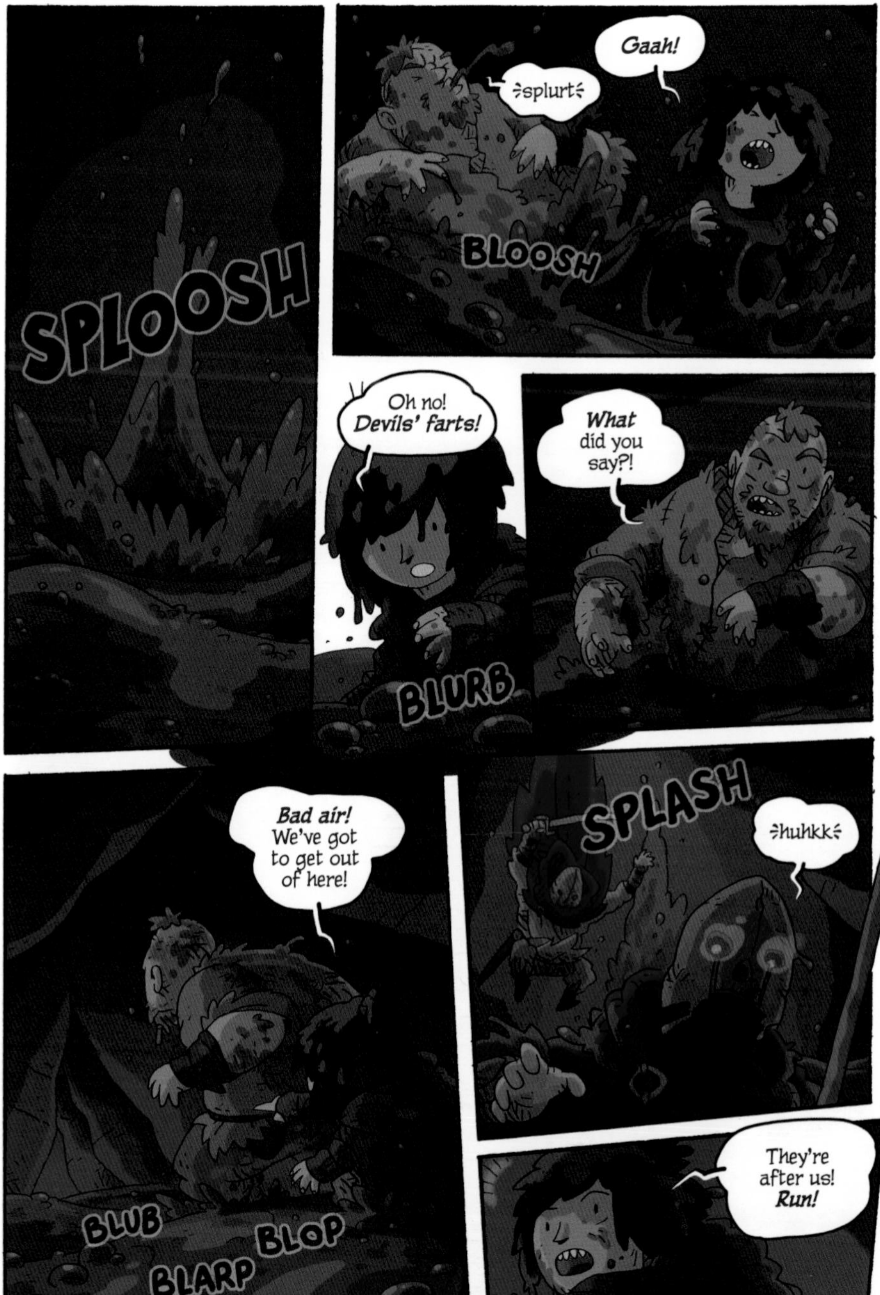
SPLOOSH
Gaah!
splurt
BLOOSH
Oh no! *Devils' farts!*
BLURB
What did you say?!
Bad air! We've got to get out of here!
BLUB
BLARP
BLOP
SPLASH
huhkk
They're after us! *Run!*

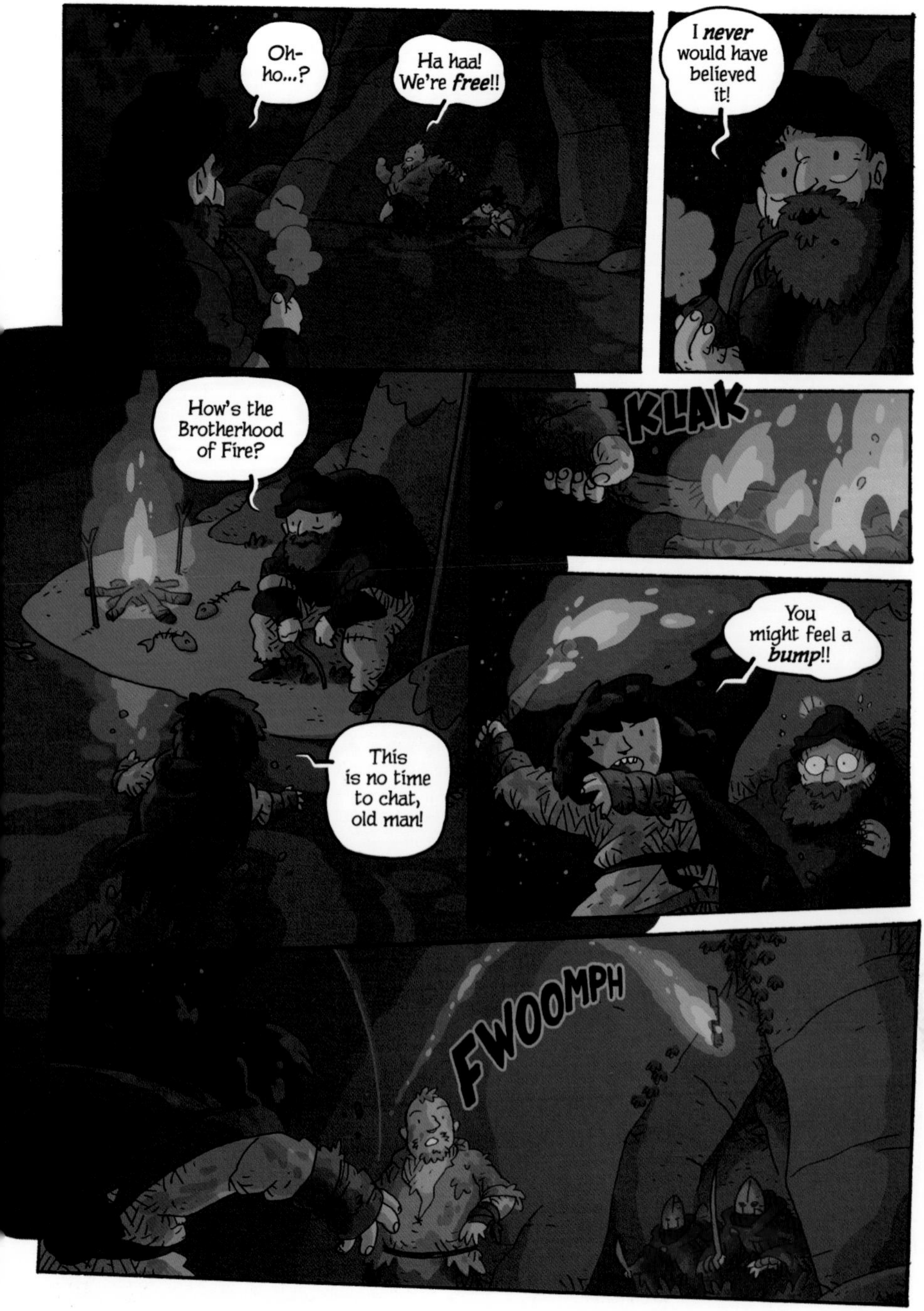

Oh-ho...?
Ha haa! We're *free*!!
I *never* would have believed it!
How's the Brotherhood of Fire?
This is no time to chat, old man!
KLAK
You might feel a *bump*!!
FWOOMPH

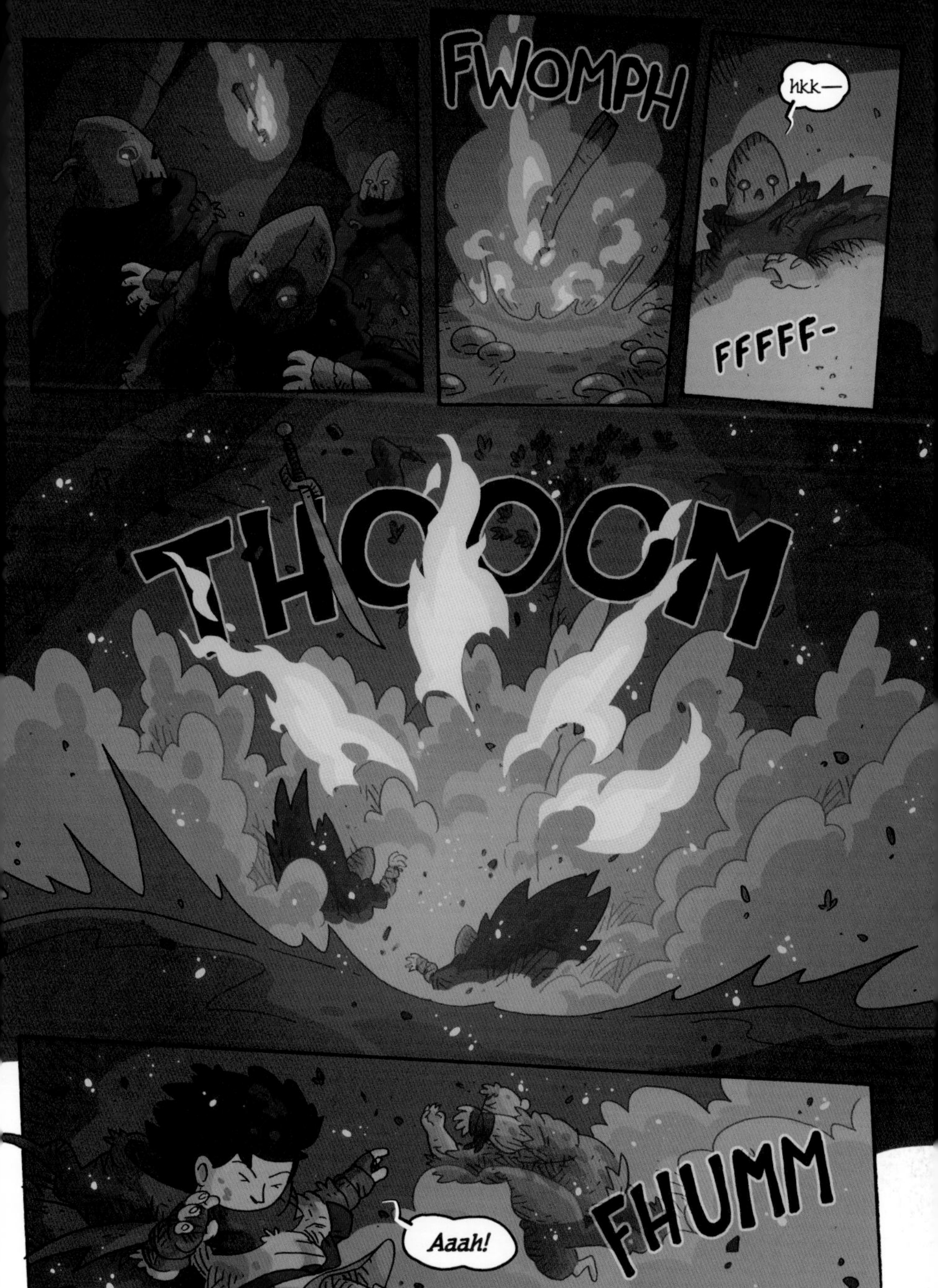
FWOMPH
hkk—
FFFFF-
THOOOM
Aaah!
FHUMM

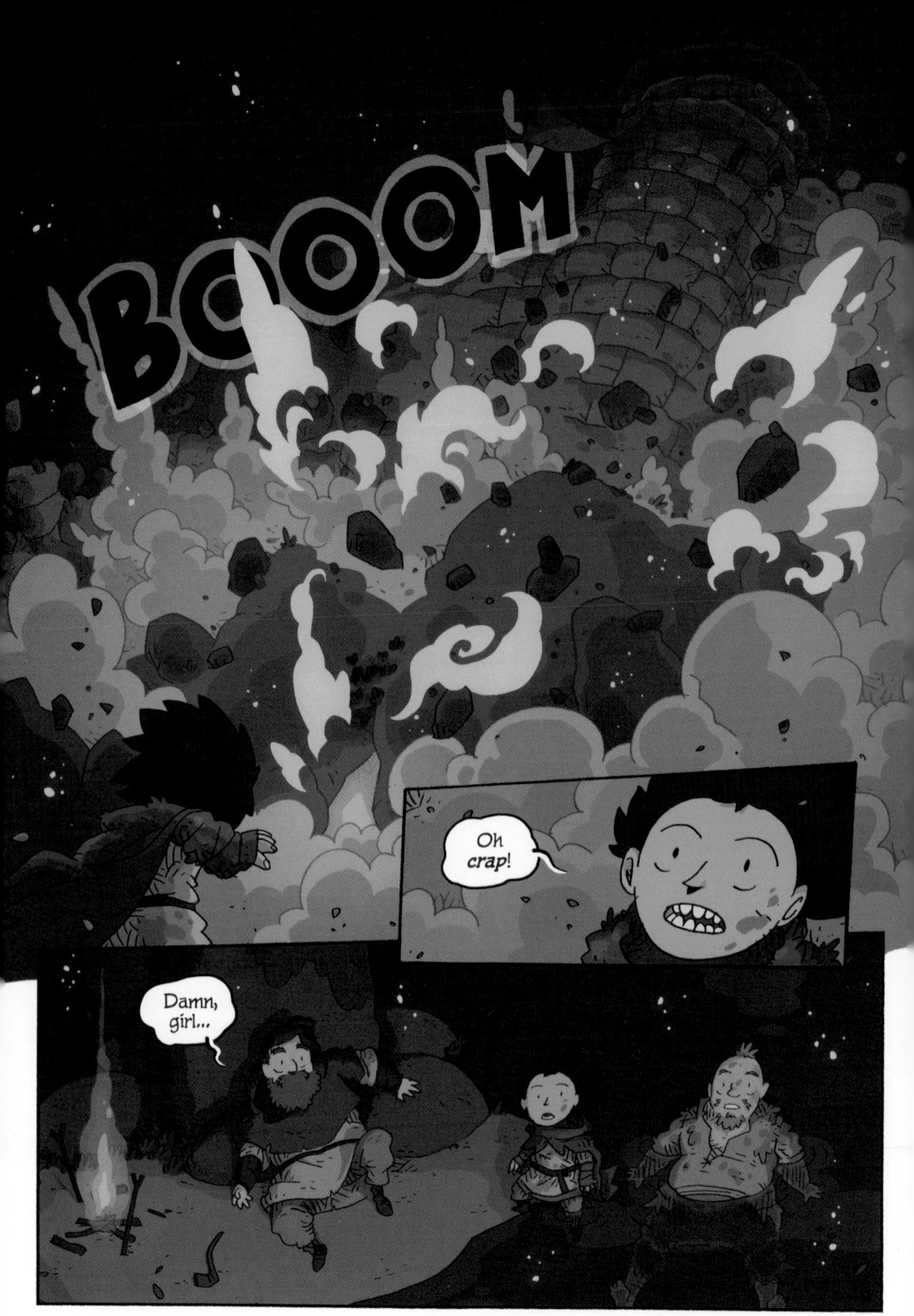
BOOOM
Oh crap!
Damn, girl...

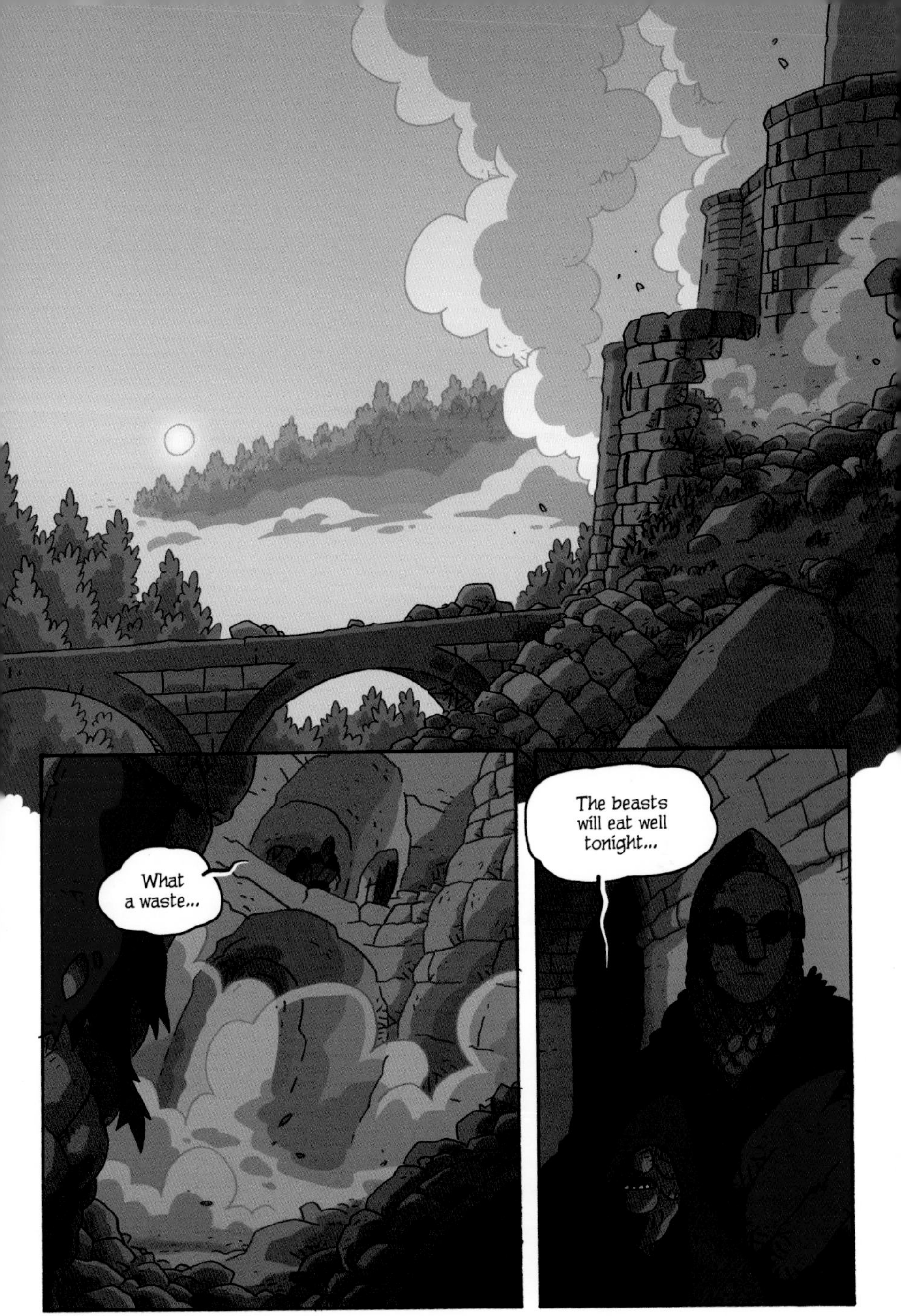
What a waste...
The beasts will eat well tonight...

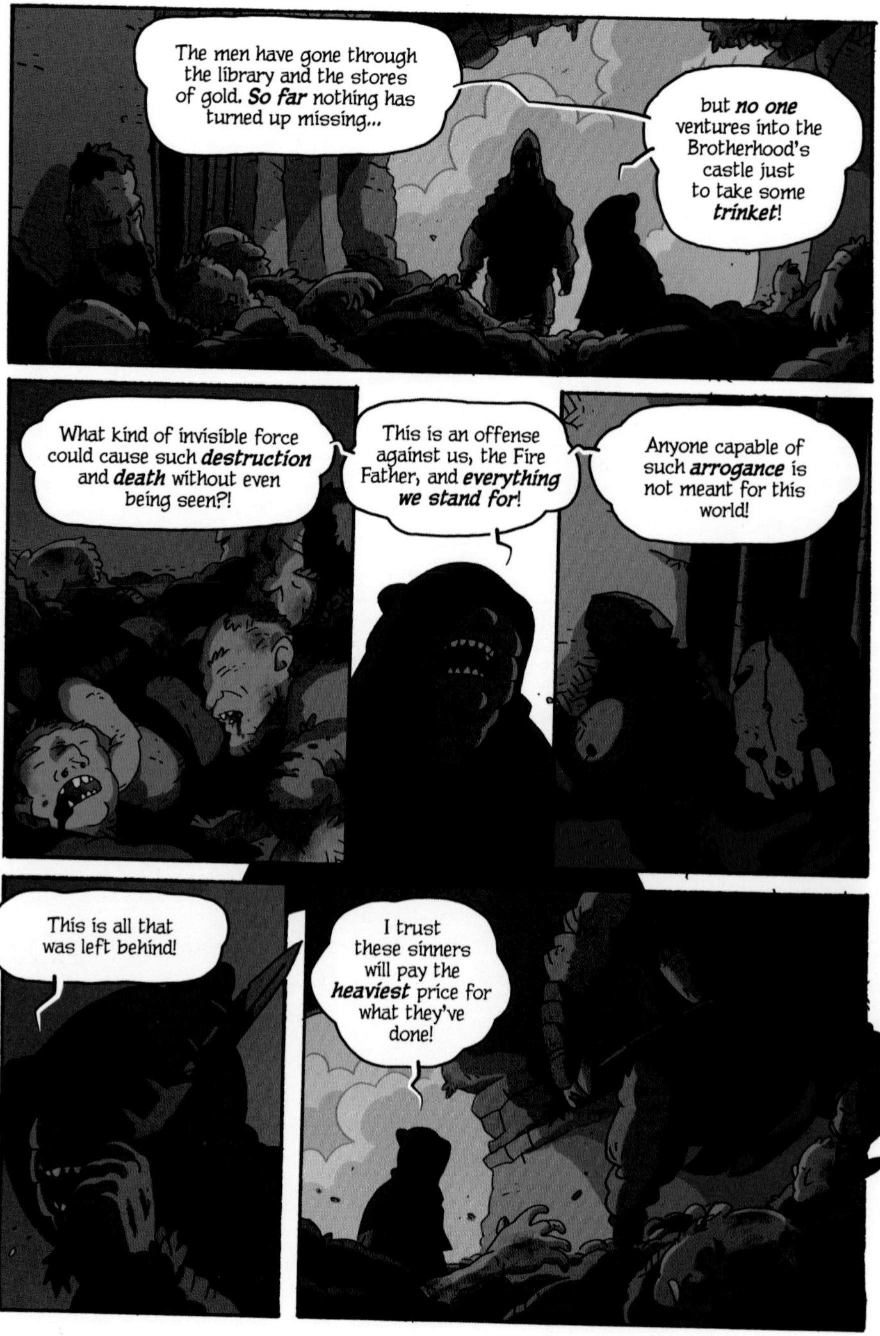
The men have gone through the library and the stores of gold. So far nothing has turned up missing...
but no one ventures into the Brotherhood's castle just to take some trinket!
What kind of invisible force could cause such destruction and death without even being seen?!
This is an offense against us, the Fire Father, and everything we stand for!
Anyone capable of such arrogance is not meant for this world!
This is all that was left behind!
I trust these sinners will pay the heaviest price for what they've done!

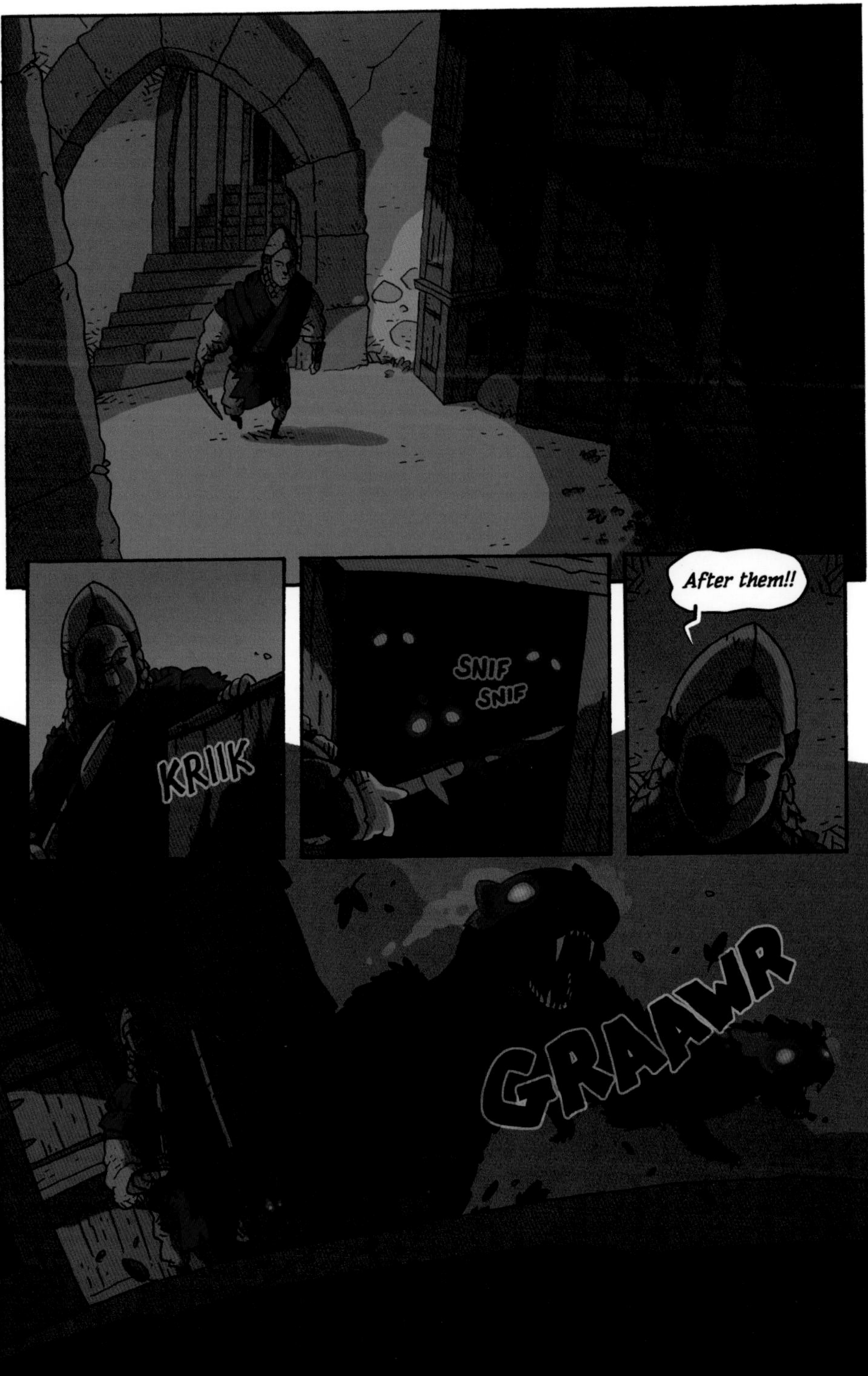
KRIIK
SNIF
SNIF
After them!!
GRAAWR

Each man against the march of days,
The old marching to the grave,
Legends and spells forgotten,
Never chanted or remembered,
The stories lost like dying embers,
Till all belongs to one.

5

The Trail

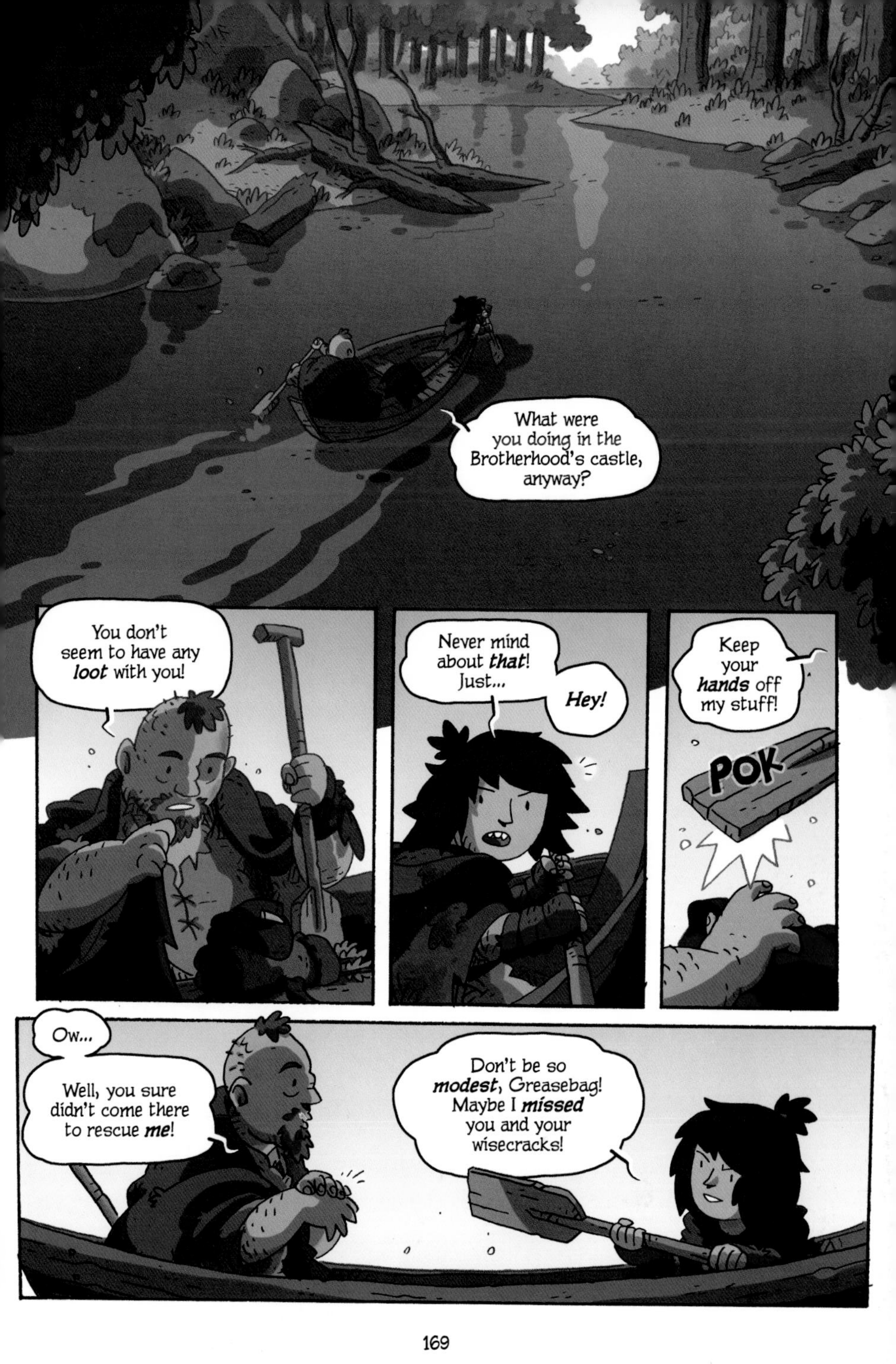
What were you doing in the Brotherhood's castle, anyway?
You don't seem to have any *loot* with you!
Never mind about *that*! Just...
Hey!
Keep your *hands* off my stuff!
POK
Ow...
Well, you sure didn't come there to rescue *me*!
Don't be so *modest*, Greasebag! Maybe I *missed* you and your wisecracks!

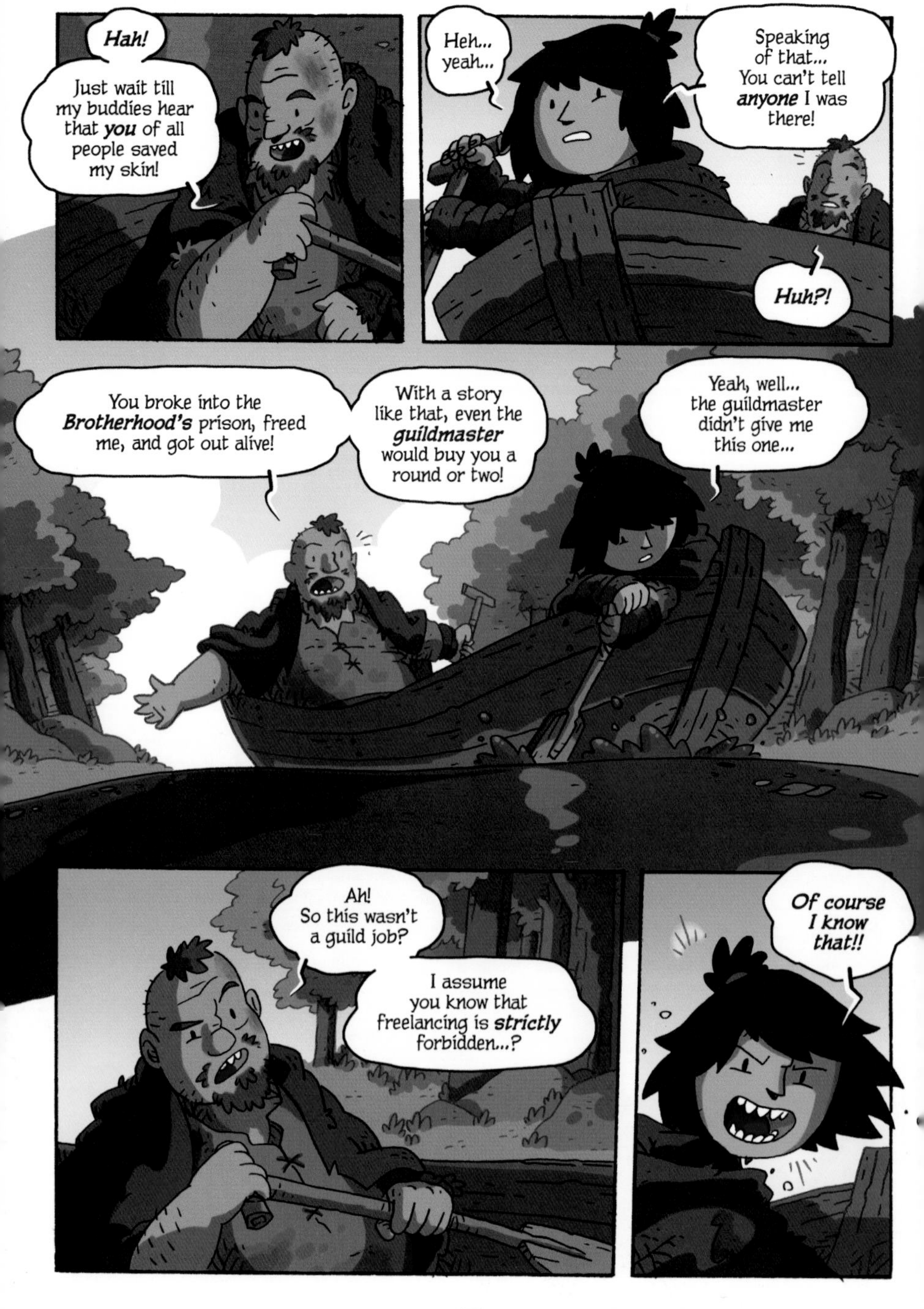

Hah!
Just wait till my buddies hear that **you** of all people saved my skin!
Heh... yeah...
Speaking of that... You can't tell **anyone** I was there!
Huh?!
You broke into the **Brotherhood's** prison, freed me, and got out alive!
With a story like that, even the **guildmaster** would buy you a round or two!
Yeah, well... the guildmaster didn't give me this one...
Ah! So this wasn't a guild job?
I assume you know that freelancing is **strictly** forbidden...?
Of course I know that!!

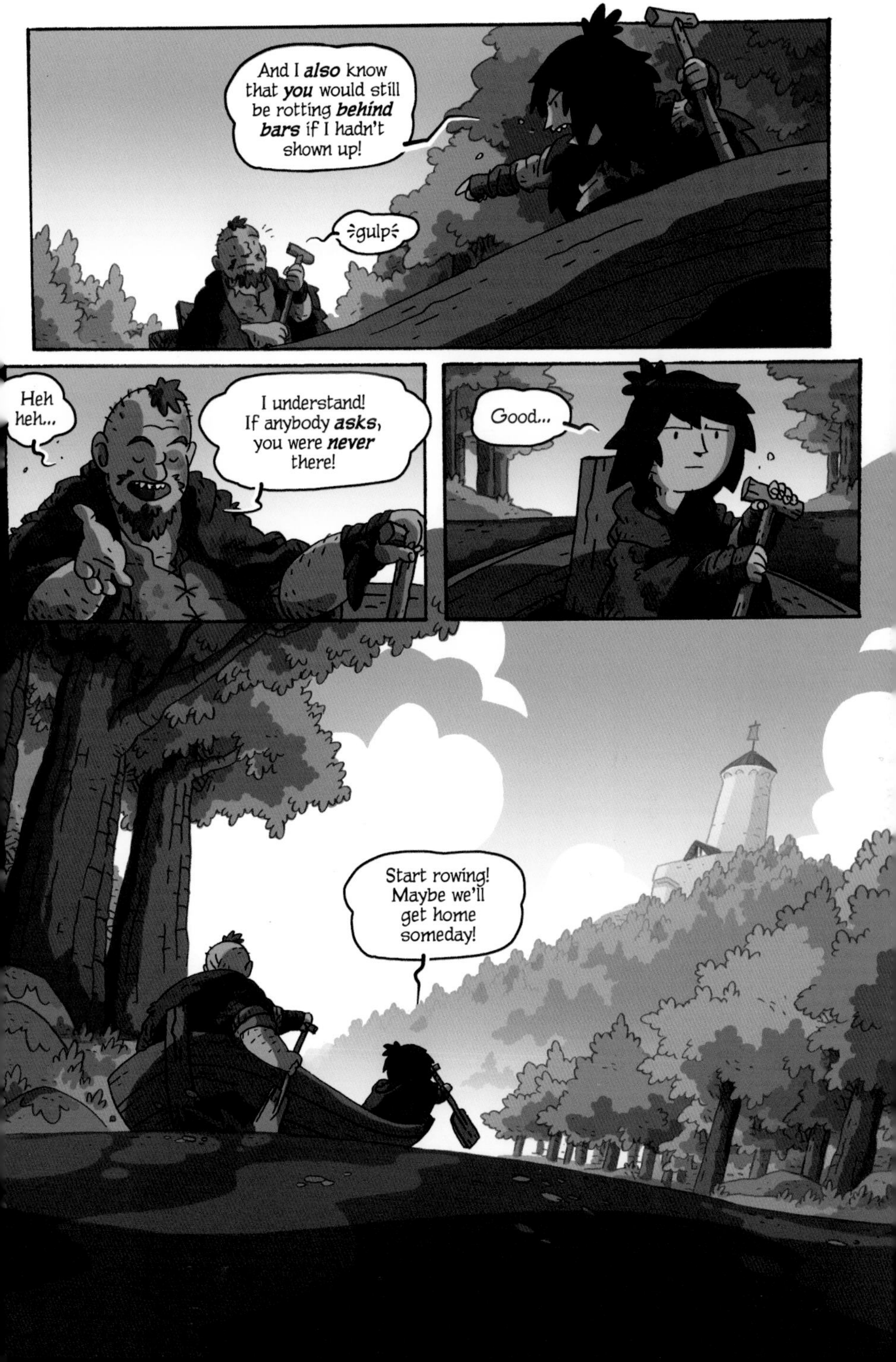
And I also know that you would still be rotting behind bars if I hadn't shown up!
gulp
Heh heh...
I understand! If anybody asks, you were never there!
Good...
Start rowing! Maybe we'll get home someday!

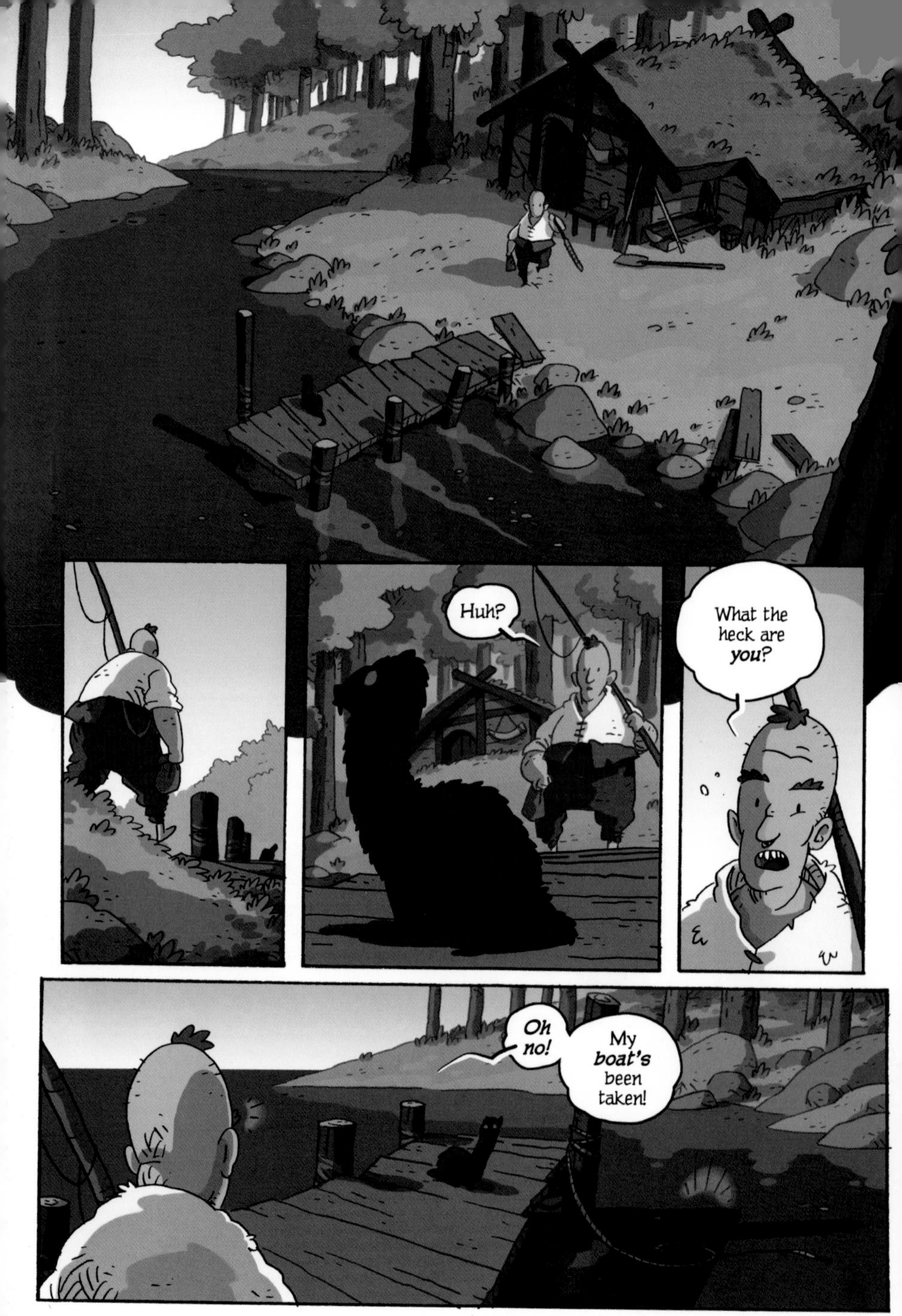
Huh?
What the heck are *you*?
Oh no!
My *boat's* been taken!

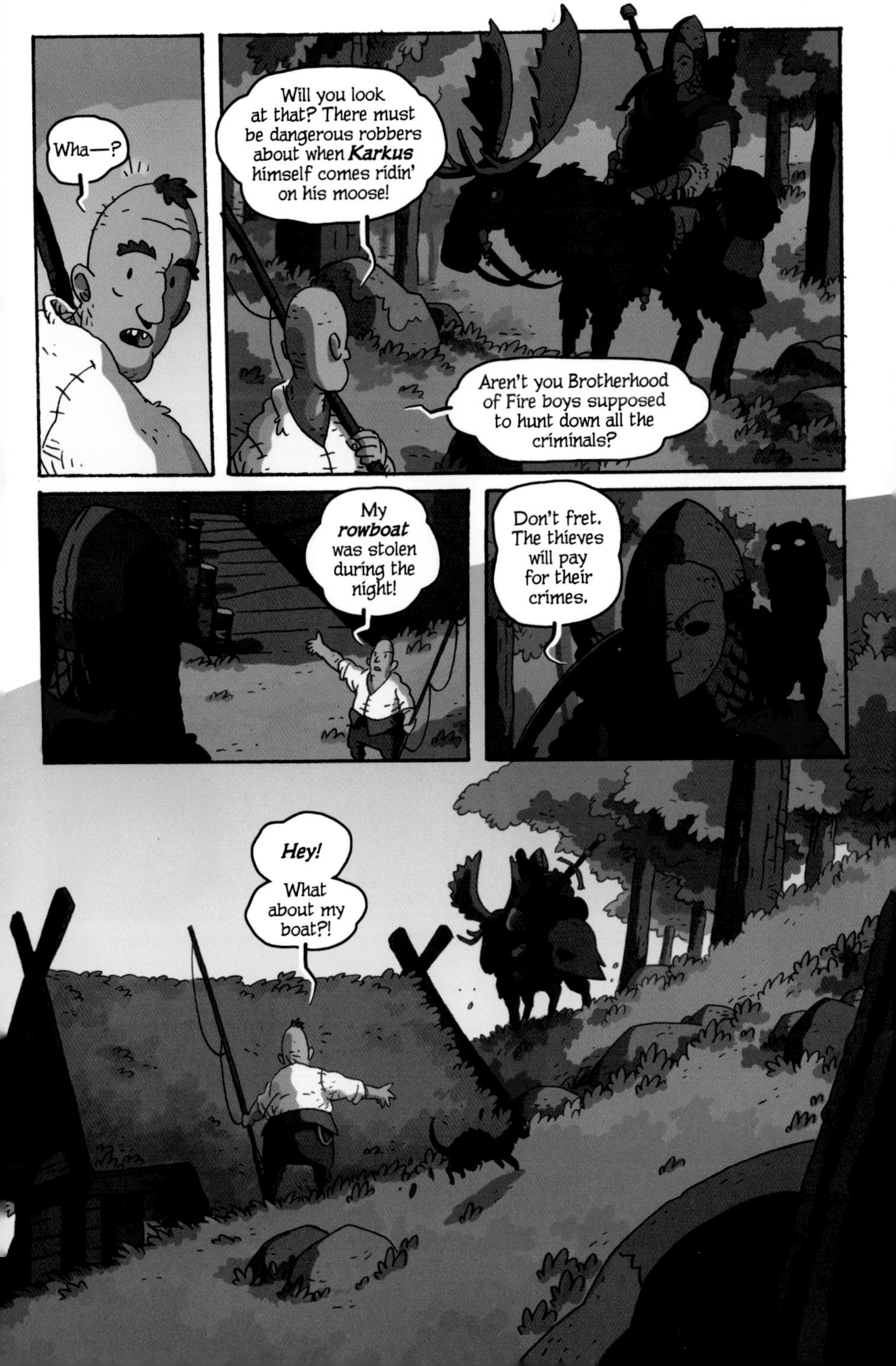
Wha—?
Will you look at that? There must be dangerous robbers about when *Karkus* himself comes ridin' on his moose!
Aren't you Brotherhood of Fire boys supposed to hunt down all the criminals?
My *rowboat* was stolen during the night!
Don't fret. The thieves will pay for their crimes.
Hey!
What about my boat?!

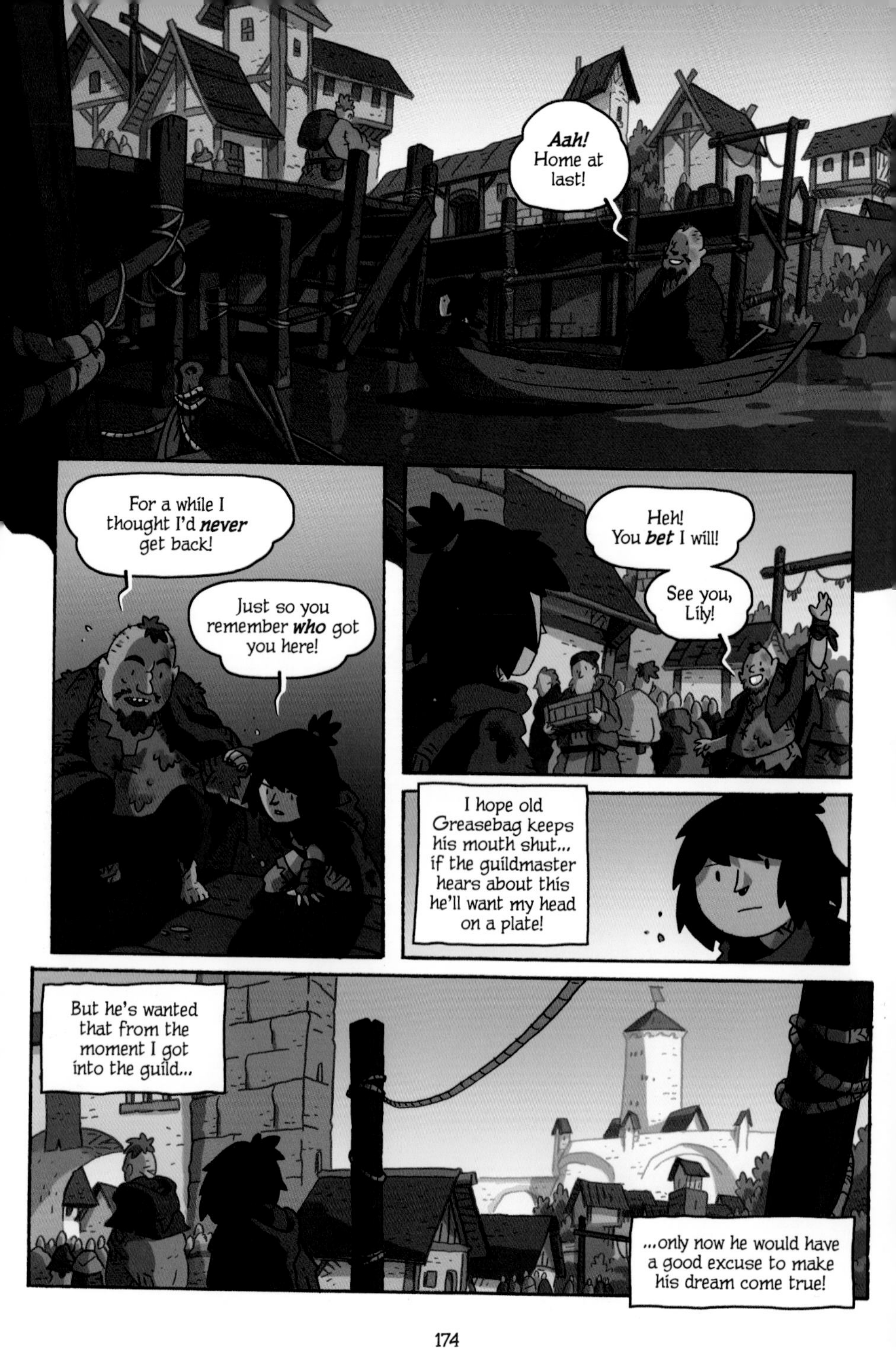
Aah! Home at last!
For a while I thought I'd ***never*** get back!
Just so you remember ***who*** got you here!
Heh! You ***bet*** I will!
See you, Lily!
I hope old Greasebag keeps his mouth shut... if the guildmaster hears about this he'll want my head on a plate!
But he's wanted that from the moment I got into the guild...
...only now he would have a good excuse to make his dream come true!

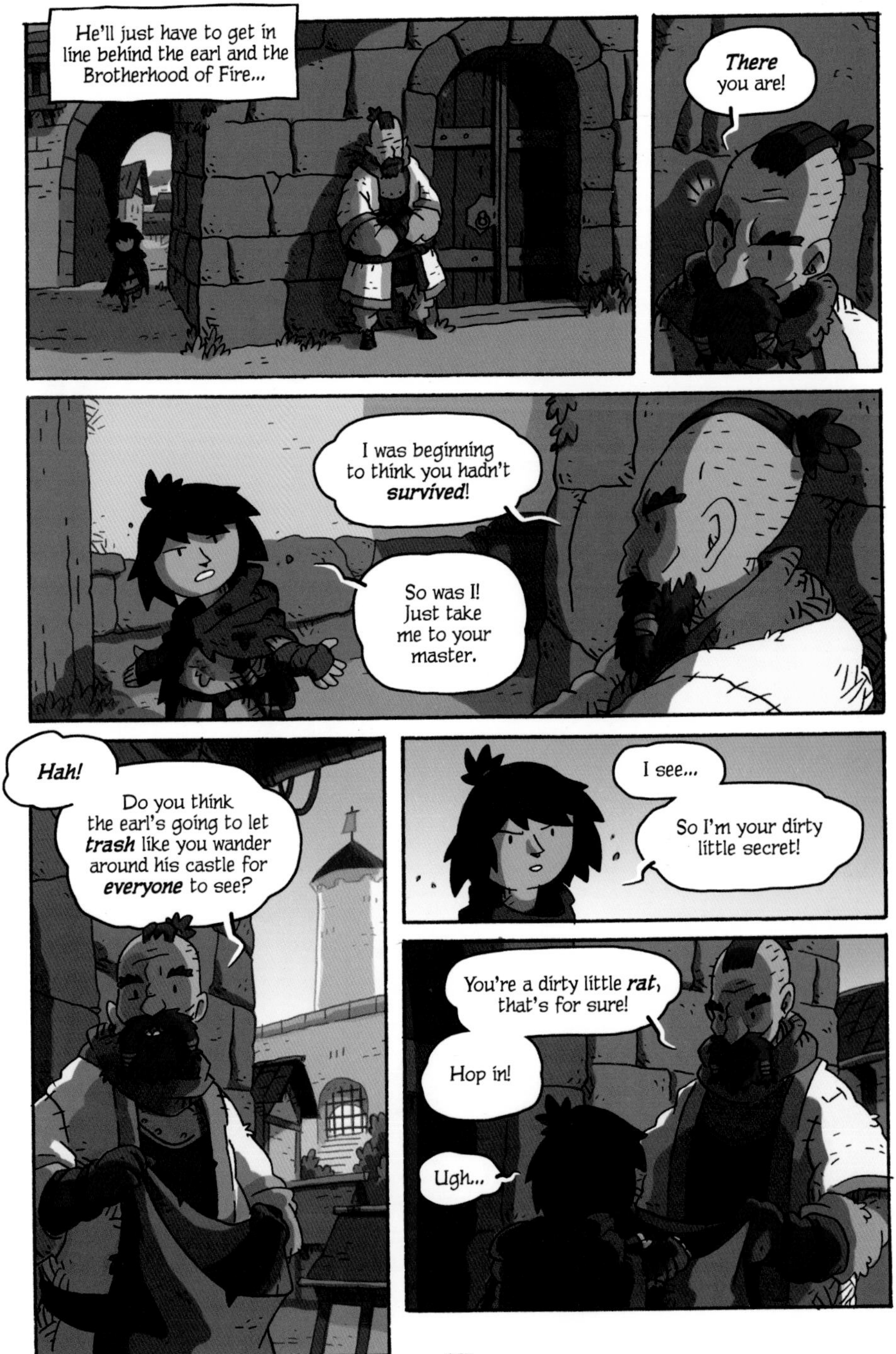

He'll just have to get in line behind the earl and the Brotherhood of Fire...
There you are!
I was beginning to think you hadn't ***survived***!
So was I! Just take me to your master.
Hah!
Do you think the earl's going to let ***trash*** like you wander around his castle for ***everyone*** to see?
I see...
So I'm your dirty little secret!
You're a dirty little ***rat***, that's for sure!
Hop in!
Ugh...

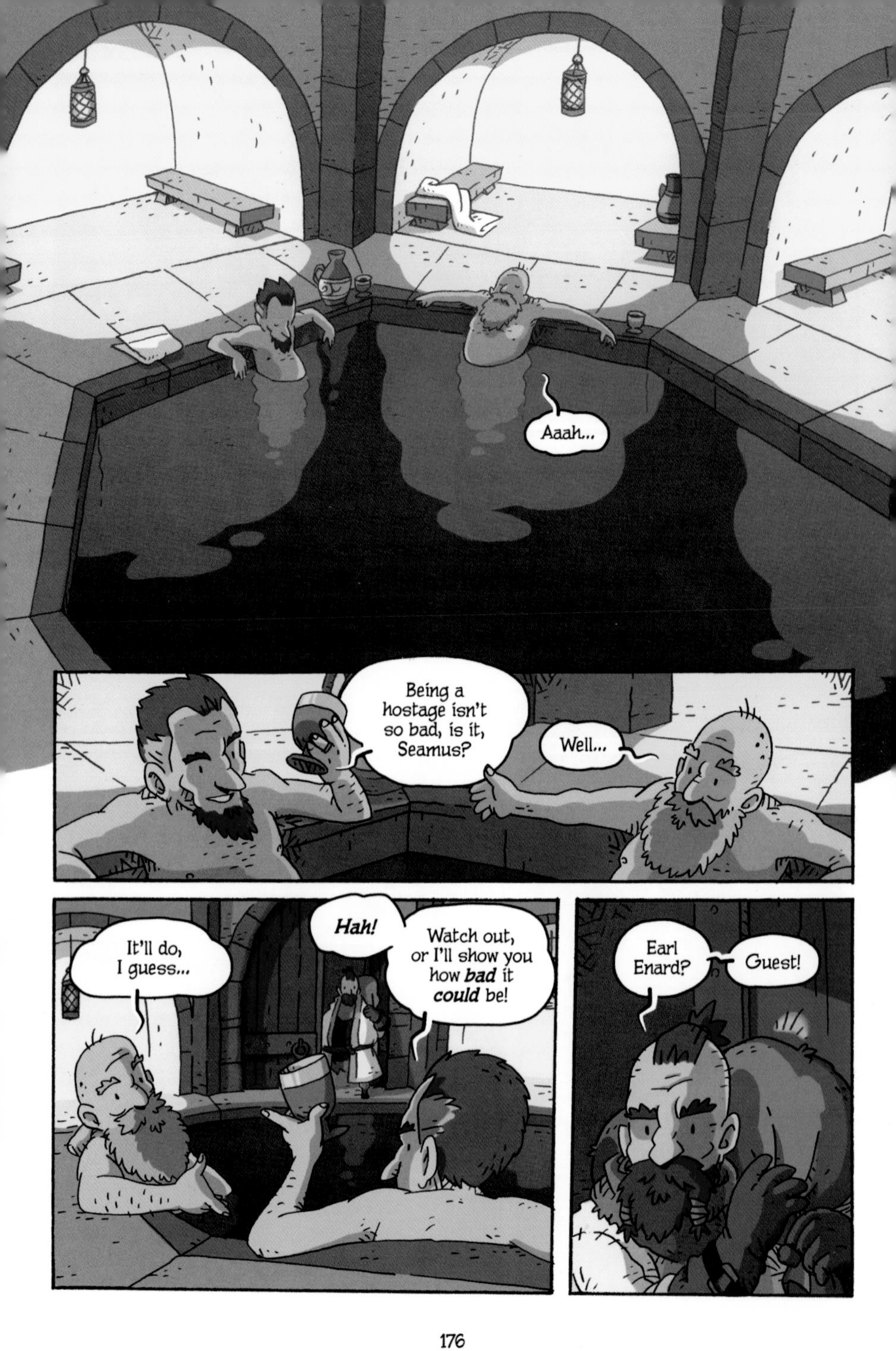
Aaah...
Being a hostage isn't so bad, is it, Seamus?
Well...
It'll do, I guess...
Hah!
Watch out, or I'll show you how bad it could be!
Earl Enard?
Guest!

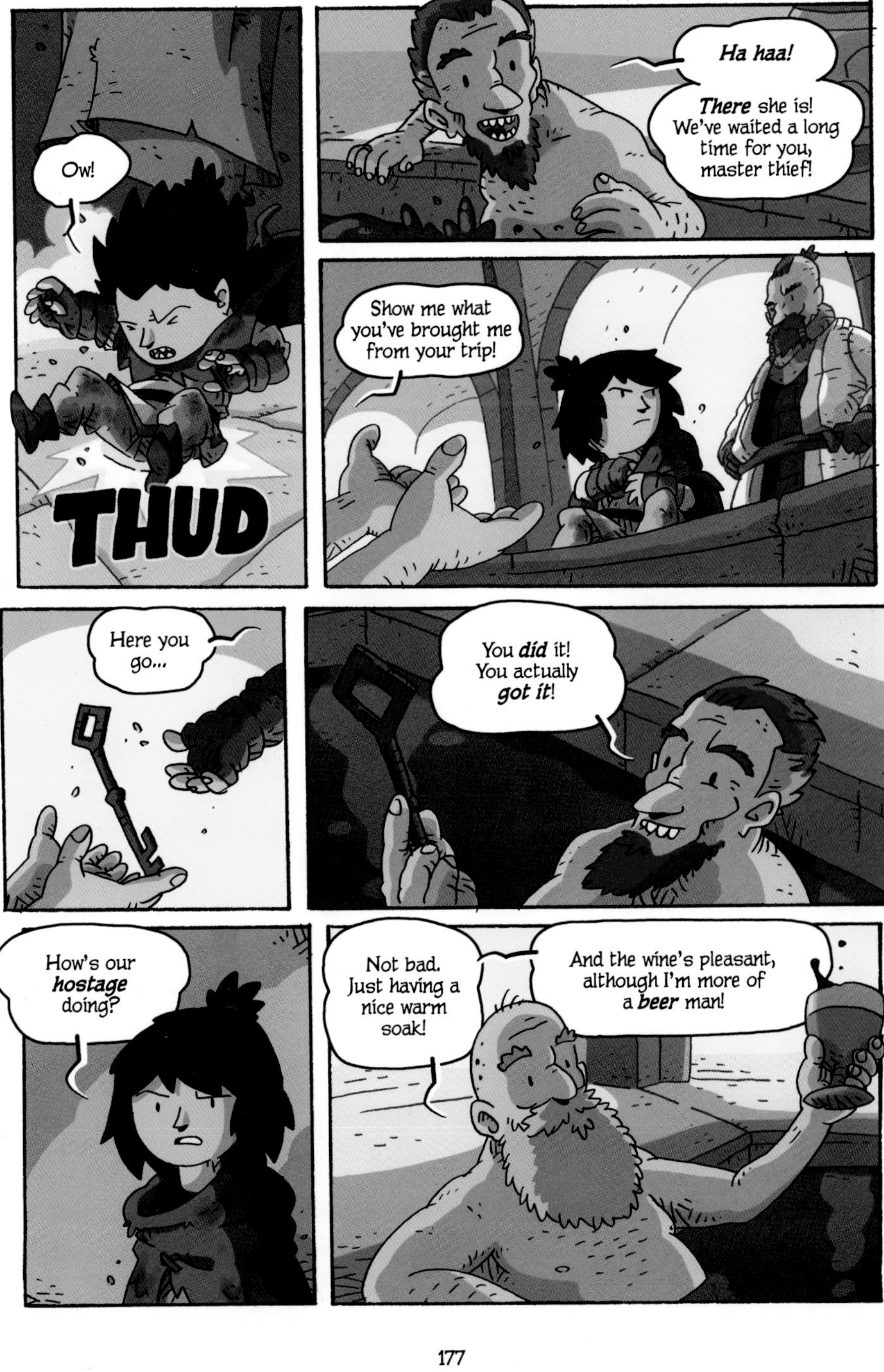
Ow!
THUD
Ha haa!
There she is! We've waited a long time for you, master thief!
Show me what you've brought me from your trip!
Here you go...
You did it! You actually got it!
How's our hostage doing?
Not bad. Just having a nice warm soak!
And the wine's pleasant, although I'm more of a beer man!

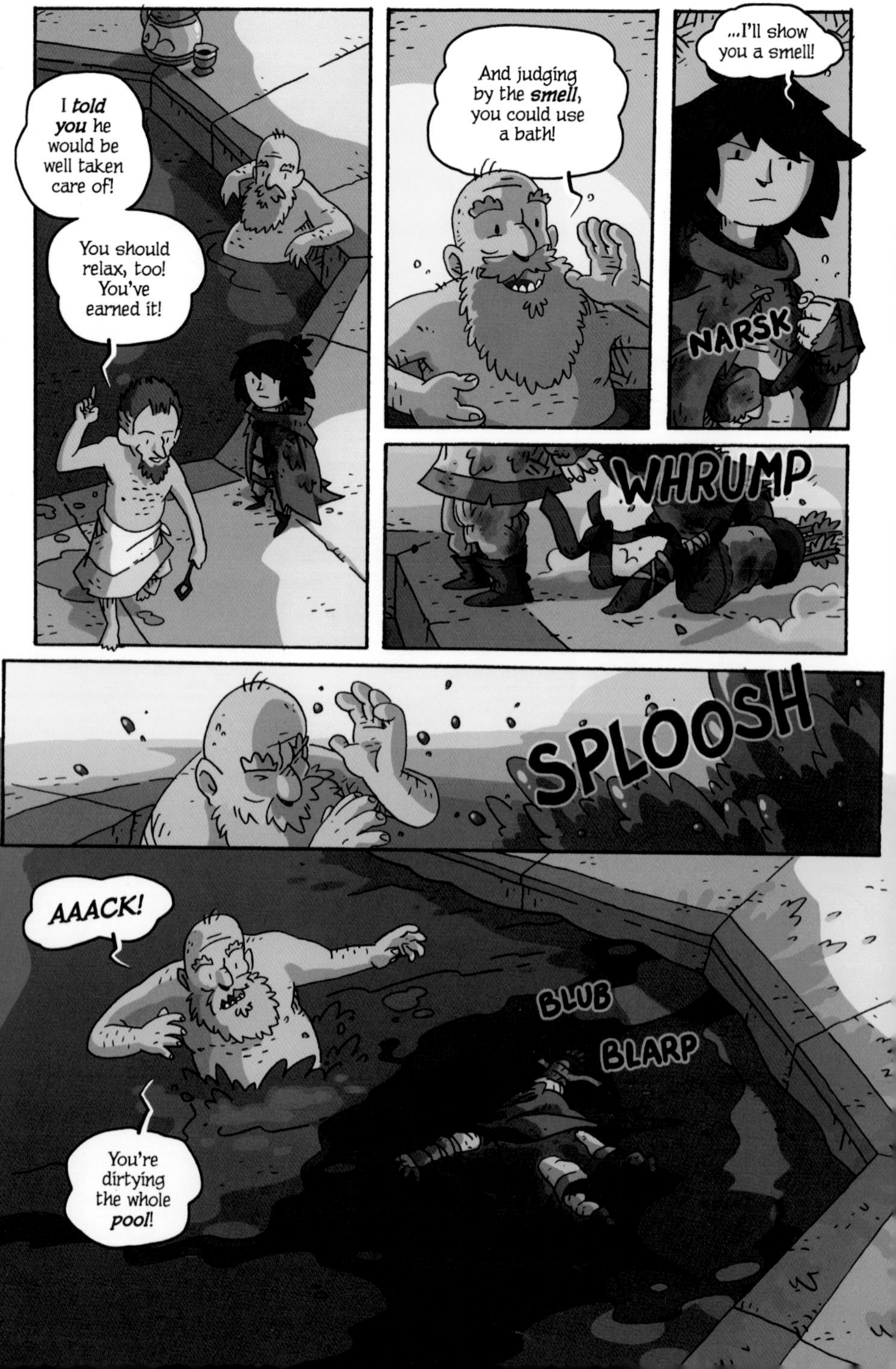
I *told you* he would be well taken care of!
You should relax, too! You've earned it!
And judging by the ***smell***, you could use a bath!
...I'll show you a smell!
NARSK
WHRUMP
SPLOOSH
AAACK!
BLUB
BLARP
You're dirtying the whole ***pool***!

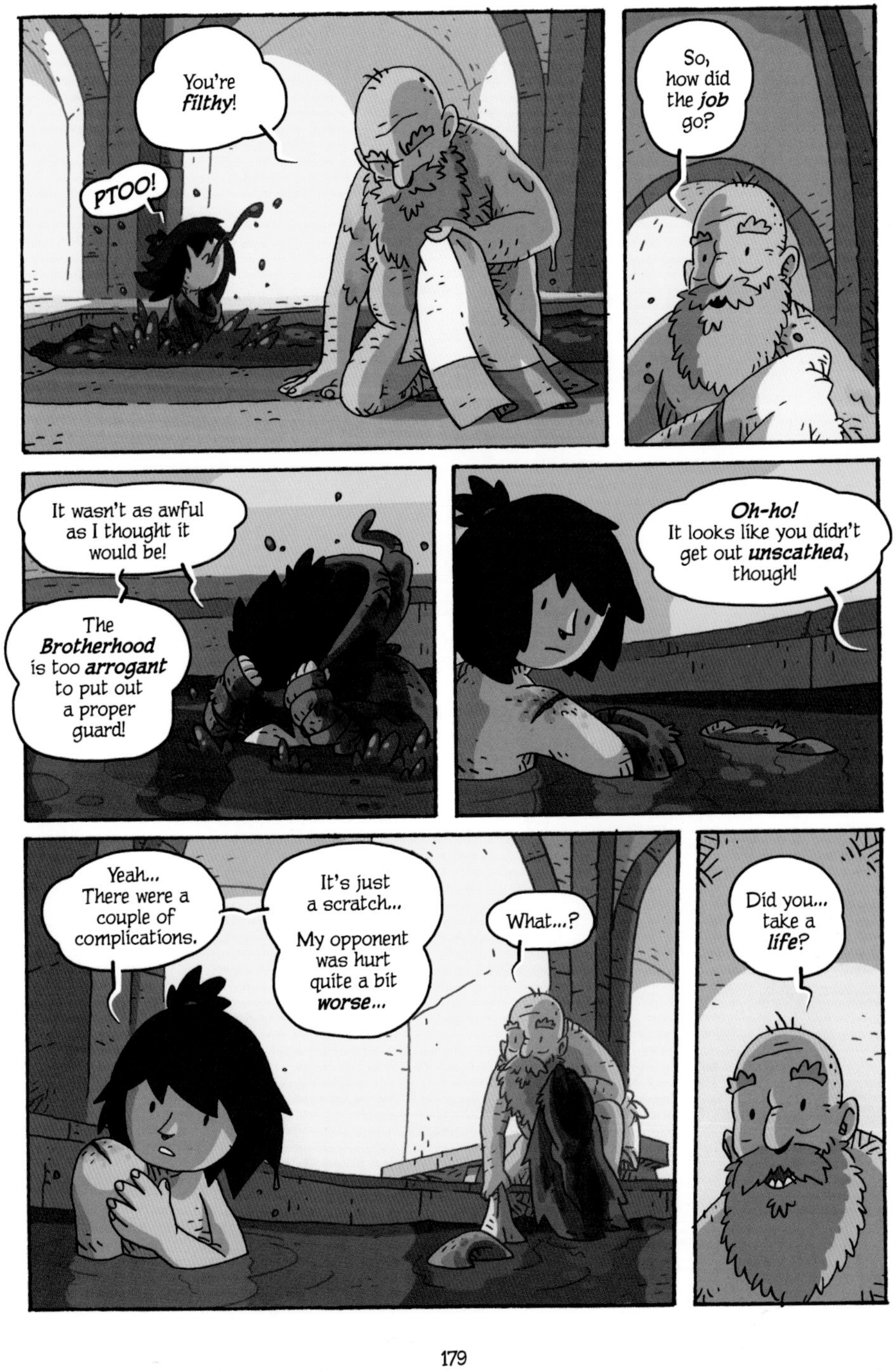
You're filthy!
PTOO!
So, how did the job go?
It wasn't as awful as I thought it would be!
The Brotherhood is too arrogant to put out a proper guard!
Oh-ho! It looks like you didn't get out unscathed, though!
Yeah... There were a couple of complications.
It's just a scratch...
My opponent was hurt quite a bit worse...
What...?
Did you... take a life?

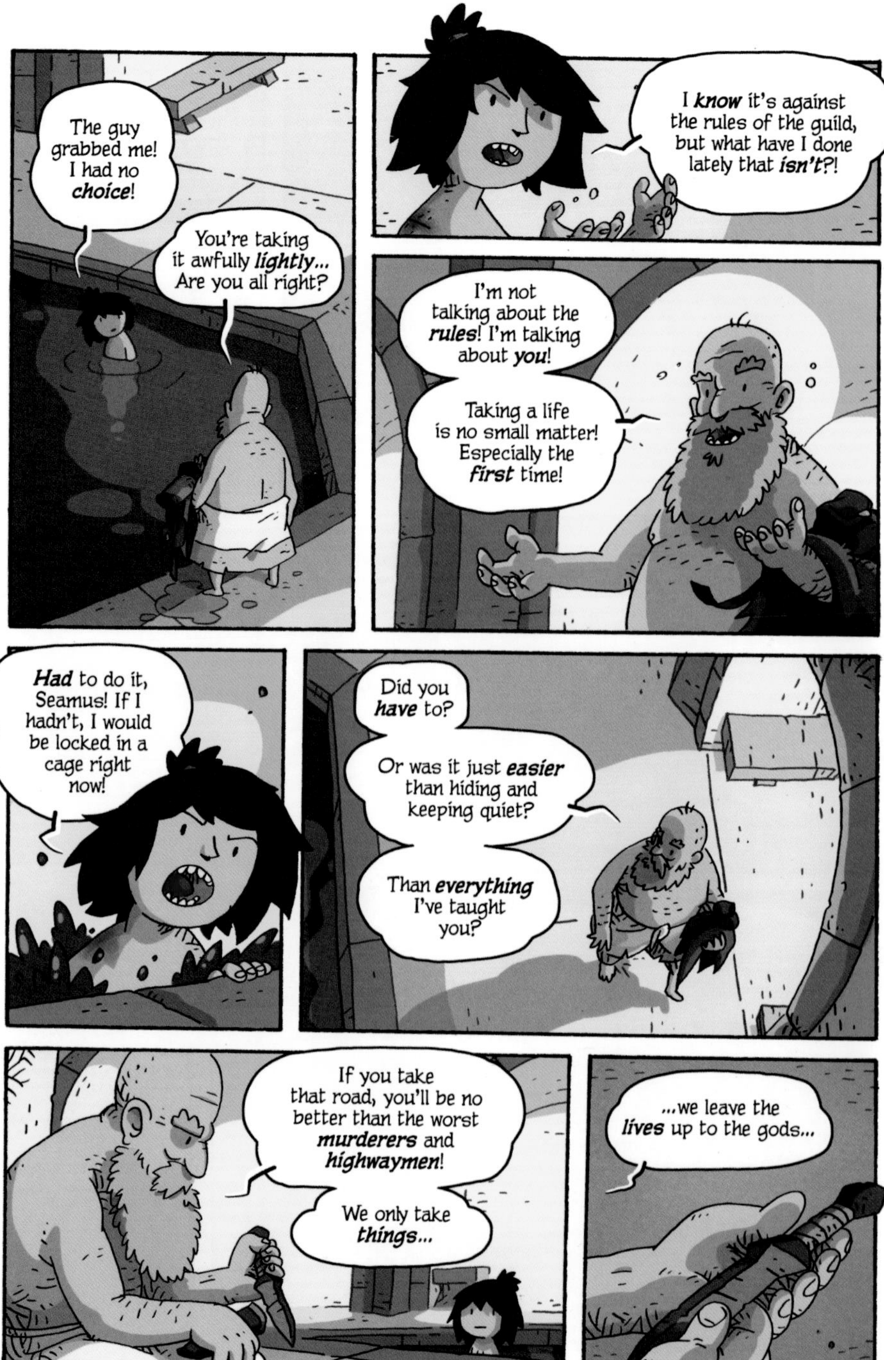
The guy grabbed me! I had no *choice*!
You're taking it awfully *lightly*... Are you all right?
I *know* it's against the rules of the guild, but what have I done lately that *isn't*?!
I'm not talking about the *rules*! I'm talking about *you*!
Taking a life is no small matter! Especially the *first* time!
Had to do it, Seamus! If I hadn't, I would be locked in a cage right now!
Did you *have* to?
Or was it just *easier* than hiding and keeping quiet?
Than *everything* I've taught you?
If you take that road, you'll be no better than the worst *murderers* and *highwaymen*!
We only take *things*...
...we leave the *lives* up to the gods...

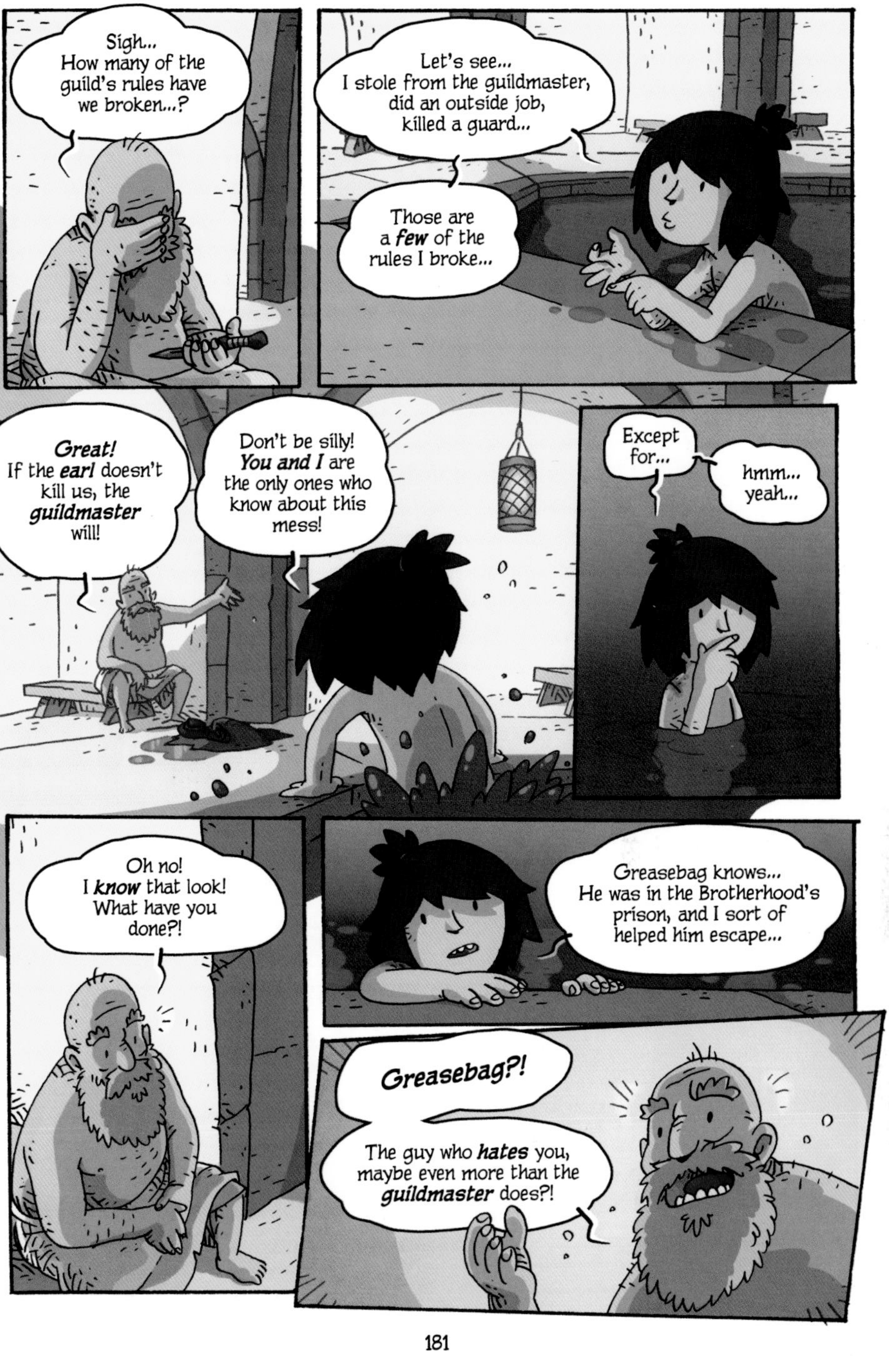
Sigh...
How many of the guild's rules have we broken...?
Let's see...
I stole from the guildmaster, did an outside job, killed a guard...
Those are a few of the rules I broke...
Great!
If the earl doesn't kill us, the guildmaster will!
Don't be silly!
You and I are the only ones who know about this mess!
Except for...
hmm... yeah...
Oh no!
I know that look!
What have you done?!
Greasebag knows...
He was in the Brotherhood's prison, and I sort of helped him escape...
Greasebag?!
The guy who hates you, maybe even more than the guildmaster does?!

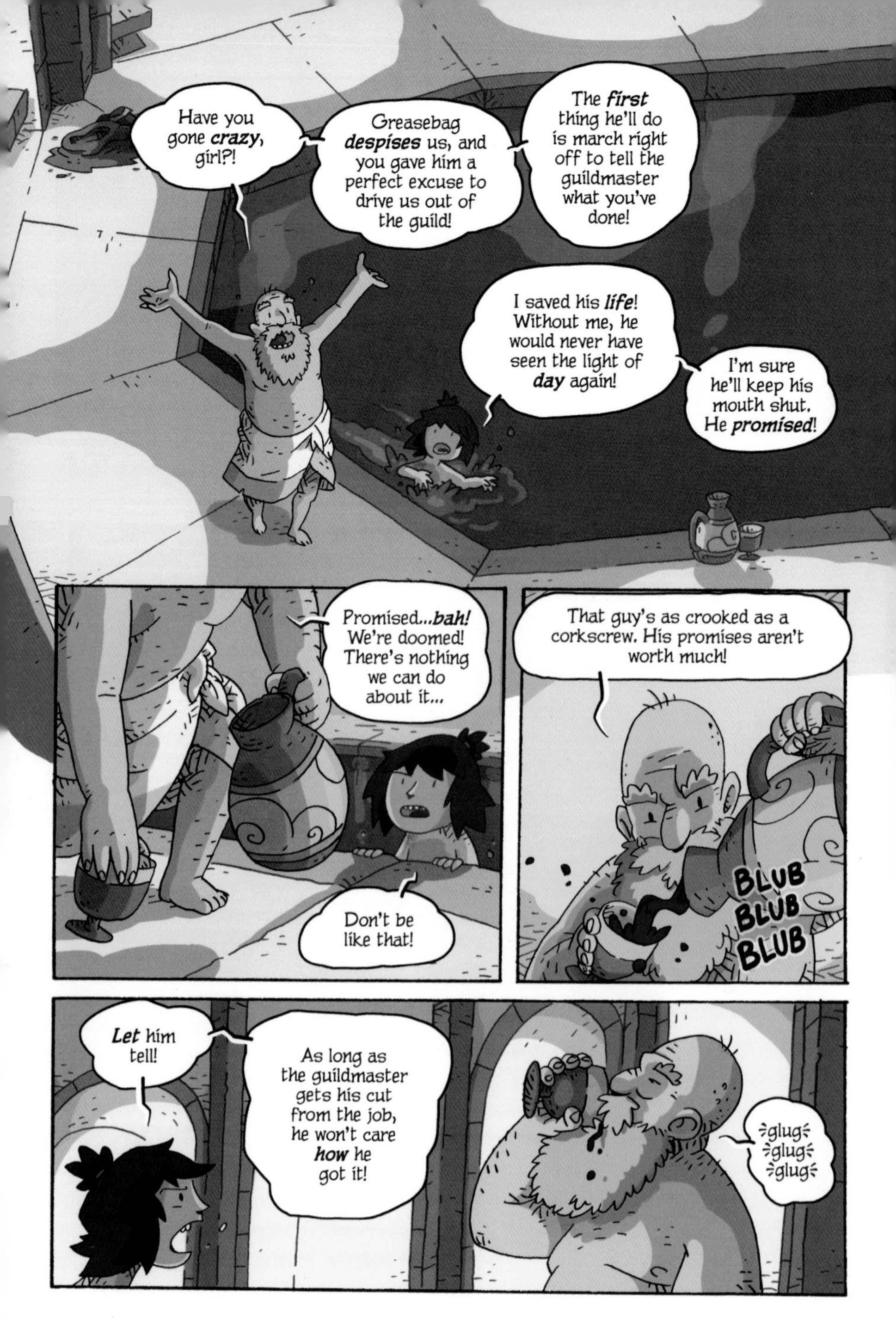

Have you gone *crazy*, girl?!
Greasebag *despises* us, and you gave him a perfect excuse to drive us out of the guild!
The *first* thing he'll do is march right off to tell the guildmaster what you've done!
I saved his *life*! Without me, he would never have seen the light of *day* again!
I'm sure he'll keep his mouth shut. He *promised*!
Promised...*bah!* We're doomed! There's nothing we can do about it...
Don't be like that!
That guy's as crooked as a corkscrew. His promises aren't worth much!
BLUB BLUB BLUB
Let him tell!
As long as the guildmaster gets his cut from the job, he won't care *how* he got it!
glug glug glug

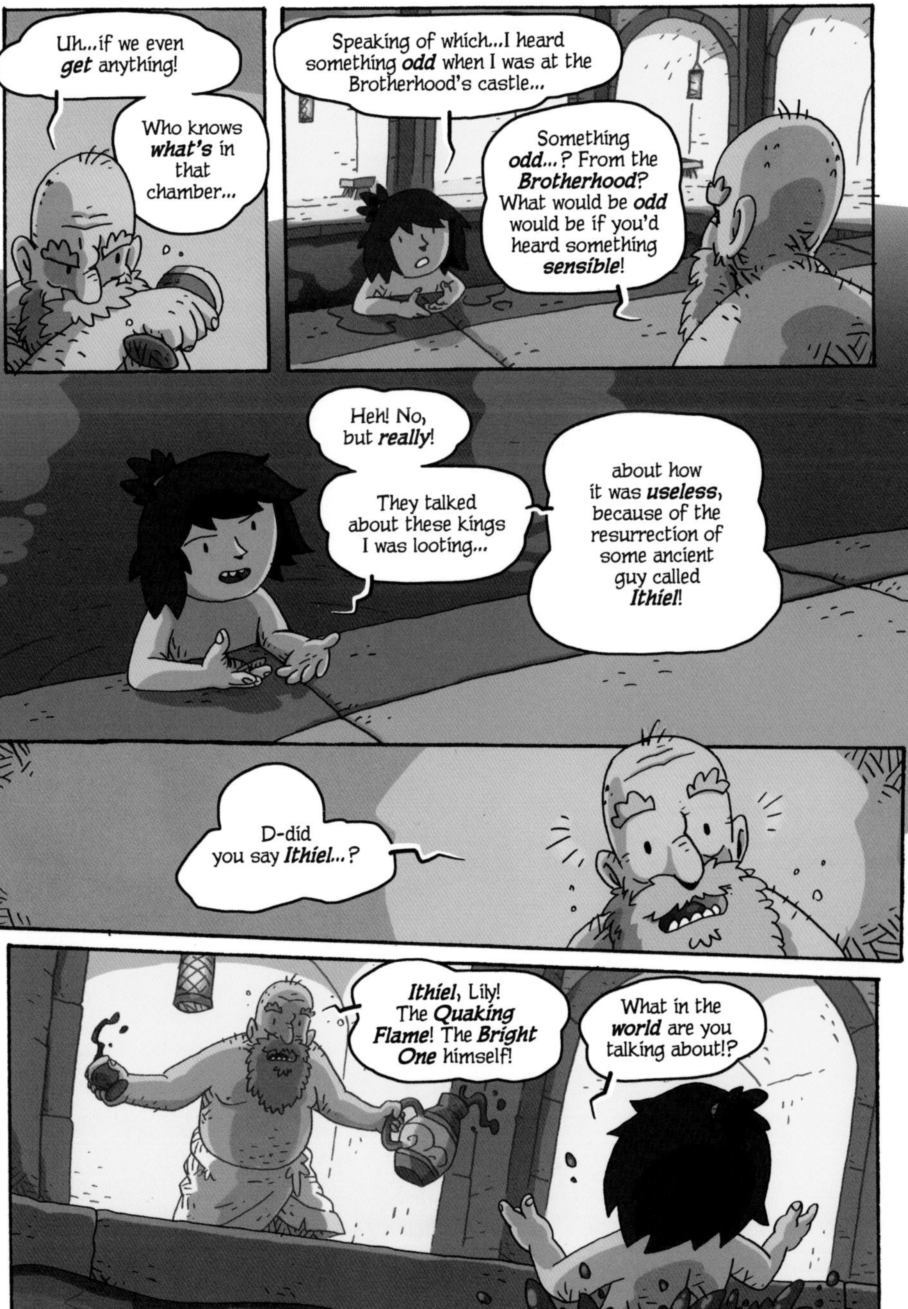
Uh...if we even *get* anything!
Who knows *what's* in that chamber...
Speaking of which...I heard something *odd* when I was at the Brotherhood's castle...
Something *odd*...? From the *Brotherhood*? What would be *odd* would be if you'd heard something *sensible*!
Heh! No, but *really*!
They talked about these kings I was looting...
about how it was *useless*, because of the resurrection of some ancient guy called *Ithiel*!
D-did you say *Ithiel*...?
Ithiel, Lily! The *Quaking Flame*! The *Bright One* himself!
What in the *world* are you talking about!?

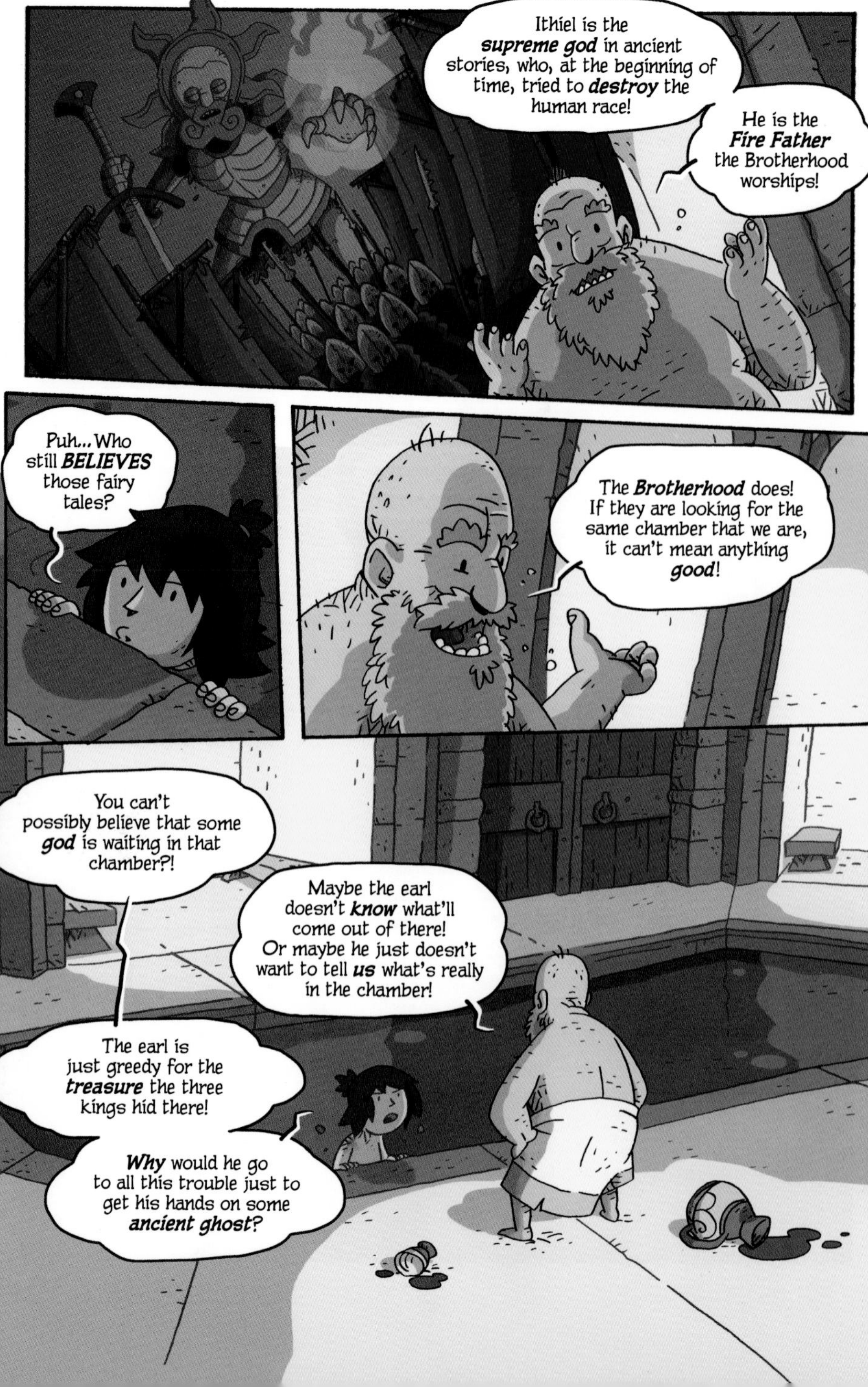

Ithiel is the supreme god in ancient stories, who, at the beginning of time, tried to destroy the human race!
He is the Fire Father the Brotherhood worships!
Puh... Who still BELIEVES those fairy tales?
The Brotherhood does! If they are looking for the same chamber that we are, it can't mean anything good!
You can't possibly believe that some god is waiting in that chamber?!
Maybe the earl doesn't know what'll come out of there! Or maybe he just doesn't want to tell us what's really in the chamber!
The earl is just greedy for the treasure the three kings hid there!
Why would he go to all this trouble just to get his hands on some ancient ghost?

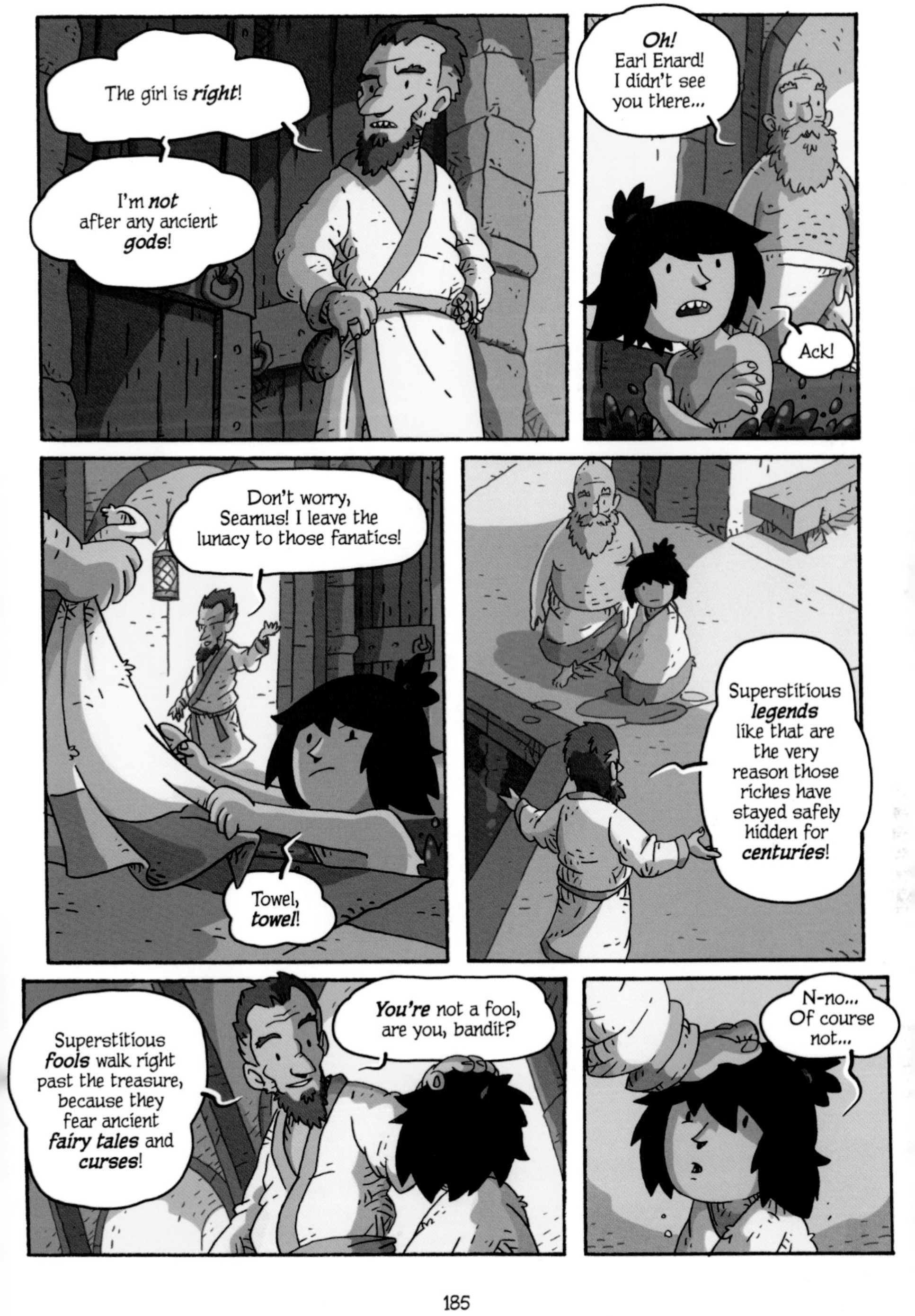

The girl is *right*!
I'm *not* after any ancient *gods*!
Oh! Earl Enard! I didn't see you there...
Ack!
Don't worry, Seamus! I leave the lunacy to those fanatics!
Towel, *towel*!
Superstitious *legends* like that are the very reason those riches have stayed safely hidden for *centuries*!
Superstitious *fools* walk right past the treasure, because they fear ancient *fairy tales* and *curses*!
You're not a fool, are you, bandit?
N-no... Of course not...

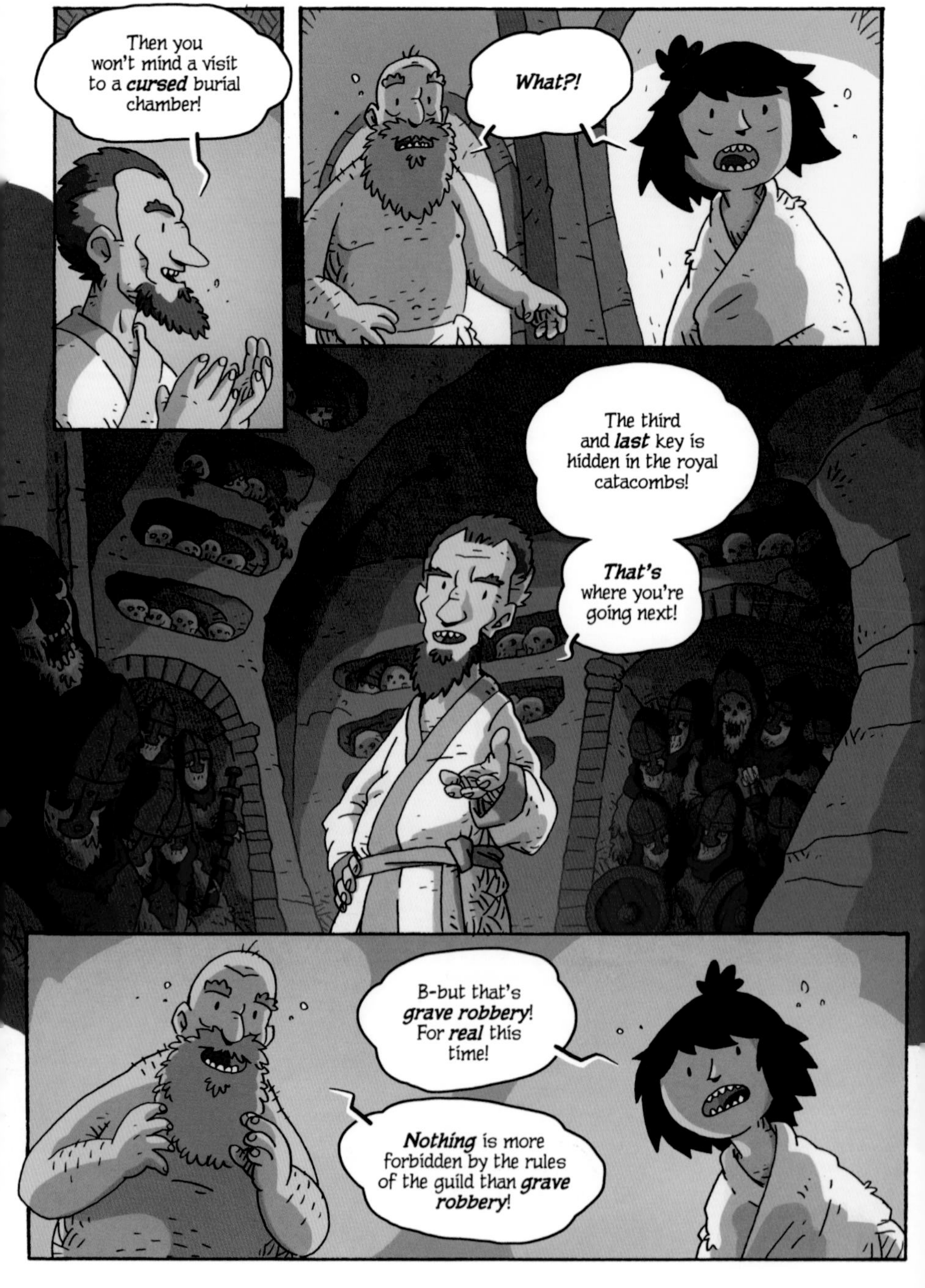
Then you won't mind a visit to a ***cursed*** burial chamber!
What?!
The third and ***last*** key is hidden in the royal catacombs!
That's where you're going next!
B-but that's ***grave robbery***! For ***real*** this time!
Nothing is more forbidden by the rules of the guild than ***grave robbery***!

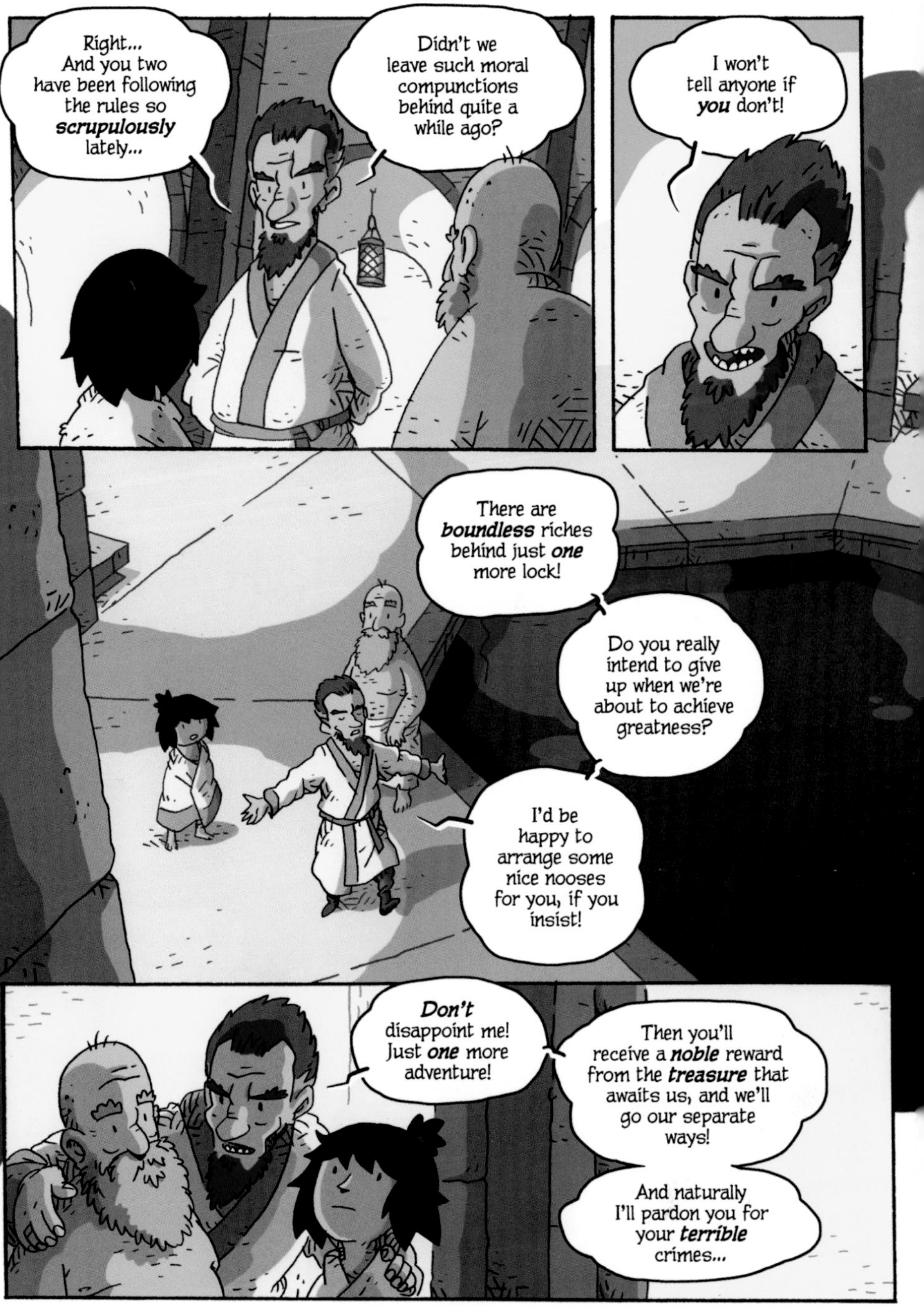
Right... And you two have been following the rules so *scrupulously* lately...
Didn't we leave such moral compunctions behind quite a while ago?
I won't tell anyone if *you* don't!
There are *boundless* riches behind just *one* more lock!
Do you really intend to give up when we're about to achieve greatness?
I'd be happy to arrange some nice nooses for you, if you insist!
Don't disappoint me! Just *one* more adventure!
Then you'll receive a *noble* reward from the *treasure* that awaits us, and we'll go our separate ways!
And naturally I'll pardon you for your *terrible* crimes...

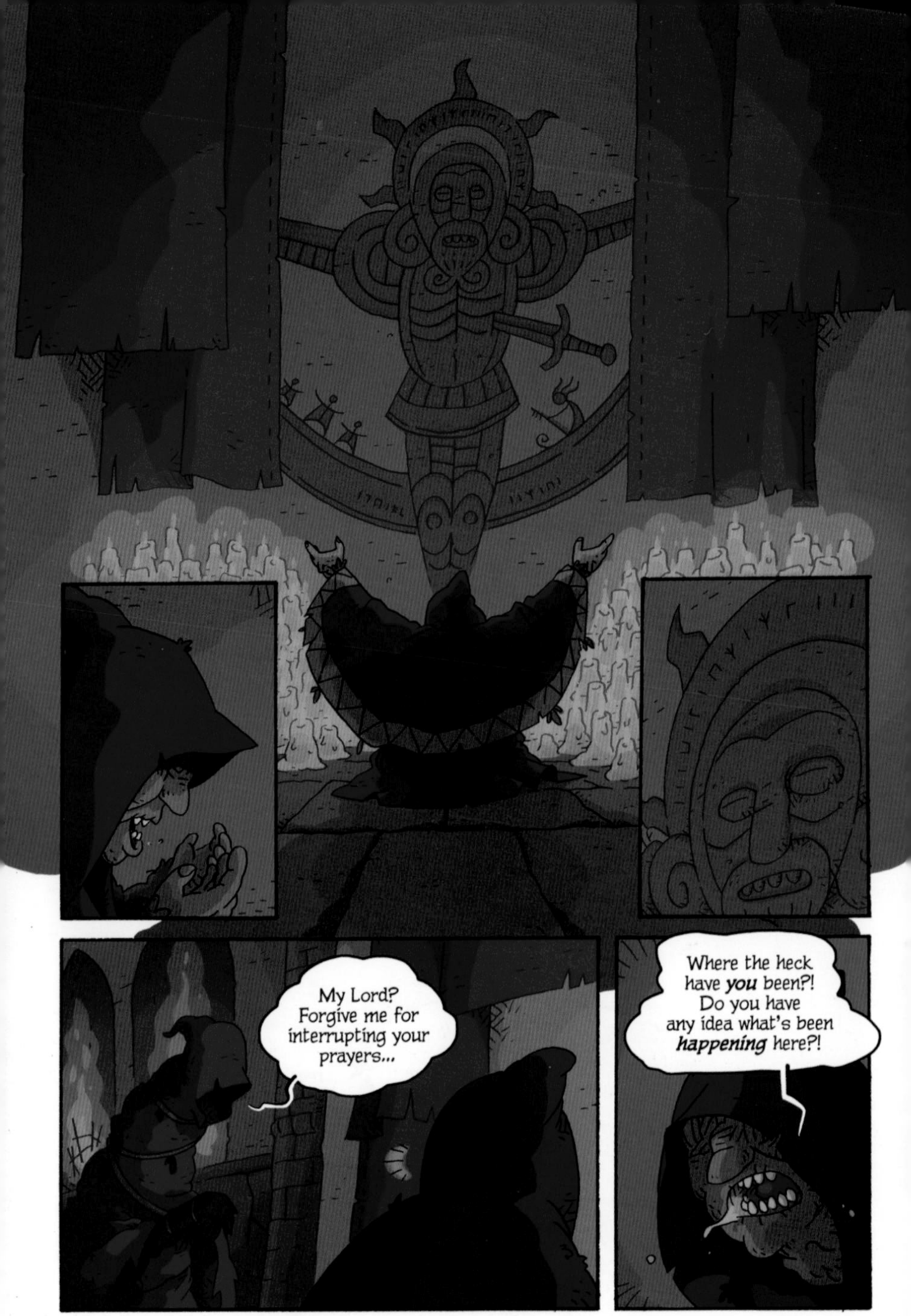
My Lord? Forgive me for interrupting your prayers...
Where the heck have ***you*** been?! Do you have any idea what's been ***happening*** here?!

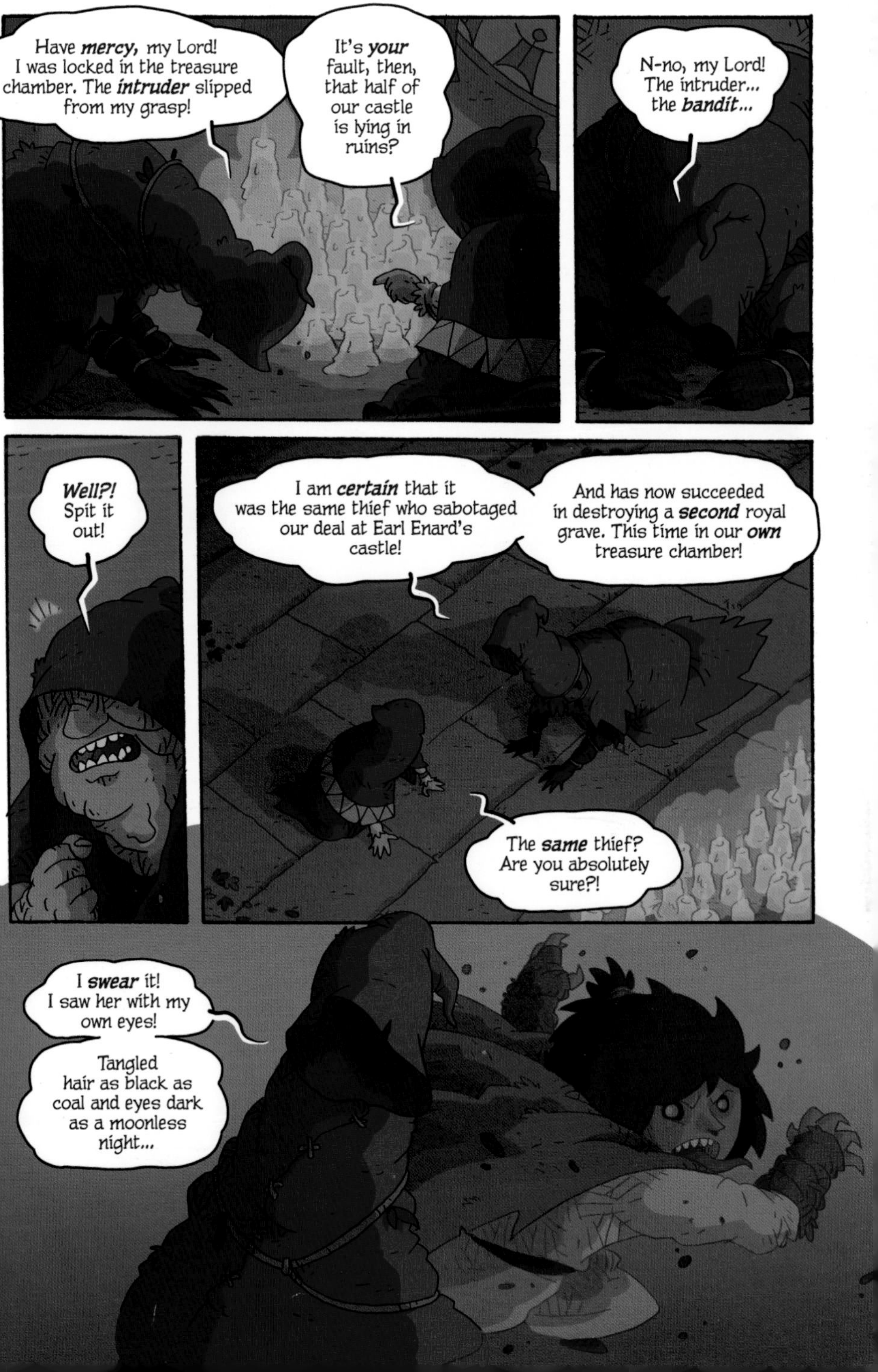
Have *mercy,* my Lord! I was locked in the treasure chamber. The *intruder* slipped from my grasp!
It's *your* fault, then, that half of our castle is lying in ruins?
N-no, my Lord! The intruder... the *bandit...*
Well?! Spit it out!
I am *certain* that it was the same thief who sabotaged our deal at Earl Enard's castle!
And has now succeeded in destroying a *second* royal grave. This time in our *own* treasure chamber!
The *same* thief? Are you absolutely sure?!
I *swear* it! I saw her with my own eyes!
Tangled hair as black as coal and eyes dark as a moonless night...

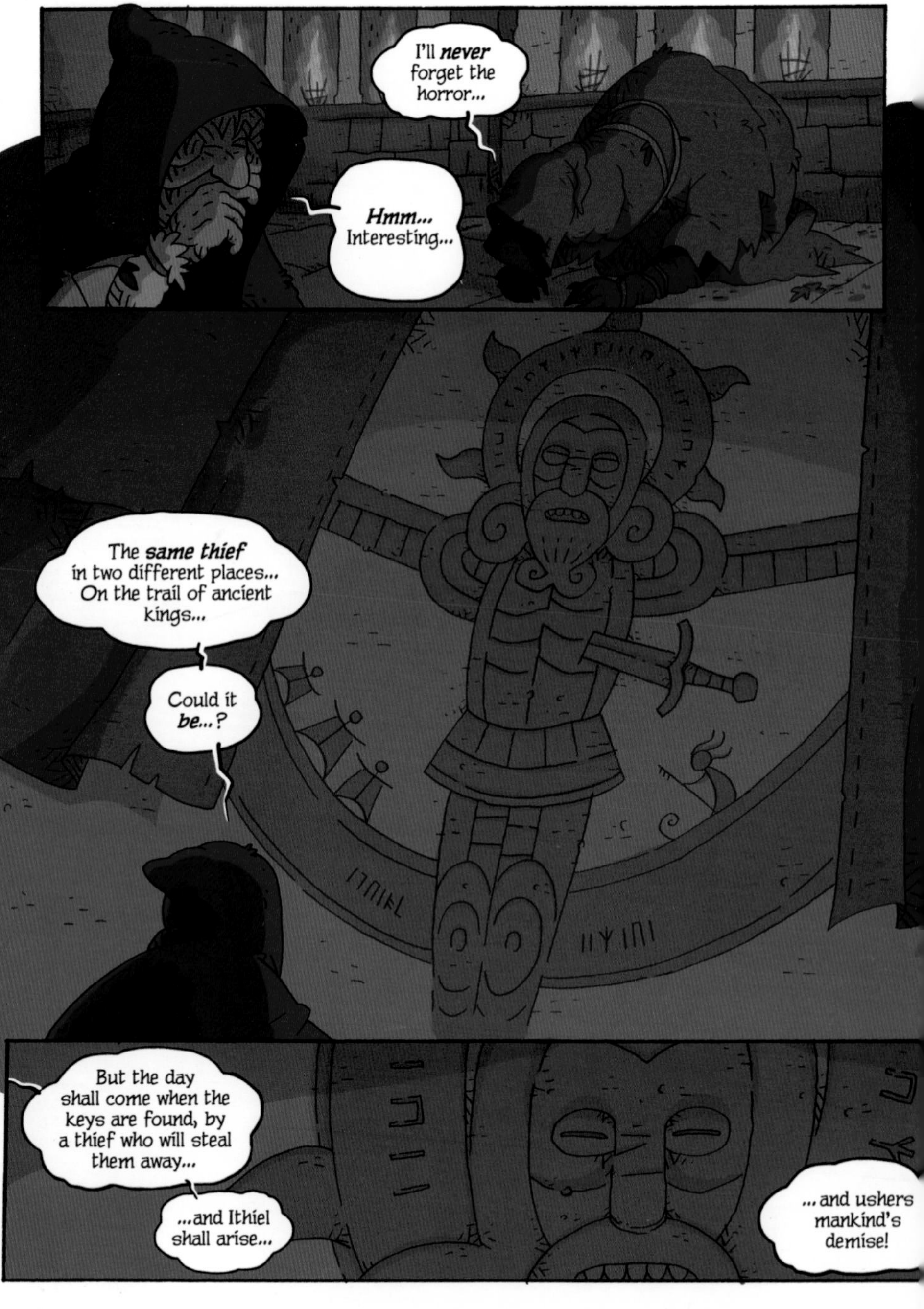
I'll **never** forget the horror...
Hmm... Interesting...
The **same thief** in two different places... On the trail of ancient kings...
Could it **be**...?
But the day shall come when the keys are found, by a thief who will steal them away...
...and Ithiel shall arise...
...and ushers mankind's demise!

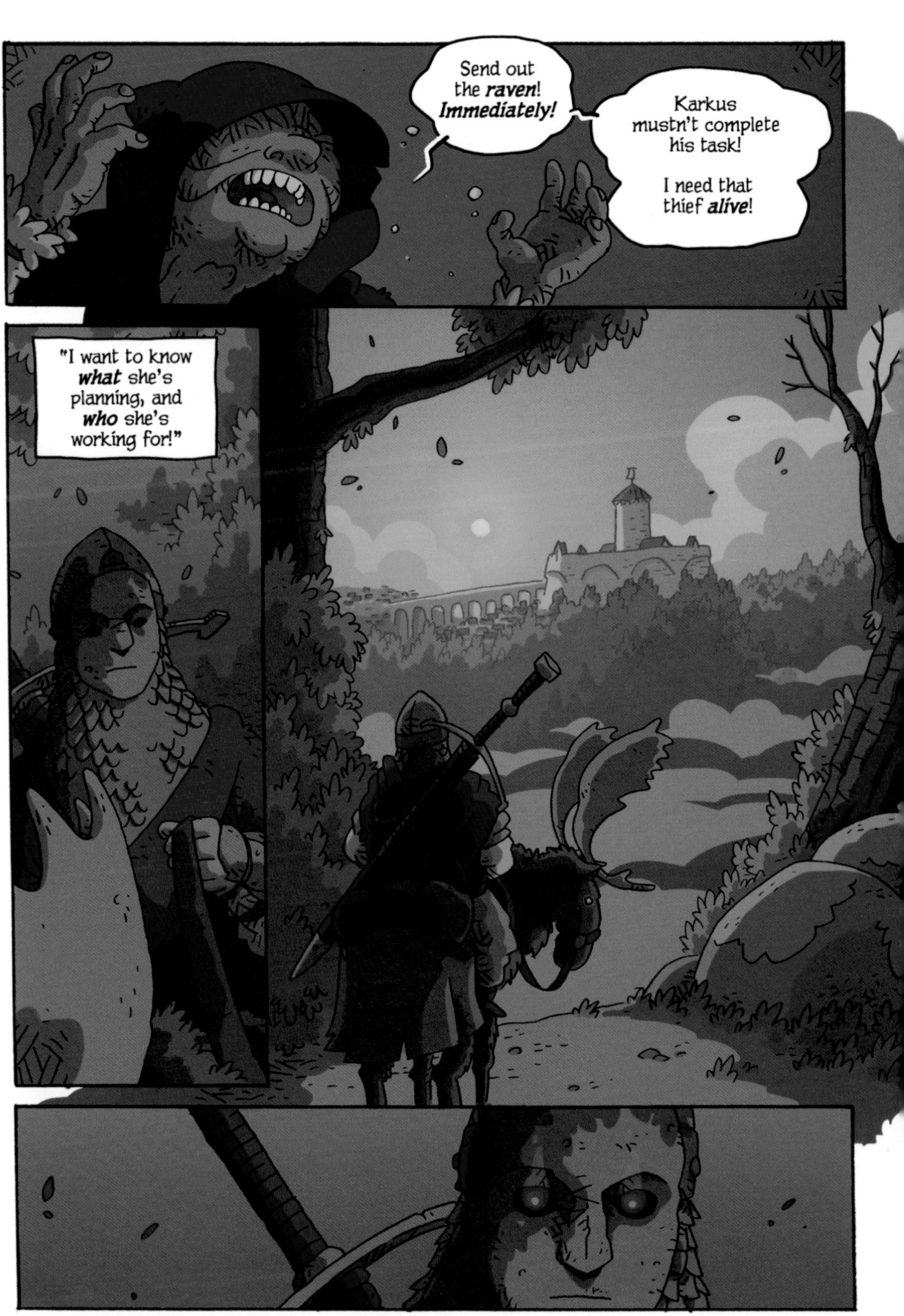
Send out the raven! Immediately!
Karkus mustn't complete his task!
I need that thief alive!
"I want to know what she's planning, and who she's working for!"

No brightness without darkness,
No darkness without light,
But what lies between them,
Is clamoring and clattering,
Rattling and battling in the night.

The **Dead**

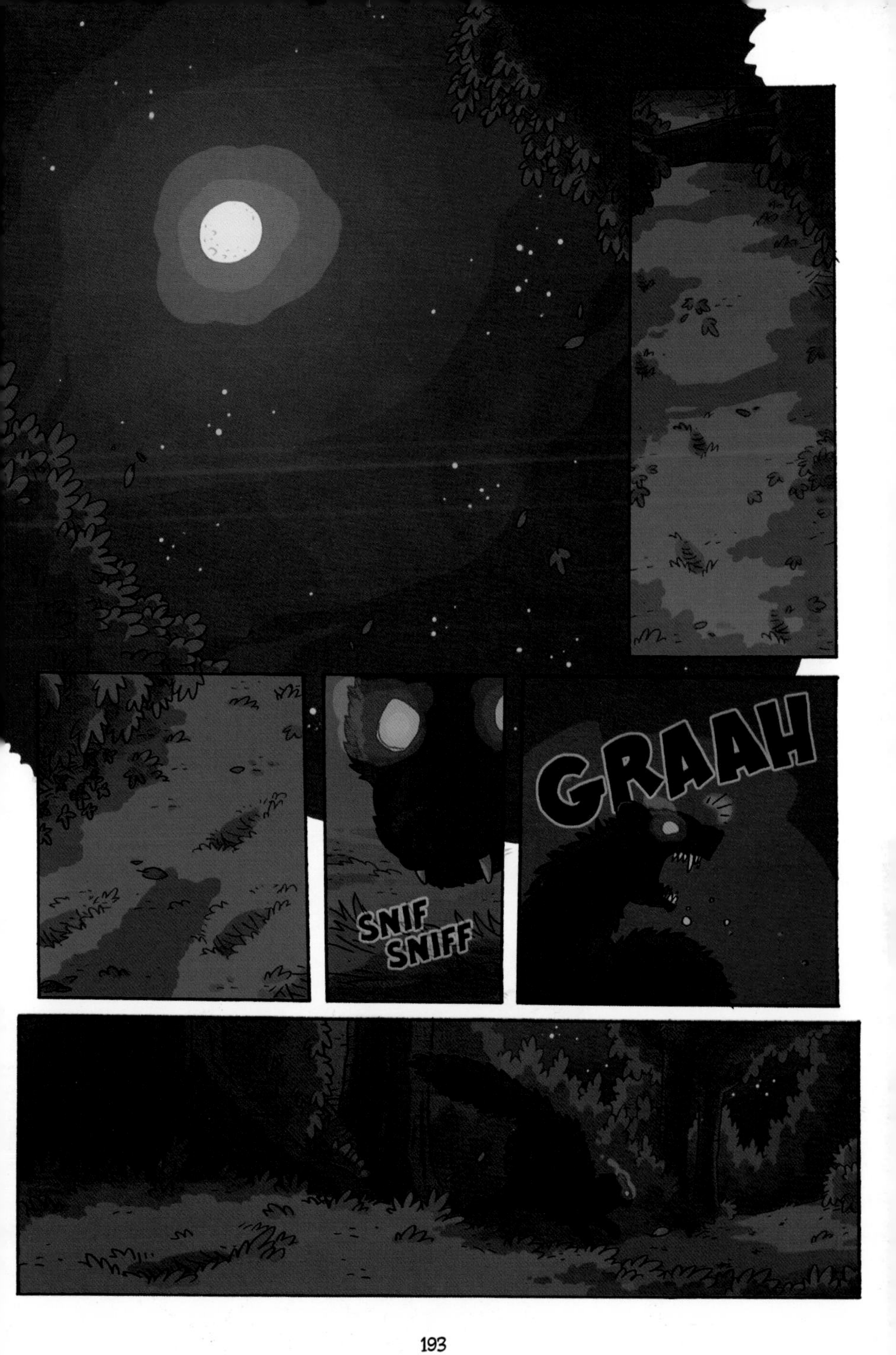
SNIF
SNIFF
GRAAH

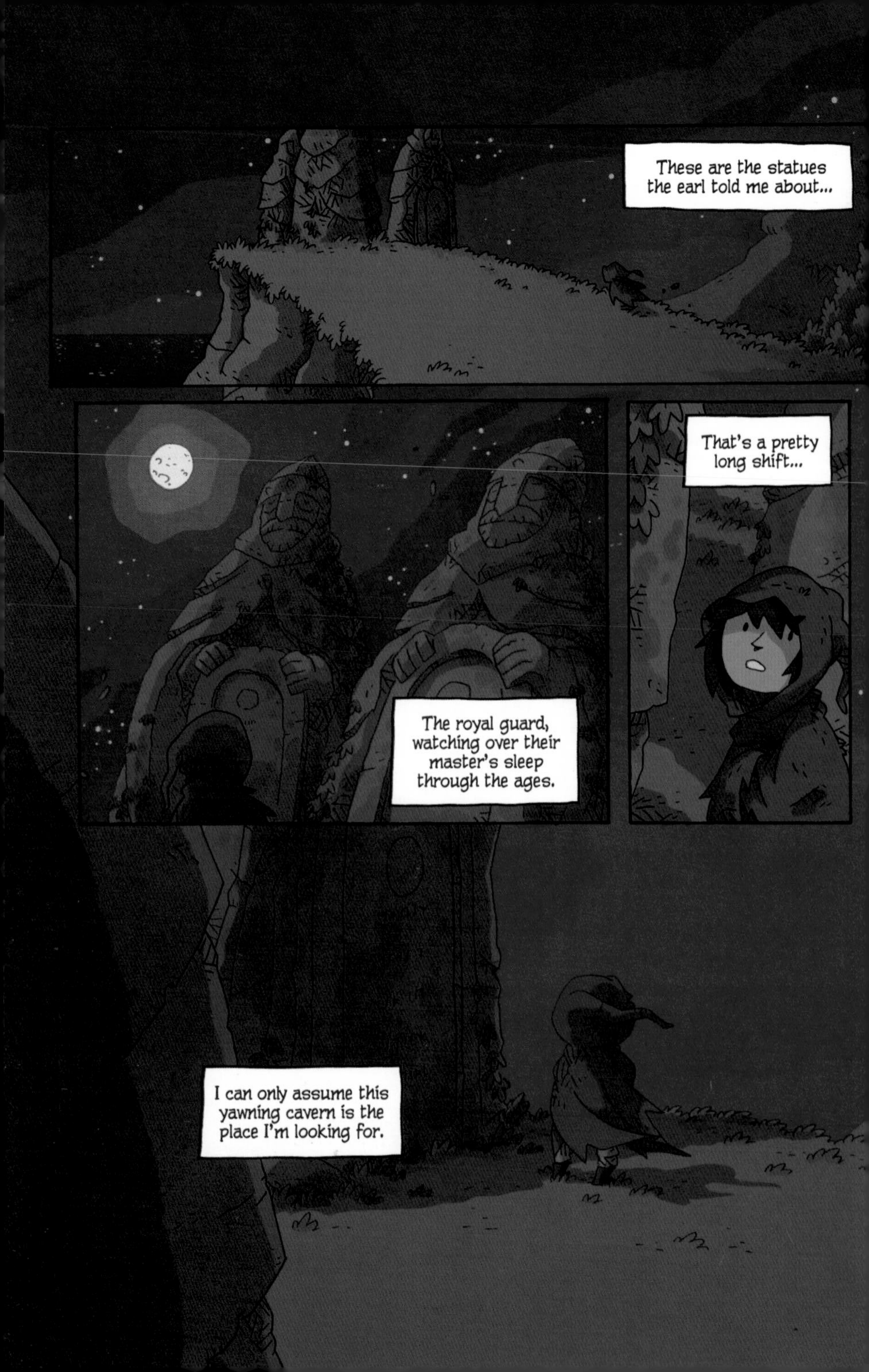
These are the statues the earl told me about...
The royal guard, watching over their master's sleep through the ages.
That's a pretty long shift...
I can only assume this yawning cavern is the place I'm looking for.

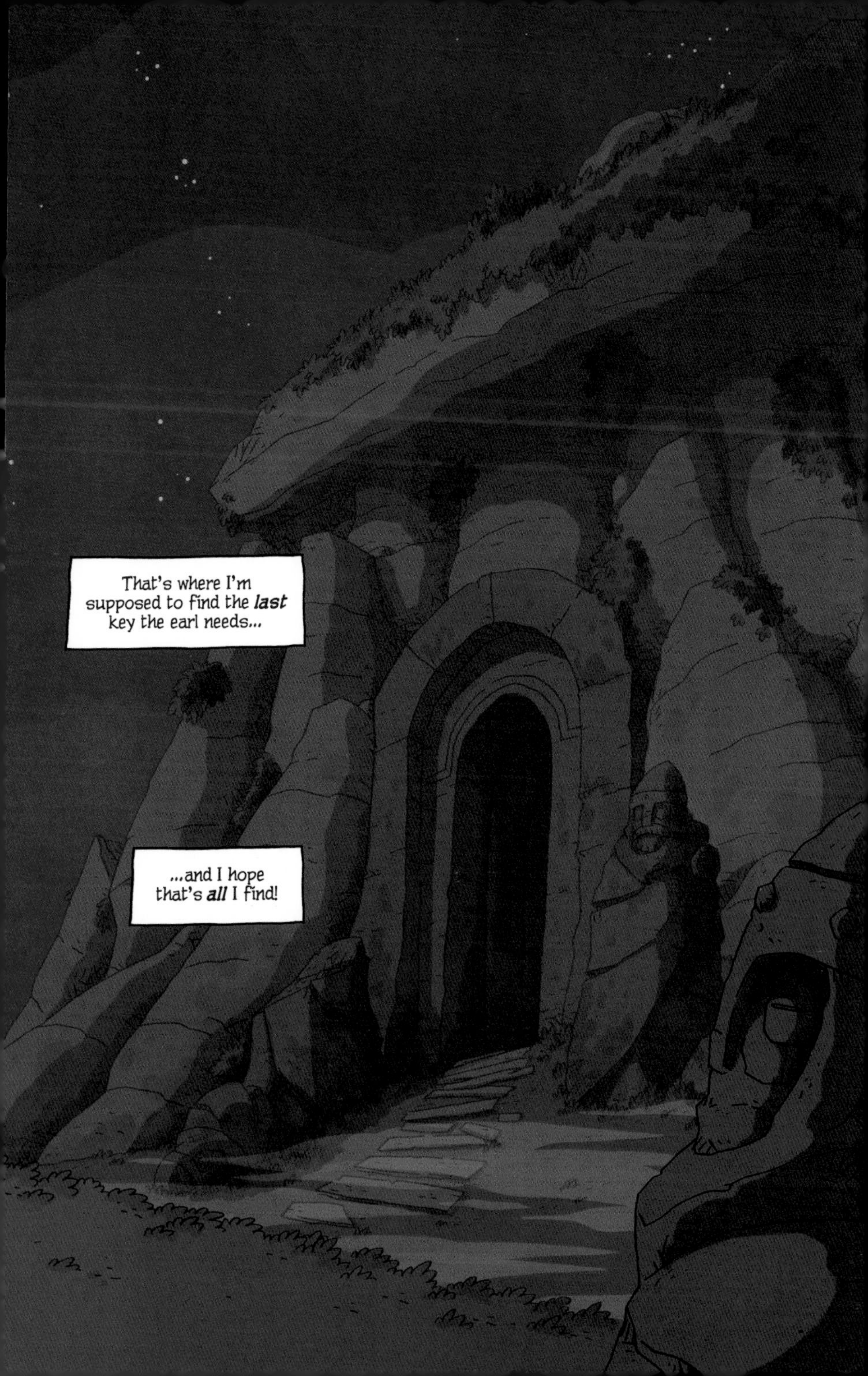
That's where I'm supposed to find the *last* key the earl needs...
...and I hope that's *all* I find!

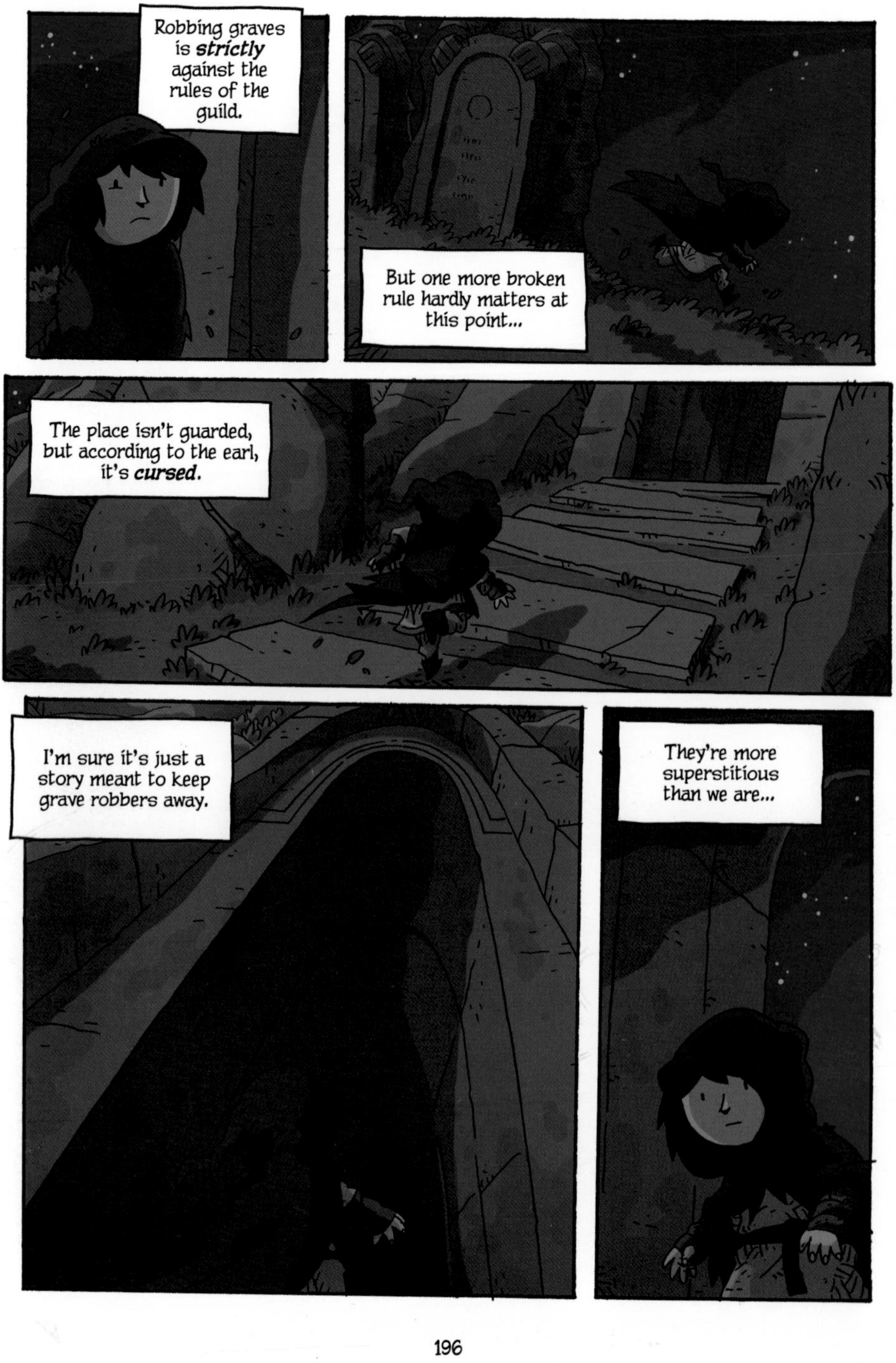
Robbing graves is **strictly** against the rules of the guild.
But one more broken rule hardly matters at this point...
The place isn't guarded, but according to the earl, it's ***cursed.***
I'm sure it's just a story meant to keep grave robbers away.
They're more superstitious than we are...

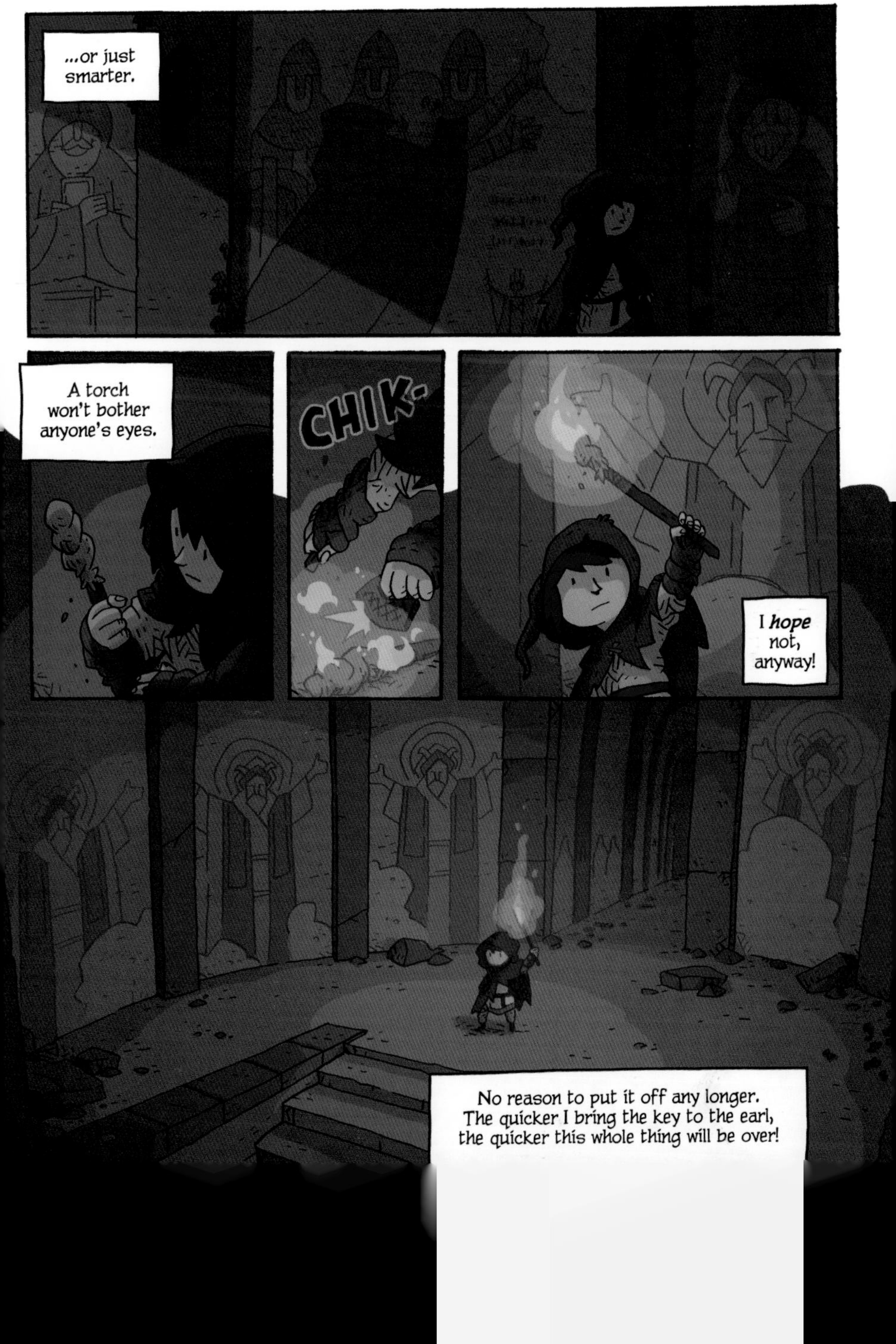
...or just smarter.
A torch won't bother anyone's eyes.
CHIK-
I *hope* not, anyway!
No reason to put it off any longer. The quicker I bring the key to the earl, the quicker this whole thing will be over!

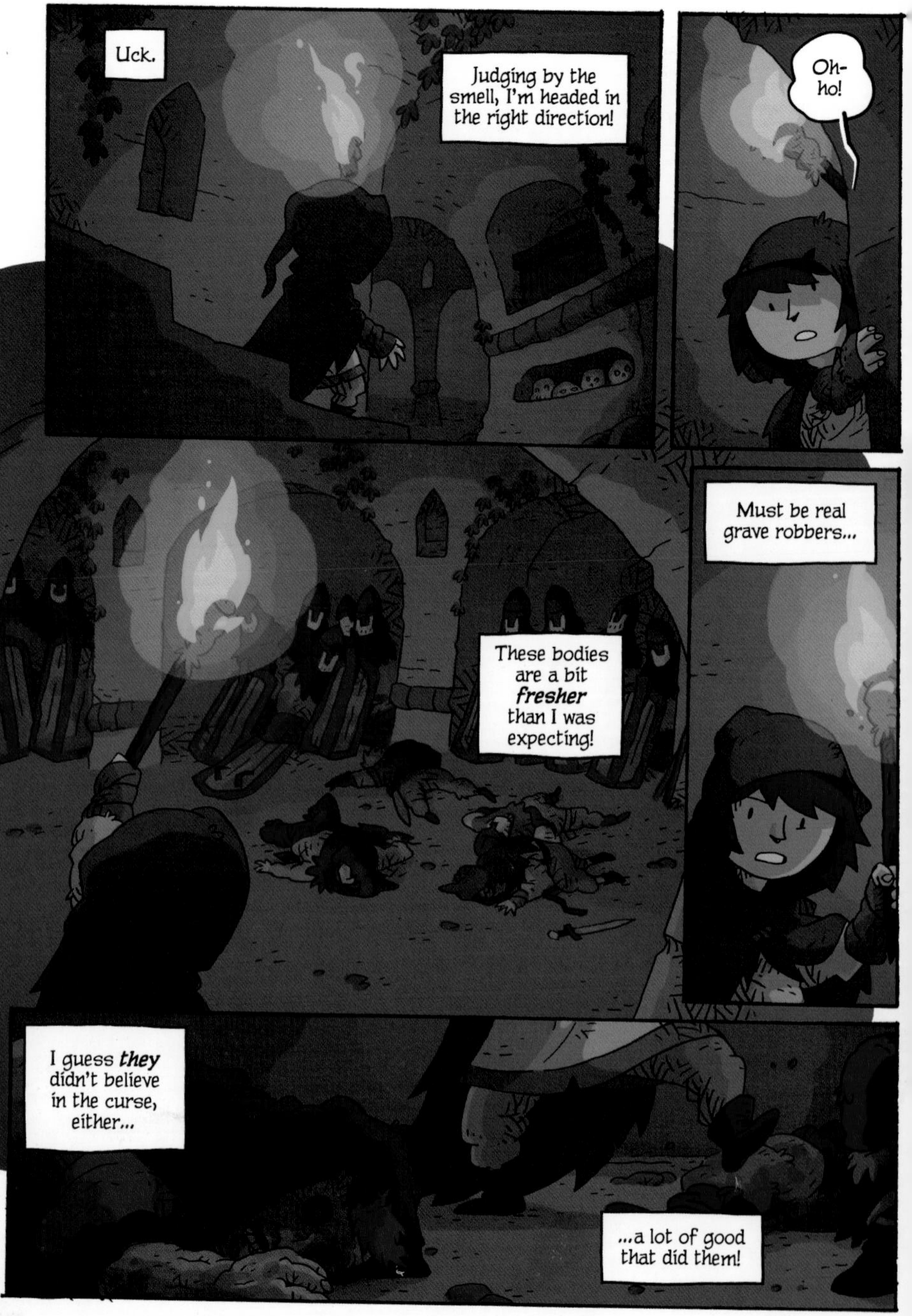
Uck.
Judging by the smell, I'm headed in the right direction!
Oh-ho!
Must be real grave robbers...
These bodies are a bit ***fresher*** than I was expecting!
I guess ***they*** didn't believe in the curse, either...
...a lot of good that did them!

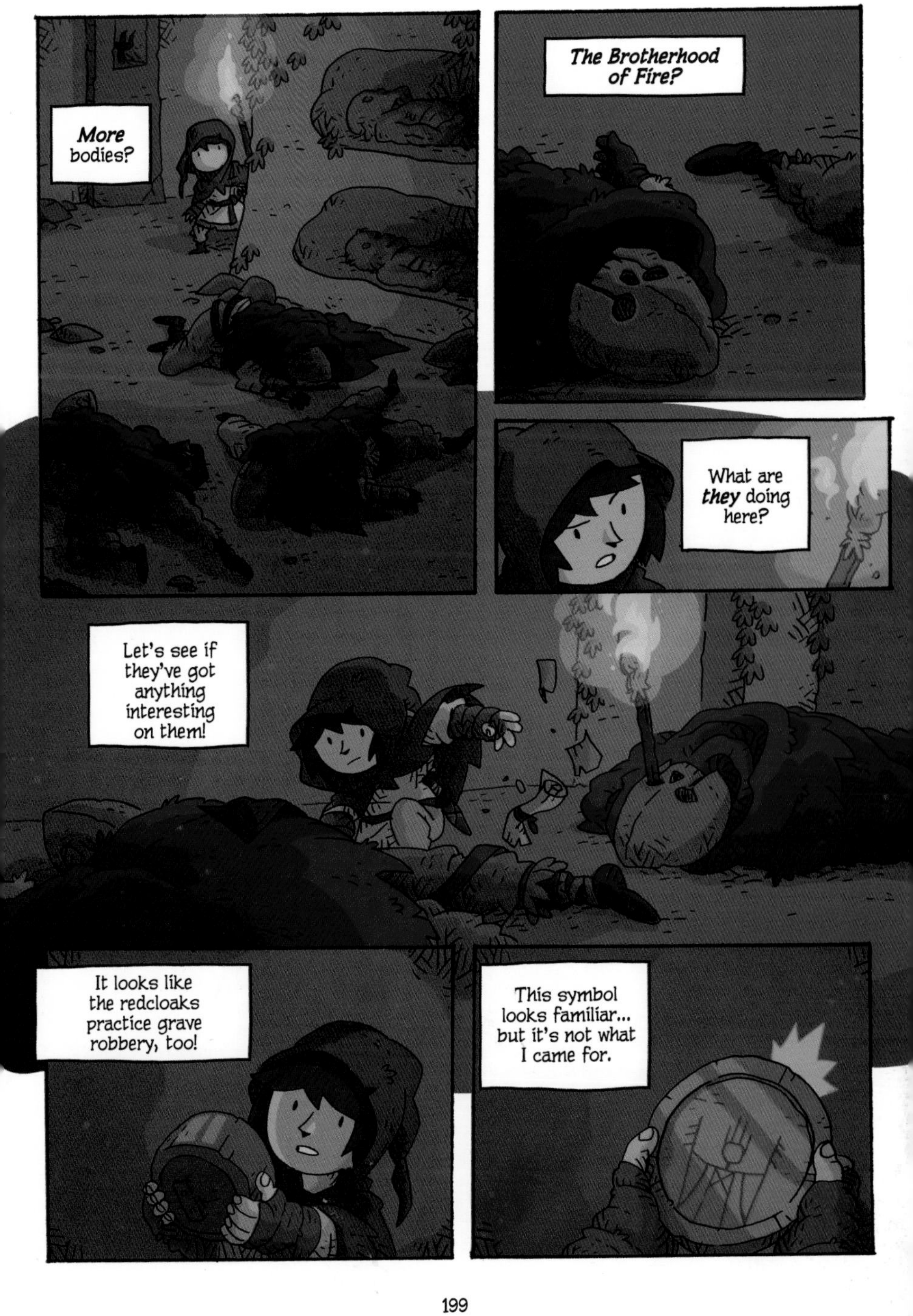
More bodies?
The Brotherhood of Fire?
What are they doing here?
Let's see if they've got anything interesting on them!
It looks like the redcloaks practice grave robbery, too!
This symbol looks familiar... but it's not what I came for.

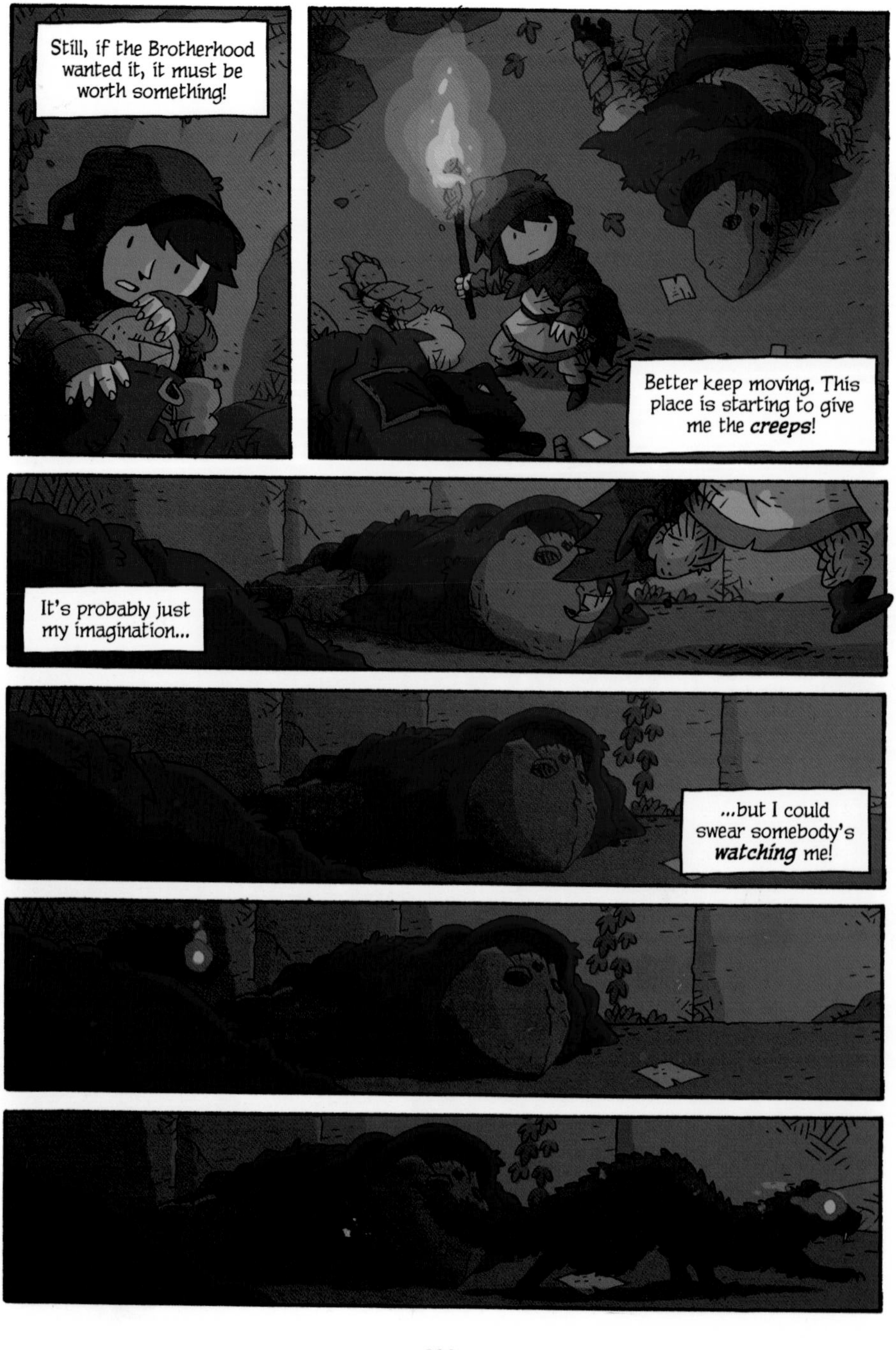
Still, if the Brotherhood wanted it, it must be worth something!
Better keep moving. This place is starting to give me the creeps!
It's probably just my imagination...
...but I could swear somebody's watching me!

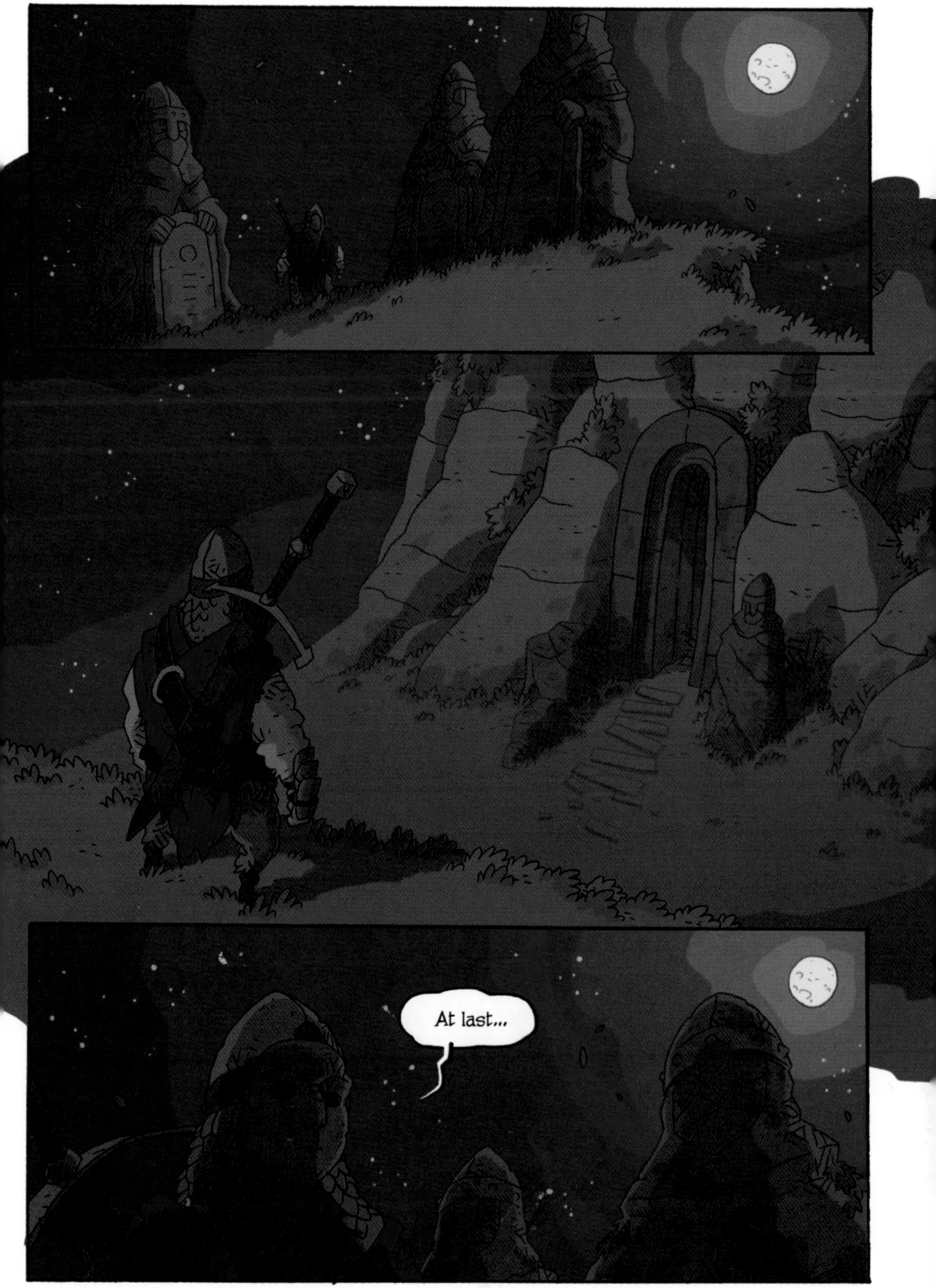
At last...

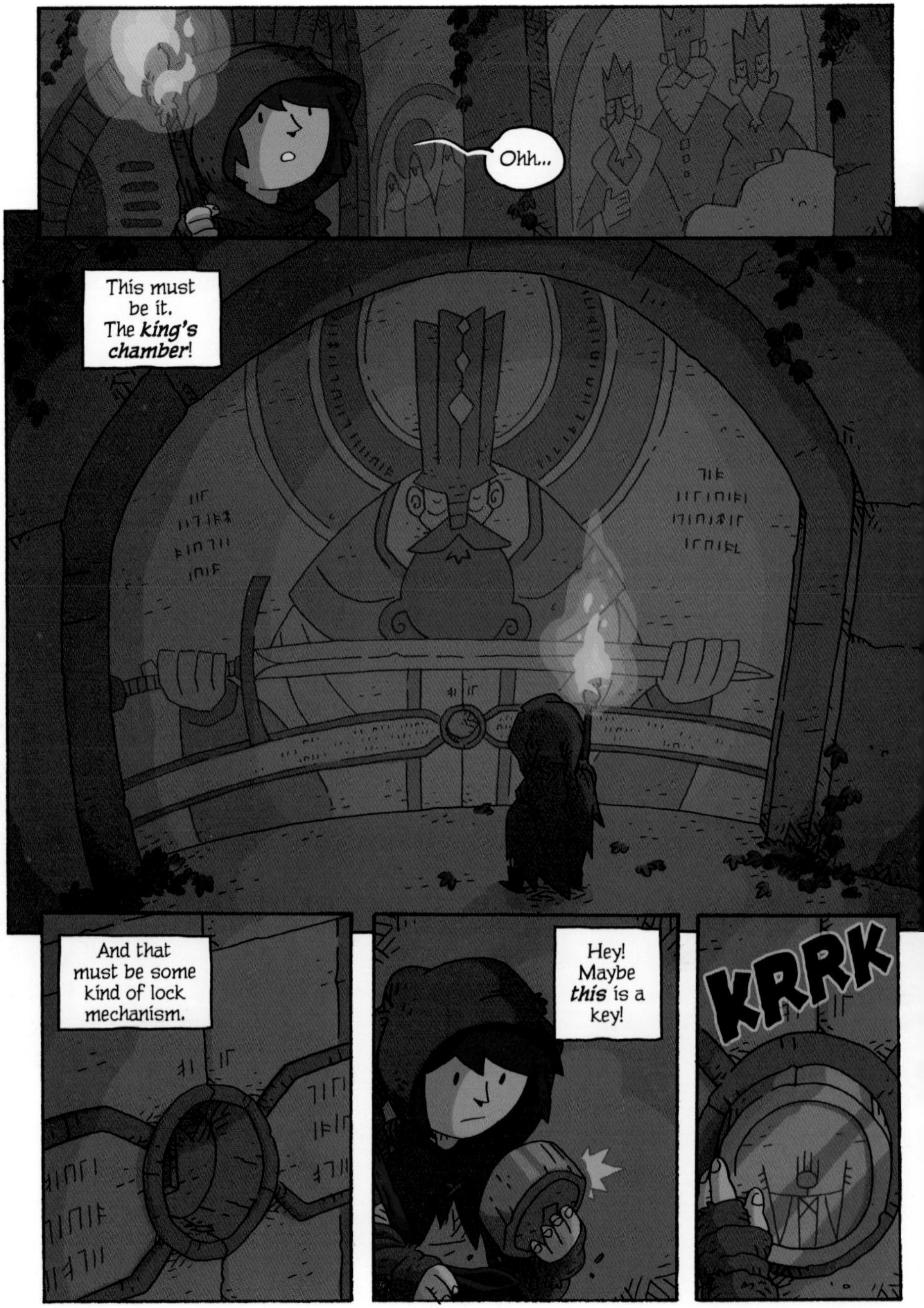
Ohh...
This must be it. The *king's chamber*!
And that must be some kind of lock mechanism.
Hey! Maybe *this* is a key!
KRRK

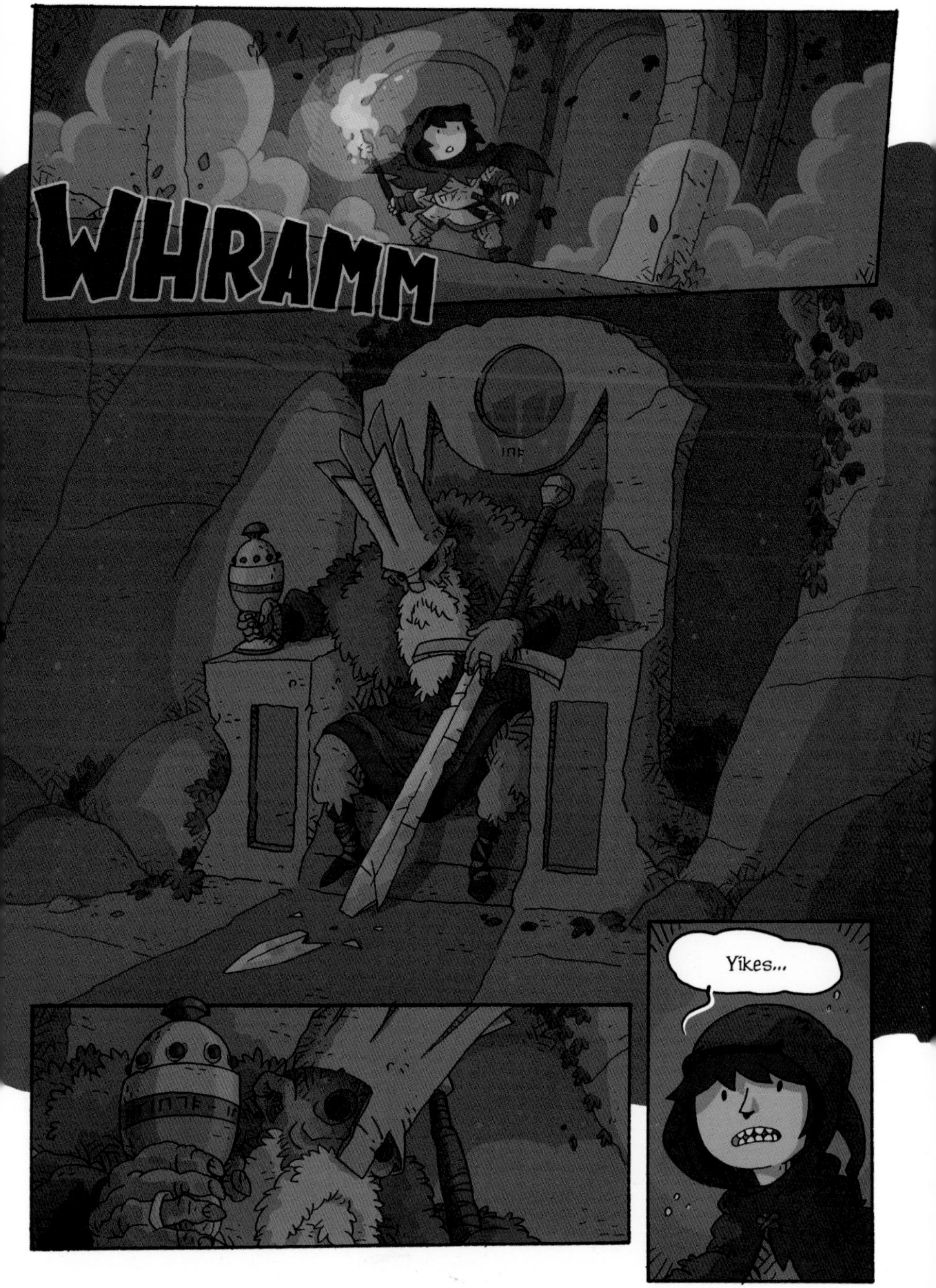
WHRAMM
Yikes...

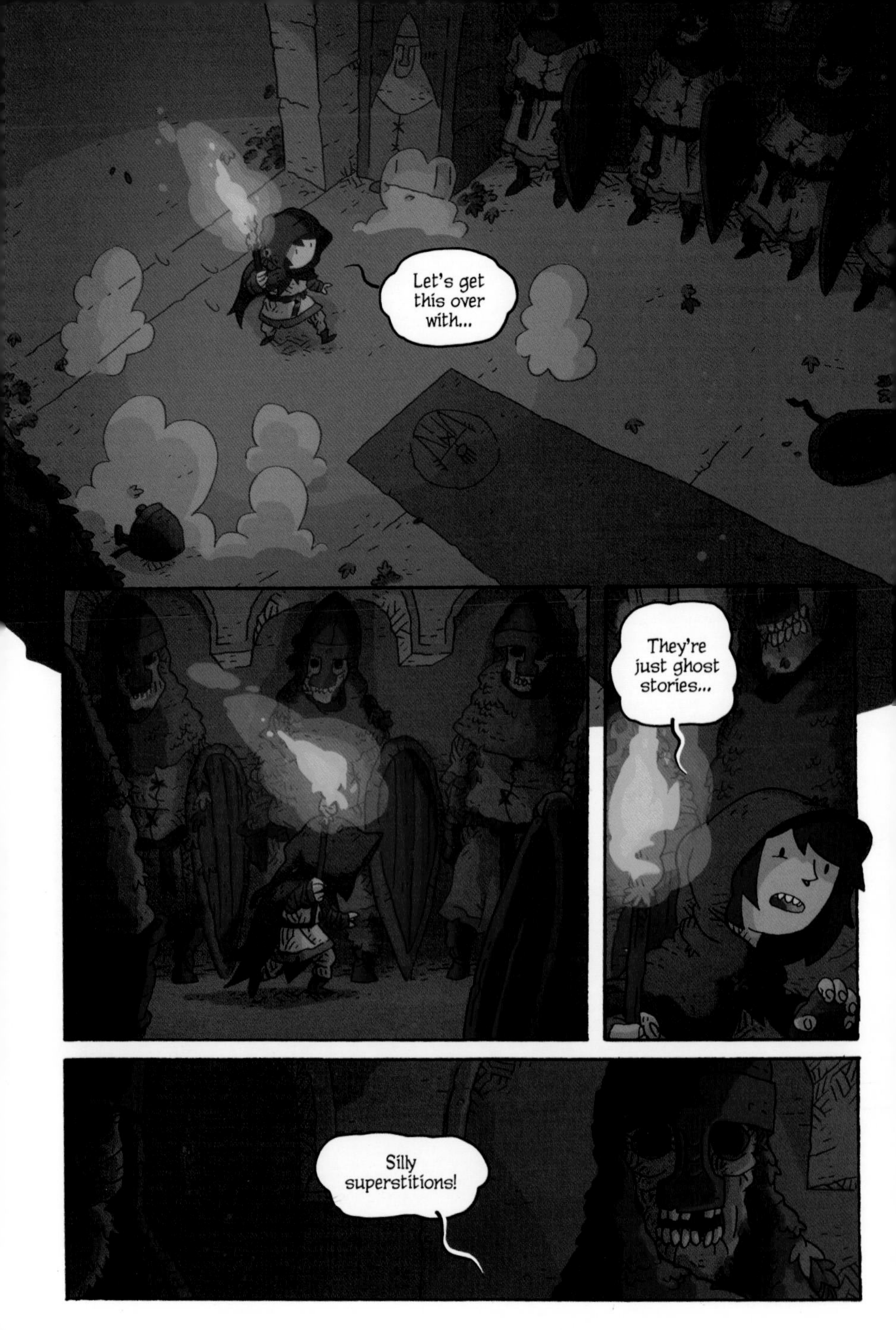
Let's get this over with...
They're just ghost stories...
Silly superstitions!

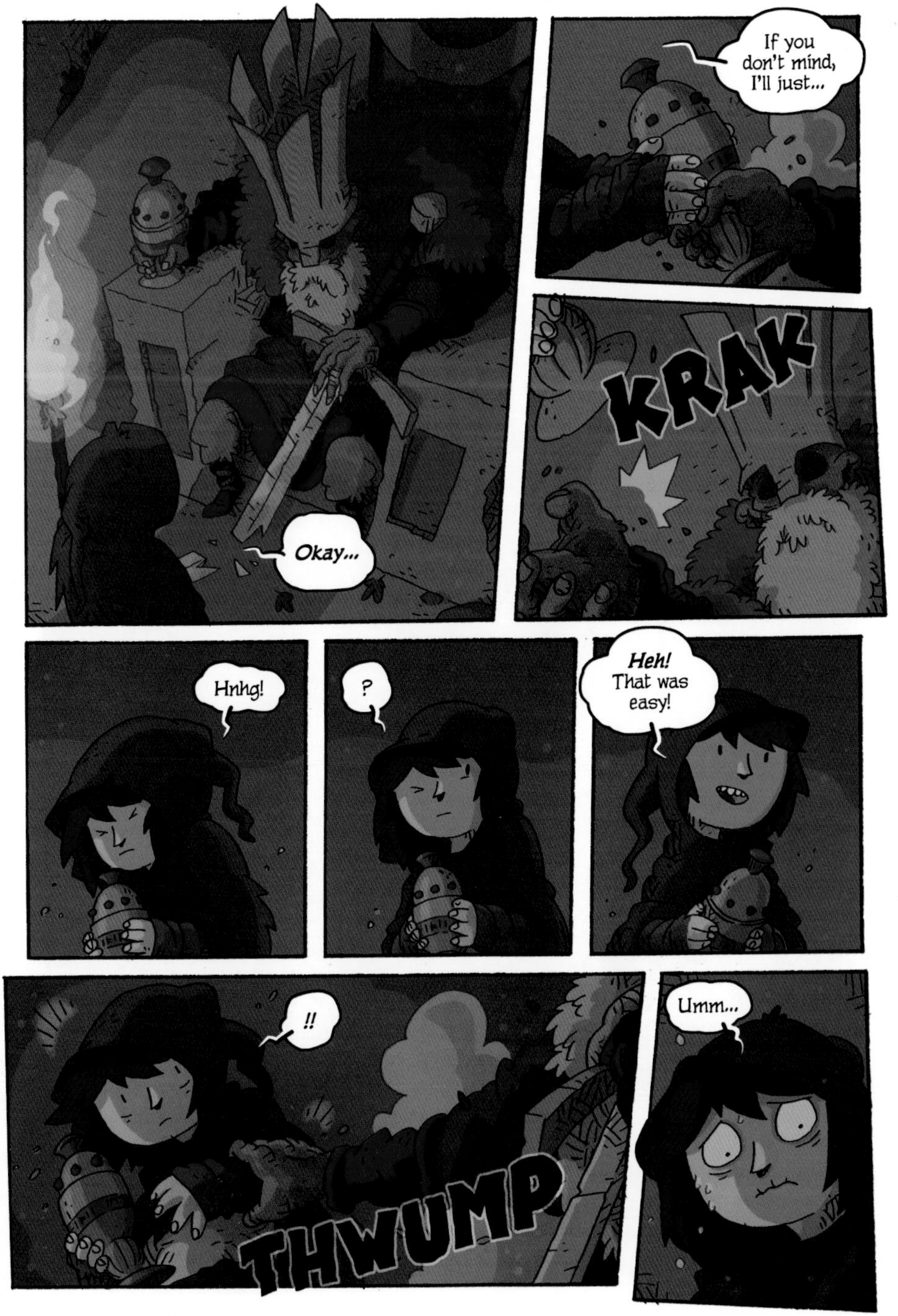

Okay...
If you don't mind, I'll just...
KRAK
Hnhg!
?
Heh! That was easy!
!!
THWUMP
Umm...

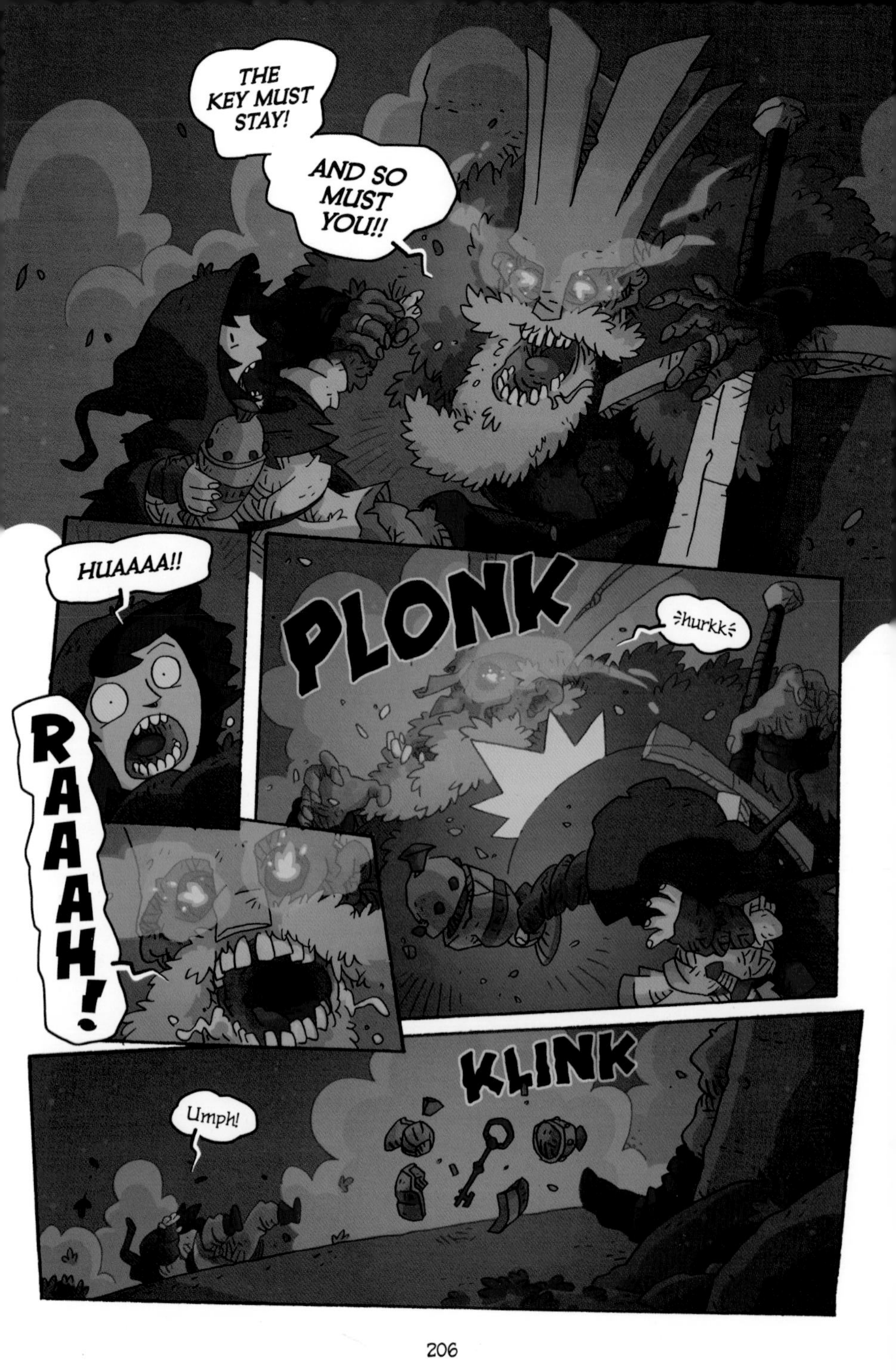
THE KEY MUST STAY!
AND SO MUST YOU!!
HUAAAA!!
RAAAAH!
PLONK
hurkk
KLINK
Umph!

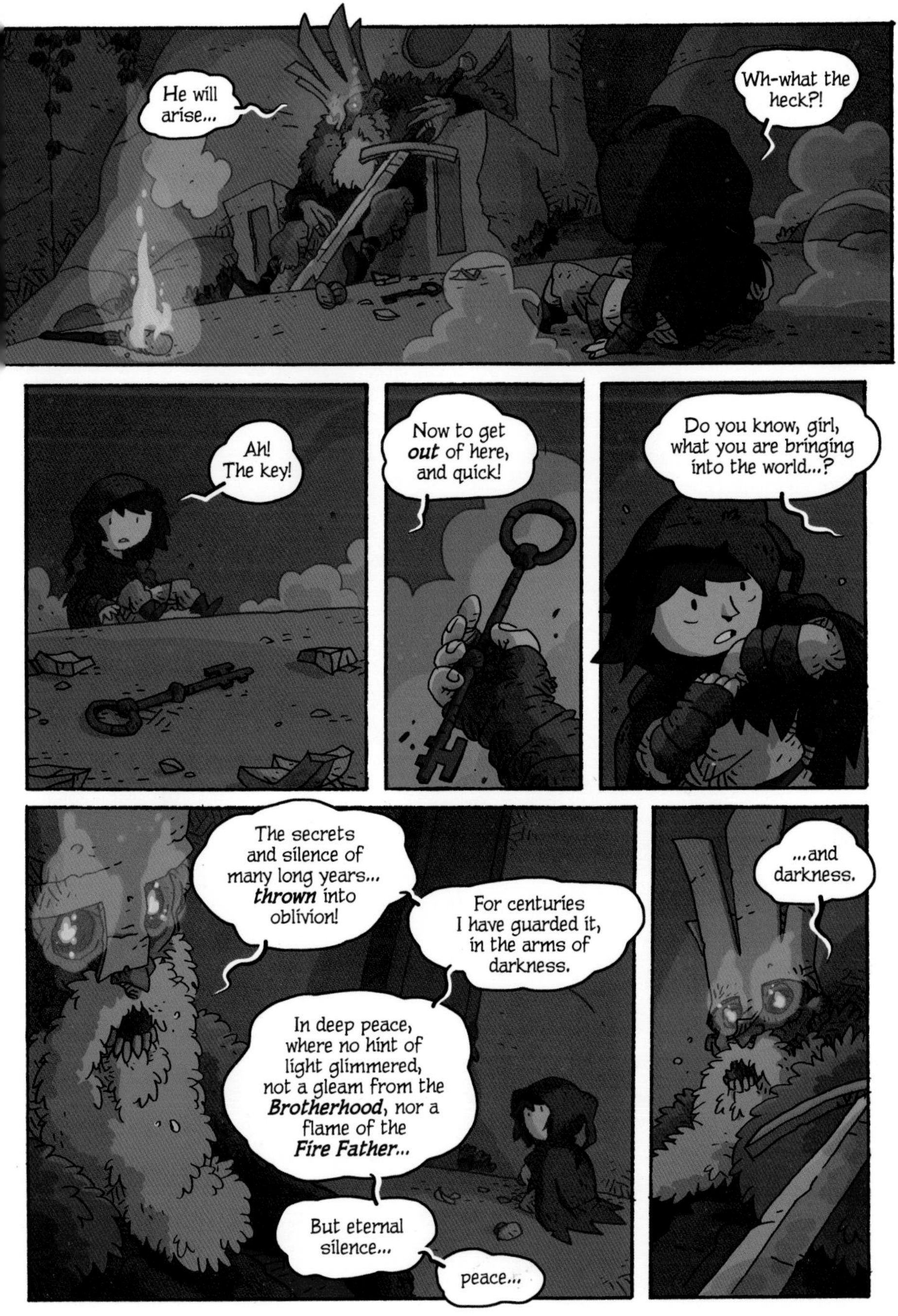
He will arise...
Wh-what the heck?!
Ah! The key!
Now to get *out* of here, and quick!
Do you know, girl, what you are bringing into the world...?
The secrets and silence of many long years... *thrown* into oblivion!
For centuries I have guarded it, in the arms of darkness.
In deep peace, where no hint of light glimmered, not a gleam from the *Brotherhood*, nor a flame of the *Fire Father*...
But eternal silence...
peace...
...and darkness.

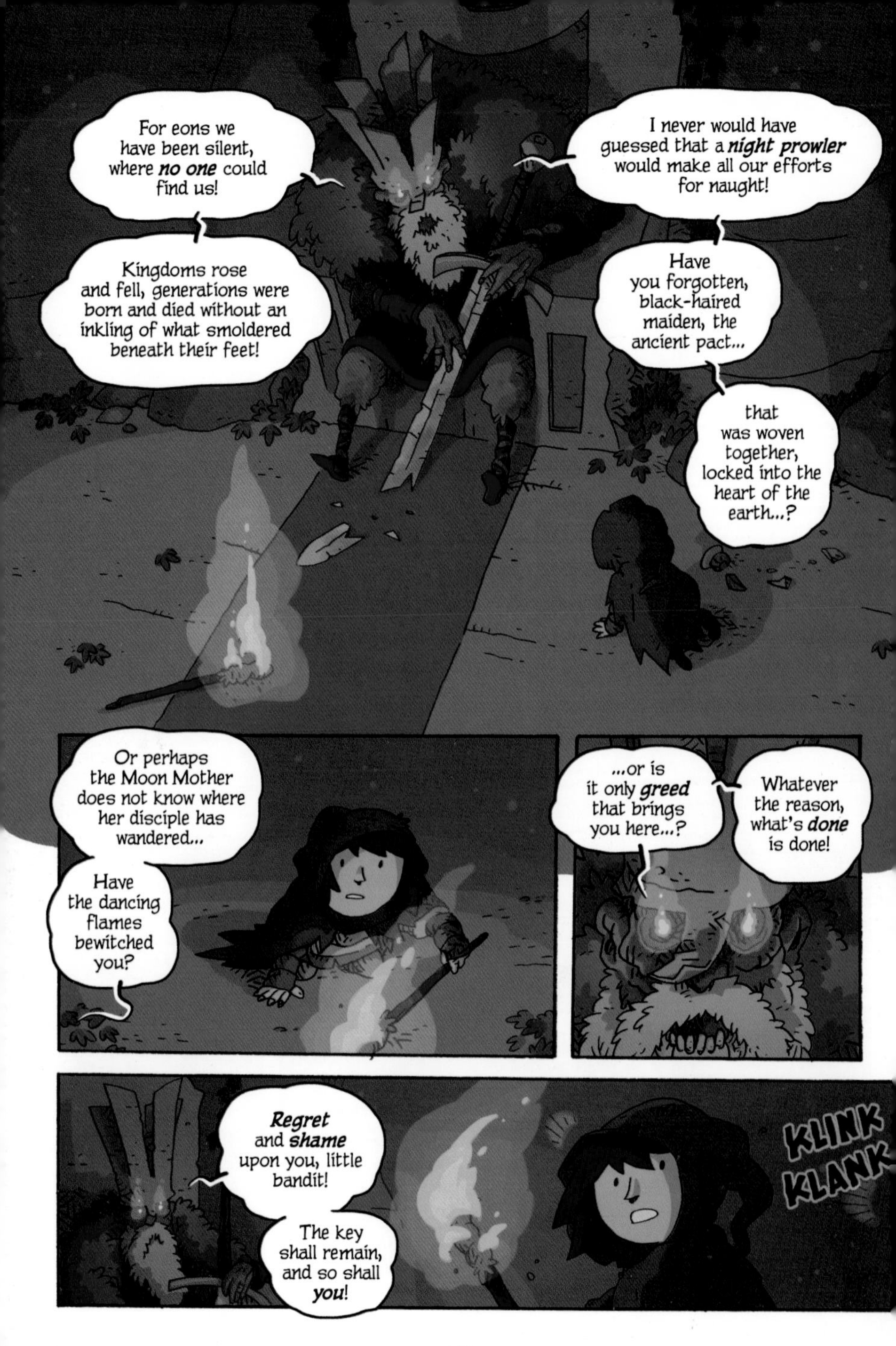
For eons we have been silent, where *no one* could find us!
Kingdoms rose and fell, generations were born and died without an inkling of what smoldered beneath their feet!
I never would have guessed that a *night prowler* would make all our efforts for naught!
Have you forgotten, black-haired maiden, the ancient pact...
that was woven together, locked into the heart of the earth...?
Or perhaps the Moon Mother does not know where her disciple has wandered...
Have the dancing flames bewitched you?
...or is it only *greed* that brings you here...?
Whatever the reason, what's *done* is done!
Regret and *shame* upon you, little bandit!
The key shall remain, and so shall *you*!
KLINK KLANK

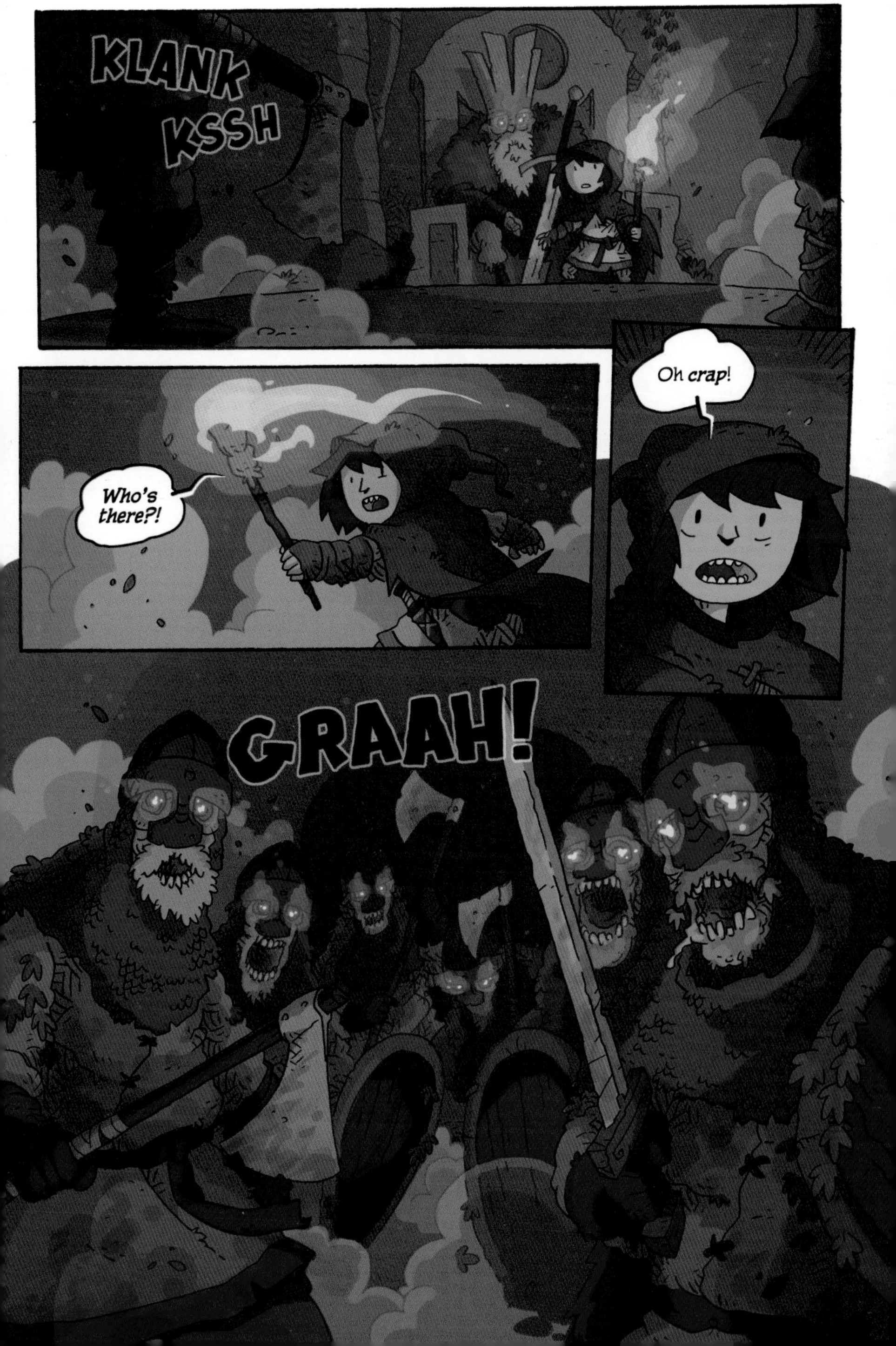
KLANK
KSSH
Who's there?!
Oh crap!
GRAAH!

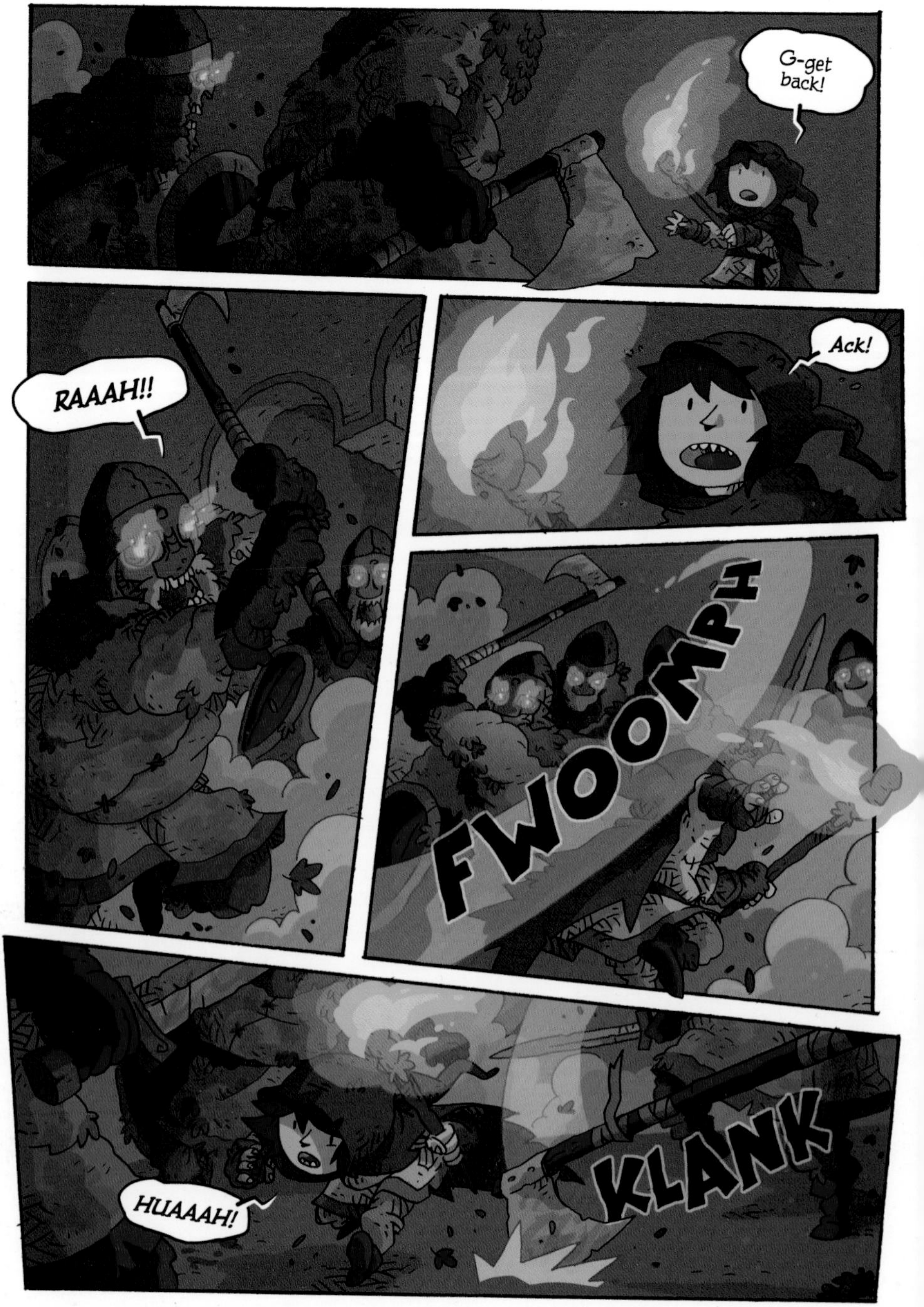
G-get back!
RAAAH!!
Ack!
FWOOMPH
HUAAAH!
KLANK

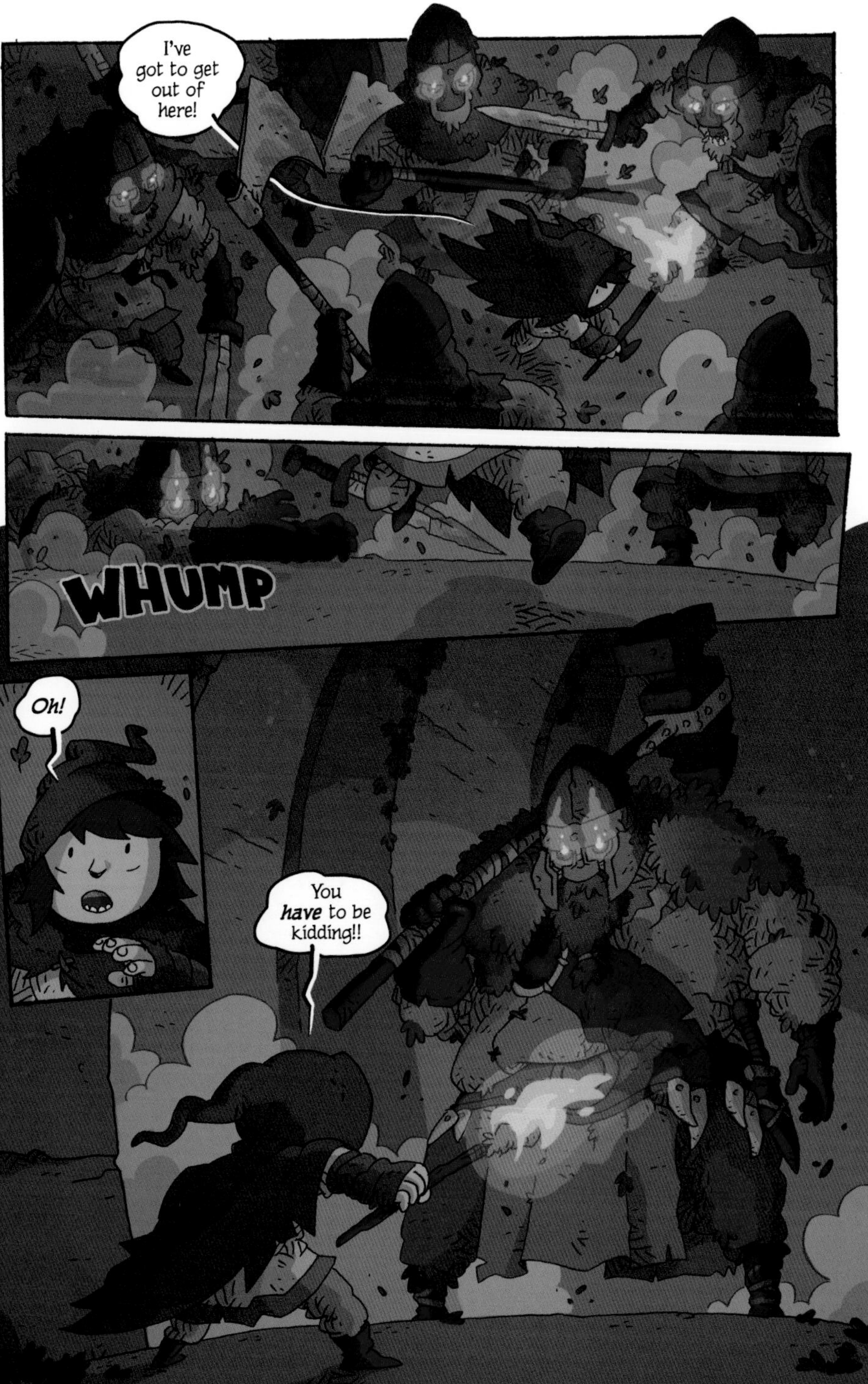
I've got to get out of here!
WHUMP
Oh!
You *have* to be kidding!!

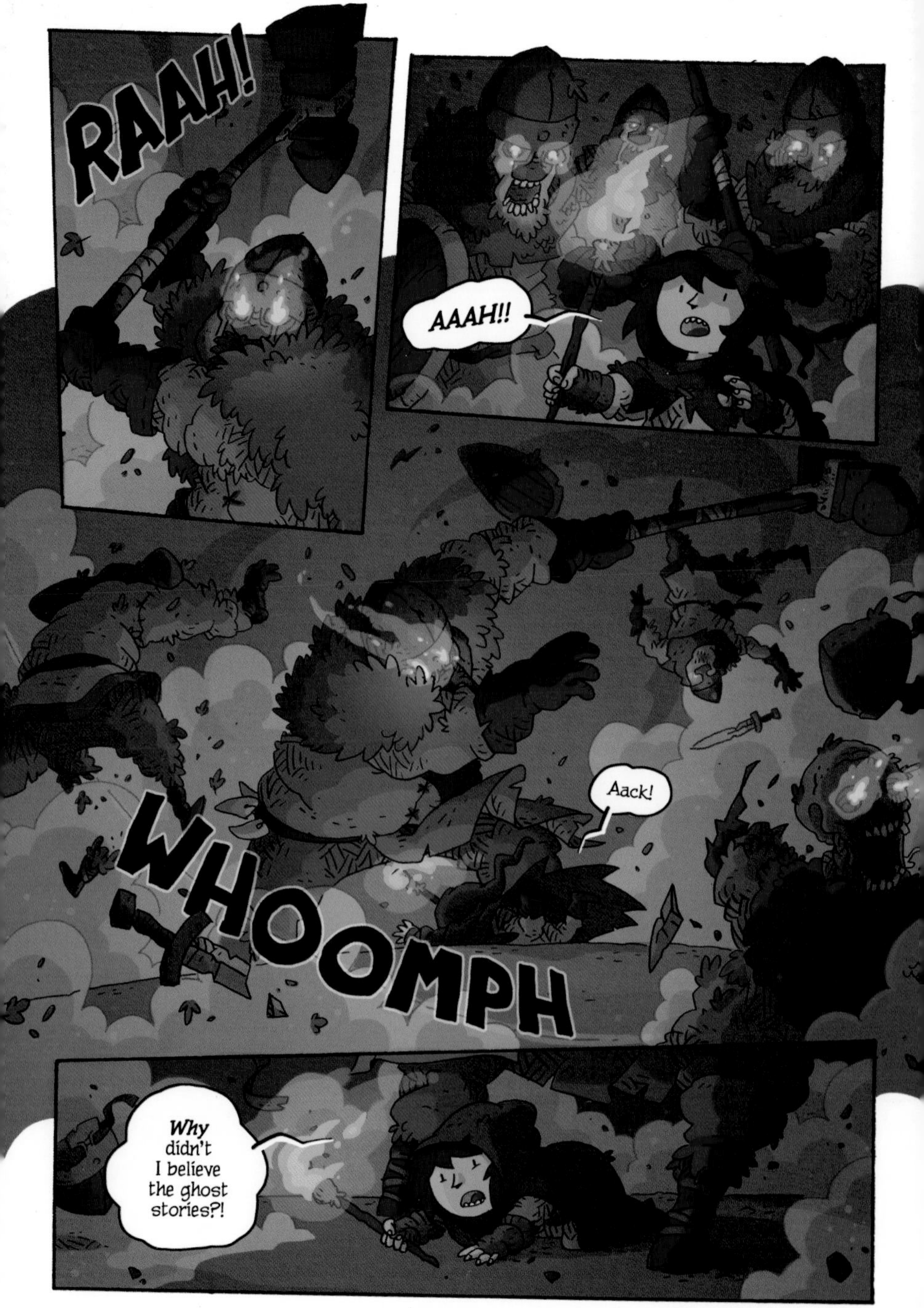
RAAH!
AAAH!!
Aack!
WHOOMPH
Why didn't I believe the ghost stories?!

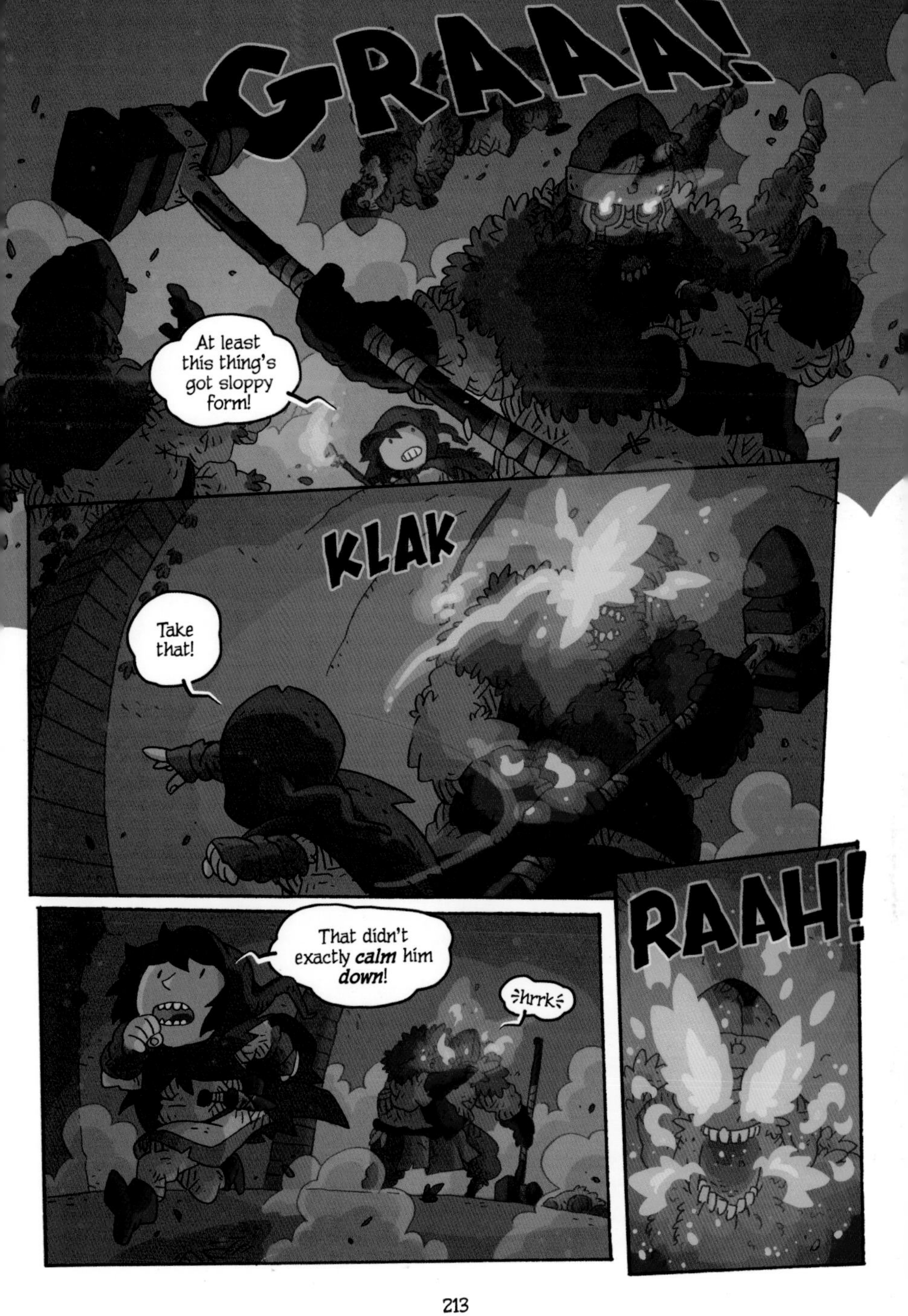
GRAAA!
At least this thing's got sloppy form!
KLAK
Take that!
That didn't exactly *calm* him *down*!
hrrk
RAAH!

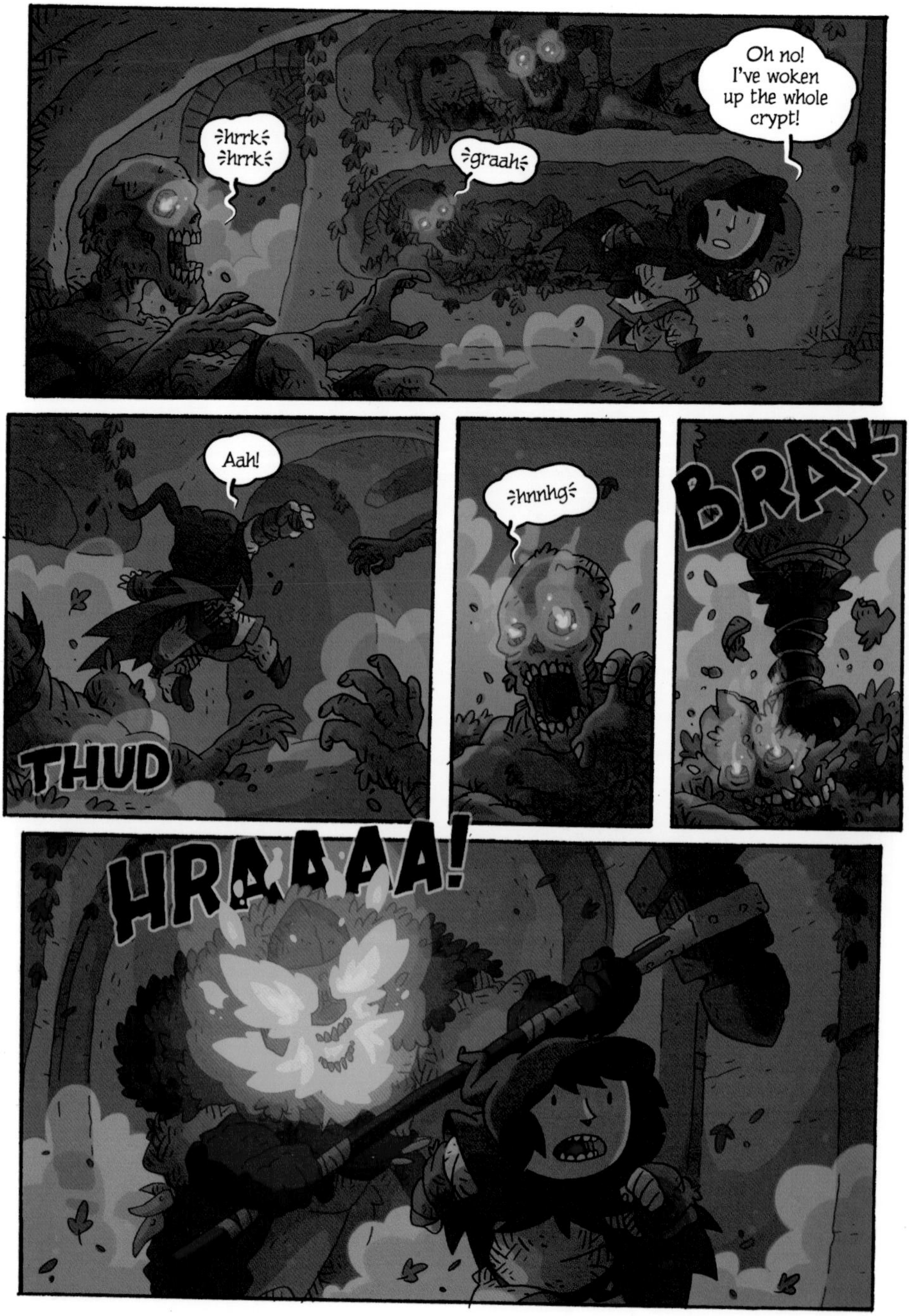
hrrk hrrk
graah
Oh no! I've woken up the whole crypt!
Aah!
THUD
hnnhg
BRAK
HRAAAA!

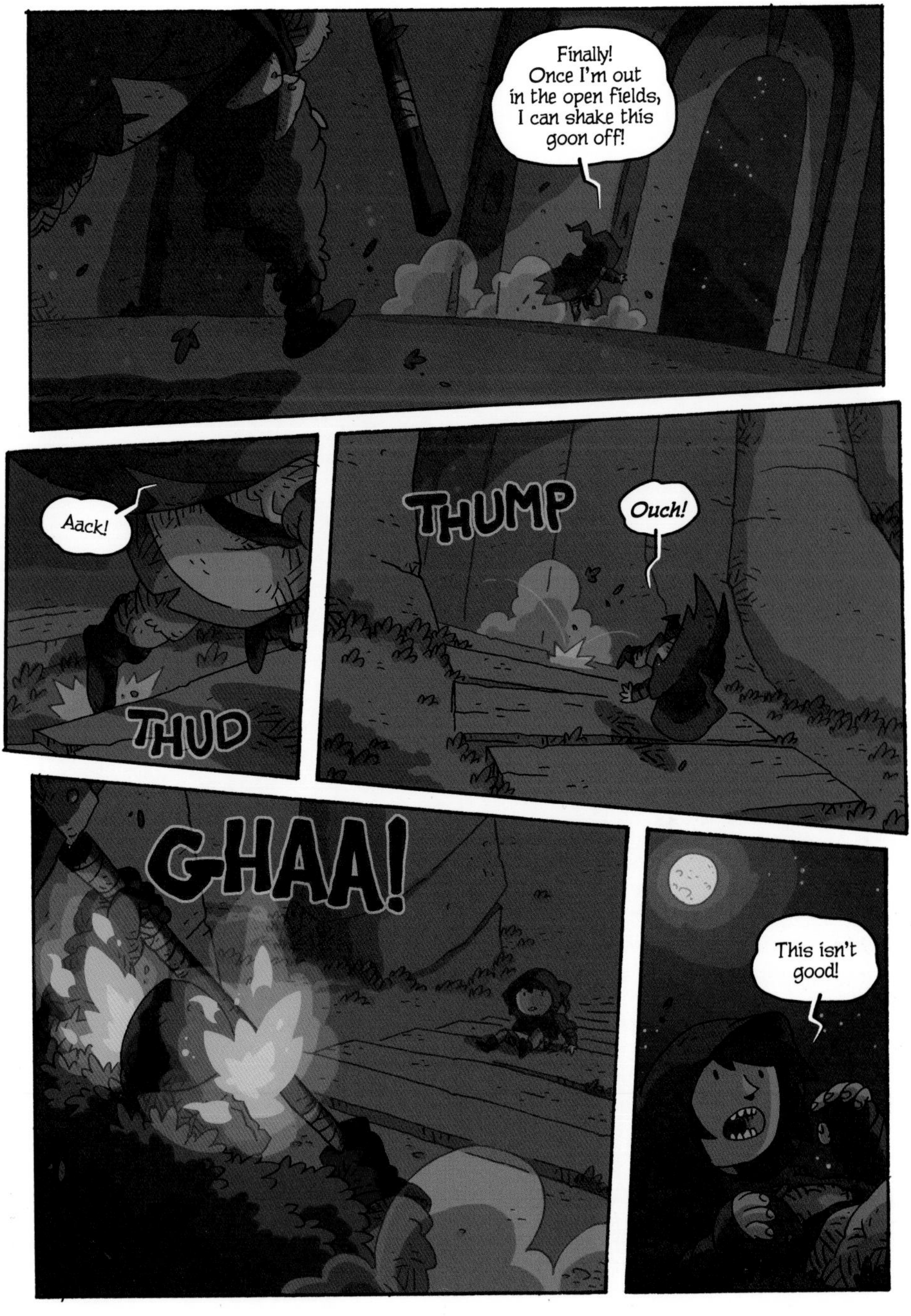
Finally! Once I'm out in the open fields, I can shake this goon off!
Aack!
THUD
THUMP
Ouch!
GHAA!
This isn't good!

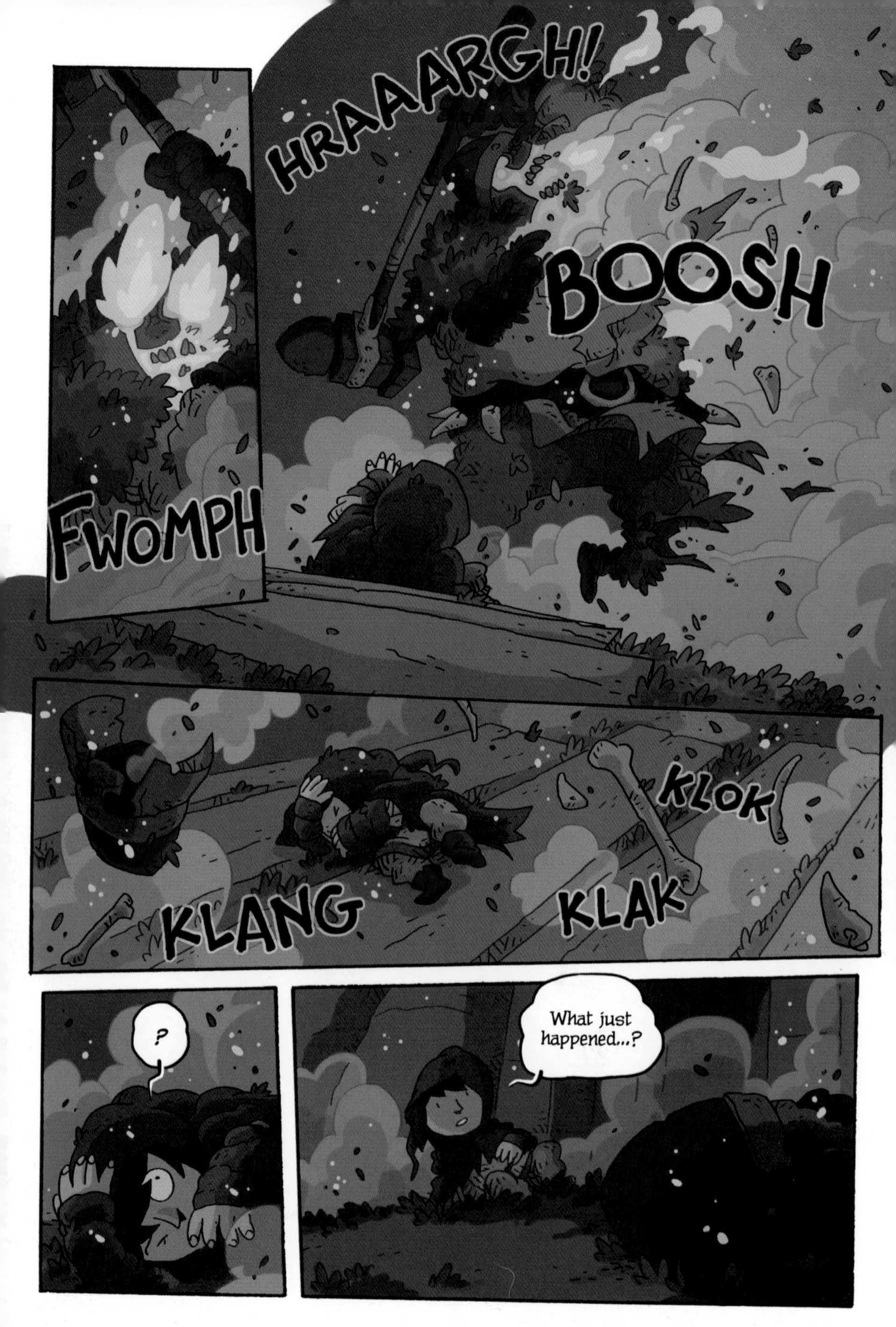
HRAAARGH!
FWOMPH
BOOSH
KLOK
KLANG
KLAK
?
What just happened...?

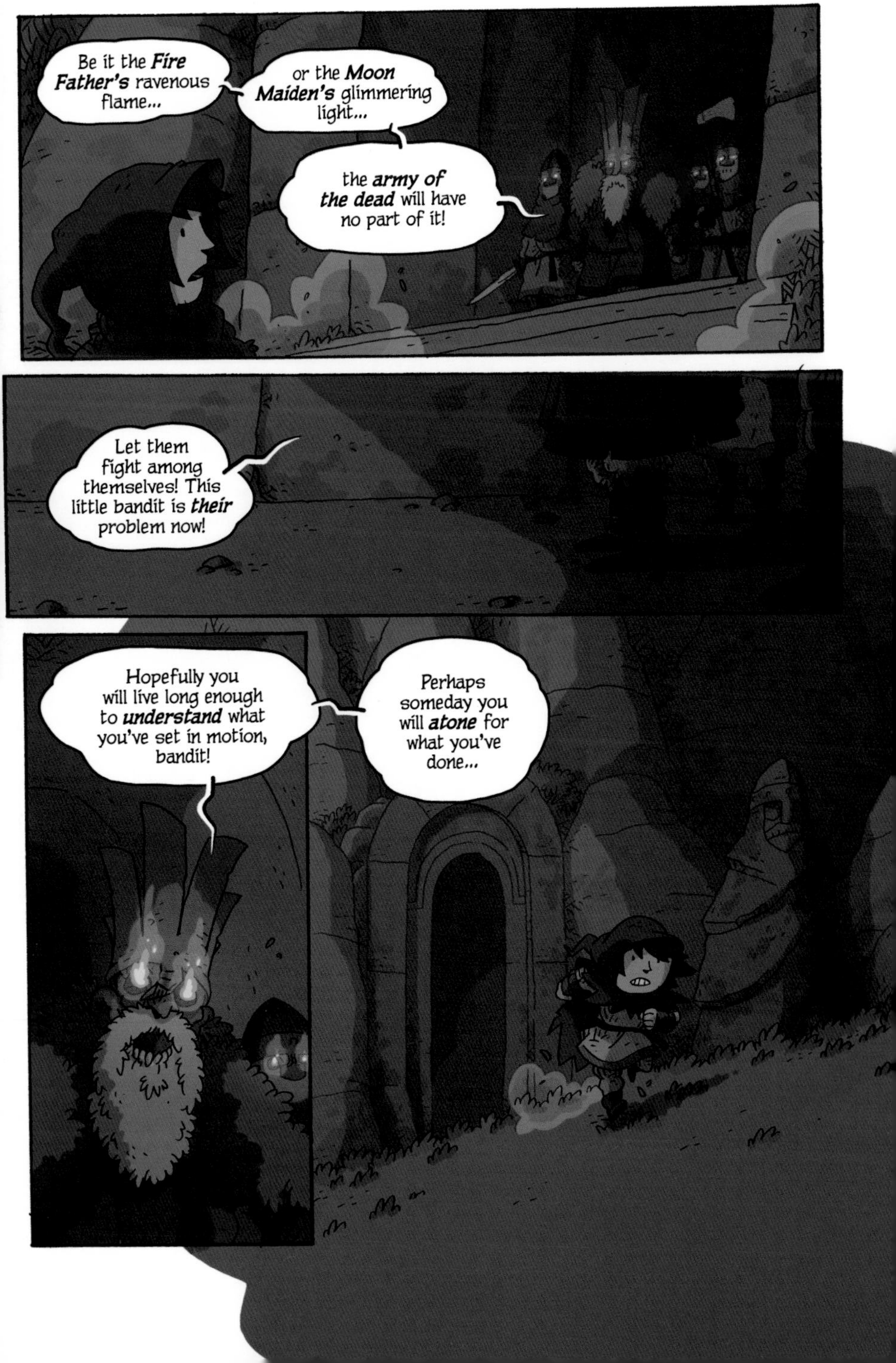
Be it the Fire Father's ravenous flame...
or the Moon Maiden's glimmering light...
the army of the dead will have no part of it!
Let them fight among themselves! This little bandit is their problem now!
Hopefully you will live long enough to understand what you've set in motion, bandit!
Perhaps someday you will atone for what you've done...

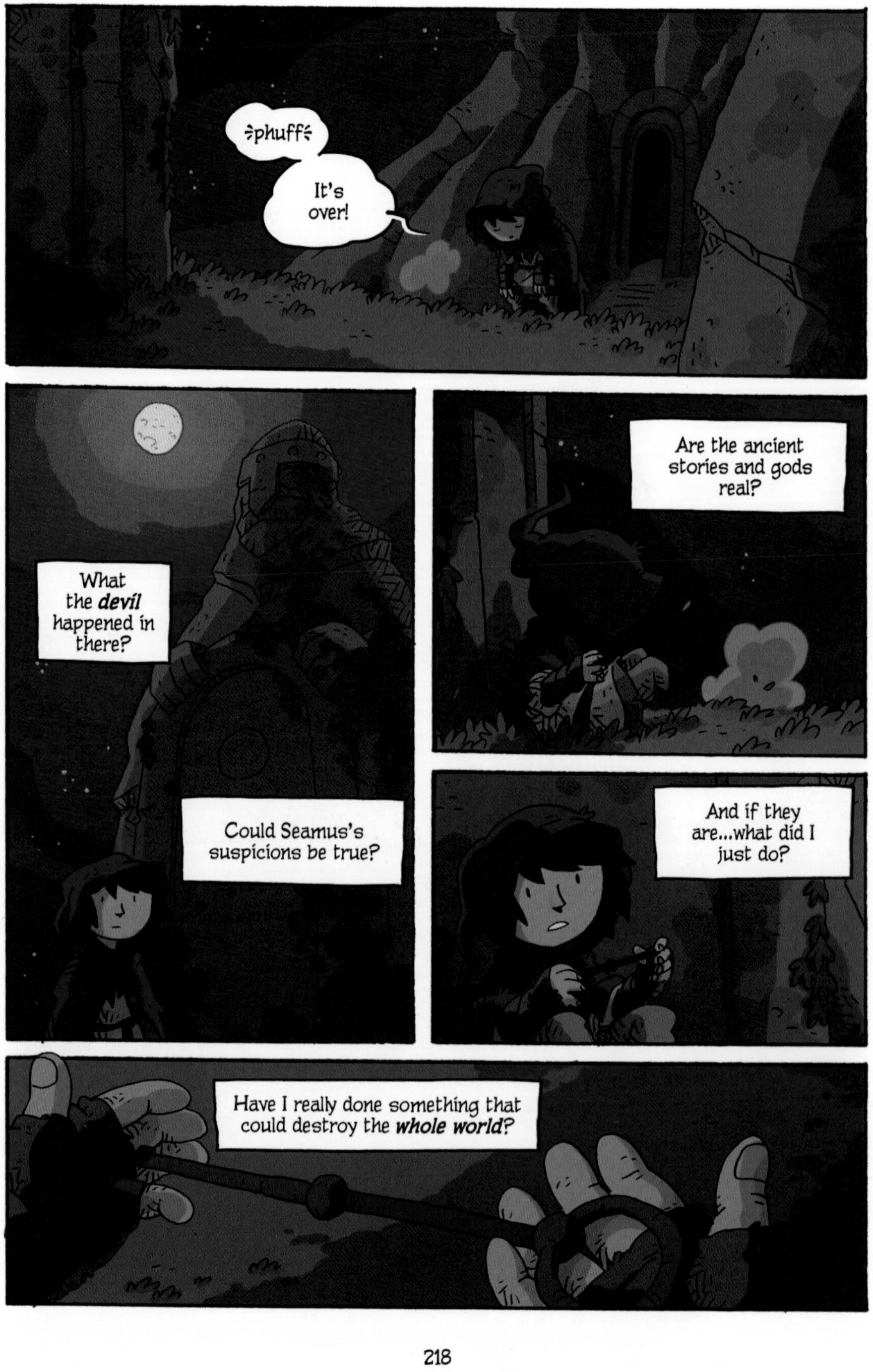

phuff
It's over!
What the *devil* happened in there?
Could Seamus's suspicions be true?
Are the ancient stories and gods real?
And if they are...what did I just do?
Have I really done something that could destroy the *whole world*?

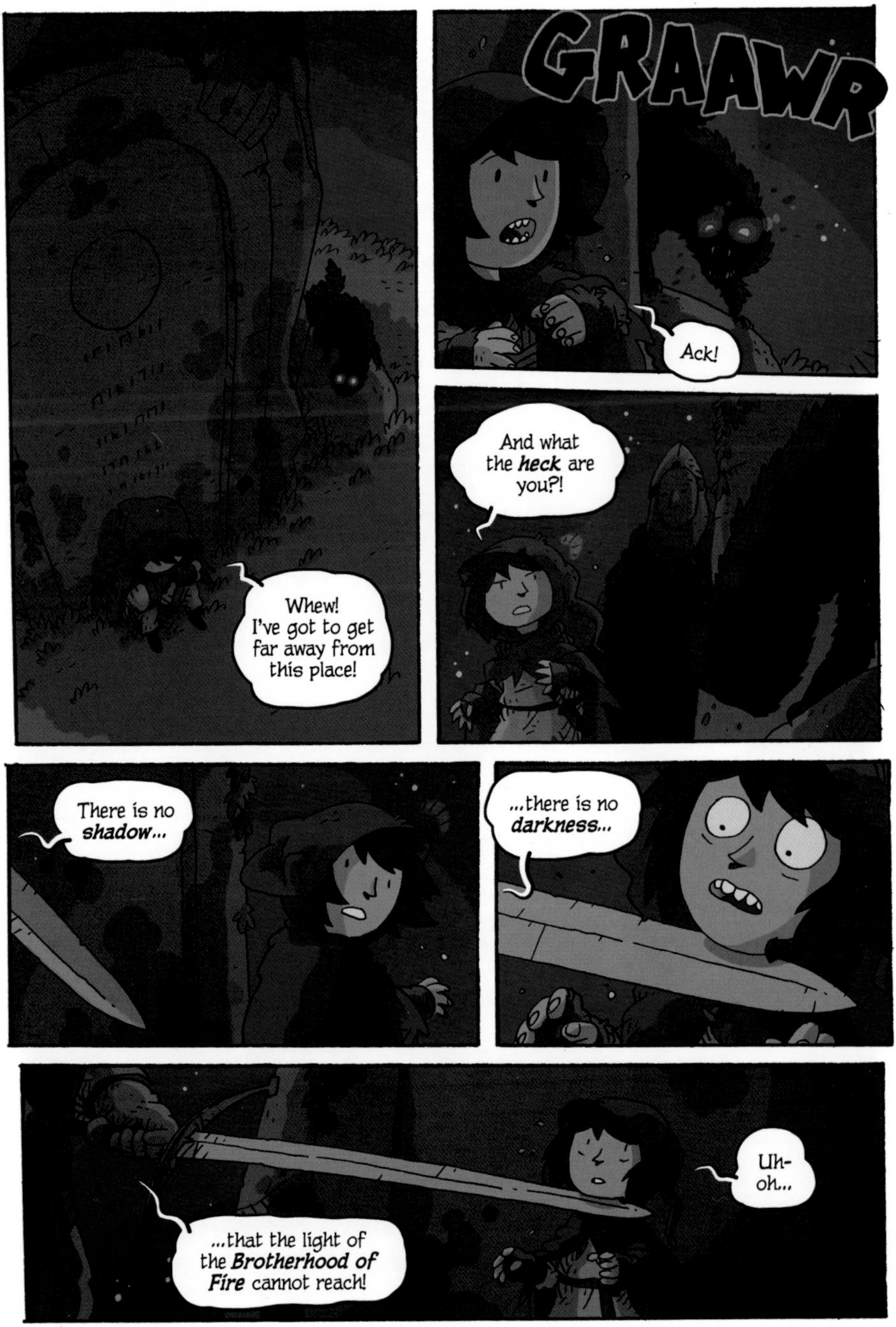

Whew!
I've got to get far away from this place!
GRAAWR
Ack!
And what the heck are you?!
There is no shadow...
...there is no darkness...
...that the light of the Brotherhood of Fire cannot reach!
Uh-oh...

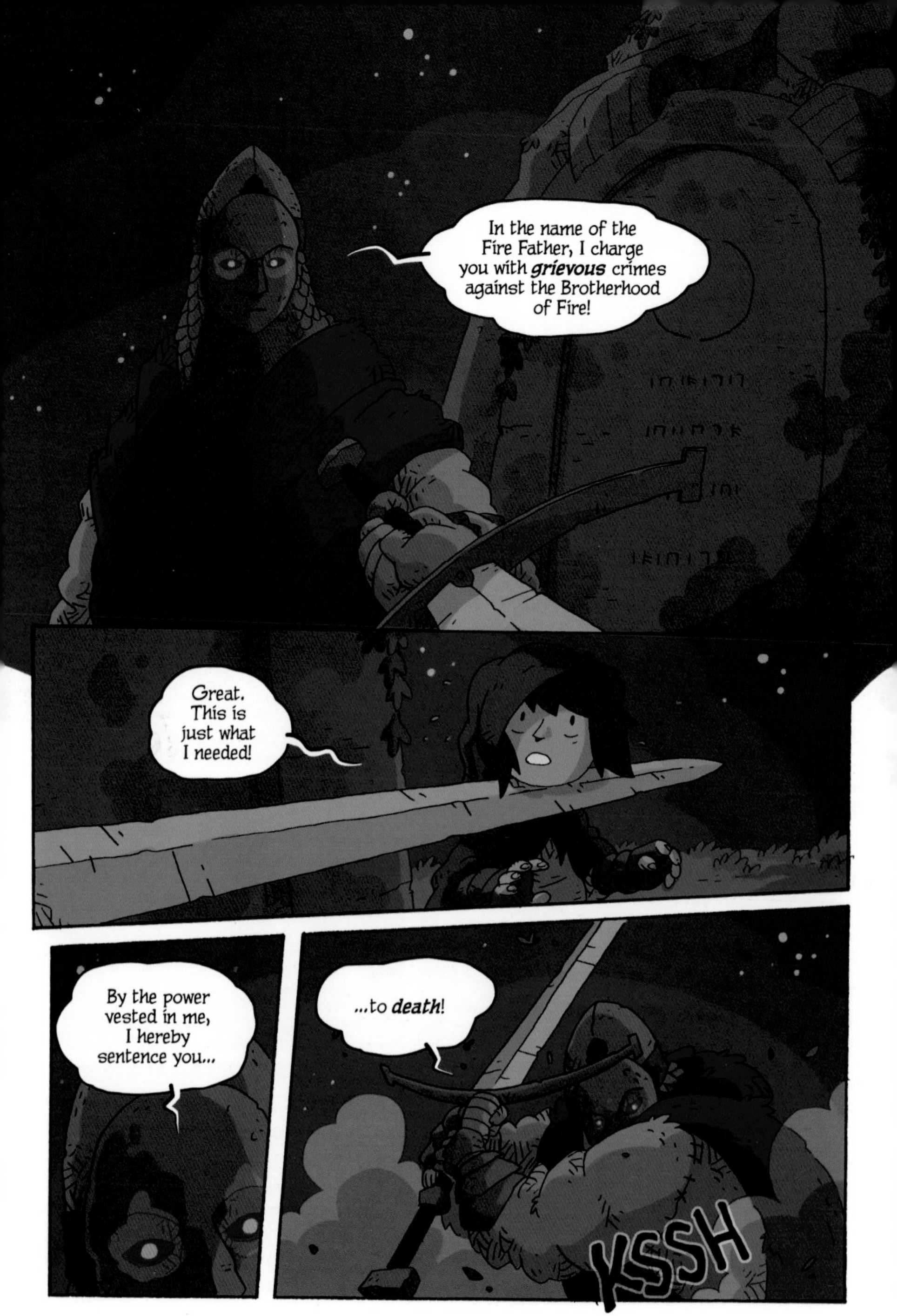
In the name of the Fire Father, I charge you with **grievous** crimes against the Brotherhood of Fire!
Great. This is just what I needed!
By the power vested in me, I hereby sentence you...
...to **death**!
KSSH

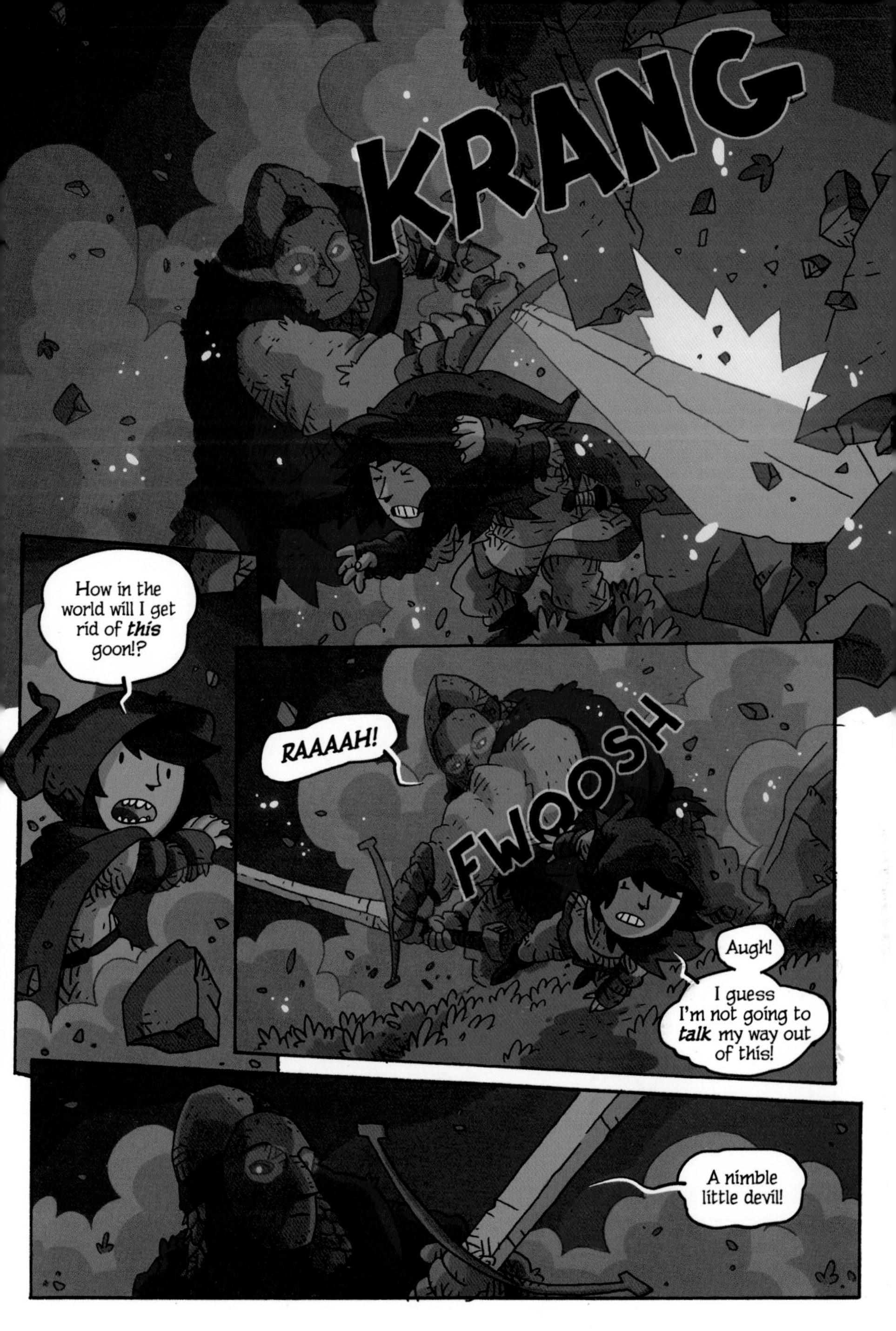
KRANG
How in the world will I get rid of *this* goon!?
RAAAAH!
FWOOSH
Augh!
I guess I'm not going to *talk* my way out of this!
A nimble little devil!

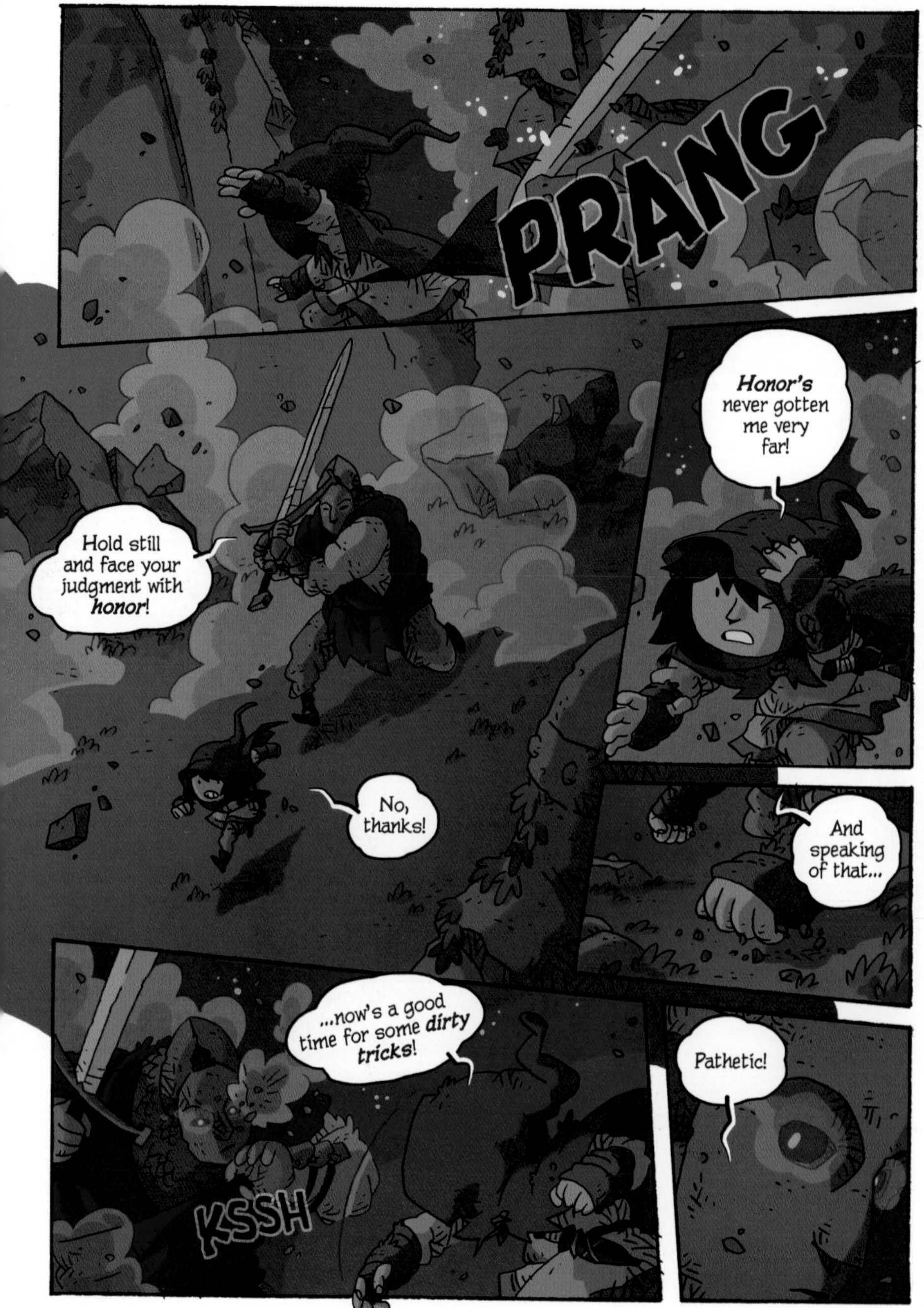
PRANG
Hold still and face your judgment with honor!
No, thanks!
Honor's never gotten me very far!
And speaking of that...
...now's a good time for some dirty tricks!
KSSH
Pathetic!

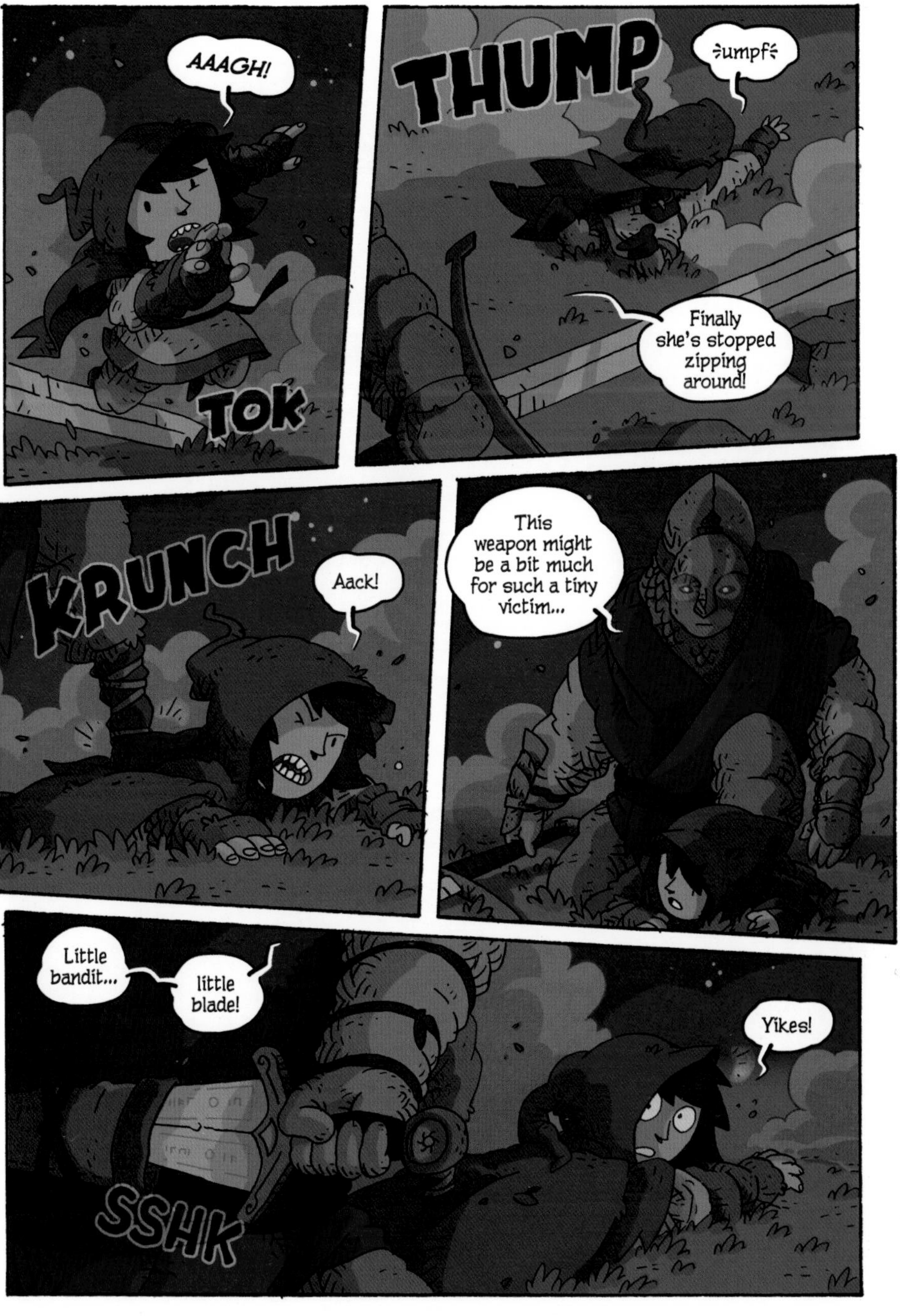
AAAGH!
TOK
THUMP
umpf
Finally she's stopped zipping around!
KRUNCH
Aack!
This weapon might be a bit much for such a tiny victim...
Little bandit...
little blade!
SSHK
Yikes!

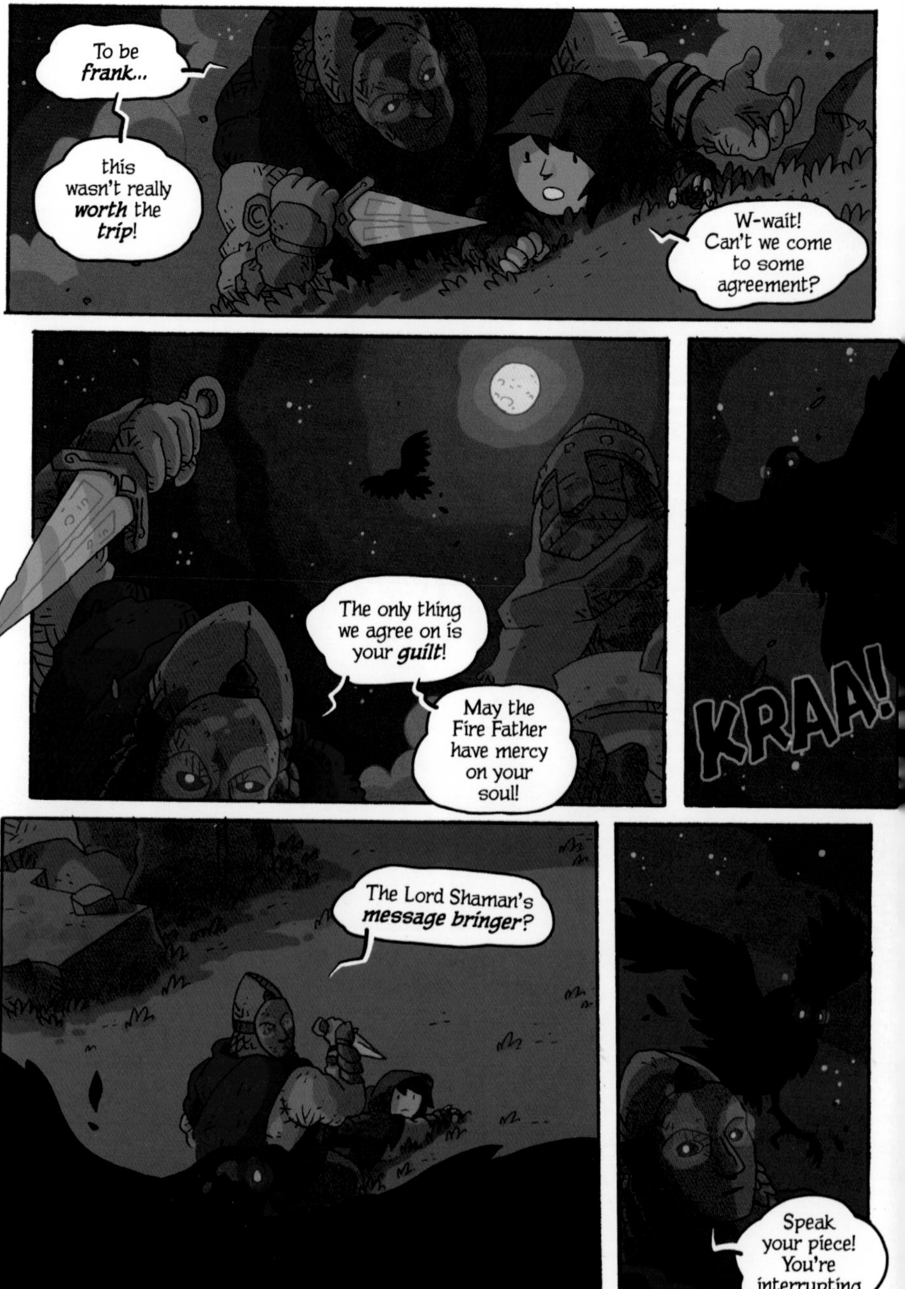
To be *frank*...
this wasn't really *worth* the *trip*!
W-wait! Can't we come to some agreement?
The only thing we agree on is your *guilt*!
May the Fire Father have mercy on your soul!
KRAA!
The Lord Shaman's *message bringer*?
Speak your piece! You're interrupting me!

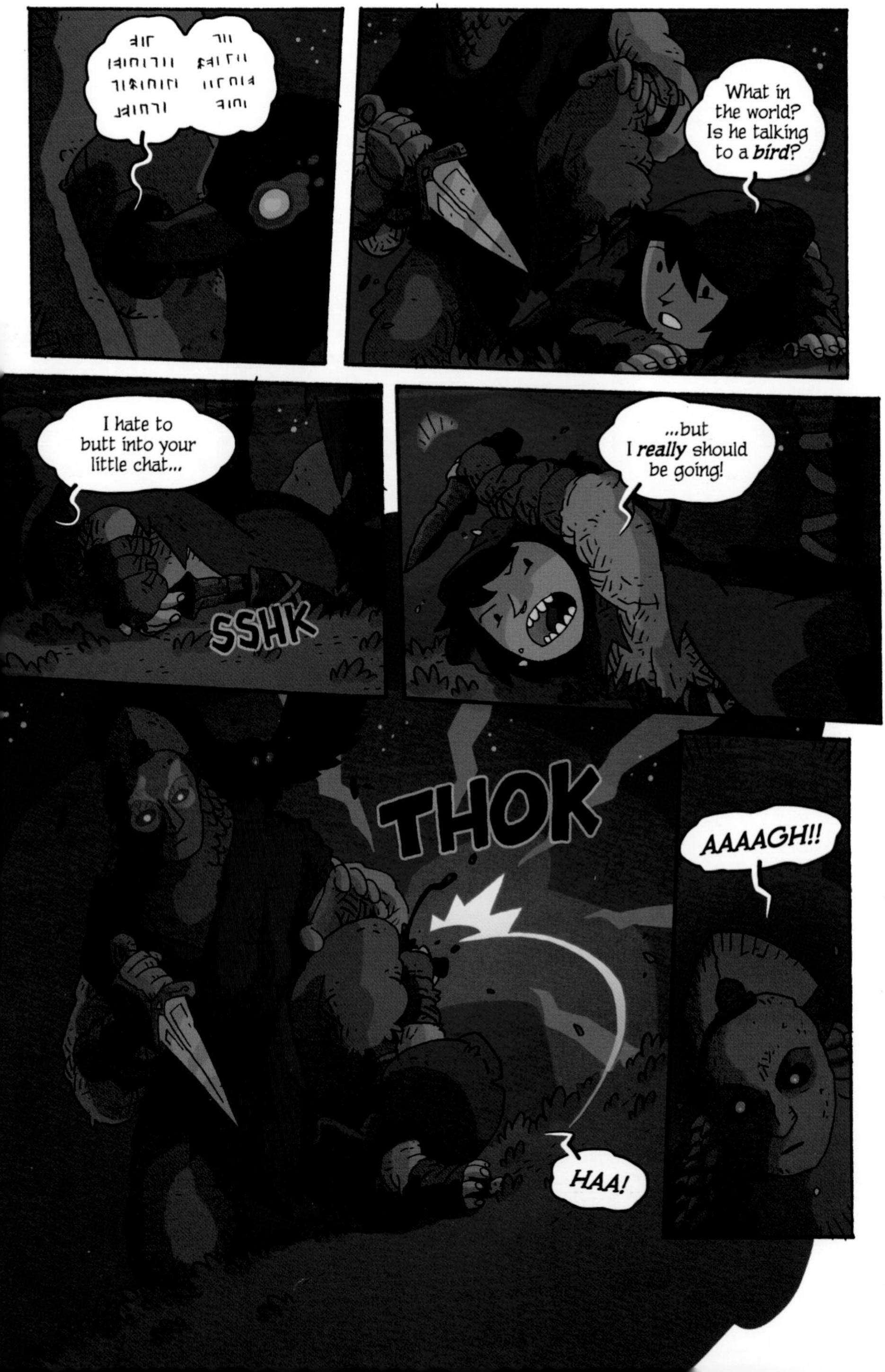
What in the world? Is he talking to a *bird*?
I hate to butt into your little chat...
SSHK
...but I *really* should be going!
THOK
AAAAGH!!
HAA!

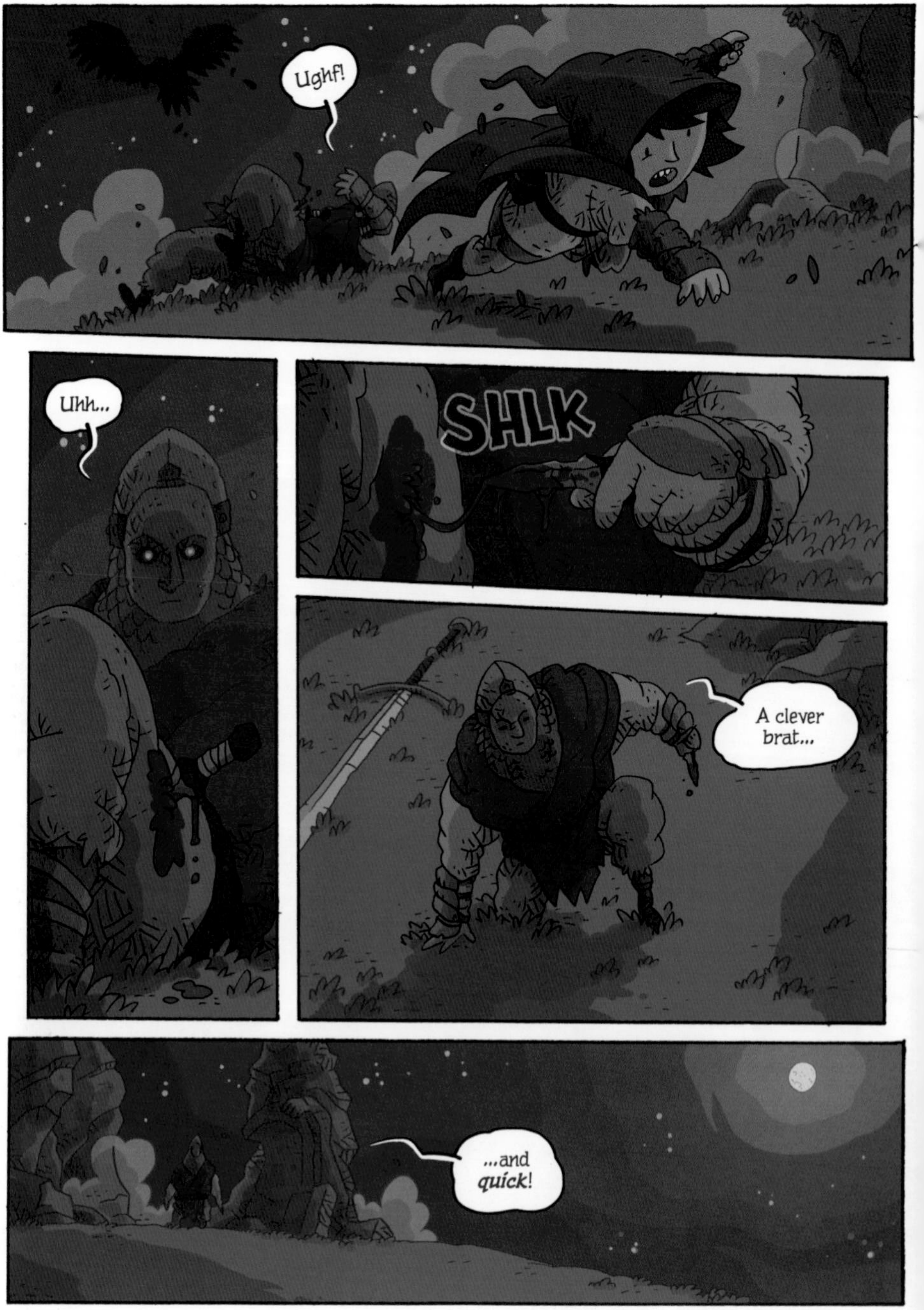
Ughf!
Uhh...
SHLK
A clever brat...
...and quick!

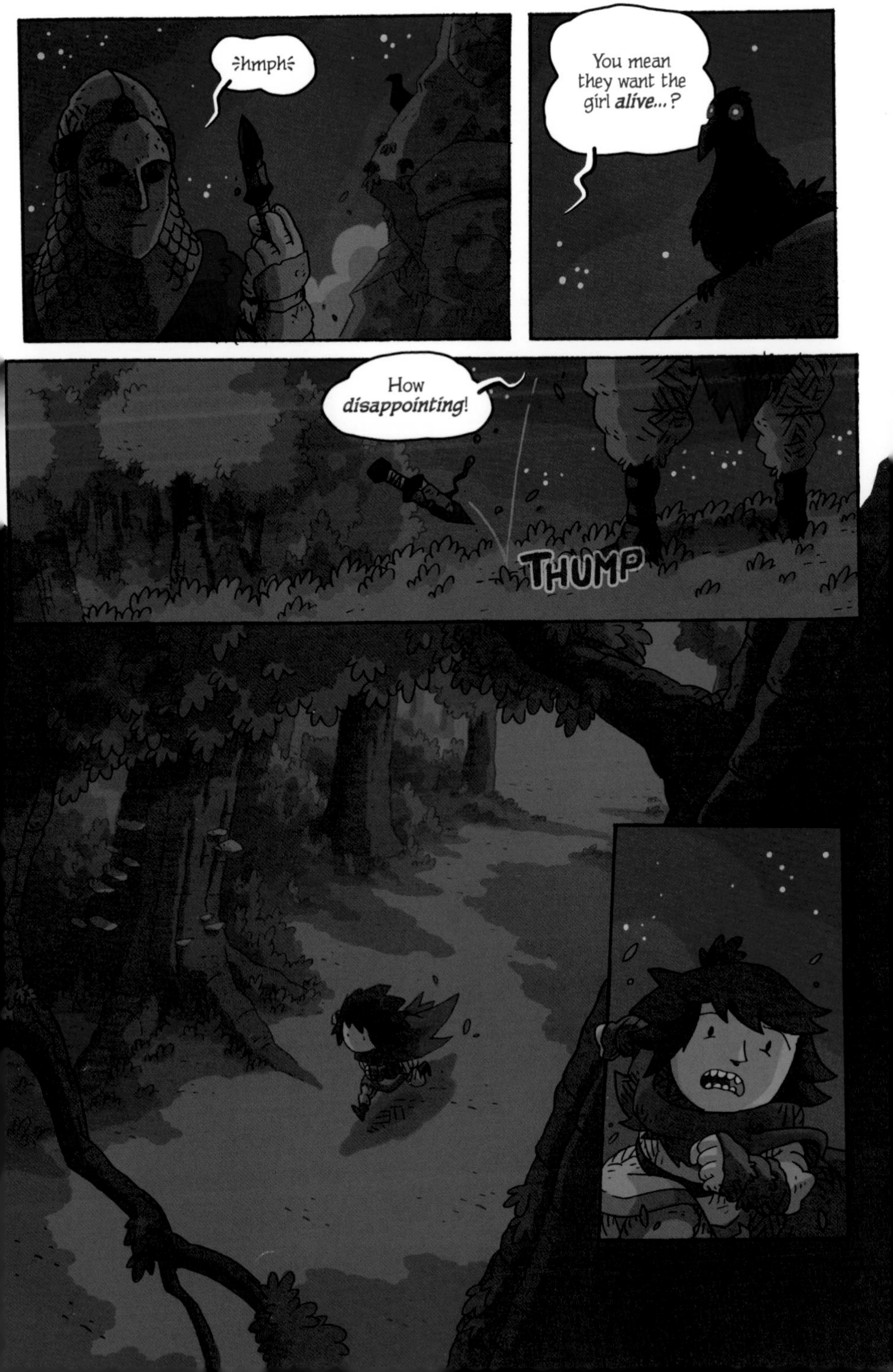

hmph
You mean they want the girl *alive*...?
How *disappointing*!
THUMP

But the day shall come,
When the keys are found,
By a thief who will steal them away,
And Ithiel shall arise,
And many men shall die,
On that fateful day.

7

The King's Treasure

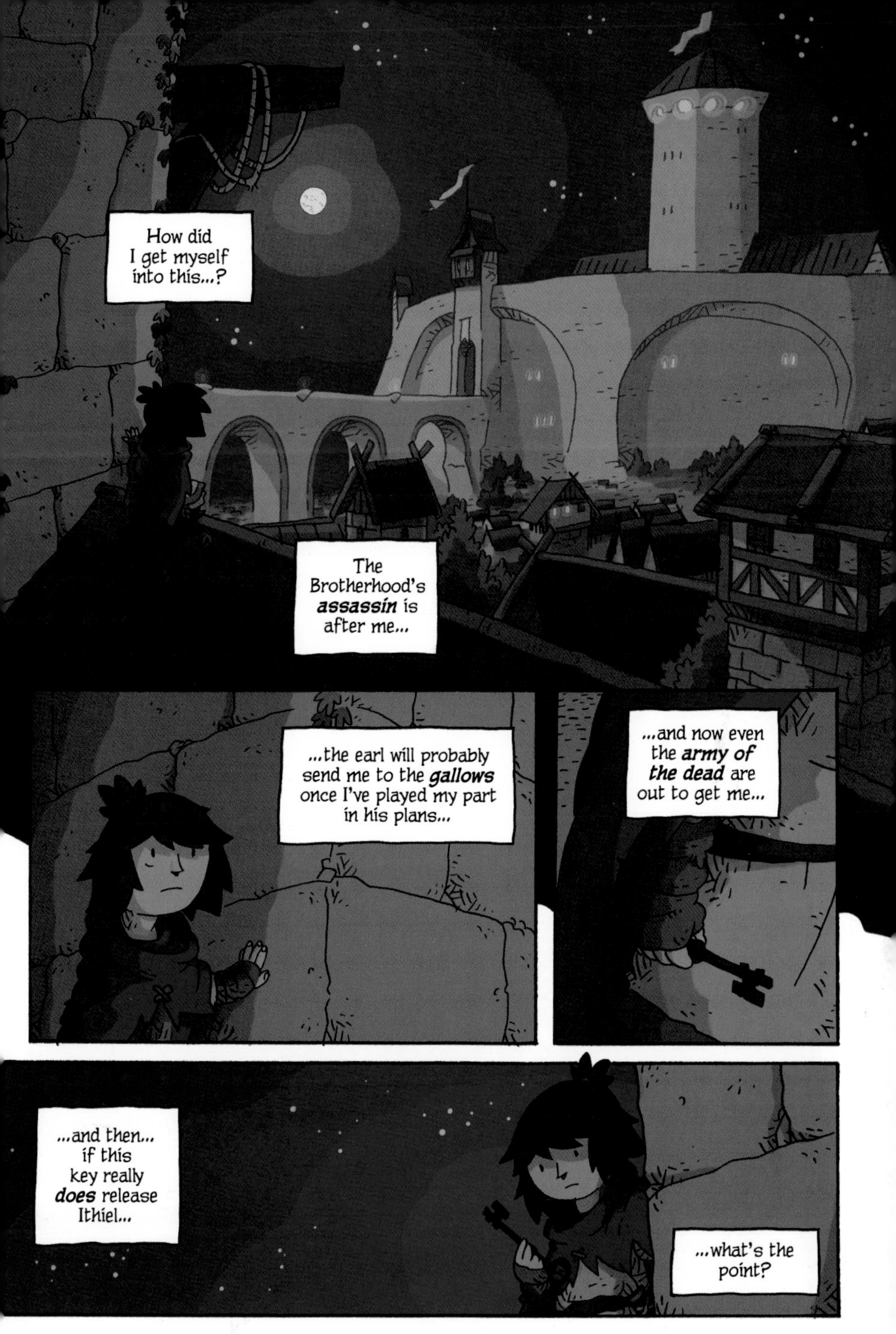
How did I get myself into this...?
The Brotherhood's **assassin** is after me...
...the earl will probably send me to the **gallows** once I've played my part in his plans...
...and now even the **army of the dead** are out to get me...
...and then... if this key really **does** release Ithiel...
...what's the point?

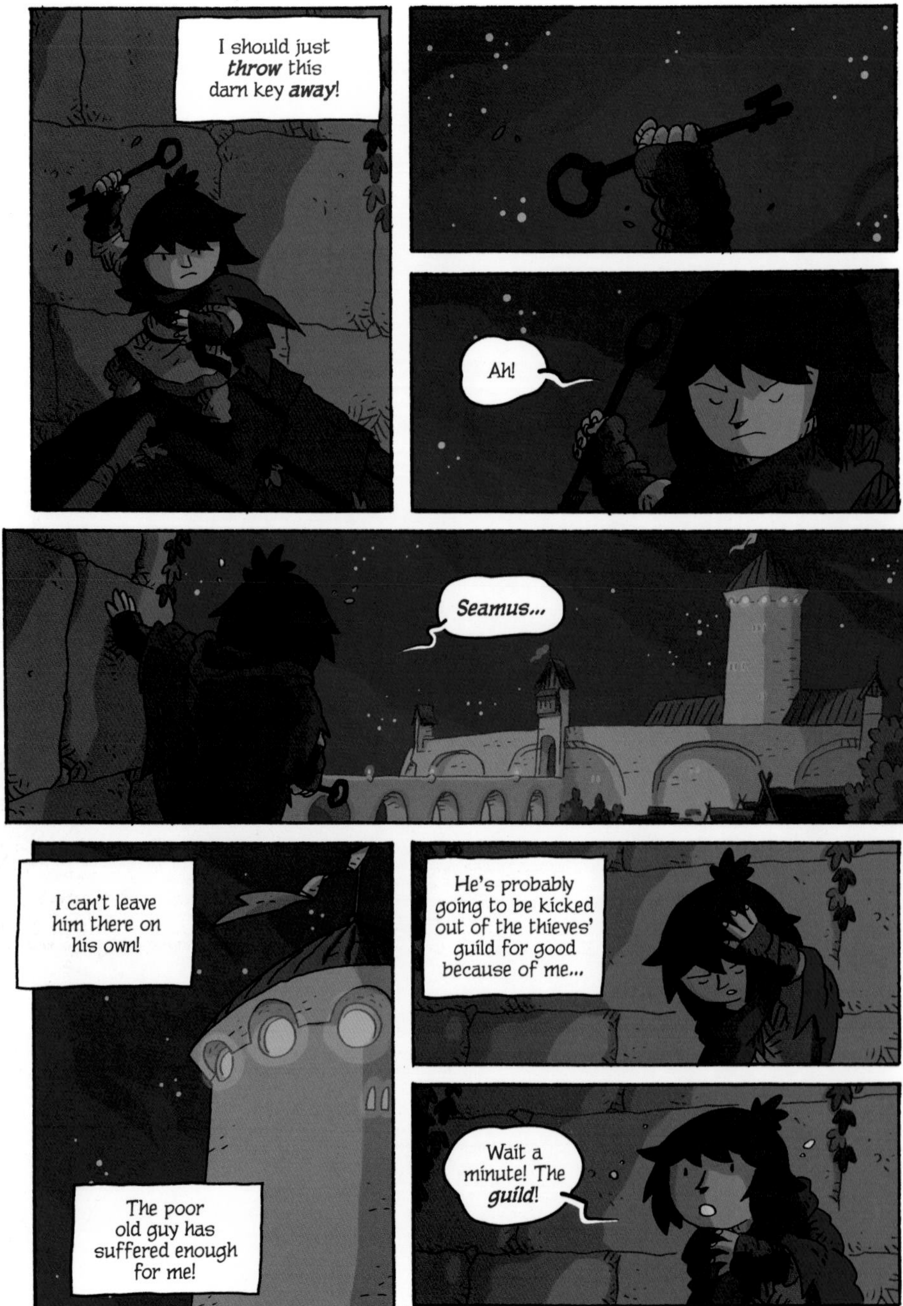
I should just *throw* this darn key *away*!
Ah!
Seamus...
I can't leave him there on his own!
The poor old guy has suffered enough for me!
He's probably going to be kicked out of the thieves' guild for good because of me...
Wait a minute! The *guild*!

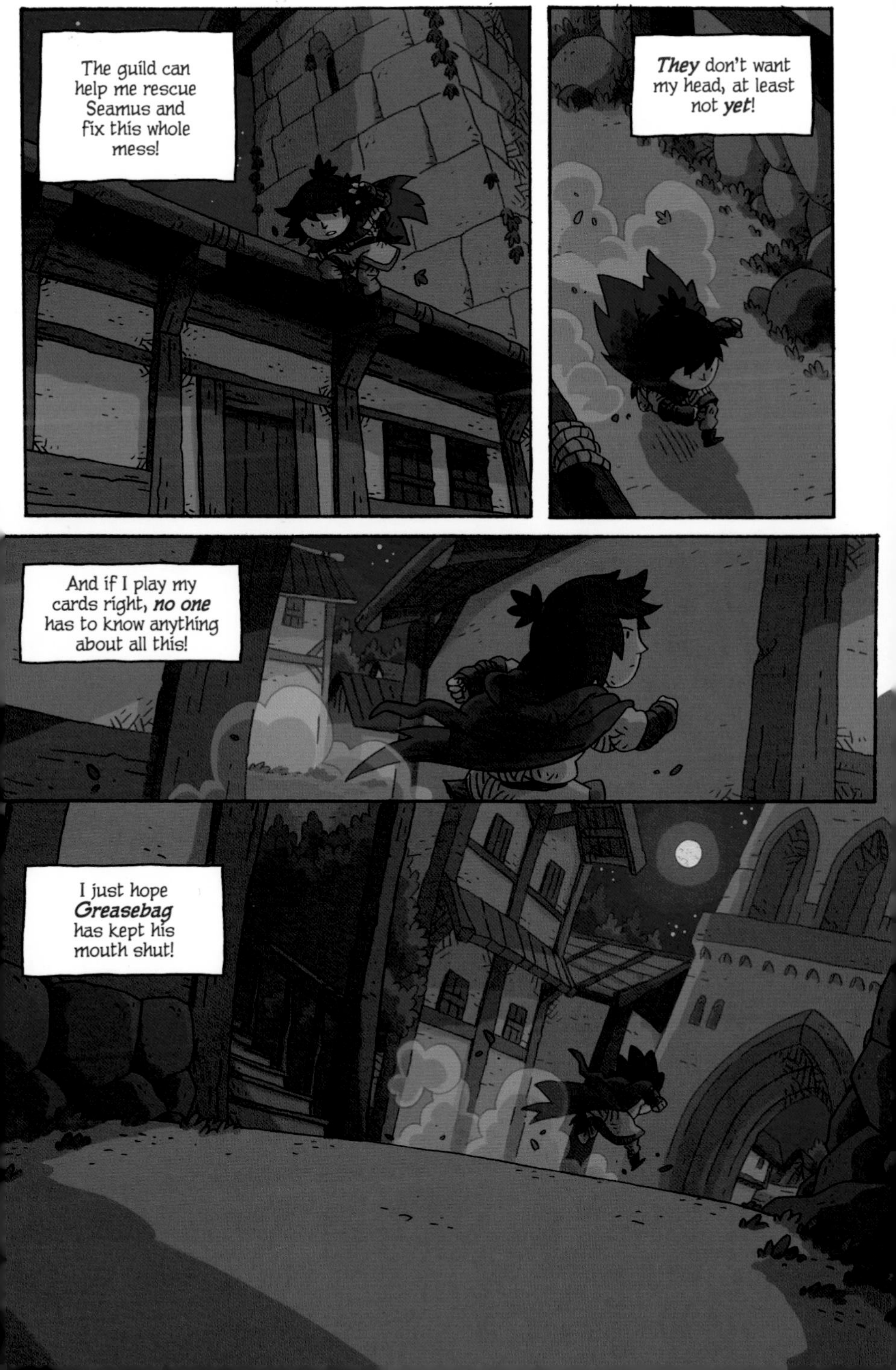
The guild can help me rescue Seamus and fix this whole mess!
They don't want my head, at least not ***yet***!
And if I play my cards right, ***no one*** has to know anything about all this!
I just hope ***Greasebag*** has kept his mouth shut!

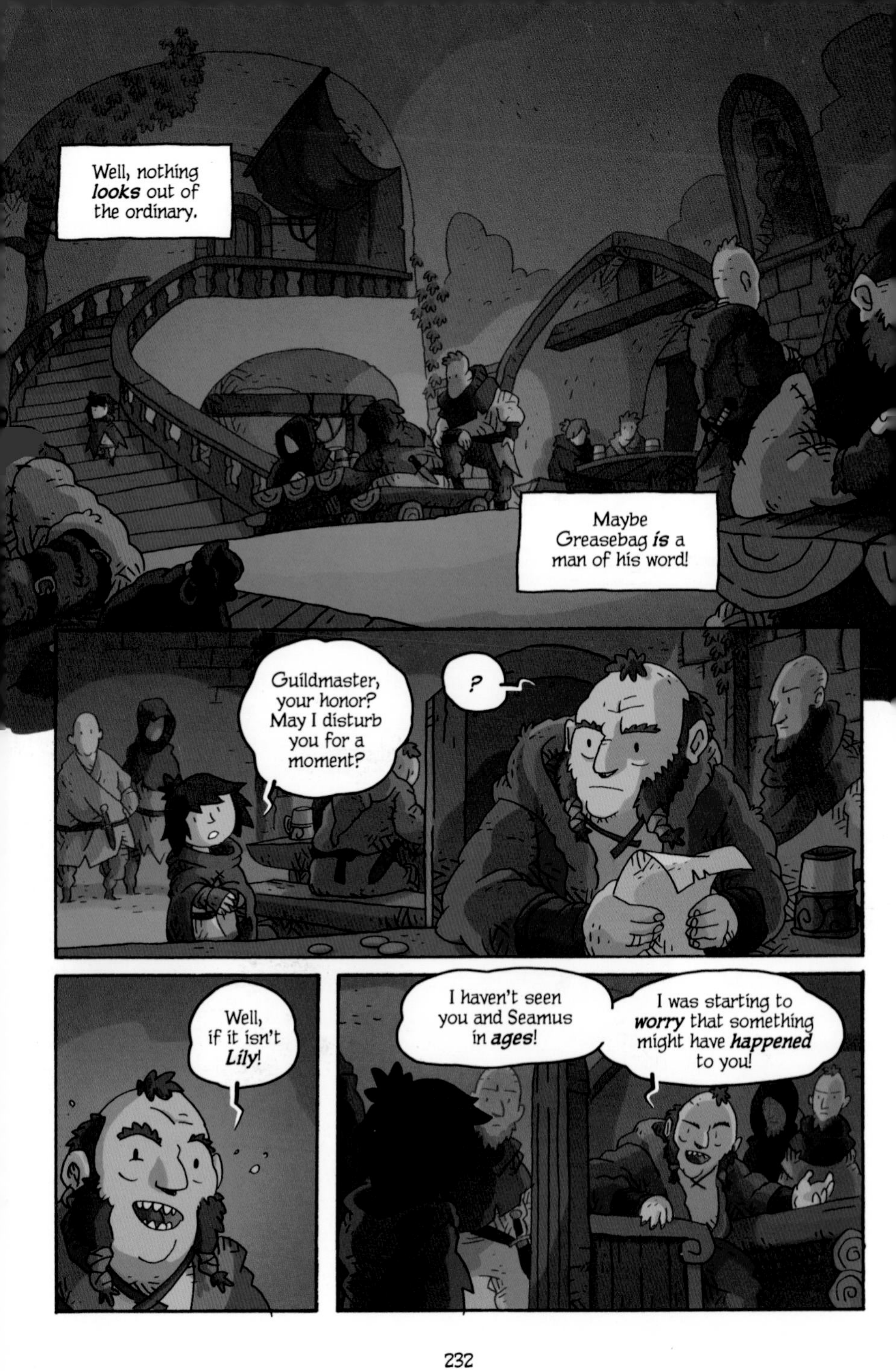
Well, nothing *looks* out of the ordinary.
Maybe Greasebag *is* a man of his word!
Guildmaster, your honor? May I disturb you for a moment?
?
Well, if it isn't *Lily*!
I haven't seen you and Seamus in *ages*!
I was starting to *worry* that something might have *happened* to you!

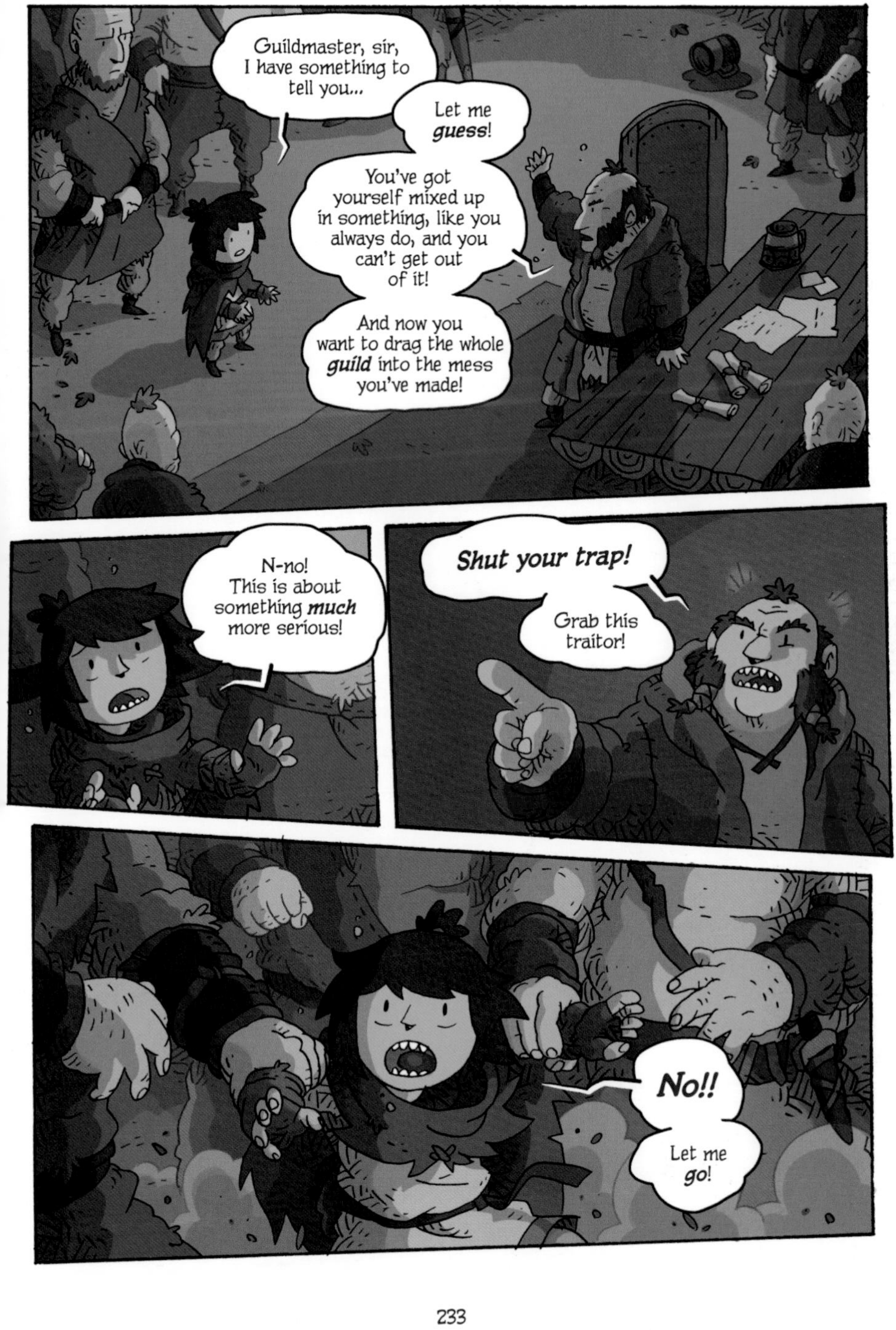
Guildmaster, sir, I have something to tell you...
Let me *guess*!
You've got yourself mixed up in something, like you always do, and you can't get out of it!
And now you want to drag the whole *guild* into the mess you've made!
N-no! This is about something *much* more serious!
Shut your trap!
Grab this traitor!
No!!
Let me *go*!

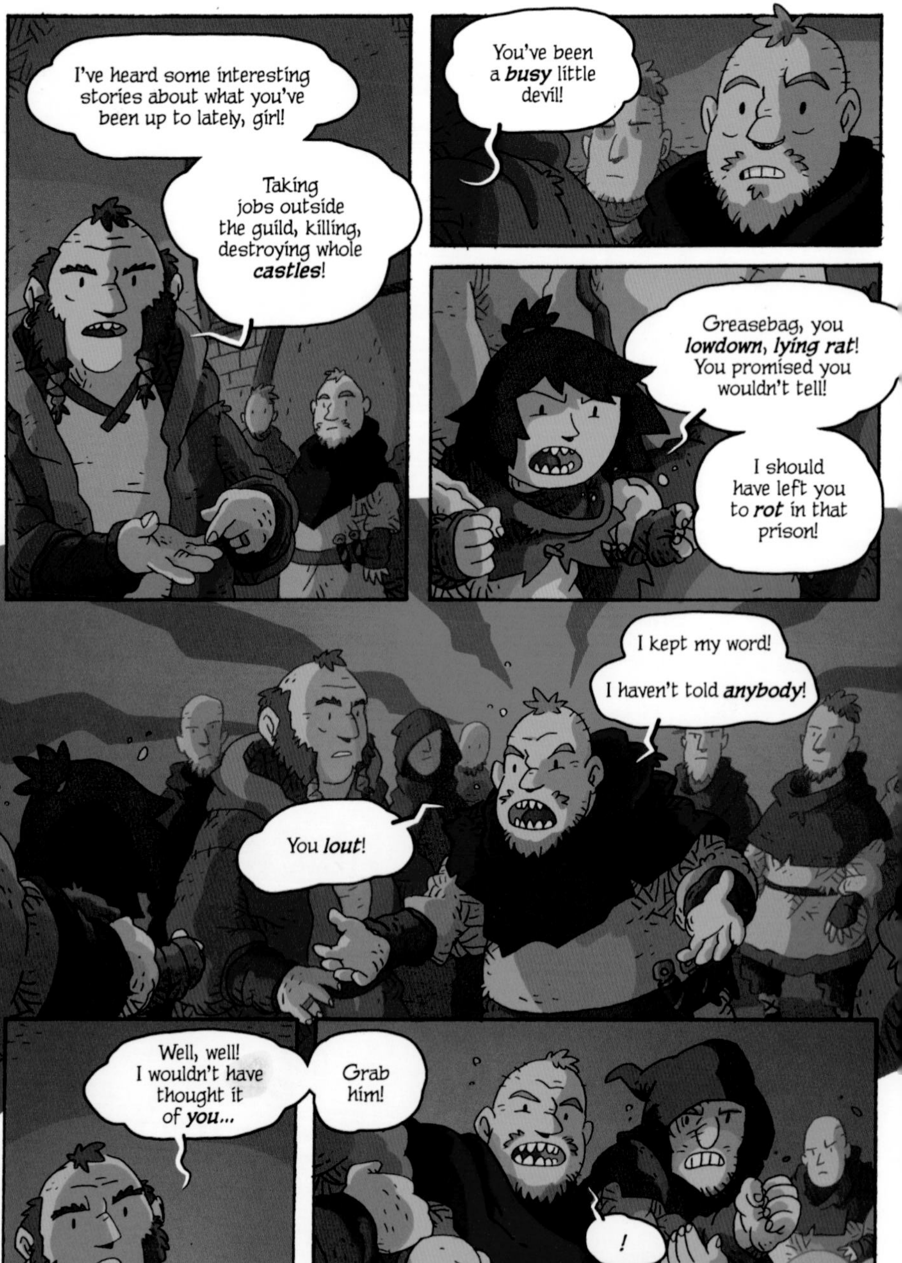
I've heard some interesting stories about what you've been up to lately, girl!
Taking jobs outside the guild, killing, destroying whole *castles*!
You've been a *busy* little devil!
Greasebag, you *lowdown, lying rat*! You promised you wouldn't tell!
I should have left you to *rot* in that prison!
I kept my word!
I haven't told *anybody*!
You *lout*!
Well, well! I wouldn't have thought it of *you*...
Grab him!
!

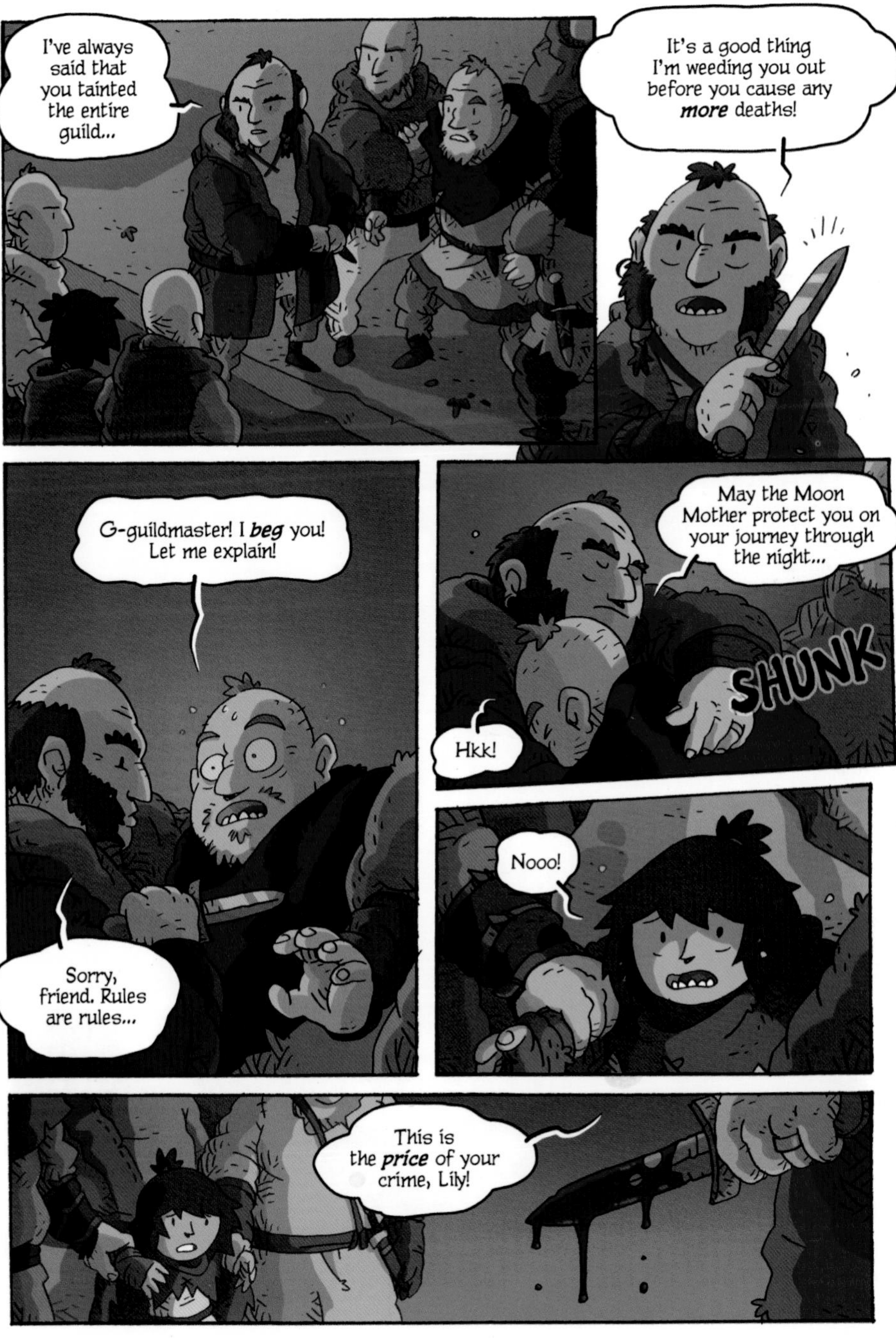
I've always said that you tainted the entire guild...
It's a good thing I'm weeding you out before you cause any *more* deaths!
G-guildmaster! I *beg* you! Let me explain!
Sorry, friend. Rules are rules...
May the Moon Mother protect you on your journey through the night...
SHUNK
Hkk!
Nooo!
This is the *price* of your crime, Lily!

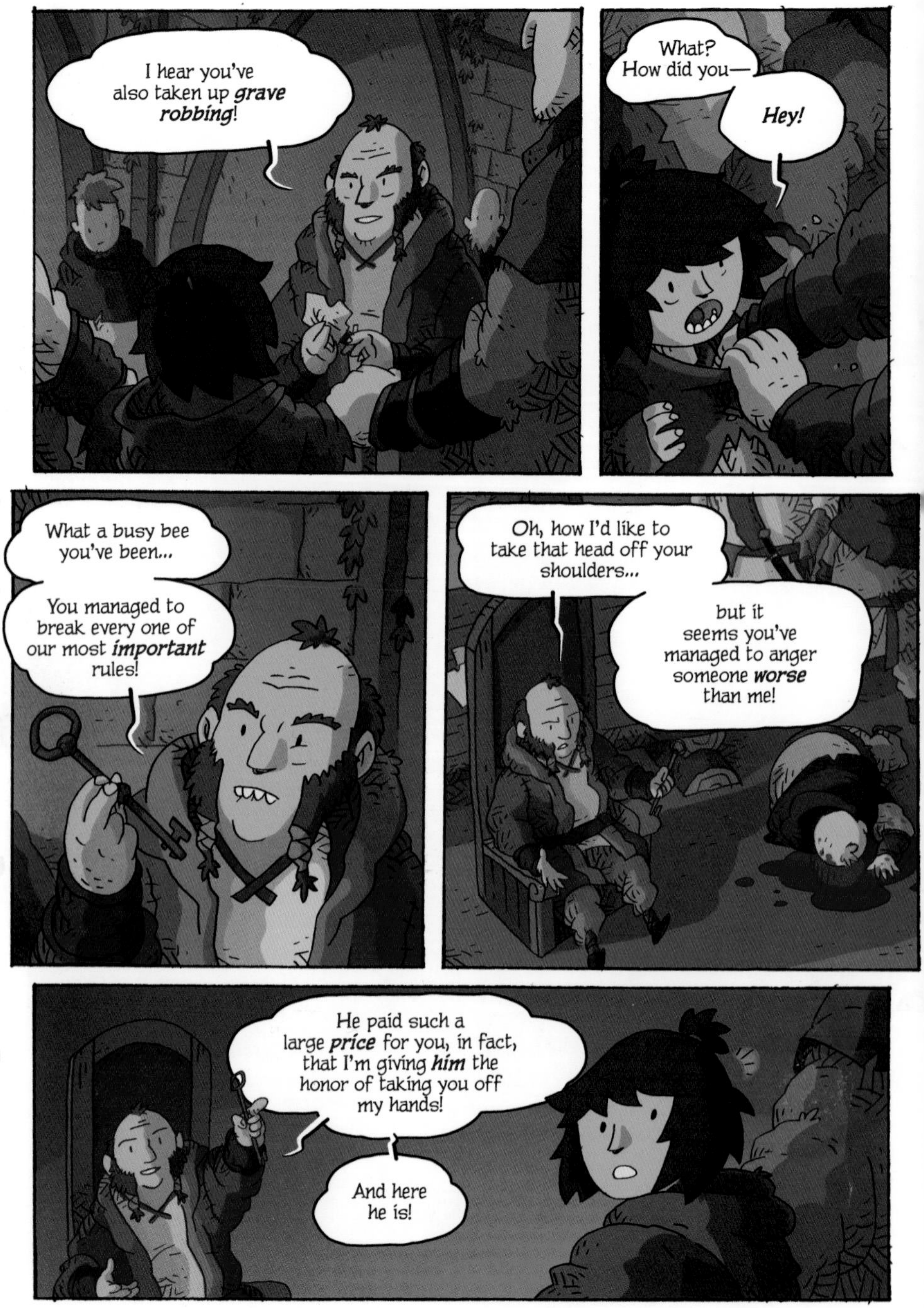
I hear you've also taken up *grave robbing*!
What? How did you—
Hey!
What a busy bee you've been...
You managed to break every one of our most *important* rules!
Oh, how I'd like to take that head off your shoulders...
but it seems you've managed to anger someone *worse* than me!
He paid such a large *price* for you, in fact, that I'm giving *him* the honor of taking you off my hands!
And here he is!

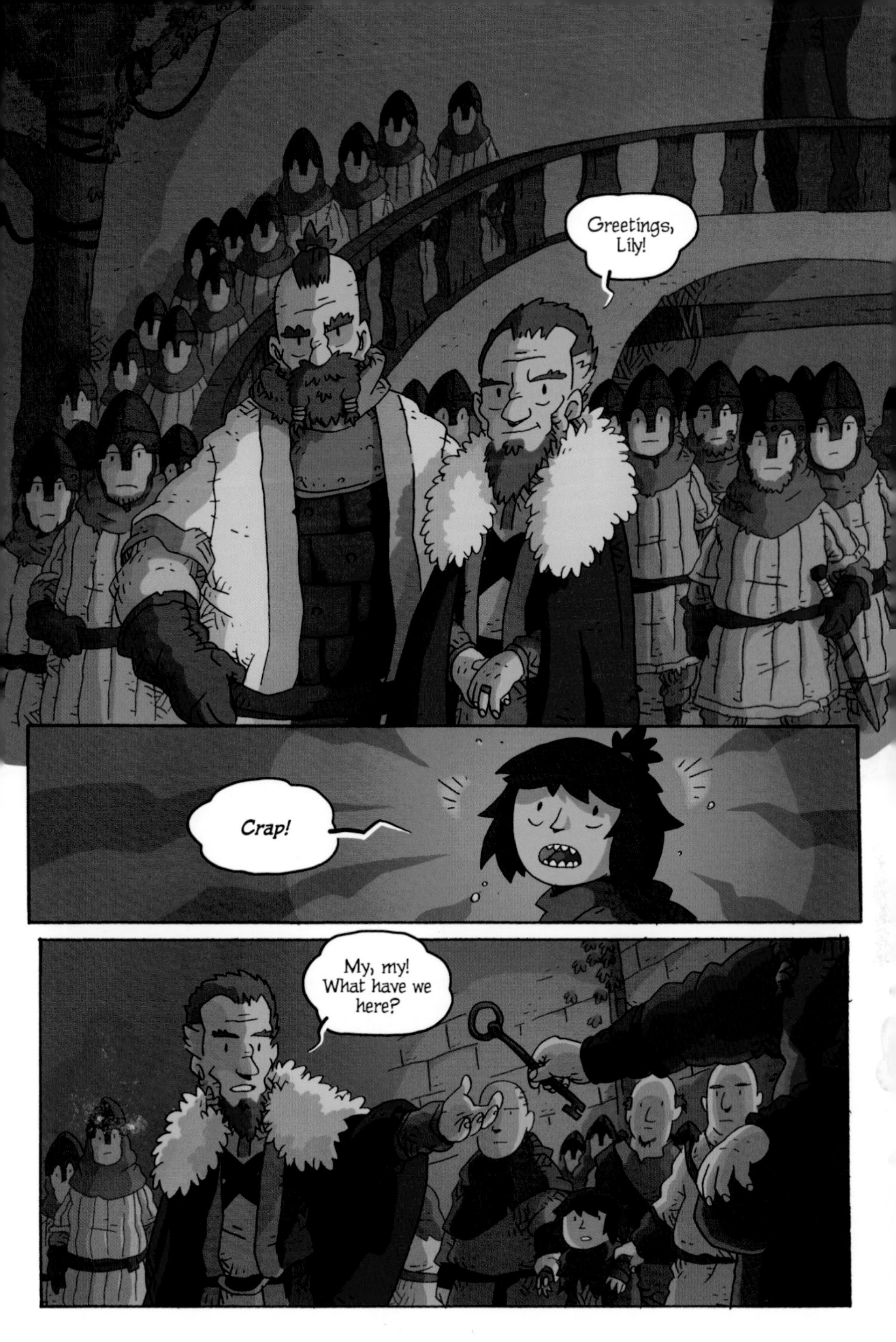
Greetings, Lily!
Crap!
My, my! What have we here?

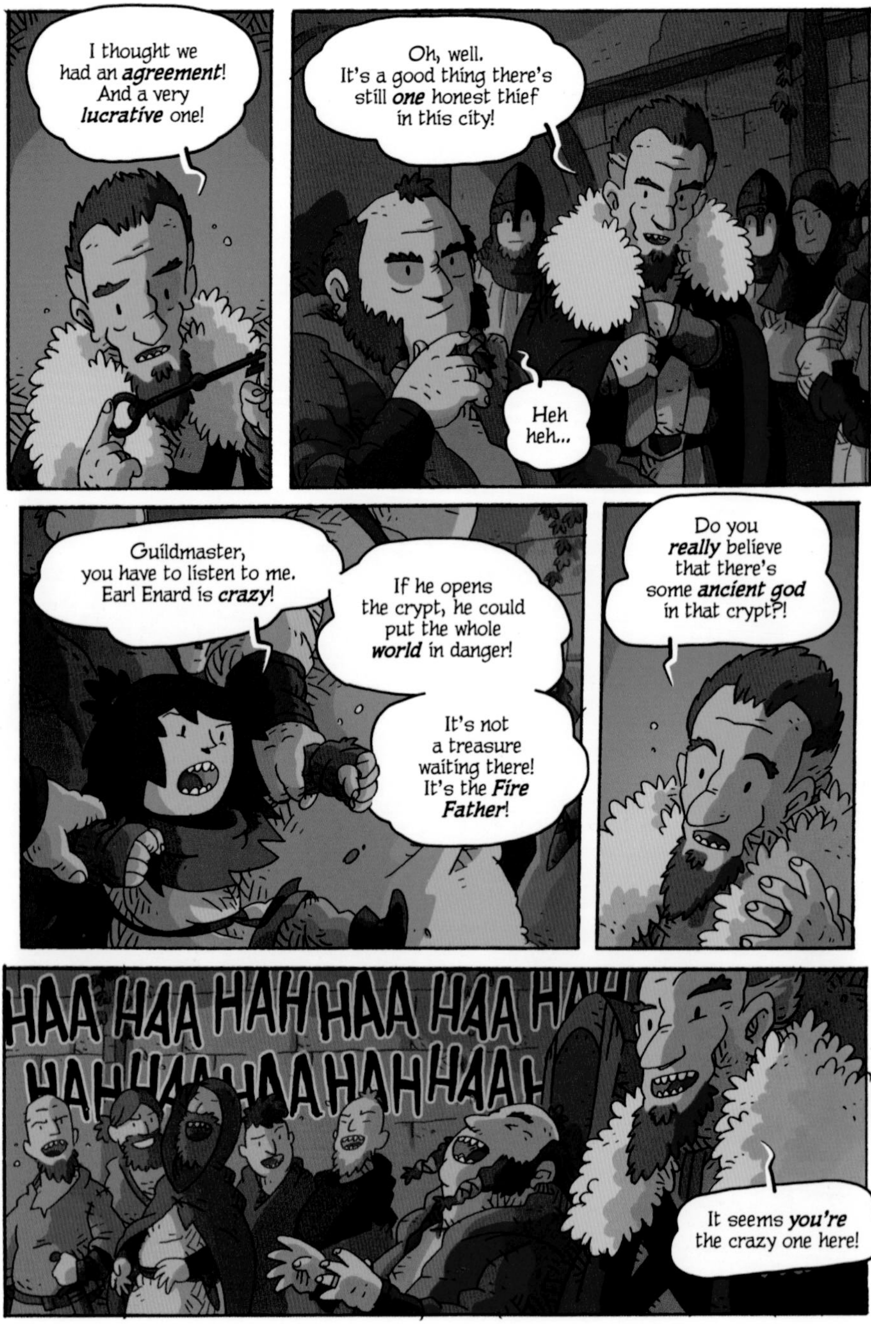

I thought we had an *agreement*! And a very *lucrative* one!
Oh, well. It's a good thing there's still *one* honest thief in this city!
Heh heh...
Guildmaster, you have to listen to me. Earl Enard is *crazy*!
If he opens the crypt, he could put the whole *world* in danger!
It's not a treasure waiting there! It's the *Fire Father*!
Do you *really* believe that there's some *ancient god* in that crypt?!
HAA HAA HAH HAA HAA HAH
HAH HAA HAA HAH HAA
It seems *you're* the crazy one here!

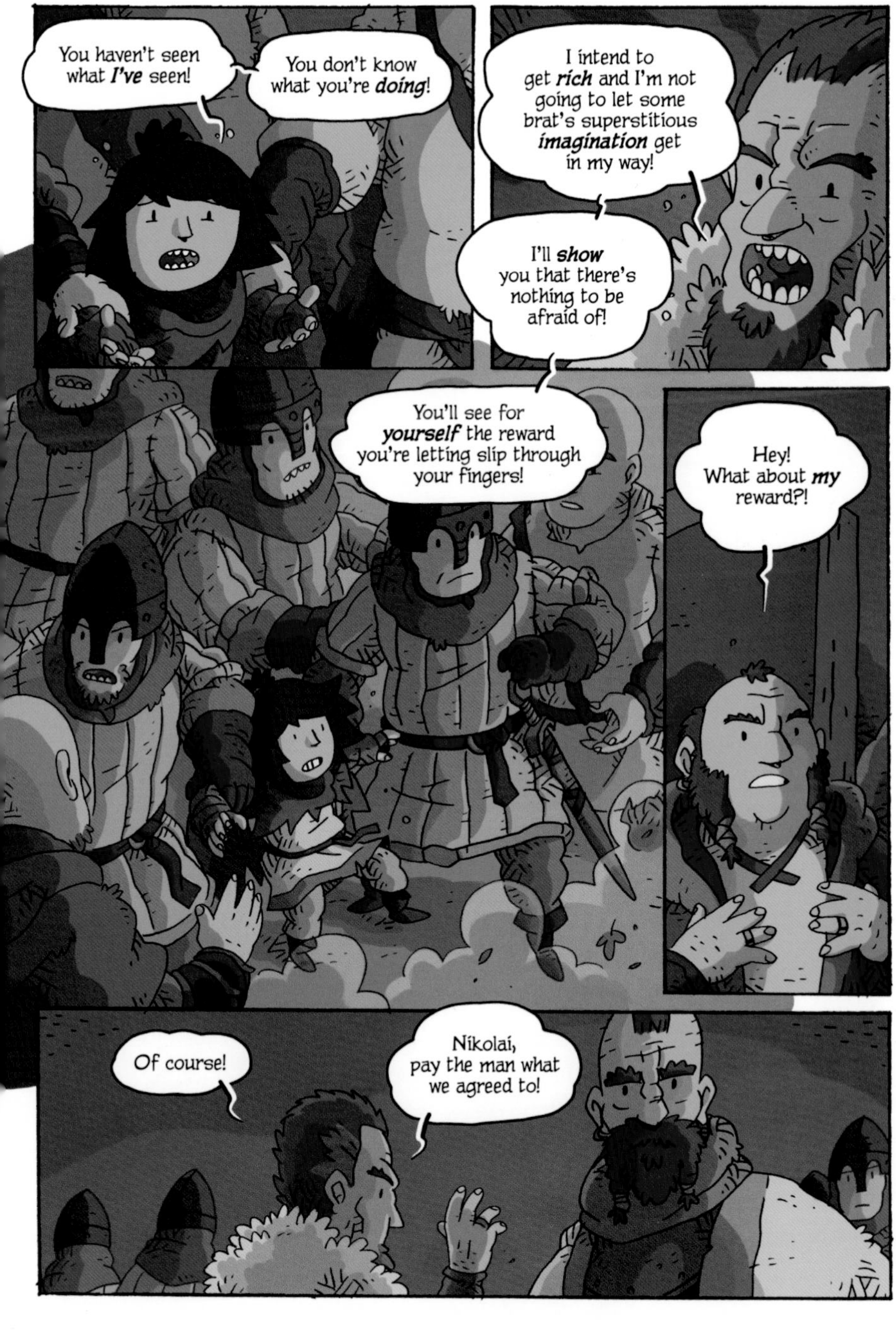

You haven't seen what ***I've*** seen!
You don't know what you're ***doing***!
I intend to get ***rich*** and I'm not going to let some brat's superstitious ***imagination*** get in my way!
I'll ***show*** you that there's nothing to be afraid of!
You'll see for ***yourself*** the reward you're letting slip through your fingers!
Hey! What about ***my*** reward?!
Of course!
Nikolai, pay the man what we agreed to!

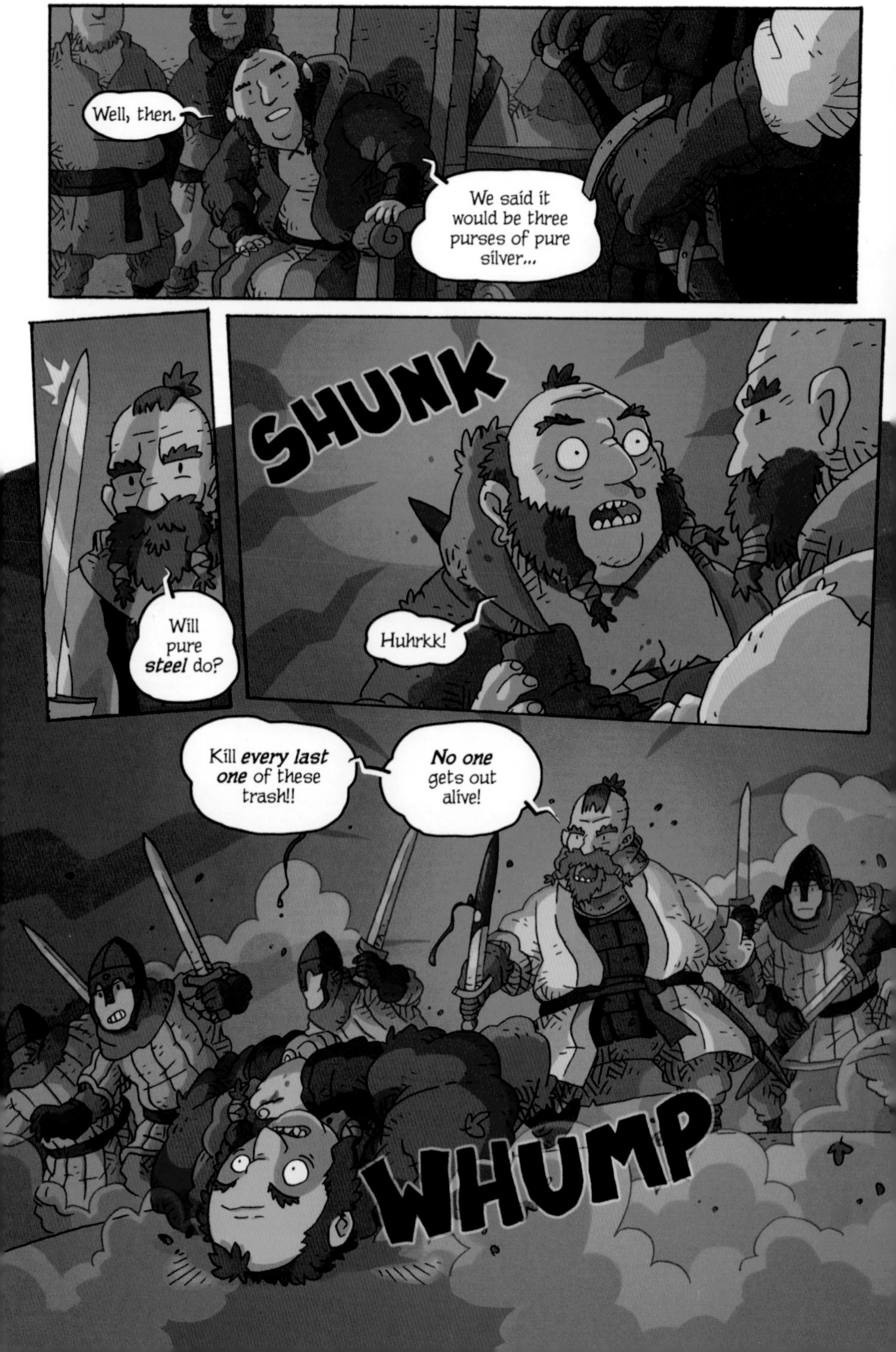
Well, then.
We said it would be three purses of pure silver...
Will pure *steel* do?
SHUNK
Huhrkk!
Kill *every last one* of these trash!!
No one gets out alive!
WHUMP

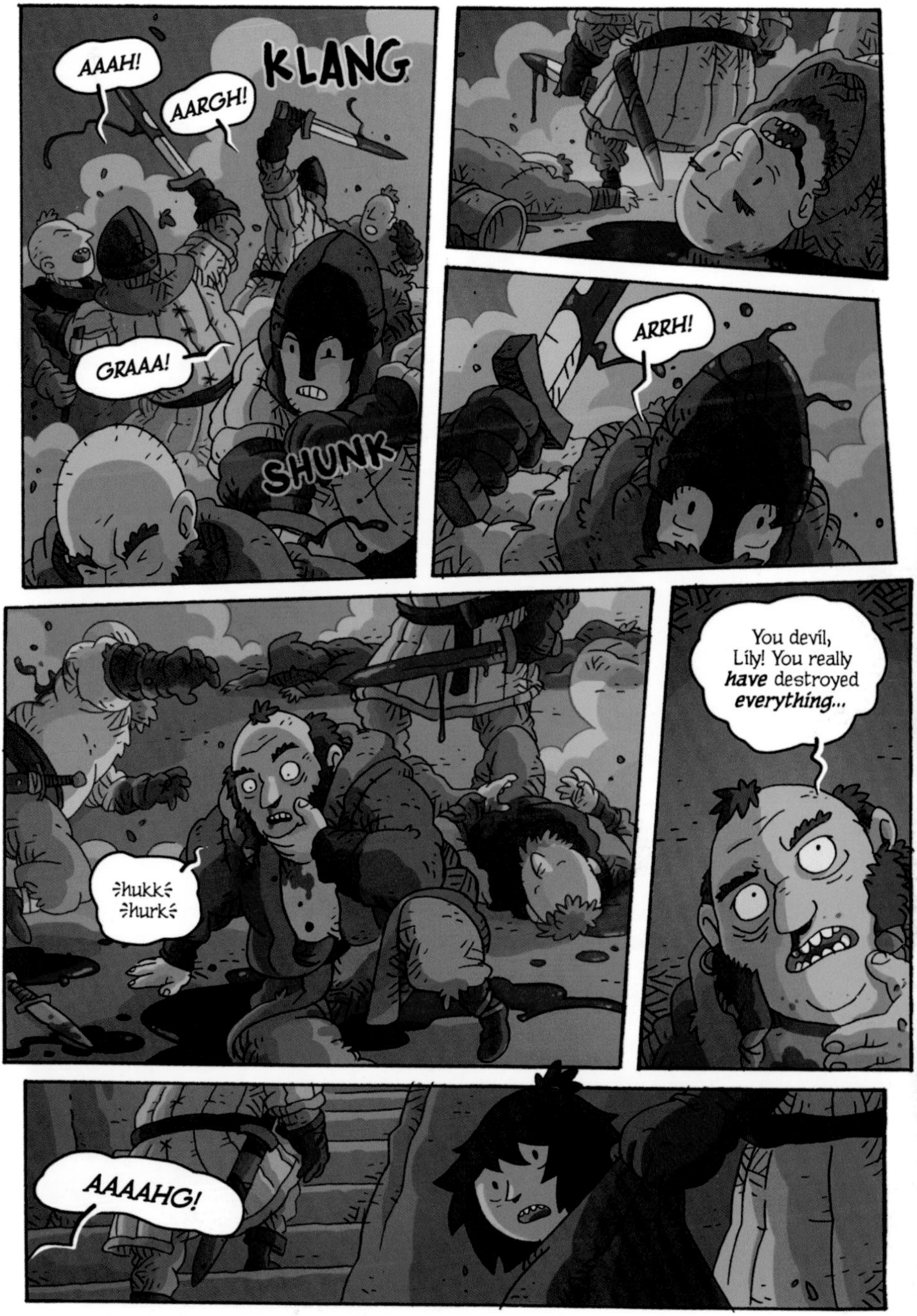
AAAH!
AARGH!
KLANG
GRAAA!
SHUNK
ARRH!
hukk
hurk
You devil, Lily! You really *have* destroyed *everything*...
AAAAHG!

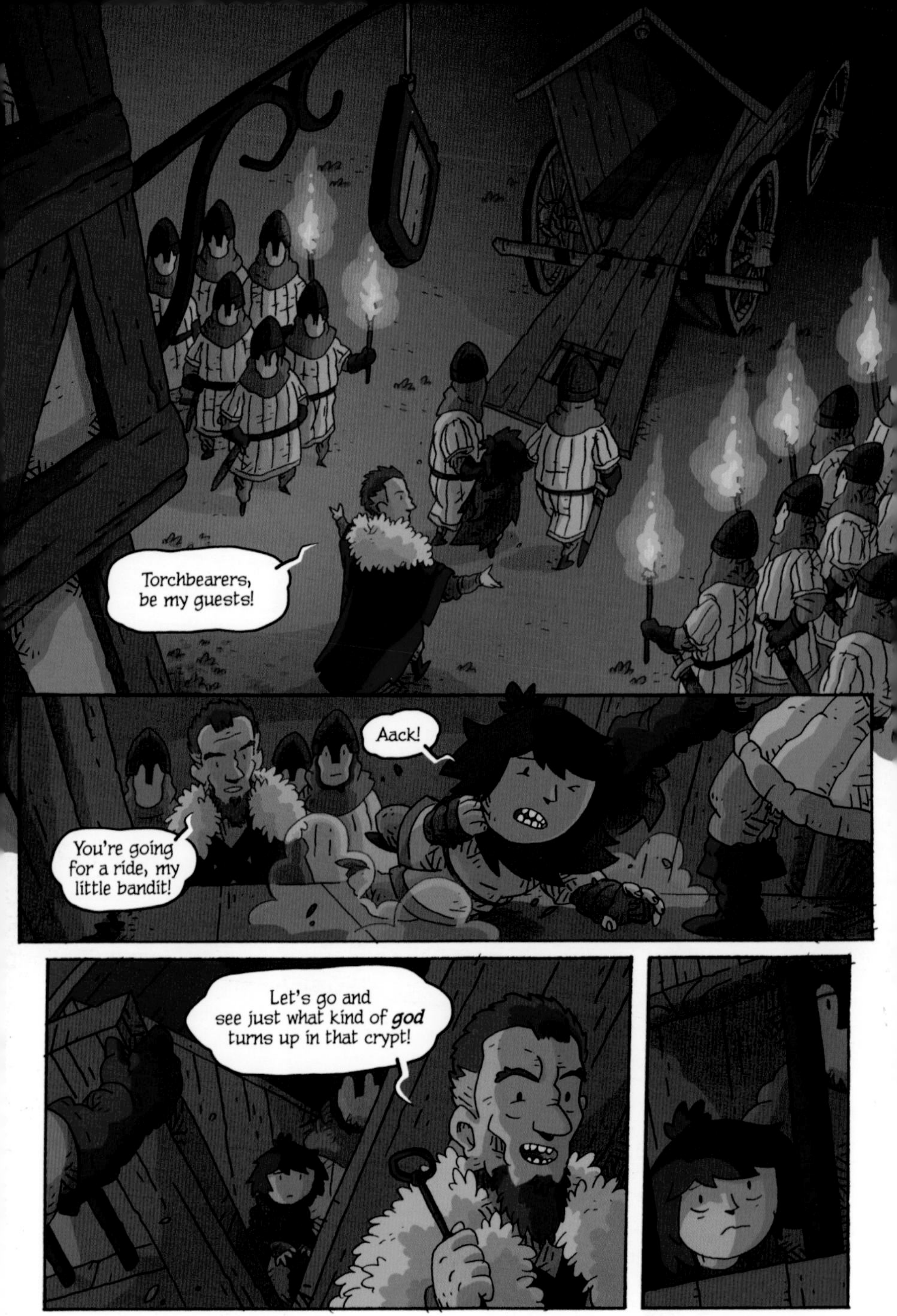

Torchbearers, be my guests!
Aack!
You're going for a ride, my little bandit!
Let's go and see just what kind of *god* turns up in that crypt!

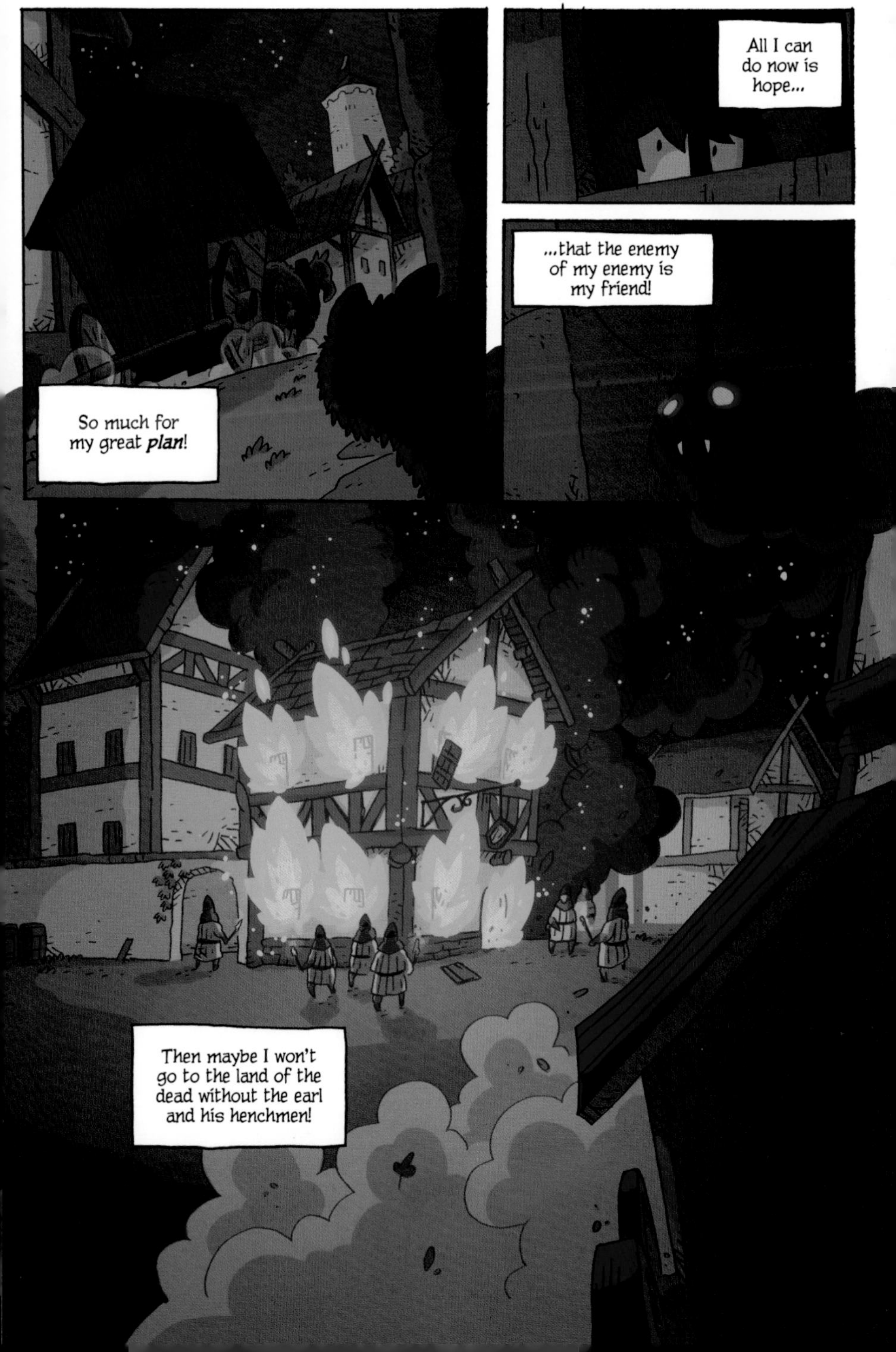

So much for my great *plan*!
All I can do now is hope...
...that the enemy of my enemy is my friend!
Then maybe I won't go to the land of the dead without the earl and his henchmen!

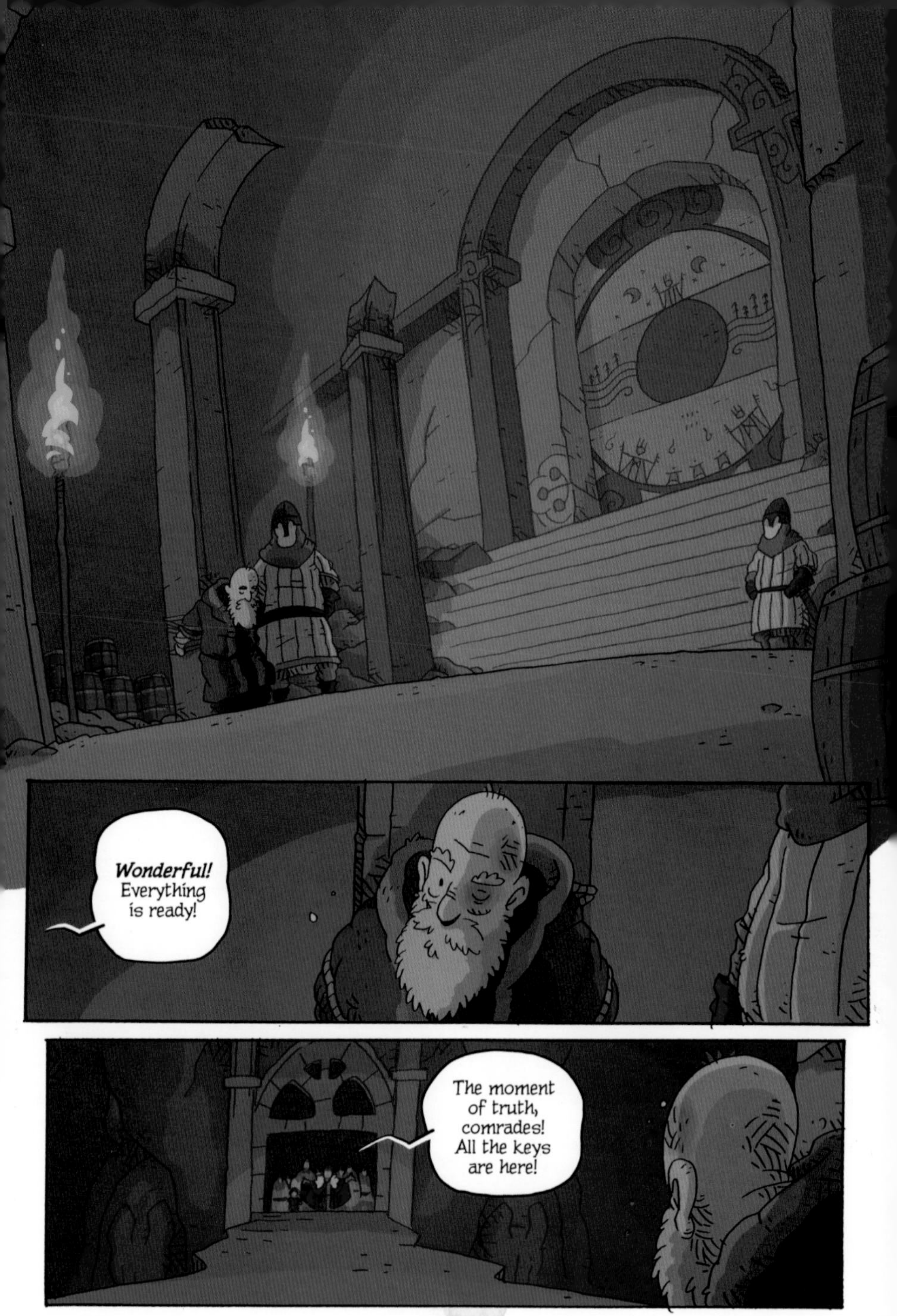
Wonderful! Everything is ready!
The moment of truth, comrades! All the keys are here!

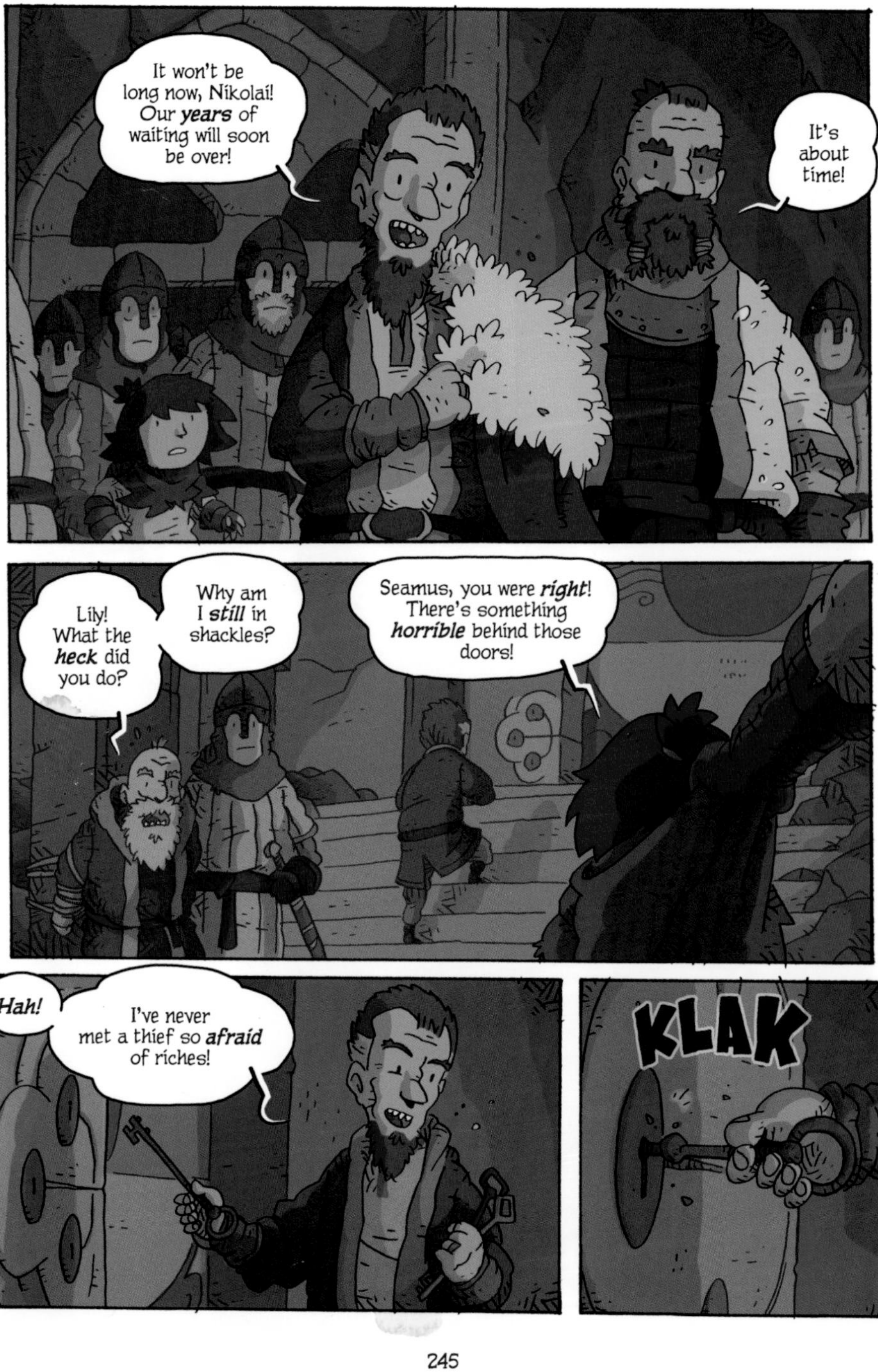
It won't be long now, Nikolai! Our *years* of waiting will soon be over!
It's about time!
Lily! What the *heck* did you do?
Why am I *still* in shackles?
Seamus, you were *right*! There's something *horrible* behind those doors!
Hah!
I've never met a thief so *afraid* of riches!
KLAK

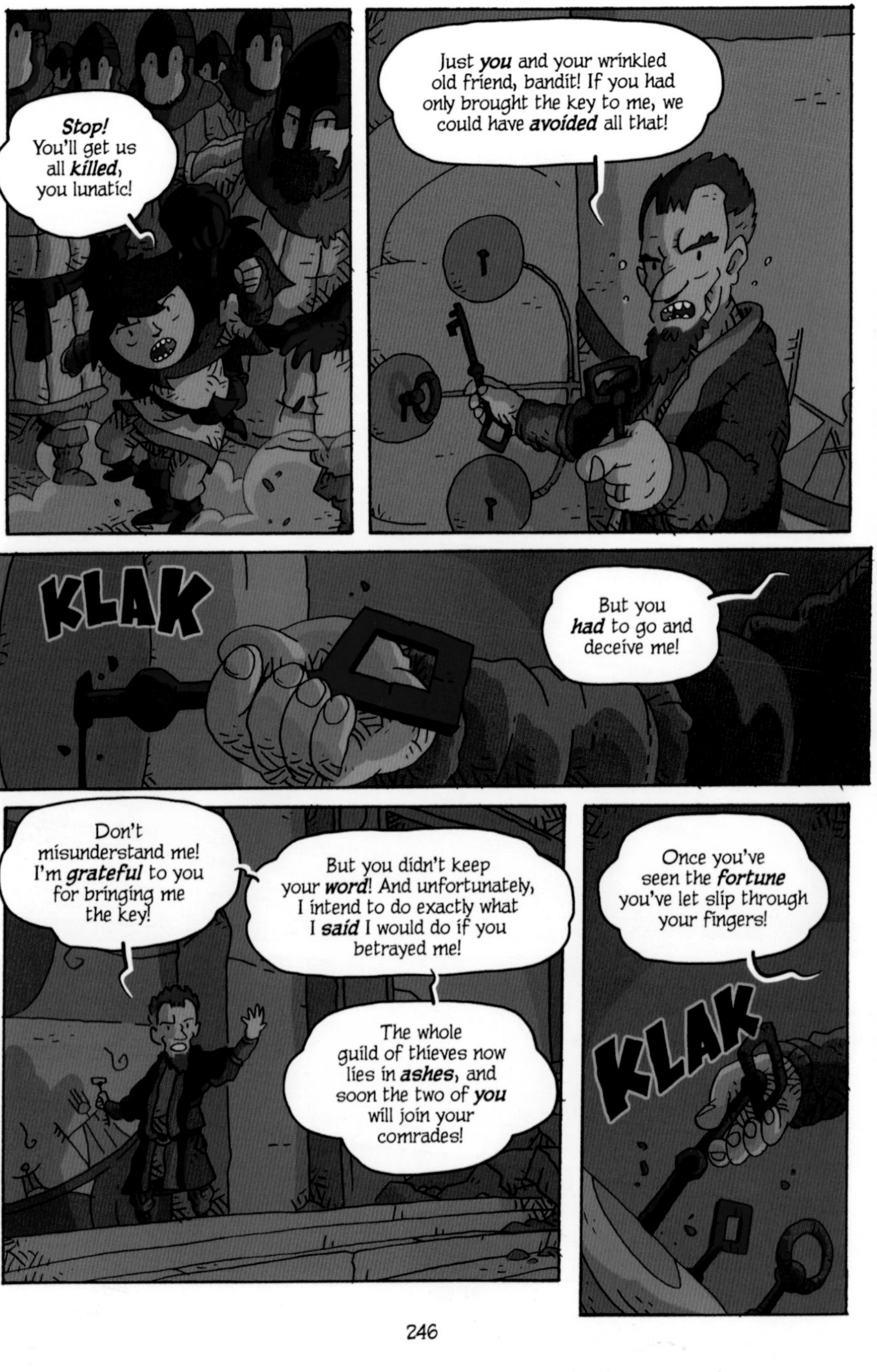
Stop! You'll get us all killed, you lunatic!
Just you and your wrinkled old friend, bandit! If you had only brought the key to me, we could have avoided all that!
KLAK
But you had to go and deceive me!
Don't misunderstand me! I'm grateful to you for bringing me the key!
But you didn't keep your word! And unfortunately, I intend to do exactly what I said I would do if you betrayed me!
The whole guild of thieves now lies in ashes, and soon the two of you will join your comrades!
Once you've seen the fortune you've let slip through your fingers!
KLAK

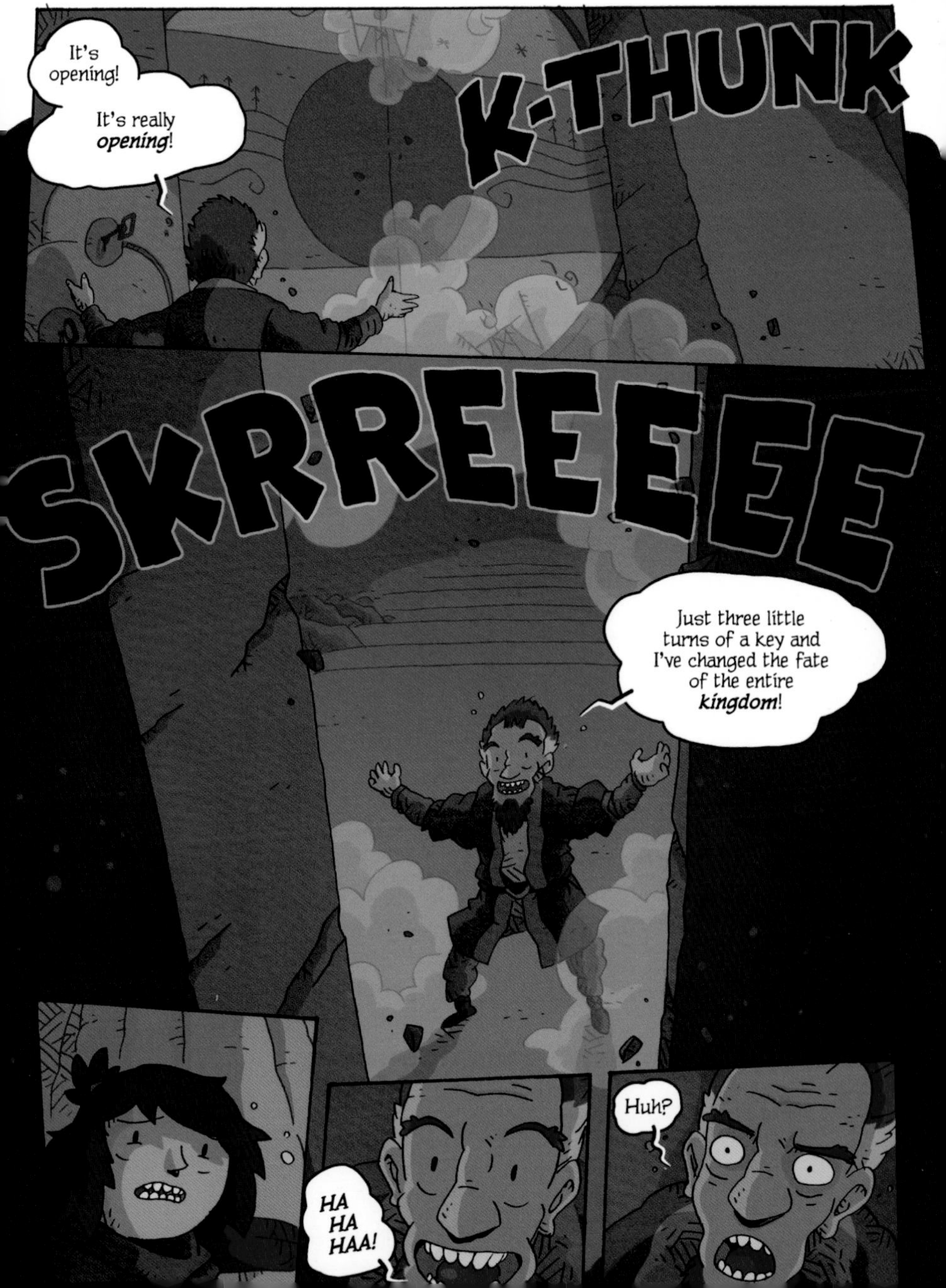
It's opening!
It's really *opening*!
K-THUNK
SKRREEEEE
Just three little turns of a key and I've changed the fate of the entire *kingdom*!
HA HA HAA!
Huh?

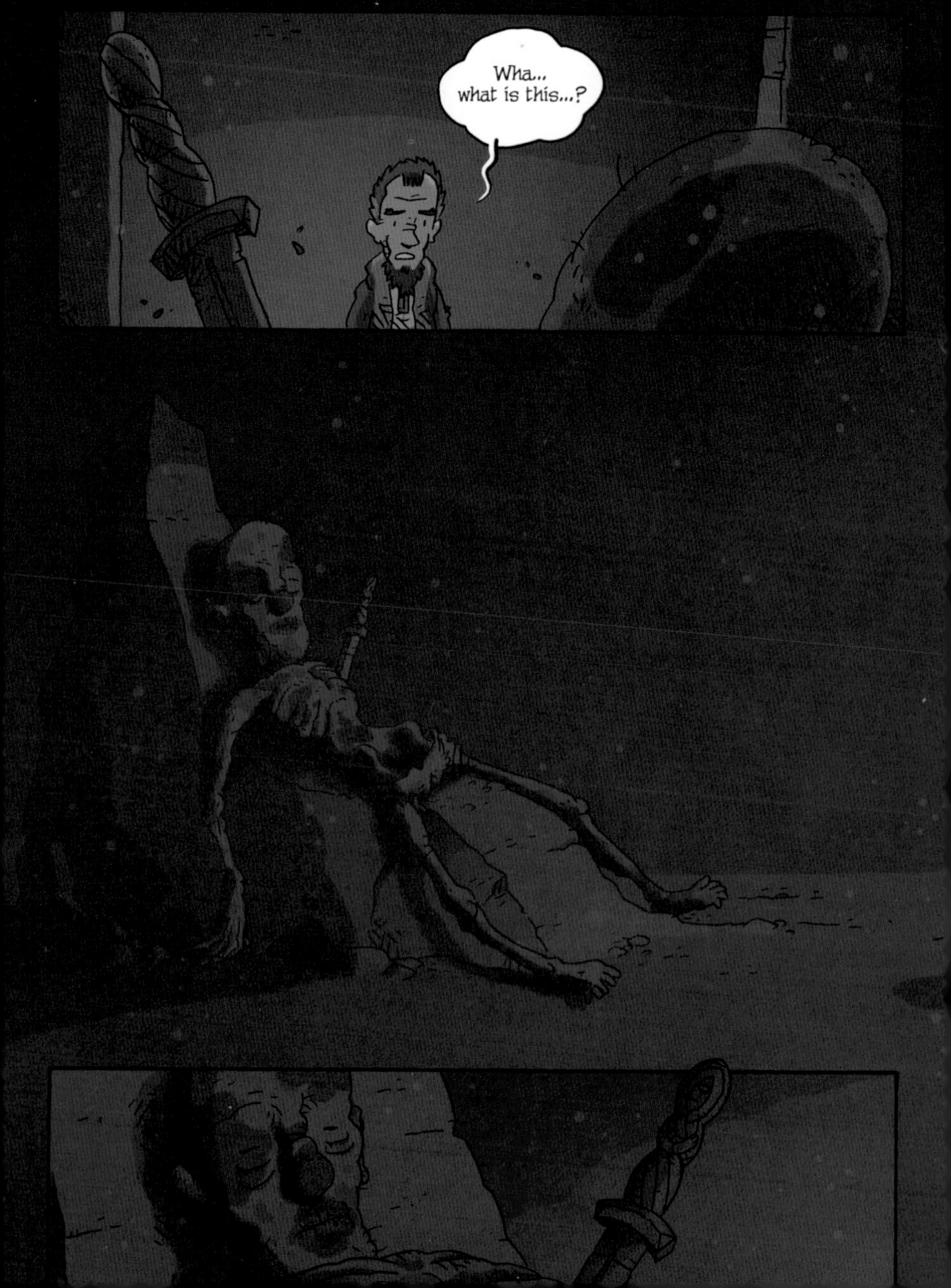
Wha... what is this...?

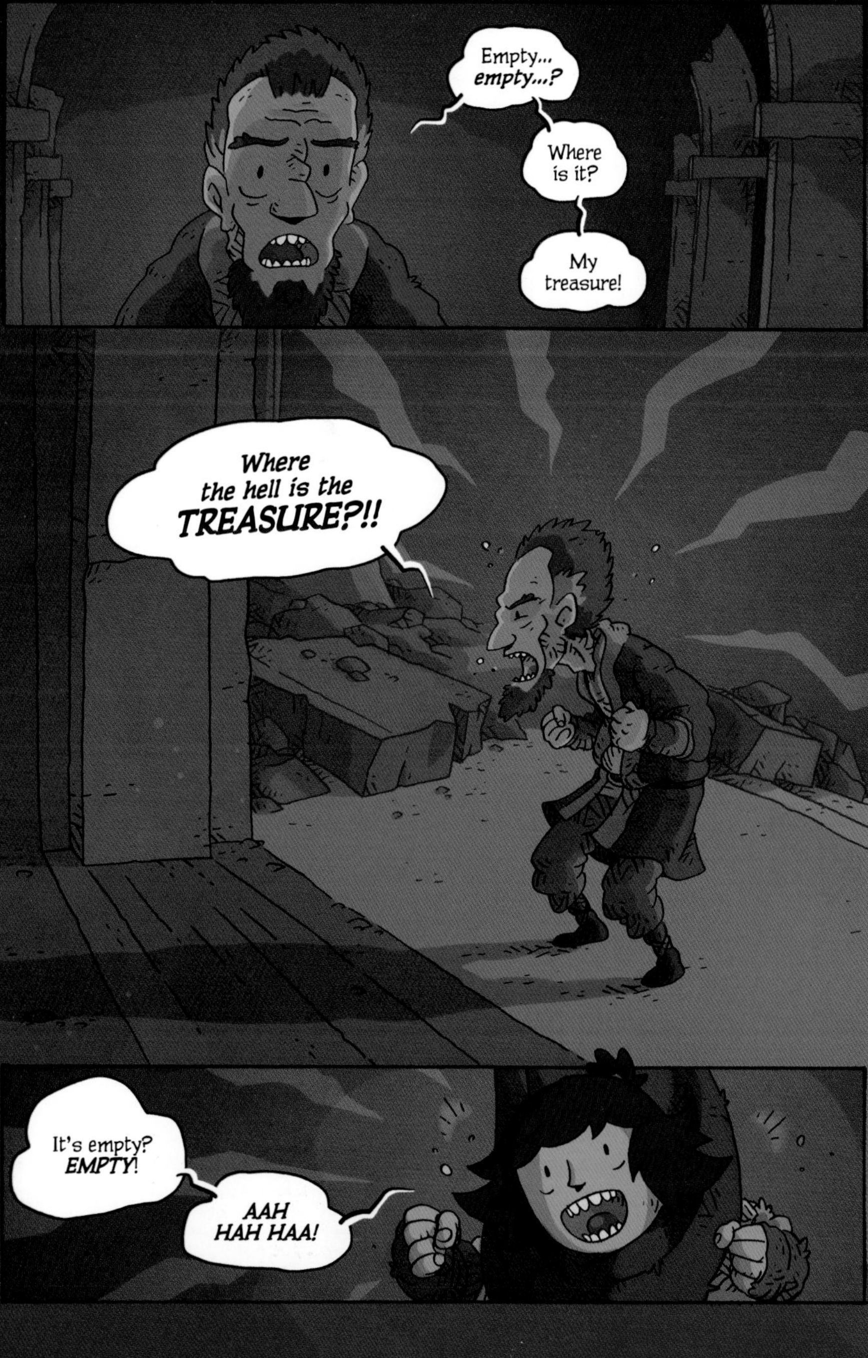
Empty... *empty...?*
Where is it?
My treasure!
Where the hell is the ***TREASURE?!!***
It's empty? ***EMPTY!***
AAH HAH HAA!

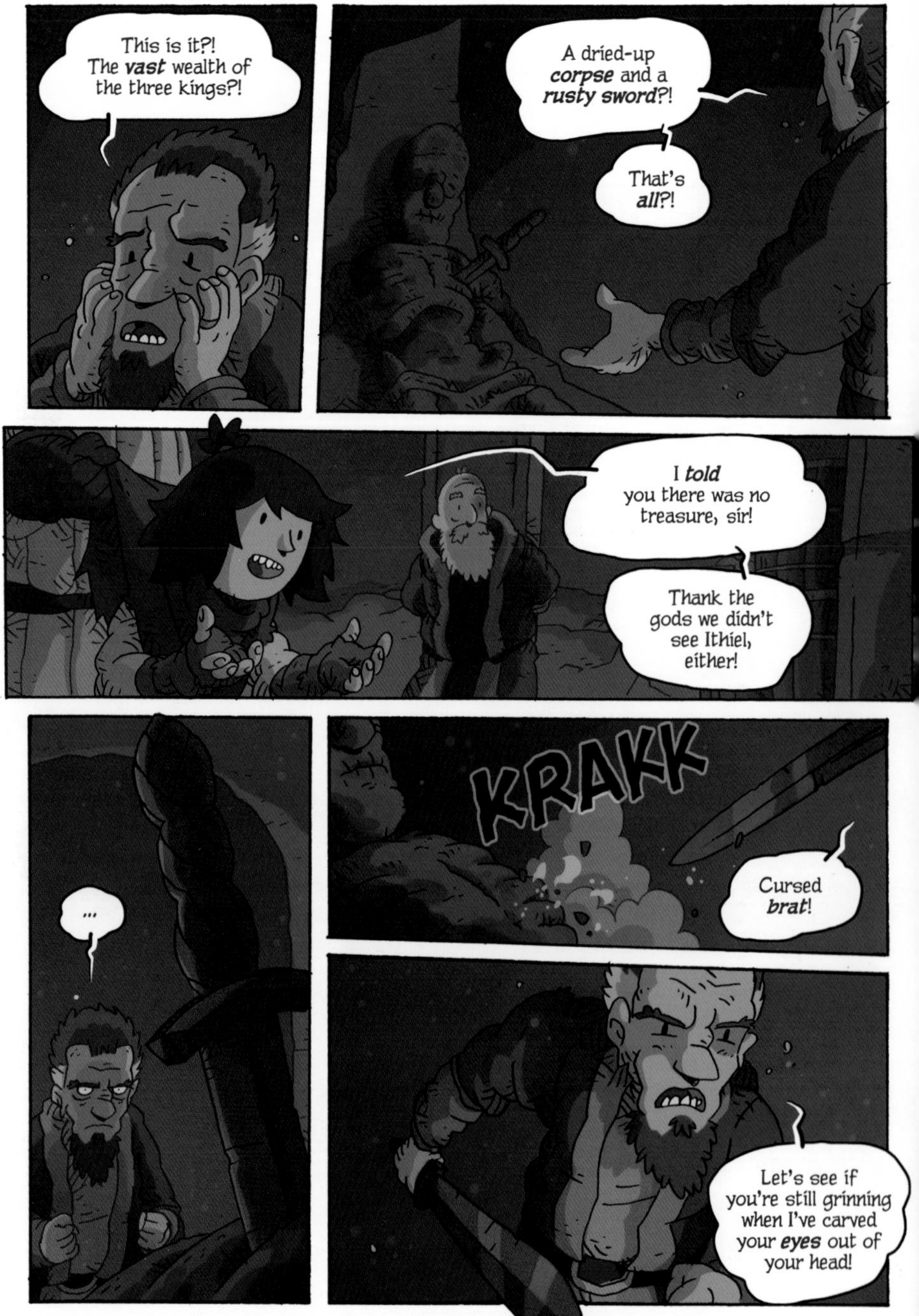
This is it?! The vast wealth of the three kings?!
A dried-up corpse and a rusty sword?!
That's all?!
I told you there was no treasure, sir!
Thank the gods we didn't see Ithiel, either!
...
KRAKK
Cursed brat!
Let's see if you're still grinning when I've carved your eyes out of your head!

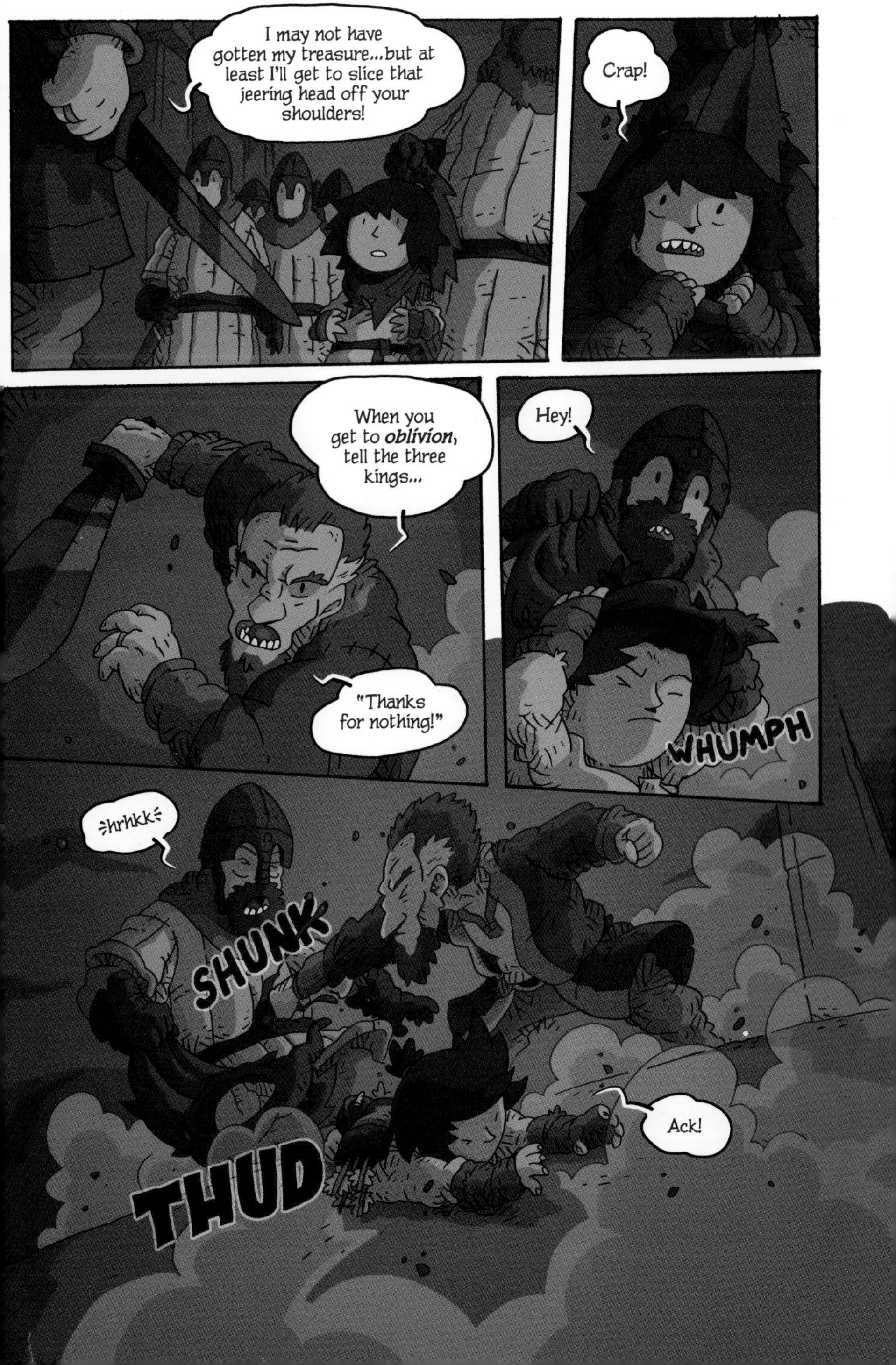
I may not have gotten my treasure...but at least I'll get to slice that jeering head off your shoulders!
Crap!
When you get to *oblivion*, tell the three kings...
"Thanks for nothing!"
Hey!
WHUMPH
hrhkk
SHUNK
THUD
Ack!

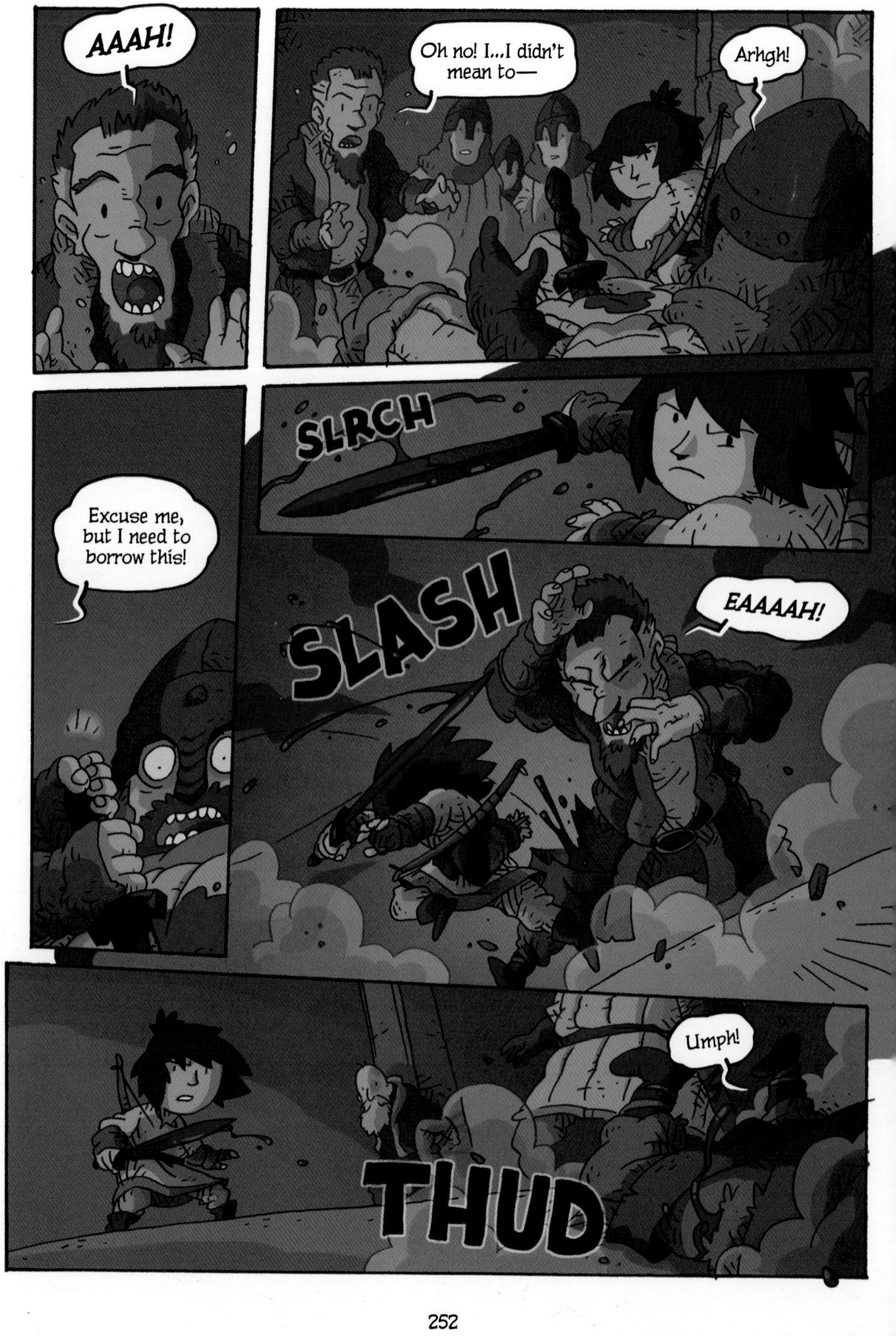
AAAH!
Oh no! I...I didn't mean to—
Arhgh!
SLRCH
Excuse me, but I need to borrow this!
SLASH
EAAAAH!
Umph!
THUD

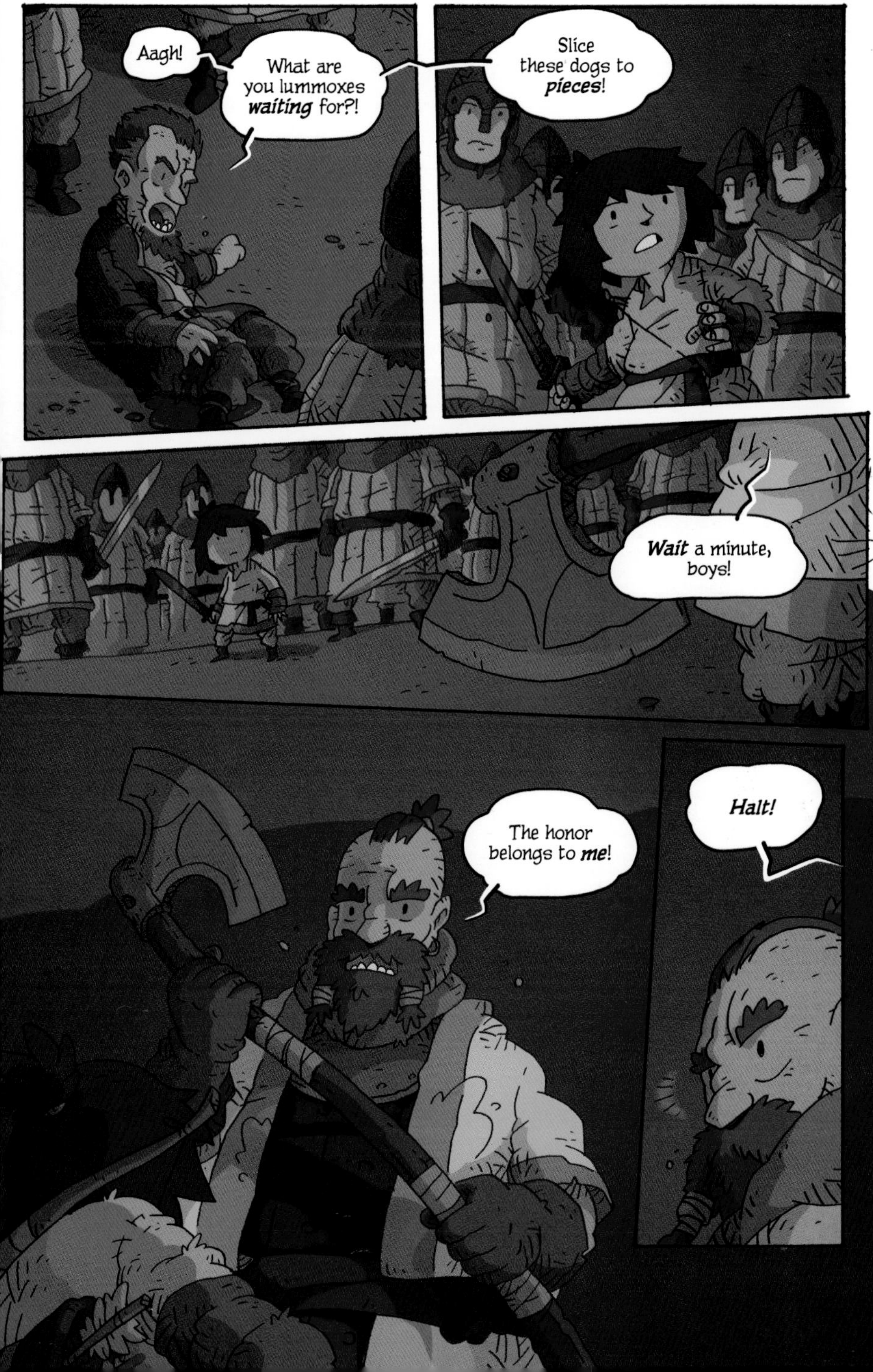
Aagh!
What are you lummoxes *waiting* for?!
Slice these dogs to *pieces*!
Wait a minute, boys!
The honor belongs to *me*!
Halt!

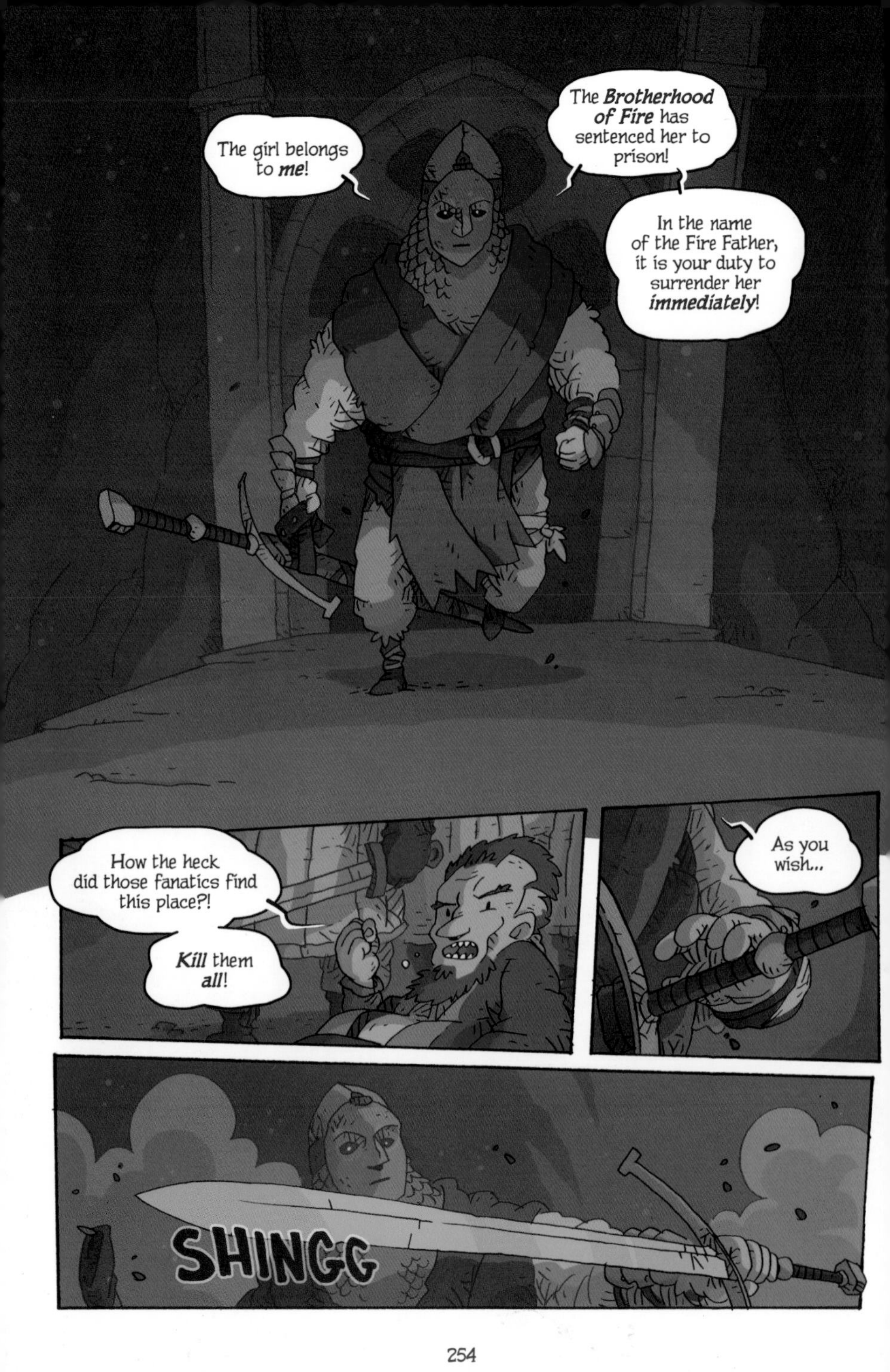
The girl belongs to *me*!
The *Brotherhood of Fire* has sentenced her to prison!
In the name of the Fire Father, it is your duty to surrender her *immediately*!
How the heck did those fanatics find this place?!
Kill them *all*!
As you wish...
SHINGG

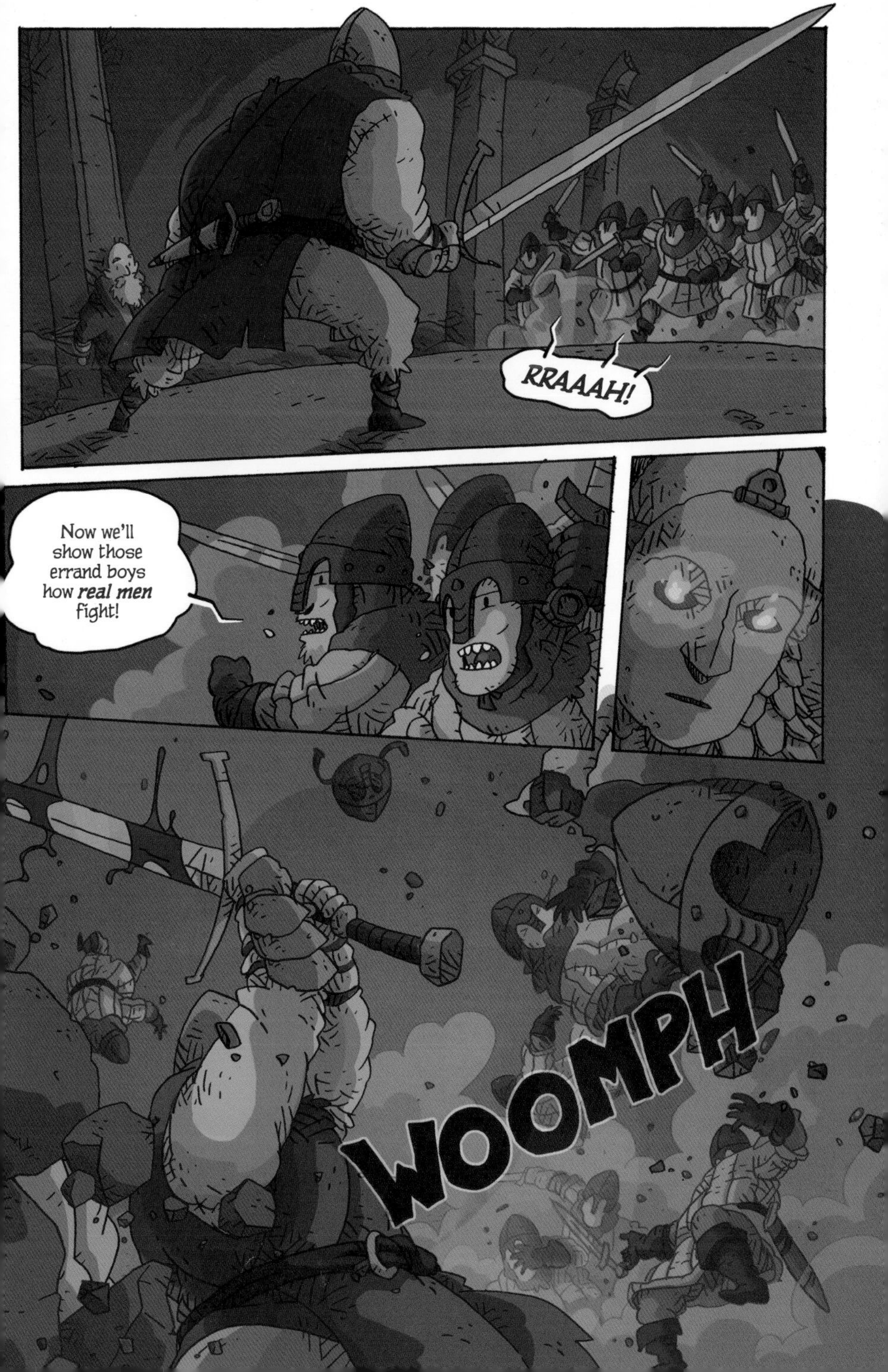
RRAAAH!
Now we'll show those errand boys how **real men** fight!
WOOMPH

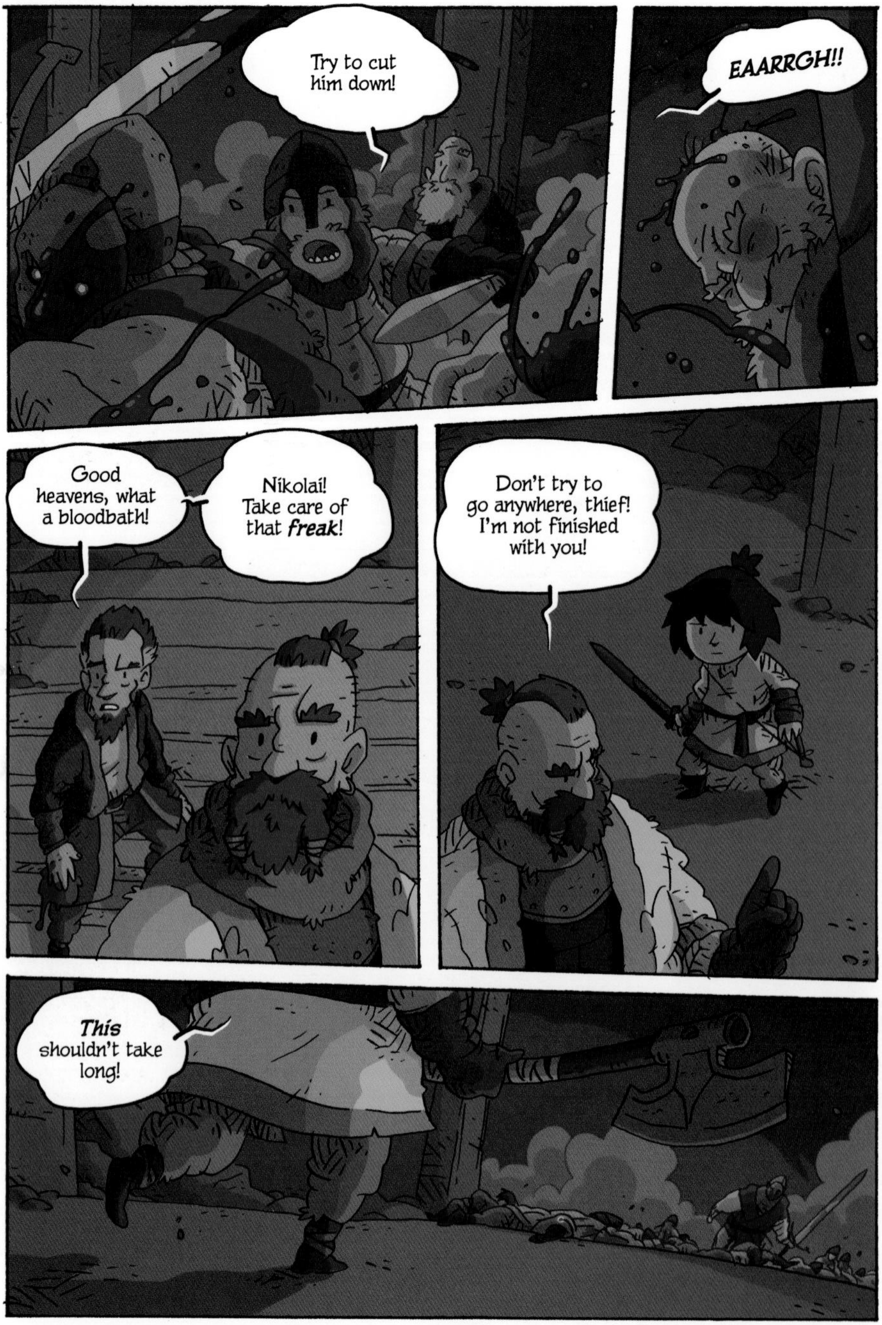
Try to cut him down!
EAARRGH!!
Good heavens, what a bloodbath!
Nikolai! Take care of that *freak*!
Don't try to go anywhere, thief! I'm not finished with you!
This shouldn't take long!

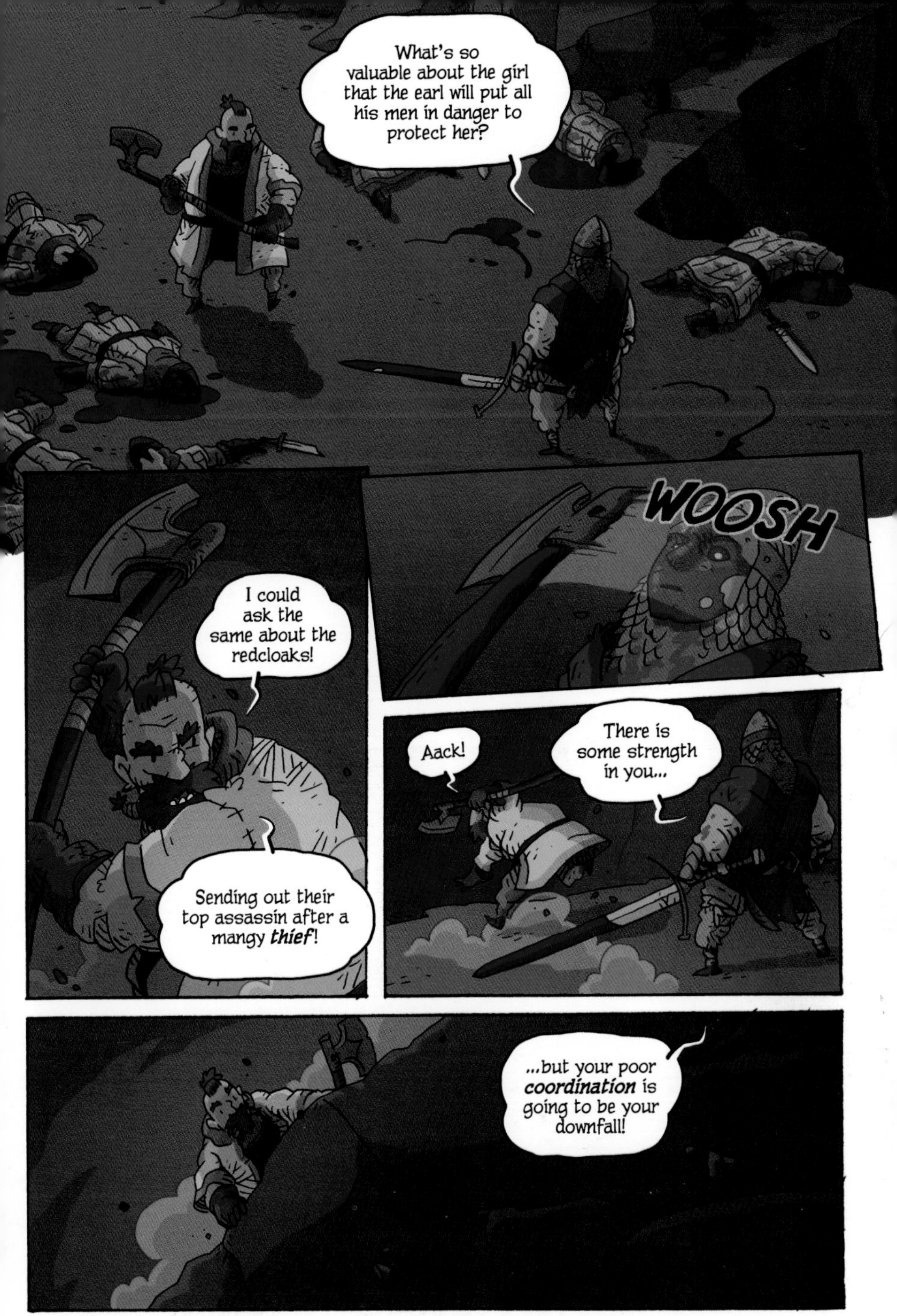
What's so valuable about the girl that the earl will put all his men in danger to protect her?
I could ask the same about the redcloaks!
Sending out their top assassin after a mangy *thief*!
WOOSH
Aack!
There is some strength in you...
...but your poor **coordination** is going to be your downfall!

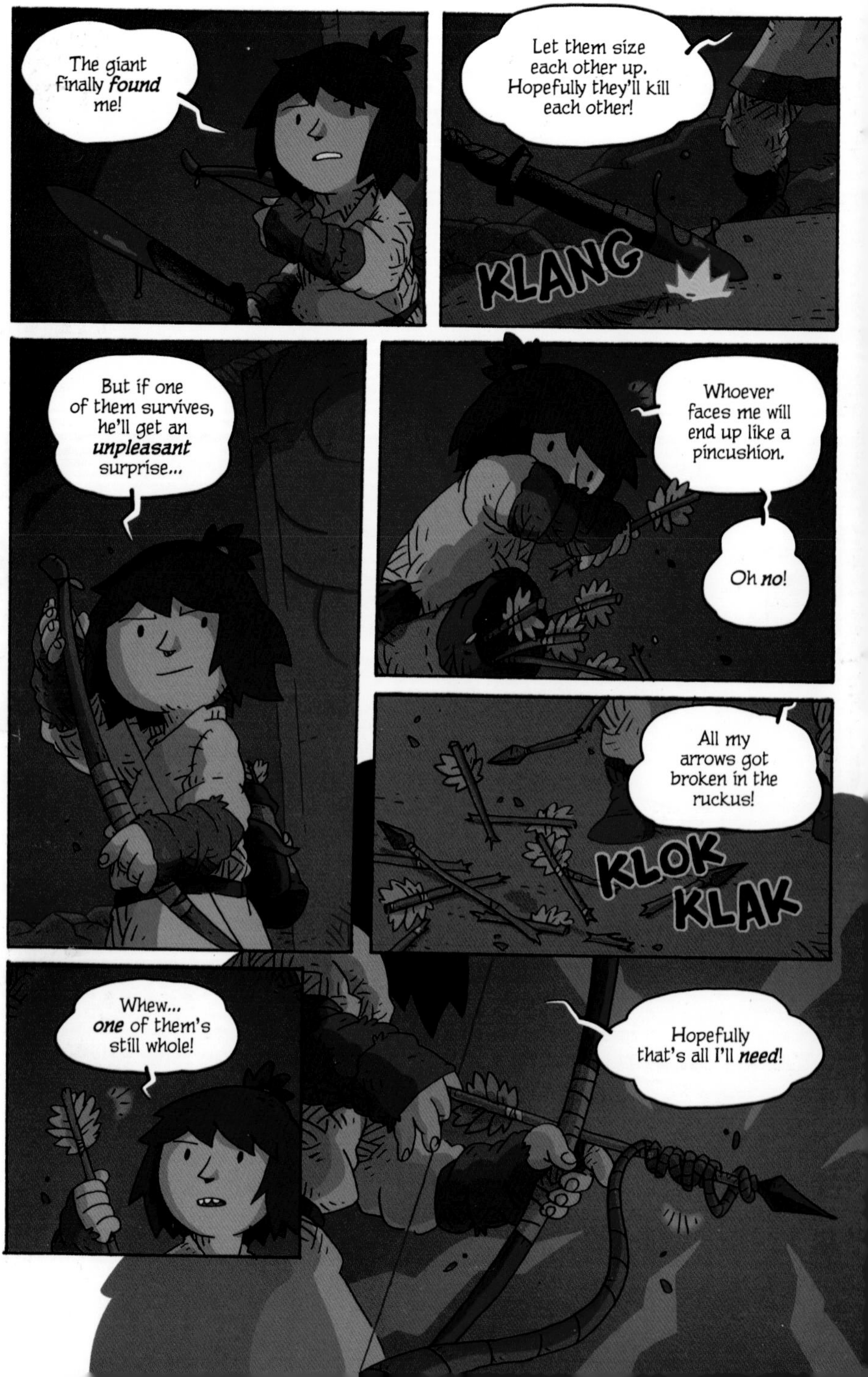
The giant finally *found* me!
Let them size each other up. Hopefully they'll kill each other!
KLANG
But if one of them survives, he'll get an *unpleasant* surprise...
Whoever faces me will end up like a pincushion.
Oh *no*!
All my arrows got broken in the ruckus!
KLOK
KLAK
Whew... *one* of them's still whole!
Hopefully that's all I'll *need*!

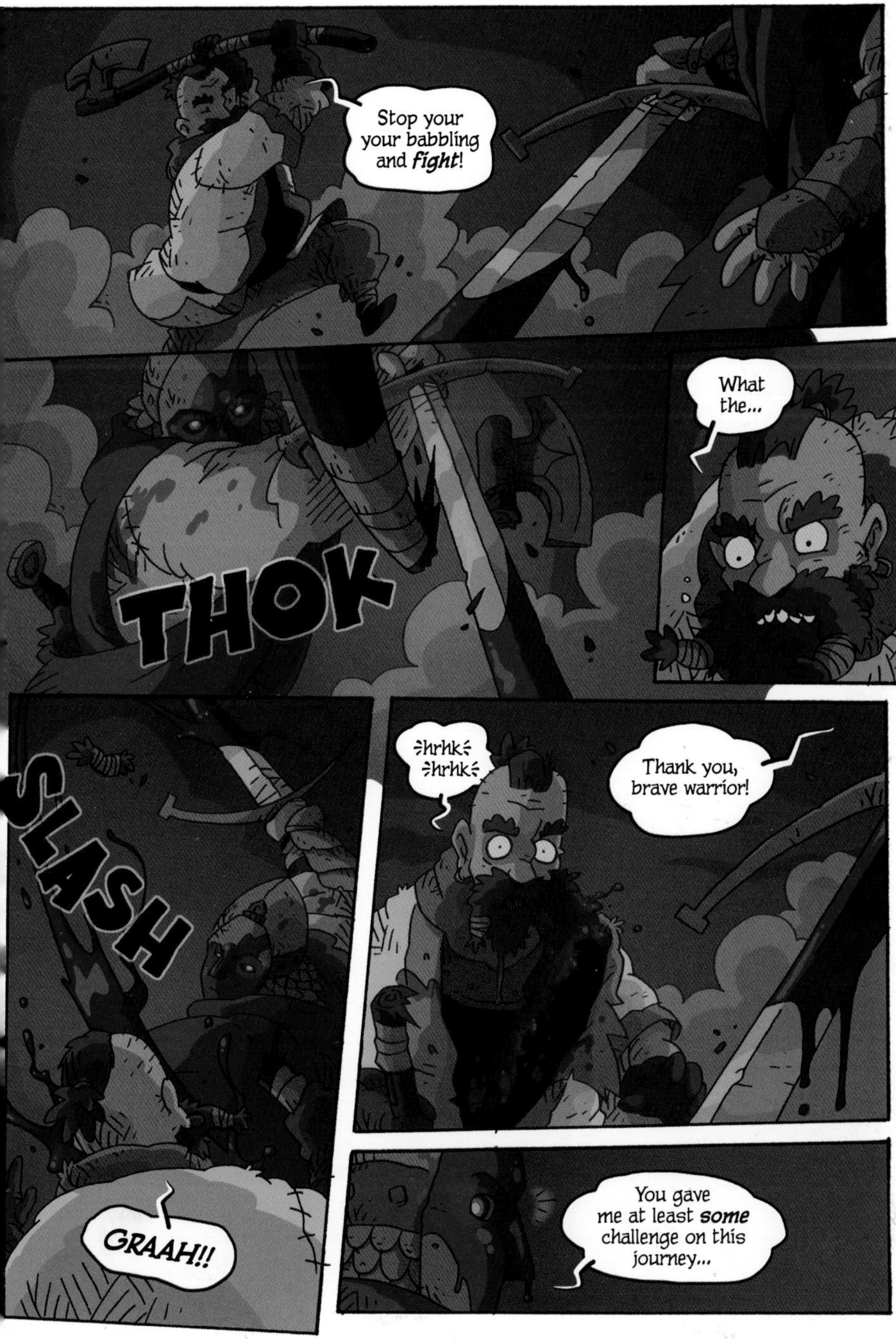
Stop your
your babbling
and *fight*!
What the...
THOK
SLASH
GRAAH!!
hrhk hrhk
Thank you, brave warrior!
You gave me at least **some** challenge on this journey...

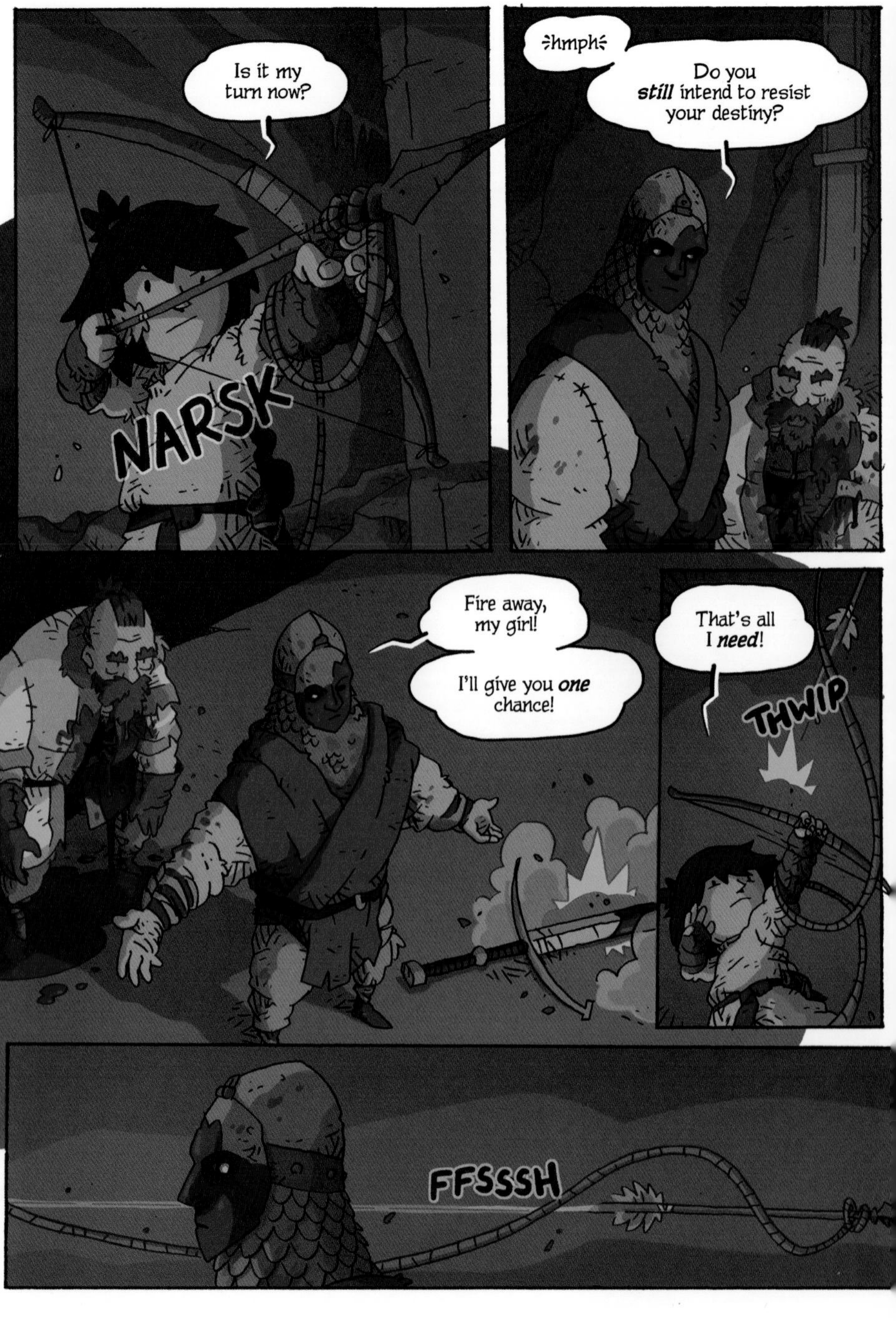
Is it my turn now?
NARSK
hmph
Do you *still* intend to resist your destiny?
Fire away, my girl!
I'll give you *one* chance!
That's all I *need*!
THWIP
FFSSSH

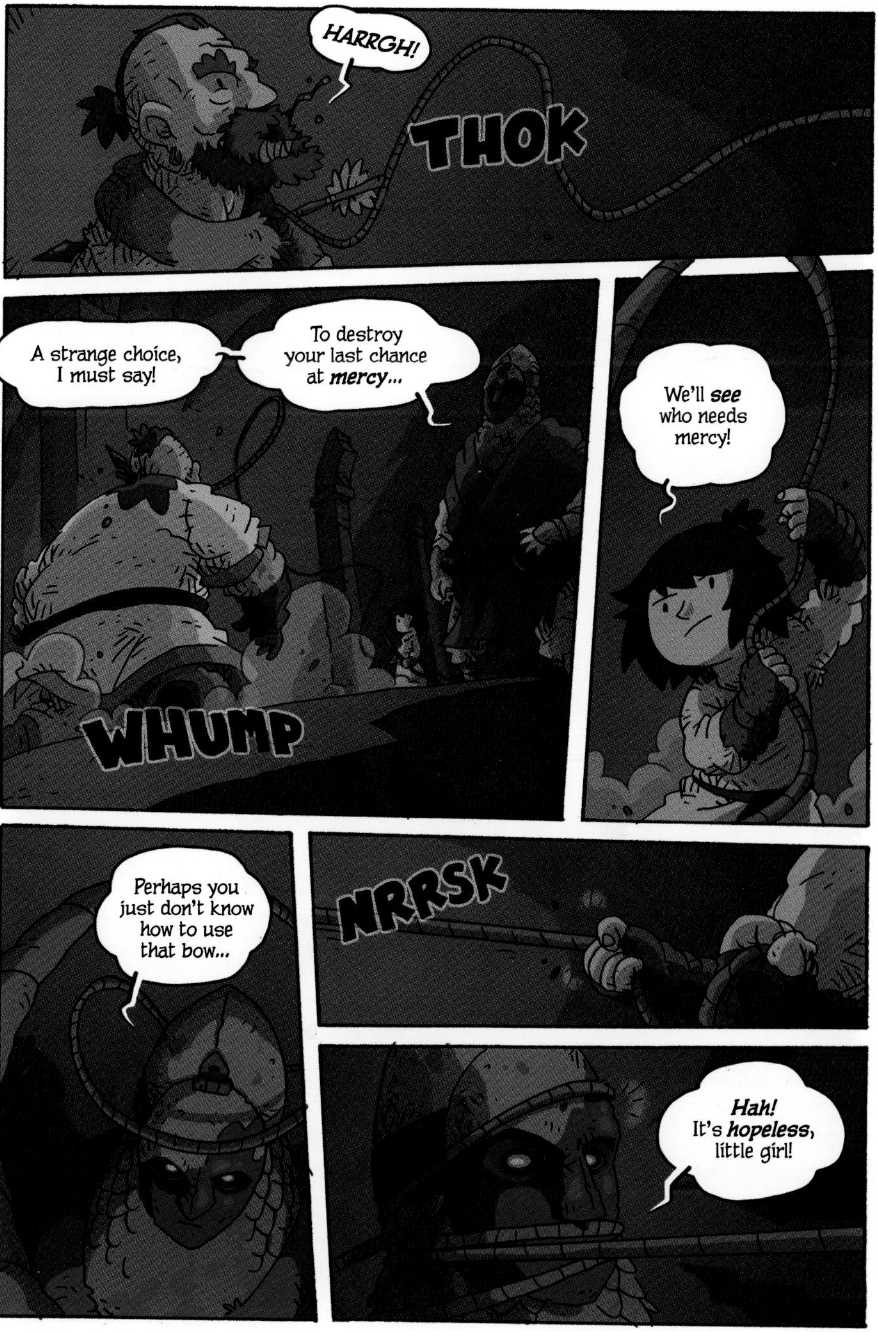
HARRGH!
THOK
A strange choice, I must say!
To destroy your last chance at *mercy*...
WHUMP
We'll *see* who needs mercy!
Perhaps you just don't know how to use that bow...
NRRSK
Hah! It's *hopeless*, little girl!

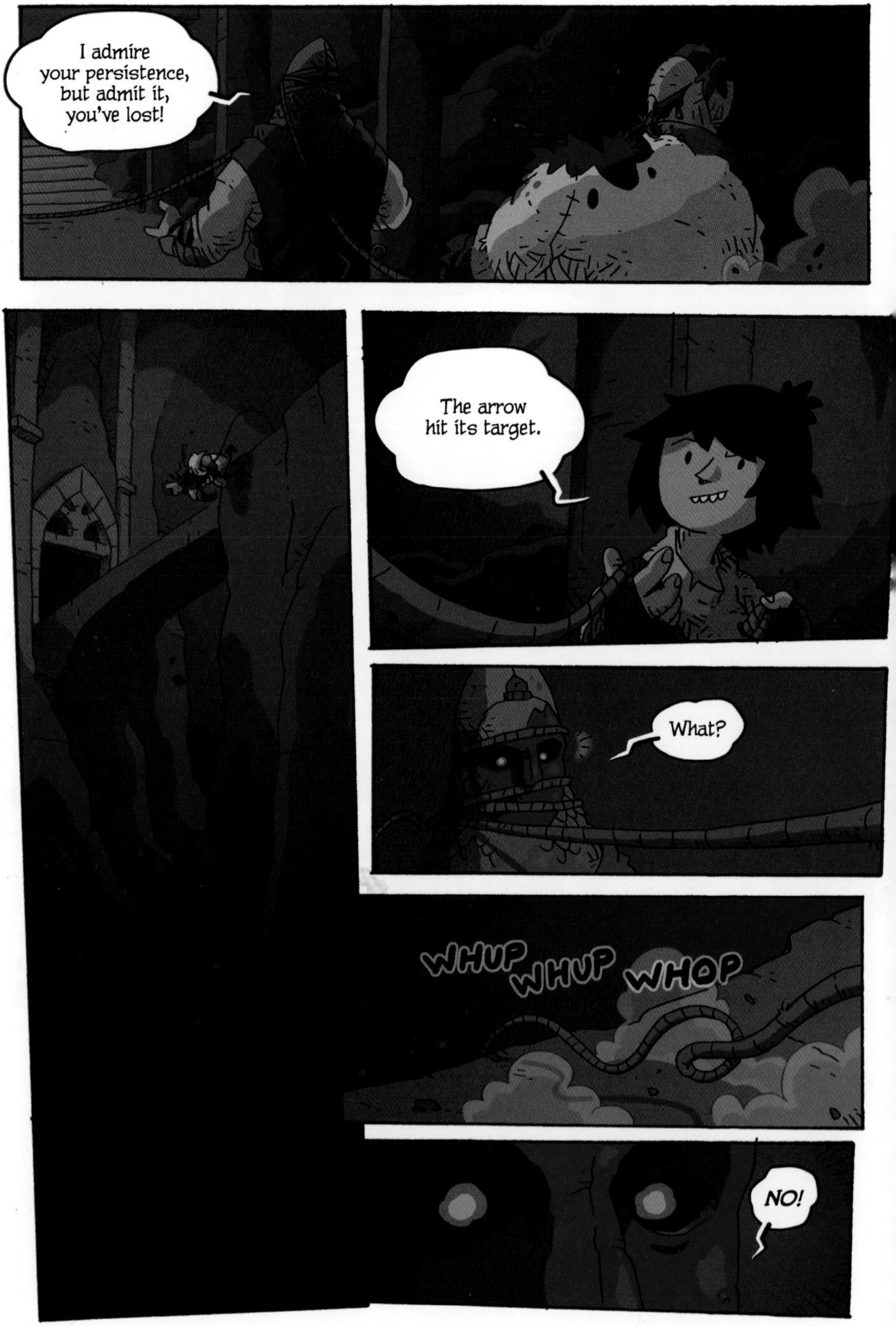
I admire your persistence, but admit it, you've lost!
The arrow hit its target.
What?
WHUP WHUP WHOP
NO!

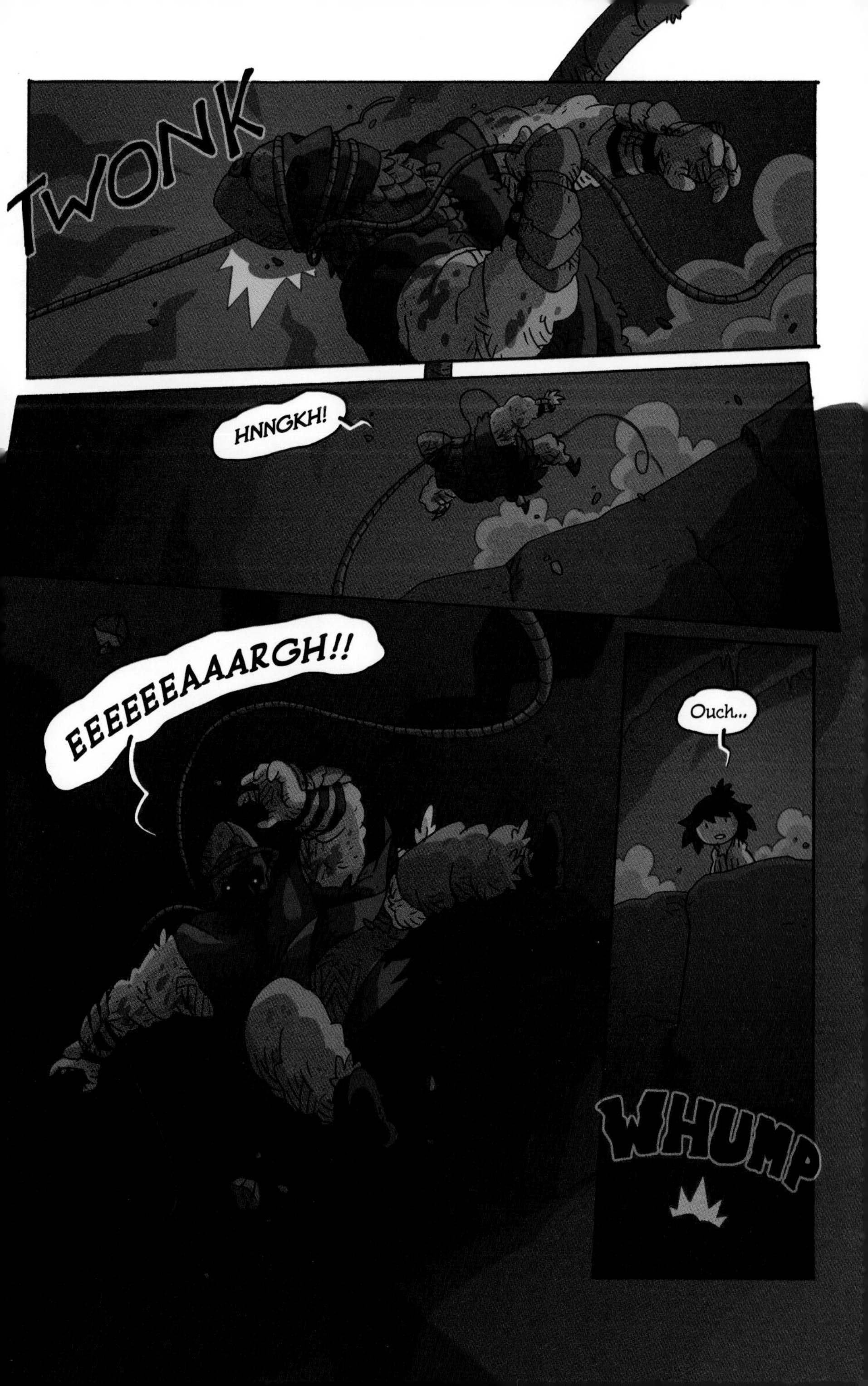
TWONK
HNNGKH!
EEEEEEAAARGH!!
Ouch...
WHUMP

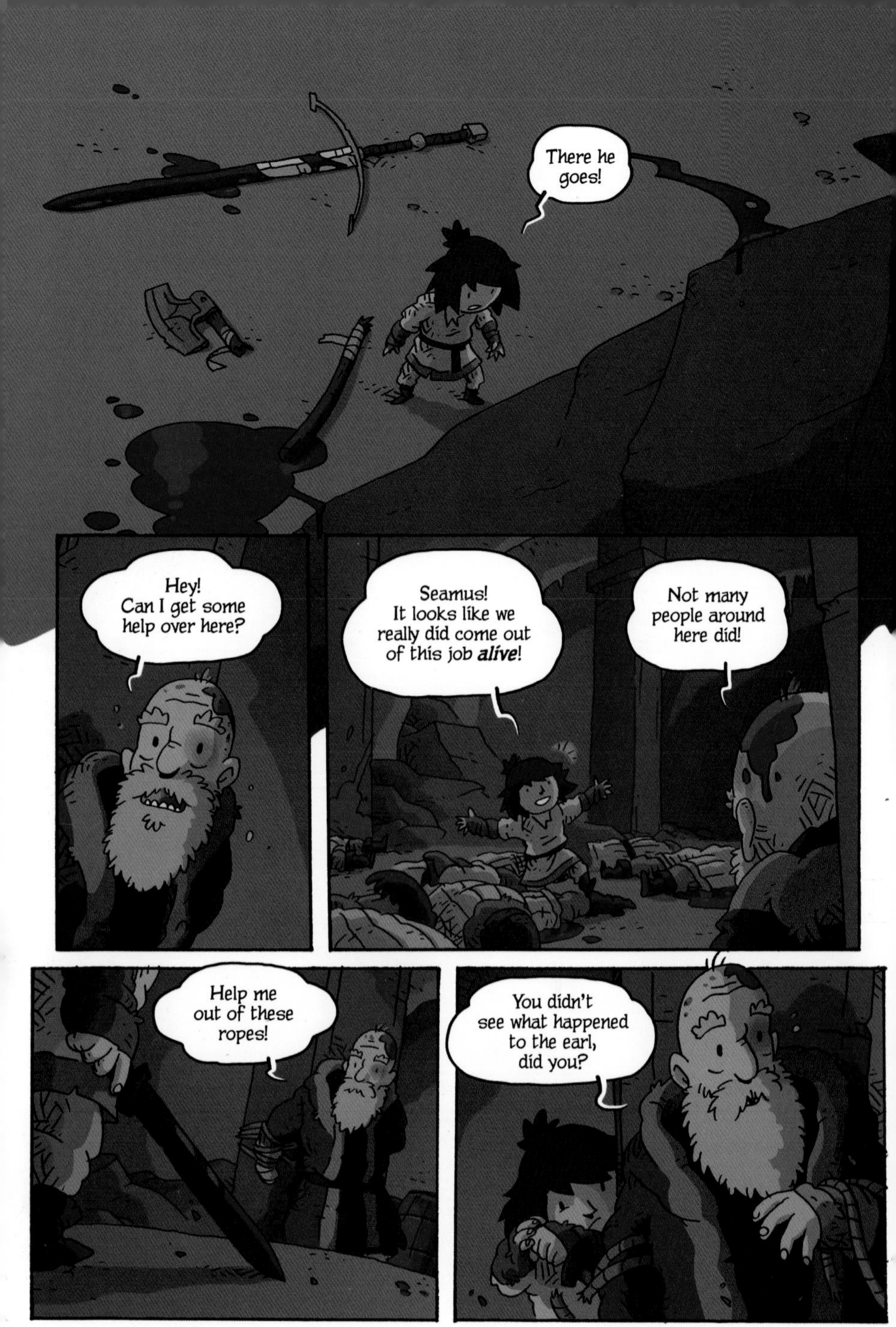

There he goes!
Hey! Can I get some help over here?
Seamus! It looks like we really did come out of this job *alive*!
Not many people around here did!
Help me out of these ropes!
You didn't see what happened to the earl, did you?

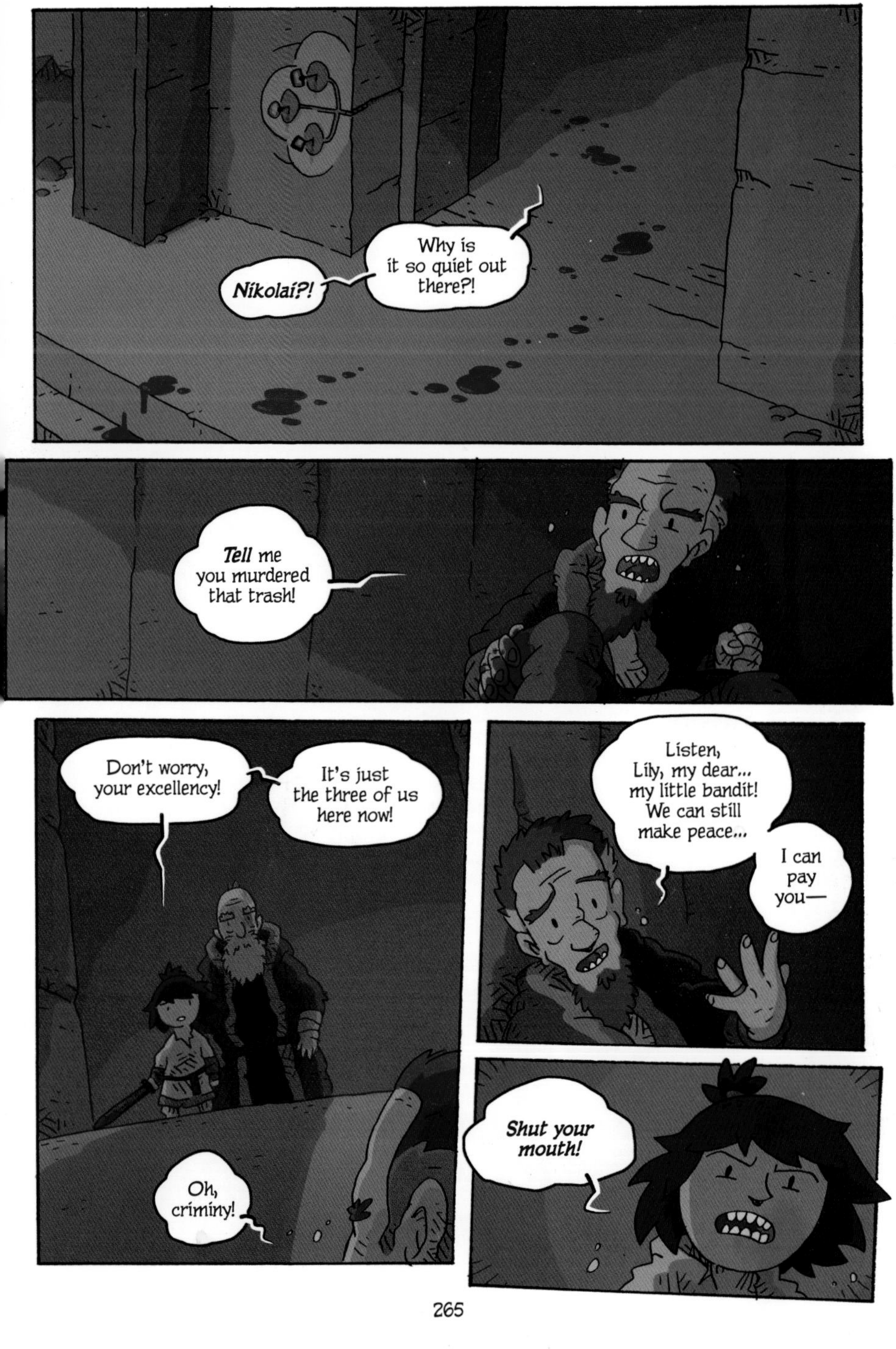
Nikolai?!
Why is it so quiet out there?!
Tell me you murdered that trash!
Don't worry, your excellency!
It's just the three of us here now!
Oh, criminy!
Listen, Lily, my dear... my little bandit! We can still make peace...
I can pay you—
Shut your mouth!

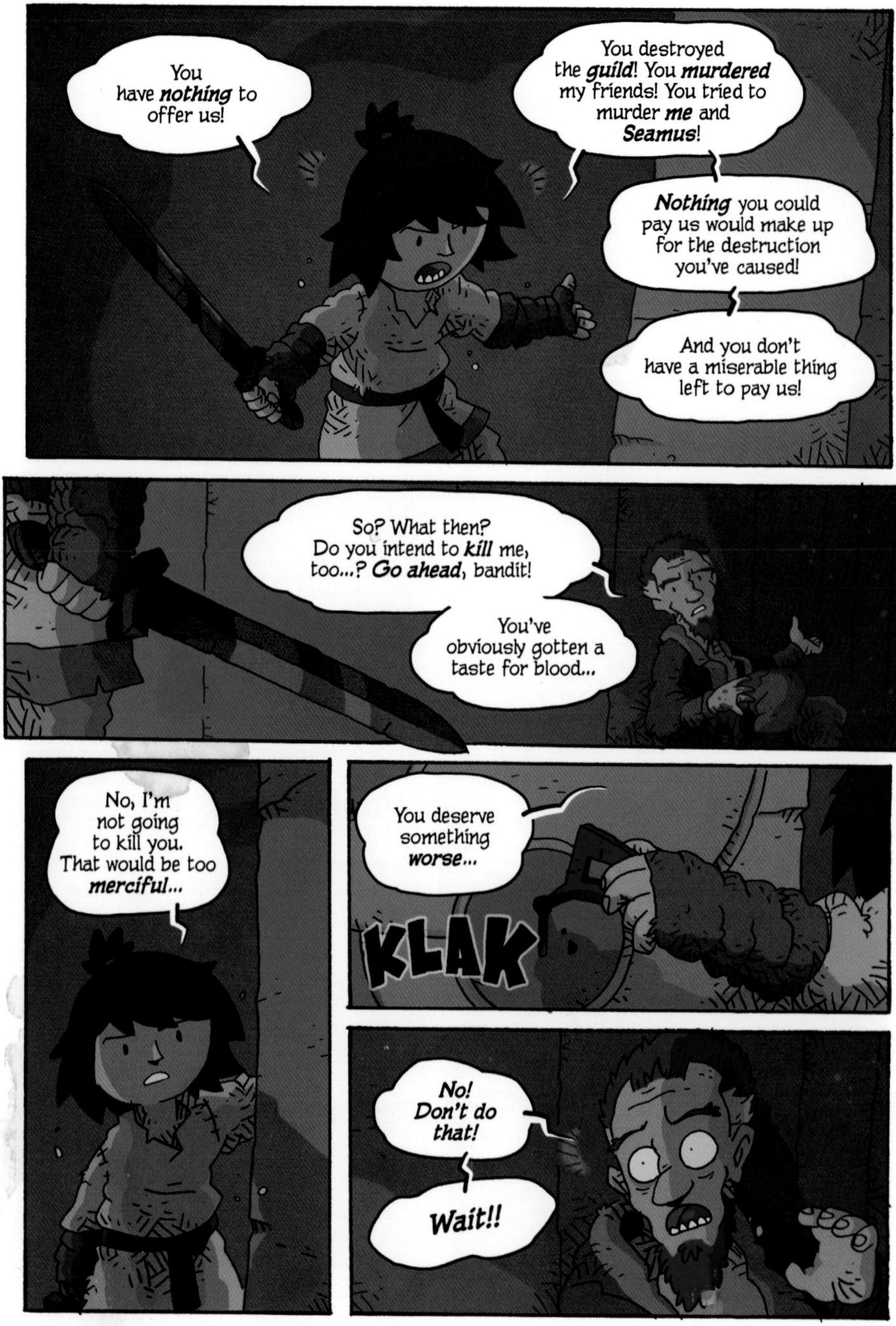
You have **nothing** to offer us!
You destroyed the **guild**! You **murdered** my friends! You tried to murder **me** and **Seamus**!
Nothing you could pay us would make up for the destruction you've caused!
And you don't have a miserable thing left to pay us!
So? What then? Do you intend to **kill** me, too...? **Go ahead**, bandit!
You've obviously gotten a taste for blood...
No, I'm not going to kill you. That would be too **merciful**...
You deserve something **worse**...
KLAK
No! Don't do that!
Wait!!

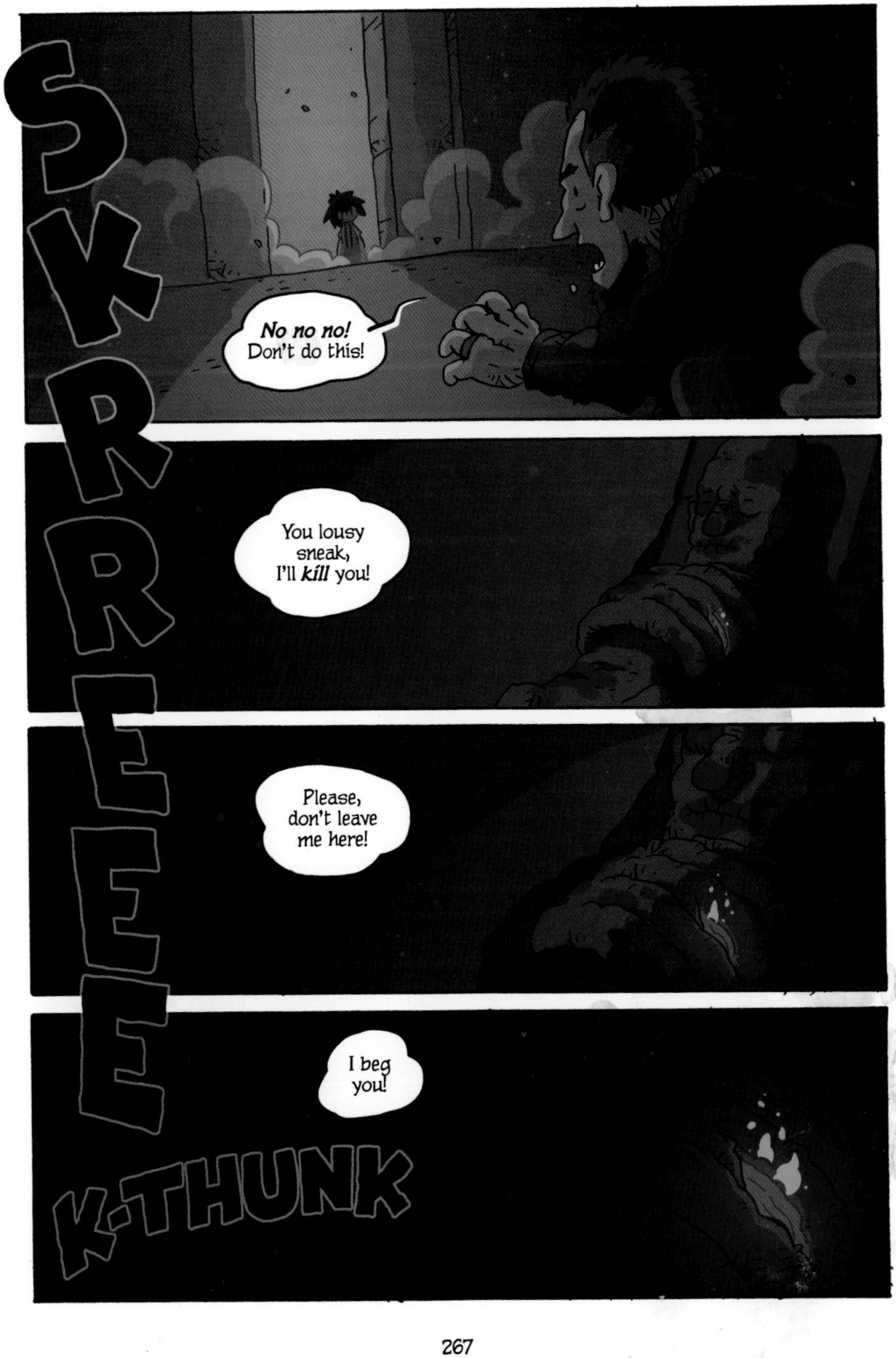
SKRREEEE
No no no! Don't do this!
You lousy sneak, I'll ***kill*** you!
Please, don't leave me here!
I beg you!
K-THUNK

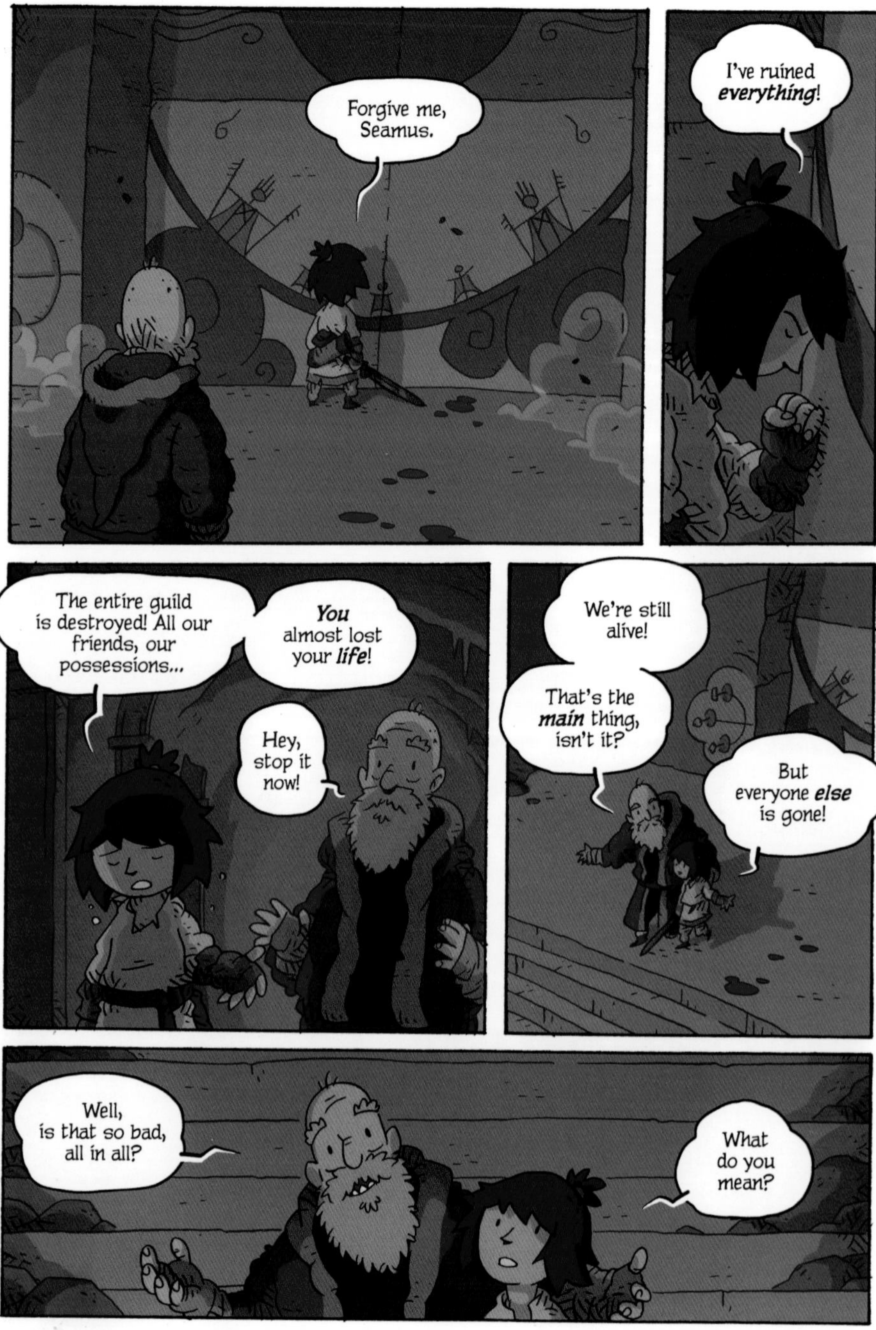
Forgive me, Seamus.
I've ruined *everything*!
The entire guild is destroyed! All our friends, our possessions...
You almost lost your *life*!
Hey, stop it now!
We're still alive!
That's the *main* thing, isn't it?
But everyone *else* is gone!
Well, is that so bad, all in all?
What do you mean?

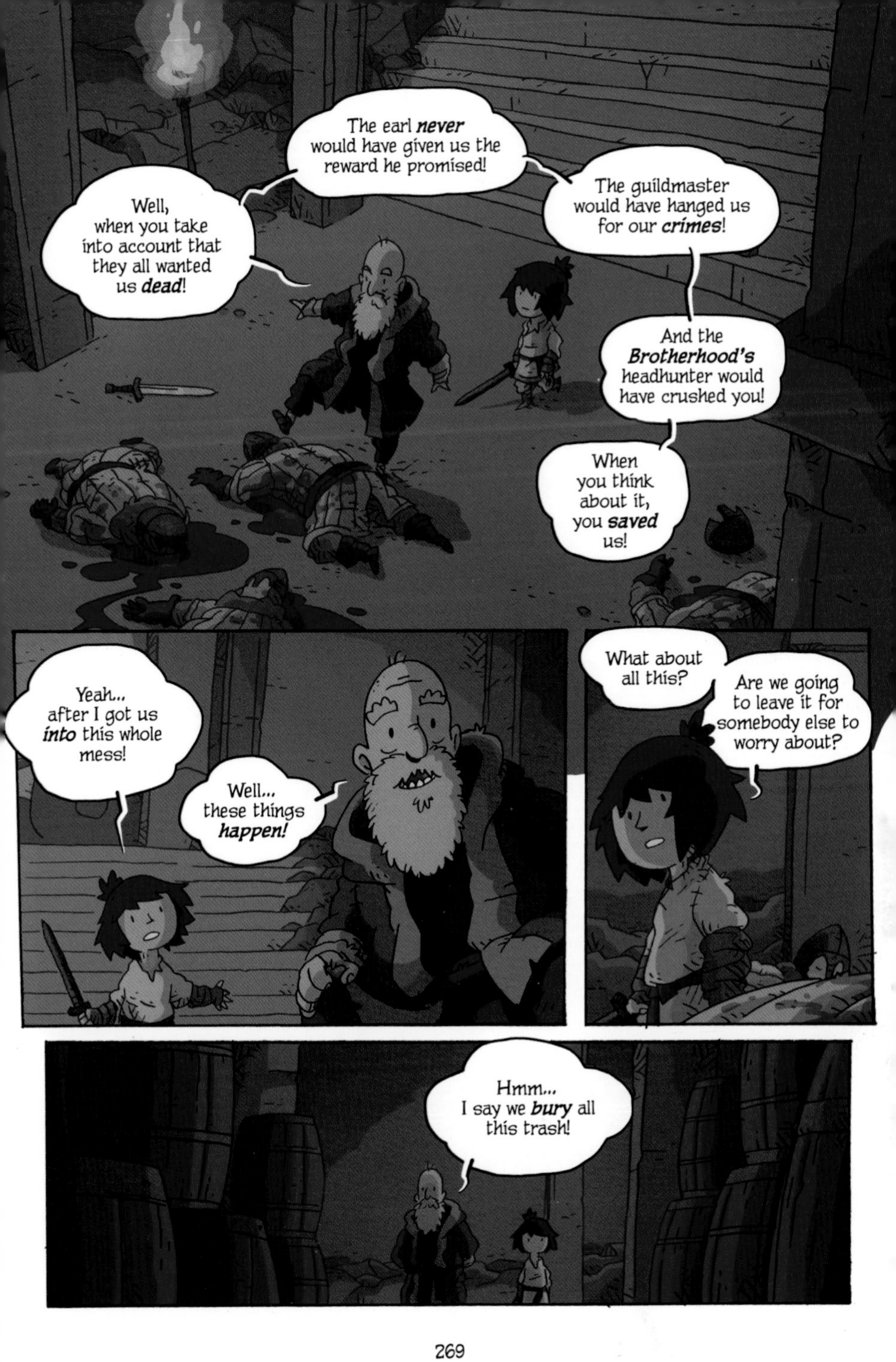
The earl ***never*** would have given us the reward he promised!
Well, when you take into account that they all wanted us ***dead***!
The guildmaster would have hanged us for our ***crimes***!
And the ***Brotherhood's*** headhunter would have crushed you!
When you think about it, you ***saved*** us!
Yeah... after I got us ***into*** this whole mess!
Well... these things ***happen!***
What about all this?
Are we going to leave it for somebody else to worry about?
Hmm... I say we ***bury*** all this trash!

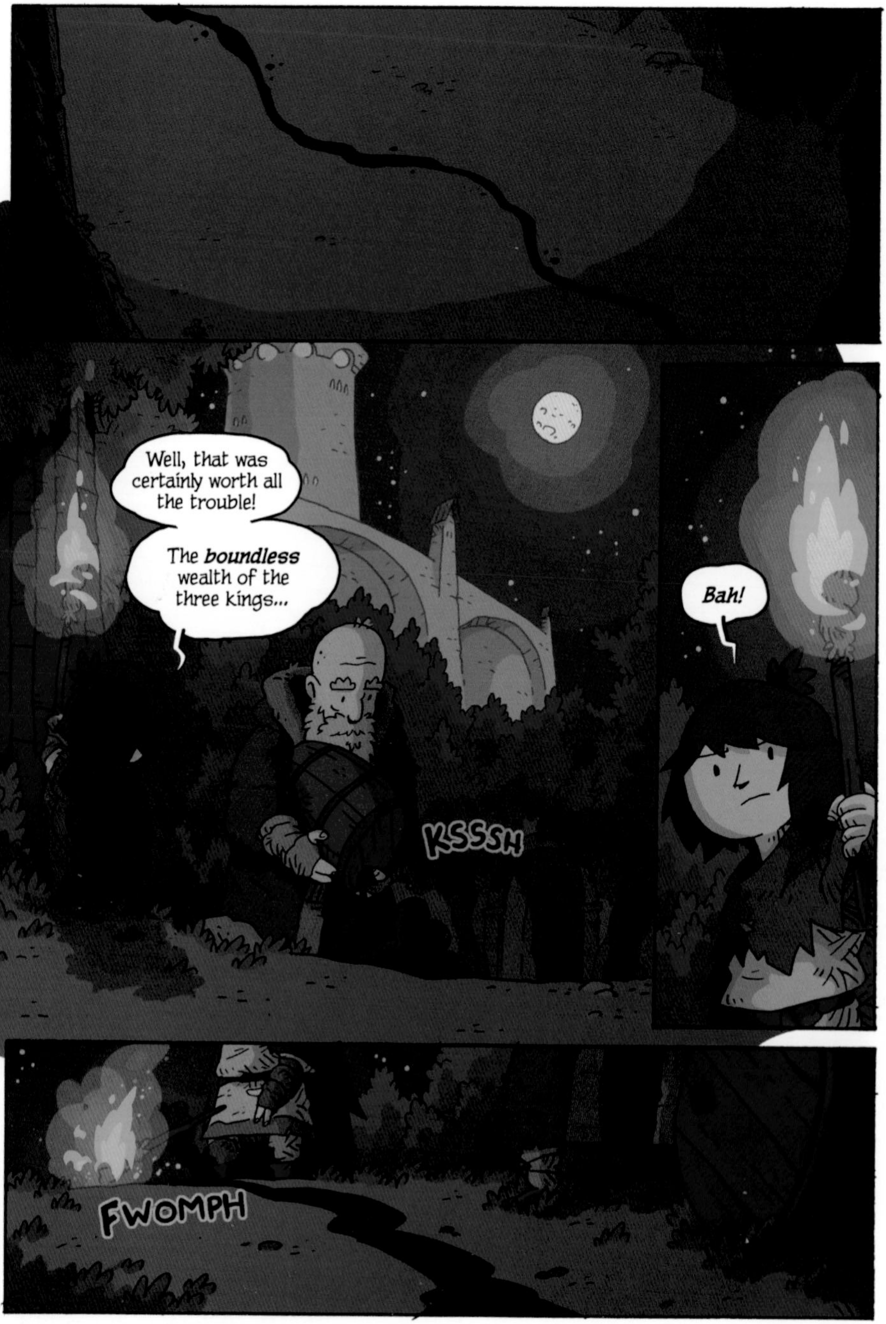

Well, that was certainly worth all the trouble!
The **boundless** wealth of the three kings...
Bah!
KSSSH
FWOMPH

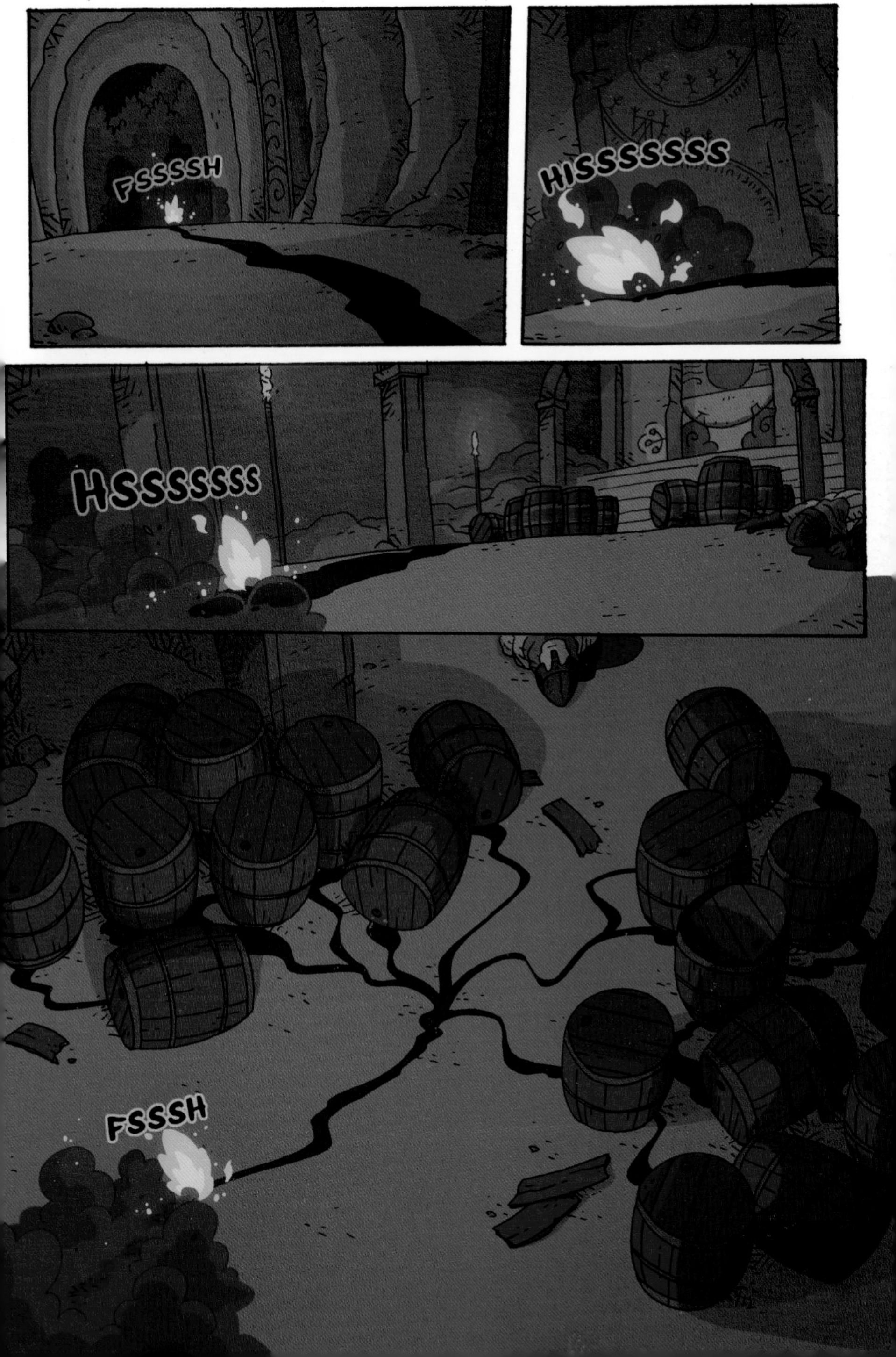
FSSSSH
HISSSSSSS
HSSSSSSS
FSSSH

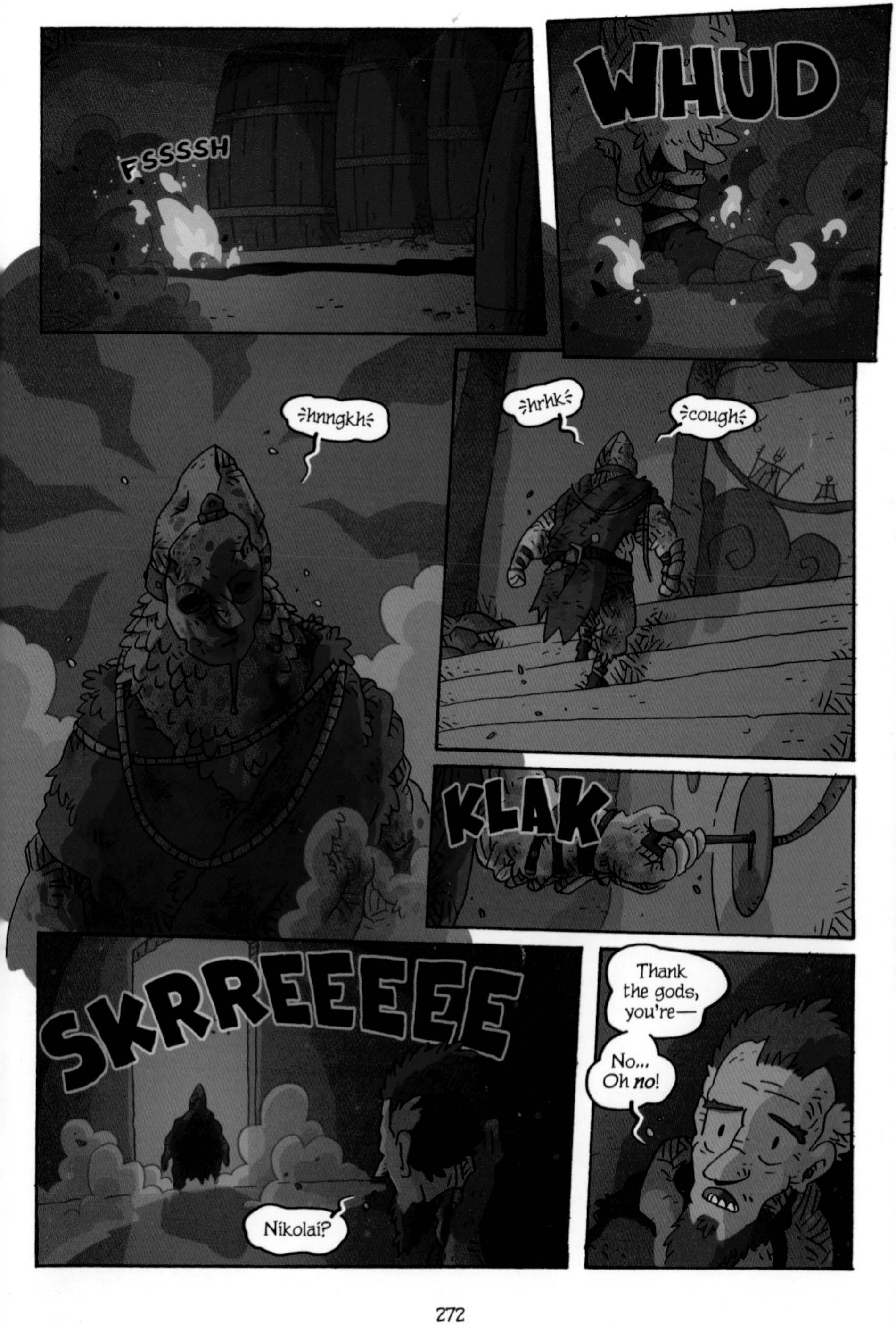
FSSSSH
WHUD
hnngkh
hrhk
cough
KLAK
SKRREEEEEE
Nikolai?
Thank the gods, you're—
No... Oh no!

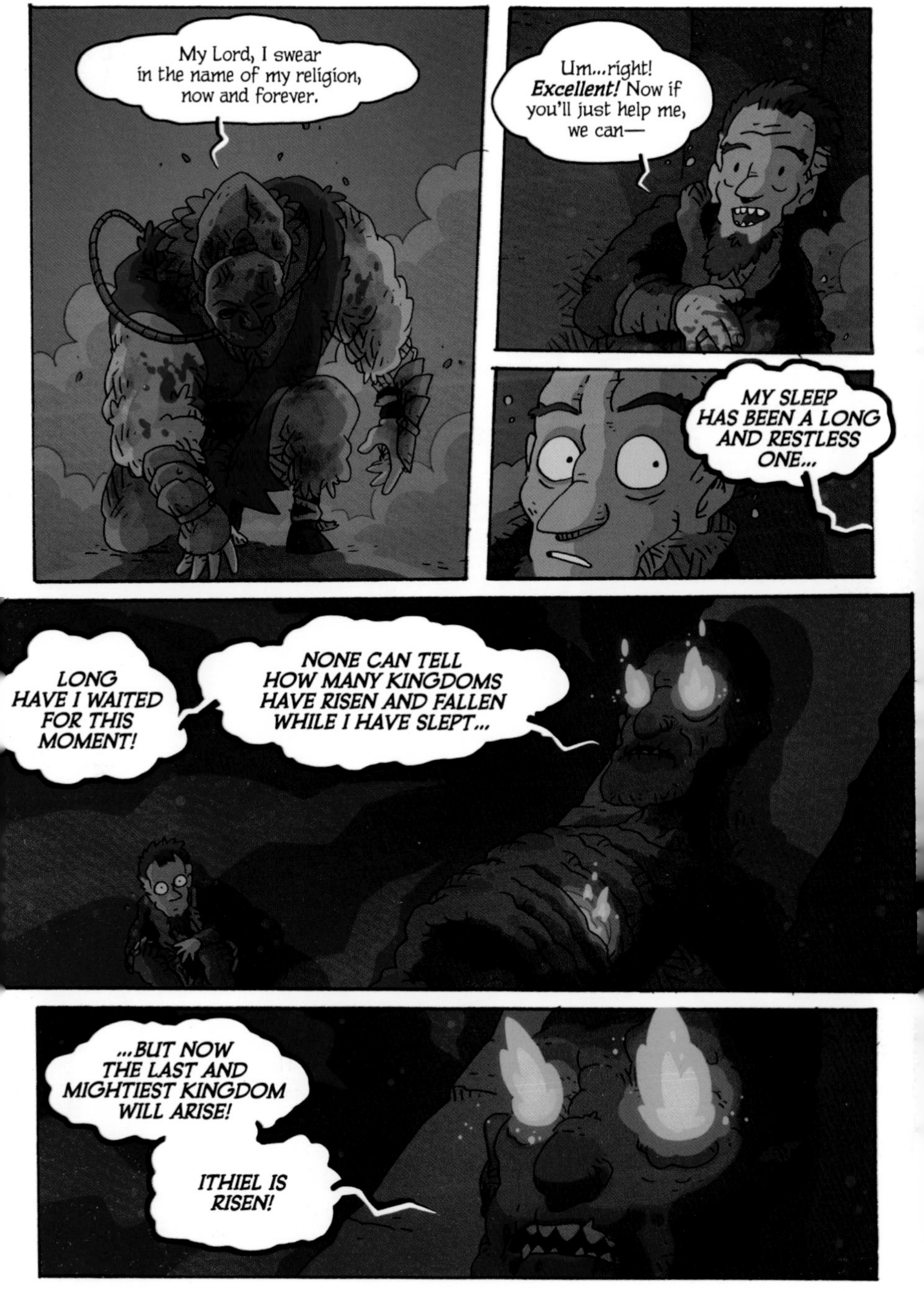
My Lord, I swear in the name of my religion, now and forever.
Um...right! Excellent! Now if you'll just help me, we can—
MY SLEEP HAS BEEN A LONG AND RESTLESS ONE...
LONG HAVE I WAITED FOR THIS MOMENT!
NONE CAN TELL HOW MANY KINGDOMS HAVE RISEN AND FALLEN WHILE I HAVE SLEPT...
...BUT NOW THE LAST AND MIGHTIEST KINGDOM WILL ARISE!
ITHIEL IS RISEN!

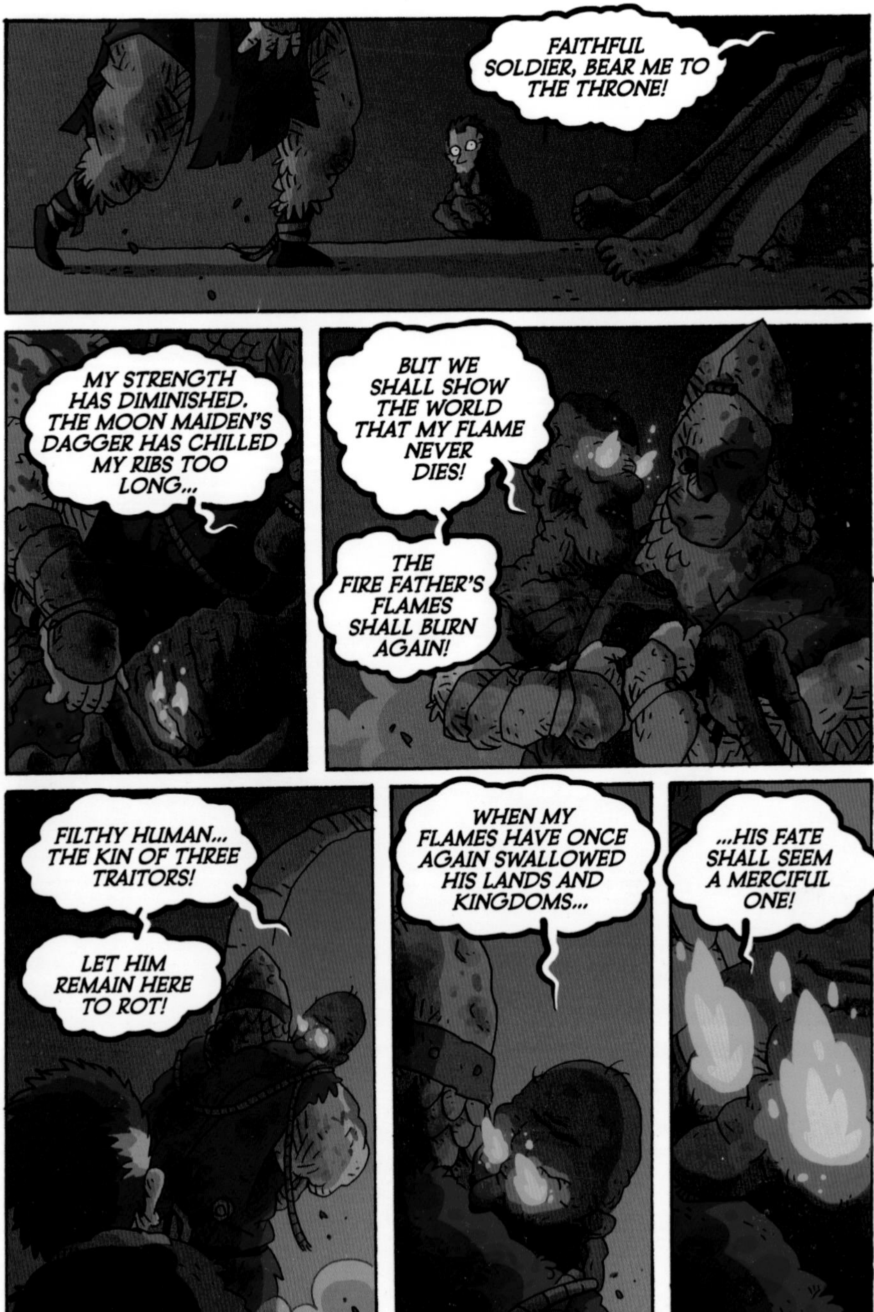
FAITHFUL SOLDIER, BEAR ME TO THE THRONE!
MY STRENGTH HAS DIMINISHED. THE MOON MAIDEN'S DAGGER HAS CHILLED MY RIBS TOO LONG...
BUT WE SHALL SHOW THE WORLD THAT MY FLAME NEVER DIES!
THE FIRE FATHER'S FLAMES SHALL BURN AGAIN!
FILTHY HUMAN... THE KIN OF THREE TRAITORS!
LET HIM REMAIN HERE TO ROT!
WHEN MY FLAMES HAVE ONCE AGAIN SWALLOWED HIS LANDS AND KINGDOMS...
...HIS FATE SHALL SEEM A MERCIFUL ONE!

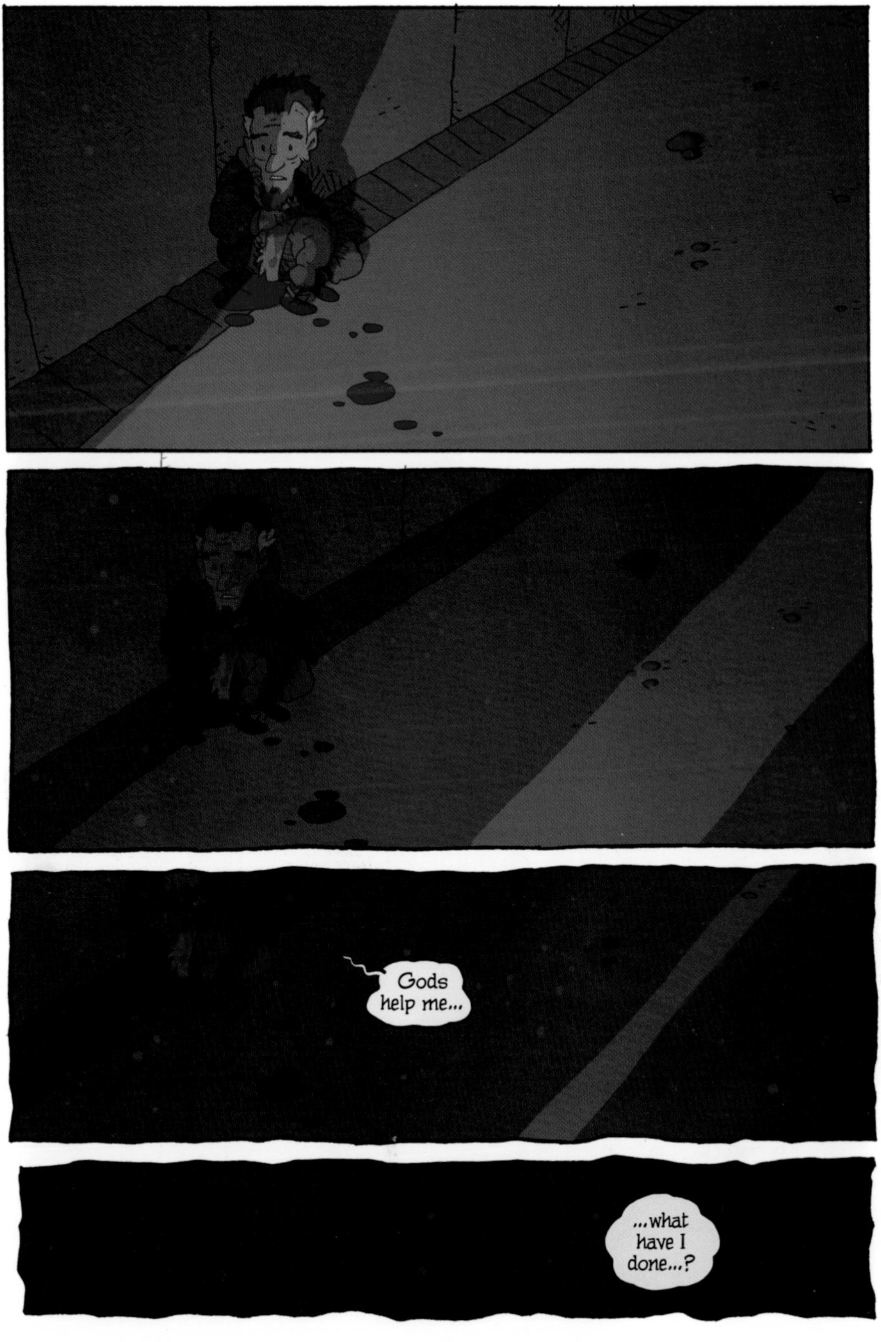
Gods help me...
...what have I done...?

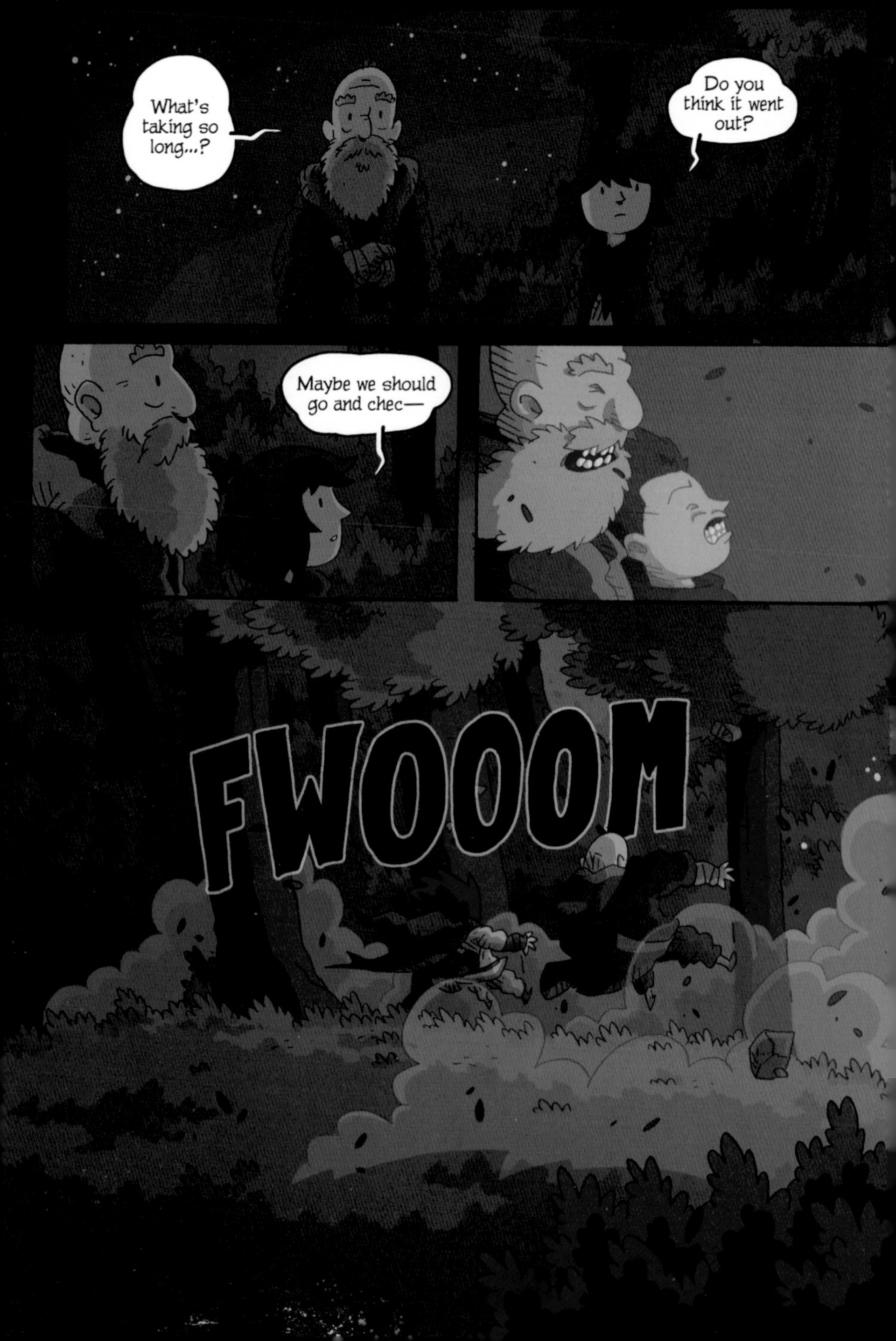
What's taking so long...?
Do you think it went out?
Maybe we should go and chec—
FWOOOM

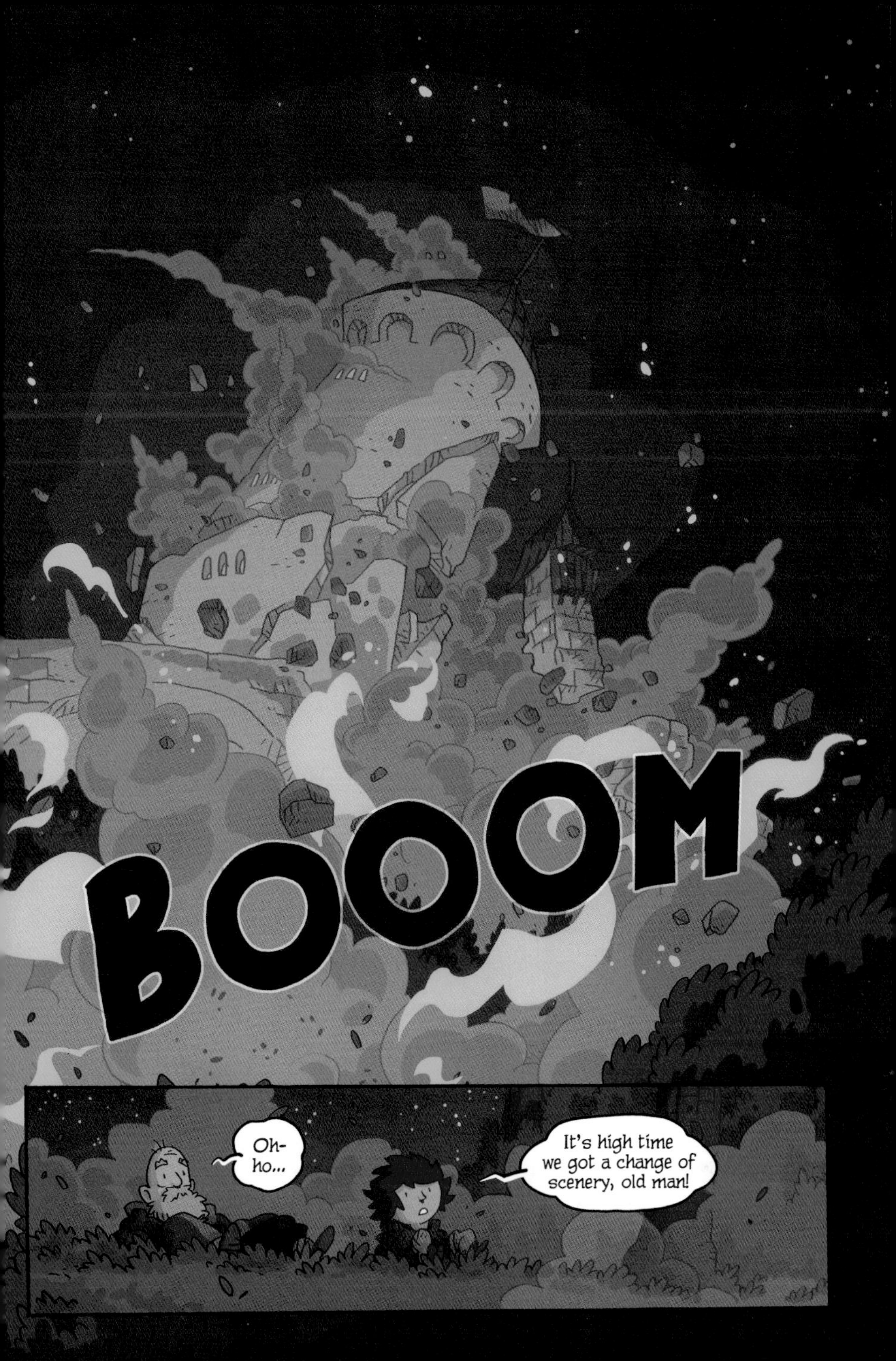
BOOOM
Oh-ho...
It's high time we got a change of scenery, old man!

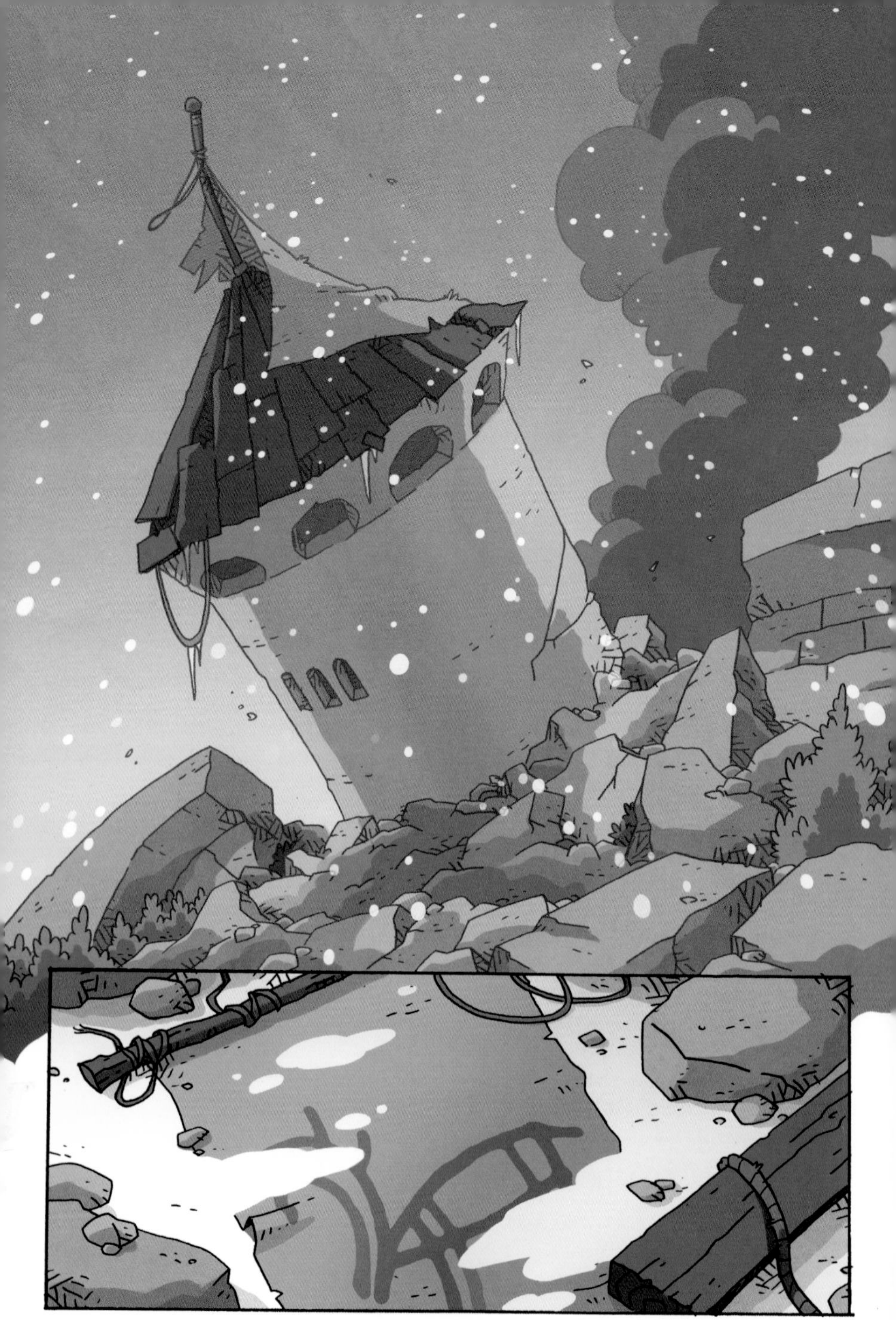

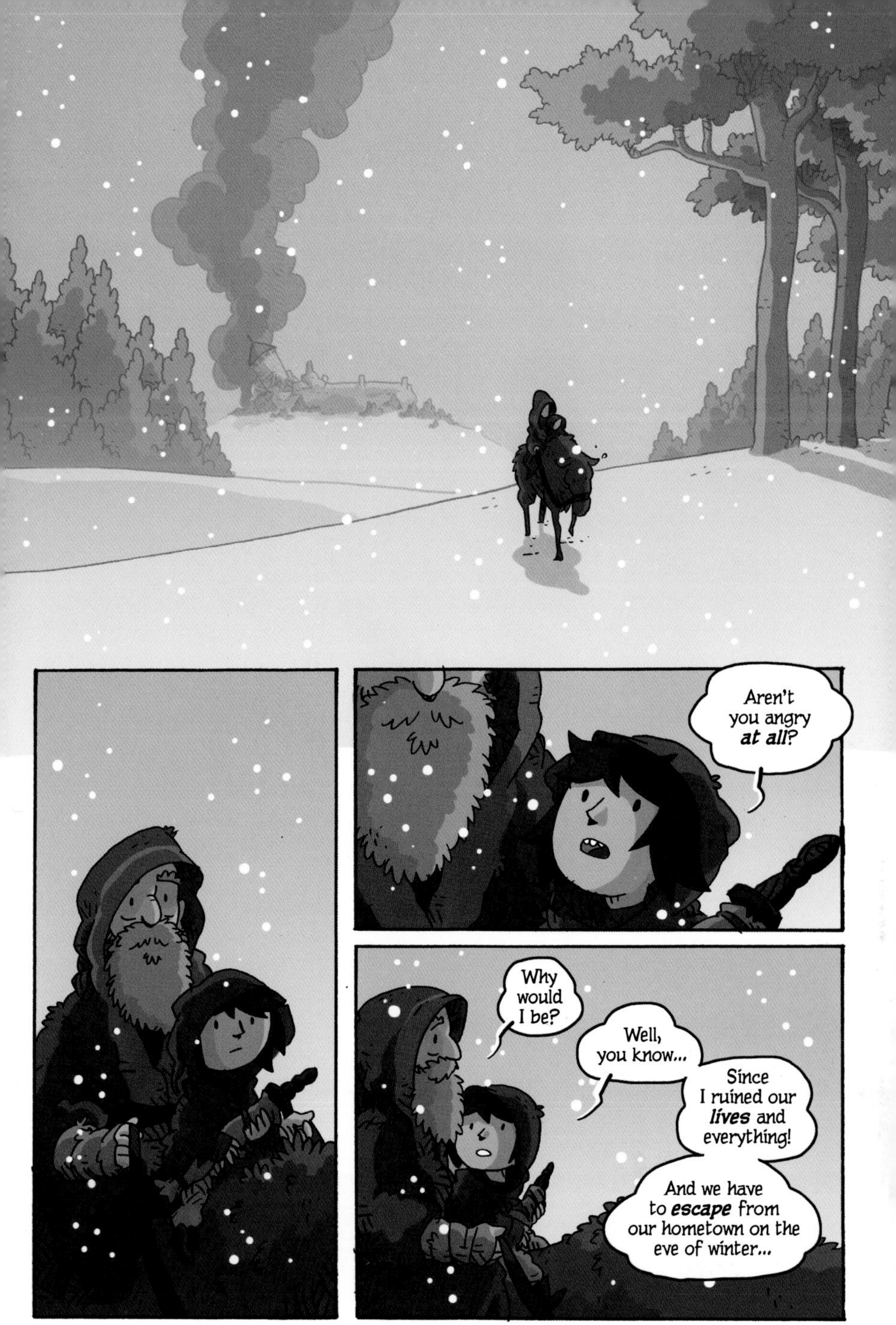

Aren't you angry *at all*?
Why would I be?
Well, you know...
Since I ruined our *lives* and everything!
And we have to *escape* from our hometown on the eve of winter...

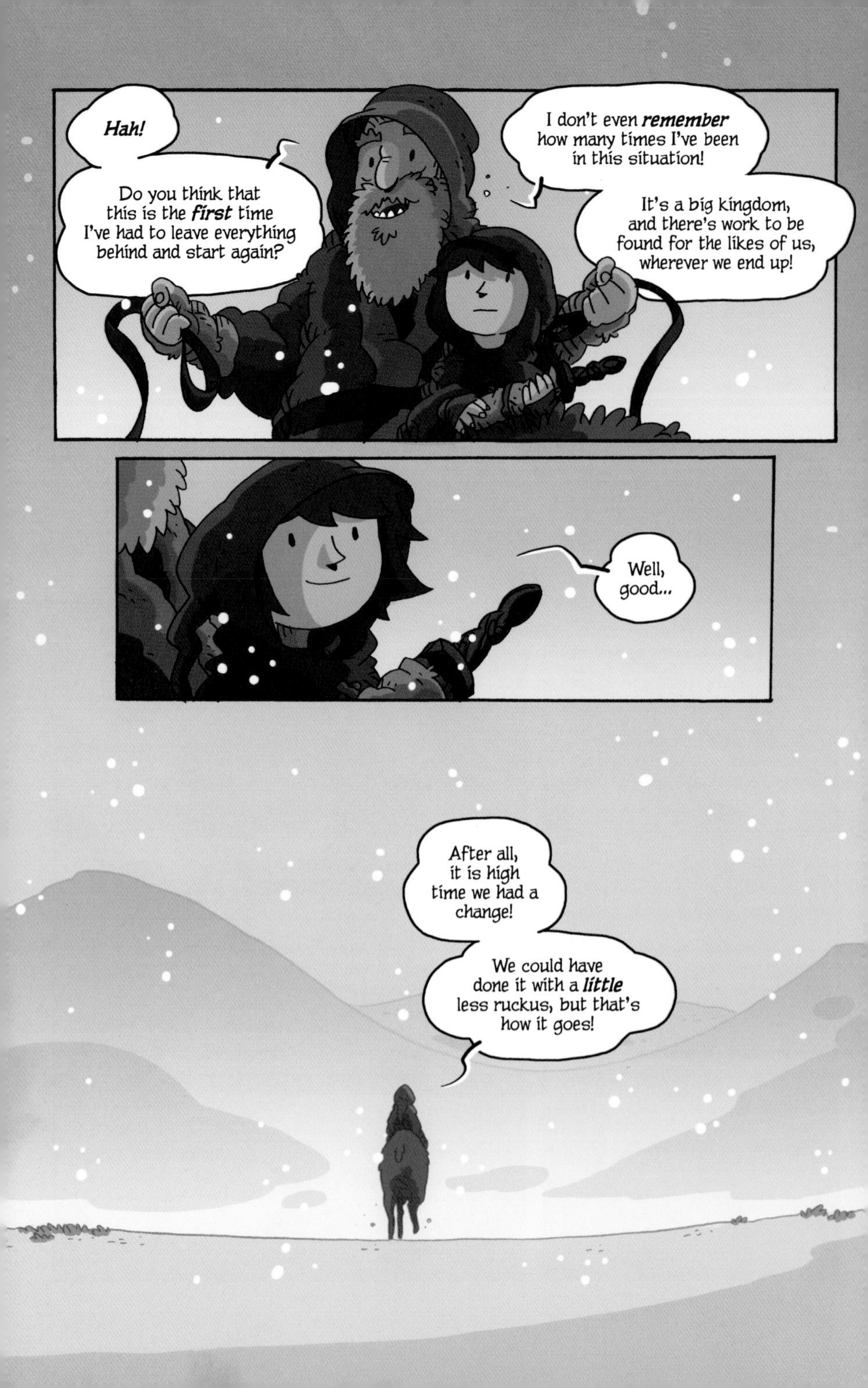
Hah!
Do you think that this is the *first* time I've had to leave everything behind and start again?
I don't even *remember* how many times I've been in this situation!
It's a big kingdom, and there's work to be found for the likes of us, wherever we end up!
Well, good...
After all, it is high time we had a change!
We could have done it with a *little* less ruckus, but that's how it goes!

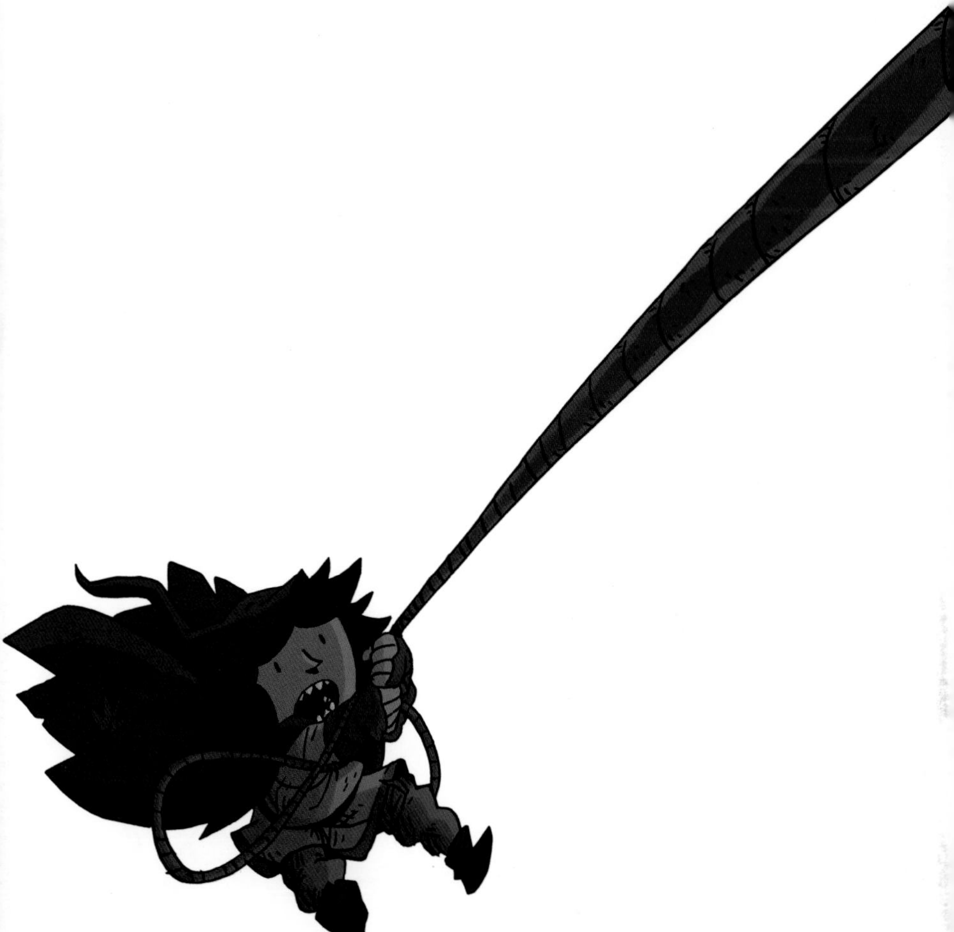

Sketch Gallery

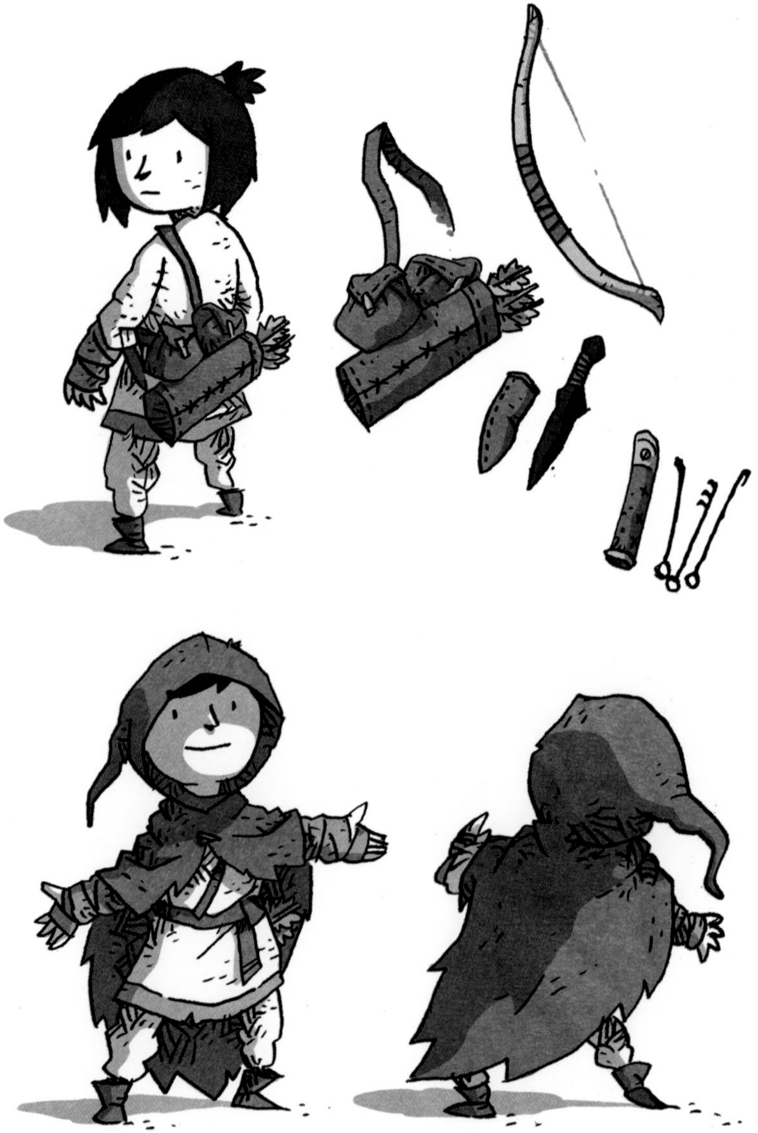

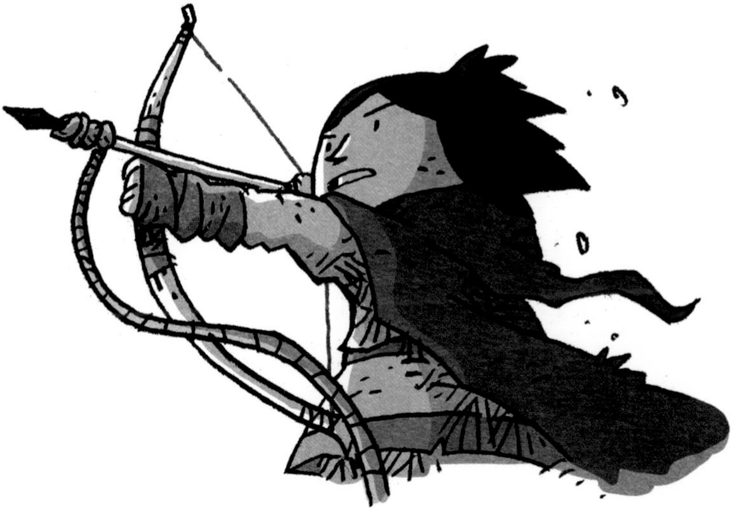

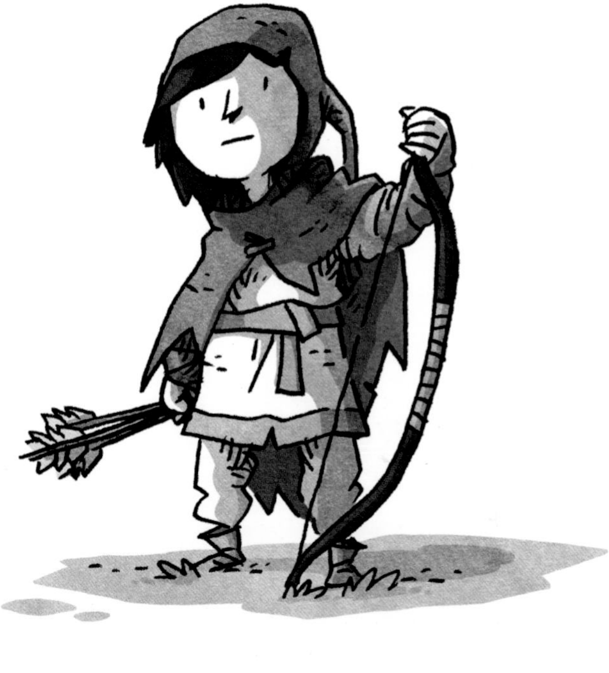

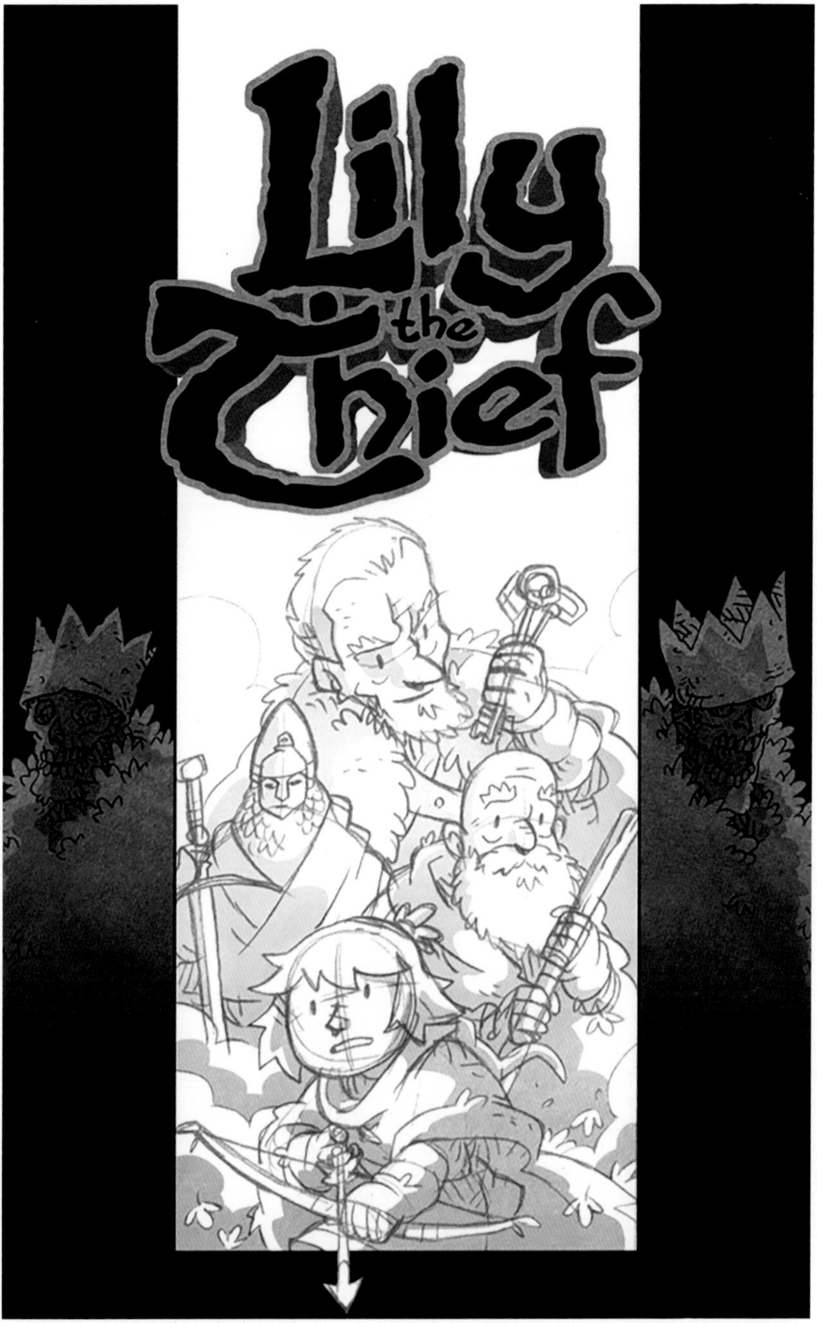
Lily the Thief

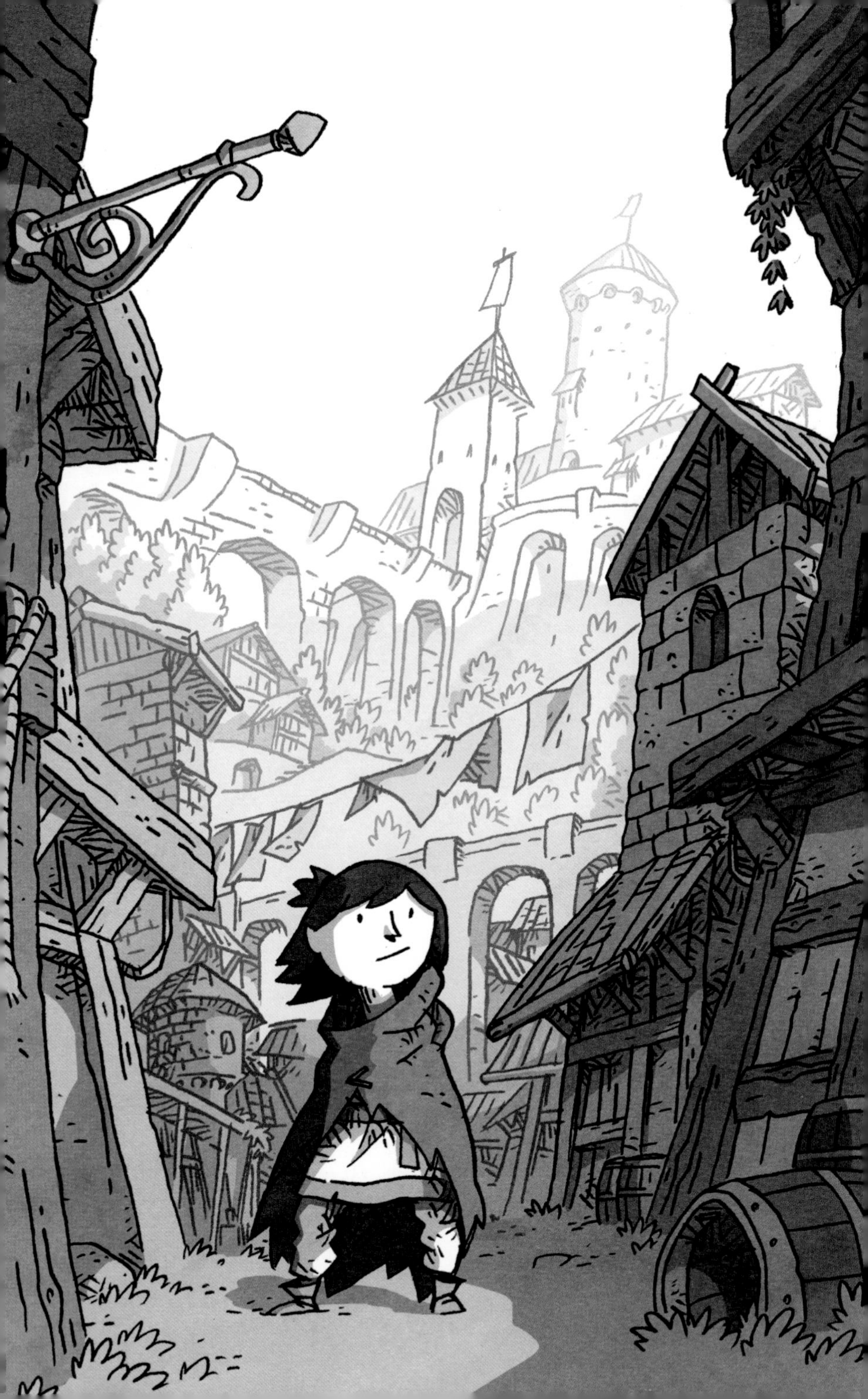

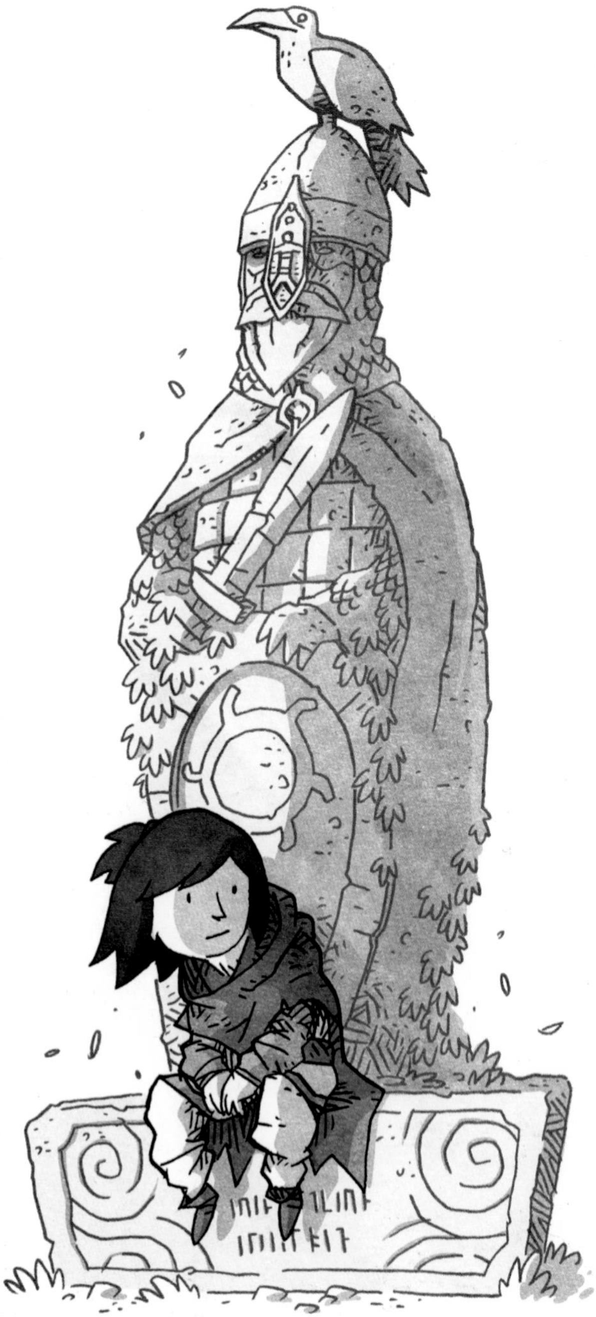

First Second

English translation by Lola Rogers
English translation copyright © 2019 by Roaring Brook Press

Published by First Second
First Second is an imprint of Roaring Brook Press,
a division of Holtzbrinck Publishing Holdings Limited Partnership
120 Broadway, New York, NY 10271

Don't miss your next favorite book from First Second! For the latest updates go to
firstsecondnewsletter.com and sign up for our enewsletter.

Library of Congress Control Number: 2018953656

Paperback ISBN: 978-1-250-19697-2
Hardcover ISBN: 978-1-250-19355-1

Our books may be purchased in bulk for promotional, educational, or business use.
Please contact your local bookseller or the Macmillan Corporate and Premium Sales Department
at (800) 221-7945 ext. 5442 or by email at MacmillanSpecialMarkets@macmillan.com.

Finnish text and illustrations copyright © 2016 by Janne Kukkonen
Originally published in 2016 in Finnish by Like Kustannus Oy as Voro
Coloring by Kévin Bazot copyright © 2019 by Casterman
First American Edition, 2019

Edited by Mark Seigel and Casey Gonzalez
Cover design by Andrew Arnold
Interior book design by Chris Dickey
Printed in China by 1010 Printing International Limited, North Point, Hong Kong

Sketched on a Foldermate sketchbook with a light blue Prismacolor Col-Erase pencil,
finished with Staedtler H pencil. Colored digitally.

Paperback: 10 9 8 7 6 5 4 3 2 1
Hardcover: 10 9 8 7 6 5 4 3 2 1